WORLD WITHOUT END

KEN FOLLETT was only twenty-seven when he wrote the award-winning *Eye of the Needle*, which became an international bestseller. He has since written several equally successful novels, including, most recently, *Whiteout*. *World Without End* is the long-awaited sequel to the worldwide bestselling *The Pillars of the Earth*, the epic of family drama, violent conflict and vaulting ambition set around the building of a great cathedral. Ken Follett is also the author of a non-fiction bestseller, *On Wings of Eagles*. He lives with his family in London and Hertfordshire.

WORLD WITHOUT END

'Follett excels in telling a yarn. Intrigue, double-twists, exciting, satisfying . . . you won't be able to put it down'
Independent

'This is a huge book in every way, sweeping and yet detailed, a powerful story packed with superbly drawn characters and which brilliantly evokes the period that saw the devastating Black Death plague and the birth of modern medicine'
Choice

THE PILLARS OF THE EARTH

'Enormous and brilliant . . . this mammoth tale seems to touch all human emotion – love and hate, loyalty and treachery, hope and despair. See for yourself. This is truly a novel to get lost in'
Cosmopolitan

'A historical saga of such breadth and density . . . Follett succeeds brilliantly in combining hugeness and detail to create a novel imbued with the rawness, violence and blind faith of the era'
Sunday Express

KEN FOLLETT

WORLD WITHOUT END

PAN BOOKS

First published 2007 by Macmillan

This edition published 2008 by Pan Books
an imprint of Pan Macmillan, a division of Macmillan Publishers Limited
Pan Macmillan, 20 New Wharf Road, London N1 9RR
Basingstoke and Oxford
Associated companies throughout the world
www.panmacmillan.com

ISBN 978-0-330-45692-0

Copyright © Ken Follett 2007

The right of Ken Follett to be identified as the
author of this work has been asserted by him in accordance
with the Copyright, Designs and Patents Act 1988.

All rights reserved. No part of this publication may be
reproduced, stored in or introduced into a retrieval system, or
transmitted, in any form, or by any means (electronic, mechanical,
photocopying, recording or otherwise) without the prior written
permission of the publisher. Any person who does any unauthorized
act in relation to this publication may be liable to criminal
prosecution and civil claims for damages.

5 7 9 8 6

A CIP catalogue record for this book is available from
the British Library.

Typeset by SetSystems Ltd, Saffron Walden, Essex
Printed and bound in the UK by CPI Mackays, Chatham ME5 8TD

This book is sold subject to the condition that it shall not,
by way of trade or otherwise, be lent, re-sold, hired out,
or otherwise circulated without the publisher's prior consent
in any form of binding or cover other than that in which
it is published and without a similar condition including this
condition being imposed on the subsequent purchaser.

Visit **www.panmacmillan.com** to read more about all our books
and to buy them. You will also find features, author interviews and
news of any author events, and you can sign up for e-newsletters
so that you're always first to hear about our new releases.

For Barbara

Part One

1 November, 1327

I

GWENDA WAS EIGHT YEARS OLD, but she was not afraid of the dark.

When she opened her eyes she could see nothing, but that was not what scared her. She knew where she was. She was at Kingsbridge Priory, in the long stone building they called the hospital, lying on the floor in a bed of straw. Her mother lay next to her, and Gwenda could tell, by the warm milky smell, that Ma was feeding the new baby, who did not yet have a name. Beside Ma was Pa, and next to him Gwenda's older brother, Philemon, who was twelve.

The hospital was crowded, and though she could not see the other families lying along the floor, squashed together like sheep in a pen, she could smell the rank odour of their warm bodies. When dawn broke it would be All Hallows, a Sunday this year and therefore an especially holy day. By the same token the night before was All Hallows' Eve, a dangerous time when evil spirits roamed freely. Hundreds of people had come to Kingsbridge from the surrounding villages, as Gwenda's family had, to spend Halloween in the sanctified precincts of the priory, and to attend the All Hallows service at daybreak.

Gwenda was wary of evil spirits, like every sensible person; but she was more scared of what she had to do during the service.

She stared into the gloom, trying not to think about what frightened her. She knew that the wall opposite her had an arched window. There was no glass – only the most important buildings had glass windows – but a linen blind kept out the cold autumn air. However, she could not see even a faint patch of grey where the window should be. She was glad. She did not want the morning to come.

She could see nothing, but there was plenty to listen to. The

3

straw that covered the floor whispered constantly as people stirred and shifted in their sleep. A child cried out, as if woken by a dream, and was quickly silenced by a murmured endearment. Now and again someone spoke, uttering the half-formed words of sleep talk. Somewhere there was the sound of two people doing the thing parents did but never spoke of, the thing Gwenda called Grunting because she had no other word for it.

Too soon, there was a light. At the eastern end of the long room, behind the altar, a monk came through the door carrying a single candle. He put the candle down on the altar, lit a taper from it, and went around touching the flame to the wall lamps, his long shadow reaching up the wall each time like a reflection, his taper meeting the shadow taper at the wick of the lamp.

The strengthening light illuminated rows of humped figures on the floor, wrapped in their drab cloaks or huddled up to their neighbours for warmth. Sick people occupied the cots near the altar, where they could get the maximum benefit from the holiness of the place. At the opposite end, a staircase led to the upper floor where there were rooms for aristocratic visitors: the earl of Shiring was there now with some of his family.

The monk leaned over Gwenda to light the lamp above her head. He caught her eye and smiled. She studied his face in the shifting light of the flame and recognized him as Brother Godwyn. He was young and handsome, and last night he had spoken kindly to Philemon.

Beside Gwenda was another family from her village: Samuel, a prosperous peasant with a large landholding, and his wife and two sons, the younger of whom, Wulfric, was an annoying six-year-old who thought that throwing acorns at girls then running away was the funniest thing in the world.

Gwenda's family was not prosperous. Her father had no land at all, and hired himself out as a labourer to anyone who would pay him. There was always work in the summer but, after the harvest was gathered in and the weather began to turn cold, the family often went hungry.

That was why Gwenda had to steal.

She imagined being caught: a strong hand grabbing her arm,

holding her in an unbreakable grip while she wriggled helplessly; a deep, cruel voice saying, 'Well, well, a little thief'; the pain and humiliation of a whipping; and then, worst of all, the agony and loss as her hand was chopped off.

Her father had suffered this punishment. At the end of his left arm was a hideous wrinkled stump. He managed well with one hand – he could use a shovel, saddle a horse and even make a net to catch birds – but all the same he was always the last labourer to be hired in the spring, and the first to be laid off in the autumn. He could never leave the village and seek work elsewhere, because the amputation marked him as a thief, so that people would refuse to hire him. When travelling, he tied a stuffed glove to the stump, to avoid being shunned by every stranger he met; but that did not fool people for long.

Gwenda had not witnessed Pa's punishment – it had happened before she was born – but she had often imagined it, and now she could not help thinking about the same thing happening to her. In her mind she saw the blade of the axe coming down on her wrist, slicing through her skin and her bones, and severing her hand from her arm, so that it could never be reattached; and she had to clamp her teeth together to keep from screaming out loud.

People were standing up, stretching and yawning and rubbing their faces. Gwenda got up and shook out her clothes. All her garments had previously belonged to her older brother. She wore a woollen shift that came down to her knees and a tunic over it, gathered at the waist with a belt made of hemp cord. Her shoes had once been laced, but the eyelets were torn and the laces gone, and she tied them to her feet with plaited straw. When she had tucked her hair into a cap made of squirrel tails, she had finished dressing.

She caught her father's eye, and he pointed surreptitiously to a family across the way, a couple in middle age with two sons a little older than Gwenda. The man was short and slight, with a curly red beard. He was buckling on a sword, which meant he was a man-at-arms or a knight: ordinary people were not allowed to wear swords. His wife was a thin woman with a brisk manner and a grumpy face. As Gwenda scrutinized them, Brother Godwyn nodded respectfully and said: 'Good morning, Sir Gerald, Lady Maud.'

Gwenda saw what had attracted her father's notice. Sir Gerald had a purse attached to his belt by a leather thong. The purse bulged. It looked as if it contained several hundred of the small, thin silver pennies, halfpennies and farthings that were the English currency – as much money as Pa could earn in a year if he had been able to find employment. It would be more than enough to feed the family until the spring ploughing. The purse might even contain a few foreign gold coins, florins from Florence or ducats from Venice.

Gwenda had a small knife in a wooden sheath hanging from a cord around her neck. The sharp blade would quickly cut the thong and cause the fat purse to fall into her small hand – unless Sir Gerald felt something strange and grabbed her before she could do the deed . . .

Godwyn raised his voice over the rumble of talk. 'For the love of Christ, who teaches us charity, breakfast will be provided after the All Hallows service,' he said. 'Meanwhile, there is pure drinking water in the courtyard fountain. Please remember to use the latrines outside – no pissing indoors!'

The monks and nuns were strict about cleanliness. Last night, Godwyn had caught a six-year-old boy peeing in a corner, and had expelled the whole family. Unless they had a penny for a tavern, they would have had to spend the cold October night shivering on the stone floor of the cathedral's north porch. There was also a ban on animals. Gwenda's three-legged dog, Hop, had been banished. She wondered where he had spent the night.

When all the lamps were lit, Godwyn opened the big wooden door to the outside. The night air bit sharply at Gwenda's ears and the tip of her nose. The overnight guests pulled their coats around them and began to shuffle out. When Sir Gerald and his family moved off, Pa and Ma fell into line behind them, and Gwenda and Philemon followed suit.

Philemon had done the stealing until now, but yesterday he had almost been caught, at Kingsbridge Market. He had palmed a small jar of expensive oil from the booth of an Italian merchant, then he had dropped the jar, so that everyone saw it. Mercifully, it had not broken when it hit the ground. He had been forced to pretend that he had accidentally knocked it off the stall.

Until recently Philemon had been small and unobtrusive, like Gwenda, but in the last year he had grown several inches, developed a deep voice, and become awkward and clumsy, as if he could not get used to his new, larger body. Last night, after the incident with the jar of oil, Pa had announced that Philemon was now too big for serious thieving, and henceforth it was Gwenda's job.

That was why she had lain awake for so much of the night.

Philemon's name was really Holger. When he was ten years old, he had decided he was going to be a monk, so he told everyone he had changed his name to Philemon, which sounded more religious. Surprisingly, most people had gone along with his wish, though Ma and Pa still called him Holger.

They passed through the door and saw two lines of shivering nuns holding burning torches to light the pathway from the hospital to the great west door of Kingsbridge Cathedral. Shadows flickered at the edges of the torchlight, as if the imps and hobgoblins of the night were cavorting just out of sight, kept at a distance only by the sanctity of the nuns.

Gwenda half expected to see Hop waiting outside, but he was not there. Perhaps he had found somewhere warm to sleep. As they walked to the church, Pa made sure they stayed close to Sir Gerald. From behind, someone tugged painfully at Gwenda's hair. She squealed, thinking it was a goblin; but when she turned she saw Wulfric, her six-year-old neighbour. He darted out of her reach, laughing. Then his father growled 'Behave!' and smacked his head, and the little boy began to cry.

The vast church was a shapeless mass towering above the huddled crowd. Only the lowest parts were distinct, arches and mullions picked out in orange and red by the uncertain torchlight. The procession slowed as it approached the cathedral entrance, and Gwenda could see a group of townspeople coming from the opposite direction. There were hundreds of them,

Gwenda thought, maybe thousands, although she was not sure how many people made a thousand, for she could not count that high.

The crowd inched through the vestibule. The restless light of the torches fell on the sculpted figures around the walls, making them dance madly. At the lowest level were demons and monsters. Gwenda stared uneasily at dragons and griffins, a bear with a man's head, a dog with two bodies and one muzzle. Some of the demons struggled with humans: a devil put a noose around a man's neck, a fox-like monster dragged a woman by her hair, an eagle with hands speared a naked man. Above these scenes the saints stood in a row under sheltering canopies; over them the apostles sat on thrones; then, in the arch over the main door, St Peter with his key and St Paul with a scroll looked adoringly upwards at Jesus Christ.

Gwenda knew that Jesus was telling her not to sin, or she would be tortured by demons; but humans frightened her more than demons. If she failed to steal Sir Gerald's purse, she would be whipped by her father. Worse, there would be nothing for the family to eat but soup made with acorns. She and Philemon would be hungry for weeks on end. Ma's breasts would dry up, and the new baby would die, as the last two had. Pa would disappear for days, and come back with nothing for the pot but a scrawny heron or a couple of squirrels. Being hungry was worse than being whipped – it hurt longer.

She had been taught to pilfer at a young age: an apple from a stall, a new-laid egg from under a neighbour's hen, a knife dropped carelessly on a tavern table by a drunk. But stealing money was different. If she were caught robbing Sir Gerald it would be no use bursting into tears and hoping to be treated as a naughty child, as she had once after thieving a pair of dainty leather shoes from a soft-hearted nun. Cutting the strings of a knight's purse was no childish peccadillo, it was a real grown-up crime, and she would be treated accordingly.

She tried not to think about it. She was small and nimble and quick, and she would take the purse stealthily, like a ghost – provided she could keep from trembling.

The wide church was already thronged with people. In the

side aisles, hooded monks held torches that cast a restless red glow. The marching pillars of the nave reached up into darkness. Gwenda stayed close to Sir Gerald as the crowd pushed forward towards the altar. The red-bearded knight and his thin wife did not notice her. Their two boys paid no more attention to her than to the stone walls of the cathedral. Gwenda's family fell back and she lost sight of them.

The nave filled up quickly. Gwenda had never seen so many people in one place: it was busier than the cathedral green on market day. People greeted one another cheerfully, feeling safe from evil spirits in this holy place, and the sound of all their conversations mounted to a roar.

Then the bell tolled, and they fell silent.

Sir Gerald was standing by a family from the town. They all wore cloaks of fine cloth, so they were probably rich wool dealers. Next to the knight stood a girl about ten years old. Gwenda stood behind Sir Gerald and the girl. She tried to make herself inconspicuous but, to her dismay, the girl looked at her and smiled reassuringly, as if to tell her not to be frightened.

Around the edges of the crowd the monks extinguished their torches, one by one, until the great church was in utter darkness.

Gwenda wondered if the rich girl would remember her later. She had not merely glanced at Gwenda then ignored her, as most people did. She had noticed her, had thought about her, had anticipated that she might be scared, and had given her a friendly smile. But there were hundreds of children in the cathedral. She could not have got a very clear impression of Gwenda's features in the dim light ... could she? Gwenda tried to put the worry out of her mind.

Invisible in the darkness, she stepped forward and slipped noiselessly between the two figures, feeling the soft wool of the girl's cloak on one side and the stiffer fabric of the knight's old surcoat on the other. Now she was in a position to get at the purse.

She reached into her neckline and took the little knife from its sheath.

The silence was broken by a terrible scream. Gwenda had been expecting it – Ma had explained what was going to happen during the service – but, all the same, she was shocked. It sounded like someone being tortured.

Then there was a harsh drumming sound, as of someone beating on a metal plate. More noises followed: wailing, mad laughter, a hunting horn, a rattle, animal noises, a cracked bell. In the congregation, a child started to cry, and others joined in. Some of the adults laughed nervously. They knew the noises were made by the monks, but all the same it was a hellish cacophony.

This was not the moment to take the purse, Gwenda thought fearfully. Everyone was tense, alert. The knight would be sensitive to any touch.

The devilish noise grew louder, then a new sound intervened: music. At first it was so soft that Gwenda was not sure she had really heard it, then gradually it grew louder. The nuns were singing. Gwenda felt her body flood with tension. The moment was approaching. Moving like a spirit, imperceptible as the air, she turned so that she was facing Sir Gerald.

She knew exactly what he was wearing. He had on a heavy wool robe gathered at the waist by a broad studded belt. His purse was tied to the belt with a leather thong. Over the robe he wore an embroidered surcoat, costly but worn, with yellowing bone buttons down the front. He had done up some of the buttons, but not all, probably out of sleepy laziness, or because the walk from the hospital to the church was so short.

With a touch as light as possible, Gwenda put one small hand on his coat. She imagined her hand was a spider, so weightless that he could not possibly feel it. She ran her spider hand across the front of his coat and found the opening. She slipped her hand under the edge of the coat and along his heavy belt until she came to the purse.

The pandemonium faded as the music grew louder. From the front of the congregation came a murmur of awe. Gwenda could see nothing, but she knew that a lamp had been lit on the altar, illuminating a reliquary, an elaborately carved ivory-and-gold box holding the bones of St Adolphus, that had not been there when the lights went out. The crowd surged forward, everyone trying to get closer to the holy remains. As Gwenda felt herself squashed between Sir Gerald and the man in front of him, she brought up her right hand and put the edge of the knife to the thong of his purse.

The leather was tough, and her first stroke did not cut it. She sawed frantically with the knife, hoping desperately that Sir Gerald was too interested in the scene at the altar to notice what was happening under his nose. She glanced upwards and realized she could just about see the outlines of people around her: the monks and nuns were lighting candles. The light would get brighter every moment. She had no time left.

She gave a fierce yank on the knife, and felt the thong give. Sir Gerald grunted quietly: had he felt something, or was he reacting to the spectacle at the altar? The purse dropped, and landed in her hand; but it was too big for her to grasp easily, and it slipped. For a terrifying moment she thought she was going to drop it and lose it on the floor among the heedless feet of the crowd; then she got a grip on it and held it.

She felt a moment of joyous relief: she had the purse.

But she was still in terrible danger. Her heart was beating so loudly she felt as if everyone must be able to hear it. She turned quickly so that her back was to the knight. In the same movement, she stuffed the heavy purse down the front of her tunic. She could feel that it made a bulge that would be conspicuous, hanging over her belt like an old man's belly. She shifted it around to her side, where it was partly covered by her arm. It would still be visible when the lights brightened, but she had nowhere else to put it.

She sheathed the knife. Now she had to get away quickly, before Sir Gerald noticed his loss – but the crush of worshippers, which had helped her take the purse unnoticed, now hindered her escape. She tried to step backwards, hoping to force a gap in the bodies behind her, but everyone was still pressing forward to look at the bones of the saint. She was trapped, unable to move, right in front of the man she had robbed.

A voice in her ear said: 'Are you all right?'

It was the rich girl. Gwenda fought down panic. She needed to be invisible. A helpful older child was the last thing she wanted. She said nothing.

'Be careful,' the girl said to the people around. 'You're squashing this little girl.'

Gwenda could have screamed. The rich girl's thoughtfulness would get Gwenda's hand chopped off.

Desperate to get away, she put her hands on the man in front and shoved, pushing herself backwards. She succeeded only in getting the attention of Sir Gerald. 'You can't see anything down there, can you?' said her victim in a kindly voice; and, to her horror, he grasped her under the arms and lifted her up.

She was helpless. His big hand in her armpit was only an inch from the purse. She faced forward, so that he could see only the back of her head, and looked over the crowd to the altar, where the monks and nuns were lighting more candles and singing to the long-dead saint. Beyond them, a faint light showed through the big rose window at the east end of the building: dawn was breaking, chasing the evil spirits away. The clangour had stopped, now, and the singing swelled. A tall, good-looking monk stepped up to the altar, and Gwenda recognized him as Anthony, the prior of Kingsbridge. Raising his hands in a blessing, he said loudly: 'And so, once again, by the grace of Christ Jesus, the evil and darkness of this world are banished by the harmony and light of God's holy church.'

The congregation gave a triumphant roar, then began to relax. The climax of the ceremony had passed. Gwenda wriggled, and Sir Gerald got the message and put her down. Keeping her face turned away from him, she pushed past him, heading towards the back of the crowd. People were no longer so eager to see the altar, and she was now able to force her way between the bodies. The farther back she went, the easier it became, until at last she found herself by the great west door, and saw her family.

Pa looked expectantly at her, ready to be angry if she had failed. She pulled the purse out of her shirt and thrust it at him, glad to get rid of it. He grabbed it, turned slightly, and furtively looked inside. She saw him grin with delight. Then he passed the purse to Ma, who quickly shoved it into the folds of the blanket that wrapped the baby.

The ordeal was over, but the risk had not yet passed. 'A rich girl noticed me,' Gwenda said, and she could hear the shrill fear in her own voice.

Pa's small, dark eyes flashed anger. 'Did she see what you did?'

'No, but she told the others not to squash me, then the knight picked me up so I could see better.'

Ma gave a low groan.

Pa said: 'He saw your face, then.'

'I tried to keep it turned away.'

'Still, better if he doesn't come across you again,' Pa said. 'We won't return to the monks' hospital. We'll go to a tavern for our breakfast.'

Ma said: 'We can't hide away all day.'

'No, but we can melt into the crowd.'

Gwenda started to feel better. Pa seemed to think there was no real danger. Anyway, she was reassured just by his being in charge again, and taking the responsibility from her.

'Besides,' he went on, 'I fancy bread and meat, instead of the monks' watery porridge. I can afford it now!'

They went out of the church. The sky was pearly grey with dawn light. Gwenda wanted to hold Ma's hand, but the baby started to cry, and Ma was distracted. Then she saw a small three-legged dog, white with a black face, come running into the cathedral close with a familiar lopsided stride. 'Hop!' she cried, and picked him up and hugged him.

2

MERTHIN WAS ELEVEN, a year older than his brother Ralph; but, to his intense annoyance, Ralph was taller and stronger.

This caused trouble with the parents. Their father, Sir Gerald, was a soldier, and could not conceal his disappointment when Merthin proved unable to lift the heavy lance, or became exhausted before the tree was chopped down, or came home crying after losing a fight. Their mother, Lady Maud, made matters worse, embarrassing Merthin by being over-protective, when what he needed her to do was pretend not to notice. When Father showed his pride in Ralph's strength, Mother tried to compensate by criticizing Ralph's stupidity. Ralph was a bit slow on the uptake, but he could not help it, and being nagged about it only made him angry, so that he got into fights with other boys.

Both parents were tetchy on the morning of All Hallows' Day. Father had not wanted to come to Kingsbridge at all. But he had been compelled. He owed money to the priory, and he could not pay. Mother said they would take away his lands: he was lord of three villages near Kingsbridge. Father reminded her that he was directly descended from the Thomas who became earl of Shiring in the year that Archbishop Becket was murdered by King Henry II. That Earl Thomas had been the son of Jack Builder, the architect of Kingsbridge Cathedral, and Lady Aliena of Shiring – a near-legendary couple whose story was told, on long winter evenings, along with the heroic tales of Charlemagne and Roland. With such ancestry, Sir Gerald could not have his land confiscated by any monk, he bellowed, least of all that old woman Prior Anthony. When he started shouting, a look of tired resignation came over Maud's face, and she turned away – though Merthin had heard her mutter: 'The Lady Aliena had a brother, Richard, who was no good for anything but fighting.'

Prior Anthony might be an old woman, but he had at least been man enough to complain about Sir Gerald's unpaid debts. He had gone to Gerald's overlord, the present earl of Shiring, who happened also to be Gerald's second cousin. Earl Roland had summoned Gerald to Kingsbridge today to meet with the prior and work out some resolution. Hence Father's bad temper.

Then Father was robbed.

He discovered the loss after the All Hallows service. Merthin had enjoyed the drama: the darkness, the weird noises, the music beginning so quietly and then swelling until it seemed to fill the huge church, and finally the slow illumination of candles. He had also noticed, as the lights began to come on, that some people had been taking advantage of the darkness to commit minor sins for which they could now be forgiven: he had seen two monks hastily stop kissing, and a sly merchant remove his hand from the plump breast of a smiling woman who appeared to be someone else's wife. Merthin was still in an excited mood when they returned to the hospital.

As they were waiting for the nuns to serve breakfast, a kitchen boy passed through the room and went up the stairs carrying a tray with a big jug of ale and a platter of hot salt beef. Mother said grumpily: 'I would think your relative, the earl, might invite us to breakfast with him in his private room. After all, your grandmother was sister to his grandfather.'

Father replied: 'If you don't want porridge, we can go to the tavern.'

Merthin's ears pricked up. He liked tavern breakfasts of new bread and salt butter. But Mother said: 'We can't afford it.'

'We can,' Father said, feeling for his purse; and that was when he realized it was gone.

At first he looked around the floor, as if it might have fallen; then he noticed the cut ends of the leather thong, and he roared with indignation. Everyone looked at him except Mother, who turned away, and Merthin heard her mutter: 'That was all the money we had.'

Father glared accusingly at the other guests in the hospital. The long scar that ran from his right temple to his left eye seemed to darken with rage. The room went quiet with tension:

an angry knight was dangerous, even one who was evidently down on his luck.

Then Mother said: 'You were robbed in the church, no doubt.'

Merthin guessed that must be right. In the darkness, people had been stealing more than kisses.

'Sacrilege, too!' said Father.

'I expect it happened when you picked up that little girl,' Mother went on. Her face was twisted, as if she had swallowed something bitter. 'The thief probably reached around your waist from behind.'

'He must be found!' Father roared.

The young monk called Godwyn spoke up. 'I'm very sorry this has happened, Sir Gerald,' he said. 'I will go and tell John Constable right away. He can look out for a poor townsman who has suddenly become rich.'

That seemed to Merthin a very unpromising plan. There were thousands of townspeople and hundreds more visitors. The constable could not observe them all.

But Father was slightly mollified. 'The rogue shall hang!' he said in a voice a little less loud.

'And, meanwhile, perhaps you and Lady Maud, and your sons, would do us the honour of sitting at the table that is being set up in front of the altar,' Godwyn said smoothly.

Father grunted. He was pleased, Merthin knew, to be accorded higher status than the mass of guests, who would eat sitting on the floor where they had slept.

The moment of potential violence passed, and Merthin relaxed a little; but, as the four of them took their seats, he wondered anxiously what would happen to the family now. His father was a brave soldier – everyone said that. Sir Gerald had fought for the old king at Boroughbridge, where a Lancashire rebel's sword had given him the scar on his forehead. But he was unlucky. Some knights came home from battle with booty: plundered jewels, a cartload of costly Flemish cloth and Italian silk, or the beloved father of a noble family who could be ransomed for a thousand pounds. Sir Gerald never seemed to get much loot. But he still had to buy weapons, armour, and an expensive warhorse to enable him to do his duty and serve the king; and somehow the rents from his lands were never enough. So, against Mother's will, he had started to borrow.

The kitchen hands brought in a steaming cauldron. Sir Gerald's family were served first. The porridge was made with barley and flavoured with rosemary and salt. Ralph, who did not understand the family crisis, started to talk excitedly about the All Hallows service, but the glum silence in which his comments were received shut him up.

When the porridge was eaten, Merthin went to the altar. Behind it he had stashed his bow and arrows. People would hesitate to steal something from an altar. They might overcome their fears, if the reward were tempting enough, but a homemade bow was not much of a prize; and, sure enough, it was still there.

He was proud of it. It was small, of course: to bend a full-size, six-foot bow took all the strength of a grown man. Merthin's was four foot long, and slender, but in other respects it was just like the standard English longbow that had killed so many Scots mountain men, Welsh rebels, and French knights in armour.

Father had not previously commented on the bow, and now he looked at it as if seeing it for the first time. 'Where did you get the stave?' he said. 'They're costly.'

'Not this one – it's too short. A bowyer gave it me.'

Father nodded. 'Apart from that it's a perfect stave,' he said. 'It's taken from the inside of the yew, where the sapwood meets the heartwood.' He pointed to the two different colours.

'I know,' Merthin said eagerly. He did not often get the chance to impress his father. 'The stretchy sapwood is best for the front of the bow, because it pulls back to its original shape; and the hard heartwood is best for the inside of the curve, because it pushes back when the bow is bent inwards.'

'Exactly,' Father said. He handed the bow back. 'But remember, this is not a nobleman's weapon. Knights' sons do not become archers. Give it to some peasant boy.'

Merthin was crestfallen. 'I haven't even tried it yet!'

Mother intervened. 'Let them play,' she said. 'They're only boys.'

'True,' Father said, losing interest. 'I wonder if those monks would bring us a jug of ale?'

'Off you go,' Mother said. 'Merthin, take care of your brother.'
Father grunted. 'More likely to be the other way around.'

Merthin was stung. Father had no idea what went on.
Merthin could look after himself, but Ralph on his own would
get into fights. However, Merthin knew better than to take issue
with his father in this mood, and he left the hospital without
saying anything. Ralph trailed behind him.

It was a clear, cold November day, and the sky was roofed
with high pale-grey cloud. They left the cathedral close and
walked down the main street, passing Cookshop Street, Leather
Yard and Fish Lane. At the bottom of the hill they crossed the
wooden bridge over the river, leaving the old city for the suburb
called Newtown. Here the streets of timber houses ran between
pastures and gardens. Merthin led the way to a meadow called
Lovers' Field. There, the town constable and his deputies had set
up butts – targets for archery. Shooting practice after church was
compulsory for all men, by order of the king.

Enforcement was not much needed: it was no hardship to
loose off a few arrows on a Sunday morning, and a hundred or so
of the young men of the town were lining up for their turn,
watched by women, children, and men who considered
themselves too old, or too dignified, to be archers. Some had their
own weapons. For those too poor to afford a bow, John Constable
had inexpensive practice bows made of ash or hazel.

It was like a feast day. Dick Brewer was selling tankards of
ale from a barrel on a cart, and Betty Baxter's four adolescent
daughters were walking around with trays of spiced buns for sale.
The wealthier townspeople were done up in fur caps and new
shoes, and even the poorer women had dressed their hair and
trimmed their cloaks with new braid.

Merthin was the only child carrying a bow, and he
immediately attracted the attention of other children. They
crowded around him and Ralph, the boys asking envious
questions, the girls looking admiring or disdainful according to
temperament. One of the girls said: 'How did you know how
to make it?'

Merthin recognized her: she had stood near him in the
cathedral. She was about a year younger than himself, he thought,

and she wore a dress and cloak of expensive, close-woven wool. Merthin usually found girls of his own age tiresome: they giggled a lot and refused to take anything seriously. But this one looked at him and his bow with a frank curiosity that he liked. 'I just guessed,' he said.

'That's clever. Does it work?'

'I haven't tried it. What's your name?'

'Caris, from the Wooler family. Who are you?'

'Merthin. My father is Sir Gerald.' Merthin pushed back the hood of his cape, reached inside it and took out a coiled bowstring.

'Why do you keep the string in your hat?'

'So it won't get wet if there's rain. It's what the real archers do.' He attached the twine to the notches at either end of the stave, bending the bow slightly so that the tension would hold the string in place.

'Are you going to shoot at the targets?'

'Yes.'

Another boy said: 'They won't let you.'

Merthin looked at him. He was about twelve, tall and thin with big hands and feet. Merthin had seen him last night in the priory hospital with his family: his name was Philemon. He had been hanging around the monks, asking questions and helping to serve supper. 'Of course they'll let me,' Merthin told him. 'Why shouldn't they?'

'Because you're too young.'

'That's stupid.' Even as he spoke, Merthin knew he should not be so sure: adults often were stupid. But Philemon's assumption of superior knowledge irritated him, especially after he had shown confidence in front of Caris.

He left the children and walked over to a group of men waiting to use a target. He recognized one of them: an exceptionally tall, broad-shouldered man called Mark Webber. Mark noticed the bow and spoke to Merthin in a slow, amiable voice. 'Where did you get that?'

'I made it,' Merthin said proudly.

'Look at this, Elfric,' Mark said to his neighbour. 'He's made a nice job of it.'

Elfric was a brawny man with a sly look. He gave the bow a cursory glance. 'It's too small,' he said dismissively. 'That'll never fire an arrow to penetrate a French knight's armour.'

'Perhaps not,' Mark said mildly. 'But I expect the lad's got a year or two to go before he has to fight the French.'

John Constable called out: 'We're ready, let's get started. Mark Webber, you're first.' The giant stepped up to the line. He picked up a stout bow and tested it, bending the thick wood effortlessly.

The constable noticed Merthin for the first time. 'No boys,' he said.

'Why not?' Merthin protested.

'Never mind why not, just get out of the way.'

Merthin heard some of the other children snigger. 'There's no reason for it!' he said indignantly.

'I don't have to give reasons to children,' John said. 'All right, Mark, take your shot.'

Merthin was mortified. The oily Philemon had proved him wrong in front of everyone. He turned away from the targets.

'I told you so,' said Philemon.

'Oh, shut up and go away.'

'You can't make me go away,' said Philemon, who was six inches taller than Merthin.

Ralph put in: 'I could, though.'

Merthin sighed. Ralph was unfailingly loyal, but he did not see that for him to fight Philemon would only make Merthin look like a weakling as well as a fool.

'I'm leaving anyway,' said Philemon. 'I'm going to help Brother Godwyn.' He walked off.

The rest of the children began to drift away, seeking other curiosities. Caris said to Merthin: 'You could go somewhere else to try the bow.' She was obviously keen to see what would happen.

Merthin looked around. 'But where?' If he was seen shooting unsupervised, the bow might be taken from him.

'We could go into the forest.'

Merthin was surprised. Children were forbidden to go into the forest. Outlaws hid there, men and women who lived by stealing. Children might be stripped of their clothes, or made into slaves, and there were worse dangers that parents only hinted at. Even if they escaped such perils, the children were liable to be flogged by their fathers for breaking the rule.

But Caris did not seem to be afraid, and Merthin was reluctant to appear less bold than she. Besides, the constable's curt dismissal had made him feel defiant. 'All right,' he said. 'But we'll have to make sure no one sees us.'

She had the answer to that. 'I know a way.'

She walked towards the river. Merthin and Ralph followed. A small three-legged dog tagged along. 'What's your dog's name?' Merthin asked Caris.

'He's not mine,' she said. 'But I gave him a piece of mouldy bacon, and now I can't shake him off.'

They walked along the muddy bank of the river, past warehouses and wharves and barges. Merthin covertly studied this girl who had so effortlessly become the leader. She had a square, determined face, neither pretty nor ugly, and there was mischief in her eyes, which were a greenish colour with brown flecks. Her light-brown hair was done in two plaits, as was the fashion among affluent women. Her clothes were costly, but she wore practical leather boots rather than the embroidered fabric shoes preferred by noble ladies.

She turned away from the river and led them through a timber yard, and suddenly they were in scrubby woodland. Merthin felt a pang of unease. Now that he was in the forest, where there might be an outlaw lurking behind any oak tree, he regretted his bravado; but he would be ashamed to back out.

They walked on, looking for a clearing big enough for archery. Suddenly Caris spoke in a conspiratorial voice. 'You see that big holly bush?'

'Yes.'

'As soon as we're past it, crouch down with me and keep silent.'

'Why?'

'You'll see.'

A moment later Merthin, Ralph and Caris squatted behind

the bush. The three-legged dog sat with them and looked hopefully at Caris. Ralph began to ask a question, but Caris hushed him.

A minute later a little girl came by. Caris jumped out and grabbed her. The girl screamed.

'Be quiet!' Caris said. 'We're not far from the road, and we don't want to be heard. Why are you following us?'

'You've got my dog, and he won't come back!' the child sobbed.

'I know you, I met you in church this morning,' Caris said to her in a softer voice. 'All right, there's nothing to cry about, we aren't going to do you any harm. What's your name?'

'Gwenda.'

'And the dog?'

'Hop.' Gwenda picked up the dog, and he licked her tears.

'Well, you've got him now. You'd better come with us, in case he runs off again. Besides, you might not be able to find your way back to town on your own.'

They went on. Merthin said: 'What has eight arms and eleven legs?'

'I give up,' Ralph said immediately. He always did.

'I know,' said Caris with a grin. 'It's us. Four children and the dog.' She laughed. 'That's good.'

Merthin was pleased. People did not always get his jokes; girls almost never did. A moment later he heard Gwenda explaining it to Ralph: 'Two arms, and two arms, and two arms, and two arms makes eight,' she said. 'Two legs...'

They saw no one, which was good. The small number of people who had legitimate business in the forest – woodcutters, charcoal burners, iron smelters – would not be working today, and it would be unusual to see an aristocratic hunting party on a Sunday. Anyone they met was likely to be an outlaw. But the chances were slim. It was a big forest, stretching for many miles. Merthin had never travelled far enough to see the end of it.

They came to a wide clearing and Merthin said: 'This will do.'

There was an oak tree with a broad trunk on the far edge, about fifty feet away. Merthin stood side-on to the target, as he had seen the men do. He took out one of his three arrows and fitted the notched end to the bowstring. The arrows had been as difficult to make as the bow. The wood was ash, and they had goose-feather flights. He had not been able to get iron for the points, so he had simply sharpened the ends then scorched the wood to harden it. He sighted on the tree, then pulled back on the bowstring. It took a great effort. He released the arrow.

It fell to the ground well short of the target. Hop the dog scampered across the clearing to fetch it.

Merthin was taken aback. He had expected the arrow to go winging through the air and embed its point in the tree. He realized that he had not bent the bow sufficiently.

He tried the bow in his right hand and the arrow in his left. He was unusual in this respect, that he was neither right-handed nor left-handed, but a mixture. With the second arrow, he pulled on the bowstring and pushed the bow with all his might, and succeeded in bending them farther than before. This time, the arrow almost reached the tree.

For his third shot he aimed the bow upwards, hoping the arrow would fly through the air in an arc and come down into the trunk. But he overcompensated, and the arrow went into the branches, and fell to the ground amid a flurry of dry brown leaves.

Merthin was embarrassed. Archery was more difficult than he had imagined. The bow was probably all right, he guessed: the problem was his own proficiency, or lack of it.

Once again, Caris seemed not to notice his discomfiture. 'Let me have a go,' she said.

'Girls can't shoot,' Ralph said, and he snatched the bow from Merthin. Standing sideways-on to the target, as Merthin had, he did not shoot straight away, but flexed the bow several times, getting the feel of it. Like Merthin, he found it harder than he had at first expected, but after a few moments he seemed to get the hang of it.

Hop had dropped all three arrows at Gwenda's feet, and now the little girl picked them up and handed them to Ralph.

He took aim without drawing the bow, sighting the arrow at the tree trunk, while there was no pressure on his arms. Merthin realized he should have done the same. Why did these things come so naturally to Ralph, who could never answer a riddle? Ralph drew the bow, not effortlessly but with a fluid motion, seeming to take the strain with his thighs. He released the arrow and it hit the trunk of the oak tree, sinking an inch or more into the soft outer wood. Ralph laughed triumphantly.

Hop scampered after the arrow. When he reached the tree he stopped, baffled.

Ralph was drawing the bow again. Merthin realized what he was intending to do. 'Don't—' he said, but he was a moment too late. Ralph shot at the dog. The arrow hit the back of its neck and sunk in. Hop fell forward and lay twitching.

Gwenda screamed. Caris said: 'Oh, no!' The two girls ran to the dog.

Ralph was grinning. 'What about that?' he said proudly.

'You shot her dog!' Merthin said angrily.

'Doesn't matter – it only had three legs.'

'The little girl was fond of it, you idiot. Look at her crying.'

'You're just jealous because you can't shoot.' Something caught Ralph's eye. With a smooth movement he notched another arrow, swept the bow round in an arc and fired while it was still moving. Merthin did not see what he was shooting at until the arrow met its target, and a fat hare jumped into the air with the shaft sticking deep into its hindquarters.

Merthin could not hide his admiration. Even with practice, not everyone could hit a running hare. Ralph had a natural gift. Merthin *was* jealous, although he would never admit it. He longed to be a knight, bold and strong, and fight for the king as his father did; and it dismayed him when he turned out to be hopeless at things such as archery.

Ralph found a stone and crushed the hare's skull, putting it out of its misery.

Merthin knelt beside the two girls and Hop. The dog was not breathing. Caris gently drew the arrow out of its neck and handed it to Merthin. There was no gush of blood: Hop was dead.

For a moment no one spoke. In the silence, they heard a man shout.

Merthin sprang to his feet, heart thudding. He heard another shout, a different voice: there was more than one person. Both sounded aggressive and angry. Some kind of fight was going on. He was terrified, and so were the others. As they stood frozen, listening, they heard another sound, the noise made by a man running headlong through woodland, snapping fallen branches, flattening saplings, trampling dead leaves.

He was coming their way.

Caris spoke first. 'The bush,' she said, pointing to a big cluster of evergreen shrubs – probably the home of the hare Ralph had shot, Merthin thought. A moment later she was flat on her belly, crawling into the thicket. Gwenda followed, cradling the body of Hop. Ralph picked up the dead hare and joined them. Merthin was on his knees when he realized that they had left a tell-tale arrow sticking out of the tree trunk. He dashed across the clearing, pulled it out, ran back and dived under the bush.

They heard the man breathing before they saw him. He was panting hard as he ran, drawing in ragged lungfuls of air in a way that suggested he was almost done in. The shouts were coming from his pursuers, calling to each other: 'This way – over here!' Merthin recalled that Caris had said they were not far from the road. Was the fleeing man a traveller who had been set upon by thieves?

A moment later he burst into the clearing.

He was a knight in his early twenties, with both a sword and a long dagger attached to his belt. He was well dressed, in a leather travelling tunic and high boots with turned-over tops. He stumbled and fell, rolled over, got up, then stood with his back to the oak tree, gasping for breath, and drew his weapons.

Merthin glanced at his playmates. Caris was white with fear, biting her lip. Gwenda was hugging the corpse of her dog as if that made her feel safer. Ralph looked scared, too, but he was not too frightened to pull the arrow out of the hare's rump and stuff the dead animal down the front of his tunic.

For a moment the knight seemed to stare at the bush, and Merthin felt, with terror, that he must have seen the hiding children. Or perhaps he had noticed broken branches and crushed leaves where they had pushed through the foliage. Out of the corner of his eye, Merthin saw Ralph notch an arrow to the bow.

Then the pursuers arrived. They were two men-at-arms,

strongly built and thuggish-looking, carrying drawn swords. They wore distinctive two-coloured tunics, the left side yellow and the right green. One had a surcoat of cheap brown wool, the other a grubby black cloak. All three men paused, catching their breath. Merthin was sure he was about to see the knight hacked to death, and he suffered a shameful impulse to burst into tears. Then, suddenly, the knight reversed his sword and offered it, hilt first, in a gesture of surrender.

The older man-at-arms, in the black cloak, stepped forward and reached out with his left hand. Warily, he took the proffered sword, handed it to his partner, then accepted the knight's dagger. Then he said: 'It's not your weapons I want, Thomas Langley.'

'You know me, but I don't know you,' said Thomas. If he was feeling any fear, he had it well under control. 'By your coats, you must be the queen's men.'

The older man put the point of his sword to Thomas's throat and pushed him up against the tree. 'You've got a letter.'

'Instructions from the earl to the sheriff on the subject of taxes. You're welcome to read it.' This was a joke. The men-at-arms were almost certainly unable to read. Thomas had a cool nerve, Merthin thought, to mock men who seemed ready to kill him.

The second man-at-arms reached under the sword of the first and grasped the wallet attached to Thomas's belt. Impatiently, he cut the belt with his sword. He threw the belt aside and opened the wallet. He took out a smaller bag made of what appeared to be oiled wool, and drew from that a sheet of parchment, rolled into a scroll and sealed with wax.

Could this fight be about nothing more than a letter? Merthin wondered. If so, what was written on the scroll? It was not likely to be routine instructions about taxes. Some terrible secret must be inscribed there.

'If you kill me,' the knight said, 'the murder will be witnessed by whoever is hiding in that bush.'

The tableau froze for a split second. The man in the black cloak kept his sword point pressed to Thomas's throat and resisted the temptation to look over his shoulder. The one in green hesitated, then looked at the bush.

At that point, Gwenda screamed.

The man in the green surcoat raised his sword and took two long strides across the clearing to the bush. Gwenda stood up and ran, bursting out of the foliage. The man-at-arms leaped after her, reaching out to grab her.

Ralph stood up suddenly, raised the bow and drew it in one fluid motion, and shot an arrow at the man. It went through his eye and sank several inches into his head. His left hand came up, as if to grasp the arrow and pull it out; then he went limp and fell like a dropped sack of grain, hitting the ground with a thump Merthin could feel.

Ralph ran out of the bush and followed Gwenda. At the edge of his vision Merthin perceived Caris going after them. Merthin wanted to flee too, but his feet seemed stuck to the ground.

There was a shout from the other side of the clearing, and Merthin saw that Thomas had knocked aside the sword that threatened him and had drawn, from somewhere about his person, a small knife with a blade as long as a man's hand. But the man-at-arms in the black cloak was alert, and jumped back out of reach. Then he raised his sword and swung at the knight's head.

Thomas dodged aside, but not fast enough. The edge of the blade came down on his left forearm, slicing through the leather jerkin and sinking into his flesh. He roared with pain, but did not fall. With a quick motion that seemed extraordinarily graceful, he swung his right hand up and thrust the knife into his opponent's throat; then, his hand continuing in an arc, he pulled the knife sideways, severing most of the neck.

Blood came like a fountain from the man's throat. Thomas staggered back, dodging the splash. The man in black fell to the ground, his head hanging from his body by a strip.

Thomas dropped the knife from his right hand and clutched his wounded left arm. He sat on the ground, suddenly looking weak.

Merthin was alone with the wounded knight, two dead men-at-arms, and the corpse of a three-legged dog. He knew he should run after the other children, but his curiosity kept him there. Thomas now seemed harmless, he told himself.

The knight had sharp eyes. 'You can come out,' he called. 'I'm no danger to you in this state.'

Hesitantly, Merthin got to his feet and pushed his way out of the bush. He crossed the clearing and stopped several feet away from the sitting knight.

Thomas said: 'If they find out you've been playing in the forest, you'll be flogged.'

Merthin nodded.

'I'll keep your secret, if you'll keep mine.'

Merthin nodded again. In agreeing to the bargain, he was making no concessions. None of the children would tell what they had seen. There would be untold trouble if they did. What would happen to Ralph, who had killed one of the queen's men?

'Would you be kind enough to help me bind up this wound?' said Thomas. Despite all that had happened, he spoke courteously, Merthin observed. The knight's poise was remarkable. Merthin felt he wanted to be like that when he was grown up.

At last Merthin's constricted throat managed to produce a word. 'Yes.'

'Pick up that broken belt, then, and wrap it around my arm, if you would.'

Merthin did as he was told. Thomas's undershirt was soaked with blood, and the flesh of his arm was sliced open like something on a butcher's slab. Merthin felt a little nauseated, but he forced himself to twist the belt around Thomas's arm so that it pulled the wound closed and slowed the bleeding. He made a knot, and Thomas used his right hand to pull it tight.

Then Thomas struggled to his feet.

He looked at the dead men. 'We can't bury them,' he said. 'I'd bleed to death before the graves were dug.' Glancing at Merthin, he added: 'Even with you helping me.' He thought for a moment. 'On the other hand, I don't want them to be discovered by some courting couple looking for a place to ... be alone. Let's lug the guts into that bush where you were hiding. Green coat first.'

They approached the body.

'One leg each,' said Thomas. With his right hand he grasped the dead man's left ankle. Merthin took the other limp foot in both hands and heaved. Together they hauled the corpse into the shrubbery, next to Hop.

'That will do,' said Thomas. His face was white with pain. After a moment, he bent down and pulled the arrow out of the corpse's eye. 'Yours?' he said with a raised eyebrow.

Merthin took the arrow and wiped it on the ground to get rid of some of the blood and brains adhering to the shaft.

In the same way they dragged the second body across the clearing, its loosely attached head trailing behind, and left it beside the first.

Thomas picked up the two men's dropped swords and threw them into the bush with the bodies. Then he found his own weapons.

'Now,' said Thomas, 'I have a great favour to ask.' He proffered his dagger. 'Would you dig me a small hole?'

'All right.' Merthin took the dagger.

'Just here, right in front of the oak tree.'

'How big?'

Thomas picked up the leather wallet that had been attached to his belt. 'Big enough to hide this for fifty years.'

Screwing up his courage, Merthin said: 'Why?'

'Dig, and I'll tell you as much of it as I can.'

Merthin scratched a square on the ground and began to loosen the cold earth with the dagger, then scoop it up with his hands.

Thomas picked up the scroll and put it into the wool bag, then fastened the bag inside the wallet. 'I was given this letter to deliver to the earl of Shiring,' he said. 'But it contains a secret so dangerous that I realized the bearer is sure to be killed, to make certain he can never speak of it. So I needed to disappear. I decided I would take sanctuary in a monastery, become a monk. I've had enough of fighting, and I've a lot of sins to repent. As soon as I went missing, the people who gave me the letter started to search for me – and I was unlucky. I was spotted in a tavern in Bristol.'

'Why did the queen's men come after you?'

'She, too, would like to prevent the spread of this secret.'

When Merthin's hole was eighteen inches deep, Thomas said: 'That will do.' He dropped the wallet inside.

Merthin shovelled the earth back into the hole on top of the wallet, and Thomas covered the freshly turned earth with leaves and twigs until it was indistinguishable from the ground around it.

'If you hear that I've died,' said Thomas, 'I'd like you to dig up this letter and give it to a priest. Would you do that for me?'

'All right.'

'Until that happens, you must tell no one. While they know I've got the letter, but they don't know where it is, they'll be afraid to do anything. But if you tell the secret, two things will happen. First, they will kill me. Then they will kill you.'

Merthin was aghast. It seemed unfair that he should be in so much danger just because he helped a man by digging a hole.

'I'm sorry to scare you,' said Thomas. 'But, then, it's not entirely my fault. After all, I didn't ask you to come here.'

'No.' Merthin wished with all his heart that he had obeyed his mother's orders and stayed out of the forest.

'I'm going to return to the road. Why don't you go back the way you came? I bet you'll find your friends waiting somewhere not far from here.'

Merthin turned to go.

'What's your name?' the knight called after him.

'Merthin, son of Sir Gerald.'

'Really?' Thomas said, as if he knew Father. 'Well, not a word, even to him.'

Merthin nodded and left.

When he had gone fifty yards he vomited. After that he felt slightly better.

As Thomas had predicted, the others were waiting for him, right at the edge of the wood, near the timber yard. They crowded around him, touching him as if to make sure he was all right, looking relieved yet ashamed, as if they were guilty about having left him. They were all shaken, even Ralph. 'That man,' he said. 'The one I shot. Was he badly hurt?'

'He's dead,' Merthin said. He showed Ralph the arrow, still stained with blood.

'Did you pull it out of his eye?'

Merthin would have liked to say he had, but he decided to tell the truth. 'The knight pulled it out.'

'What happened to the other man-at-arms?'

'The knight cut his throat. Then we hid the bodies in the bush.'

'And he just let you go?'

'Yes.' Merthin said nothing about the buried letter.

'We have to keep this secret,' Caris urged. 'There will be terrible trouble if anyone finds out.'

Ralph said: 'I'll never tell.'

'We should swear an oath,' Caris said.

They stood in a little ring. Caris stuck out her arm so that her hand was in the centre of the circle. Merthin placed his hand over hers. Her skin was soft and warm. Ralph added his hand, then Gwenda did the same, and they swore by the blood of Jesus.

Then they walked back into the town.

Archery practice was over, and it was time for the midday meal. As they crossed the bridge, Merthin said to Ralph: 'When I grow up, I want to be like that knight – always courteous, never frightened, deadly in a fight.'

'Me, too,' said Ralph. 'Deadly.'

In the old city, Merthin felt an irrational sense of surprise that normal life was going on all around: the sound of babies crying, the smell of roasting meat, the sight of men drinking ale outside taverns.

Caris stopped outside a big house on the main street, just opposite the entrance to the priory precincts. She put an arm around Gwenda's shoulders and said: 'My dog at home has had puppies. Do you want to see them?'

Gwenda still looked frightened and close to tears, but she nodded emphatically. 'Yes, please.'

That was clever as well as kind, Merthin thought. The puppies would be a comfort to the little girl – and a distraction, too. When she returned to her family, she would talk about the puppies and be less likely to speak of going into the forest.

They said goodbye, and the girls went into the house. Merthin found himself wondering when he would see Caris again.

Then his other troubles came back to him. What was his father going to do about his debts? Merthin and Ralph turned into the cathedral close, Ralph still carrying the bow and the dead hare. The place was quiet.

The guest house was empty but for a few sick people. A nun said to them: 'Your father is in the church, with the earl of Shiring.'

They went into the great cathedral. Their parents were in the vestibule. Mother was sitting at the foot of a pillar, on the outjutting corner where the round column met the square base. In the cold light that came through the tall windows, her face was still and serene, almost as if she were carved of the same grey stone as the pillar against which she leaned her head. Father stood beside her, his broad shoulders slumped in an attitude of resignation. Earl Roland faced them. He was older than Father, but with his black hair and vigorous manner he seemed more youthful. Prior Anthony stood beside the earl.

The two boys hung back at the door, but Mother beckoned them. 'Come here,' she said. 'Earl Roland has helped us come to an arrangement with Prior Anthony that solves all our problems.'

Father grunted, as if he was not as grateful as she for what the earl had done. 'And the priory gets my lands,' he said. 'There'll be nothing for you two to inherit.'

'We're going to live here, in Kingsbridge,' Mother went on brightly. 'We'll be corrodiaries of the priory.'

Merthin said: 'What's a corrodiary?'

'It means the monks will provide us with a house to live in and two meals a day, for the rest of our lives. Isn't that wonderful?'

Merthin could tell that she did not really think it was wonderful. She was pretending to be pleased. Father was clearly ashamed to have lost his lands. There was more than a hint of disgrace in this, Merthin realized.

Father addressed the earl. 'What about my boys?'

Earl Roland turned and looked at them. 'The big one looks promising,' he said. 'Did you kill that hare, lad?'

'Yes, lord,' Ralph said proudly. 'Shot it with an arrow.'

'He can come to me as a squire in a few years' time,' the earl said briskly. 'We'll teach him to be a knight.'

Father looked pleased.

Merthin felt bewildered. Big decisions were being made too quickly. He was outraged that his younger brother should be so favoured while no mention was made of himself. 'That's not fair!' he burst out. 'I want to be a knight, too!'

His mother said: 'No!'

'But I made the bow!'

Father gave a sigh of exasperation and looked disgusted.

'You made the bow, did you, little one?' the earl said, and his face showed disdain. 'In that case, you shall be apprenticed to a carpenter.'

3

CARIS'S HOME WAS A LUXURIOUS wood-frame building with
stone floors and a stone chimney. There were three separate
rooms on the ground floor: the hall with the big dining table,
the small parlour where Papa could discuss business privately,
and the kitchen at the back. When Caris and Gwenda walked
in, the house was full of the mouth-watering smell of a ham
boiling.

Caris led Gwenda through the hall and up the internal
staircase.

'Where are the puppies?' said Gwenda.

'I want to see my mother first,' Caris replied. 'She's ill.'

They went into the front bedroom, where Mama lay on the
carved wooden bedstead. She was small and frail: Caris was
already the same height. Mama looked paler than usual, and her
hair was not yet dressed, so it stuck to her damp cheeks. 'How
are you feeling?' Caris said.

'A little weak, today.' The effort of speaking made Mama
breathless.

Caris felt a familiar, painful jumble of anxiety and
helplessness. Her mother had been ill for a year. It had started
with pains in her joints. Soon she had ulcers inside her mouth
and unaccountable bruises on her body. She had felt too weak to
do anything. Last week she had caught a cold. Now she was
running a fever, and had trouble in catching her breath.

'Is there anything you need?' Caris asked.

'No, thank you.'

It was the usual answer, but Caris felt maddened by
powerlessness each time she heard it. 'Should I fetch Mother
Cecilia?' The prioress of Kingsbridge was the only person able to
bring Mama some comfort. She had an extract of poppies that she

mixed with honey and warm wine that eased the pain for a while. Caris regarded Cecilia as better than an angel.

'No need, dear,' Mama said. 'How was the All Hallows service?'

Caris noticed how pale her mother's lips were. 'Scary,' she said.

Mama paused, resting, then said: 'What have you been doing this morning?'

'Watching the archery.' Caris held her breath, frightened that Mama might guess her guilty secret, as she often did.

But Mama looked at Gwenda. 'Who is your little friend?'

'Gwenda. I've brought her to see the puppies.'

'That's lovely.' Mama suddenly looked tired. She closed her eyes and turned her head aside.

The girls crept out quietly.

Gwenda was looking shocked. 'What's wrong with her?'

'A wasting disease.' Caris hated to talk about it. Her mother's illness gave her the unnerving feeling that nothing was certain, anything could happen, there was no safety in the world. It was even more frightening than the fight they had witnessed in the forest. If she thought about what might happen, and the possibility that her mother might die, she suffered a panicky fluttering sensation in her chest that made her want to scream.

The middle bedroom was used in summer by the Italians, wool buyers from Florence and Prato who came to do business with Papa. Now it was empty. The puppies were in the back bedroom, which belonged to Caris and her sister, Alice. They were seven weeks old, ready to leave their mother, who was growing impatient with them. Gwenda gave a sigh of joy and immediately got down on the floor with them.

Caris picked up the smallest of the litter, a lively female, always going off on her own to explore the world. 'This is the one I'm going to keep,' she said. 'She's called Scrap.' Holding the little dog soothed her, and helped her forget about the things that troubled her.

The other four clambered all over Gwenda, sniffing her and chewing her dress. She picked up an ugly brown dog with a long muzzle and eyes set too close together. 'I like this one,' she said. The puppy curled up in her lap.

Caris said: 'Would you like to keep him?'

Tears came to Gwenda's eyes. 'Could I?'

'We're allowed to give them away.'

'Really?'

'Papa doesn't want any more dogs. If you like him, you can have him.'

'Oh, yes,' Gwenda said in a whisper. 'Yes, please.'

'What will you name him?'

'Something that reminds me of Hop. Perhaps I'll call him Skip.'

'That's a good name.' Skip had already gone to sleep in Gwenda's lap, Caris saw.

The two girls sat quietly with the dogs. Caris thought about the boys they had met, the little red-haired one with the golden-brown eyes and his tall, handsome younger brother. What had made her take them into the forest? It was not the first time she had yielded to a stupid impulse. It tended to happen when someone in authority ordered her not to do something. Her Aunt Petranilla was a great rule-maker. 'Don't feed that cat, we'll never get rid of it. No ball games in the house. Stay away from that boy, his family are peasants.' Rules that constrained her behaviour seemed to drive Caris crazy.

But she had never done something this foolish. She felt shaky when she thought of it. Two men had died. But what might have happened was worse. The four children might have been killed too.

She wondered what the fight had been about, and why the men-at-arms had been chasing the knight. Obviously it was not a simple robbery. They had spoken about a letter. But Merthin had said no more about that. Probably he had learned nothing further. It was just another of the mysteries of adult life.

Caris had liked Merthin. His boring brother, Ralph, was just like every other boy in Kingsbridge, boastful and aggressive and stupid, but Merthin seemed different. He had intrigued her right from the start.

Two new friends in one day, she thought, looking at Gwenda. The little girl was not pretty. She had dark brown eyes set close together above a beaky nose. She had picked a dog that looked a bit like her, Caris realized with amusement. Gwenda's clothes were old, and must have been worn by many children before her. Gwenda was calmer now. She no longer looked as if she might burst into tears at any moment. She, too, had been soothed by the puppies.

There was a familiar lopsided tread in the hall below, and a moment later a voice bellowed: 'Bring me a flagon of ale, for the love of the saints, I've got a thirst like a carthorse.'

'It's my father,' Caris said. 'Come and meet him.' Seeing that Gwenda looked anxious, she added: 'Don't worry, he always shouts like that, but he's really nice.'

The girls went downstairs with their puppies. 'What's happened to all my servants?' Papa roared. 'Have they run away to join the fairy folk?' He came stomping out of the kitchen, trailing his twisted right leg as always, carrying a big wooden cup slopping over with ale. 'Hello, my little buttercup,' he said to Caris in a softer voice. He sat on the big chair at the head of the table and took a long draft from the cup. 'That's better,' he said, wiping his straggly beard with his sleeve. He noticed Gwenda. 'A little daisy to go with my buttercup?' he said. 'What's your name?'

'Gwenda, from Wigleigh, my lord,' she said, awestruck.

'I gave her a puppy,' Caris explained.

'That's a good idea!' Papa said. 'Puppies need affection, and no one can love a puppy the way a little girl does.'

On the stool beside the table Caris saw a cloak of scarlet cloth. It had to be imported, for English dyers did not know how to achieve such a bright red. Following her eye, Papa said: 'It's for your mother. She's always wanted a coat of Italian red. I'm hoping it will encourage her to get well enough to wear it.'

Caris touched it. The wool was soft and close-woven, as only the Italians could make it. 'It's beautiful,' she said.

Aunt Petranilla entered from the street. She bore some resemblance to Papa, but was purse-mouthed where he was hearty. She was more like her other brother Anthony, the prior of Kingsbridge: they were both tall, imposing figures, whereas Papa was short, barrel-chested and lame.

Caris disliked Petranilla. She was clever as well as mean, a deadly combination in an adult: Caris was never able to outwit her. Gwenda sensed Caris's dislike, and looked apprehensively at the newcomer. Only Papa was pleased to see her. 'Come in, sister,' he said. 'Where are all my servants?'

'I can't think why you imagine I should know that, having just come from my own house at the other end of the street, but if I had to guess, Edmund, I should say that your cook is in the henhouse, hoping to find an egg to make you a pudding, and your maid is upstairs, helping your wife to a close-stool, which she generally requires about midday. As for your apprentices, I hope they are both on guard duty at the warehouse by the riverside, making sure that no holiday revellers take it into their drunken heads to light a bonfire within a spark's fly of your wool store.'

She often spoke like this, giving a little sermon in answer to a simple question. Her manner was supercilious, as always, but Papa did not mind, or pretended not to. 'My remarkable sister,' he said. 'You're the one who inherited our father's wisdom.'

Petranilla turned to the girls. 'Our father was descended from Tom Builder, the stepfather and mentor of Jack Builder, architect of Kingsbridge Cathedral,' she said. 'Father vowed to give his firstborn to God but, unfortunately, his firstborn was a girl – me. He named me after St Petranilla – who was the daughter of St Peter, as I'm sure you know – and he prayed for a boy next time. But his first son was born deformed, and he did not want to give God a flawed gift, so he brought Edmund up to take over the wool business. Happily, his third child was our brother Anthony, a well-behaved and God-fearing child, who entered the monastery as a boy and is now, we are all proud to say, the prior.'

She would have become a priest, had she been a man, but as it was she had done the next best thing and brought up her son, Godwyn, to be a monk at the priory. Like Grandfather Wooler, she had given a child to God. Caris had always felt sorry for Godwyn, her older cousin, for having Petranilla as a mother.

Petranilla noticed the red coat. 'Whose is this?' she said. 'It's the most expensive Italian cloth!'

'I bought it for Rose,' said Papa.

Petranilla stared at him for a moment. Caris could tell she

thought he was a fool to buy such a coat for a woman who had not left the house for a year. But all she said was: 'You're very good to her,' which might have been a compliment or not.

Father did not care. 'Go up and see her,' he urged. 'You'll cheer her up.'

Caris doubted that, but Petranilla suffered no such misgivings, and she went up the stairs.

Caris's sister, Alice, came in from the street. She was eleven, a year older than Caris. She stared at Gwenda and said: 'Who's she?'

'My new friend Gwenda,' said Caris. 'She's going to take a puppy.'

'But she's got the one I wanted!' Alice protested.

She had not said that before. 'Ooh – you never picked one!' Caris said, outraged. 'You're just saying that to be mean.'

'Why should she have one of our puppies?'

Papa intervened. 'Now, now,' he said. 'We've got more puppies than we need.'

'Caris should have asked me which one I wanted first!'

'Yes, she should,' Papa said, even though he knew perfectly well that Alice was only making trouble. 'Don't do it again, Caris.'

'Yes, Papa.'

The cook came in from the kitchen with jugs and cups. When Caris was learning to talk she had called the cook Tutty, no one knew why, but the name had stuck. Papa said: 'Thank you, Tutty. Sit at the table, girls.' Gwenda hesitated, not sure if she was invited, but Caris nodded at her, knowing that Papa intended her to be included – he generally asked everyone within his range of vision to come to dinner.

Tutty refilled Papa's cup with ale, then gave Alice, Caris and Gwenda ale mixed with water. Gwenda drank all of hers immediately, with relish, and Caris guessed she did not often get ale: poor people drank cider made from crab apples.

Next, the cook put in front of each of them a thick slice of rye bread a foot square. Gwenda picked hers up to eat it, and Caris realized she had never dined at a table before. 'Wait,' she said quietly, and Gwenda put the bread down again. Tutty brought in the ham on a board and a dish of cabbage. Papa took a big knife and cut slices off the ham, piling it on their bread trenchers. Gwenda stared big-eyed at the quantity of meat she was given. Caris spooned cabbage leaves on top of the ham.

The chambermaid, Elaine, came hurrying down the stairs. 'The mistress seems worse,' she said. 'Mistress Petranilla says we should send for Mother Cecilia.'

'Then run to the priory and beg her to come,' Papa said.

The maid hurried off.

'Eat up, children,' said Papa, and he speared a slice of hot ham with his knife; but Caris could see that the dinner now had no relish for him, and he seemed to be looking at something far away.

Gwenda ate some cabbage and whispered: 'This is food from heaven.' Caris tried it. The cabbage was cooked with ginger. Gwenda had probably never tasted ginger: only rich people could afford it.

Petranilla came down, put some ham on a wooden platter, and took it up for Mama; but she came back a few moments later with the food untouched. She sat at the table to eat it herself, and the cook brought her a bread trencher. 'When I was a girl, we were the only family in Kingsbridge who had meat for dinner every day,' she said. 'Except on fast days – my father was very devout. He was the first wool merchant in town to deal directly with the Italians. Everyone does now – although my brother Edmund is still the most important.'

Caris had lost her appetite, and she had to chew for a long time before she could swallow. At last Mother Cecilia arrived, a small, vital woman with a reassuringly bossy manner. With her was Sister Juliana, a simple person with a warm heart. Caris felt better as she watched them climb the stairs, a chirpy sparrow with a hen waddling behind. They would wash Mama in rose water to cool her fever, and the fragrance would lift her spirits.

Tutty brought in apples and cheese. Papa peeled an apple absent-mindedly with his knife. Caris remembered how, when she was younger, he used to feed her peeled slices then eat the skin himself.

Sister Juliana came downstairs, a worried look on her podgy face. 'The prioress wants Brother Joseph to come and see Mistress

Rose,' she said. Joseph was the senior physician at the monastery: he had trained with the masters at Oxford. 'I'll just go and fetch him,' Juliana said, and she ran out through the door to the street.

Papa put his peeled apple down uneaten.

Caris said: 'What is going to happen?'

'I don't know, buttercup. Will it rain? How many sacks of wool do the Florentines need? Will the sheep catch a murrain? Is the baby a girl, or a boy with a twisted leg? We never know, do we? That's...' He looked away. 'That's what makes it so hard.'

He gave her the apple. Caris gave it to Gwenda, who ate it entire, core and pips too.

Brother Joseph arrived a few minutes later with a young assistant whom Caris recognized as Saul Whitehead, so called because his hair – what little he had left after his monkish haircut – was ash-blond.

Cecilia and Juliana came downstairs, no doubt to make room for the two men in the small bedroom. Cecilia sat at the table, but did not eat. She had a small face with sharp features: a little pointed nose, bright eyes, a chin like the prow of a boat. She looked with curiosity at Gwenda. 'Well, now,' she said brightly, 'who is this little girl, and does she love Jesus and His Holy Mother?'

Gwenda said: 'I'm Gwenda, I'm Caris's friend.' She looked anxiously at Caris, as if she feared it might have been presumptuous of her to claim friendship.

Caris said: 'Will the Virgin Mary make my mama better?'

Cecilia raised her eyebrows. 'Such a direct question. I could have guessed you're Edmund's daughter.'

'Everyone prays to her, but not everyone gets well,' Caris said. 'And do you know why that is?'

'Perhaps she never helps anyone, and it's just that the strong people get well and the weak don't.'

'Now, now, don't be silly,' said Papa. 'Everyone knows the Holy Mother helps us.'

'That's all right,' Cecilia told him. 'It's normal for children to ask questions – especially the bright ones. Caris, the saints are always powerful, but some prayers are more effective than others. Do you understand that?'

Caris nodded reluctantly, feeling not convinced so much as outwitted.

'She must come to our school,' Cecilia said. The nuns had a school for the daughters of the nobility and of the more prosperous townspeople. The monks ran a separate school for boys.

Papa looked stubborn. 'Rose has taught both girls their letters,' he said. 'And Caris knows her numbers as well as I do – she helps me in the business.'

'She should learn more than that. Surely you don't want her to spend her life as your servant?'

Petranilla put in: 'She has no need of book learning. She will marry extremely well. There will be crowds of suitors for both sisters. Sons of merchants, even sons of knights, will be eager to marry into this family. But Caris is a wilful child: we must take care she doesn't throw herself away on some penniless minstrel boy.'

Caris noticed that Petranilla did not anticipate trouble with obedient Alice, who would probably marry whomever they picked for her.

Cecilia said: 'God might call Caris to his service.'

Papa said grumpily: 'God has already called two from this family – my brother and my nephew. I'd have thought He would be satisfied by now.'

Cecilia looked at Caris. 'What do you think?' she said. 'Will you be a wool merchant, a knight's wife, or a nun?'

The idea of being a nun horrified Caris. She would have to obey someone else's orders every hour of the day. It would be like remaining a child all your life, and having Petranilla for a mother. Being the wife of a knight, or of anyone else, seemed almost as bad, for women had to obey their husbands. Helping Papa, then perhaps taking over the business when he was too old, was the least unattractive option, but on the other hand it was not exactly her dream. 'I don't want to be any of those,' she said.

'Is there something you would like?' Cecilia asked.

There was, although Caris had not told anyone before, in fact had not fully realized it until now; but the ambition seemed fully formed, and suddenly she knew without doubt that it was her destiny. 'I'm going to be a doctor,' she said.

There was a moment of silence, then they all laughed.

Caris flushed, not knowing what was so funny.

Papa took pity and said: 'Only men can be doctors. Didn't you know that, buttercup?'

Caris was bewildered. She turned to Cecilia. 'But what about you?'

'I'm not a physician,' Cecilia said. 'We nuns care for the sick, of course, but we follow the instructions of trained men. The monks who have studied under the masters understand the humours of the body, the way they go out of balance in sickness, and how to bring them back to their correct proportions for good health. They know which vein to bleed for migraine, leprosy or breathlessness; where to cup and cauterize; whether to poultice or bathe.'

'Couldn't a woman learn those things?'

'Perhaps, but God has ordained it otherwise.'

Caris felt frustrated with the way adults trotted out this truism every time they were stuck for an answer. Before she could say anything, Brother Saul came downstairs with a bowl of blood, and went through the kitchen to the back yard to get rid of it. The sight made Caris feel weepy. All doctors used bloodletting as a cure, so it must be effective, she supposed; but all the same she hated to see her mother's life force in a bowl to be thrown away.

Saul returned to the sick room, and a few moments later he and Joseph came down. 'I've done what I can for her,' Joseph said solemnly to Papa. 'And she has confessed her sins.'

Confessed her sins! Caris knew what that meant. She began to cry.

Papa took six silver pennies from his purse and gave them to the monk. 'Thank you, brother,' he said. His voice was hoarse.

As the monks left, the two nuns went back upstairs.

Alice sat on Papa's lap and buried her face in his neck. Caris cried and hugged Scrap. Petranilla ordered Tutty to clear the table. Gwenda watched everything with wide eyes. They sat around the table in silence, waiting.

4

BROTHER GODWYN WAS HUNGRY. He had eaten his dinner, a stew of sliced turnips with salt fish, and it had not satisfied him. The monks nearly always had fish and weak ale for dinner, even when it was not a fast day.

Not all the monks, of course: Prior Anthony had a privileged diet. He would dine especially well today, for the prioress, Mother Cecilia, was to be his guest. She was accustomed to rich food. The nuns, who always seemed to have more money than the monks, killed a pig or a sheep every few days and washed it down with Gascon wine.

It was Godwyn's job to supervise the dinner, a hard task when his own stomach was rumbling. He spoke to the monastery cook, and checked on the fat goose in the oven and the pot of apple sauce bubbling on the fire. He asked the cellarer for a jug of cider from the barrel, and got a loaf of rye bread from the bakery – stale, for there was no baking on Sunday. He took the silver platters and goblets from the locked chest and set them on the table of the hall in the prior's house.

The prior and prioress dined together once a month. The monastery and the nunnery were separate institutions, with their own premises, and different sources of income. Prior and prioress were independently responsible to the bishop of Kingsbridge. Nevertheless they shared the great cathedral and several other buildings including the hospital, where monks worked as doctors and nuns as nurses. So there were always details to discuss: cathedral services, hospital guests and patients, town politics. Anthony often tried to get Cecilia to pay costs that should, strictly speaking, have been divided equally – glass windows for the chapter house, bedsteads for the hospital, the repainting of the cathedral's interior – and she usually agreed.

Today, however, the talk was likely to centre on politics. Anthony had returned yesterday from two weeks in Gloucester, where he had assisted at the interment of King Edward II, who had lost his throne in January and his life in September. Mother Cecilia would want to hear the gossip, while pretending to be above it all.

Godwyn had something else on his mind. He wanted to talk to Anthony about his future. He had been anxiously awaiting the right moment ever since the prior returned home. He had rehearsed his speech, but had not yet found the opportunity to deliver it. He hoped to get a chance this afternoon.

Anthony entered the hall as Godwyn was putting a cheese and a bowl of pears on the sideboard. The prior looked like an older version of Godwyn. Both were tall, with regular features and light-brown hair, and like all the family they had greenish eyes with flecks of gold. Anthony stood by the fire – the room was cold and the old building let in freezing draughts. Godwyn poured him a cup of cider. 'Father Prior, today is my birthday,' he said as Anthony drank. 'I'm twenty-one.'

'So it is,' said Anthony. 'I remember your birth very well. I was fourteen years old. My sister Petranilla screamed like a boar with an arrow in its guts as she brought you into the world.' He raised his goblet in a toast, looking fondly at Godwyn. 'And now you're a man.'

Godwyn decided that this was his moment. 'I've been at the priory ten years,' he said.

'Is it that long?'

'Yes – as schoolboy, novice and monk.'

'My goodness.'

'I hope I've been a credit to my mother and to you.'

'We're both very proud of you.'

'Thank you.' Godwyn swallowed. 'And now I want to go to Oxford.'

The city of Oxford had long been a centre for masters of theology, medicine and law. Priests and monks went there to study and debate with teachers and other students. In the last century the masters had been incorporated into a company, or university, that had royal permission to set examinations and award degrees. Kingsbridge Priory maintained a branch or cell in the city, known as Kingsbridge College, where eight monks could carry on their lives of worship and self-denial while they studied.

'Oxford!' said Anthony, and an expression of anxiety and distaste came over his face. 'Why?'

'To study. It's what monks are supposed to do.'

'I never went to Oxford – and I'm prior.'

It was true, but Anthony was sometimes at a disadvantage with his senior colleagues in consequence. The sacrist, the treasurer and several other monastic officials, or obedientiaries, were graduates of the university, as were all the physicians. They were quick-thinking and skilled in argument, and Anthony sometimes appeared bumbling by comparison, especially in chapter, the daily meeting of all the monks. Godwyn longed to acquire the sharp logic and confident superiority he observed in the Oxford men. He did not want to be like his uncle.

But he could not say that. 'I want to learn,' he said.

'Why learn heresy?' Anthony said scornfully. 'Oxford students question the teachings of the church!'

'In order to understand them better.'

'Pointless and dangerous.'

Godwyn asked himself why Anthony was making this fuss. The prior had never appeared concerned about heresy before, and Godwyn was not in the least interested in challenging accepted doctrines. He frowned. 'I thought you and my mother had ambitions for me,' he said. 'Don't you want me to advance, and become an obedientiary, and perhaps one day prior?'

'Eventually, yes. But you don't have to leave Kingsbridge to achieve that.'

You don't want me to advance too fast, in case I outstrip you; and you don't want me to leave town, in case you lose control of me, Godwyn thought in a flash of insight. He wished he had anticipated this resistance to his plans. 'I don't want to study theology,' he said.

'What, then?'

'Medicine. It's such an important part of our work here.'

Anthony pursed his lips. Godwyn had seen the same disapproving expression on his mother's face. 'The monastery can't afford to pay for you,' Anthony said. 'Do you realize that just one book costs at least fourteen shillings?'

Godwyn was taken by surprise. Students could hire books by the page, he knew; but that was not the main point. 'What about the students already there?' he said. 'Who pays for them?'

'Two are supported by their families, and one by the nuns. The priory pays for the other three, but we can't afford any more. In fact there are two places vacant in the college for lack of funds.'

Godwyn knew the priory was in financial difficulties. On the other hand, it had vast resources: thousands of acres of land; mills and fishponds and woodland; and the enormous income from Kingsbridge market. He could not believe his uncle was refusing him the money to go to Oxford. He felt betrayed. Anthony was his mentor as well as a relative. He had always favoured Godwyn over other young monks. But now he was trying to hold Godwyn back.

'Physicians bring money in to the priory,' he argued. 'If you don't train young men, eventually the old ones will die and the priory will be poorer.'

'God will provide.'

This infuriating platitude was always Anthony's answer. For some years the priory's income from the annual Fleece Fair had been declining. The townspeople had urged Anthony to invest in better facilities for the wool traders – tents, booths, latrines, even a wool exchange building – but he always refused, pleading poverty. And when his brother, Edmund, told him the fair would eventually decline to nothing, he said: 'God will provide.'

Godwyn said: 'Well, then, perhaps he will provide the money for me to go to Oxford.'

'Perhaps he will.'

Godwyn felt painfully disappointed. He had an urge to get away from his home town and breathe a different air. At Kingsbridge College he would be subject to the same monastic discipline, of course – but nevertheless he would be far from his uncle and his mother, and that prospect was alluring.

He was not yet ready to give up the argument. 'My mother will be very disappointed if I don't go.'

Anthony looked uneasy. He did not want to incur the wrath of his formidable sister. 'Then let her pray for the money to be found.'

'I may be able to get it elsewhere,' Godwyn said, extemporizing.

'How would you do that?'

He cast about for an answer, and found inspiration. 'I could do what you do, and ask Mother Cecilia.' It was possible. Cecilia made him nervous – she could be as intimidating as Petranilla – but she was more susceptible to his boyish charm. She might be persuaded to pay for a bright young monk's education.

The suggestion took Anthony by surprise. Godwyn could see him trying to think of an objection. But he had been arguing as if money were the main consideration, and it was difficult now for him to shift his ground.

While Anthony hesitated, Cecilia came in.

She wore a heavy cloak of fine wool, her only indulgence – she hated to be cold. After greeting the prior, she turned to Godwyn. 'Your Aunt Rose is gravely ill,' she said. Her voice was musically precise. 'She may not last the night.'

'May God be with her.' Godwyn felt a pang of pity. In a family where everyone was a leader, Rose was the only follower. Her petals seemed the more fragile for being surrounded by brambles. 'It's not a shock,' he added. 'But my cousins, Alice and Caris, will be sad.'

'Fortunately, they have your mother to console them.'

'Yes.' Consolation was not Petranilla's strong point, Godwyn thought – she was better at stiffening your spine and preventing you from backsliding – but he did not correct the prioress. Instead he poured her a goblet of cider. 'Is it a little chilly in here, Reverend Mother?'

'Freezing,' she said bluntly.

'I'll build up the fire.'

Anthony said slyly: 'My nephew Godwyn is being attentive because he wants you to pay for him to go to Oxford.'

Godwyn glared furiously at him. Godwyn would have planned a careful speech and chosen the best time to deliver it. Now

Anthony had blurted out the request in the most charmless fashion.

Cecilia said: 'I don't think we can afford to finance *two* more.'

It was Anthony's turn to be surprised. 'Someone else has asked you for money to go to Oxford?'

'Perhaps I shouldn't say,' Cecilia replied. 'I don't want to get anyone into trouble.'

'It's of no consequence,' Anthony said huffily; then he recollected himself and added: 'We are always grateful for your generosity.'

Godwyn put more wood on the fire then went out. The prior's house was on the north side of the cathedral. The cloisters, and all the other priory buildings, were to the south of the church. Godwyn walked shivering across the cathedral green to the monastery kitchen.

He had thought Anthony might quibble about Oxford, saying he should wait until he was older, or until one of the existing students graduated – for Anthony was a quibbler by nature. But he was Anthony's protégé, and he had been confident that in the end his uncle would support him. Anthony's flat opposition had left him feeling shocked.

He asked himself who else had petitioned the prioress for support. Of the twenty-six monks, six were around Godwyn's age: it could be any one of them. In the kitchen the sub-cellarer, Theodoric, was helping the cook. Could he be the rival for Cecilia's money? Godwyn watched him put the goose on a platter with a bowl of apple sauce. Theodoric had brains enough to study. He could be a contender.

Godwyn carried the dinner back to the prior's house, feeling worried. If Cecilia decided to help Theodoric, he did not know what he would do. He had no fall-back plan.

He wanted to be prior of Kingsbridge one day. He felt sure he could do the job better than Anthony. And if he was a successful prior, he might rise higher: bishop, archbishop, or perhaps a royal official or counsellor. He had only a vague idea of what he would do with such power, but he felt strongly that he belonged in some elevated position in life. However, there were only two routes to such heights. One was aristocratic birth; the other, education. Godwyn came from a family of wool merchants: his only hope was the university. And for that, he was going to need Cecilia's money.

He put the dinner on the table. Cecilia was saying: 'But how did the king die?'

'He suffered a fall,' Anthony said.

Godwyn carved the goose. 'May I give you some of the breast, Reverend Mother?'

'Yes, please. A fall?' she said sceptically. 'You make the king sound like a doddering old man. He was forty-three!'

'It's what his jailers say.' Having been deposed, the ex-king had been a prisoner at Berkeley Castle, a couple of days' ride from Kingsbridge.

'Ah, yes, his jailers,' Cecilia said. 'Mortimer's men.' She disapproved of Roger Mortimer, the earl of March. Not only had he led the rebellion against Edward II, he had also seduced the king's wife, Queen Isabella.

They began to eat. Godwyn wondered whether there would be any left over.

Anthony said to Cecilia: 'You sound as if you suspect something sinister.'

'Of course not – but others do. There has been talk...'

'That he was murdered? I know. But I saw the corpse, naked. There were no marks of violence on the body.'

Godwyn knew he should not interrupt, but he could not resist. 'Rumour says that when the king died his screams of agony were heard by everyone in the village of Berkeley.'

Anthony looked censorious. 'When a king dies, there are always rumours.'

'This king did not merely die,' Cecilia said. 'He was first deposed by Parliament – something that has never happened before.'

Anthony lowered his voice. 'The reasons were powerful. There were sins of impurity.'

He was being enigmatic, but Godwyn knew what he meant. Edward had had 'favourites' – young men he seemed unnaturally fond of. The first, Peter Gaveston, had been given so much power and privilege that he aroused jealousy and resentment among the barons, and in the end he had been executed for treason. But then there had been others. It was no wonder, people said, that the queen took a lover.

'I cannot believe such a thing,' said Cecilia, who was a passionate royalist. 'It may be true that outlaws in the forest give themselves up to such foul practices, but a man of royal blood could never sink so low. Is there any more of that goose?'

'Yes,' Godwyn said, concealing his disappointment. He cut the last of the meat from the bird and gave it to the prioress.

Anthony said: 'At least there is now no challenge to the new king.' The son of Edward II and Queen Isabella had been crowned as King Edward III.

'He is fourteen years old, and he has been put on the throne by Mortimer,' said Cecilia. 'Who will be the real ruler?'

'The nobles are glad to have stability.'

'Especially those of them who are Mortimer's cronies.'

'Such as Earl Roland of Shiring, you mean?'

'He seemed ebullient today.'

'You're not suggesting...'

'That he had something to do with the king's "fall"? Certainly not.' The prioress ate the last of the meat. 'Such an idea would be dangerous to speak of, even among friends.'

'Indeed.'

There was a tap at the door, and Saul Whitehead came in. He was the same age as Godwyn. Could he be the rival? He was intelligent and capable, and he had the great advantage of being a distant relation of the earl of Shiring; but Godwyn doubted whether he had the ambition to go to Oxford. He was devout and shy, the kind of man for whom humility was no virtue because it came naturally. But anything was possible.

'A knight has come into the hospital with a sword wound,' Saul said.

'Interesting,' said Anthony, 'but hardly shocking enough to justify interrupting the prior and the prioress at dinner.'

Saul looked scared. 'I beg your pardon, Father Prior,' he stammered. 'But there is a disagreement about the treatment.'

Anthony sighed. 'Well, the goose is all gone,' he said, and he got to his feet.

Cecilia went with him, and Godwyn and Saul followed. They entered the cathedral by the north transept and walked through the crossing, out by the south transept, across the cloisters and into the hospital. The wounded knight lay on the bed nearest the altar, as befitted his rank.

Prior Anthony uttered an involuntary grunt of surprise. For a moment he showed shock and fear. But he recovered his composure quickly, and made his face expressionless.

However, Cecilia missed nothing. 'Do you know this man?' she asked Anthony.

'I believe I do. He is Sir Thomas Langley, one of the earl of Monmouth's men.'

He was a handsome man in his twenties, broad-shouldered and long-legged. He was naked to the waist, showing a muscular torso criss-crossed with the scars of earlier fights. He looked pale and exhausted.

'He was attacked on the road,' Saul explained. 'He managed to fight off his assailants, but then he had to drag himself a mile or more to the town. He's lost a lot of blood.'

The knight's left forearm was split from elbow to wrist, a clean cut obviously made by a sharp sword.

The monastery's senior physician, Brother Joseph, stood beside the patient. Joseph was in his thirties, a small man with a big nose and bad teeth. He said: 'The wound should be kept open and treated with an ointment to bring on a pus. That way, evil humours will be expelled and the wound will heal from the inside out.'

Anthony nodded. 'So where is the disagreement?'

'Matthew Barber has another idea.'

Matthew was a barber-surgeon from the town. He had been standing back deferentially, but now he stepped forward, holding the leather case that contained his expensive, sharp knives. He was a small, thin man with bright blue eyes and a solemn expression.

Anthony did not acknowledge Matthew, but said to Joseph: 'What's he doing here?'

'The knight knows him and sent for him.'

Anthony spoke to Thomas. 'If you want to be butchered, why did you come to the priory hospital?'

The ghost of a smile flickered across the knight's white face, but he seemed too tired to reply.

Matthew spoke up with surprising confidence, apparently undeterred by Anthony's scorn. 'I've seen many wounds like this on the battlefield, Father Prior,' he said. 'The best treatment is the simplest: wash the wound with warm wine, then stitch it closed and bandage it.' He was not as deferential as he looked.

Mother Cecilia interrupted. 'I wonder if our two young monks have opinions on the question?' she asked.

Anthony looked impatient, but Godwyn realized what she was up to. This was a test. Perhaps Saul was the rival for her money.

The answer was easy, so Godwyn got in first. 'Brother Joseph has studied the ancient masters,' he said. 'He must know best. I don't suppose Matthew can even read.'

'I can, Brother Godwyn,' Matthew protested. 'And I have a book.'

Anthony laughed. The idea of a barber with a book was silly, like a horse with a hat. 'What book?'

'The Canon of Avicenna, the great Islamic physician. Translated from Arabic into Latin. I have read it all, slowly.'

'And is your remedy proposed by Avicenna?'

'No, but—'

'Well, then.'

Matthew persisted. 'But I learned more about healing by travelling with armies and treating the wounded than I ever did from the book.'

Mother Cecilia said: 'Saul, what's your view?'

Godwyn expected Saul to give the same answer, so that the contest would be indecisive. But, although he looked nervous and shy, Saul contradicted Godwyn. 'The barber may be right,' he said. Godwyn was delighted. Saul went on arguing for the wrong side. 'The treatment proposed by Brother Joseph might be more suitable for crushing or hammering injuries, such as we get on building sites, where the skin and flesh all around the cut is damaged, and to close the wound prematurely might seal evil humours inside the body. This is a clean cut, and the sooner it is closed the faster it will heal.'

'Nonsense,' said Prior Anthony. 'How could a town barber be right and an educated monk be wrong?'

Godwyn smothered a triumphant grin.

The door flew open, and a young man in the robes of a priest strode in. Godwyn recognized Richard of Shiring, the younger of the two sons of Earl Roland. His nod to the prior and prioress was so perfunctory as to be impolite. He went straight to the bedside and spoke to the knight. 'What the devil has happened?' he said.

Thomas lifted a weak hand and beckoned Richard closer. The young priest leaned over the patient. Thomas whispered in his ear.

Father Richard drew away as if shocked. 'Absolutely not!' he said.

Thomas beckoned again, and the process was repeated: another whisper, another outraged reaction. This time, Richard said: 'But why?'

Thomas did not reply.

Richard said: 'You are asking for something that is not in our power to give.'

Thomas nodded firmly, as if to say: Yes, it is.

'You're giving us no choice.'

Thomas shook his head weakly from side to side.

Richard turned to Prior Anthony. 'Sir Thomas wishes to become a monk here at the priory.'

There was a moment of surprised silence. Cecilia was the first to react. 'But he's a man of violence!'

'Come on, it's not unknown,' Richard said impatiently. 'A fighting man sometimes decides to abandon his life of warfare and seek forgiveness for his sins.'

'In old age, perhaps,' Cecilia said. 'This man is not yet twenty-five. He's fleeing some danger.' She looked hard at Richard. 'Who threatens his life?'

'Curb your curiosity,' Richard said rudely. 'He wants to be a monk, not a nun, so you need not inquire further.' It was a shocking way to talk to a prioress, but the sons of earls could get away with such rudeness. He turned to Anthony. 'You must admit him.'

Anthony said: 'The priory is too poor to take on any more monks – unless there were to be a gift that would pay the costs ...'

'It will be arranged.'

'It would have to be adequate to the need—'

'It will be arranged!'

'Very well.'

Cecilia was suspicious. She said to Anthony: 'Do you know more about this man than you're telling me?'

'I see no reason to turn him away.'

'What makes you think he's a genuine penitent?'

Everyone looked at Thomas. His eyes had closed.

Anthony said: 'He will have to prove his sincerity during his novitiate, like anyone else.'

She was clearly dissatisfied, but for once Anthony was not asking her for the money, so there was nothing she could do. 'We'd better get on with treating this wound,' she said.

Saul said: 'He refused Brother Joseph's treatment. That's why we had to fetch the Father Prior.'

Anthony leaned over the patient. In a loud voice, as if speaking to someone deaf, he said: 'You must have the treatment prescribed by Brother Joseph. He knows best.'

Thomas appeared unconscious.

Anthony turned to Joseph. 'He is no longer objecting.'

Matthew Barber said: 'He could lose his arm!'

'You'd better leave,' Anthony told him.

Looking angry, Matthew went out.

Anthony said to Richard: 'Perhaps you would come to the prior's house for a cup of cider.'

'Thank you.'

As they left, Anthony said to Godwyn: 'Stay here and help the Mother Prioress. Come to me before Vespers and tell me how the knight is recovering.'

Prior Anthony did not normally worry about the progress of individual patients. Clearly he had a special interest in this one.

Godwyn watched as Brother Joseph applied ointment to the

arm of the now-unconscious knight. He thought he had probably ensured Cecilia's financial support by giving the correct answer to the question, but he was keen to get her explicit agreement. When Brother Joseph had done, and Cecilia was bathing Thomas's forehead with rose water, he said: 'I hope you will consider my request favourably.'

She gave him a sharp look. 'I might as well tell you now that I have decided to give the money to Saul.'

Godwyn was shocked. 'But I gave the right answer!'

'Did you?'

'Surely you didn't agree with the barber?'

She raised her eyebrows. 'I won't be interrogated by you, Brother Godwyn.'

'I'm sorry,' he said immediately. 'I just don't understand it.'

'I know.'

If she was going to be enigmatic there was no point in talking to her. Godwyn turned away, shaking with frustration and disappointment. She was giving the money to Saul! Was it because he was related to the earl? Godwyn thought not: she was too independent-minded. It was Saul's showy piety that had tipped the balance, he decided. But Saul would never be leader of anything. What a waste. Godwyn wondered how he was going to break this news to his mother. She would be furious – but who would she blame? Anthony? Godwyn himself? A familiar feeling of dread came over him as he pictured his mother's wrath.

As he thought of her, he saw her enter the hospital by the door at the far end, a tall woman with a prominent bust. She caught his eye and stood by the door, waiting for him to come to her. He walked slowly, trying to figure out what to say.

'Your Aunt Rose is dying,' Petranilla said as soon as he was close.

'May God bless her soul. Mother Cecilia told me.'

'You look shocked – but you know how ill she is.'

'It's not Aunt Rose. I've had other bad news.' He swallowed. 'I can't go to Oxford. Uncle Anthony won't pay for it, and Mother Cecilia turned me down too.'

She did not explode immediately, to his great relief. However, her mouth tightened into a grim line. 'But why?' she said.

'He hasn't got the money, and she is sending Saul.'

'Saul Whitehead? He'll never amount to anything.'

'Well, at least he's going to be a physician.'

She looked him in the eye, and he shrivelled. 'I think you handled this badly,' she said. 'You should have discussed it with me beforehand.'

He had feared she would take this line. 'How can you say I mishandled it?' he protested.

'You should have let me speak to Anthony first. I would have softened him.'

'He still might have said no.'

'And before you approached Cecilia, you should have found out whether anyone else had asked her. Then you could have undermined Saul before speaking to her.'

'How?'

'He must have a weakness. You could have found out what it is, and made sure it was brought to her attention. Then, when she was feeling disillusioned, you could have approached her yourself.'

He saw the sense of what she was saying. 'I never thought of that,' he said. He bowed his head.

With controlled anger she said: 'You have to plan these things, the way earls plan battles.'

'I see that now,' he said, not meeting her eye. 'I'll never make the same mistake again.'

'I hope not.'

He looked at her. 'What am I going to do?'

'I'm not giving up.' A familiar expression of determination came over her face. 'I shall provide the money,' she said.

Godwyn felt a surge of hope, but he could not imagine how his mother would fulfil such a promise. 'Where will you get it?' he asked.

'I'll give up my house, and move in with my brother Edmund.'

'Will he have you?' Edmund was a generous man, but he sometimes clashed with his sister.

'I think he will. He's going to be a widower soon, and he'll need a housekeeper. Not that Rose was ever very effective in that role.'

Godwyn shook his head. 'You'll still need money.'

'For what? Edmund will give me bed and board, and pay for the few small necessities I may require. In return, I'll manage his servants and raise his daughters. And you shall have the money I inherited from your father.'

She spoke firmly, but Godwyn could see the bitterness of regret expressed in the twist of her mouth. He knew what a sacrifice this would be for her. She was proud of her independence. She was one of the town's prominent women, the daughter of a wealthy man and the sister of the leading wool merchant, and she prized that status. She loved to invite the powerful men and women of Kingsbridge to dine with her and drink the best wine. Now she was proposing to move into her brother's house and live as a poor relation, working as a kind of servant and dependent on him for everything. It would be a terrible comedown. 'It's too much to sacrifice,' Godwyn said. 'You can't do it.'

Her face hardened, and she gave a little shake of the shoulders, as if preparing to take the weight of a heavy burden. 'Oh, yes, I can,' she said.

5

GWENDA TOLD HER FATHER EVERYTHING.

She had sworn on the blood of Jesus that she would keep the secret, so now she was going to hell, but she was more frightened of her father than of hell.

He began by asking her where she got Skip, the new puppy, and she was forced to explain how Hop had died; and in the end the whole story came out.

To her surprise, she was not whipped. In fact Pa seemed pleased. He made her take him to the clearing in the forest where the killings had happened. It was not easy to find the place again, but she got there, and they found the bodies of the two men-at-arms dressed in green-and-yellow livery.

First Pa opened their purses. Both contained twenty or thirty pennies. He was even more pleased with their swords, which were worth more than a few pennies. He began to strip the dead men, which was difficult for him with one hand, so he made Gwenda help him. The lifeless bodies were awkwardly heavy, so strange to touch. Pa made her take off everything they wore, even their muddy hose and their soiled underdrawers.

He wrapped their weapons in the clothing, making what looked like a bundle of rags. Then he and Gwenda dragged the naked corpses back into the evergreen bush.

He was in high spirits as they walked back into Kingsbridge. He took her to Slaughterhouse Ditch, a street near the river, and they went into a large but dirty tavern called the White Horse. He bought Gwenda a cup of ale to drink while he disappeared into the back of the house with the innkeeper, whom he addressed as 'Davey boy'. It was the second time Gwenda had drunk ale in one day. Pa reappeared a few minutes later without the bundle.

They returned to the main street and found Ma, Philemon and the baby at the Bell inn, next to the priory gates. Pa winked broadly at Ma and gave her a big handful of money to hide in the baby's blankets.

It was mid-afternoon, and most visitors had left to return to their villages; but it was too late to set out for Wigleigh, so the family would spend the night at the inn. As Pa kept saying, they could afford it now; although Ma said nervously: 'Don't let people know you've got money!'

Gwenda felt weary. She had got up early and walked a long way. She lay down on a bench and quickly fell asleep.

She was awakened by the inn door banging open violently. She looked up, startled, to see two men-at-arms walk in. At first she thought they were the ghosts of the men who had been killed in the forest, and she suffered a moment of sheer terror. Then she realized they were different men wearing the same uniform, yellow on one side and green on the other. The younger of the two carried a familiar-looking bundle of rags.

The older spoke directly to Pa. 'You're Joby from Wigleigh, aren't you.'

Gwenda instantly felt frightened again. There was a tone of serious menace in the man's voice. He was not posturing, just determined, but he gave her the impression he would do anything to get his way.

'No,' Pa replied, lying automatically. 'You've got the wrong man.'

They ignored that. The second man put the bundle on the table and spread it out. It consisted of two yellow-and-green tunics wrapped around two swords and two daggers. He looked at Pa and said: 'Where did these come from?'

'I've never seen them before, I swear by the Cross.'

He was stupid to deny it, Gwenda thought fearfully: they would get the truth out of him, just as he had got the truth out of her.

The older man-at-arms said: 'Davey, the landlord of the White Horse, says he bought these from Joby Wigleigh.' His voice hardened with threat, and the handful of other customers in the room all got up from their seats and quickly slipped out of the inn, leaving only Gwenda's family.

'Joby left here a while ago,' Pa said desperately.

The man nodded. 'With his wife, two children, and a baby.'

'Yes.'

The man moved with sudden speed. He grabbed Pa's tunic in a strong hand and pushed him up against the wall. Ma screamed, and the baby began to cry. Gwenda saw that the man's right hand bore a padded glove covered with chain-mail. He drew back his arm and punched Pa in the stomach.

Ma shouted: 'Help! Murder!' Philemon began to cry.

Pa's face turned white with pain, and he went limp, but the man held him up against the wall, preventing him from falling, and punched him again, this time in the face. Blood spurted from Pa's nose and mouth.

Gwenda wanted to scream, and her mouth was open wide, but no noise would come from her throat. She thought her father was all-powerful – even though he often slyly pretended to be weak, or craven, in order to get sympathy, or turn aside anger – and it terrified her to see him so helpless.

The innkeeper appeared in the doorway that led to the back of the house. He was a big man in his thirties. A plump little girl peeped from behind him. 'What's this?' he said in a voice of authority.

The man-at-arms did not look at him. 'You keep out of it,' he said, and he punched Pa in the stomach again.

Pa vomited blood.

'Stop that,' said the innkeeper.

The man-at-arms said: 'Who do you think you are?'

'I'm Paul Bell, and this is my house.'

'Well, then, Paul Bell, you mind your own business, if you know what's good for you.'

'I suppose you think you can do what you like, wearing that uniform.' There was contempt in Paul's voice.

'That's about right.'

'Whose livery is it, anyway?'

'The queen's.'

Paul spoke over his shoulder. 'Bessie, run and fetch John Constable. If a man is going to be murdered in my tavern, I want the constable to witness it.' The little girl disappeared.

'There'll be no killing here,' the man-at-arms said. 'Joby has changed his mind. He's decided to lead me to the place where he robbed two dead men – haven't you, Joby?'

Pa could not speak, but he nodded. The man let him go, and he fell to his knees, coughing and retching.

The man looked at the rest of the family. 'And the child that witnessed the fight...?'

Gwenda screamed: 'No!'

He nodded in satisfaction. 'The rat-faced girl, obviously.'

Gwenda ran to her mother. Ma said: 'Mary, Mother of God, save my child.'

The man grabbed Gwenda's arm and roughly pulled her away from her mother. She cried out. He said harshly: 'Shut your noise, or you'll get the same as your miserable father.'

Gwenda clamped her jaws together to stop herself screaming.

'Get up, Joby.' The man dragged Pa to his feet. 'Pull yourself together, you're going for a ride.'

The second man picked up the clothes and the weapons.

As they left the inn, Ma called out frantically: 'Just do everything they ask!'

The men had horses. Gwenda rode in front of the older man, and Pa was mounted in the same position on the other horse. Pa was helpless, groaning, so Gwenda directed them, remembering the way clearly now that she had followed it twice. They made rapid progress on horseback, but all the same the afternoon was darkening when they reached the clearing.

The younger man held on to Gwenda and Pa while the leader pulled the bodies of their comrades out from under the bush.

'That Thomas must be a rare fighter, to kill Harry and Alfred together,' the older man mused, looking at the corpses. Gwenda realized that these men did not know about the other children. She would have confessed that she had not been alone, and that Ralph had killed one of the men, but she was too terrified to speak. 'He's nearly cut Alfred's head off,' the man went on. He turned and looked at Gwenda. 'Was anything said about a letter?'

'I don't know!' she said, finding her voice. 'I had my eyes shut because I was frightened, and I couldn't hear what they were saying! It's true, I'd tell you if I knew!'

'If they got the letter from him in the first place, he would have taken it back after he killed them anyway,' the man said to his comrade. He looked at the trees around the clearing, as if the letter might have been hanging among the dying leaves. 'He probably has it now, at the priory, where we can't get at him without violating the sanctity of the monastery.'

The second man said: 'At least we can report exactly what happened, and take the bodies home for a Christian burial.'

There was a sudden commotion. Pa wrenched himself out of the grasp of the second man and dashed across the clearing. His captor moved to go after him, but was stopped by the older man-at-arms. 'Let him go – what's the point in killing him now?'

Gwenda began to cry quietly.

'What about this child?' said the younger man.

They were going to murder her, Gwenda felt sure. She could see nothing through her tears, and she was sobbing too hard to plead for her life. She would die and go to hell. She waited for the end.

'Let her go,' said the older man. 'I wasn't born to kill little girls.'

The younger man released her and gave her a shove. She stumbled and fell to the ground. She got up, wiped her eyes so that she could see, and stumbled off.

'Go on, run away,' the man called after her. 'It's your lucky day!'

*

CARIS COULD NOT SLEEP. She got up from her bed and went into Mama's room. Papa was sitting on a stool, staring at the still figure in the bed.

Mama's eyes were closed and her face glistened, in the candlelight, with a film of perspiration. She seemed to be hardly breathing. Caris took her pale hand: it was terribly cold. She held it between her own, trying to warm it.

She said: 'Why did they take her blood?'

'They think illness sometimes comes from an excess of one of the humours. They hope to take it away with the blood.'

'But it didn't make her better.'

'No. In fact, she seems worse.'

Tears came to Caris's eyes. 'Why did you let them do it, then?'

'Priests and monks study the works of the ancient philosophers. They know more than we do.'

'I don't believe that.'

'It's hard to know what to believe, little buttercup.'

'If I was a doctor, I'd only do things that made people better.'

Papa was not listening. He was looking more intently at Mama. He leaned forward and slipped his hand under the blanket to touch her chest just below her left breast. Caris could see the shape of his big hand under the fine wool. He made a small choking sound in his throat, then moved his hand and pressed down more firmly. He held it there for a few moments.

He closed his eyes.

He seemed to fall slowly forward, until he was on his knees beside the bed, as if praying, with his big forehead resting on Mama's thigh, and his hand still on her chest.

She realized he was crying. It was the most frightening thing that had ever happened to her, much more frightening than seeing a man killed in the forest. Children cried, women cried, weak and helpless people cried, but Papa never cried. She felt as if the world was ending.

She had to get help. She let Mama's cold hand slip out of her own on to the blanket, where it lay motionless. She went back to her bedroom and shook the shoulder of the sleeping Alice. 'You've got to wake up!' she said.

At first Alice would not open her eyes.

'Papa is crying!' Caris said.

Alice sat upright. 'He can't be,' she said.

'Get up!'

Alice got out of bed. Caris took her older sister's hand and they went together into Mama's room. Papa was standing up, now, looking down at the still face on the pillow, his face wet with tears. Alice stared at him in shock. Caris whispered: 'I told you so.'

On the other side of the bed stood Aunt Petranilla.

Papa saw the girls standing in the doorway. He left his station by the bed and came to them. He put one arm around each of them, drew them both to him, and hugged them. 'Your Mama has gone to be with the angels,' he said quietly. 'Pray for her soul.'

'Be brave, girls,' said Petranilla. 'From now on, I will be your mama.'

Caris wiped the tears from her eyes and looked up at her aunt. 'Oh, no, you won't,' she said.

Part Two

Part Two

8 to 14 June, 1337

6

On Whit Sunday in the year that Merthin was twenty-one, a river of rain fell on Kingsbridge Cathedral.

Great globules of water bounced off the slate roof; streams flooded the gutters; fountains gushed from the mouths of gargoyles; sheets of water unfolded down the buttresses; and torrents ran over the arches and down the columns, soaking the statues of the saints. The sky, the great church and the town round about were all shades of wet grey paint.

Whit Sunday commemorated the moment when the Holy Spirit descended on the disciples of Jesus. The seventh Sunday after Easter, it fell in May or June, soon after most of England's sheep had been sheared; and so it was always the first day of the Kingsbridge Fleece Fair.

As Merthin splashed through the downpour to the cathedral for the morning service, pulling his hood forward over his brow in a vain attempt to keep his face dry, he had to pass through the fair. On the broad green to the west of the church, hundreds of traders had set out their stalls – then hastily covered them with sheets of oiled sacking or felted cloth to keep the rain off. Wool traders were the key figures in the fair, from the small operators who collected the produce of a few scattered villagers, to the big dealers such as Edmund who had a warehouse full of woolsacks to sell. Around them clustered subsidiary stalls selling just about everything else money could buy: sweet wine from the Rhineland, silk brocade threaded with gold from Lucca, glass bowls from Venice, ginger and pepper from places in the East that few people could even name. And finally there were the workaday tradespeople who supplied visitors and stallholders with their commonplace needs: bakers, brewers, confectioners, fortune-tellers and prostitutes.

The stallholders responded bravely to the rain, joking with one another, trying to create the carnival atmosphere; but the weather would be bad for their profits. Some people had to do business, rain or shine: Italian and Flemish buyers needed soft English wool for thousands of busy looms in Florence and Bruges. But more casual customers would stay at home: a knight's wife would decide she could manage without nutmeg and cinnamon; a prosperous peasant would make his old coat last another winter; a lawyer would judge that his mistress did not really need a gold bangle.

Merthin was not going to buy anything. He had no money. He was an unpaid apprentice, living with his master, Elfric Builder. He was fed at the family table, he slept on the kitchen floor, and he wore Elfric's cast-off clothes, but he got no wages. In the long winter evenings he carved ingenious toys that he sold for a few pennies – a jewel box with secret compartments, a cockerel whose tongue poked out when its tail was pressed – but in summer there was no spare time, for craftsmen worked until dark.

However, his apprenticeship was almost over. In less than six months, on the first day of December, he would become a full member of the carpenters' guild of Kingsbridge, at the age of twenty-one. He could hardly wait.

The great west doors of the cathedral were open to admit the thousands of townspeople and visitors who would attend today's service. Merthin stepped inside, shaking the rain off his clothes. The stone floor was slippery with water and mud. On a fine day, the interior of the church would be bright with shafts of sunlight, but today it was murky, the stained-glass windows dim, the congregation shrouded in dark, wet clothes.

Where did all the rain go? There were no drainage ditches around the church. The water – thousands and thousands of gallons of it – just soaked into the ground. Did it go on down, farther and farther, until it fell as rain again in hell? No. The cathedral was built on a slope. The water travelled underground, seeping down the hill from north to south. The foundations of large stone buildings were designed to let water flow through, for a build-up was dangerous. All this rain eventually passed into the river on the southern boundary of the priory grounds.

Merthin imagined he could feel the underground rush of the water, its drumming vibration transmitted through the foundations and the tiled floor and sensed by the soles of his feet.

A small black dog scampered up to him, wagging its tail, and greeted him joyfully. 'Hello, Scrap,' he said, and patted her. He looked up to see the dog's mistress, Caris; and his heart skipped a beat.

She wore a cloak of bright scarlet that she had inherited from her mother. It was the only splash of colour in the gloom. Merthin smiled broadly, happy to see her. It was hard to say what made her so beautiful. She had a small round face with neat, regular features; mid-brown hair; and green eyes flecked with gold. She was not so different from a hundred other Kingsbridge girls. But she wore her hat at a jaunty angle, there was a mocking intelligence in her eyes, and she looked at him with a mischievous grin that promised vague but tantalizing delights. He had known her for ten years, but it was only in the last few months that he had realized he loved her.

She drew him behind a pillar and kissed him on the mouth, the tip of her tongue running lightly across his lips.

They kissed every chance they got: in church, in the market place, when they met on the street, and – best of all – when he was at her house and they found themselves alone. He lived for those moments. He thought about kissing her before he went to sleep and again as soon as he woke up.

He visited her house two or three times a week. Her father, Edmund, liked him, though her aunt Petranilla did not. A convivial man, Edmund often invited Merthin to stay for supper, and Merthin accepted gratefully, knowing it would be a better meal than he would get at Elfric's house. He and Caris would play chess or draughts, or just sit talking. He liked to watch her while she told a story or explained something, her hands drawing pictures in the air, her face expressing amusement or astonishment, acting every part in a pageant. But, most of the time, he was waiting for those moments when he could steal a kiss.

He glanced around the church: no one was looking their way. He slipped his hand inside her coat, and touched her through the soft linen of her dress. Her body was warm. He held her breast in his palm, small and round. He loved the way her flesh yielded to the press of his fingertips. He had never seen her naked, but he knew her breasts intimately.

In his dreams they went farther. Then, they were alone somewhere, a clearing in the woods or the big bedchamber of a castle; and they were both naked. But, strangely, his dreams always ended a moment too soon, just before he entered her; and he would wake up frustrated.

One day, he would think; one day.

They had not yet spoken about marriage. Apprentices could not marry, so he had to wait. Caris must, surely, have asked herself what they were going to do when he finished his term; but she had not voiced those thoughts. She seemed content to take life one day at a time. And he had a superstitious fear of talking about their future together. It was said that pilgrims should not spend too much time planning their journey, for they might learn of so many hazards that they would decide not to go.

A nun walked past, and Merthin withdrew his hand guiltily from Caris's bosom; but the nun did not notice them. People did all sorts of things in the vast space of the cathedral. Last year Merthin had seen a couple having sexual congress up against the wall of the south aisle, in the darkness of the Christmas Eve service – although they had been thrown out for it. He wondered if he and Caris could stay here throughout the service, dallying discreetly.

But she had other ideas. 'Let's go to the front,' she said. She took his hand and led him through the crowd. He knew many of the people there, though not all: Kingsbridge was one of the larger cities in England, with about seven thousand inhabitants, and no one knew everybody. He followed Caris to the crossing, where the nave met the transepts. There they came up against a wooden barrier blocking entrance to the eastern end, or chancel, which was reserved for clergy.

Merthin found himself standing next to Buonaventura Caroli,

the most important of the Italian merchants, a heavy-set man in a richly embroidered coat of thick wool cloth. He came originally from Florence – which he said was the greatest city in the Christian world, more than ten times the size of Kingsbridge – but he now lived in London, managing the large business his family had with English wool producers. The Carolis were so rich they loaned money to kings, but Buonaventura was amiable and unpretentious – though people said that in business he could be implacably hard.

Caris greeted the man in a casually familiar way: he was staying at her house. He gave Merthin a friendly nod, even though he must have guessed, from Merthin's age and hand-me-down clothing, that he was a mere apprentice.

Buonaventura was looking at the architecture. 'I have been coming to Kingsbridge for five years,' he said, making idle conversation, 'but until today I have never noticed that the windows of the transepts are much bigger than those in the rest of the church.' He spoke French with an admixture of words from the dialect of the Italian region of Tuscany.

Merthin had no trouble understanding. He had grown up, like most sons of English knights, speaking Norman French to his parents and English to his playmates; and he could guess the meanings of many Italian words because he had learned Latin in the monks' school. 'I can tell you why the windows are like that,' he said.

Buonaventura raised his eyebrows, surprised that an apprentice should claim such knowledge.

'The church was built two hundred years ago, when these narrow lancet windows in the nave and chancel were a revolutionary new design,' Merthin went on. 'Then, a hundred years later, the bishop wanted a taller tower, and he rebuilt the transepts at the same time, putting in the bigger windows that had by then come into fashion.'

Buonaventura was impressed. 'And how do you happen to know this?'

'In the monastery library there is a history of the priory, called Timothy's Book, that tells all about the building of the cathedral. Most of it was written in the time of the great Prior Philip, but later writers have added to it. I read it as a boy at the monks' school.'

Buonaventura looked hard at Merthin for a moment, as if memorizing his face, then he said casually: 'It's a fine building.'

'Are the buildings very different in Italy?' Merthin was fascinated by talk of foreign countries, their life in general and their architecture in particular.

Buonaventura looked thoughtful. 'I believe the principles of building are the same everywhere. But in England I have never seen domes.'

'What's a dome?'

'A round roof, like half a ball.'

Merthin was astonished. 'I never heard of such a thing! How is it built?'

Buonaventura laughed. 'Young man, I am a wool merchant. I can tell whether a fleece comes from a Cotswold sheep or a Lincoln sheep, just by rubbing the wool between my finger and thumb, but I don't know how a henhouse is built, let alone a dome.'

Merthin's master, Elfric, arrived. He was a prosperous man, and he wore expensive clothes, but they always looked as if they belonged to someone else. An habitual sycophant, he ignored Caris and Merthin, but made a deep bow to Buonaventura and said: 'Honoured to have you in our city once again, sir.'

Merthin turned away.

'How many languages do you think there are?' Caris said to him.

She was always saying crazy things. 'Five,' Merthin replied without thinking.

'No, be serious,' she said. 'There's English, and French, and Latin, that's three. Then the Florentines and the Venetians speak differently, though they have words in common.'

'You're right,' he said, entering into the game. 'That's five already. Then there's Flemish.' Few people could make out the tongue of the traders who came to Kingsbridge from the weaving towns of Flanders: Ypres, Bruges, Ghent.

'And Danish.'

'The Arabs have their own language and, when they write, they don't even use the same letters as we do.'

'And Mother Cecilia told me that all the barbarians have their own tongues that no one even knows how to write down – Scots, Welsh, Irish, and probably others. That makes eleven, and there might be people we haven't even heard of!'

Merthin grinned. Caris was the only person he could do this with. Among their friends of the same age, no one understood the thrill of imagining strange people and different ways of life. She would ask a random question: What is it like to live at the edge of the world? Are the priests wrong about God? How do you know you're not dreaming, right now? And they would be off on a speculative voyage, competing to come up with the most outlandish notions.

The roar of conversation in the church suddenly quietened, and Merthin saw that the monks and nuns were seating themselves. The choirmaster, Blind Carlus, came in last. Although he could not see, he walked without assistance in the church and the monastic buildings, moving slowly, but as confident as a sighted man, familiar with every pillar and flagstone. Now he sang a note in his rich baritone, and the choir began a hymn.

Merthin was quietly sceptical about the clergy. Priests had power that was not always matched by their knowledge – rather like his employer, Elfric. However, he liked going to church. The services induced a kind of trance in him. The music, the architecture and the Latin incantations enchanted him, and he felt as if he were asleep with his eyes open. Once again he had the fanciful sensation that he could feel the rainwater flowing in torrents far beneath his feet.

His gaze roamed over the three levels of the nave – arcade, gallery and clerestory. He knew that the columns were made by placing one stone on top of another, but they gave a different impression, at least at first glance. The stone blocks were carved so that each column looked like a bundle of shafts. He traced the rise of one of the four giant piers of the crossing, from the huge square foot on which it stood, up to where one shaft branched north to form an arch across the side aisle, on up to the tribune level where another shaft branched west to form the arcade of the gallery, on up to the westward springing of a clerestory arch, until the last remaining shafts separated, like a spray of flowers, and became the curving ribs of the ceiling vault far above. From the central boss at the highest point of the vault, he followed a rib all the way down again to the matching pier on the opposite corner of the crossing.

As he did so, something odd happened. His vision seemed momentarily to blur, and it looked as if the east side of the transept moved.

There was a low rumbling sound, so deep it was almost inaudible, and a tremor underfoot, as if a tree had fallen nearby.

The singing faltered.

In the chancel, a crack appeared in the south wall, right next to the pier Merthin had been looking at.

He found himself turning towards Caris. Out of the corner of his eye he saw masonry falling in the choir and the crossing. Then there was nothing but noise: women screaming, men shouting, and the deafening crash of huge stones hitting the floor. It lasted a long moment. When silence descended, Merthin found he was holding Caris, his left arm around her shoulders pressing her to him, his right arm protectively covering her head, his body interposed between her and the place where a part of the great church lay in ruins.

*

IT WAS OBVIOUSLY a miracle that no one died.

The worst of the damage was in the south aisle of the chancel, which had been empty of people during the service. The congregation was not admitted to the chancel, and the clergy had all been in the central part, called the choir. Several monks had had narrow escapes, which only heightened the talk of miracles, and others had bad cuts and bruises from flying chips of stone. The congregation suffered no more than a few scratches. Evidently, they had all been supernaturally protected by St Adolphus, whose bones were preserved under the high altar, and whose deeds included many instances of curing the sick and saving people from death. However, it was generally agreed that

God had sent the people of Kingsbridge a warning. What he was warning them about was not yet clear.

An hour later, four men were inspecting the damage. Brother Godwyn, the cousin of Caris, was the sacrist, responsible for the church and all its treasures. Under him as matricularius, in charge of building operations and repairs, was Brother Thomas, who had been Sir Thomas Langley ten years ago. The contract for cathedral maintenance was held by Elfric, a carpenter by training and a general builder by trade. And Merthin tagged along as Elfric's apprentice.

The east end of the church was divided by pillars into four sections, called bays. The collapse had affected the two bays nearest the crossing. The stone vaulting over the south aisle was destroyed completely in the first bay and partially in the second. There were cracks in the tribune gallery, and stone mullions had fallen from the windows of the clerestory.

Elfric said: 'Some weakness in the mortar allowed the vault to crumble, and that in turn caused the cracks at higher levels.'

That did not sound right to Merthin, but he lacked an alternative explanation.

Merthin hated his master. He had first been apprenticed to Elfric's father, Joachim, a builder of wide experience who had worked on churches and bridges in London and Paris. The old man had delighted in explaining to Merthin the lore of the masons – what they called their 'mysteries', which were mostly arithmetical formulas for building, such as the ratio between the height of a building and the depth of its foundations. Merthin liked numbers and lapped up everything Joachim could teach him.

Then Joachim died, and Elfric took over. Elfric believed the main thing an apprentice had to learn was obedience. Merthin found this difficult to accept, and Elfric punished him with short rations, thin clothing and outdoor work in frosty weather. To make matters worse, Elfric's chubby daughter Griselda, the same age as Merthin, was always well fed and warmly dressed.

Three years ago Elfric's wife had died, and he had married Alice, the older sister of Caris. People thought Alice was the prettier sister, and it was true that she had more regular features, but she lacked Caris's captivating ways, and Merthin found her dull. Alice had always seemed to like Merthin almost as much as her sister did, and so he had hoped she would make Elfric treat him better. But the reverse happened. Alice seemed to think it was her wifely duty to join with Elfric in tormenting him.

Merthin knew that many other apprentices suffered in the same way, and they all put up with it because apprenticeship was the only way into a well-paid trade. The craft guilds efficiently kept out upstarts. No one could do business in a town without belonging to a guild. Even a priest, a monk or a woman who wanted to deal in wool or brew ale for sale would have to get into a guild. And outside the towns there was little business to be done: peasants built their own houses and sewed their own shirts.

At the end of the apprenticeship, most boys would remain with the master, working as journeymen for a wage. A few would end up partners, taking over the enterprise when the old man died. That would not be Merthin's destiny. He hated Elfric too much. He would leave the moment he could.

'Let's look at it from above,' said Godwyn.

They walked towards the east end. Elfric said: 'It's good to see you back from Oxford, Brother Godwyn. But you must miss the company of all those learned people.'

Godwyn nodded. 'The masters are truly astonishing.'

'And the other students – they must be remarkable young men, I imagine. Though we hear tales of bad behaviour, too.'

Godwyn looked rueful. 'I'm afraid some of those stories are true. When a young priest or monk is away from home for the first time, he may suffer temptation.'

'Still – we're fortunate to have the benefit of university-trained men here in Kingsbridge.'

'Very kind of you to say so.'

'Oh, but it's true.'

Merthin wanted to say: Shut up, for pity's sake. But this was Elfric's way. He was a poor craftsman, his work inaccurate and his judgement shaky, but he knew how to ingratiate himself. Merthin had watched him do it, time and again – for Elfric could be as charming to people from whom he wanted something as he could be rude to those who had nothing he needed.

Merthin was more surprised at Godwyn. How could an intelligent and educated man fail to see through Elfric? Perhaps it was less obvious to the person who was the object of the compliments.

Godwyn opened a small door and led the way up a narrow spiral staircase concealed in the wall. Merthin felt excited. He loved to enter the hidden passageways of the cathedral. He was also curious about the dramatic collapse, and eager to figure out its cause.

The aisles were single-storey structures that stuck out either side of the main body of the church. They had rib-vaulted stone ceilings. Above the vault, a lean-to roof rose from the outer edge of the aisle up to the base of the clerestory. Under that sloping roof was a triangular void, its floor the hidden side, or extrados, of the aisle's vaulted ceiling. The four men climbed into this void to look at the damage from above.

It was lit by window openings into the interior of the church, and Thomas had had the foresight to bring an oil lamp. The first thing Merthin noticed was that the vaults, viewed from above, were not exactly the same in each bay. The easternmost formed a slightly flatter curve than its neighbour, and the next one – partly destroyed – looked as though it was different again.

They walked along the extrados, staying close to the edge where the vault was strongest, until they were as near as they dared go to the collapsed portion. The vault was constructed in the same way as the rest of the church, of stones mortared together, except that ceiling stones were very thin and light. The vault was almost vertical at its springing but, as it rose, it leaned inwards, until it met the stonework coming up from the opposite edge.

Elfric said: 'Well, the first thing to do is obviously to rebuild the vaulting over the first two bays of the aisle.'

Thomas said: 'It's a long time since anyone in Kingsbridge built rib-vaulting.' He turned to Merthin. 'Could you make the formwork?'

Merthin knew what he meant. At the edge of the vault, where the masonry was almost upright, the stones would stay in place by their own weight; but, higher up, as the curve turned towards the horizontal, some support was needed to keep everything in place while the mortar dried. The obvious method was to make a wooden frame, called formwork or centering, and lay the stones on top of that.

It was a challenging job for a carpenter, for the curves had to be just right. Thomas knew the quality of Merthin's craftsmanship, having closely supervised the work Merthin and Elfric carried out at the cathedral over several years. However, it was tactless of Thomas to address the apprentice rather than the boss, and Elfric reacted quickly. 'Under my supervision he can do it, yes,' he said.

'I can make the formwork,' Merthin said, already thinking about how the frame would be supported by the scaffolding, and the platform on which the masons would have to stand. 'But these vaults were not built with formwork.'

'Don't talk nonsense, boy,' Elfric said. 'Of course they were. You know nothing about it.'

Merthin knew it was unwise to argue with his employer. On the other hand, in six months he would be competing with Elfric for work, and he needed people such as Brother Godwyn to believe in his competence. Also, he was stung by the scorn in Elfric's voice, and he felt an irresistible desire to prove his master wrong. 'Look at the extrados,' he said indignantly. 'Having finished one bay, surely the masons would have re-used the same formwork for the next. In which case, all the vaults would have the same curve. But, in fact, they're all different.'

'Obviously they didn't re-use their formwork,' Elfric said irritably.

'Why wouldn't they?' Merthin persisted. 'They must have wanted to save on timber, not to mention the wages of skilled carpenters.'

'Anyway, it's not possible to build vaulting without formwork.'

'Yes, it is,' Merthin said. 'There's a method—'

'That's enough,' Elfric said. 'You're here to learn, not teach.'

Godwyn put in: 'Just a minute, Elfric. If the boy is right, it could save the priory a lot of money.' He looked at Merthin. 'What were you going to say?'

Merthin was half wishing he had not raised this subject. There would be hell to pay later. But he was committed now. If he backed off, they would think he did not know what he was talking about. 'It's described in a book in the monastery library, and it's very simple,' he said. 'As each stone is laid, a rope is draped over it. One end of the rope is tied to the wall, the other weighted with a lump of wood. The rope forms a right angle over the edge of the stone, and keeps it from slipping off its bed of mortar and falling to the ground.'

There was a moment of silence as they all concentrated, trying to visualize the arrangements. Then Thomas nodded. 'It could work,' he said.

Elfric looked furious.

Godwyn was intrigued. 'What book is this?'

'It's called Timothy's Book,' Merthin told him.

'I know of it, but I've never studied it. Obviously I should.' Godwyn addressed the others. 'Have we seen enough?'

Elfric and Thomas nodded. As the four men left the roof space, Elfric muttered to Merthin: 'Do you realize you've just talked yourself out of several weeks' work? You won't do that when you're your own master, I'll bet.'

Merthin had not thought of that. Elfric was right: by proving that formwork was unnecessary, he had also done himself out of a job. But there was something badly wrong with Elfric's way of thinking. It was unfair to allow someone to spend money unnecessarily, just to keep yourself in work. Merthin did not want to live by cheating people.

They went down the spiral staircase into the chancel. Elfric said to Godwyn: 'I'll come to you tomorrow with a price for the work.'

'Good.'

Elfric turned to Merthin. 'You stay here and count the stones in an aisle vault. Bring me the answer at home.'

'Yes.'

Elfric and Godwyn left, but Thomas lingered. 'I got you into trouble,' he said.

'You were trying to boost me.'

The monk shrugged, and made a what-can-you-do gesture with his right arm. His left arm had been amputated at the elbow ten years ago, after infection set in to the wound he received in the fight Merthin had witnessed.

Merthin hardly ever thought about that strange scene in the forest – he had become used to Thomas in a monk's robe – but he recalled it now: the men-at-arms, the children hiding in the bush, the bow and arrow, the buried letter. Thomas was always kind to him, and he guessed it was because of what happened that day. 'I've never told anyone about that letter,' he said quietly.

'I know,' Thomas replied. 'If you had, you'd be dead.'

*

MOST LARGE TOWNS were run by a guild merchant, an organization of the leading citizens. Under the guild merchant were numerous craft guilds, each dedicated to a particular trade: masons, carpenters, leather tanners, weavers, tailors. Then there were the parish guilds, small groups centred on local churches, formed to raise money for priestly robes and sacred ornaments, and for the support of widows and orphans.

Cathedral towns were different. Kingsbridge, like St Albans and Bury St Edmunds, was ruled by the monastery, which owned almost all the land in and around the town. The priors had always refused permission for a guild merchant. However, the most important craftsmen and traders belonged to the parish guild of St Adolphus. No doubt this had started out, in the distant past, as a pious group that raised money for the cathedral, but it was now the most important organization in town. It made rules for the conduct of business, and elected an alderman and six wardens to enforce them. In the guild hall were kept the measures that standardized the weight of a woolsack, the width of a bolt of cloth, and the volume of a bushel for all Kingsbridge trade. Nevertheless, the merchants could not hold courts and dispense justice the way they did in borough towns – the Kingsbridge prior retained those powers for himself.

On the afternoon of Whit Sunday, the parish guild gave a banquet at the guild hall for the most important visiting buyers.

Edmund Wooler was the alderman, and Caris went with him to be hostess, so Merthin had to amuse himself without her.

Fortunately, Elfric and Alice were also at the banquet, so he could sit in the kitchen, listening to the rain and thinking. The weather was not cold, but there was a small fire for cooking, and its red glow was cheerful.

He could hear Elfric's daughter, Griselda, moving about upstairs. It was a fine house, although smaller than Edmund's. There was just a hall and a kitchen downstairs. The staircase led to an open landing, where Griselda slept, and a closed bedroom for the master and his wife. Merthin slept in the kitchen.

There had been a time, three or four years ago, when Merthin had been tormented at night by fantasies of climbing the stairs and slipping under the blankets next to Griselda's warm, plump body. But she considered herself superior to him, treating him like a servant, and she had never given him the least encouragement.

Sitting on a bench, Merthin looked into the fire and visualized the wooden scaffolding he would build for the masons who would reconstruct the collapsed vaulting in the cathedral. Wood was expensive, and long tree trunks were rare – the owners of woodland usually yielded to the temptation of selling the timber before it was fully mature. So builders tried to minimize the amount of scaffolding. Rather than build it up from floor level, they saved timber by suspending it from the existing walls.

While he was thinking, Griselda came into the kitchen and took a cup of ale from the barrel. 'Would you like some?' she said. Merthin accepted, amazed by her courtesy. She surprised him again by sitting on a stool opposite him to drink.

Griselda's paramour, Thurstan, had disappeared three weeks ago. No doubt she now felt lonely, which would be why she wanted Merthin's company. The drink warmed his stomach and relaxed him. Searching for something to say, he asked: 'What happened to Thurstan?'

She tossed her head like a frisky mare. 'I told him I didn't want to marry him.'

'Why not?'

'He's too young for me.'

That did not sound right to Merthin. Thurstan was seventeen, Griselda twenty, but Griselda was not notably mature. More likely, he thought, Thurstan was too low-class. He had arrived in Kingsbridge from nowhere a couple of years ago, and had worked as an unskilled labourer for several of the town's craftsmen. He had probably got bored, with Griselda or with Kingsbridge, and simply moved on.

'Where did he go?'

'I don't know, and I don't care. I should marry someone my own age, someone with a sense of responsibility – perhaps a man who could take over my father's enterprise one day.'

It occurred to Merthin that she might mean him. Surely not, he thought; she's always looked down on me. Then she got up from her stool and came and sat on the bench beside him.

'My father is spiteful to you,' she said. 'I've always thought that.'

Merthin was astonished. 'Well, it's taken you long enough to say so – I've been living here six and a half years.'

'It's hard for me to go against my family.'

'Why is he so vile to me, anyway?'

'Because you think you know better than him, and you can't hide it.'

'Maybe I do know better.'

'See what I mean?'

He laughed. It was the first time she had ever made him laugh.

She shifted closer on the bench, so that her thigh in the woollen dress was pressed against his. He was in his worn linen shirt, which came to mid-thigh, with the undershorts that all men wore, but he could feel the warmth of her body through their clothes. What had brought this on? He looked incredulously at her. She had glossy dark hair and brown eyes. Her face was attractive in a fleshy way. She had a nice mouth for kissing.

She said: 'I like being indoors in a rainstorm. It feels cosy.'

He felt himself becoming aroused, and looked away from her. What would Caris think, he asked himself, if she walked in here now? He tried to quell his desire, but that only made it worse.

He looked back at Griselda. Her lips were moist and slightly parted. She leaned towards him. He kissed her. Immediately, she thrust her tongue into his mouth. It was a sudden, shocking intimacy that he found thrilling, and he responded in the same way. This was not like kissing Caris—

That thought arrested him. He tore himself away from Griselda and stood up.

She said: 'What's the matter?'

He did not want to tell her the truth, so he said: 'You never seemed to like me.'

She looked annoyed. 'I've told you, I had to side with my father.'

'You've changed very suddenly.'

She stood up and moved towards him. He stepped away until his back was to the wall. She took his hand and pressed it to her bosom. Her breasts were round and heavy, and he could not resist the temptation to feel them. She said: 'Have you ever done it – the real thing – with a girl?'

He found he could not speak, but he nodded.

'Have you thought about doing it with me?'

'Yes,' he managed.

'You can do it to me now, if you like, while they're out. We can go upstairs and lie on my bed.'

'No.'

She pressed her body to his. 'Kissing you has made me go all hot and slippery inside.'

He pushed her away. The shove was rougher than he intended, and she fell backwards, landing on her well-cushioned bottom. 'Leave me alone,' he said.

He was not sure he meant it, but she took him at his word. 'Go to hell, then,' she swore. She got to her feet and stomped upstairs.

He stayed where he was, panting. Now that he had rejected her, he regretted it.

Apprentices were not very attractive to young women, who did not want to be forced to wait years before marrying. All the same, Merthin had courted several Kingsbridge girls. One, Kate Brown, had been sufficiently fond of him to let him go all the way, one warm summer afternoon a year ago, in her father's orchard. Then her father had died suddenly, and her mother had taken the family to live in Portsmouth. It was the only time Merthin had lain with a woman. Was he mad to turn down Griselda's offer?

He told himself he had had a lucky escape. Griselda was a mean-spirited girl who did not really like him. He should be proud of having resisted temptation. He had not followed his instinct like a dumb beast; he had made a decision, like a man.

Then Griselda started to cry.

Her weeping was not loud, but all the same he could hear everything. He went to the back door. Like every house in town, Elfric's had a long, narrow strip of land at the back with a privy and a rubbish tip. Most householders kept chickens and a pig, and grew vegetables and fruits, but Elfric's yard was used to store stacks of lumber and stones, coils of rope, buckets and barrows and ladders. Merthin stared at the rain falling on the yard, but Griselda's sobbing still reached his ears.

He decided to leave the house, and got as far as the front door, but then he could not think where to go. At Caris's house there was only Petranilla, who would not welcome him. He thought of going to his parents, but they were the last people he wanted to see when he was in this state. He could have talked to his brother, but Ralph was not due to arrive in Kingsbridge until later in the week. Besides, he realized, he could not leave the house without a coat – not because of the rain, he did not mind getting wet, but because of the bulge in front of his clothing that would not subside.

He tried to think of Caris. She would be sipping wine, he thought, and eating roast beef and wheat bread. He asked himself what she was wearing. Her best dress was a soft pinkish-red with a square-cut neckline that showed off the pale skin of her slender neck. But Griselda's crying kept intruding on his thoughts. He wanted to comfort her, to tell her he was sorry to make her feel spurned, and explain to her that she was an attractive person but they were not right for one another.

He sat down, then stood up again. It was hard to listen to a woman in distress. He could not think about scaffolding while that sound filled the house. Can't stay, can't leave, can't sit still.

He went upstairs.

She was lying face down on the straw-filled palliasse that was her bed. Her dress was rucked up around her chubby thighs. The skin on the back of her legs was very white and looked soft.

'I'm sorry,' he said.

'Go away.'

'Don't cry.'

'I hate you.'

He knelt down and patted her back. 'I can't sit in the kitchen and listen to you crying.'

She rolled over and looked at him, her face wet with tears. 'I'm ugly and fat, and you hate me.'

'I don't hate you.' He wiped her wet cheeks with the back of his hand.

She took his wrist and drew him to her. 'Don't you? Truly?'

'No. But...'

She put her hand behind his head, pulled him down, and kissed him. He groaned, more aroused than ever. He lay beside her on the mattress. I will leave her in a moment, he told himself. I'll just comfort her a little more, then I'll get up and go down the stairs.

She took his hand and pushed it up her skirt, placing it between her legs. He felt the wiry hair, the soft skin beneath, and the moist divide, and he knew he was lost. He stroked her roughly, his finger slipping inside. He felt as if he would burst. 'I can't stop,' he said.

'Quickly,' she said, panting. She pulled up his shirt and pushed down his drawers, and he rolled on to her.

He felt himself losing control as she guided him inside her. The remorse hit him before it was over. 'Oh, no,' he said. The explosion began with his first thrust, and in an instant it was finished. He slumped on top of her, his eyes closed. 'Oh, God,' he said. 'I wish I was dead.'

7

BUONAVENTURA CAROLI made his shock announcement at breakfast on Monday, the day after the big banquet at the guild hall.

Caris felt a little unwell as she took her seat at the oak table in the dining hall of her father's house. She had a headache and a touch of nausea. She ate a small dish of warm bread-and-milk to settle her stomach. Recalling that she had enjoyed the wine at the banquet, she wondered whether she had drunk too much of it. Was this the morning-after feeling that men and boys joked about when they boasted how much strong drink they could take?

Father and Buonaventura were eating cold mutton, and Aunt Petranilla was telling a story. 'When I was fifteen, I was betrothed to a nephew of the earl of Shiring,' she said. 'It was considered a good match: his father was a knight of the middling sort, and mine a wealthy wool merchant. Then the earl and his only son both died in Scotland, at the battle of Loudon Hill. My fiancé, Roland, became the earl – and broke off the engagement. He is still the earl today. If I had married Roland before the battle, I would now be the countess of Shiring.' She dipped toast in her ale.

'Perhaps it was not the will of God,' said Buonaventura. He threw a bone to Scrap, who pounced on it as if she had not seen food for a week. Then he said to Papa: 'My friend, there is something I should tell you before we begin the day's business.'

Caris felt, from his tone of voice, that he had bad news; and her father must have had the same intuition, for he said: 'This sounds ominous.'

'Our trade has been shrinking for the last few years,' Buonaventura went on. 'Each year my family sells a little less cloth, each year we buy a little less wool from England.'

'Business is always like that,' said Edmund. 'It goes up, it goes down, no one knows why.'

'But now your king has interfered.'

It was true. Edward III had seen the money being made in wool and had decided that more of it must go to the crown. He had introduced a new tax of one pound per woolsack. A sack was standardized at 364 pounds weight, and sold for about four pounds in money; so the extra tax was a quarter of the value of the wool, a huge slice.

Buonaventura went on: 'What is worse, he has made it difficult to export wool from England. I have had to pay large bribes.'

'The ban on exports will be lifted shortly,' Edmund said. 'The merchants of the Wool Company in London are negotiating with royal officials—'

'I hope you are right,' Buonaventura said. 'But, with things as they are, my family feels I no longer need to visit two separate wool fairs in this part of the country.'

'Quite right!' said Edmund. 'Come here, and forget about the Shiring Fair.'

The town of Shiring was two days' travel from Kingsbridge. It was about the same size, and while it did not have a cathedral or a priory, it boasted the sheriff's castle and the county court. It held a rival Wool Fair once a year.

'I'm afraid I can't find the range of wool here. You see, the Kingsbridge Fleece Fair seems to be declining. More and more sellers go to Shiring. Their fair offers a greater variety of types and qualities.'

Caris was dismayed. This could be disastrous for her father. She put in: 'Why would sellers prefer Shiring?'

Buonaventura shrugged. 'The guild merchant there has made the fair attractive. There's no long queue to enter the city gate; the dealers can hire tents and booths; there's a wool exchange building where everyone can do business when it rains like this...'

'We could do all that,' she said.

Her father snorted. 'If only.'

'Why not, Papa?'

'Shiring is an independent borough, with a royal charter. The guild merchant there has the power to organize things for the benefit of the wool merchants. Kingsbridge belongs to the priory—'

Petranilla put in: 'For the glory of God.'

'No doubt,' Edmund said. 'But our parish guild can't do anything without the priory's approval – and priors are cautious and conservative people, my brother being no exception. The upshot is that most improvement plans get rejected.'

Buonaventura went on: 'Because of my family's long association with you, Edmund, and your father before you, we have continued to come to Kingsbridge; but in hard times we can't afford to be sentimental.'

'Then let me ask you a small favour, for the sake of that long association,' Edmund said. 'Don't make a final decision yet. Keep an open mind.'

That was clever, Caris thought. She was struck – as she often was – by how shrewd her father could be in a negotiation. He did not argue that Buonaventura should reverse his decision, for that would just make him dig his heels in. The Italian was much more likely to agree not to make the decision final. That committed him to nothing, but left the door open.

Buonaventura found it hard to refuse. 'All right, but to what end?'

'I want the chance to improve the fair, and especially that bridge,' Edmund replied. 'If we could offer better facilities here at Kingsbridge than they have at Shiring, and attract more sellers, you would continue to visit us, wouldn't you?'

'Of course.'

'Then that's what we'll have to do.' He stood up. 'I'll go and see my brother now. Caris, come with me. We'll show him the queue at the bridge. No, wait, Caris, go and fetch your clever young builder, Merthin. We might need his expertise.'

'He'll be working.'

Petranilla said: 'Just tell his master that the alderman of the parish guild wants the boy.' Petranilla was proud that her brother was alderman, and mentioned it at every opportunity.

But she was right. Elfric would have to release Merthin. 'I'll go and find him,' Caris said.

She put on a cape with a hood and went out. It was still raining, though not as heavily as yesterday. Elfric, like most of the leading citizens, lived on the main street that ran from the bridge up to the priory gates. The broad street was crowded with carts and people heading for the fair, splashing through puddles and streamlets of rain.

She was eager to see Merthin, as always. She had liked him ever since All Hallows' Day ten years ago, when he had appeared at archery practice with his home-made bow. He was clever and funny. Like her, he knew that the world was a bigger and more fascinating place than most Kingsbridge citizens could conceive. But six months ago they had discovered something that was even more fun than being friends.

Caris had kissed boys before Merthin, though not often: she had never really seen the point. With him it was different, exciting and sexy. He had an impish streak that made everything he did seem mildly wicked. She liked it when he touched her body, too. She wanted to do more – but she tried not to think about that. 'More' meant marriage, and a wife had to be subordinate to her husband, who was her master – and Caris hated that idea. Fortunately she was not forced to think about it yet, for Merthin could not marry until his apprenticeship was over, and that was half a year away.

She reached Elfric's house and stepped inside. Her sister, Alice, was in the front room, at the table, with her stepdaughter, Griselda. They were eating bread with honey. Alice had changed in the three years since she had married Elfric. Her nature had always been harsh, like Petranilla's, and under the influence of her husband she had become more suspicious, resentful and ungenerous.

But she was pleasant enough today. 'Sit down, sister,' she said. 'The bread is fresh this morning.'

'I can't, I'm looking for Merthin.'

Alice looked disapproving. 'So early?'

'Father wants him.' Caris went through the kitchen to the

back door and looked into the yard. Rain fell on a dismal landscape of builder's junk. One of Elfric's labourers was putting wet stones into a barrow. There was no sign of Merthin. She went back inside.

Alice said: 'He's probably at the cathedral. He's been making a door.'

Caris recalled that Merthin had mentioned this. The door in the north porch had rotted, and Merthin was working on a replacement.

Griselda added: 'He's been carving virgins.' She grinned, then put more bread-and-honey into her mouth.

Caris knew this, too. The old door was decorated with carvings illustrating the story Jesus told on the Mount of Olives, about the wise and foolish virgins, and Merthin had to copy it. But there was something unpleasant about Griselda's grin, Caris thought; almost as if she were laughing at Caris for being a virgin herself.

'I'll try the cathedral,' Caris said, and with a perfunctory wave she left.

She climbed the main street and entered the cathedral close. As she threaded her way through the market stalls, it seemed to her that a dismal air hung over the fair. Was she imagining it, because of what Buonaventura had said? She thought not. When she recalled the Fleece Fairs of her childhood, it seemed to her that they had been busier and more crowded. In those days, the priory precincts had not been large enough to contain the fair, and the streets all around had been obstructed by unlicensed stalls – often just a small table covered with trinkets – plus hawkers with trays, jugglers, fortune tellers, musicians, and itinerant friars calling sinners to redemption. Now it seemed to her there might have been room for a few more stalls within the precincts. 'Buonaventura must be right,' she said to herself. 'The fair is shrinking.' A trader gave her a strange look, and she realized she had spoken her thoughts out loud. It was a bad habit: people thought she was talking to spirits. She had taught herself not to do it, but she sometimes forgot, especially when she was anxious.

She walked around the great church to the north side.

Merthin was working in the porch, a roomy space where people often held meetings. He had the door standing upright in a stout wooden frame that held it still while he carved. Behind the new work, the old door was still in place in the archway, cracked and crumbling. Merthin stood with his back to her, so that the light fell over his shoulders on to the wood in front of him. He did not see her, and the sound of the rain drowned her footsteps, so she was able to study him for a few moments unnoticed.

He was a small man, not much taller than she. He had a large, intelligent head on a wiry body. His small hands moved deftly across the carving, shaving fine curls of wood with a sharp knife as he shaped the images. He had white skin and a lot of bushy red hair. 'He's not very handsome,' Alice had said, with a twist of her lip, when Caris admitted she had fallen in love with him. It was true that Merthin did not have the dashing good looks of his brother, Ralph, but Caris thought his face was quite marvellous: irregular and quirky and wise and full of laughter, just as he was.

'Hello,' she said, and he jumped. She laughed. 'It's not like you to be so easily spooked.'

'You startled me.' He hesitated, then kissed her. He seemed a little awkward, but that sometimes happened when he was concentrating on his work.

She looked at the carving. There were five virgins on each side of the door, the wise ones feasting at the wedding, and the foolish ones outside, holding their lamps upside down to show that they were empty of oil. Merthin had copied the design of the old door, but with subtle changes. The virgins stood in rows, five on one side and five on the other, like the arches in the cathedral; but, in the new door, they were not exactly alike. Merthin had given each girl a sign of individuality. One was pretty, another had curly hair, one wept, another closed one eye in a mischievous wink. He had made them real, and the scene on the old door now looked stiff and lifeless by comparison. 'It's wonderful,' Caris said. 'But I wonder what the monks will think.'

'Brother Thomas likes it,' Merthin replied.

'What about Prior Anthony?'

'He hasn't seen it. But he'll accept it. He won't want to pay twice.'

That was true, Caris thought. Her uncle Anthony was unadventurous, but parsimonious too. The mention of the prior reminded her of her errand. 'My father wants you to meet him and the prior at the bridge.'

'Did he say why?'

'I think he's going to ask Anthony to build a new bridge.'

Merthin put his tools into a leather satchel, and quickly swept the floor, brushing sawdust and wood shavings out of the porch. Then he and Caris walked in the rain through the fair and down the main street to the wooden bridge. Caris told him what Buonaventura had said at the breakfast table. Merthin felt, as she did, that recent fairs had not been as bustling as those he remembered from childhood.

Despite that, there was a long queue of people and carts waiting to get into Kingsbridge. At the near end of the bridge was a small gatehouse where a monk sat taking a fee of one penny from every trader who entered the city with goods for sale. The bridge was narrow, so it was not possible for anyone to jump the queue, and in consequence people who did not need to pay – residents of the town, mainly – also had to stand in line. In addition, some of the boards that formed the surface were twisted and broken, so carts had to move slowly as they crossed. The result was that the queue stretched away along the road between the suburban hovels and disappeared into the rain.

The bridge was also too short. Once, no doubt, both its ends had given on to dry land. But either the river had widened or, more likely, the passage of carts and people over decades and centuries had flattened the banks, so that now people had to wade across muddy beaches on both sides.

Caris saw that Merthin was studying its structure. She knew that look in his eyes: he was thinking about how it stayed upright. She often caught him staring at something in that way, usually in the cathedral, but sometimes in front of a house or even something natural, a thorn tree in blossom or a sparrowhawk hovering. He became very still, his gaze bright and sharp, as if he were shining a light into a murky place, trying to make out what was there. If she asked him, he told her he was trying to see the insides of things.

She followed his gaze and strained to imagine what he perceived in the old bridge. It was sixty yards from end to end, the longest bridge she had ever seen. The roadbed was supported by massive oak piers in two rows, like the pillars that marched either side of the nave of the cathedral. There were five pairs of piers. The end ones, where the water was shallow, were quite short, but the three central pairs stood fifteen feet above the water line.

Each pier consisted of four oak beams in a cluster, held together by plank braces. Legend said that the king had given Kingsbridge Priory the twenty-four best oak trees in England to build the three central pairs of piers. The tops were linked by beams in two parallel lines. Shorter beams crossed from one line to the other, forming the roadbed; and longitudinal planks had been laid on top to form the road surface. On each side was a wooden railing that served as a flimsy parapet. Every couple of years a drunk peasant would drive a cart through the rail and kill himself and his horse in the river.

'What are you looking at?' Caris asked Merthin.

'The cracks.'

'I don't see any.'

'The timbers on either side of the central pier are splitting. You can see where Elfric has reinforced them with iron braces.'

Now that he pointed them out, Caris could see the flat metal strips nailed across the cracks. 'You look worried,' she said to him.

'I don't know why the timbers cracked in the first place.'

'Does it matter?'

'Of course it does.'

He was not very talkative this morning. She was about to ask him why, when he said: 'Here comes your father.'

She looked along the street. The two brothers made an odd pair. Tall Anthony fastidiously held up the skirts of his monkish robe and stepped gingerly around the puddles, wearing an expression of distaste on his pale indoor face. Edmund, more vigorous despite being the elder, had a red face and a long untidy grey beard, and he walked carelessly, dragging his withered leg through the mud, speaking argumentatively and gesturing extravagantly with both arms. When Caris saw her father at a distance, the way a stranger might see him, she always felt a surge of love.

The dispute was in full swing when they got to the bridge, and they continued without pause. 'Look at that queue!' Edmund shouted. 'Hundreds of people *not* trading at the fair because they haven't got there yet! And you can be sure half of them will meet a buyer or seller while waiting, and conduct their business right then and there, then go home without even entering the city!'

'That's forestalling, and it's against the law,' said Anthony.

'You could go and tell them that, if you could get across the bridge, but you can't, because it's too narrow! Listen, Anthony. If the Italians pull out, the Fleece Fair will never be the same again. Your prosperity and mine are based on the fair – we must not just let it go!'

'We can't force Buonaventura to do business here.'

'But we can make our fair more attractive than Shiring's. We need to announce a big, symbolic project, right now, this week, something to convince them all that the Fleece Fair isn't finished. We have to tell them we're going to tear down this old bridge and build a new one, twice as wide.' Without warning, he turned to Merthin. 'How long would it take, young lad?'

Merthin looked startled, but he answered. 'Finding the trees would be the hard part. You need very long timbers, well seasoned. Then the piers have to be driven into the river bed – that's tricky, because you're working in running water. After that it's just carpentry. You could finish it by Christmas.'

Anthony said: 'There's no certainty the Caroli family will change its plans if we build a new bridge.'

'They will,' Edmund said forcefully. 'I guarantee it.'

'Anyway, I can't afford to build a bridge. I don't have the money.'

'You can't afford *not* to build a bridge,' Edmund shouted. 'You'll ruin yourself as well as the town.'

'It's out of the question. I don't even know where I'm going to get the money for the repairs in the south aisle.'

'So what will you do?'

'Trust in God.'

'Those who trust in God and sow a seed may reap a harvest. But you're not sowing the seed.'

Anthony got irritated. 'I know this is difficult for you to understand, Edmund, but Kingsbridge Priory is not a commercial enterprise. We're here to worship God, not to make money.'

'You won't worship God for long if you've nothing to eat.'

'God will provide.'

Edmund's red face flushed with anger, turning a purplish colour. 'When you were a boy, our father's business fed you and clothed you and paid for your education. Since you've been a monk, the citizens of this town and the peasants of the surrounding countryside have kept you alive by paying you rents, tithes, charges for market stalls, bridge tolls, and a dozen other different fees. All your life you've lived like a flea on the backs of hard working people. And now you have the nerve to tell us that God provides.'

'That's perilously close to blasphemy.'

'Don't forget that I've known you since you were born, Anthony. You always had a talent for avoiding work.' Edmund's voice, so often raised in a shout, now dropped – a sign, Caris knew, that he was really furious. 'When it was time to empty out the privy, you went off to bed, so that you would be rested for school the next day. Father's gift to God, you always had the best of everything, and never lifted your hand to earn it. Strengthening food, the warmest bedroom, the best clothes – I was the only boy who wore his younger brother's cast-off outfits!'

'And you never let me forget it.'

Caris had been waiting for the opportunity to halt the flow, and now she took it. 'There ought to be a way around this.'

They both looked at her, surprised to be interrupted.

She went on: 'For example, couldn't the townspeople build a bridge?'

'Don't be ridiculous,' said Anthony. 'The town belongs to the priory. A servant doesn't furnish his master's house.'

'But if your permission was sought, you would have no reason to refuse it.'

Anthony did not immediately contradict that, which was

encouraging; but Edmund was shaking his head. 'I don't think I could persuade them to put up the money,' he said. 'It would be in their interests, long term, of course; but people are very reluctant to think in the long term when being asked to part with their money.'

'Ha!' said Anthony. 'Yet you expect me to think long term.'

'You deal with eternal life, don't you?' Edmund shot back. 'You of all people ought to be able to see beyond the end of next week. Besides, you get a penny toll from everyone who crosses the bridge. You'd get your money back *and* you'd benefit from the improvement in business.'

Caris said: 'But Uncle Anthony is a spiritual leader, and he feels it's not his role.'

'But he owns the town!' Papa protested. 'He's the only one who can do it!' Then he gave her an inquiring look, realizing that she would not have contradicted him without a reason. 'What are you thinking?'

'Suppose the townspeople built a bridge, and were repaid out of the penny tolls?'

Edmund opened his mouth to express an objection, but could not think of one.

Caris looked at Anthony.

Anthony said: 'When the priory was new, its only income came from that bridge. I can't give it away.'

'But think what you would gain, if the Fleece Fair and the weekly market began to return to their former size: not just the bridge tolls, but stallholders' fees, the percentage you take of all transactions at the fair, and gifts to the cathedral too!'

Edmund added: 'And the profits on your own sales: wool, grain, hides, books, statues of the saints—'

Anthony said: 'You planned this, didn't you?' He pointed an accusing finger at his older brother. 'You told your daughter what to say, and the lad. He would never think up a scheme like this, and she's just a woman. It has your mark on it. This is all a plot to cheat me of my bridge tolls. Well, it's failed. Praise God, I'm not that stupid!' He turned away and splashed off through the mud.

Edmund said: 'I don't know how my father ever sired someone with so little sense.' And he, too, stomped off.

Caris turned to Merthin. 'Well,' she said, 'what did you think of all that?'

'I don't know.' He looked away, avoiding her eye. 'I'd better get back to work.' He went without kissing her.

'Well!' she said when he was out of earshot. 'What on earth has got into him?'

8

THE EARL OF SHIRING came to Kingsbridge on the Tuesday of
Fleece Fair week. He brought with him both his sons, various
other family members, and an entourage of knights and squires.
The bridge was cleared by his advance men, and no one was
permitted to cross for an hour before his arrival, lest he should
suffer the indignity of being made to wait alongside the common
people. His followers wore his red-and-black livery, and they all
splashed into town with banners flying, their horses' hooves
spattering the citizens with rainwater and mud. Earl Roland had
prospered in the last ten years – under Queen Isabella and, later,
her son Edward III – and he wanted the world to know it, as rich
and powerful men generally did.

In his company was Ralph, son of Sir Gerald and brother of
Merthin. At the same time as Merthin had been apprenticed to
Elfric's father, Ralph had become a squire in the household of
Earl Roland, and he had been happy ever since. He had been well
fed and clothed, he had learned to ride and fight, and he had
spent most of his time hunting and playing sports and games. In
six and a half years no one had asked him to read or write a
word. As he rode behind the earl through the huddled stalls of
the Fleece Fair, watched by faces both envious and fearful, he
pitied the merchants and tradesmen grubbing for pennies in the
mud.

The earl dismounted at the prior's house, on the north side of
the cathedral. His younger son, Richard, did the same. Richard
was bishop of Kingsbridge and the cathedral was, theoretically,
his church. However, the bishop's palace was in the county town
of Shiring, two days' journey away. This suited the bishop, whose
duties were political as much as religious; and it suited the monks,
who preferred not to be too closely supervised.

Richard was only twenty-eight, but his father was a close ally of the king, and that counted for more than seniority.

The rest of the entourage rode to the south end of the cathedral close. The earl's elder son, William, lord of Caster, told the squires to stable the horses while half a dozen knights settled in to the hospital. Ralph moved quickly to help William's wife, Lady Philippa, get down from her horse. She was a tall, attractive woman with long legs and deep breasts, and Ralph nurtured a hopeless love for her.

When the horses were settled, Ralph went to visit his mother and father. They lived rent-free in a small house in the south-west quarter of the town, by the river, in a neighbourhood made malodorous by the work of leather tanners. As he approached the house, Ralph felt himself shrivelling with shame inside his red-and-black uniform. He was grateful that Lady Philippa could not see the indignity of his parents' situation.

He had not seen them for a year, and they seemed older. There was a lot of grey in his mother's hair, and his father was losing his eyesight. They gave him cider made by the monks and wild strawberries Mother had gathered in the woods. Father admired his livery. 'Has the earl made you a knight yet?' he asked eagerly.

It was the ambition of every squire to become a knight, but Ralph felt it more keenly than most. His father had never got over the humiliation, ten years ago, of being degraded to the position of pensioner of the priory. An arrow had pierced Ralph's heart that day. The pain would not be eased until he had restored the family honour. But not all squires became knights. Nevertheless, Father always talked as if it were only a matter of time for Ralph.

'Not yet,' Ralph said. 'But we're likely to go to war with France before long, and that will be my chance.' He spoke lightly, not wishing to show how badly he yearned for the chance to distinguish himself in battle.

Mother was disgusted. 'Why do kings always want war?'

Father laughed. 'It's what men were made for.'

'No, it's not,' she said sharply. 'When I gave birth to Ralph in pain and suffering, I didn't intend that he should live to have his head cut off by a Frenchman's sword or his heart pierced by a bolt from a crossbow.'

Father flapped a hand at her in a dismissive gesture and said to Ralph: 'What makes you say there will be war?'

'King Philip of France has confiscated Gascony.'

'Ah. We can't have that.'

English kings had ruled the western French province of Gascony for generations. They had given trade privileges to the merchants of Bordeaux and Bayonne, who did more business with London than with Paris. Still, there was always trouble.

Ralph said: 'King Edward has sent ambassadors to Flanders to form alliances.'

'Allies may want money.'

'That's why Earl Roland has come to Kingsbridge. The king wants a loan from the wool merchants.'

'How much?'

'The talk is of two hundred thousand pounds, nationwide, as an advance against the wool tax.'

Mother said bleakly: 'The king should take care not to tax the wool merchants to death.'

Father said: 'The merchants have plenty of money – just look at their fine clothes.' There was bitterness in his tone, and Ralph observed that he had on a worn linen undershirt and old shoes. 'Anyway, they want us to stop the French navy interfering with their trade.' Over the last year, French ships had raided towns on the south coast of England, sacking the ports and setting fire to ships in the harbours.

'The French attack us, so we attack the French,' said Mother. 'What is the sense of it?'

'Women will never understand,' Father replied.

'That's the truth,' she said crisply.

Ralph changed the subject. 'How is my brother?'

'He's a fine craftsman,' said his father, and he sounded, Ralph thought, like a horse salesman saying that an undersized pony was a good mount for a woman.

Mother said: 'He's smitten with Edmund Wooler's daughter.'

'Caris?' Ralph smiled. 'He always liked her. We played

together as children. She was a bossy little minx, but Merthin never seemed to mind. Will he marry her?'

'I expect so,' Mother said. 'When he finishes his apprenticeship.'

'He'll have his hands full.' Ralph got up. 'Where do you think he is now?'

'He's working in the north porch of the cathedral,' Father said. 'But he might be having his dinner.'

'I'll find him.' Ralph kissed them both and went out.

He returned to the priory and wandered through the fair. The rain had stopped and the sun was shining fitfully, glinting in the puddles and raising steam off the stallholders' wet covers. He saw a familiar profile, and the regular footsteps of his heart faltered. It was the straight nose and strong jaw of Lady Philippa. She was older than Ralph, about twenty-five, he guessed. She was standing at a stall, looking at bolts of silk from Italy, and he drank in the way her light summer dress draped itself lasciviously over the curves of her hips. He made her an unnecessarily elaborate bow.

She glanced up and gave a perfunctory nod.

'Beautiful materials,' he said, trying to open a conversation.

'Yes.'

At that moment, a diminutive figure with untidy carrot-coloured hair approached: Merthin. Ralph was delighted to see him. 'This is my clever older brother,' he said to Philippa.

Merthin said to Philippa: 'Buy the pale green – it matches your eyes.'

Ralph winced. Merthin should not have addressed her in such a familiar way.

However, she did not seem to mind too much. She spoke in a tone of mild reproof, saying: 'When I want a boy's opinion, I'll ask my son,' but as she said it she gave him a smile that was almost flirtatious.

Ralph said: 'This is the Lady Philippa, you fool! I apologize for my brother's cheek, my lady.'

'What's his name, anyway?'

'I'm Merthin Fitzgerald, at your service any time you find yourself hesitating over silks.'

Ralph took his arm and led him away before he could say anything else indiscreet. 'I don't know how you do it!' he said, with exasperation and admiration equally mixed. 'It matches her eyes, does it? If I said something like that, she'd have me flogged.' He was exaggerating, but it was true that Philippa usually responded sharply to insolence. He did not know whether to be amused or angry that she had been indulgent to Merthin.

'That's me,' Merthin said. 'Every woman's dream.'

Ralph detected bitterness in his tone. 'Is anything wrong?' he said. 'How's Caris?'

'I've done something stupid,' Merthin replied. 'I'll tell you later. Let's look around while the sun's out.'

Ralph noticed a stall where a monk with ash-blond hair was selling cheese. 'Watch this,' he said to Merthin. He approached the stall and said: 'This looks tasty, brother – where does it come from?'

'We make it at St-John-in-the-Forest. It's a small cell, or branch, of Kingsbridge Priory. I'm the prior there – my name is Saul Whitehead.'

'It makes me hungry to look at it. I wish I could buy some – but the earl keeps us squires penniless.'

The monk cut a slice off the wheel of cheese and gave it to Ralph. 'Then you shall have some for nothing, in the name of Jesus,' he said.

'Thank you, Brother Saul.'

As they walked away, Ralph grinned at Merthin and said: 'See? As easy as taking an apple from a child.'

'And about as admirable,' Merthin said.

'But what a fool, to give his cheese away to anyone with a sob story!'

'He probably thinks it's better to risk being made a fool of than to deny food to a starving man.'

'You're a bit sour today. How come you're allowed to cheek a noblewoman, but I can't talk a stupid monk into giving me free cheese?'

Merthin surprised him with a grin. 'Just like when we were boys, eh?'

'Exactly!' Now Ralph did not know whether to be angry or amused. Before he could make up his mind, a pretty girl approached him with eggs on a tray. She was slim, with a small bust under a homespun dress, and he imagined her breasts to be pale and round like the eggs. He smiled at her: 'How much?' he said, though he had no need of eggs.

'A penny for twelve.'

'Are they good?'

She pointed at a nearby stall. 'They're from these hens.'

'And have the hens been well serviced by a healthy rooster?' Ralph saw Merthin roll up his eyes in mock despair at this sally.

However, the girl played along. 'Yes, sir,' she said with a smile.

'Lucky hens, eh?'

'I don't know.'

'Of course not. A maid understands little of these things.' Ralph scrutinized her. She had fair hair and a turned-up nose. She was about eighteen, he guessed.

She batted her eyelids and said: 'Don't stare at me, please.'

From behind the stall a peasant – no doubt the girl's father – had called: 'Annet! Come here.'

'So your name is Annet,' Ralph said.

She ignored the summons.

Ralph said: 'Who is your father?'

'Perkin from Wigleigh.'

'Really? My friend Stephen is lord of Wigleigh. Is Stephen good to you?'

'Lord Stephen is just and merciful,' she said dutifully.

Her father called again. 'Annet! You're wanted here.'

Ralph knew why Perkin was trying to get her away. He would not mind if a squire wanted to marry his daughter: that would be a step up the social ladder for her. But he feared that Ralph wanted to dally with her then discard her. And he was right.

'Don't go, Annet Wigleigh,' Ralph said.

'Not until you've bought what I'm offering.'

Beside them, Merthin groaned: 'One is as bad as the other.'

Ralph said: 'Why don't you put down the eggs and come with me. We could stroll along the river bank.' Between the river and the wall of the priory grounds there was a wide bank, covered at this time of year with wild flowers and bushes, where courting couples traditionally went.

But Annet was not that easy. 'My father would be displeased,' she said.

'Let's not worry about him.' There was not much a peasant could do to oppose the will of a squire, especially when the squire was wearing the livery of a great earl. It was an insult to the earl to lay hands on one of his servants. The peasant might try to dissuade his daughter, but it would be risky for him to restrain her forcibly.

However, someone else came to Perkin's aid. A youthful voice said: 'Hello, Annet, is all well?'

Ralph turned to the newcomer. He looked about sixteen, but he was almost as tall as Ralph, with broad shoulders and big hands. He was strikingly handsome, with regular features that might have been carved by a cathedral sculptor. He had thick tawny hair and the beginnings of a beard the same colour.

Ralph said: 'Who the hell are you?'

'I'm Wulfric from Wigleigh, sir.' Wulfric was deferential, but not afraid. He turned back to Annet and said: 'I've come to help you sell some eggs.'

The boy's muscular shoulder came between Ralph and Annet, his stance protecting the girl and at the same time excluding Ralph. It was mildly insolent, and Ralph felt a stirring of anger. 'Get out of the way, Wulfric Wigleigh,' he said. 'You're not wanted here.'

Wulfric turned again and gave him a level look. 'I'm betrothed to this woman, sir,' he said. Once again, the tone was respectful but the attitude fearless.

Perkin spoke up. 'That's true, sir – they are to be married.'

'Don't talk to me about your peasant customs,' Ralph said contemptuously. 'I don't care if she's married to the oaf.' It angered him to be spoken to this way by his inferiors. It was not their place to tell him what to do.

Merthin butted in. 'Let's go, Ralph,' he said. 'I'm hungry, and Betty Baxter is selling hot pies.'

'Pies?' Ralph said. 'I'm more interested in eggs.' He picked up one of the eggs on her tray and fondled it suggestively, then he put it down and touched her left breast. It was firm to his fingertips, and egg-shaped.

'What do you think you're doing?' She sounded indignant, but she did not move away.

He squeezed gently, enjoying the sensation. 'Examining the goods on offer.'

'Take your hands off me.'

'In a minute.'

Then Wulfric shoved him violently.

Ralph was taken by surprise. He had not expected to be attacked by a peasant. He staggered back, stumbled, and fell to the ground with a thump. He heard someone laugh, and amazement gave way to humiliation. He sprang to his feet, enraged.

He was not wearing his sword, but he had a long dagger at his belt. However, it would be undignified to use weapons on an unarmed peasant: he could lose the respect of the earl's knights and the other squires. He would have to punish Wulfric with his fists.

Perkin stepped from behind his stall, speaking rapidly. 'A clumsy mistake, sir, not intended, the lad is deeply sorry, I assure you—'

However, his daughter seemed unafraid. 'Boys, boys!' she said in a tone of mock reprimand, but she seemed more pleased than anything else.

Ralph ignored them both. He took one step towards Wulfric and raised his right fist. Then, when Wulfric lifted both arms to defend his face from the blow, Ralph drove his left fist into the boy's belly.

It was not as soft as he had expected. All the same, Wulfric bent forward, his face twisted in agony, both hands going to his midriff; whereupon Ralph hit him full in the face with his right fist, catching him high on the cheekbone. The punch hurt his hand but brought joy to his soul.

To his astonishment, Wulfric hit him back.

Instead of crumpling to the floor and lying there waiting to be kicked, the peasant boy came back with a right-handed punch that had all the strength of his shoulders behind it. Ralph's nose seemed to explode in blood and pain. He roared with anger.

Wulfric stepped back, seeming to realize what a terrible thing he had done, and he dropped both arms, holding his palms upwards.

But it was too late to be sorry. Ralph hit him with both fists on the face and body, a storm of blows that Wulfric feebly tried to ward off by holding up his arms and ducking his head. As he punched him, Ralph wondered vaguely why the boy did not run away, and guessed he was hoping to take his punishment now rather than face worse later. He had guts, Ralph realized; but that made him even angrier. He hit him harder, again and again, and he was filled with an emotion that was both rage and ecstasy. Merthin tried to intervene. 'For the love of Christ, enough,' he said, putting a hand on Ralph's shoulder; but Ralph shook him off.

At last Wulfric's hands fell to his sides and he staggered, dazed, his handsome face covered in blood, his eyes closing; then he fell down. Ralph started to kick him. Then a burly man in leather trousers appeared and spoke with a voice of authority: 'Now then, young Ralph, don't murder the boy.'

Ralph recognized John, the town constable, and said indignantly: 'He attacked me!'

'Well, he's not attacking you any more, is he, sir? Lying on the ground like that with his eyes shut.' John put himself in front of Ralph. 'I'd rather do without the trouble of a coroner's inquiry.'

People crowded around Wulfric: Perkin; Annet, who was flushed with excitement; the Lady Philippa; and several bystanders.

The ecstatic feeling left Ralph, and his nose hurt like hell. He could breathe only through his mouth. He tasted blood. 'That animal punched my nose,' he said, and he sounded like a man with a heavy cold.

'Then he shall be punished,' said John.

Two men who looked like Wulfric appeared: his father and his elder brother, Ralph guessed. They helped Wulfric to his feet, shooting angry glances at Ralph.

Perkin spoke up. He was a fat man with a sly face. 'The squire threw the first punch,' he said.

Ralph said: 'The peasant deliberately shoved me!'

'The squire insulted Wulfric's wife-to-be.'

The constable said: 'No matter what the squire may have said, Wulfric should know better than to lay hands on a servant of Earl Roland. I should think the earl will expect him to be severely dealt with.'

Wulfric's father spoke up. 'Is there a new law, John Constable, that says a man in livery may do what he likes?'

There was a mutter of agreement from the small crowd now gathered. Young squires caused a lot of trouble, and often escaped punishment because they were wearing the colours of some baron; and this was deeply resented by law-abiding tradesmen and peasants.

Lady Philippa intervened. 'I'm the earl's daughter-in-law, and I saw the whole thing,' she said. Her voice was low and melodious, but she spoke with the authority of high rank. Ralph expected her to take his side, but to his dismay she went on: 'I'm sorry to say that this was entirely Ralph's fault. He fondled the girl's body in a most outrageous way.'

'Thank you, my lady,' John Constable said deferentially. He lowered his voice to confer with her. 'But I think the earl might not want the peasant lad to go unpunished.'

She nodded thoughtfully. 'We don't want this to be the start of a lengthy dispute. Put the boy in the stocks for twenty-four hours. It won't do him much harm, at his age, but everyone will know that justice has been done. That will satisfy the earl – I'll answer for him.'

John hesitated. Ralph could see that the constable did not like taking orders from anyone but his master, the prior of Kingsbridge. However, Philippa's decision would surely satisfy all parties. Ralph himself would have liked to see Wulfric flogged, but he was beginning to suspect that he did not come out of this as a hero, and he would look worse if he demanded a harsh punishment. After a moment John said: 'Very well, Lady Philippa, if you're willing to take responsibility.'

'I am.'

'Right.' John took Wulfric by the arm and led him away. The lad had recovered fast, and was able to walk normally. His family followed. Perhaps they would bring him food and drink while he was in the stocks, and make sure he was not pelted.

Merthin said to Ralph: 'How are you?'

Ralph felt as if the middle of his face were swelling like an inflated bladder. His vision was blurred, his speech was a nasal honk, and he was in pain. 'I'm fine,' he said. 'Never better.'

'Let's get a monk to look at your nose.'

'No.' Ralph was not afraid of fights, but he hated the things physicians did: bleeding and cupping and lancing boils. 'All I need is a bottle of strong wine. Take me to the nearest tavern.'

'All right,' Merthin said, but he did not move. He was giving Ralph a queer look.

Ralph said: 'What's the matter with you?'

'You don't change, do you?'

Ralph shrugged. 'Does anyone?'

9

GODWYN WAS COMPLETELY fascinated by Timothy's Book. It was a history of Kingsbridge Priory and, like most such histories, it began with the creation by God of heaven and earth. But mostly it recounted the era of Prior Philip, two centuries ago, when the cathedral was built – a time now regarded by the monks as a golden age. The author, Brother Timothy, claimed that the legendary Philip had been a stern disciplinarian as well as a man of compassion. Godwyn was not sure how you could be both.

On the Wednesday of Fleece Fair week, in the study hour before the service of Sext, Godwyn sat on a high stool in the monastery library, the book open on a lectern before him. This was his favourite place in the priory: a spacious room, well lit by high windows, with almost a hundred books in a locked cupboard. It was normally hushed, but today he could hear, from the far side of the cathedral, the muffled roar of the fair – a thousand people buying and selling, haggling and quarrelling, calling their wares, and shouting encouragement at cock-fighting and bear-baiting.

At the back of the book, later authors had tracked the descendants of the cathedral builders down to the present day. Godwyn was pleased – and frankly surprised – to find confirmation of his mother's theory that she was descended from Tom Builder through Tom's daughter Martha. He wondered what family traits might have come down from Tom. A mason needed to be a shrewd businessman, he supposed, and Godwyn's grandfather and his uncle Edmund had that quality. His cousin Caris also showed signs of the same flair. Perhaps Tom had also had the green eyes flecked with yellow that they all shared.

Godwyn also read about Tom Builder's stepson, Jack, the architect of Kingsbridge Cathedral, who had married the Lady

Aliena and fathered a dynasty of earls of Shiring. He was the ancestor of Caris's sweetheart, Merthin Fitzgerald. That made sense: young Merthin was already showing unparalleled ability as a carpenter. Timothy's Book even mentioned Jack's red hair, which had been inherited by Sir Gerald and Merthin, though not Ralph.

What interested him most was the book's chapter on women. It seemed there had been no nuns at Kingsbridge in Prior Philip's day. Women had been strictly forbidden to enter the monastery buildings. The author, quoting Philip, said that if possible a monk should never look at a female, for his own peace of mind. Philip disapproved of combined monastery-nunneries, saying the advantages of shared facilities were outweighed by the opportunities for the devil to introduce temptation. Where there was a double house, the separation of monks and nuns should be as rigid as possible, he added.

Godwyn felt the thrill of finding authoritative support for a pre-existing conviction. At Oxford he had enjoyed the all-male environment of Kingsbridge College. The university teachers were men, as were the students, without exception. He had hardly spoken to a female for seven years and, if he kept his eyes on the ground as he walked through the city, he could even avoid looking at them. On his return to the priory, he had found it disturbing to see nuns so frequently. Although they had their own cloisters, refectory, kitchen and other buildings, he met them constantly in the church, the hospital, and other communal areas. At this moment there was a pretty young nun called Mair just a few feet away, consulting an illustrated book on medicinal herbs. It was even worse to encounter girls from the town, with their close-fitting clothes and alluring hairstyles, casually walking through the priory grounds on everyday errands, bringing supplies to the kitchen or visiting the hospital.

Clearly, he thought, the priory had fallen from Philip's high standards – another example of the slackness that had crept in under the rule of Anthony, Godwyn's uncle. But perhaps there was something he could do about this.

The bell rang for Sext, and he closed the book. Sister Mair

did the same, and smiled at him, her red lips forming a sweet curve as she did so. He looked away and hurried out of the room.

The weather was improving, the sun shining fitfully between showers of rain. In the church, the stained-glass windows brightened and faded as patchy clouds blew across the sky. Godwyn's mind was equally restless, distracted from his prayers by thoughts of how he could best use Timothy's Book to inspire a revival in the priory. He decided he would raise the subject at chapter, the daily meeting of all the monks.

The builders were getting on quickly with the repairs to the chancel after last Sunday's collapse, he noted. The rubble had been cleared away and the area had been roped off. There was a growing stack of thin, lightweight stones in the transept. The men did not stop work when the monks began to sing – there were so many services during the course of a normal day that the repairs would have been severely delayed. Merthin Fitzgerald, who had temporarily abandoned his work on the new door, was in the south aisle, constructing an elaborate spider web of ropes, branches and hurdles on which the masons would stand as they rebuilt the vaulted ceiling. Thomas Langley, whose job it was to supervise the builders, was standing in the south transept with Elfric, pointing with his one arm at the collapsed vault, obviously discussing Merthin's work.

Thomas was effective as matricularius: he was decisive, and he never let things slip. Any morning the builders failed to show up – a frequent irritation – Thomas would go and find them and demand to know why. If he had a fault, it was that he was too independent: he rarely reported progress or asked Godwyn's opinion, but got on with the work as if he were his own master rather than Godwyn's subordinate. Godwyn had an annoying suspicion that Thomas doubted his ability. Godwyn was younger, but only slightly: he was thirty-one, Thomas thirty-four. Perhaps Thomas thought that Godwyn had been promoted by Anthony under pressure from Petranilla. However, he showed no other sign of resentment. He just did things his own way.

As Godwyn watched, murmuring the responses of the service automatically, Thomas's conversation with Elfric was interrupted.

Lord William of Caster came striding into the church. He was a tall, black-bearded figure very like his father, and equally harsh, though people said he was sometimes softened by his wife, Philippa. He approached Thomas and waved Elfric away. Thomas turned to William, and something in his stance reminded Godwyn that Thomas had once been a knight, and had first arrived at the priory bleeding from the sword wound that had eventually necessitated the amputation of his left arm at the elbow.

Godwyn wished he could hear what Lord William was saying. William was leaning forward, speaking aggressively, pointing a finger. Thomas, unafraid, answered with equal vigour. Godwyn suddenly remembered Thomas having just such an intense, combative conversation ten years ago, on the day he arrived here. On that occasion, he had been arguing with William's younger brother, Richard – then a priest, now the bishop of Kingsbridge. Perhaps it was fanciful, but Godwyn imagined they were quarrelling about the same thing today. What could it be? Could there really be an issue between a monk and a noble family that was still a cause of anger after ten years?

Lord William stamped off, evidently unsatisfied, and Thomas turned back to Elfric.

The argument ten years ago had resulted in Thomas's joining the priory. Godwyn recalled that Richard had promised a donation to secure Thomas's admittance. Godwyn had never heard any more about that donation. He wondered if it had ever been paid.

In all that time, no one at the priory seemed to have learned much about Thomas's former life. That was curious: monks gossiped constantly. Living closely together in a small group – there were twenty-six at present – they tended to know almost everything about one another. What lord had Thomas served? Where had he lived? Most knights ruled over a few villages, receiving rents that enabled them to pay for horses, armour and weapons. Had Thomas had a wife and children? If so, what had become of them? No one knew.

Apart from the mystery of his background, Thomas was a good monk, devout and hard-working. It seemed as if this existence suited him better than his life as a knight. Despite his former career of violence, there was something of the woman about him, as there was about many monks. He was very close to Brother Matthias, a sweet-natured man a few years younger than he. But, if they were committing sins of impurity, they were very discreet about it, for no accusation had ever been made.

Towards the end of the service Godwyn glanced into the deep gloom of the nave and saw his mother, Petranilla, standing as still as one of the pillars, a shaft of sunlight illuminating her proud grey head. She was alone. He wondered how long she had been there, watching. Lay people were not encouraged to attend the weekday services, and Godwyn guessed she was here to see him. He felt the familiar mixture of pleasure and apprehension. She would do anything for him, he knew. She had sold her house and become her brother Edmund's housekeeper just so that he could study at Oxford; when he thought of the sacrifice that entailed for his proud mother, he wanted to weep with gratitude. Yet her presence always made him anxious, as if he were going to be reprimanded for some transgression.

As the monks and nuns filed out, Godwyn peeled off from the procession and approached her. 'Good morning, Mama.'

She kissed his forehead. 'You look thin,' she said with maternal anxiety. 'Aren't you getting enough to eat?'

'Salt fish and porridge, but there's plenty of it,' he said.

'What are you so excited about?' She could always read his mood.

He told her about Timothy's Book. 'I could read the passage during chapter,' he said.

'Would others support you?'

'Theodoric and the younger monks would. A lot of them find it disturbing to see women all the time. After all, they have all chosen to live in an all-male community.'

She nodded approvingly. 'This casts you in the role of leader. Excellent.'

'Besides, they like me because of the hot stones.'

'Hot stones?'

'I introduced a new rule in the winter. On frosty nights,

when we go into church for Matins, each monk is given a hot stone wrapped in a rag. It prevents them getting chilblains in their feet.'

'Very clever. All the same, check your support before you make your move.'

'Of course. But it fits in with what the masters teach at Oxford.'

'Which is?'

'Mankind is fallible, so we should not rely on our own reasoning. We cannot hope to understand the world – all we can do is stand amazed at God's creation. True knowledge comes only from revelation. We should not question received wisdom.'

Mother looked sceptical, as lay people often did when educated men tried to explain high philosophy. 'And this is what bishops and cardinals believe?'

'Yes. The University of Paris has actually banned the works of Aristotle and Aquinas because they are based on rationality rather than faith.'

'Will this way of thinking help you find favour with your superiors?'

That was all she really cared about. She wanted her son to be prior, bishop, archbishop, even cardinal. He wanted the same, but he hoped he was not as cynical as she. 'I'm sure of it,' he replied.

'Good. But that's not why I came to see you. Your uncle Edmund has suffered a blow. The Italians are threatening to take their custom to Shiring.'

Godwyn was shocked. 'That will ruin his business.' But he was not sure why she had made a special visit to tell him.

'Edmund thinks he can win them back if we improve the Fleece Fair, and in particular if we tear down the old bridge and build a new, wider one.'

'Let me guess: Uncle Anthony refused.'

'But Edmund has not given up.'

'You want me to talk to Anthony?'

She shook her head. 'You can't persuade him. But, if the subject comes up in chapter, you should support the proposal.'

'And go against Uncle Anthony?'

'Whenever a sensible proposal is opposed by the old guard, you must be identified as leader of the reformers.'

Godwyn smiled admiringly. 'Mama, how do you know so much about politics?'

'I'll tell you.' She looked away, her eyes focusing on the great rose window at the east end, her mind in the past. 'When my father started to trade with the Italians, he was treated as an upstart by the leading citizens of Kingsbridge. They turned up their noses at him and his family, and did everything they could to prevent him implementing his new ideas. My mother was dead by then, and I was an adolescent, so I became his confidante, and he told me everything.' Her face, normally fixed in an expression of frozen calm, twisted now into a mask of bitterness and resentment: her eyes narrowed, her lip curled, and her cheek flushed with remembered shame. 'He decided he would never be free of them until he took control of the parish guild. So that's what he set out to do, and I helped him.' She drew a deep breath, as if once again gathering her strength for a long war. 'We divided the ruling group, set one faction against the other, made alliances then shifted them, ruthlessly undermined our opponents, and used our supporters until it suited us to discard them. It took us ten years and, at the end of it, he was alderman of the guild and the richest man in town.'

She had told him the story of his grandfather before, but never in quite such bluntly honest terms. 'So you were his aide, as Caris is to Edmund?'

She gave a short, harsh laugh. 'Yes. Except that, by the time Edmund took over, we were the leading citizens. My father and I climbed the mountain, and Edmund just had to walk down the other side.'

They were interrupted by Philemon. He came into the church from the cloisters, a tall, scrawny-necked man of twenty-two, walking like a bird with short, pigeon-toed steps. He carried a broom: he was employed by the priory as a cleaner. He seemed excited. 'I've been looking for you, Brother Godwyn.'

Petranilla ignored his obvious hurry. 'Hello, Philemon, haven't they made you a monk yet?'

'I can't raise the necessary donation, Mistress Petranilla. I come from a humble family.'

'But it's not unknown for the priory to waive the donation in the case of an applicant who shows devotion. And you've been a servant of the priory, paid and unpaid, for years.'

'Brother Godwyn has proposed me, but some of the older monks argued against me.'

Godwyn put in: 'Blind Carlus hates Philemon – I don't know why.'

Petranilla said: 'I'll speak to my brother Anthony. He should overrule Carlus. You're a good friend to my son – I'd like to see you get on.'

'Thank you, mistress.'

'Well, you're obviously bursting to tell Godwyn something that can't be said in front of me, so I'll take my leave.' She kissed Godwyn. 'Remember what I said.'

'I will, Mama.'

Godwyn felt relieved, as if a storm cloud had passed overhead and gone on to drench some other town.

As soon as Petranilla was out of earshot, Philemon said: 'It's Bishop Richard!'

Godwyn raised his eyebrows. Philemon had a way of learning people's secrets. 'What have you found out?'

'He's in the hospital, right now, in one of the private rooms upstairs – with his cousin Margery!'

Margery was a pretty girl of sixteen. Her parents – a younger brother of Earl Roland, and a sister of the countess of Marr – were both dead, and she was Roland's ward. He had arranged for her to marry a son of the earl of Monmouth, in a political alliance that would greatly strengthen Roland's position as the leading nobleman of south-west England. 'What are they doing?' Godwyn said, though he could guess.

Philemon lowered his voice. 'Kissing!'

'How do you know?'

'I'll show you.'

Philemon led the way out of the church via the south transept, through the monks' cloisters, and up a flight of steps to the dormitory. It was a plain room with two rows of simple wooden bedsteads, each having a straw mattress. It shared a party wall with the hospital. Philemon went to a large cupboard that contained blankets. With an effort, he pulled it forward. In the wall behind it there was a loose stone. Momentarily Godwyn wondered how Philemon had come across this peephole, and guessed he might have hidden something in the gap. Philemon lifted the stone out, careful to make no noise, and whispered: 'Look, quick!'

Godwyn hesitated. In a low voice he said: 'How many other guests have you observed from here?'

'All of them,' Philemon replied, as if that should have been obvious.

Godwyn thought he knew what he was going to see, and he did not relish it. Peeping at a misbehaving bishop might be all right for Philemon, but it seemed shamefully underhand. However, his curiosity urged him on. In the end he asked himself what his mother would advise, and knew immediately that she would tell him to look.

The hole in the wall was a little below eye level. He stooped and peeked through.

He was looking into one of the two private guest rooms upstairs at the hospital. In one corner stood a prie-dieu facing a wall painting of the crucifixion. There were two comfortable chairs and a couple of stools. When there was a crowd of important guests, the men took one room and the women the other; and this was clearly the women's room, for on a small table were several distinctly feminine articles: combs, ribbons, and mysterious small jars and vials.

On the floor were two straw mattresses. Richard and Margery lay on one of them. They were doing more than kissing.

Bishop Richard was an attractive man with wavy mid-brown hair and regular features. Margery was not much more than half his age, a slender girl with white skin and dark eyebrows. They lay side by side. Richard was kissing her face and speaking into her ear. A smile of pleasure played upon his fleshy lips. Margery's dress was pushed up around her waist. She had beautiful long white legs. His hand was between her thighs, moving with a practised, regular motion: although Godwyn had no experience of women, somehow he knew what Richard was doing. Margery looked at Richard adoringly, her mouth half open, panting with excitement, her face flushed with passion. Perhaps it was mere prejudice, but Godwyn sensed intuitively that Richard saw Margery as a plaything of the moment, whereas Margery believed Richard was the love of her life.

Godwyn stared at them for a horrified moment. Richard moved his hand, and suddenly Godwyn was looking at the triangle of coarse hair between Margery's thighs, dark against her white skin, like her eyebrows. Quickly, he looked away.

'Let me see,' said Philemon.

Godwyn moved away from the wall. This was shocking, but what should he do about it – if anything?

Philemon looked through the hole and gave a gasp of excitement. 'I can see her cunt!' he whispered. 'He's rubbing it!'

'Come away from there,' Godwyn said. 'We've seen enough – too much.'

Philemon hesitated, fascinated; then, reluctantly, he moved away and replaced the loose stone. 'We must expose the bishop's fornication at once!' he said.

'Shut your mouth and let me think,' Godwyn said. If he did as Philemon suggested he would make enemies of Richard and his powerful family – and to no purpose. But surely there was a way something like this could be turned to advantage? Godwyn tried to think about it as his mother would. If there was nothing to be gained by revealing Richard's sin, was it possible to make a virtue of concealing it? Perhaps Richard would be grateful to Godwyn for keeping it secret.

That was more promising. But for it to work, Richard had to know that Godwyn was protecting him.

'Come with me,' Godwyn said to Philemon.

Philemon moved the cupboard back into place. Godwyn wondered whether the sound of the wood scraping on the floor was audible in the next room. He doubted it – and, anyway, Richard and Margery were surely too absorbed in what they were doing to notice noises from beyond the wall.

Godwyn led the way down the stairs and through the cloisters. There were two staircases to the private rooms: one led up from the hospital's ground floor, and the other was outside the building, permitting important guests to come and go without passing through the common people's quarters. Godwyn hurried up the outside stairs.

He paused outside the room where Richard and Margery were and spoke to Philemon quietly. 'Follow me in,' he said. 'Do nothing. Say nothing. Leave when I leave.'

Philemon put down his broom.

'No,' Godwyn said. 'Carry it.'

'All right.'

Godwyn threw open the door and strode in. 'I want this chamber immaculately clean,' he said loudly. 'Sweep every corner – oh! I beg your pardon! I thought the room was empty!'

In the time it had taken Godwyn and Philemon to rush from the dormitory to the hospital, the lovers had progressed. Richard now lay on top of Margery, his long clerical robe lifted in front. Her shapely white legs stuck straight up in the air either side of the bishop's hips. There was no mistaking what they were doing.

Richard ceased his thrusting motion and looked at Godwyn, his expression a mixture of angry frustration and frightened guilt. Margery gave a cry of shock and she, too, stared at Godwyn with fear in her eyes.

Godwyn drew the moment out. 'Bishop Richard!' he said, feigning bewilderment. He wanted Richard to be in no doubt that he had been recognized. 'But how ... and Margery?' He pretended to understand suddenly. 'Forgive me!' He spun on his heel. He shouted at Philemon: 'Get out! Now!' Philemon scuttled back through the door, still clutching his broom.

Godwyn followed, but he turned at the door, to make sure Richard got a good look at him. The two lovers remained frozen in position, locked in sexual congress, but their faces had changed. Margery's hand had flown to her mouth in the eternal gesture of surprised guilt. Richard's expression had become frantically calculating. He wanted to speak but he could not think what to say. Godwyn decided to put them out of their misery. He had done everything he needed to do.

He stepped out – then, before he could close the door, a shock made him stop. A woman was coming up the stairs. He suffered a moment of panic. It was Philippa, the wife of the earl's other son.

He realized instantly that Richard's guilty secret would lose its value if someone else knew it. He had to warn Richard. 'Lady Philippa!' he said in a loud voice. 'Welcome to Kingsbridge Priory!'

Urgent scuffling noises came from behind him. Out of the corner of his eye, he saw Richard leap to his feet.

Luckily, Philippa did not march straight past, but stopped and spoke to Godwyn. 'Perhaps you can help me.' From where she stood, she could not quite see into the room, he thought. 'I've lost a bracelet. It's not precious, just carved wood, but I'm fond of it.'

'What a shame,' Godwyn said sympathetically. 'I'll ask all the monks and nuns to look out for it.'

Philemon said: 'I haven't seen it.'

Godwyn said to Philippa: 'Perhaps it slipped from your wrist.'

She frowned. 'The odd thing is, I haven't actually worn it since I got here. I took it off when I arrived, and put it on the table, and now I can't find it.'

'Perhaps it rolled into a dark corner. Philemon here will look for it. He cleans the guest rooms.'

Philippa looked at Philemon. 'Yes, I saw you as I was leaving, an hour or so ago. You didn't spot it when you swept the room?'

'I didn't sweep. Miss Margery came in just as I was getting started.'

Godwyn said: 'Philemon has just come back to clean your room, but Miss Margery is –' he looked into the room – 'at prayer,' he finished. Margery was kneeling on the prie-dieu, eyes closed – begging forgiveness for her sin, Godwyn hoped. Richard stood behind her, head bowed, hands clasped, lips moving in a murmur.

Godwyn stepped aside to let Philippa enter the room. She gave her brother-in-law a suspicious look. 'Hello, Richard,' she said. 'It's not like you to pray on a weekday.'

He put his finger to his lips in a shushing gesture, and pointed to Margery on the prayer stool.

Philippa said briskly: 'Margery can pray as much as she likes, but this is the women's room, and I want you out.'

Richard concealed his relief and left, closing the door on the two women.

He and Godwyn stood face to face in the hallway. Godwyn could tell that Richard did not know what line to take. He might be inclined to say: How dare you burst into a room without knocking? However, he was so badly in the wrong that he probably could not summon up the nerve to bluster. On the other hand, he could hardly beg Godwyn to keep quiet about what he had seen, for that would be to acknowledge himself in Godwyn's power. It was a moment of painful awkwardness.

While Richard hesitated, Godwyn spoke. 'No one shall hear of this from me.'

Richard looked relieved, then glanced at Philemon. 'What about him?'

'Philemon wants to be a monk. He is learning the virtue of obedience.'

'I'm in your debt.'

'A man should confess his own sins, not those of others.'

'All the same, I'm grateful, Brother . . . ?'

'Godwyn, the sacrist. I'm the nephew of Prior Anthony.' He wanted Richard to know that he was sufficiently well connected to make serious trouble. But, to take the edge off the threat, he added: 'My mother was betrothed to your father, many years ago, before your father became the earl.'

'I've heard that story.'

Godwyn wanted to add: And your father spurned my mother, just as you're planning to spurn the wretched Margery. But instead he said pleasantly: 'We might have been brothers.'

'Yes.'

The bell rang for dinner. Relieved of their embarrassment, the three men parted company: Richard to Prior Anthony's house, Godwyn to the monks' refectory, and Philemon to the kitchen to help serve.

Godwyn was thoughtful as he walked through the cloisters. He was upset by the animal scene he had witnessed, but he felt he had handled it well. At the end, Richard had seemed to trust him.

In the refectory Godwyn sat next to Theodoric, a bright monk a couple of years younger than he. Theodoric had not studied at Oxford, and in consequence he looked up to Godwyn. Godwyn treated him as an equal, which flattered Theodoric. 'I've just read something that will interest you,' Godwyn said. He summarized what he had read about the revered Prior Philip's attitude to women in general and nuns in particular. 'It's what you've always said,' he finished. In fact, Theodoric had never expressed an opinion on the subject, but he always agreed when Godwyn complained about Prior Anthony's slackness.

'Of course,' Theodoric said. He had blue eyes and fair skin, and now he flushed with excitement. 'How can we have pure thoughts when we are constantly distracted by females?'

'But what can we do about it?'

'We must confront the prior.'

'In chapter, you mean,' Godwyn said, as if it were Theodoric's idea rather than his own. 'Yes, excellent plan. But would others support us?'

'The younger monks would.'

Young men probably agreed with more or less any criticism of their elders, Godwyn thought. But he also knew that many monks shared his own preference for a life in which women were absent or, at least, invisible. 'If you talk to anyone between now and chapter, let me know what they say,' he said. That would encourage Theodoric to go around whipping up support.

The dinner arrived, a stew of salt fish and beans. Before Godwyn could begin to eat, he was prevented by Friar Murdo.

Friars were monks who lived among the people instead of secluding themselves in monasteries. They felt that their self-denial was more rigorous than that of institutional monks, whose vow of poverty was compromised by their splendid buildings and extensive landholdings. Traditionally friars had no property, not even churches – although many had slipped from this ideal after pious admirers gave them land and money. Those who still lived by the original principles scrounged their food and slept on kitchen floors. They preached in market places and outside taverns, and were rewarded with pennies. They did not hesitate to sponge on ordinary monks for food and lodging any time it suited their convenience. Not surprisingly, their assumption of superiority was resented.

Friar Murdo was a particularly unpleasant example: fat, dirty, greedy, often drunk, and sometimes seen in the company of prostitutes. But he was also a charismatic preacher who could hold a crowd of hundreds with his colourful, theologically dubious sermons.

Now he stood up, uninvited, and began to pray in a loud voice. 'Our Father, bless this food to our foul, corrupt bodies, as full of sin as a dead dog is full of maggots...'

Murdo's prayers were never short. Godwyn put down his spoon with a sigh.

*

THERE WAS ALWAYS a reading in chapter – usually from the Rule of St Benedict, but often from the Bible, and occasionally other religious books. As the monks were taking their places on the raked stone benches around the octagonal chapter house, Godwyn sought out the young monk who was due to read today and told him, quietly but firmly, that he, Godwyn, would be reading instead. Then, when the moment came, he read the crucial page from Timothy's Book.

He felt nervous. He had returned from Oxford a year ago, and he had been quietly talking to people about reforming the priory ever since; but, until this moment, he had not openly confronted Anthony. The prior was weak and lazy, and needed to be shocked out of his lethargy. Furthermore, St Benedict had written: 'All must be called to chapter, for the Lord often reveals to a younger member what is best.' Godwyn was perfectly entitled to speak out in chapter and call for stricter compliance with monastic rules. All the same, he suddenly felt he was running a risk, and wished he had taken longer to think about his tactics in using Timothy's Book.

But it was too late for regrets. He closed the book and said: 'My question, to myself and my brethren, is this: Have we slipped below the standards of Prior Philip in the matter of separation between monks and females?' He had learned, in student debates, to put his argument in the form of a question whenever he could, giving his opponent as little as possible to argue against.

The first to reply was Blind Carlus, the sub-prior, Anthony's deputy. 'Some monasteries are located far from any centre of population, on an uninhabited island, or deep in the forest, or perched on a lonely mountain top,' he said. His slow, deliberate speech made Godwyn fidget with impatience. 'In such houses, the brothers seclude themselves from all contact with the secular world,' he went on unhurriedly. 'Kingsbridge has never been like that. We're in the heart of a great city, the home of seven thousand souls. We care for one of the most magnificent cathedrals in Christendom. Many of us are physicians, because St Benedict said: "Special care must be taken of the sick, so that in very deed they be looked after as if it were Christ himself." The luxury of total isolation has not been granted to us. God has given us a different mission.'

Godwyn had expected something like this. Carlus hated furniture to be moved, for then he would stumble over it; and he opposed any other kind of change, out of a parallel anxiety about coping with the unfamiliar.

Theodoric had a quick answer to Carlus. 'All the more reason for us to be strict about the rules,' he said. 'A man who lives next door to a tavern must be extra careful to avoid drunkenness.'

There was a murmur of pleased agreement: the monks enjoyed a smart riposte. Godwyn gave a nod of approval. The fair-skinned Theodoric blushed with gratification.

Emboldened, a novice called Juley said in a loud whisper: 'Women don't bother Carlus, he can't see them.' Several monks laughed, though others shook their heads in disapproval.

Godwyn felt it was going well. He seemed to be winning the argument, so far. Then Prior Anthony said: 'Exactly what are you proposing, Brother Godwyn?' He had not been to Oxford, but he knew enough to press for his opponent's real agenda.

Reluctantly, Godwyn put his cards on the table. 'We might consider reverting to the position as it was in the time of Prior Philip.'

Anthony persisted: 'What do you mean by that, exactly? No nuns?'

'Yes.'

'But where would they go?'

'The nunnery could be removed to another location, and

become a remote cell of the priory, like Kingsbridge College, or St-John-in-the-Forest.'

That shocked them. There was a clamour of comment, which the prior suppressed with difficulty. The voice that emerged from the hubbub was that of Joseph, the senior physician. He was a clever man, but proud, and Godwyn was wary of him. 'How would we run a hospital without nuns?' he said. His bad teeth caused him to slur his sibilants, making him sound drunk, but he spoke with no less authority. 'They administer medicines, change dressings, feed the incapable, comb the hair of senile old men—'

Theodoric said: 'Monks could do all that.'

'Then what about childbirth?' Joseph said. 'We often deal with women who are having difficulty bringing a baby into the world. How could monks help them without nuns to do the actual ... handling?'

Several men voiced their agreement, but Godwyn had anticipated this question, and now he said: 'Suppose the nuns removed to the old lazar house?' The leper colony – or lazar house – was on a small island in the river on the south side of the town. In the old days it had been full of sufferers, but leprosy seemed to be dying out, and now there were only two occupants, both elderly.

Brother Cuthbert, who was a wit, muttered: 'I wouldn't want to be the one to tell Mother Cecilia she's being moved to a leper colony.' There was a ripple of laughter.

'Women should be ruled by men,' said Theodoric.

Prior Anthony said: 'And Mother Cecilia is ruled by Bishop Richard. He would have to make a decision such as this.'

'Heaven forbid that he should,' said a new voice. It was Simeon, the treasurer. A thin man with a long face, he spoke against every proposal that involved spending money. 'We could not survive without the nuns,' he said.

Godwyn was taken by surprise. 'Why not?' he said.

'We don't have enough money,' Simeon said promptly. 'When the cathedral needs repair, who do you think pays the builders? Not us – we can't afford it. Mother Cecilia pays. She buys supplies for the hospital, parchment for the scriptorium and fodder for the stables. Anything used communally by both monks and nuns is paid for by her.'

Godwyn was dismayed. 'How can this be? Why are we dependent on them?'

Simeon shrugged. 'Over the years, many devout women have given the nunnery land and other assets.'

That was not the whole story, Godwyn felt sure. The monks also had extensive resources. They collected rent and other charges from just about every citizen of Kingsbridge, and they held thousands of acres of farmland too. The way the wealth was husbanded must be a factor. But there was no point going into that now. He had lost the argument. Even Theodoric was silent.

Anthony said complacently: 'Well, that was a most interesting discussion. Thank you, Godwyn, for asking the question. And now let us pray.'

Godwyn was too angry for prayer. He had gained nothing of what he wanted, and he was unsure where he had gone wrong.

As the monks filed out, Theodoric gave him a frightened look and said: 'I didn't know the nuns paid for so much.'

'None of us knew,' Godwyn said. He realized he was glaring at Theodoric, and made amends hastily, adding: 'But you were splendid – you debated better than many an Oxford man.'

It was just the right thing to say, and Theodoric looked happy.

This was the hour for monks to read in the library or walk in the cloisters, meditating, but Godwyn had other plans. Something had been nagging him all through dinner and chapter. He had thrust it to the back of his mind, because more important things had intervened, but now it came back. He thought he knew where Lady Philippa's bracelet might be.

There were few hiding places in a monastery. The monks lived communally: no one but the prior had a room to himself. Even in the latrine they sat side by side over a trough that was continuously flushed by a stream of piped water. They were not permitted to have personal possessions, so no one had his own cupboard or even box.

But today Godwyn had seen a hiding place.

He went upstairs to the dormitory. It was empty. He pulled the blanket cupboard away from the wall and removed the loose stone, but he did not look through the hole. Instead, he put his hand into the gap, exploring. He felt the top, bottom and sides of the hole. To the right there was a small fissure. Godwyn eased his fingers inside and touched something that was neither stone nor mortar. Scrabbling with his fingertips, he drew the object out.

It was a carved wooden bracelet.

Godwyn held it to the light. It was made of some hard wood, probably oak. The inner surface was smoothly polished, but the outside was carved with an interlocking design of bold squares and diagonals, executed with pleasing precision: Godwyn could see why Lady Philippa was fond of it.

He put it back, restored the loose stone and returned the cupboard to its usual position.

What did Philemon want with such a thing? He might be able to sell it for a penny or two, though that would be dangerous because it was so recognizable. But he certainly could not wear it.

Godwyn left the dormitory and went down the stairs to the cloisters. He was in no mood for study or meditation. He needed to talk over the day's events. He felt the need to see his mother.

The thought made him apprehensive. She might berate him for his failure in chapter. But she would praise him for his handling of Bishop Richard, he felt sure, and he was eager to tell her the story. He decided to go in search of her.

Strictly speaking, this was not allowed. Monks were not supposed to roam about the streets of the town at will. They needed a reason, and in theory they were supposed to ask the prior's permission before leaving the precincts. But in practice, the obedientiaries – monastic officials – had dozens of excuses. The priory did business constantly with merchants, buying food, cloth, shoes, parchment, candles, garden tools, tack for horses, all the necessities of everyday life. The monks were landlords, owning almost the entire city. And any one of the physicians might be called to see a patient who was unable to walk to the hospital. So it was common to see monks in the streets, and Godwyn, the sacrist, was not likely to be asked to explain what he was doing out of the monastery.

Nevertheless it was wise to be discreet, and he made sure he was not observed as he left the priory. He passed through the busy fair and went quickly along the main street to his Uncle Edmund's house.

As he hoped, Edmund and Caris were out doing business, and he found his mother alone but for the servants. 'This is a treat for a mother,' she said. 'To see you twice in one day! And it gives me a chance to feed you up.' She poured him a big tankard of strong ale and told the cook to bring a plate of cold beef. 'What happened in chapter?' she said.

He told her the story. 'I was in too much of a hurry,' he said at the end.

She nodded. 'My father used to say: Never call a meeting until the outcome is a foregone conclusion.'

Godwyn smiled. 'I must remember that.'

'All the same, I don't think you've done any harm.'

That was a relief. She was not going to be angry. 'But I lost the argument,' he said.

'You also established your position as leader of the reformist younger group.'

'Even though I made a fool of myself?'

'Better than being a nonentity.'

He was not sure she was right about that but, as usual when he doubted the wisdom of his mother's advice, he did not challenge her, but resolved to think about it later. 'Something very odd happened,' he said, and he told her about Richard and Margery, leaving out the gross physical details.

She was surprised. 'Richard must be mad!' she said. 'The wedding will be called off if the earl of Monmouth finds out that Margery isn't a virgin. Earl Roland will be furious. Richard could be unfrocked.'

'But a lot of bishops have mistresses, don't they?'

'That's different. A priest may have a "housekeeper" who is his wife in all but name. A bishop may have several. But to take the virginity of a noblewoman shortly before her wedding – even the son of an earl might find it difficult to survive as a clergyman after that.'

'What do you think I should do?'

'Nothing. You've handled it perfectly so far.' He glowed with pride. She added: 'One day this information will be a powerful weapon. Just remember it.'

'There's one more thing. I wondered how Philemon had come across the loose stone, and it occurred to me that he might have used it initially as a hiding place. I was right – and I found a bracelet that Lady Philippa had lost.'

'Interesting,' she said. 'I have a strong feeling that Philemon will be useful to you. He'll do anything, you see. He has no scruples, no morals. My father had an associate who was always willing to do his dirty work – start rumours, spread poisonous gossip, foment strife. Such men can be invaluable.'

'So you don't think I should report the theft.'

'Certainly not. Make him give the bracelet back, if you think it's important – he can just say he found it while sweeping. But don't expose him. You'll reap the benefit, I guarantee.'

'So I should protect him?'

'As you would a mad dog that mauls intruders. He's dangerous, but he's worth it.'

10

ON THURSDAY, MERTHIN completed the door he was carving.

He had finished work in the south aisle, for the present. The scaffolding was in place. There was no need for him to make formwork for the masons, as Godwyn and Thomas were determined to save money by trying Merthin's method of building without it. So he returned to his carving and realized there was little left to do. He spent an hour improving a wise virgin's hair, and another on a foolish virgin's silly smile, but he was not sure he was making them any better. He found it difficult to make decisions, because his mind kept wandering to Caris and Griselda.

He had hardly been able to bring himself to speak to Caris all week. He felt so ashamed of himself. Every time he saw Caris, he thought of how he had embraced Griselda, and kissed her, and done with her the most loving act of human life – a girl he did not like, let alone love. Although he had formerly spent many happy hours imagining the moment when he would do that with Caris, now the prospect was filled with dread. There was nothing wrong with Griselda – well, there was, but that was not what disturbed him. He would have felt the same if it had been any woman other than Caris. He had taken away the meaning of the act by doing it with Griselda. And now he could not face the woman he loved.

While he was staring at his work, trying to stop thinking about Caris and decide whether the door was finished or not, Elizabeth Clerk walked into the north porch. She was a pale, thin beauty of twenty-five with a cloud of fair curls. Her father had been the bishop of Kingsbridge before Richard. He had lived, like Richard, in the bishop's palace at Shiring, but on his frequent visits to Kingsbridge he had fallen for a serving wench at the Bell

– Elizabeth's mother. Because of her illegitimacy, Elizabeth was sensitive about her social position, alert to the least slight and quick to take offence. But Merthin liked her because she was clever, and because when he was eighteen she had kissed him and let him feel her breasts, which were high on her chest and flat, as if moulded from shallow cups, with nipples that hardened at the gentlest touch. Their romance had ended over something that seemed trivial to him and unforgivable to her – a joke he had made about randy priests – but he still liked her.

She touched his shoulder and looked at the door. Her hand went to her mouth, and she drew in her breath. 'They seem alive!' she said.

He was thrilled. Her praise was not lightly given. All the same, he felt an impulse to be modest. 'It's only that I've made each one individual. On the old door, the virgins were identical.'

'It's more than that. They look as if they might step forward and talk to us.'

'Thank you.'

'But it's so different from everything else in the cathedral. What will the monks say?'

'Brother Thomas likes it.'

'What about the sacrist?'

'Godwyn? I don't know what he'll think. But if there's a fuss I'll appeal to Prior Anthony – who won't want to commission another door and pay twice.'

'Well,' she said thoughtfully, 'the Bible doesn't say that they were all alike, of course – just that five had the sense to get ready well in advance, and the other five left arrangements until the last minute and ended up missing the party. But what about Elfric?'

'It's not for him.'

'He's your master.'

'He only cares about getting the money.'

She was not convinced. 'The problem is that you're a better craftsman than he. That's been obvious for a couple of years, and everyone knows it. Elfric would never admit it, but that's why he hates you. He may make you regret this.'

'You always see the black side.'

'Do I?' She was offended. 'Well, we'll see if I'm right. I hope I'm wrong.' She turned to go.

'Elizabeth?'

'Yes.'

'I'm really pleased you think it's good.'

She did not reply, but she seemed a bit mollified. She waved goodbye and left.

Merthin decided the door was finished. He wrapped it in coarse sacking. He would have to show it to Elfric, and now was as good a time as any: the rain had stopped, for a while at least.

He got one of the labourers to help him carry the door. The builders had a technique for carrying heavy, awkward objects. They laid two stout poles on the ground, parallel, then placed boards crosswise on the poles in the centre to provide a firm base. They manhandled the object on to the boards. Then they stood between the poles, one man at each end, and lifted. The arrangement was called a stretcher, and it was also used for carrying sick people to the hospital.

Even so, the door was very heavy. However, Merthin was used to difficult lifting. Elfric had never allowed him to make an excuse of his slight stature, and the result was that he had become surprisingly strong.

The two men reached Elfric's house and carried the door inside. Griselda was sitting in the kitchen. She seemed to be getting more voluptuous by the day – her large breasts appeared to be growing even bigger. Merthin hated to be at odds with people, so he tried to be friendly. 'Do you want to see my door?' he said as they passed her.

'Why would I want to look at a door?'

'It's carved. The story of the wise and foolish virgins.'

She gave a humourless laugh. 'Don't tell me about virgins.'

They carried it through to the yard. Merthin did not understand women. Griselda had been cold to him ever since they had made love. If that was how she felt, why had she done it? She was making it clear she did not want to do it again. He could have reassured her that he felt the same way – in fact he loathed the prospect – but that would be insulting, so he said nothing.

They put down the stretcher and Merthin's helper left. Elfric was in the yard, his brawny body bent over a stack of timber, counting planks, tapping each beam with a piece of square-cut wood a couple of feet long, sticking his tongue into his cheek as he did whenever he faced a mental challenge. He glared at Merthin and carried on, so Merthin said nothing, but unwrapped the door and stood it up against a pile of stone blocks. He was extraordinarily proud of what he had done. He had followed the traditional pattern but at the same time he had done something original that made people gasp. He could hardly wait to see the door installed in the church.

'Forty-seven,' Elfric said, then he turned to Merthin.

'I finished the door,' Merthin said proudly. 'What do you think?'

Elfric looked at the door for a moment. He had a big nose, and his nostrils twitched in surprise. Then, without warning, he hit Merthin across the face with the stick he had been using to count. It was a solid piece of wood and the blow was hard. Merthin cried out in sudden agony, staggered back and fell to the ground.

'You piece of filth!' Elfric yelled. 'You defiled my daughter!'

Merthin tried to sputter a protest, but his mouth was full of blood.

'How dare you?' Elfric bellowed.

As if at a signal, Alice appeared from inside the house. 'Snake!' she screamed. 'You slithered into our home and deflowered our little girl!'

They were pretending to be spontaneous, but they must have planned this, Merthin thought. He spat blood and said: 'Deflowered? She was no virgin!'

Elfric lashed out again with his improvised club. Merthin rolled out of the way, but the blow landed painfully on his shoulder.

Alice said: 'How could you do this to Caris? My poor sister – when she finds out, it will break her heart.'

Merthin was stung into a response. 'And you'll be sure to tell her, won't you, you bitch.'

'Well, you're not going to marry Griselda in secret,' Alice said.

Merthin was astonished. 'Marry? I'm not marrying her. She hates me!'

With that, Griselda appeared. 'I certainly don't want to marry you,' she said. 'But I'll have to. I'm pregnant.'

Merthin stared at her. 'That's not possible – we only did it once.'

Elfric laughed harshly. 'It only takes once, you young fool.'

'I'm still not marrying her.'

'If you don't, you'll be sacked,' Elfric said.

'You can't do that.'

'Why not?'

'I don't care, I'm not going to marry her.'

Elfric dropped the club and picked up an axe.

Merthin said: 'Jesus Christ!'

Alice took a step forward. 'Elfric, don't commit murder.'

'Get out of the way, woman.' Elfric lifted the axe.

Merthin, still on the ground, scooted away, in fear of his life.

Elfric brought the axe down, not on Merthin, but on his door.

Merthin shouted: 'No!'

The sharp blade sank into the face of the long-haired virgin and split the wood along the grain.

Merthin yelled: 'Stop it!'

Elfric lifted the axe again and brought it down even harder. It split the door in two.

Merthin got to his feet. To his horror, he felt his eyes fill with tears. 'You have no right!' He was trying to shout, but his voice came out in a whisper.

Elfric lifted the axe and turned towards him. 'Stay back, boy – don't tempt me.'

Merthin saw a mad light in Elfric's eye, and backed away.

Elfric brought the axe down on the door again.

Merthin stood and watched with tears pouring down his face.

11

THE TWO DOGS, SKIP AND SCRAP, greeted one another with joyful enthusiasm. They were from the same litter, though they did not look similar: Skip was a brown boy dog and Scrap a small black female. Skip was a typical village dog, lean and suspicious, whereas the city-dwelling Scrap was plump and contented.

It was ten years since Gwenda had picked Skip out of a litter of mongrel puppies, on the floor of Caris's bedroom in the wool merchant's big house, the day Caris's mother died. Since then, Gwenda and Caris had become close friends. They met only two or three times a year, but they shared their secrets. Gwenda felt she could tell Caris everything and the information would never get back to her parents or anyone else in Wigleigh. She assumed Caris felt the same: because Gwenda did not talk to any other Kingsbridge girls, there could be no risk of her letting something slip in a careless moment.

Gwenda arrived in Kingsbridge on the Friday of Fleece Fair week. Her father, Joby, went to the fairground in front of the cathedral to sell the furs of squirrels he had trapped in the forest near Wigleigh. Gwenda went straight to Caris's house, and the two dogs were reunited.

As always, Gwenda and Caris talked about boys. 'Merthin is in a strange mood,' Caris said. 'On Sunday he was his normal self, kissing me in church – then, on Monday, he could hardly look me in the eye.'

'He's feeling guilty about something,' Gwenda said immediately.

'It's probably connected with Elizabeth Clerk. She's always had her eye on him, though she's a cold bitch and much too old for him.'

'Have you and Merthin done it yet?'

'Done what?'

'You know ... When I was little, I used to call it Grunting, because that was the noise grown-ups made while they were doing it.'

'Oh, that? No, not yet.'

'Why not?'

'I don't know...'

'Don't you want to?'

'Yes, but ... don't you worry about spending your life doing some man's bidding?'

Gwenda shrugged. 'I don't like the idea but, on the other hand, I don't worry about it.'

'What about you? Have you done it yet?'

'Not properly. I said yes to a boy from the next village, years ago, just to see what it was like. It's a nice warm glow, like drinking wine. That was the only time. But I'd let Wulfric do it any time he liked.'

'Wulfric? This is new!'

'I know. I mean, I've known him since we were small, when he used to pull my hair and run away. Then one day, soon after Christmas, I looked at him as he came into church, and I realized he'd become a man. Well, not just a man, but a really gorgeous man. He had snow in his hair and a sort of mustard-coloured scarf around his neck, and he just looked glowing.'

'Do you love him?'

Gwenda sighed. She did not know how to say what she felt. It was not just love. She thought about him all the time, and she did not know how she could live without him. She daydreamed about kidnapping him and locking him up in a hut deep in the forest so that he could never escape from her.

'Well, the look on your face answers my question,' Caris said. 'Does he love you?'

Gwenda shook her head. 'He never even speaks to me. I wish he'd do something to show that he knows who I am, even if it was only pulling my hair. But he's in love with Annet, the daughter of Perkin. She's a selfish cow, but he adores her. Her father and his are the two wealthiest men in the village. Her father raises laying hens and sells them, and his father has fifty acres.'

'You make it sound hopeless.'

'I don't know. What's hopeless? Annet might die. Wulfric might suddenly realize he's always loved me. My father might be made earl and order him to marry me.'

Caris smiled. 'You're right. Love is never hopeless. I'd like to see this boy.'

Gwenda stood up. 'I was hoping you'd say that. Let's go and find him.'

They left the house, the dogs following at their heels. The rainstorms that had lashed the town earlier in the week had given way to occasional showers, but the main street was still a stream of mud. Because of the fair, the mud was mixed with animal droppings, rotten vegetables, and all the litter and filth of a thousand visitors.

As they splashed through the disgusting puddles, Caris asked about Gwenda's family.

'The cow died,' Gwenda said. 'Pa needs to buy another, but I don't know how he's going to do it. He only has a few squirrel furs to sell.'

'A cow costs twelve shillings this year,' Caris said with concern. 'That's a hundred and forty-four silver pennies.' Caris always did arithmetic in her head: she had learned Arabic numbers from Buonaventura Caroli, and she said that made it easy.

'For the last few winters that cow has kept us alive – especially the little ones.' The pain of extreme hunger was familiar to Gwenda. Even with the cow to give milk, four of Ma's babies had died. No wonder Philemon had longed to be a monk, she thought: it was worth almost any sacrifice to have hearty meals provided every day without fail.

Caris said: 'What will your father do?'

'Something underhand. It's difficult to steal a cow – you can't slip it into your satchel – but he'll have a crafty scheme.' Gwenda was sounding more confident than she felt. Pa was dishonest, but not clever. He would do anything he could, legal or not, to get another cow, but he might just fail.

They passed through the priory gates into the wide fairground. The traders were wet and miserable on the sixth day of bad weather. They had exposed their stock to the rain and got little in return.

Gwenda felt awkward. She and Caris almost never talked about the disparity in wealth between the two families. Every time Gwenda visited, Caris would quietly give her a present to take home: a cheese, a smoked fish, a bolt of cloth, a jar of honey. Gwenda would thank her – and she was always profoundly grateful – but no more would be said. When Pa tried to make her take advantage of Caris's trust by stealing from the house, Gwenda would argue that she would then be unable to visit again, whereas this way she came home with something two or three times a year. Even Pa could see the sense of that.

Gwenda looked for the stall where Perkin would be selling his hens. Annet would probably be there and, wherever Annet was, Wulfric would not be far away. Gwenda was right. There was Perkin, fat and sly, greasily polite to his customers, curt to everyone else. Annet was carrying a tray of eggs, smiling coquettishly, the tray pulling her dress tight against her breasts, her fair hair straying from her hat in wisps that played around her pink cheeks and her long neck. And there was Wulfric, looking like an archangel who had lost his way and wandered among humankind by mistake.

'There he is,' Gwenda murmured. 'The tall one with—'

'I can tell which one he is,' Caris said. 'He looks good enough to eat.'

'You see what I mean.'

'He's a bit young, isn't he?'

'Sixteen. I'm eighteen. Annet is eighteen too.'

'All right.'

'I know what you're thinking,' Gwenda said. 'He's too handsome for me.'

'No—'

'Handsome men never fall for ugly women, do they?'

'You're not ugly—'

'I've seen myself in a glass.' The memory was painful, and Gwenda grimaced. 'I cried when I realized what I looked like. I have a big nose and my eyes are too close together. I resemble my father.'

Caris protested: 'You have beautiful soft brown eyes, and wonderful thick hair.'

'But I'm not in Wulfric's class.'

Wulfric was standing side-on to Gwenda and Caris, giving them a good view of his carved profile. They both admired him for a moment – then he turned, and Gwenda gasped. The other side of his face was completely different: bruised and swollen, with one eye closed.

She ran up to him. 'What happened to you?' she cried.

He was startled. 'Oh, hello, Gwenda. I had a fight.' He half turned away, obviously embarrassed.

'Who with?'

'Some squire of the earl's.'

'You're hurt!'

He looked impatient. 'Don't worry, I'm fine.'

He did not understand why she was concerned, of course. Perhaps he even thought she was revelling in his misfortune. Then Caris spoke. 'Which squire?' she said.

Wulfric looked at her with interest, realizing from her dress that she was a wealthy woman. 'His name is Ralph Fitzgerald.'

'Oh – Merthin's brother!' Caris said. 'Was he hurt?'

'I broke his nose.' Wulfric looked proud.

'Weren't you punished?'

'A night in the stocks.'

Gwenda gave a little cry of anguish. 'Poor you!'

'It wasn't so bad. My brother made sure no one pelted me.'

'Even so...' Gwenda was horrified. The idea of being imprisoned in any way seemed to her the worst kind of torture.

Annet finished with a customer and joined in the conversation. 'Oh, it's you, Gwenda,' she said coldly. Wulfric might be oblivious to Gwenda's feelings, but Annet was not, and she treated Gwenda with a mixture of hostility and scorn. 'Wulfric fought a squire who insulted me,' she said, unable to conceal her satisfaction. 'He was just like a knight in a ballad.'

Gwenda said sharply: 'I wouldn't want him to get his face hurt for my sake.'

'Fortunately, that's not very likely, is it?' Annet smiled triumphantly.

Caris said: 'One never knows what the future may hold.'

Annet looked at her, startled by the interruption, and showed surprise that Gwenda's companion was so expensively dressed.

Caris took Gwenda's arm. 'Such a pleasure to meet you Wigleigh folk,' she said graciously. 'Goodbye.'

They walked on. Gwenda giggled. 'You were terribly condescending to Annet.'

'She annoyed me. Her kind give women a bad name.'

'She was so pleased that Wulfric got beaten up for her sake! I'd like to poke out her eyes.'

Caris said thoughtfully: 'Apart from his good looks, what is he actually like?'

'Strong, proud, loyal – just the type to get into a fight on someone else's behalf. But he's the kind of man who will provide tirelessly for his family, year in and year out, until the day he drops dead.'

Caris said nothing.

Gwenda said: 'He doesn't appeal to you, does he?'

'You make him sound a bit dull.'

'If you'd grown up with my father, you wouldn't think a good provider was dull.'

'I know.' Caris squeezed Gwenda's arm. 'I think he's wonderful for you – and, to prove it, I'm going to help you get him.'

Gwenda was not expecting that. 'How?'

'Come with me.'

They left the fairground and walked to the north end of the town. Caris led Gwenda to a small house in a side street near St Mark's parish church. 'A wise woman lives here,' she said. Leaving the dogs outside, they ducked through a low doorway.

The single, narrow downstairs room was divided by a curtain. In the front half were a chair and a bench. The fireplace had to be at the back, Gwenda thought, and she wondered why someone would want to hide whatever went on in the kitchen. The room was clean, and there was a strong smell, herby and slightly acid, hardly a perfume but not unpleasant. Caris called out: 'Mattie, it's me.'

After a moment, a woman of about forty pulled aside the curtain and came through. She had grey hair and pale indoor skin. She smiled when she saw Caris. Then she gave Gwenda a hard look and said: 'I see your friend is in love – but the boy hardly speaks to her.'

Gwenda gasped: 'How did you know?'

Mattie sat on the chair heavily: she was stout, and short of breath. 'People come here for three reasons: sickness, revenge and love. You look healthy, and you're too young for revenge, so you must be in love. And the boy must be indifferent to you, otherwise you wouldn't need my help.'

Gwenda glanced at Caris, who looked pleased and said: 'I told you she was wise.' The two girls sat on the bench and looked expectantly at the woman.

Mattie went on: 'He lives close to you, probably in the same village; but his family are wealthier than yours.'

'All true.' Gwenda was amazed. No doubt Mattie was guessing, but she was so accurate it seemed as if she must have second sight.

'Is he handsome?'

'Very.'

'But he's in love with the prettiest girl in the village.'

'If you like that type.'

'And her family, too, is wealthier than yours.'

'Yes.'

Mattie nodded. 'A familiar story. I can help you. But you must understand something. I have nothing to do with the spirit world. Only God can work miracles.'

Gwenda was puzzled. Everyone knew that the spirits of the dead controlled all of life's hazards. If they were pleased with you, they would guide rabbits to your traps, give you healthy babies, and make the sun shine on your ripening corn. But if you did something to anger them, they could put worms in your apples, cause your cow to give birth to a deformed calf, and make your husband impotent. Even the physicians at the priory admitted that prayers to the saints were more efficacious than their medicines.

Mattie went on: 'Don't despair. I can sell you a love potion.'

'I'm sorry, I have no money.'

'I know. But your friend Caris is extraordinarily fond of you, and she wants you to be happy. She came here prepared to pay for the potion. However, you must administer it correctly. Can you get the boy alone for an hour?'

'I'll find a way.'

'Put the potion in his drink. Within a short time he will become amorous. That's when you must be alone with him – if there is another girl in sight he may fall for her instead. So keep him away from other women, and be very sweet to him. He will think you the most desirable woman in the world. Kiss him, tell him he's wonderful, and – if you want – make love to him. After a while, he will sleep. When he wakes up, he will remember that he spent the happiest hour of his life in your arms, and he'll want to do it again as soon as he can.'

'But won't I need another dose?'

'No. The second time, your love and desire and femininity will be enough. A woman can make any man blissfully happy if he gives her the chance.'

The very thought made Gwenda feel lustful. 'I can't wait.'

'Then let's make up the mixture.' Mattie heaved herself out of the chair. 'You can come behind the curtain,' she said. Gwenda and Caris followed her. 'It's only there for the ignorant.'

The kitchen had a clean stone floor and a big fireplace equipped with stands and hooks for cooking and boiling, far more than one woman would need for her own food. There was a heavy old table, stained and scorched but scrubbed clean; a shelf with a row of pottery jars; and a locked cupboard, presumably containing the more precious ingredients used in Mattie's potions. Hanging on the wall was a large slate with numbers and letters scratched on it, presumably recipes. 'Why do you need to hide all this behind a curtain?' Gwenda said.

'A man who makes ointments and medicines is called an apothecary, but a woman who does the same runs the risk of being called a witch. There's a woman in town called Crazy Nell who goes around shouting about the devil. Friar Murdo has accused her of heresy. Nell is mad, it's true, but there's no harm in her. All the same, Murdo is insisting on a trial. Men like to kill a woman, every now and again, and Murdo will give them an excuse, and collect their pennies afterwards as alms. That's why I always tell people that only God works miracles. I don't conjure spirits. I just use the herbs of the forest and my powers of observation.'

While Mattie talked, Caris was moving about the kitchen as freely as if she were at home. She put a mixing bowl and a vial on the table. Mattie handed her a key, and she opened the cupboard. 'Put three drops of essence of poppies into a spoonful of distilled wine,' Mattie said. 'We must be careful not to make the mixture over-strong, or he will go to sleep too soon.'

Gwenda was astonished. 'Are *you* going to make the potion, Caris?'

'I sometimes help Mattie. Don't say anything to Petranilla, she would disapprove.'

'I wouldn't tell her if her hair was on fire.' Caris's aunt disliked Gwenda, probably for the same reason she would disapprove of Mattie: they were both low-class, and such things mattered to Petranilla.

But why was Caris, the daughter of a wealthy man, working like an apprentice in the kitchen of a side-street medicine woman? While Caris made up the mixture, Gwenda recalled that her friend had always been intrigued by illness and cures. As a little girl, Caris had wanted to be a physician, not understanding that only priests were allowed to study medicine. Gwenda remembered her saying, after her mother had died: 'But *why* do people have to fall sick?' Mother Cecilia had told her it was because of sin; Edmund had said that no one really knew. Neither response had satisfied Caris. Perhaps she was still seeking the answer here in Mattie's kitchen.

Caris poured the liquid into a tiny jar, stoppered it, and bound the stopper tightly with cord, tying the ends in a knot. Then she handed the jar to Gwenda.

Gwenda tucked it into the leather purse attached to her belt. She wondered how on earth she was going to get Wulfric on his own for an hour. She had glibly said that she would find a way but, now that she had the love potion in her possession, the task seemed nearly impossible. He showed signs of restlessness if she merely spoke to him. He wanted to be with Annet any free time he had. What reason would Gwenda give for needing to be alone with him? 'I want to show you a place where we can get wild duck eggs.' But why would she show him and not her father? Wulfric was a little naïve, but not stupid: he would know she was up to something.

Caris gave Mattie twelve silver pennies – two weeks' wages for Pa. Gwenda said: 'Thank you, Caris. I hope you'll come to my wedding.'

Caris laughed. 'That's what I like to see – confidence!'

They left Mattie and headed back to the fair. Gwenda decided to begin by finding out where Wulfric was staying. His family were too well off to claim poverty, so they could not stay free at the priory. They would probably be lodging in a tavern. She could just casually ask him, or his brother, and follow up with a question about the standard of accommodation, as if she were interested to know which of the town's many inns was the best.

A monk passed by, and Gwenda realized with a guilty start that she had not even thought about trying to see her brother, Philemon. Pa would not visit him, for they had hated one another for years; but Gwenda was fond of him. She knew that he was sly, untruthful and malicious, but all the same he loved her. They had been through many hungry winters together. She would seek him out later, she resolved, after she had seen Wulfric again.

But, before she and Caris reached the fairground, they met Gwenda's father.

Joby was near the priory gates, outside the Bell. With him was a rough-looking man in a yellow tunic, with a pack on his back – and a brown cow.

He waved Gwenda over. 'I've found a cow,' he said.

Gwenda looked more closely. It was two years old, and thin, with a bad-tempered look, but it appeared healthy. 'It seems fine,' she said.

'This is Sim Chapman,' he said, jerking a thumb at the yellow tunic. A chapman travelled from village to village selling small necessities – needles, buckles, hand mirrors, combs. He might have stolen the cow, but that would not bother Pa, if the price was right.

Gwenda said to her father: 'Where did you get the money?'

'I'm not paying, exactly,' he replied, looking shifty.

Gwenda had expected him to have some scheme. 'What, then?'

'It's more of a swap.'

'What are you giving him in exchange for the cow?'

'You,' said Pa.

'Don't be silly,' she said, and then she felt a loop of rope dropped over her head and tightened around her body, pinning her arms to her sides.

She felt bewildered. This could not be happening. She struggled to free herself, but Sim just pulled the rope tighter.

'Now, don't make a fuss,' Pa said.

She could not believe they were serious. 'What do you think you're doing?' she said incredulously. 'You can't sell me, you fool!'

'Sim needs a woman, and I need a cow,' Pa said. 'It's very simple.'

Sim spoke for the first time. 'She's ugly enough, your daughter.'

'This is ridiculous!' Gwenda said.

Sim smiled at her. 'Don't worry, Gwenda,' he said. 'I'll be good to you, as long as you behave yourself, and do as you're told.'

They meant it, Gwenda saw. They actually thought they could make this exchange. A cold needle of fear entered her heart as she realized it might even happen.

Caris spoke up. 'This joke has gone on long enough,' she said in a loud, clear voice. 'Release Gwenda immediately.'

Sim was not intimidated by her air of command. 'And who are you, to give orders?'

'My father is alderman of the parish guild.'

'But you're not,' Sim said. 'And even if you were, you'd have no authority over me or my friend Joby.'

'You can't trade a girl for a cow!'

'Why not?' said Sim. 'It's my cow, and the girl is his daughter.'

Their raised voices attracted the attention of passers-by, who stopped to stare at the girl tied up with a rope. Someone said: 'What's happening?' Another replied: 'He's sold his daughter for a cow.' Gwenda saw a look of panic cross her father's face. He was wishing he had done this up a quiet alley – but he was not smart enough to have foreseen the public reaction. Gwenda realized the bystanders might be her only hope.

Caris waved to a monk who came out of the priory gates. 'Brother Godwyn!' she called. 'Come and settle an argument, please.' She looked triumphantly at Sim. 'The priory has jurisdiction over all bargains agreed at the Fleece Fair,' she said. 'Brother Godwyn is the sacrist. I think you'll have to accept his authority.'

Godwyn said: 'Hello, cousin Caris. What's the matter?'

Sim grunted with disgust. 'Your cousin, is he?'

Godwyn gave him a frosty look. 'Whatever the dispute is here, I shall try to give a fair judgement, as a man of God – you can depend on me for that, I hope.'

'And very glad to hear it, sir,' Sim said, becoming obsequious.

Joby was equally oily. 'I know you, brother – my son Philemon is devoted to you. You've been the soul of kindness to him.'

'All right, enough of that,' Godwyn said. 'What's going on?'

Caris said: 'Joby here wants to sell Gwenda for a cow. Tell him he can't.'

Joby said: 'She's my daughter, sir, and she's eighteen years old and a maid, so she's mine to do with what I will.'

Godwyn said: 'All the same, it seems a shameful business, selling your children.'

Joby became pathetic. 'I wouldn't do it, sir, only I've three more at home, and I'm a landless labourer, with no means to feed the children through the winter, unless I have a cow, and our old one has died.'

There was a sympathetic murmur from the growing crowd. They knew about winter hardship, and the extremes to which a man might have to go to feed his family. Gwenda began to despair.

Sim said: 'Shameful you may think it, Brother Godwyn, but is it a sin?' He spoke as if he already knew the answer, and Gwenda guessed he might have had this argument before, in a different place.

With obvious reluctance, Godwyn said: 'The Bible does appear to sanction selling your daughter into slavery. The book of Exodus, chapter twenty-one.'

'Well, there you are, then!' said Joby. 'It's a Christian act!'

Caris was outraged. 'The book of Exodus!' she said scornfully.

One of the bystanders joined in. 'We are not the children of Israel,' she said. She was a small, chunky woman with an underbite that gave her jaw a determined look. Although dressed poorly, she was assertive. Gwenda recognized her as Madge, the wife of Mark Webber. 'There is no slavery today,' Madge said.

Sim said: 'Then what of apprentices, who get no pay, and may be beaten by their master? Or novice monks and nuns? Or those who skivvy for bed and board in the palaces of the nobility?'

Madge said: 'Their life may be hard, but they can't be bought and sold – can they, Brother Godwyn?'

'I don't say that the trade is lawful,' Godwyn responded. 'I studied medicine at Oxford, not law. But I can find no reason, in Holy Scripture or the teachings of the Church, to say that what these men are doing is a sin.' He looked at Caris and shrugged. 'I'm sorry, cousin.'

Madge Webber folded her arms across her chest. 'Well, chapman, how are you going to take the girl out of town?'

'At the end of a rope,' he said. 'Same way I brought the cow in.'

'Ah, but you didn't have to get the cow past me and these people.'

Gwenda's heart leaped with hope. She was not sure how many of the bystanders supported her, but if it came to a fight they were more likely to side with Madge, who was a townswoman, than with Sim, an outsider.

'I've dealt with obstinate women before,' Sim said, and his mouth twisted as he spoke. 'They've never given me much trouble.'

Madge put her hand on the rope. 'Perhaps you've been lucky.'

He snatched the rope away. 'Keep your hands off my property and you won't get hurt.'

Deliberately, Madge put a hand on Gwenda's shoulder.

Sim shoved Madge roughly, and she staggered back; but there was a murmur of protest from the crowd.

A bystander said: 'You wouldn't do that if you'd seen her husband.'

There was a ripple of laughter. Gwenda recalled Madge's husband, Mark, a gentle giant. If only he would show up!

But it was John Constable who arrived, his well-developed nose for trouble bringing him to any crowd almost as soon as it gathered. 'We'll have no shoving,' he said. 'Are you causing trouble, chapman?'

Gwenda became hopeful again. Chapmen had a bad reputation, and the constable was assuming Sim was the cause of the trouble.

Sim turned obsequious, something he could obviously do quicker than changing his hat. 'Beg pardon, Master Constable,' he said. 'But when a man has paid an agreed price for his purchase, he must be allowed to leave Kingsbridge with his goods intact.'

'Of course.' John had to agree. A market town depended on its reputation for fair dealing. 'But what have you bought?'

'This girl.'

'Oh.' John looked thoughtful. 'Who sold her?'

'I did,' said Joby. 'I'm her father.'

Sim went on: 'And this woman with the big chin threatened to stop me taking the girl away.'

'So I did,' said Madge. 'For I've never heard of a woman being bought and sold in Kingsbridge Market, and nor has anyone else around here.'

Joby said: 'A man may do as he will with a child of his own.' He looked around the crowd appealingly. 'Is there anyone here who will disagree with that?'

Gwenda knew that no one would. Some people treated their children kindly, and some harshly, but all were agreed that the father must have absolute power over the child. She burst out angrily: 'You wouldn't stand there, deaf and dumb, if you had a father like him. How many of you were sold by your parents? How many of you were made to steal, when you were children and had hands small enough to slide into folks' wallets?'

Joby started to look worried. 'She's raving, now, Master Constable,' he said. 'No child of mine ever stole.'

'Never mind that,' said John. 'Everyone listen to me. I shall make a ruling on this. Those who disagree with my decision can complain to the prior. If there's any shoving, by anyone, or any other kind of rough stuff, I shall arrest everyone involved in it. I hope that's clear.' He looked around belligerently. No one spoke: they were eager to hear his decision. He went on: 'I know of no reason why this trade is unlawful, therefore Sim Chapman is allowed to go his way, with the girl.'

Joby said: 'I told you so, didn't—'

'Shut your damn mouth, Joby, you fool,' said the constable. 'Sim, get going, and make it quick. Madge Webber, if you raise a hand I'll put you in the stocks, and your husband won't stop me either. And not a word from you, Caris Wooler, please – you may complain to your father about me if you wish.'

Before John had finished speaking, Sim jerked hard on the rope. Gwenda was tipped forward, and stuck a foot out in front of her to keep from falling to the ground; then, somehow, she was moving along, stumbling and half running down the street. Out of the corner of her eye, she saw Caris alongside her. Then John Constable seized Caris by the arm, she turned to protest to him, and a moment later she disappeared from Gwenda's sight.

Sim walked quickly down the muddy main street, hauling on the rope, keeping Gwenda just off balance. As they approached the bridge she began to feel desperate. She tried jerking back on the rope, but he responded with an extra strong heave that threw her down in the mud. Her arms were still pinioned, so she could not use her hands to protect herself, and she fell flat, bruising her chest, her face squelching into the ooze. She struggled to her feet, giving up all resistance. Roped like an animal, hurt, frightened and covered in filthy mud, she staggered after her new owner, across the bridge and along the road that led into the forest.

*

SIM CHAPMAN LED Gwenda through the suburb of Newtown to the crossroads known as Gallows Cross, where criminals were hanged. There he took the road south, towards Wigleigh. He tied her rope to his wrist so that she could not break away, even when his attention wandered. Her dog, Skip, followed them, but Sim threw stones at him and, after one hit him full on the nose, he retreated with his tail between his legs.

After several miles, as the sun began to set, Sim turned into the forest. Gwenda had seen no feature beside the road to mark the spot, but Sim seemed to have chosen carefully for, a few hundred paces into the trees, they came upon a pathway. Looking down, Gwenda could see the neat impressions of dozens of small hooves in the earth, and she realized it was a deer path. It would lead to water, she guessed. Sure enough, they came to a little brook, the vegetation on either side trodden into mud.

Sim knelt beside the stream, filled his cupped hands with clear water, and drank. Then he moved the rope so that it was around her neck, freeing her hands, and motioned her to the water.

She washed her hands in the stream then drank thirstily.

'Wash your face,' he ordered. 'You're ugly enough by nature.'

She did as she was told, wondering wearily why he cared how she looked.

The path continued on the farther side of the drinking hole. They walked on. Gwenda was a strong girl, capable of walking all day, but she was defeated and miserable and scared, and that made her feel exhausted. Whatever fate awaited her at their destination, it was probably worse than this, but all the same she yearned to get there so that she could sit down.

Darkness was falling. The deer path wound through trees for a mile then petered out at the foot of a hill. Sim stopped beside a particularly massive oak tree and gave a low whistle.

A few moments later, a figure materialized out of the half-lit woodland and said: 'All right, Sim.'

'All right, Jed.'

'What you got there, a fruit tart?'

'You shall have a slice, Jed, same as the others, so long as you've got sixpence.'

Gwenda realized what Sim had planned. He was going to prostitute her. The realization hit her like a blow, and she staggered and fell to her knees.

'Sixpence, eh?' Jed's voice seemed to come from far away, but all the same she could hear the excitement in his voice. 'How old is she?'

'Her father claimed she was eighteen.' Sim jerked on the rope. 'Stand up, you lazy cow, we're not there yet.'

Gwenda got to her feet. That's why he wanted me to wash my face, she thought, and for some reason the realization made her cry.

She wept hopelessly as she stumbled along in Sim's footsteps until they came to a clearing with a fire in the middle. Through her tears, she perceived fifteen or twenty people lying around the edge of the clearing, most of them wrapped in blankets or cloaks. Almost all those watching her in the firelight were male, but she caught sight of a white female face, hard in expression but smooth-chinned, that stared at her briefly then disappeared back into a bundle of ragged bedding. An upturned wine barrel and a scattering of wooden cups testified to a drunken party.

Gwenda realized that Sim had brought her to a den of outlaws.

She groaned. How many of them would she be forced to submit to?

As soon as she asked herself the question, she knew the answer: all of them.

Sim dragged her across the clearing to a man who was sitting upright, his back against a tree. 'All right, Tam,' said Sim.

Gwenda knew instantly who the man must be: the most famous outlaw in the county, he was called Tam Hiding. He had a handsome face, though it was reddened by drink. People said he was noble-born, but they always said that about famous outlaws. Looking at him, Gwenda was surprised by his youth: he was in his mid-twenties. But then, to kill an outlaw was no crime so, in all probability, few lived to be old.

Tam said: 'All right, Sim.'

'I traded Alwyn's cow for a girl.'

'Well done.' Tam's speech was only slightly slurred.

'We're going to charge the boys sixpence, but of course you can have a free go. I expect you'd like to be first.'

Tam peered at her with bloodshot eyes. Perhaps it was wishful thinking, but she imagined she saw a hint of pity in his look. He said: 'No, thanks, Sim. You go ahead and let the boys have a good time. Though you might want to leave it until tomorrow. We got a barrel of good wine from a pair of monks who were taking it to Kingsbridge, and most of the lads are dead drunk now.'

Gwenda's heart leaped with hope. Perhaps her torture would be postponed.

'I'll have to consult Alwyn,' Sim said doubtfully. 'Thanks, Tam.' He turned away, pulling Gwenda behind him.

A few yards away, a broad-shouldered man was struggling to his feet. Sim said: 'All right, Alwyn.' The phrase seemed to serve the outlaws as a greeting and a recognition code.

Alwyn was at the bad-tempered phase of drunkenness. 'What have you got?'

'A fresh young girl.'

Alwyn took Gwenda's chin in his hand, gripping unnecessarily hard, and turned her face to the firelight. She was forced to look into his eyes. He was young, like Tam Hiding, but with the same unhealthy air of dissipation. His breath smelled of drink. 'By Christ, you picked an ugly one,' he said.

For once Gwenda was happy to be thought ugly: perhaps Alwyn would not want to do anything to her.

'I took what I could get,' Sim said testily. 'If the man had a beautiful daughter he wouldn't sell her for a cow, would he? He'd marry her to the son of a rich wool merchant instead.'

The thought of her father made Gwenda angry. He must have known, or suspected, that this would happen. How could he do it to her?

'All right, all right, it doesn't matter,' Alwyn said to Sim. 'With only two women in the group, most of the lads are desperate.'

'Tam said we should wait until tomorrow, because they're all too drunk tonight – but it's up to you.'

'Tam's right. Half of them are asleep already.'

Gwenda's fear retreated a little. Anything could happen overnight.

'Good,' Sim said. 'I'm dog-tired anyway.' He looked at Gwenda. 'Lie down, you.' He never called her by her name.

She lay down, and he used the rope to tie her feet together

and her hands behind her back. Then he and Alwyn lay down either side of her. In a few moments, both men were asleep.

Gwenda was exhausted, but she had no thought of sleep. With her arms behind her back, every position was painful. She tried to move her wrists within the rope, but Sim had pulled it tight and knotted it well. All she achieved was to break her skin, so that the rope burned her flesh.

Despair turned to helpless rage, and she pictured herself taking revenge on her captors, lashing them all with a whip as they cowered in front of her. It was a pointless fantasy. She turned her mind to practical means of escape.

First she would have to make them untie her. That done, she would have to get away. Ideally, she would somehow ensure they could not follow her and recapture her.

It seemed impossible.

12

GWENDA WAS COLD when she woke up. It was midsummer, but the weather was cool, and she had no covering but her light dress. The sky was turning from black to grey. She looked around the clearing in the faint light: no one was moving.

She needed to pee. She thought of doing it there, and soaking her dress. If she made herself disgusting, so much the better. Almost as soon as the thought occurred to her she dismissed it. That would be giving up. She was not giving up.

But what was she going to do?

Alwyn was sleeping beside her, with his long dagger in its sheath still attached to his belt, and that gave her the glimmer of an idea. She was not sure she had the nerve to carry out the plan that was forming in her mind. But she refused to think about how scared she was. She just had to do it.

Although her ankles were tied together, she could move her legs. She kicked Alwyn. At first he did not seem to feel it. She kicked him again, and he moved. The third time, he sat upright. 'Was that you?' he said blearily.

'I have to pee,' she said.

'Not in the clearing. It's one of Tam's rules. Go twenty paces for a piss, fifty for a shit.'

'So, even outlaws live by rules.'

He stared uncomprehendingly at her. The irony escaped him. He was not a clever man, she realized. That was helpful. But he was strong, and mean. She would have to be very cautious.

She said: 'I can't go anywhere tied up.'

Grumbling, he undid the rope around her ankles.

The first part of her plan had worked. Now she was even more frightened.

She struggled to her feet. All the muscles of her legs ached from a night of constriction. She took a step, stumbled, and fell down again. 'It's so hard with my hands tied,' she said.

He ignored that.

The second part of her plan had not worked.

She would have to keep trying.

She got up again and walked into the trees, with Alwyn following her. He was counting paces on his fingers. The first time he got to ten, he started again. The second time, he said: 'Far enough.'

She looked at him helplessly. 'I can't lift my dress,' she said.

Would he fall for this?

He stared dumbly at her. She could almost hear his brain working, rumbling like the gears of a water mill. He could lift her dress while she peed, but that was the kind of thing a mother did for a toddler, and he would find it humiliating. Alternatively, he could untie her hands. With hands and feet free, she might make a run for it. But she was small, weary and cramped: there was no way she could outrun a man with long, muscular legs. He must be thinking that the risk was not serious.

He untied the rope around her wrists.

She looked away from him, so that he would not see her look of triumph.

She rubbed her forearms to restore the circulation. She wanted to poke his eyeballs out with her thumbs, but instead she smiled as sweetly as she could and said: 'Thank you,' as if he had performed an act of kindness.

He said nothing, but stood watching her, waiting.

She expected him to look away when she hitched up the skirt of her dress and squatted, but he only stared more intensely. She held his gaze, unwilling to act ashamed while she did what was natural. His mouth opened slightly and she could tell he was breathing harder.

Now came the hardest part.

She stood up slowly, letting him get a good look before she dropped her dress. He licked his lips, and she knew she had him.

She went closer and stood in front of him. 'Will you be my protector?' she said, using a little-girl voice that did not come naturally to her.

He showed no sign of suspicion. He did not speak, but grasped her breast in his rough hand and squeezed.

She gasped with pain. 'Not so hard!' She took his hand in hers. 'Be more gentle.' She moved his hand against her breast, rubbing the nipple so that it stood up. 'It's nicer if you're gentle.'

He grunted, but continued to rub softly. Then he took the neckline of her dress in his left hand and drew his dagger. The knife was a foot long, with a point, and the blade gleamed with recent sharpening. He obviously intended to cut her dress off. That would not do – it would leave her naked.

She took his wrist in a light grip, restraining him momentarily. 'You don't need the knife,' she said. 'Look.' She stepped back, undid her belt and, with a quick movement, pulled the dress off over her head. It was her only garment.

She stretched it out on the ground then lay on it. She tried to smile at him. She felt sure the result was a horrible grimace. Then she parted her legs.

He hesitated only for a moment.

Keeping the knife in his right hand, he pushed down his underdrawers and knelt between her thighs. He pointed the dagger at her face and said: 'Any trouble, and I'll slice your cheek open.'

'You won't need to do that,' she said. She was trying desperately to think what words such a man would like to hear from a woman. 'My big, strong protector,' she said.

He showed no reaction to that.

He lay over her, thrusting blindly. 'Not so fast,' she said, gritting her teeth against the pain of his clumsy stabs. She reached between her legs and guided him inside, throwing her legs up to make the entrance easier.

He reared over her, taking his weight on his arms. He put the dagger on the grass beside her head, covering the hilt with his right hand. He groaned as he moved inside her. She moved with him, keeping up the pretence of willingness, watching his face, forcing herself not to glance sideways at the dagger, waiting for her moment. She was both scared and disgusted, but a small part of her mind remained calm and calculating.

He closed his eyes and lifted his head like an animal scenting the breeze. His arms were straight, holding him up. She risked a look at the knife. He had moved his hand slightly, so that it only partly covered the hilt. She could grab it now, but how fast would he react?

She looked at his face again. His mouth was twisted in a rictus of concentration. He thrust faster, and she matched his motion.

To her dismay, she felt a glow spread through her loins. She was appalled at herself. The man was a murdering outlaw, little better than a beast, and he was planning to prostitute her for sixpence a time. She was doing this to save her life, not for enjoyment! Yet there was a gush of moisture inside her, and he thrust faster.

She sensed that his moment of climax was near. It was now or never. He gave a groan that sounded like surrender, and she moved.

She snatched the knife from under his hand. There was no change in the expression of ecstasy on his face: he had not noticed her movement. Terrified that he would see what she was doing and stop her at the last moment, she did not hesitate but jabbed upwards, jerking her shoulders up from the lying position as she did so. He sensed her movement and opened his eyes. Shock and fear showed on his face. Stabbing wildly, she stuck the knife into his throat just below the jaw. She cursed, knowing she had missed the most vulnerable parts of the neck – the breathing-pipe and the jugular vein. He roared with pain and rage, but he was not incapacitated, and she knew she was as close to death as she had ever been.

She moved instinctively, without forethought. Using her left arm, she struck at the inside of his elbow. He could not prevent the bending of his arm, and involuntarily he slumped. She pushed harder at the foot-long dagger, and his weight dragged him down on to the blade. As the knife entered his head from below, blood gushed from his open mouth, falling on her face, and she jerked her head aside reflexively; but she kept pushing on the knife. The blade met resistance for a moment, then slipped through, until his eyeball seemed to explode, and she saw the point emerge from the eye socket in a spray of blood and brains. He slumped on top of her, dead or nearly so. His weight knocked the breath out of her. It was like being stuck under a fallen tree. For a moment she was helpless to move.

To her horror, she felt him ejaculate inside her.

She was filled with superstitious terror. He was more frightening like this than when he had threatened her with a knife. Panicking, she wriggled out from under him.

She scrambled to her feet shakily, breathing hard. She had his blood on her breasts and his seed on her thighs. She glanced fearfully towards the outlaws' camp. Had anyone been awake to hear Alwyn's shout? If they had all been asleep, had the sound wakened any of them?

Trembling, she pulled her dress over her head and buckled her belt. She had her wallet and her own small knife, mainly used for eating. She hardly dared take her eyes off Alwyn: she had a dreadful feeling he might still be alive. She knew she should finish him off, but she could not bring herself to do it. A sound from the direction of the clearing startled her. She needed to get away fast. She looked around, getting her bearings, then headed in the direction of the road.

There was a sentry near the big oak tree, she recalled with a sudden start of fear. She walked softly through the woods, careful to make no sound, as she approached the tree. Then she saw the sentry – Jed, his name was – fast asleep on the ground. She tiptoed past him. It took all her will power not to break into a mad run. But he did not stir.

She found the deer path and followed it to the brook. It seemed there was no one on her tail. She washed the blood off her face and chest, then splashed cold water on her private parts. She drank deeply, knowing she had a long walk ahead.

Feeling slightly less frantic, she continued along the deer path. As she walked, she listened. How soon would the outlaws find Alwyn? She had not even tried to conceal the body. When they figured out what had happened they would surely come after her, for they had given a cow for her, and that was worth twelve shillings, half a year's pay for a labourer such as her father.

She reached the road. For a woman travelling alone, the open road was almost as hazardous as a forest track. Tam Hiding's group were not the only outlaws, and there were plenty of other men – squires, peasant boys, bands of men-at-arms – who might take advantage of a defenceless woman. But her first priority was to get away from Sim Chapman and his cronies, so speed was paramount.

Which direction should she take? If she went home to Wigleigh, Sim might follow her there and claim her back – and there was no telling how her father would deal with that. She needed friends she could trust. Caris would help her.

She set off for Kingsbridge.

It was a clear day, but the road was muddy from many days of rain, and walking was that much more difficult. After a while she reached the top of a hill. Looking back, she could see along the road for about a mile. At the far limit of her vision, she saw a lone figure striding along. He wore a yellow tunic.

Sim Chapman.

She broke into a run.

*

THE CASE AGAINST Crazy Nell was heard in the north transept of the cathedral on Saturday at noon. Bishop Richard presided over the ecclesiastical court, with Prior Anthony on his right and, on his left, his personal assistant, Archdeacon Lloyd, a dour black-haired priest who was said to do all the actual work of the bishopric.

There was a big crowd of townspeople. A heresy trial was good entertainment, and Kingsbridge had not seen one for years. Many craftsmen and labourers finished work at midday on Saturdays. Outside, the Fleece Fair was coming to an end, tradespeople dismantling their stalls and packing up their unsold goods, buyers preparing for the journey home, or arranging to consign their purchases by raft downriver to the sea port of Melcombe.

Waiting for the trial to begin, Caris thought gloomily of Gwenda. What was she doing now? Sim Chapman would force her to have sex with him, for sure – but that might not be the worst thing to happen to her. What else would she have to do as his slave? Caris had no doubt Gwenda would try to escape – but would she succeed? And, if she failed, how would Sim punish her? Caris realized she might never find out.

It had been a strange week. Buonaventura Caroli had not changed his mind: the Florentine buyers would not return to Kingsbridge, at least until the priory improved facilities for the Fleece Fair. Caris's father and the other leading wool merchants had spent half the week shut up with Earl Roland. Merthin continued in a strange mood, withdrawn and gloomy. And it was raining again.

Nell was dragged into church by John Constable and Friar Murdo. Her only garment was a sleeveless surcoat, fastened at the front but revealing her bony shoulders. She had no hat or shoes. She struggled feebly in the men's grasp, shouting imprecations.

When they got her quietened down, a series of townspeople came forward to attest that they had heard her call upon the devil. They were telling the truth. Nell threatened people with the devil all the time – for refusing to give her a handout, for standing in her way on the street, for wearing a good coat, or for no reason at all.

Each witness related some misfortune that had followed the curse. A goldsmith's wife had lost a valuable brooch; an innkeeper's chickens had all died; a widow developed a painful boil on her bottom – a complaint that caused laughter, but also carried conviction, for witches were known to have a malicious sense of humour.

While this was going on, Merthin appeared beside Caris. 'This is so stupid,' Caris said to him indignantly. 'Ten times the number of witnesses could come forward to say that Nell cursed them and nothing bad ensued.'

Merthin shrugged. 'People just believe what they want to believe.'

'Ordinary people, perhaps. But the bishop and the prior should know better – they are educated.'

'I've got something to tell you,' Merthin said.

Caris perked up. Perhaps she was about to learn the reason for his bad mood. She had been looking at him sidelong, but now she turned and saw that he had a huge bruise on the left side of his face. 'What happened to you?'

The crowd roared with laughter at some interjection of Nell's, and Archdeacon Lloyd had to call repeatedly for quiet. When Merthin could be heard again he said: 'Not here. Can we go somewhere quiet?'

She almost turned to leave with him, but something stopped her. All week long he had bewildered and wounded her by his coldness. Now, at last, he had decided he was ready to say what was on his mind – and she was expected to jump at his command. Why should he set the timetable? He had made her wait five days – why should she not make him wait an hour or so? 'No,' she said. 'Not now.'

He looked surprised. 'Why not?'

'Because it doesn't suit my convenience,' she said. 'Now let me listen.' As she turned from him, she saw a hurt look cross his face, and straight away she wished she had not been so cold; but it was too late, and she was not going to apologize.

The witnesses had finished. Bishop Richard said: 'Woman, do you say that the devil rules the earth?'

Caris was outraged. Heretics worshipped Satan because they believed he had jurisdiction over the earth, and God only ruled heaven. Crazy Nell could not even understand such a sophisticated credo. It was disgraceful that Richard was going along with Friar Murdo's ridiculous accusation.

Nell shouted back: 'You can shove your prick up your arse.'

The crowd laughed, delighted by this coarse insult to the bishop.

Richard said: 'If that's her defence . . .'

Archdeacon Lloyd intervened. 'Someone should speak on her behalf,' he said. He spoke respectfully, but he seemed comfortable correcting his superior. No doubt the lazy Richard relied on Lloyd to remind him of the rules.

Richard looked around the transept. 'Who will speak for Nell?' he called out.

Caris waited, but no one volunteered. She could not allow this to happen. Someone must point out how irrational this whole procedure was. When no one else spoke, Caris stood up. 'Nell is mad,' she said.

Everyone looked around, wondering who was foolish enough to side with Nell. There was a murmur of recognition – most people knew Caris – but no great sense of surprise, for she had a reputation for doing the unexpected.

Prior Anthony leaned over and said something in the bishop's ear. Richard said: 'Caris, the daughter of Edmund Wooler, tells us that the accused woman is mad. We had reached that conclusion without her assistance.'

Caris was goaded by his cool sarcasm. 'Nell has no idea what she is saying! She calls upon the devil, the saints, the moon and the stars. It has no more meaning than the barking of a dog. You might as well hang a horse for neighing at the king.' She could not keep the note of scorn from her voice, though she knew it was unwise to let your contempt show when addressing the nobility.

Some of the crowd murmured agreement. They liked a spirited argument.

Richard said: 'But you have heard people testify to the damage done by her curses.'

'I lost a penny yesterday,' Caris rejoined. 'I boiled an egg, and it was bad. My father lay awake all night coughing. But no one cursed us. Bad things just happen.'

There was much head-shaking at this. Most people believed there was some malign influence behind every misfortune, great or small. Caris had lost the support of the crowd.

Prior Anthony, her uncle, knew her views, and had argued with her before. Now he leaned forward and said: 'Surely you don't believe that God is responsible for illness and misfortune and loss?'

'No—'

'Who, then?'

Caris imitated Anthony's prissy tone. 'Surely you don't believe that every misfortune in life is the responsibility of either God or Crazy Nell?'

Archdeacon Lloyd said sharply: 'Speak respectfully to the

prior.' He did not realize Anthony was Caris's uncle. The townspeople laughed: they knew the prim prior and his independent-minded niece.

Caris finished: 'I believe Nell is harmless. Mad, yes, but harmless.'

Suddenly Friar Murdo was on his feet. 'My lord bishop, men of Kingsbridge, friends,' he said in his sonorous voice. 'The evil one is everywhere among us, tempting us to sin – to lying, greed of food, drunkenness with wine, puffed-up pride and fleshly lust.' The crowd liked this: Murdo's descriptions of sin called to the imagination delightful scenes of indulgence that were sanctified by his brimstone disapproval. 'But he cannot go unobserved,' Murdo went on, his voice rising with excitement. 'As the horse presses his hoofprints into the mud, as the kitchen mouse makes dainty tracks across the butter, as the lecher deposits his vile seed to grow in the womb of the deceived maid, so the devil must leave – his mark!'

They shouted their approval. They knew what he meant, and so did Caris.

'The servants of the evil one may be known by the mark he leaves upon them. For he sucks their hot blood as a child sucks the sweet milk from its mother's swollen breasts. And, like the child, he needs a teat from which to suck – a third nipple!'

He had the audience rapt, Caris observed. He began each sentence in a low, quiet voice, then built it up, piling one emotive phrase on another to his climax; and the crowd responded eagerly, listening in silence while he spoke, then shouting their approval at the end.

'This mark is dark in colour, ridged like a nipple, and rises from the clear skin around it. It may be on any part of the body. Sometimes it lies in the soft valley between a woman's breasts, the unnatural manifestation cruelly mimicking the natural. But the devil best likes it to be in the secret places of the body: in the groin, on the private parts, especially—'

Bishop Richard said loudly: 'Thank you, Friar Murdo, you need go no farther. You are demanding that the woman's body be examined for the Devil's Mark.'

'Yes, my lord bishop, for—'

'All right, no need for further argument, your point is well made.' He looked around. 'Is Mother Cecilia close by?'

The prioress was sitting on a bench on one side of the court, with Sister Juliana and some of the senior nuns. Crazy Nell's naked body could not be examined by men, so women would have to do it in private and report back. The nuns were the obvious choice.

Caris did not envy them their task. Most townspeople washed their hands and faces every day, and the smellier parts of their bodies once a week. All-over bathing was at best a twice-a-year ritual, necessary though dangerous to the health. However, Crazy Nell never seemed to wash at all. Her face was grimy, her hands were filthy, and she smelled like a dunghill.

Cecilia stood up. Richard said: 'Please take this woman to a private room, remove her clothing, examine her body carefully, and come back to report faithfully what you find.'

The nuns got up immediately and approached Nell. Cecilia spoke soothingly to the mad woman, and took her gently by the arm. But Nell was not fooled. She twisted away, throwing her arms into the air.

At that point, Friar Murdo shouted: 'I see it! I see it!'

Four of the nuns managed to hold Nell still.

The friar said: 'No need to take off her clothes. Just look under her right arm.' As Nell started to wriggle again, he strode over to her and lifted her arm himself, holding it high above her head. 'There!' he said, pointing into her armpit.

The crowd surged forward. 'I see it!' someone shouted, and others repeated the cry. Caris could see nothing other than normal armpit hair, and she was unwilling to commit the indignity of peering. She had no doubt that Nell had some kind of blemish or growth there. Lots of people had marks on their skin, especially the elderly.

Archdeacon Lloyd called for order, and John Constable beat the crowd back with a stick. When at last the church was quiet, Richard stood up. 'Crazy Nell of Kingsbridge, I find you guilty of heresy,' he said. 'You shall now be tied to the back of a cart and whipped through the town, then taken to the place known as

Gallows Cross, where you shall be hanged by the neck until you die.'

The crowd cheered. Caris turned away in disgust. With justice like this, no woman was safe. Her eye lit on Merthin, waiting patiently for her. 'All right,' she said bad-temperedly. 'What is it?'

'It's stopped raining,' he said. 'Come down to the river.'

*

THE PRIORY HAD a string of ponies for the senior monks and nuns to use when travelling, plus some carthorses for transporting goods. These were kept, along with the mounts of prosperous visitors, in a run of stone stables at the south end of the cathedral close. The nearby kitchen garden was manured with the straw from the stalls.

Ralph was in the stable yard, with the rest of Earl Roland's entourage. Their horses were saddled ready to begin the two-day journey back to Roland's residence at Earlscastle, near Shiring. They were waiting only for the earl.

Ralph was holding his horse, a bay called Griff, and talking to his parents. 'I don't know why Stephen was made lord of Wigleigh while I got nothing,' he said. 'We're the same age, and he's no better than I am at riding or jousting or fencing.'

Every time they met, Sir Gerald asked the same hopeful questions, and Ralph had to give him the same inadequate answers. Ralph could have borne his disappointment more easily had it not been for his father's pathetic eagerness to see him elevated.

Griff was a young horse. He was a hunter: a mere squire did not merit a costly warhorse. But Ralph liked him. He responded gratifyingly well when Ralph urged him on in the hunt. Griff was excited by all the activity in the yard, and impatient to get going. Ralph murmured in his ear: 'Quiet, my lovely lad, you shall stretch your legs later.' The horse calmed down at the sound of his voice.

'Be constantly on the alert for ways to please the earl,' Sir Gerald said. 'Then he will remember you when there is a post to be filled.'

That was all very well, Ralph thought, but the real

opportunities came only in battle. However, war might be a little nearer today than it had been a week ago. Ralph had not been in on the meetings between the earl and the wool merchants, but he gathered that the merchants were willing to lend money to King Edward. They wanted the king to take some decisive action against France, in retaliation for French attacks on the south coast ports.

Meanwhile, Ralph longed for some way to distinguish himself and begin to win back the honour the family had lost ten years ago – not just for his father, but for his own pride.

Griff stamped and tossed his head. To calm him, Ralph began to walk him up and down, and his father walked with him. His mother stood apart. She was upset about his broken nose.

With Father he walked past Lady Philippa, who was holding the bridle of a spirited courser with a firm hand while she talked to her husband, Lord William. She wore close-fitting clothes, which were suitable for a long ride but also emphasized her full bosom and long legs. Ralph was always on the lookout for excuses to talk to her, but it did him no good: he was just one of her father-in-law's followers, and she never spoke to him unless she had to.

As Ralph watched, she smiled at her husband and tapped him on the chest with the back of her hand in a gesture of mock reprimand. Ralph was filled with resentment. Why should it not be him with whom she was sharing such a moment of private amusement? No doubt she would if he were lord of forty villages, as William was.

Ralph felt that his life was all aspiration. When would he actually achieve something? He and his father walked the length of the yard then turned and came back.

He saw a one-armed monk come out of the kitchen and cross the yard, and was struck by how familiar the man looked. A moment later, he remembered how he knew the face. This was Thomas Langley, the knight who had killed one of the men-at-arms in the forest ten years ago. Ralph had not seen the man since that day, but his brother Merthin had, for the knight-become-monk was now responsible for supervising repairs to the priory buildings. Thomas wore a drab robe instead of the fine clothes of a knight, and had his head shaved in the monkish tonsure. He was heavier around the waist, but still carried himself like a fighting man.

As Thomas walked past, Ralph said casually to Lord William: 'There he goes – the mystery monk.'

William said sharply: 'What do you mean?'

'Brother Thomas. He used to be a knight, and no one knows why he joined the monastery.'

'What the devil do you know of him?' William's tone showed anger, although Ralph had said nothing offensive. Perhaps he was in a bad mood, despite the affectionate smiles of his beautiful wife.

Ralph wished he had not begun the conversation. 'I was here the day he came to Kingsbridge,' he said. He hesitated, recalling the oath the children had sworn that afternoon. Because of that, and because of William's inexplicable annoyance, Ralph did not tell the whole story. 'He staggered into town bleeding from a sword wound,' he went on. 'A boy remembers such things.'

Philippa said: 'How curious.' She looked at her husband. 'Do you know what Brother Thomas's story is?'

'Certainly not,' William snapped. 'How would I know a thing like that?'

She shrugged and turned away.

Ralph walked on, glad to get away. 'Lord William was lying,' he said to his father in a low voice. 'I wonder why?'

'Don't ask any more questions about that monk,' Father said anxiously. 'It's obviously a touchy subject.'

At last Earl Roland appeared. Prior Anthony was with him. The knights and squires mounted up. Ralph kissed his parents and swung himself into the saddle. Griff danced sideways, eager to be off. The motion made Ralph's broken nose hurt like fire. He gritted his teeth: there was nothing he could do but endure it.

Roland went up to his horse, Victory, a black stallion with a white patch over one eye. He did not mount, but took the bridle and began to walk, still in conversation with the prior. William called out: 'Sir Stephen Wigleigh and Ralph Fitzgerald, ride ahead and clear the bridge.'

Ralph and Stephen rode across the cathedral green. The grass was trampled and the ground muddy from the Fleece Fair. A few stalls were still doing business, but most were closing, and many had already gone. They passed out through the priory gates.

On the main street, Ralph saw the boy who had given him a broken nose. Wulfric, his name was, and he came from Stephen's village of Wigleigh. The left side of his face was bruised and swollen where Ralph had repeatedly punched him. Wulfric was outside the Bell inn with his father, mother and brother. They appeared to be about to leave.

You'd better hope you never meet me again, Ralph thought.

He tried to think of some insult to shout, but he was distracted by the sound of a crowd.

As he and Stephen rode down the main street, their horses stepping adroitly through the mud, they saw ahead of them a mob of people. Half way down the hill, they were forced to stop.

The street was jammed by hundreds of men, women and children shouting, laughing and jostling for space. They all had their backs to Ralph. He looked over their heads.

At the front of this unruly procession was a cart drawn by an ox. Tied to the back of the cart was a half-naked woman. Ralph had seen this kind of thing before: to be whipped through the town was a common punishment. The woman wore only a skirt of rough wool secured at the waist by a cord. Her face, when he could see it, was begrimed, and her hair was filthy, so that at first he thought she was old. Then he saw her breasts and realized she was only in her twenties.

Her hands were bound together and attached by the same rope to the back end of the cart. She stumbled along behind it, sometimes falling and being dragged writhing through the mud until she managed to get back on her feet. The town constable followed, vigorously lashing her bare back with a bull whip, a strip of leather at the end of a stick.

The crowd, led by a knot of young men, were taunting the woman, shouting insults, laughing, and throwing mud and rubbish. She delighted them by responding, screaming imprecations and spitting at anyone who got near her.

Ralph and Stephen urged their horses into the crowd. Ralph

raised his voice. 'Clear the way!' he shouted at the top of his voice. 'Make way for the earl!'

Stephen did the same.

No one took any notice.

＊

To the south of the priory, the ground sloped steeply down to the river. The bank on that side was rocky, unsuitable for loading barges and rafts, so all the wharves were on the more accessible south side, in the suburb of Newtown. The quiet north side bloomed at this time of year with shrubbery and wild flowers. Merthin and Caris sat on a low bluff overlooking the water.

The river was swollen with rain. It moved faster than it used to, Merthin noticed, and he could see why: the channel was narrower than formerly. That was because of the development of the riverside. When he was a child, most of the south bank had been a wide, muddy beach with a swampy field beyond. The river then had flowed at a stately pace, and as a boy he had floated on his back from one side to the other. But the new wharves, protected from flooding by stone walls, squeezed the same quantity of water into a smaller funnel, through which it hurried as if eager to get past the bridge. Beyond the bridge, the river widened and slowed around Leper Island.

'I've done something terrible,' Merthin said to Caris.

Unfortunately, she looked particularly lovely today. She wore a dark red linen dress, and her skin seemed to glow with vitality. She had been angry at the trial of Crazy Nell, but now she just seemed worried, and that gave her a vulnerable look that tugged at Merthin's heart. She must have noticed how he had been unable to meet her eye all week. But what he had to tell her was probably worse than anything she had imagined.

He had spoken to no one about this since the row with Griselda, Elfric and Alice. No one even knew that his door had been destroyed. He was longing to unburden himself, but he had held back. He did not want to talk to his parents: his mother would be judgemental and his father would just tell him to be a man. He might have talked to Ralph, but there had been a coolness between them since the fight with Wulfric: Merthin thought Ralph had behaved like a bully, and Ralph knew it.

He dreaded telling Caris the truth. For a moment he asked himself why. It was not that he was afraid of what she would do. She might be scornful – she was good at that – but she could not say anything worse than the things he said to himself constantly.

What he truly feared, he realized, was hurting her. He could bear her anger: it was her pain he could not face.

She said: 'Do you still love me?'

He was not expecting the question, but he answered without hesitation. 'Yes.'

'And I love you. Anything else is just a problem we can solve together.'

He wished she were right. He wished it so badly that tears came to his eyes. He looked away so that she would not see. A mob of people was moving on to the bridge, following a slow-moving cart, and he realized this must be Crazy Nell being whipped through the town on her way to Gallows Cross in Newtown. The bridge was already crowded with departing stallholders and their carts, and the traffic was almost at a standstill.

'What's the matter?' Caris said. 'Are you crying?'

'I lay with Griselda,' Merthin said abruptly.

Caris's mouth dropped open. '*Griselda?*' she said unbelievingly.

'I'm so ashamed.'

'I thought it must be Elizabeth Clerk.'

'She's too proud to offer herself.'

Caris's reaction to that surprised him. 'Oh, so you would have done it with her, too, if she'd suggested it?'

'That's not what I meant!'

'Griselda! Dear St Mary, I thought I was worth more than that.'

'You are.'

'*Lupa,*' she said, using the Latin word for a whore.

'I don't even like her. I hated it.'

'Is that supposed to make me feel better? Are you saying you wouldn't be so sorry if you'd enjoyed it?'

'No!' Merthin was dismayed. Caris seemed determined to misinterpret everything he said.

'Whatever got into you?'

'She was crying.'

'Oh, for God's sake! Do you do that to every girl you see crying?'

'Of course not! I was just trying to explain to you how it happened even though I really didn't want it to.'

Her scorn got worse with everything he said. 'Don't talk rubbish,' she said. 'If you hadn't wanted it to happen, it wouldn't have.'

'Listen to me, please,' he said frustratedly. 'She asked me, and I said no. Then she cried, and I put my arm around her to comfort her, then—'

'Oh, spare me the sickening details – I don't want to know.'

He began to feel resentful. He knew he had done wrong, and he expected her to be angry, but her contempt stung. 'All right,' he said, and he shut up.

But silence was not what she wanted. She stared at him in dissatisfaction, then said: 'What else?'

He shrugged. 'What's the point in my speaking? You just pour scorn on everything I say.'

'I don't want to listen to pathetic excuses. But there's something you haven't told me – I can feel it.'

He sighed. 'She's pregnant.'

Caris's reaction surprised him again. All the anger left her. Her face, until now taut with indignation, seemed to collapse. Only sadness remained. 'A baby,' she said. 'Griselda is going to have your baby.'

'It may not happen,' he said. 'Sometimes...'

Caris shook her head. 'Griselda is a healthy girl, well fed. There's no reason she should miscarry.'

'Not that I'd wish it,' he said, though he was not quite sure that was true.

'But what will you do?' she said. 'It will be your child. You will love it, even if you hate its mother.'

'I've got to marry her.'

Caris gasped. 'Marry! But that would be for ever.'

'I've fathered a child, so I should take care of it.'

'But to spend your whole life with Griselda!'

'I know.'

'You don't have to,' she said decisively. 'Think. Elizabeth Clerk's father didn't marry her mother.'

'He was a bishop.'

'There's Maud Roberts, in Slaughterhouse Ditch – she has three children, and everyone knows the father is Edward Butcher.'

'He's already married, and has four other children with his wife.'

'I'm saying they don't always force people to marry. You could just carry on as you are.'

'No, I couldn't. Elfric would throw me out.'

She looked thoughtful. 'So, you've already talked to Elfric?'

'Talked?' Merthin touched his bruised cheek. 'I thought he was going to kill me.'

'And his wife – my sister?'

'She screamed at me.'

'So she knows.'

'Yes. She said I have to marry Griselda. She never wanted me to be with you, anyway. I don't know why.'

Caris muttered: 'She wanted you for herself.'

That was news to Merthin. It seemed unlikely that the haughty Alice would be attracted to a lowly apprentice. 'I never saw any sign of that.'

'Only because you never looked at her. That's what made her so cross. She married Elfric in frustration. You broke my sister's heart – and now you're breaking mine.'

Merthin looked away. He barely recognized this picture of himself as a heartbreaker. How had things gone so wrong? Caris went quiet. Merthin stared moodily along the river to the bridge.

The crowd had come to a standstill, he saw. A heavy cart loaded with woolsacks was stuck at the southern end, probably with a broken wheel. The cart pulling Nell had stopped, unable to pass. The crowd were swarming around both carts, and some people had climbed on to the woolsacks for a better view. Earl Roland was also trying to leave. He was at the town end of the bridge, on horseback, with his entourage; but even they were having trouble getting the citizens to give way. Merthin spotted his brother Ralph on his horse, chestnut-coloured with a black mane and tail. Prior Anthony, who had evidently come to see the earl off, stood wringing his hands with anxiety while Roland's men forced their horses into the mob, trying in vain to clear a passage.

Merthin's intuition rang an alarm. Something was badly wrong, he felt sure, though at first he did not know what. He looked more closely at the bridge. He had noticed, on Monday, that the massive oak beams stretching from one piling to another across the length of the bridge were showing cracks on the upstream side; and that the beams had been strengthened with iron braces nailed across the cracks. Merthin had not been involved in this job, which was why he had not previously looked hard at the work. On Monday he had wondered why the beams were cracking. The weakness was not half way between the uprights, as he would have expected if the timbers had simply deteriorated over time. Rather, the cracks were near the central pier, where the strain should have been less.

He had not thought about it since Monday – there was too much else on his mind – but now an explanation occurred to him. It was almost as if that central pier was not supporting the beams, but dragging them down. That would mean that something had undermined the foundation beneath the pier – and, as soon as that thought occurred to him, he realized how it could have happened. It must be the faster flow of the river, scouring the river bed from under the pier.

He remembered walking barefoot on a sandy beach, as a child, and noticing that when he stood at the sea's edge, letting the water wash over his feet, the outgoing waves would suck the sand from under his toes. That kind of phenomenon had always fascinated him.

If he was right the central pier, with nothing underneath to support it, was now hanging from the bridge – hence the cracks. Elfric's iron braces had not helped; in fact, they might have worsened the problem, by making it impossible for the bridge to settle slowly into a new, stable position.

Merthin guessed that the other pier of the pair – on the farther, downstream side of the bridge – was still grounded. The current surely spent most of its force on the upstream pier, and attacked the second of the pair with reduced violence. Only one pier was affected; and it seemed that the rest of the structure was knitted together strongly enough for the entire bridge to stay upright – as long as it was not subjected to extraordinary strain.

But the cracks seemed wider today than on Monday. And it was not difficult to guess why. Hundreds of people were on the bridge, a much greater load than it normally took; and there was a heavily laden wool cart, with twenty or thirty people sitting on the sacks of wool to add to the burden.

Fear gripped Merthin's heart. He did not think the bridge could withstand that level of strain for long.

He was vaguely aware that Caris was speaking, but her meaning did not penetrate his thoughts until she raised her voice and said: 'You're not even listening!'

'There's going to be a terrible accident,' he said.

'What do you mean?'

'We have to get everyone off the bridge.'

'Are you mad? They're all tormenting Crazy Nell. Even Earl Roland can't get them to move. They're not going to listen to you.'

'I think it could collapse.'

'Oh, look!' said Caris, pointing. 'Can you see someone running along the road from the forest, approaching the south end of the bridge?'

Merthin wondered what that had to do with anything, but he followed her pointing finger. Sure enough, he saw the figure of a young woman running, her hair flying.

Caris said: 'It looks like Gwenda.'

Behind her, in hot pursuit, was a man in a yellow tunic.

*

GWENDA WAS MORE tired than she had ever been in her life.

She knew that the fastest way to cover a long distance was to run twenty paces then walk twenty paces. She had started to do that half a day ago, when she spotted Sim Chapman a mile behind her. For a while she lost sight of him, but when once again the road provided her with a long rearward view, she saw that he, too, was walking and running alternately. As mile succeeded mile and hour followed hour he gained on her. By mid-morning she had known that at this rate he would catch her before she reached Kingsbridge.

In desperation, she had taken to the forest. But she could not stray far from the road for fear of losing her way. Eventually she heard running steps and heavy breathing, and peered through the undergrowth to see Sim go by on the road. She realized that as soon as he came to a long clear stretch he would guess what she had done. Sure enough, some time later she saw him come back.

She had pressed on through the forest, stopping every few minutes to stand in silence and listen. For a long time she had evaded him, and she knew he would have to search the woods on both sides of the road to make sure she was not in hiding. But her progress was also slow, for she had to fight her way through the summer undergrowth, and keep checking that she had not strayed too far from the road.

When she heard the sound of a distant crowd she knew she could not be far from the city, and she thought she was going to escape after all. She made her way to the road and cautiously looked out from a bush. The way was clear in both directions – and, a quarter of a mile to the north, she could see the tower of the cathedral.

She was almost there.

She heard a familiar bark and her dog, Skip, emerged from the bushes at the side of the road. She bent to pat him, and he wagged joyfully, licking her hands. Tears came to her eyes.

Sim was not in sight, so she risked the open road. She wearily resumed her twenty paces of running and twenty of walking, now with Skip trotting happily beside her, thinking this was a new game. Each time she switched, she looked back over her shoulder. The third time she did so, she saw Sim.

He was only a couple of hundred yards behind.

Despair washed over her like a tidal wave. She wanted to lie down and die. But she was in the suburbs, now, and the bridge was only a quarter of a mile away. She forced herself to keep going.

She tried to sprint, but her legs refused to obey orders. A staggering jog was the best she could manage. Her feet hurt. Looking down, she saw blood seeping through the holes in her tattered shoes. As she turned the corner at Gallows Cross, she saw a huge crowd on the bridge ahead of her. They were all looking at something, and no one noticed her running for her life, with Sim Chapman close behind.

She had no weapons other than her eating knife, which would just about cut through a baked hare, but would hardly disable a man. She wished with all her heart that she had had the nerve to pull Alwyn's long dagger out of his head and bring it away with her. Now she was virtually defenceless.

She had a row of small houses on one side of her – the suburban homes of people too poor to live in the city – and, on the other side, the pasture called Lovers' Field, owned by the priory. Sim was so close behind her that she could hear his breathing, harsh and ragged like her own. Terror gave her a last burst of energy. Skip barked, but there was more fear than defiance in his note – he had not forgotten the stone that hit him on the nose.

The approach to the bridge was a swamp of sticky mud, churned up by boots, hooves and cartwheels. Gwenda waded through it, desperately hoping that the heavier Sim would be hampered even more than she.

At last she reached the bridge. She pushed into the crowd, which was less dense at this end. They were all looking the other way, where a heavy cart loaded with wool was blocking the passage of an ox-cart. She had to get to Caris's house, almost in sight now on the main street. 'Let me through!' she screamed, fighting her way forward. Only one person seemed to hear her. A head turned to look, and she saw the face of her brother Philemon. His mouth dropped open in alarm, and he tried to move towards her, but the crowd resisted him as it resisted her.

Gwenda tried to push past the team of oxen drawing the wool cart, but an ox tossed its massive head and knocked her sideways.

She lost her footing – and, at that moment, a big hand grasped her arm in a powerful grip, and she knew she was recaptured.

'I've got you, you bitch,' Sim gasped. He pulled her to him and slapped her across the face as hard as he could. She had no strength left to resist him. Skip snapped ineffectually at his heels. 'You won't get away from me again,' he said.

Despair engulfed her. It had all been for nothing: seducing Alwyn, murdering him, running for miles. She was back where she had started, the captive of Sim.

Then the bridge seemed to move.

13

MERTHIN SAW THE BRIDGE BEND.

Over the central pier on the near side, the entire roadbed sagged like a horse with a broken back. The people tormenting Nell suddenly found the surface beneath their feet unsteady. They staggered, grabbing their neighbours for support. One fell backwards over the parapet into the river; then another, then another. The shouts and catcalls directed at Nell were quickly drowned out by yells of warning and screams of fright.

Merthin said: 'Oh, no!'

Caris screamed: 'What's happening?'

All those people, he wanted to say – people we grew up with, women who have been kind to us, men we hate, children who admire us; mothers and sons, uncles and nieces; cruel masters and sworn enemies and panting lovers – they're going to die. But he could not get any words out.

For a moment – less than a breath – Merthin hoped the structure might stabilize in the new position; but he was disappointed. The bridge sagged again. This time, the interlocked timbers began to tear free of their joints. The longitudinal planks on which the people were standing sprang from their wooden pegs; the transverse joints that supported the roadbed twisted out of their sockets; and the iron braces that Elfric had hammered across the cracks were ripped out of the wood.

The central part of the bridge seemed to lurch downward on the side nearest Merthin, the upstream side. The wool cart tilted, and the spectators standing and sitting on the piled woolsacks were hurled into the river. Great timbers snapped and flew through the air, killing everyone they struck. The insubstantial parapet gave way, and the cart slid slowly off the edge, its helpless oxen lowing in terror. It fell with nightmare slowness through the air and hit the water with a thunderclap. Suddenly there were dozens of people jumping or falling into the river, then scores of them. Those already in the water were struck by the falling bodies of those who came after, and by the disintegrating timbers, some small, some huge. Horses fell, with and without riders, and carts fell on top of them.

Merthin's first thought was of his parents. Neither of them had gone to the trial of Crazy Nell, and they would not have wanted to watch her punishment: his mother thought such public spectacles beneath her dignity, and his father was not interested when there was no more at stake than the life of a mad woman. Instead, they had gone to the priory to say goodbye to Ralph.

But Ralph was now on the bridge.

Merthin could see his brother fighting to control his horse, Griff, which was rearing and kicking out with its front hooves. 'Ralph!' he yelled uselessly. Then the timbers under Griff fell into the water. 'No!' Merthin shouted as horse and rider disappeared from view.

Merthin's gaze flashed to the other end, where Caris had spotted Gwenda, and he saw her struggling with a man in a yellow tunic. Then that part gave way, and both ends of the bridge were dragged into the water by the collapsing middle.

The river was now a mass of writhing people, panicking horses, splintered timbers, smashed carts and bleeding bodies. Merthin realized that Caris was no longer by his side when he saw her hurrying along the bank towards the bridge, clambering over rocks and running along the muddy strand. She looked back at him and yelled: 'Hurry up! What are you waiting for? Come and help!'

*

THIS MUST BE what a battlefield is like, Ralph thought: the screaming, the random violence, the people falling, the horses mad with fear. It was the last thought he had before the ground dropped away beneath him.

He suffered a moment of sheer terror. He did not understand what had happened. The bridge had been there, under his horse's hooves, but now it was not, and he and his mount were tumbling through the air. Then he could no longer feel the familiar bulk of Griff between his thighs, and he realized they had separated. An instant later he hit the cold water.

He went under and held his breath. The panic left him. Now he felt scared, but calm. He had played in the sea as a child – a seaside village had been among his father's domains – and he knew he would rise to the surface, though it might seem to take a long time. He was weighed down by his thick travelling clothes, now saturated, and by his sword. If he had been wearing armour, he would have sunk to the bottom and stayed there for ever. But at last his head broke the surface and he gasped for breath.

He had swum a good deal as a boy, but that was many years ago. All the same, the technique came back to him, more or less, and he was able to keep his head above water. He began to thrash his way towards the north bank. Beside him, he recognized the chestnut coat and black mane of Griff, doing the same as he was, swimming for the nearest shore.

The horse's gait changed, and he realized it had found its footing. Ralph let his feet drift down to the river bed and found that he, too, could stand. He waded through the shallows. The sticky mud of the bottom seemed to be trying to suck him back into midstream. Griff hauled himself on to a narrow strip of beach below the priory wall. Ralph did the same.

He turned and looked back. There were several hundred people in the water, many bleeding, many screaming, many dead. Near the edge he saw a figure wearing the red-and-black livery of the earl of Shiring, floating face down. He stepped back into the water, grabbed the man by the belt, and hauled him ashore.

He turned the heavy body over, and his heart lurched with recognition. It was his friend Stephen. The face was unmarked, but Stephen's chest appeared to have caved in. His eyes were wide open, showing no sign of life. There was no breath. The body was too damaged even for Ralph to feel for a heartbeat. A few minutes ago I was envying him, Ralph thought. Now I'm the lucky one.

Feeling irrationally guilty, he closed Stephen's eyes.

He thought of his parents. Only a few minutes ago he had

left them in the stable yard. Even if they had followed him, they could not have reached the bridge yet. They must be safe.

Where was Lady Philippa? Ralph cast his mind back to the scene on the bridge just before the collapse. Lord William and Philippa had been at the rear of the earl's procession, and had not yet ridden on to the bridge.

But the earl had.

Ralph could picture the scene quite clearly. Earl Roland had been close behind him, impatiently urging his horse, Victory, forward through the gap in the crowd made by Ralph on Griff. Roland must have fallen close to Ralph.

Ralph heard again his father's words: 'Be constantly on the alert for ways to please the earl.' Perhaps this was the big chance he had been looking for, he thought excitedly. He might not have to wait for a war. He could distinguish himself today. He would save Earl Roland – or even just Victory.

The thought energized him. He scanned the river. The earl had been wearing a distinctive purple robe and a black velvet surcoat. It was hard to pick out an individual in the seething mass of bodies, alive and dead. Then he saw a black stallion with a distinctive white patch over one eye, and his heart leaped: it was Roland's mount. Victory was thrashing around in the water, apparently unable to swim in a straight line, probably having broken one or more legs.

Floating next to the horse was a tall figure in a purple robe.

This was Ralph's moment.

He threw off his outer clothing: it would hamper his swimming. Wearing only his underdrawers, he plunged back into the river and swam towards the earl. He had to force his way through a mass of men, women and children. Many of the living grabbed desperately at him, delaying his progress. He fought them off ruthlessly with merciless blows of his fists.

At last he reached Victory. The beast's struggles were weakening. It was still for a moment, and started to sink; then, when its head dipped into the water, it began to struggle again. 'Easy, boy, easy,' Ralph said into its ear; but he felt sure it was going to drown.

Roland was floating on his back, eyes closed, unconscious or dead. One foot was caught in a stirrup, and that seemed to be what was keeping his body from going down. He had lost his hat, and the top of his head was a bloody mess. Ralph could not see how a man could live after such an injury. All the same, he would rescue him. There would surely be some reward just for the corpse, when it was that of an earl.

He tried to pull Roland's foot from the stirrup, but he found the strap was twisted tight around the ankle. He felt for his knife and realized it was attached to his belt, which he had left on the shore with the rest of his outer clothing. But the earl had weapons. Ralph fumbled Roland's dagger from its sheath.

Victory's convulsions made it difficult for Ralph to cut the strap. Each time he caught hold of the stirrup, the dying horse jerked it from his grasp before he could bring the knife to bear on the leather. He cut the back of his own hand in the struggle. Finally he braced himself against the horse's side with both feet, for stability, and in that position he was able to slice through the stirrup strap.

Now he had to drag the unconscious earl to the bank. Ralph was not a strong swimmer, and he was already panting with exhaustion. To make matters worse, he could not breathe through his broken nose, so his mouth kept filling with river water. He paused for a moment, leaning his weight on the doomed Victory, trying to catch his breath; but the earl's body, now unsupported, began to sink, and Ralph realized he could not rest.

He grabbed Roland's ankle in his right hand and started to swim for the shore. He found it harder to keep his head above the surface when he had only one hand free for swimming. He did not look back at Roland: if the earl's head went under water there was nothing Ralph could do about it. After a few seconds he was gasping for air and his limbs were aching.

He was not used to this. He was young and strong, and his whole life was spent hunting, jousting and fencing. He could ride all day then win a wrestling match the same evening. But now he seemed to be relying on disused muscles. His neck hurt from the effort of keeping his head up. He could not help breathing water in, and that made him cough and choke. He flapped his left arm madly and just managed to keep himself afloat. He heaved at the bulky body of the earl, made heavier by its water-soaked clothing. He approached the shore with agonizing slowness.

At last he was close enough to put his feet on the river bed. Gulping air, he began to wade, still dragging Roland. When the water was thigh-high he turned and picked up the earl in his arms, and carried him the last few steps to the shore.

He put the body on the ground and collapsed beside it, exhausted. With the last of his energy, he felt the chest. There was a strong heartbeat.

Earl Roland was alive.

*

THE COLLAPSE OF the bridge paralysed Gwenda with fear. Then, an instant later, the sudden immersion in cold water shocked her back to normal.

When her head came above the surface, she found herself surrounded by brawling, yelling people. Some had found a piece of wood to keep them afloat, but every other man tried to keep himself above water by leaning on someone else. Those leaned upon felt themselves being pushed under, and lashed out with their fists to get free. Many of the blows missed. Those that connected were returned. It was like being outside a Kingsbridge tavern at midnight. It would have been comical, except that people were dying.

Gwenda gasped air and went under. She could not swim.

She came up again. To her horror, Sim Chapman was immediately in front of her, blowing water out of his mouth like a fountain. He began to go under, obviously as unable to swim as she was. In desperation, he grabbed her shoulder and tried to use her for support. She immediately sank. Finding her inadequate to keep him on the surface, he let her go.

Under the water, holding her breath, fighting off panic, she thought: I can't drown now, after all I've been through.

Next time she surfaced, she felt herself shoved aside by a heavy body and she saw, out of the corner of her eye, the ox that had knocked her over a moment before the bridge fell apart. It was apparently unharmed and swimming strongly. She reached out, kicking her feet, and managed to get hold of one of its horns. She pulled its head sideways for a moment, then the powerful neck pulled back and its head came upright again.

Gwenda managed to hang on.

Her dog, Skip, appeared beside her, swimming effortlessly, and yelped for joy to see her face.

The ox was heading for the suburban shore. Gwenda clung to its horn, even though her arm felt as if it was about to drop off.

Someone grabbed her, and she looked over her shoulder to see Sim again. Trying to use her to keep himself afloat, he pulled her under. Without letting go of the ox, she pushed Sim off with her free hand. He dropped back, his head close to her feet. Taking careful aim, she kicked him as hard as she could in the face. He gave a cry of pain that was quickly silenced as his head went under.

The ox found its footing and lumbered out of the water, splashing and snorting. Gwenda let go as soon as she could stand on the bottom.

Skip gave a frightened bark, and Gwenda looked around warily. Sim was not on the bank. She scanned the river, looking for the flash of a yellow tunic among the bodies and the floating timbers.

She saw him, keeping himself afloat by holding on to a plank, kicking with his legs and coming straight towards her.

She could not run. She had no strength left, and her dress was waterlogged. On this side of the river, there was no place to hide. And, now that the bridge was down, there was no way to cross to the Kingsbridge side.

But she was not going to let him take her.

She saw that he was struggling, and that gave her hope. The plank would have kept him afloat if he had remained still, but he was kicking for the shore, and his thrashing destabilized him. He would push down on the plank to lift himself up, then kick to swim for shore, and his head would go under again. He might not make it to the bank.

She realized she could make certain of that.

She looked around quickly. The water was full of bits of wood, from huge load-bearing timbers to splinters. Her eye lit on a stout timber about a yard long. She stepped into the water and grabbed it. Then she waded out into the river to meet her owner.

She had the satisfaction of seeing the light of fear in his eyes.

He paused in his paddling. Ahead of him was the woman he had tried to enslave – angry, determined, and wielding a formidable club. Behind him, death by drowning.

He came forward.

Gwenda stood up to her waist in water and waited for her moment.

She saw Sim pause again, and guessed from his movements that he was trying to find the bottom with his feet.

Now or never.

Gwenda raised the wood over her head and stepped forward. Sim saw what she was about to do, and scrabbled desperately to get out of the way; but he was off balance, neither swimming nor wading, and he could not dodge. Gwenda brought the timber down on top of his head with all her might.

Sim's eyes rolled up and he slumped unconscious.

She reached forward and grabbed him by the yellow tunic. She was not going to let him float away – he might survive. She pulled him to her, then took his head in both hands and pushed it under the water.

It was more difficult than she had imagined to keep a body under, even though he was out cold. His greasy hair was slippery. She had to grasp his head under her arm then lift her feet off the bottom, so that her weight carried them both down.

She began to feel she might have overcome him. How long did it take to drown a man? She had no idea. Sim's lungs must be filling with water already. How would she know when she could let go?

Suddenly he twisted. She tightened her grip on his head. For a moment she struggled to hold him. She was not sure whether he had come round, or was undergoing an unconscious convulsion. His spasms were strong, but seemed random. Her feet found the bottom again and she braced herself and held on.

She looked around. No one was watching: they were all too busy saving themselves.

After a few moments, Sim's movements became weaker. Soon

he was still. Gradually she relaxed her grip. Sim sank slowly to the bottom.

He did not come up again.

Panting for breath, Gwenda waded to the shore. She sat down heavily on the muddy ground. She felt for the leather purse on her belt: it was still there. The outlaws had not got around to stealing it from her, and she had kept it through all her trials. It contained the precious love potion made by Mattie Wise. She opened the purse to check – and found nothing but shards of pottery. The little vial had been smashed.

She started to cry.

*

THE FIRST PERSON Caris saw doing anything sensible was Merthin's brother, Ralph. He was wearing nothing but a soaking wet pair of underdrawers. He was uninjured, apart from his red and swollen nose, which he had had before. Ralph pulled the earl of Shiring out of the water and laid him on the shore next to a body in the earl's livery. The earl had a grisly head injury that might be fatal. Ralph appeared exhausted by his efforts and unsure what to do next. Caris considered what she should tell him.

She looked around. On this side, the river bank consisted of small muddy beaches separated by rocky outcrops. There was not much room to lay out the dead and injured here: they would have to be taken elsewhere.

A few yards away, a flight of stone steps led up from the river to a gate in the priory wall. Caris made a decision. Pointing, she said to Ralph: 'Take the earl that way into the priory. Lay him down carefully in the cathedral, then run to the hospital. Tell the first nun you see to fetch Mother Cecilia immediately.'

Ralph seemed glad to have someone decisive to obey, and did as he was told right away.

Merthin started to wade into the water, but Caris stopped him. 'Look at that crowd of idiots,' she said, pointing to the city end of the ruined bridge. Dozens of people were standing gawping at the scene of carnage in front of them. 'Get all the strong men down here,' she went on. 'They can start pulling people out of the water and carrying them to the cathedral.'

He hesitated. 'They can't get down here from there.'

Caris saw his point. They would have to clamber over the wreckage, and that would probably lead to more injuries. But the houses on this side of the main street had gardens that backed up against the priory walls; and the house on the corner, belonging to Ben Wheeler, had a small door in the wall so that he could come to the river directly from his garden.

Merthin was thinking the same. He said: 'I'll bring them through Ben's house and across his yard.'

'Good.'

He clambered over the rocks, pushed open the door and disappeared.

Caris looked across the water. A tall figure was wading on to the bank nearby, and she recognized Philemon. Gasping, he said: 'Have you seen Gwenda?'

'Yes – just before the bridge collapsed,' Caris replied. 'She was running from Sim Chapman.'

'I know – but where is she now?'

'I don't see her. The best thing you can do is start pulling people out of the water.'

'I want to find my sister.'

'If she's alive, she'll be among those who need to get out of the river.'

'All right.' Philemon splashed back into the water.

Caris was desperate to find out where her own family were – but there was too much to do here. She promised herself she would look for her father as soon as possible.

Ben Wheeler emerged from his gate. A squat man with big shoulders and a thick neck, he was a carter, and got through life more by the use of his muscles than his brain. He scrambled down to the beach, then looked around, not knowing what to do.

On the ground at Caris's feet was one of Earl Roland's men, wearing the red-and-black livery, apparently dead. She said: 'Ben, carry this man into the cathedral.'

Ben's wife, Lib, appeared, carrying a toddler. She was a little brighter than her husband, and she asked: 'Shouldn't we deal with the living first?'

'We have to get them out of the water before we can tell whether they're dead or alive – and we can't leave bodies here on the bank because they will get in the way of rescuers. Take him to the church.'

Lib saw the sense of that. 'You'd better do as Caris says, Ben,' she said.

Ben picked up the body effortlessly and moved off.

Caris realized they could move the bodies more quickly if they carried them on the kind of stretchers the builders used. The monks could organize those. Where were the monks? She had told Ralph to alert Mother Cecilia, but so far no one had appeared. The injured would need wound dressings, ointments and cleansing fluids: every nun and monk would be needed. Matthew Barber must be summoned: there would be many broken bones to set. And Mattie Wise, to give potions to the injured to ease their pain. Caris needed to raise the alarm, but she was reluctant to leave the riverside before the rescue operation was properly organized. Where was Merthin?

A woman was crawling to the shore. Caris stepped into the water and pulled her to her feet. It was Griselda. Her wet dress clung to her, and Caris could see her full breasts and the swell of her thighs. Knowing that she was pregnant, Caris said anxiously: 'Are you all right?'

'I think so.'

'You're not bleeding?'

'No.'

'Thank God.' Caris looked around and was grateful to see Merthin coming from Ben Wheeler's garden at the head of a line of men, some of them wearing the earl's livery. She called to him: 'Take Griselda's arm. Help her up the steps to the priory. She should sit down and rest for a while.' She added reassuringly: 'She's all right, though.'

Both Merthin and Griselda looked at her strangely, and she realized in a flash how peculiar this situation was. The three of them stood for a moment in a frozen triangle: the mother-to-be, the father of her child, and the woman who loved him.

Then Caris turned away, breaking the spell, and began to give orders to the men.

*

GWENDA CRIED FOR a few moments, then stopped. It was not really the broken vial that made her so sad: Mattie could make up another love potion, and Caris would pay for it, if either of them was still alive. Her tears were for everything she had been through in the last twenty-four hours, from her father's treachery to her bleeding feet.

She had no regrets about the two men she had killed. Sim and Alwyn had tried to enslave her then prostitute her. They deserved to die. Killing them was not even murder, for it was no crime to do away with an outlaw. All the same, she could not stop her hands shaking. She was exultant that she had beaten her enemies and won her freedom, and at the same time she felt sickened by what she had done. She would never forget the way the dying body of Sim had twitched at the end. And she feared that the vision of Alwyn with the point of his own knife sticking out of his eye socket might appear in her dreams. She could not help trembling in the grip of such strong contradictory feelings.

She tried to put the killings out of her mind. Who else was dead? Her parents had been planning to leave Kingsbridge yesterday. But what about her brother, Philemon? Caris, her greatest friend? Wulfric, the man she loved?

She looked across the river and was immediately reassured about Caris. She was on the far side with Merthin, and they appeared to be organizing a gang of men to pull people out of the water. Gwenda felt a surge of gratitude: at least she had not been left completely alone in the world.

But what about Philemon? He was the last person she had seen before the collapse. He should have fallen near her, all other things being equal; but she could not see him now.

And where was Wulfric? She doubted whether he would have cared to watch the spectacle of a witch being flogged through the town. However, he had been planning to return home to Wigleigh with his family today, and it was possible – God forbid, she thought – that they had been crossing the bridge on their way home when the collapse happened. She scanned the surface frantically, looking for his distinctive tawny hair, praying that she would see him swimming vigorously for the shore, rather than floating face down. But she could not see him at all.

She decided to cross over. She could not swim, but she thought that if she had a sizeable piece of wood to keep her afloat she might be able to kick herself across. She found a plank, pulled it from the water, and walked fifty yards upstream, to get well clear of the mass of bodies. Then she re-entered the water. Skip followed fearlessly. It was more taxing than she had expected, and her wet dress was a drag on progress, but she reached the far shore.

She ran to Caris, and they embraced. Caris said: 'What happened?'

'I escaped.'

'And Sim?'

'He was an outlaw.'

'Was?'

'He's dead.'

Caris looked startled.

Gwenda added hastily: 'Killed when the bridge collapsed.' She did not want even her best friend to know the exact circumstances. She went on: 'Have you seen any of my family?'

'Your parents left town yesterday. I saw Philemon a few moments ago – he's looking for you.'

'Thank God! What about Wulfric?'

'I don't know. He hasn't been brought out of the river. His fiancée left yesterday, but his parents and his brother were in the cathedral this morning, at the trial of Crazy Nell.'

'I have to look for him.'

'Good luck.'

Gwenda ran up the steps to the priory and across the green. A few of the stallholders were still packing up their effects, and it seemed incredible to her that they could go about their normal business when hundreds of people had just been killed in an accident – until she realized that they probably did not yet know: it had happened only minutes ago, though it felt like hours.

She passed through the priory gates into the main street.

Wulfric and his family had been staying at the Bell. She ran inside.

An adolescent boy stood beside the ale barrel, looking frightened.

Gwenda said: 'I'm looking for Wulfric Wigleigh.'

'There's no one here,' the boy said. 'I'm the apprentice, they left me to guard the beer.'

Someone had summoned everyone to the riverside, Gwenda guessed.

She ran out again. As she passed through the doorway, Wulfric appeared.

She was so relieved that she threw her arms around him. 'You're alive – thank God!' she cried.

'Someone said the bridge collapsed,' he said. 'Is it true, then?'

'Yes – it's dreadful. Where are the rest of your family?'

'They left a while ago. I stayed behind to collect a debt.' He held up a small leather money bag. 'I hope they weren't on the bridge when it fell.'

'I know how we can find out,' Gwenda said. 'Come with me.'

She took his hand. He let her lead him into the priory precincts without withdrawing his hand. She had never touched him for so long. His hand was large, the fingers rough with work, the palm soft. It sent thrills through her, despite all that had happened.

She took him across the green and inside the cathedral. 'They're pulling people out of the river and bringing them here,' she explained.

There were already twenty or thirty bodies on the stone floor of the nave, with more arriving continually. A handful of nuns attended to the injured, dwarfed by the mighty pillars around them. The blind monk who normally led the choir seemed to be in charge. 'Put the dead on the north side,' he called out as Gwenda and Wulfric entered the nave. 'Wounded to the south.'

Suddenly Wulfric let out a cry of shock and dismay. Gwenda followed his gaze, and saw David, his brother, lying among the wounded. They both knelt beside him on the floor. David was a couple of years older than Wulfric, and the same large build. He was breathing, and his eyes were open, but he seemed not to see them. Wulfric spoke to him. 'Dave!' he said in a low, urgent voice. 'Dave, it's me, Wulfric.'

Gwenda felt something sticky, and realized David was lying in a pool of blood.

Wulfric said: 'Dave – where are Ma and Pa?'

There was no response.

Gwenda looked around and saw Wulfric's mother. She was on the far side of the nave, in the north aisle, where Blind Carlus was telling people to put the dead. 'Wulfric,' Gwenda said quietly.

'What?'

'Your ma.'

He stood up and looked. 'Oh, no,' he said.

They crossed the wide church. Wulfric's mother was lying next to Sir Stephen, the lord of Wigleigh – his equal, now. She was a petite woman – it was amazing that she had given birth to two such big sons. In life she had been wiry and full of energy, but now she looked like a fragile doll, white and thin. Wulfric put his hand on her chest, feeling for a heartbeat. When he pressed down, a trickle of water came from her mouth.

'She drowned,' he whispered.

Gwenda put her arm around his wide shoulders, trying to console him with her touch. She could not tell whether he noticed.

A man-at-arms wearing Earl Roland's red-and-black livery came up carrying the lifeless body of a big man. Wulfric gasped again: it was his father.

Gwenda said: 'Lay him here, next to his wife.'

Wulfric was stunned. He said nothing, seeming unable to take it in. Gwenda herself was bewildered. What could she say to the man she loved in these circumstances? Every phrase that came to mind seemed stupid. She was desperate to give him some kind of comfort, but she did not know how.

As Wulfric stared at the bodies of his mother and father, Gwenda looked across the church at his brother. David seemed very still. She walked quickly to his side. His eyes were staring up blindly, and he was no longer breathing. She felt his chest: no heartbeat.

How could Wulfric bear it?

She wiped tears from her own eyes and returned to him. There was no point in hiding the truth. 'David is dead, too,' she said.

Wulfric looked blank, as if he did not understand. The dreadful thought occurred to Gwenda that the shock might have caused him to lose his mind.

But he spoke at last. 'All of them,' he said in a whisper. 'All three. All dead.' He looked at Gwenda, and she saw tears come to his eyes.

She put her arms around him, and felt his big body shake with helpless sobs. She squeezed him tightly. 'Poor Wulfric,' she said. 'Poor, beloved Wulfric.'

'Thank God I've still got Annet,' he said.

*

AN HOUR LATER, the bodies of the dead and wounded covered most of the floor of the nave. Blind Carlus, the sub-prior, stood in the middle of it all with thin-faced Simeon, the treasurer, beside him to be his eyes. Carlus was in charge because Prior Anthony was missing. 'Brother Theodoric, is that you?' he said, apparently recognizing the tread of the fair-skinned, blue-eyed monk who had just walked in. 'Find the gravedigger. Tell him to get six strong men to help him. We're going to need at least a hundred new graves, and in this season we don't want to delay burial.'

'Right away, brother,' said Theodoric.

Caris was impressed by how effectively Carlus could organize things despite his blindness.

Caris had left Merthin efficiently managing the rescue of bodies from the water. She had made sure the nuns and monks were alerted to the disaster, then she had found Matthew Barber and Mattie Wise. Finally she had checked on her own family.

Only Uncle Anthony and Griselda had been on the bridge at the time of the collapse. She had found her father at the guild hall with Buonaventura Caroli. Edmund had said: 'They'll have to build a new bridge now!' Then he had gone limping down to the river bank to help pull people out of the water. The others were safe: Aunt Petranilla had been at home, cooking; Caris's sister Alice had been with Elfric at the Bell inn; her cousin Godwyn had been in the cathedral, checking on the repairs to the south side of the chancel.

Griselda had now gone home to rest. Anthony was still unaccounted for. Caris was not fond of her uncle, but she would not wish him dead, and she looked anxiously for him every time a new body was brought into the nave from the river.

Mother Cecilia and the nuns were washing wounds, applying honey as an antiseptic, affixing bandages and giving out restorative cups of hot spiced ale. Matthew Barber, the briskly efficient battlefield surgeon, was working with a panting, overweight Mattie Wise, Mattie administering a calming medicine a few minutes before Matthew set the broken arms and legs.

Caris walked to the south transept. There, away from the noise, the bustle and the blood in the nave, the senior physician-monks were clustered around the still-unconscious figure of the earl of Shiring. His wet clothes had been removed, and he had been covered with a heavy blanket. 'He's alive,' said Brother Godwyn. 'But his injury is very serious.' He pointed to the back of the head. 'Part of his skull has shattered.'

Caris peered over Godwyn's shoulder. She could see the skull, like a broken pie crust, stained with blood. Through the gaps she could see grey matter underneath. Surely nothing could be done for such a dreadful injury?

Brother Joseph, the oldest of the physicians, felt the same. He rubbed his large nose and spoke through a mouth full of bad teeth. 'We must bring the relics of the saint,' he said, slurring his sibilants like a drunk, as always. 'They are his best hope for recovery.'

Caris had little faith in the power of the bones of a long-dead saint to heal a living man's broken head. She said nothing, of course: she knew she was peculiar in this respect, and she kept her views to herself most of the time.

The earl's sons, Lord William and Bishop Richard, stood looking on. William, with his tall, soldierly figure and black hair, was a younger version of the unconscious man on the table. Richard was fairer and rounder. Merthin's brother, Ralph, was with them. 'I pulled the earl out of the water,' he said. It was the second time Caris had heard him say it.

'Yes, well done,' said William.

William's wife, Philippa, was as dissatisfied as Caris with Brother Joseph's pronouncement. 'Isn't there something *you* can do to help the earl?' she said.

Godwyn replied: 'Prayer is the most effective cure.'

The relics were kept in a locked compartment under the high altar. As soon as Godwyn and Joseph left to fetch them, Matthew Barber bent over the earl, peering at the head wound. 'It will never heal like that,' he said. 'Not even with the help of the saint.'

William said sharply: 'What do you mean?' Caris thought he sounded just like his father.

'The skull is a bone like any other,' Matthew answered. 'It can mend itself, but the pieces need to be in the right place. Otherwise it will grow back crooked.'

'Do you think you know better than the monks?'

'My lord, the monks know how to call upon the help of the spirit world. I only set broken bones.'

'And where did you get this knowledge?'

'I was surgeon with the king's armies for many years. I marched alongside your father, the earl, in the Scottish wars. I have seen broken heads before.'

'What would you do for my father now?'

Matthew was nervous under William's aggressive questioning, Caris felt; but he seemed sure of what he was saying. 'I would take the pieces of broken bone out of the brain, clean them, and try to fit them together again.'

Caris gasped. She could hardly imagine such a bold operation. How did Matthew have the nerve to propose it? And what if it went wrong?

William said: 'And he would recover?'

'I don't know,' Matthew replied. 'Sometimes a head wound has strange effects, impairing a man's ability to walk, or speak. All I can do is mend his skull. If you want miracles, ask the saint.'

'So you can't promise success.'

'Only God is all-powerful. Men must do what they can and hope for the best. But I believe your father will die of this injury if it remains untreated.'

'But Joseph and Godwyn have read the books written by the ancient medical philosophers.'

'And I have seen wounded men die or recover on the battlefield. It's for you to decide whom to trust.'

William looked at his wife. Philippa said: 'Let the barber do what he can, and ask St Adolphus to help him.'

William nodded. 'All right,' he said to Matthew. 'Go ahead.'

'I want the earl lying on a table,' Matthew said decisively. 'Near the window, where a strong light will fall on his injury.'

William snapped his fingers at two novice monks. 'Do whatever this man asks,' he ordered.

Matthew said: 'All I need is a bowl of warm wine.'

The monks brought a trestle table from the hospital and set it up below the big window in the south transept. Two squires lifted Earl Roland on to the table.

'Face down, please,' said Matthew.

They turned him over.

Matthew had a leather satchel containing the sharp tools from which barbers got their name. He first took out a small pair of scissors. He bent over the earl's head and began to cut away the hair around the wound. The earl had thick black hair that was naturally oily. Matthew snipped the locks and tossed them aside so that they landed on the floor. When he had clipped a circle around the wound, the damage was more clearly visible.

Brother Godwyn reappeared, carrying the reliquary, the carved ivory-and-gold box containing the skull of St Adolphus and the bones of one arm and a hand. When he saw Matthew operating on Earl Roland, he said indignantly: 'What is going on here?'

Matthew looked up. 'If you would place the holy relics on the earl's back, as close as possible to his head, I believe the saint will steady my hands.'

Godwyn hesitated, clearly angry that a mere barber had taken charge.

Lord William said: 'Do as he says, brother, or the death of my father may be laid at your door.'

Still Godwyn did not obey. Instead he spoke to Blind Carlus, standing a few yards away. 'Brother Carlus, I am ordered by Lord William to—'

'I heard what Lord William said,' Carlus interrupted. 'You'd better do as he wishes.'

It was not the answer Godwyn had been hoping for. His face showed angry frustration. With evident distaste, he placed the sacred container on Earl Roland's broad back.

Matthew picked up a fine pair of forceps. With a delicate touch, he grasped the visible edge of a piece of bone and lifted it, without touching the grey matter beneath. Caris watched, entranced. The bone came right away from the head, with skin and hair attached. Matthew put it gently into the bowl of warm wine.

He did the same with two more small pieces of bone. The noise from the nave – the groans of the wounded and the sobs of the bereaved – seemed to recede into the background. The people watching Matthew stood silent and still in a circle around him and the unconscious earl.

Next, he worked on the shards that remained attached to the rest of the skull. In each case he snipped away the hair, washed the area carefully with a piece of linen dipped in wine, then used the forceps to press the bone gently into what he thought was its original position.

Caris could hardly breathe, the tension was so great. She had never admired anyone as much as she admired Matthew Barber at this moment. He had such courage, such skill, such confidence. And he was performing this inconceivably delicate operation on an earl! If it went wrong they would probably hang him. Yet his hands were as steady as the hands of the angels carved in stone over the cathedral doorway.

Finally he replaced the three detached shards that he had put in the bowl of wine, fitting them together as if he were mending a broken jar.

He pulled the skin of the scalp across the wound and sewed it together with swift, precise stitches.

Now Roland's skull was complete.

'The earl must sleep for a day and a night,' he said. 'If he wakes, give him a strong dose of Mattie Wise's sleeping draught. Then he must lie still for forty days and forty nights. If necessary, strap him down.'

Then he asked Mother Cecilia to bandage the head.

*

GODWYN LEFT THE cathedral and ran down to the river bank, feeling frustrated and annoyed. There was no firm authority: Carlus was letting everyone do as they wished. Prior Anthony was weak, but he was better than Carlus. He had to be found.

Most of the bodies were out of the water now. Those who were merely bruised and shocked had walked away. Most of the dead and wounded had been carried to the cathedral. Those left were somehow entangled with the wreckage.

Godwyn was both excited and frightened by the thought that Anthony might be dead. He longed for a new regime at the priory: a stricter interpretation of Benedict's rule, along with meticulous management of the finances. But, at the same time, he knew that Anthony was his patron, and that under another prior he might not continue to be promoted.

Merthin had commandeered a boat. He and two other young men were out in midstream, where most of what had been the bridge was now floating in the water. Wearing only their underdrawers, the three were trying to lift a heavy beam in order to free someone. Merthin was small in stature, but the other two looked strong and well fed, and Godwyn guessed they were squires from the earl's entourage. Despite their evident fitness, they were finding it difficult to get leverage on the heavy timbers, standing as they were in the well of a small rowing-boat.

Godwyn stood with a crowd of townspeople, watching, torn by fear and hope, as the two squires raised a heavy beam and Merthin pulled a body from beneath it. After a short examination, he called out: 'Marguerite Jones – dead.'

Marguerite was an elderly woman of no account. Impatiently, Godwyn shouted out: 'Can't you see Prior Anthony?'

A look passed between the men on the boat, and Godwyn

realized he had been too peremptory. But Merthin called back: 'I can see a monk's robe.'

'Then it's the prior!' Godwyn shouted. Anthony was the only monk still unaccounted for. 'Can you tell how he is?'

Merthin leaned over the side of the boat. Apparently unable to get close enough from there, he eased himself into the water. Eventually he called out: 'Still breathing.'

Godwyn felt both elated and disappointed. 'Then get him out, quickly!' he shouted. 'Please,' he added.

There was no acknowledgement of what he said, but he saw Merthin duck under a partly submerged plank, then relay instructions to the other two. They eased the beam they were holding to one side, letting it slip gently into the water, then they leaned over the prow of the little boat to get hold of the plank Merthin was under. Merthin seemed to be struggling to detach Anthony's clothing from a tangle of boards and splinters.

Godwyn watched, frustrated that he could do nothing to speed the process. He spoke to two of the bystanders. 'Go to the priory and get two monks to bring a stretcher. Tell them Godwyn sent you.' The two men went up the steps and into the priory grounds.

At last Merthin managed to pull the unconscious figure from the wreckage. He drew him close, then the other two heaved the prior into the boat. Merthin scrambled in after, and they poled to the bank.

Eager volunteers took Anthony from the boat and put him on the stretcher brought by the monks. Godwyn examined the prior quickly. He was breathing, but his pulse was weak. His eyes were closed and his face was ominously white. His head and chest were only bruised, but his pelvis seemed smashed, and he was bleeding.

The monks picked him up. Godwyn led the way across the priory grounds into the cathedral. 'Make way!' he shouted. He took the prior along the nave and into the chancel, the holiest part of the church. He told the monks to lay the body in front of the high altar. The sodden robe clearly outlined Anthony's hips and legs, which were twisted so far out of shape that only his top half looked human.

Within a few moments, all the monks had gathered around

the unconscious body of their prior. Godwyn retrieved the reliquary from Earl Roland and placed it at Anthony's feet. Joseph placed a jewelled crucifix on his chest and wrapped Anthony's hands around it.

Mother Cecilia knelt beside Anthony. She wiped his face with a cloth soaked in some soothing liquid. She said to Joseph: 'He seems to have broken many bones. Do you want Matthew Barber to look at him?'

Joseph shook his head silently.

Godwyn was glad. The barber would have defiled the holy sanctuary. Better to leave the outcome to God.

Brother Carlus performed the last rites, then led the monks in a hymn.

Godwyn did not know what to hope for. For some years he had been looking forward to the end of Priory Anthony's rule. But in the last hour he had got a glimpse of what might replace Anthony: joint rule by Carlus and Simeon. They were Anthony's cronies, and would be no better.

Suddenly he saw Matthew Barber at the edge of the crowd, looking over the monks' shoulders, studying Anthony's lower half. Godwyn was about to order him indignantly to leave the chancel, when he gave an almost imperceptible shake of the head and walked away.

Anthony opened his eyes.

Brother Joseph cried: 'Praise God!'

The prior seemed to want to speak. Mother Cecilia, who was still kneeling beside him, leaned over his face to catch his words. Godwyn saw Anthony's mouth move, and wished he could hear. After a moment, the prior fell silent.

Cecilia looked shocked. 'Is that true?' she said.

They all stared. Godwyn said: 'What did he say, Mother Cecilia?'

She did not answer.

Anthony's eyes closed. A subtle change came over him. He went very still.

Godwyn bent over his body. There was no breath. He placed a hand over Anthony's heart, and felt no beat. He grasped the wrist, feeling for a pulse: nothing.

He stood up. 'Prior Anthony has left this world,' he said. 'May God bless his soul and welcome him into His holy presence.'

All the monks said: 'Amen.'

Godwyn thought: Now there will have to be an election.

Part Three

June to December, 1337

Part Three

14

Kingsbridge Cathedral was a place of horror. Wounded people groaned in pain and cried out for help to God, or the saints, or their mothers. Every few minutes, someone searching for a loved one would find him or her dead, and would scream with the shock of sudden grief. The living and the dead were grotesquely twisted with broken bones, covered in blood, their clothing ripped and sodden. The stone floor of the church was slippery with water, blood and riverside mud.

In the middle of the horror, a small zone of calm and efficiency was centred on the figure of Mother Cecilia. Like a small quick bird, she went from one horizontal figure to the next. She was followed by a little flock of hooded nuns, among them her long-time assistant, Sister Juliana, now respectfully known as Old Julie. As she examined each patient, she gave orders: for washing, for ointments, for bandages, for herbal medicines. In the more serious cases she would summon Mattie Wise, Matthew Barber or Brother Joseph. She always spoke quietly but clearly, her instructions simple and decisive. She left most patients soothed, and their relatives reassured and hopeful.

It reminded Caris, with dreadful vividness, of the day her mother died. There had been terror and confusion then, though only in her heart. In the same way, Mother Cecilia had seemed to know what to do. Mama had died despite Cecilia's help, just as many of today's wounded would die; but there had been an orderliness about the death, a sense that everything possible had been done.

Some people appealed to the Virgin and the saints when someone was sick, but that only made Caris more uncertain and frightened, for there was no way to know if the spirits would help, or even whether they had heard. Mother Cecilia was not as powerful as the saints, the ten-year-old Caris had known; but all the same her assured, practical presence had given Caris both hope and resignation, in a combination that brought peace to her soul.

Now Caris became part of Cecilia's entourage, without really making a decision or even thinking about it. She followed the commands of the most assertive person in the vicinity, just as people had obeyed her directions at the riverside immediately after the collapse, when no one else seemed to know what to do. Cecilia's brisk practicality was infectious, and those around her acquired some of the same cool competence. Caris found herself holding a small bowl of vinegar, while a beautiful novice nun called Mair dipped a rag in it and washed the blood from the face of Susanna Chepstow, the timber merchant's wife.

After that it was non-stop until well after dark. Thanks to the long summer evening, all the floating bodies were retrieved from the river before nightfall – though perhaps no one would ever know how many drowned people had sunk to the bottom or drifted downstream. There was no trace of Crazy Nell, who must have been pulled under by the cart to which she was tied. Unjustly, Friar Murdo had survived, having suffered nothing worse than a twisted ankle, and had limped off to the Bell to recuperate with hot ham and strong ale.

However, the treatment of the injured continued, after nightfall, by candlelight. Some of the nuns became exhausted and had to stop; others were overwhelmed by the scale of the tragedy and fell apart, misunderstanding what they were told and becoming clumsy, so that they had to be dismissed; but Caris and a small core group carried on until there was no more to do. It must have been midnight when the last knot was tied in the last bandage, and Caris staggered across the green to her father's house.

Papa and Petranilla sat together in the dining hall, holding hands, grieving for the death of their brother Anthony. Edmund's eyes were wet with tears, and Petranilla was crying inconsolably. Caris kissed them both, but she could think of nothing to say. If she had sat down, she would have gone to sleep in the chair; so she climbed the stairs. She got into bed next to Gwenda, who was staying with her, as always. Gwenda was deep in an exhausted sleep, and did not stir.

Caris closed her eyes, her body weary and her heart aching with sorrow.

Her father was mourning one person among the many, but she felt the weight of them all. She thought of her friends, neighbours and acquaintances lying dead on the cold stone floor of the cathedral; and she imagined the sadness of their parents, their children, their brothers and sisters; and the sheer volume of grief overwhelmed her. She sobbed into her pillow. Without speaking, Gwenda put an arm around her and hugged her. After a few moments exhaustion overtook her, and she fell asleep.

She got up again at dawn. Leaving Gwenda still fast asleep, she returned to the cathedral and continued the work. Most of the injured were sent home. Those who still needed to be watched over – such as the still-unconscious Earl Roland – were moved into the hospital. The dead bodies were laid out in neat rows in the chancel, the eastern end of the church, to await burial.

The time flew by, with hardly a moment to rest. Then, late on Sunday afternoon, Mother Cecilia told Caris to take a break. She looked around and realized that most of the work was done. That was when she started to think of the future.

Until that moment she had felt, unconsciously, that ordinary life was over, and she was living in a new world of horror and tragedy. Now she realized that this, like everything else, would pass. The dead would be buried, the injured would heal, and somehow the town would struggle back to normal. And she remembered that, just before the bridge collapsed, there had been another tragedy, violent and devastating in its own way.

She found Merthin down by the river, with Elfric and Thomas Langley, organizing the clean-up with the help of fifty or more volunteers. Merthin's quarrel with Elfric had clearly been set aside in the emergency. Most of the loose timber had been retrieved from the water and stacked on the bank. But much of the woodwork was still joined together, and a mass of interlocked timber floated on the surface, moving slightly on the rise and fall of the water, with the innocent tranquillity of a great beast after it has killed and eaten.

The men were trying to break up the wreckage into manageable proportions. It was a dangerous job, with a constant risk that the bridge would collapse further and injure the volunteers. They had tied a rope around the central part of the bridge, now partly submerged, and a team of men stood on the bank hauling on the rope. In a boat in midstream were Merthin and giant Mark Webber with an oarsman. When the men on the bank rested, the boat was rowed in close to the wreckage, and Mark, directed by Merthin, attacked the beams with a huge forester's axe. Then the boat moved to a safe distance, Elfric gave a command, and the rope team pulled again.

As Caris watched, a big section of the bridge came free. Everyone cheered, and the men dragged the tangled woodwork to the shore.

The wives of some of the volunteers arrived with loaves of bread and jugs of ale. Thomas Langley ordered a break. While the men were resting, Caris got Merthin on his own. 'You can't marry Griselda,' she said without preamble.

The sudden assertion did not surprise him. 'I don't know what to do,' he said. 'I keep thinking about it.'

'Will you walk with me?'

'All right.'

They left the crowd at the riverside and went up the main street. After the bustle of the Fleece Fair, the town was graveyard quiet. Everyone was staying indoors, tending the sick or mourning the dead. 'There can't be many families in town that don't have someone dead or injured,' she said. 'There must have been a thousand people on the bridge, either trying to leave town or tormenting Crazy Nell. There are more than a hundred bodies in the church, and we've treated about four hundred wounded.'

'And five hundred lucky ones,' Merthin said.

'We could have been on the bridge, or near it. You and I might be lying on the floor of the chancel, now, cold and still. But we've been given a gift – the rest of our lives. And we mustn't waste that gift because of one mistake.'

'It's not a mistake,' he said sharply. 'It's a baby – a person, with a soul.'

'You're a person with a soul, too – an exceptional one. Look at what you've been doing just now. Three people are in charge down there at the river. One is the town's most prosperous builder. Another is the matricularius at the priory. And the third is ... a mere apprentice, not yet twenty-one. Yet the townsmen obey you as readily as they obey Elfric and Thomas.'

'That doesn't mean I can shirk my responsibilities.'

They turned into the priory close. The green in front of the cathedral was rutted and trampled by the fair, and there were boggy patches and wide puddles. In the three great west windows of the church Caris could see the reflection of a watery sun and ripped clouds, a picture divided, like a three-sided altarpiece. A bell began to ring for Evensong.

Caris said: 'Think how often you've talked of going to see the buildings of Paris and Florence. Will you give all that up?'

'I suppose so. A man can't abandon his wife and child.'

'So you're already thinking of her as your wife.'

He rounded on her. 'I'll never think of her as my wife,' he said bitterly. 'You know who I love.'

For once she could not think of a clever answer. She opened her mouth to speak, but no words came to her. Instead, she felt a constriction in her throat. She blinked away tears, and looked down to hide her emotions.

He grasped her arms and pulled her close to him. 'You know, don't you?'

She forced herself to meet his eye. 'Do I?' Her vision blurred.

He kissed her mouth. It was a new kind of kiss, different from anything she had experienced before. His lips moved gently but insistently against hers, as if he was determined to remember the moment; and she realized, with dread, that he was thinking this would be their last kiss.

She clung to him, wanting it to go on for ever, but all too soon he drew away.

'I love you,' he said. 'But I'm going to marry Griselda.'

*

LIFE AND DEATH went on. Children were born and old people died. On Sunday Emma Butcher attacked her adulterous husband Edward with his largest cleaver in a fit of jealous rage. On Monday one of Bess Hampton's chickens went missing, and was found boiling in a pot over Glynnie Thompson's kitchen fire, whereupon Glynnie was stripped and flogged by John Constable. On Tuesday Howell Tyler was working on the roof of St Mark's church when a rotten beam gave way beneath him and he fell, crashing through the ceiling to the floor below, and died immediately.

By Wednesday the wreckage of the bridge had been cleared, all but the stumps of two of the main piers, and the timber was stacked on the bank. The waterway was open, and barges and rafts were able to leave Kingsbridge for Melcombe with wool and other goods from the Fleece Fair consigned to Flanders and Italy.

When Caris and Edmund went to the riverside to check on progress, Merthin was using the salvaged timbers to build a raft to ferry people across the river. 'It's better than a boat,' he explained. 'Livestock can walk on and off, and carts can be driven on, too.'

Edmund nodded gloomily. 'It will have to do, for the weekly market. Fortunately, we should have a new bridge by the time of the next Fleece Fair.'

'I don't think so,' Merthin said.

'But you told me it would take nearly a year to build a new bridge!'

'A wooden bridge, yes. But if we build another wooden one it, too, will fall down.'

'Why?'

'Let me show you.' Merthin took them to a pile of timber. He pointed to a group of mighty posts. 'These formed the piers – they're probably the famous twenty-four best oak trees in the land, given to the priory by the king. Notice the ends.'

Caris could see that the huge posts had originally been sharpened into points, though their outlines had been softened by years under water.

Merthin said: 'A timber bridge has no foundations. The posts are simply driven into the river bed. That's not good enough.'

'But this bridge has stood for hundreds of years!' Edmund said indignantly. He always sounded quarrelsome when he argued.

Merthin was used to him, and paid no attention to his tone of voice. 'And now it has fallen down,' he said patiently. 'Something has changed. Wooden piers were once firm enough, but no longer.'

'What can have changed? The river is the river.'

'Well, for one thing you built a barn and a jetty on the bank, and protected the property with a wall. Several other merchants did the same. The old mud beach where I used to play on the south shore has mostly gone. So the river can no longer spread itself into the fields. As a result, the water flows faster than it used to – especially after the kind of heavy rain we've had this year.'

'So it will have to be a stone bridge?'

'Yes.'

Edmund looked up and saw Elfric standing by, listening. 'Merthin says a stone bridge will take three years.'

Elfric nodded. 'Three building seasons.'

Most building was done in the warmer months, Caris knew. Merthin had explained to her that stone walls could not be constructed when there was a risk that the mortar might freeze before it had begun to set.

Elfric went on: 'One season for the foundations, one for the arches, and one for the roadbed. After each stage, the mortar must be left for three or four months to set hard before the next stage can be laid on top of it.'

'Three years with no bridge,' Edmund said gloomily.

'Four years, unless you get started right away.'

'You'd better prepare an estimate of the cost for the priory.'

'I've already started, but it's a long job. It will take me another two or three days.'

'Quick as you can.'

Edmund and Caris left the riverside and walked up the main street, Edmund with his energetically lopsided stride. He would never lean on anyone's arm, despite his withered leg. To keep his balance, he swung his arms as if he were sprinting. The townspeople knew to give him plenty of room, especially when he was in a hurry. 'Three years!' he said as they walked. 'It will do terrible damage to the Fleece Fair. I don't know how long it will take us to get back to normal. Three years!'

When they got home they found Caris's sister, Alice, there. Her hair was tied up in her hat in an elaborate new style copied from Lady Philippa. She was sitting at the table with Aunt Petranilla. Caris knew immediately, from the looks on their faces, that they had been talking about her.

Petranilla went to the kitchen and came back with ale, bread and fresh butter. She filled a cup for Edmund.

Petranilla had cried on Sunday, but since then she had shown little sign of bereavement for her dead brother, Anthony. Surprisingly Edmund, who had never liked Anthony, seemed to grieve more: tears would come to his eyes at unexpected moments during the day, though they would disappear just as quickly.

Now he was full of news of the bridge. Alice was inclined to question Merthin's judgement, but Edmund dismissed that notion impatiently. 'The boy's a genius,' he said. 'He knows more than many master builders, yet he isn't out of his apprenticeship.'

Caris said bitterly: 'All the more shame that he's going to spend his life with Griselda.'

Alice leaped to the defence of her stepdaughter. 'There's nothing wrong with Griselda.'

'Yes, there is,' Caris said. 'She doesn't love him. She seduced him because her boyfriend left town, that's all.'

'Is that the story Merthin's telling you?' Alice laughed sarcastically. 'If a man doesn't want to do it, he doesn't do it – take my word.'

Edmund grunted. 'Men can be tempted,' he said.

'Oh, so you're siding with Caris, are you, Papa?' Alice said. 'I shouldn't be surprised, you usually do.'

'It's not a question of taking sides,' Edmund replied. 'A man may not want to do a thing beforehand, and he may regret it afterwards, yet for a brief moment his wishes may change – especially when a woman uses her wiles.'

'Wiles? Why do you assume that she threw herself at him?'

'I didn't say that. But I understand it began when she cried, and he comforted her.'

Caris herself had told him this.

Alice made a disgusted sound. 'You've always had a soft spot for that insubordinate apprentice.'

Caris ate some bread with butter, but she had no appetite. She said: 'I suppose they'll have half a dozen fat children, and Merthin will inherit Elfric's business, and become just another town tradesman, building houses for merchants and fawning on clergymen for contracts, just like his father-in-law.'

Petranilla said: 'And very lucky so to do! He'll be one of the leading men of the town.'

'He's worthy of a better destiny.'

'Is he, really?' Petranilla said in mock amazement. 'And him the son of a knight who fell from grace and hasn't a shilling to buy shoes for his wife! What exactly do you believe him to be destined for?'

Caris was stung by this mockery. It was true that Merthin's parents were poor corrodiaries, dependent on the priory for their food and drink. For him to inherit a successful building business would indeed mean a jump up the social ladder. Yet she still felt he deserved better. She could not say exactly what future she had in mind for him. She just knew that he was different from everyone else in town, and she could not bear the thought of his becoming like the rest.

*

ON FRIDAY, CARIS took Gwenda to see Mattie Wise.

Gwenda was still in town because Wulfric was there, attending to the burial of his family. Elaine, Edmund's housemaid, had dried Gwenda's dress in front of the fire, and Caris had bandaged her feet and given her an old pair of shoes.

Caris felt that Gwenda was not telling the full truth about her adventure in the forest. She said that Sim had taken her to the outlaws, and she had escaped; he had chased after her, and he had died in the bridge collapse. John Constable was satisfied with that story: outlaws were outside the law, as their name indicated, so there was no question of Sim bequeathing his property. Gwenda was free. But something else had happened in the forest, Caris felt sure; something Gwenda did not want to talk about. Caris did not press her friend. Some things were best buried.

Funerals were the business of the town this week. The extraordinary manner of the deaths made little difference to the rituals of interment. The bodies had to be washed, the shrouds sewn for the poor, the coffins nailed for the rich, the graves dug and the priests paid. Not all the monks were qualified as priests, but several were, and they worked in shifts, all day, every day, conducting obsequies in the cemetery on the north side of the cathedral. There were half a dozen small parish churches in Kingsbridge, and their priests were also busy.

Gwenda was helping Wulfric with the arrangements, performing the traditional woman's tasks, washing the bodies and making the shrouds, doing what she could to comfort him. He was in a kind of daze. He managed the details of the burial well enough, but spent hours gazing into space, with a slightly puzzled frown, as if trying to make sense of a massive conundrum.

By Friday the funerals were over, but the acting prior, Carlus, had announced a special service on Sunday for the souls of all those killed, so Wulfric was staying until Monday. Gwenda reported to Caris that he seemed grateful for the company of someone from his own village, but showed animation only when talking about Annet. Caris offered to buy her another love potion.

They found Mattie Wise in her kitchen, brewing medicines. The little house smelled of herbs, oil and wine. 'I used just about everything I had on Saturday and Sunday,' she said. 'I need to restock.'

'You must have made some money, anyway,' Gwenda said.

'Yes – if I can collect it.'

Caris was shocked. 'Do people welsh on you?'

'Some do. I always try to collect the fee in advance, while they're still in pain. But if they haven't got the money there and then, it's hard to refuse them treatment. Most pay up afterwards, but not all.'

Caris felt indignant on behalf of her friend. 'What do they say?'

'All sorts of things. They can't afford it, the potion did them no good, they were given it against their will, anything. But don't worry. There are enough honest people for me to continue. What's on your mind?'

'Gwenda lost her love potion in the accident.'

'That's easily remedied. Why don't you prepare it for her?'

While Caris was making up the mixture she asked Mattie: 'How many pregnancies end in a miscarriage?'

Gwenda knew why she was asking. Caris had told her all about Merthin's dilemma. The two girls had spent most of their time together discussing either Wulfric's indifference or Merthin's high principles. Caris had even been tempted to buy a love potion herself, and use it on Merthin; though something held her back.

Mattie gave her a sharp look, but answered noncommittally. 'No one knows. Many times, a woman misses one month but comes on again the next. Did she get pregnant and lose the baby, or was there some other reason? It's impossible to tell.'

'Oh.'

'Neither of you is pregnant, though, if that's what you're worried about.'

Gwenda said quickly: 'How do you know?'

'By looking at you. A woman changes almost immediately. Not just her belly and her breasts, but her complexion, her way of moving, her mood. I see these things better than most people – that's why they call me wise. So who is pregnant?'

'Griselda, Elfric's daughter.'

'Oh, yes, I've seen her. She's three months gone.'

Caris was astonished. 'How long?'

'Three months, or very nearly. Take a look at her. She was never a thin girl, but she's even more voluptuous now. So why are you so shocked? I suppose it's Merthin's baby, is it?'

Mattie always guessed these things.

Gwenda said to Caris: 'I thought you told me it happened recently.'

'Merthin didn't say exactly when, but he gave me the impression it was not long ago, and it only happened once. Now it seems he's been doing it to her for months!'

Mattie frowned. 'Why would he lie?'

'To make himself look not so bad?' Gwenda suggested.

'How could it be worse?'

'Men are peculiar, the way they think.'

'I'm going to ask him,' Caris said. 'Right now.' She put down the jar and the measuring spoon.

Gwenda said: 'What about my love potion?'

'I'll finish making it,' Mattie said. 'Caris is in too much of a hurry.'

'Thank you,' Caris said, and she went out.

She marched down to the riverside, but for once Merthin was not there. She failed to find him at Elfric's house either. She decided he must be in the mason's loft.

In the west front of the cathedral, neatly fitted into one of the towers, was a work room for the master mason. Caris reached it by climbing a narrow spiral staircase in a buttress of the tower. It was a wide room, well lit by tall lancet windows. All along one wall were stacked the beautifully shaped wooden templates used by the original cathedral stone carvers, carefully preserved and used now for repairs.

Underfoot was the tracing floor. The floorboards were covered with a layer of plaster, and the original master mason, Jack Builder, had scratched his plans in the mortar with iron drawing instruments. The marks thus made were white at first, but they faded over time, and new drawings could be scratched on top of the old. When there were so many designs that it became hard to tell the new from the old, a fresh layer of plaster was laid on top, and the process began again.

Parchment, the thin leather on which monks copied out the books of the Bible, was much too expensive to be used for drawings. In Caris's lifetime a new writing material had appeared, paper, but it came from the Arabs, so monks rejected it as a heathen Muslim invention. Anyway, it had to be imported from Italy and was no cheaper than parchment. And the tracing floor had another advantage: a carpenter could lay a piece of wood on the floor, on top of the drawing, and carve his template exactly to the lines drawn by the master mason.

Merthin was kneeling on the floor, carving a piece of oak in accordance with a drawing, but he was not making a template. He was carving a cog wheel with sixteen teeth. On the floor close by was another, smaller wheel, and Merthin stopped carving for a moment to put the two together and see how well they fitted. Caris had seen such cogs, or gears, in water mills, connecting the mill paddle to the grindstone.

He must have heard her footsteps on the stone staircase, but he was too absorbed in his work to glance up. She regarded him for a second, anger competing with love in her heart. He had the look of total concentration that she knew so well: his slight body bent over his work, his strong hands and dextrous fingers making fine adjustments, his face immobile, his gaze unwavering. He had the perfect grace of a young deer bending its head to drink from a stream. This was what a man looked like, she thought, when he was doing what he was born to do. He was in a state like happiness, but more profound. He was fulfilling his destiny.

She burst out: 'Why did you lie to me?'

His chisel slipped. He cried out in pain and looked at his finger. 'Christ,' he said, and put his finger in his mouth.

'I'm sorry,' Caris said. 'Are you hurt?'

'Nothing much. When did I lie to you?'

'You gave me the impression that Griselda seduced you one time. The truth is that the two of you have been at it for months.'

'No, we haven't.' He sucked his bleeding finger.

'She's three months pregnant.'

'She can't be, it happened two weeks ago.'

'She is, you can tell by her figure.'

'Can you?'

'Mattie Wise told me. Why did you lie?'

He looked her in the eye. 'But I didn't lie,' he said. 'It happened on the Sunday of Fleece Fair week. That was the first and only time.'

'Then how could she be sure she's pregnant, after only two weeks?'

'I don't know. How soon can women tell, anyway?'

'Don't you know?'

'I've never asked. Anyway, three months ago Griselda was still with . . .'

'Oh, God!' Caris said. A spark of hope flared in her breast. 'She was still with her old boyfriend – Thurstan.' The spark blazed into a flame. 'It must be his baby, Thurstan's – not yours. You're not the father!'

'Is it possible?' Merthin seemed hardly to dare to hope.

'Of course – it explains everything. If she had suddenly fallen in love with you, she'd be after you every chance she gets. But you said she hardly speaks to you.'

'I thought that was because I was reluctant to marry her.'

'She's never liked you. She just needed a father for her baby. Thurstan ran away – probably when she told him she was pregnant – and you were right there in the house, and stupid enough to fall for her trick. Oh, thank God!'

'Thank Mattie Wise,' said Merthin.

She caught sight of his left hand. Blood was welling from a finger. 'Oh, I made you hurt yourself!' she cried. She took his hand and examined the cut. It was small, but deep. 'I'm so sorry.'

'It's not that bad.'

'But it is,' she said, not knowing whether she was talking about the cut or something else. She kissed his hand, feeling his hot blood on her lips. She put his finger in her mouth, sucking the wound clean. It was so intimate that it felt like a sexual act, and she closed her eyes, feeling ecstatic. She swallowed, tasting his blood, and shuddered with pleasure.

*

A WEEK AFTER the bridge collapsed, Merthin had built a ferry.

It was ready at dawn on Saturday morning, in time for the weekly Kingsbridge market. He had worked on it by lamplight all Friday night, and Caris guessed he had not had time to speak to Griselda and tell her he knew the baby was Thurstan's. Caris and her father came down to the riverside to see the new sensation as the first traders arrived – women from the surrounding villages with baskets of eggs, peasants with cartloads of butter and cheese, and shepherds with flocks of lambs.

Caris admired Merthin's work. The raft was large enough to carry a horse and cart without taking the beast out of the shafts, and it had a firm wooden railing to keep sheep from falling overboard. New wooden platforms at water level on both banks made it easy for carts to roll on and off. Passengers paid a penny, collected by a monk – the ferry, like the bridge, belonged to the priory.

Most ingenious was the system Merthin had devised for moving the raft from one bank to the other. A long rope ran from the south end of the raft across the river, around a post, back across the river, around a drum and back to the raft, where it was attached again at the north end. The drum was connected by wooden gears to a wheel turned by a pacing ox: Caris had seen Merthin carving the gears yesterday. A lever altered the gears so that the drum turned in either direction, depending on whether the raft was going or coming back – and there was no need to take the ox out of its traces and turn it around.

'It's quite simple,' Merthin said when she marvelled at it – and it was, when she looked closely. The lever simply lifted one large cog wheel up out of the chain and moved into its place two smaller wheels, the effect being to reverse the direction in which the drum turned. All the same, no one in Kingsbridge had seen anything like it.

During the course of the morning, half the town came to look at Merthin's amazing new machine. Caris was bursting with pride in him. Elfric stood by, explaining the mechanism to anyone who asked, taking the credit for Merthin's work.

Caris wondered where Elfric got the nerve. He had destroyed Merthin's door – an act of violence that would have scandalized the town, had it not been overtaken by the greater tragedy of the bridge collapse. He had beaten Merthin with a stick, and Merthin still had the bruise on his face. And he had colluded in a deception intended to make Merthin marry Griselda and raise another man's child. Merthin had continued to work with him, feeling that the emergency outweighed their quarrel. But Caris did not know how Elfric could continue to hold his head up.

The ferry was brilliant – but inadequate.

Edmund pointed this out. On the far side of the river, carts and traders were queuing all along the road through the suburbs as far as the eye could see.

'It would go faster with two oxen,' Merthin said.

'Twice as fast?'

'Not quite, no. I could build another ferry.'

'There's already a second one,' Edmund said, pointing. He was right: Ian Boatman was rowing foot passengers across. Ian could not take carts, he refused livestock and he charged two pence. Normally he had trouble scraping a living: he took a monk across to Leper Island twice a day and found little other business. But today he, too, had a queue.

Merthin said: 'Well, you're right. In the end, a ferry is not a bridge.'

'This is a catastrophe,' Edmund said. 'Buonaventura's news was bad enough. But this – this could kill the town.'

'Then you must have a new bridge.'

'It's not me, it's the priory. The prior is dead, and there's no telling how long they will take to elect a new one. We'll just have to pressure the acting prior to make a decision. I'll go and see Carlus now. Come with me, Caris.'

They walked up the street and entered the priory. Most visitors had to go to the hospital and tell one of the servants that they wanted to speak to a monk; but Edmund was too important a personage, and too proud, to beg the favour of an audience in that way. The prior was lord of Kingsbridge, but Edmund was alderman of the guild, leader of the merchants who made the town what it was, and he treated the prior as a partner in the governance of the town. Besides, for the last thirteen years the prior had been his younger brother. So he went straight to the prior's house on the north side of the cathedral.

It was a timber-framed house like Edmund's, with a hall and a parlour on the ground floor and two bedrooms upstairs. There was no kitchen, for the prior's meals were prepared in the monastery kitchen. Many bishops and priors lived in palaces – and the bishop of Kingsbridge had a fine place in Shiring – but the prior of Kingsbridge lived modestly. However, the chairs were comfortable, the wall was hung with tapestries of Bible scenes, and there was a big fireplace to keep the house cosy in winter.

Caris and Edmund arrived mid-morning, the time when younger monks were supposed to labour, and their elders to read. Edmund and Caris found Blind Carlus in the hall of the prior's house, deep in conversation with Simeon, the treasurer. 'We must talk about the new bridge,' Edmund said immediately.

'Very well, Edmund,' Carlus said, recognizing him by his voice. The welcome was not warm, Caris noted, and she wondered if they had come at a bad time.

Edmund was just as sensitive as she to atmosphere, but he always blustered through. Now he took a chair and said: 'When do you think you'll hold the election for the new prior?'

'You can sit down too, Caris,' said Carlus. She had no idea how he knew she was there. 'No date has been set for the election,' he went on. 'Earl Roland has the right to nominate a candidate, but he has not yet recovered consciousness.'

'We can't wait,' Edmund said. Caris thought he was being too abrupt, but this was his way, so she said nothing. 'We have to start work on the new bridge right away,' her father continued. 'Timber's no good, we have to build in stone. It's going to take three years – four, if we delay.'

'A stone bridge?'

'It's essential. I've been talking to Elfric and Merthin. Another wooden bridge would fall down like the old.'

'But the cost!'

'About two hundred and fifty pounds, depending on the design. That's Elfric's calculation.'

Brother Simeon said: 'A new wooden bridge would cost fifty pounds, and Prior Anthony rejected that a week ago because of the price.'

'And look at the result! A hundred people dead, many more injured, livestock and carts lost, the prior dead and the earl at death's door.'

Carlus said stiffly: 'I hope you don't mean to blame all that on the late Prior Anthony.'

'We can't pretend his decision worked out well.'

'God has punished us for sin.'

Edmund sighed. Caris felt frustrated. Whenever they were in the wrong, monks would bring God into the argument. Edmund said: 'It is hard for us mere men to know God's intentions. But one thing we do know is that, without a bridge, this town will die. We're already losing out to Shiring. Unless we build a new stone bridge as fast as we possibly can, Kingsbridge will soon become a small village.'

'That may be God's plan for us.'

Edmund began to show his exasperation. 'Is it possible that God is so displeased with you monks? For, believe me, if the Fleece Fair and the Kingsbridge market die, there will not be a priory here with twenty-five monks and forty nuns and fifty employees, and a hospital and a choir and a school. There may not be a cathedral, either. The bishop of Kingsbridge has always lived in Shiring – what if the prosperous merchants there offer to build him a splendid new cathedral in their own town, out of the profits from their ever-growing market? No Kingsbridge market, no town, no cathedral, no priory – is that what you want?'

Carlus looked dismayed. Clearly it had not occurred to him that the long-term consequences of the bridge collapse could actually affect the status of the priory.

But Simeon said: 'If the priory can't afford to build a wooden bridge, there's certainly no prospect of a stone one.'

'But you must!'

'Will the masons work free?'

'Certainly not. They have to feed their families. But we've already explained how the townspeople could raise the money and lend it to the priory against the security of the bridge tolls.'

'And take away our income from the bridge!' Simeon said indignantly. 'You're back to that swindle, are you?'

Caris put in: 'You've got no bridge tolls at all, now.'

'On the contrary, we're collecting fares on the ferry.'

'You found the money to pay Elfric for that.'

'A lot less than a bridge – and even so it emptied our coffers.'

'The fares will never amount to much – the ferry is too slow.'

'The time may come, in the future, when the priory is able to build a new bridge. God will send the means, if he wishes it. And then we will still have the tolls.'

Edmund said: 'God has already sent the means. He inspired my daughter to dream up a way of raising the money that has never been thought of before.'

Carlus said primly: 'Please leave it to us to decide what God has done.'

'Very well.' Edmund stood up, and Caris did the same. 'I'm very sorry you're taking this attitude. It's a catastrophe for Kingsbridge and everyone who lives here, including the monks.'

'I must be guided by God, not you.'

Edmund and Caris turned to leave.

'One more thing, if I may,' said Carlus.

Edmund turned at the door. 'Of course.'

'It's not acceptable for lay people to enter priory buildings at will. Next time you wish to see me, please come to the hospital, and send a novice or a priory servant to seek me out, in the usual way.'

'I'm alderman of the parish guild!' Edmund protested. 'I've always had direct access to the prior.'

'No doubt the fact that Prior Anthony was your brother made him reluctant to impose the usual rules. But those days are over.'

Caris looked at her father's face. He was repressing fury. 'Very well,' he said tightly.

'God bless you.'

Edmund went out, and Caris followed.

They walked across the muddy green together, passing a pitifully small cluster of market stalls. Caris felt the weight of her father's obligations. Most people just worried about feeding their families. Edmund worried about the entire town. She glanced at him and saw that his expression was twisted into an anxious frown. Unlike Carlus, Edmund would not throw his hands in the air and say that God's will would be done. He was racking his brains for a solution to the problem. She felt a surge of compassion for him, straining to do the right thing with no help from the powerful priory. He never complained of the responsibility, he just took it on. It made her want to weep.

They left the precincts and crossed the main street. As they came to their front door, Caris said: 'What are we going to do?'

'It's obvious, isn't it?' said her father. 'We've got to make sure Carlus doesn't get elected prior.'

15

GODWYN WANTED TO BE PRIOR of Kingsbridge. He longed for it with all his heart. He itched to reform the priory's finances, tightening up the management of its lands and other assets, so that the monks no longer had to go to Mother Cecilia for money. He yearned for the stricter separation of monks from nuns, and both from townspeople, so that they might all breathe the pure air of sanctity. But as well as these irreproachable motives, there was something else. He lusted for the authority and distinction of the title. At night, in his imagination, he was already prior.

'Clean up that mess in the cloister!' he would say to a monk.

'Yes, Father Prior, right away.'

Godwyn loved the sound of *Father Prior.*

'Good day, Bishop Richard,' he would say, not obsequiously, but with friendly courtesy.

And Bishop Richard would reply, as one distinguished clergyman to another: 'And a good day to you, too, Prior Godwyn.'

'I trust everything is to your satisfaction, archbishop?' he might say, more deferentially this time, but still as a junior colleague of the great man, rather than as an underling.

'Oh, yes, Godwyn, you've done extraordinarily well here.'

'Your reverence is very kind.'

And perhaps, one day, strolling in the cloister side by side with a richly dressed potentate: 'Your majesty does us great honour to visit our humble priory.'

'Thank you, Father Godwyn, but I come to ask your advice.'

He wanted this position – but he was not sure how to get it. He pondered the question all week, as he supervised a hundred burials, and planned the big Sunday service that would be both Anthony's funeral and a remembrance for the souls of all the Kingsbridge dead.

Meanwhile, he spoke to no one of his hopes. It was only ten days ago that he had learned the price of being guileless. He had gone to the chapter with Timothy's Book and a strong argument for reform – and the old guard had turned on him with perfect coordination, as if they had rehearsed it, and squashed him like a frog under a cartwheel.

He would not let that happen again.

On Sunday morning, as the monks were filing into the refectory for breakfast, a novice whispered to Godwyn that his mother would like to see him in the north porch of the cathedral. He slipped away discreetly.

He felt apprehensive as he passed quietly through the cloisters and the church. He could guess what had happened. Something had occurred yesterday to trouble Petranilla. She had lain awake half the night worrying about it. This morning she had woken up at dawn with a plan of action – and he was part of it. She would be at her most impatient and domineering. Her plan would probably be good – but even if it was not she would insist he carried it out.

She stood in the gloom of the porch in a wet cloak – it was raining again. 'My brother Edmund came to see Blind Carlus yesterday,' she said. 'He tells me Carlus is acting as if he is already prior, and the election is a mere formality.'

There was an accusing note in her voice as if this was Godwyn's fault, and he answered defensively. 'The old guard swung behind Carlus before Uncle Anthony's body was cold. They won't hear talk of rival candidates.'

'Hm. And the youngsters?'

'They want me to run, of course. They liked the way I stood up to Prior Anthony over Timothy's Book – even though I was overruled. But I've said nothing.'

'Any other candidates?'

'Thomas Langley is the outsider. Some disapprove of him because he used to be a knight, and has killed people, by his own admission. But he's capable, does his job with quiet efficiency, never bullies the novices...'

His mother looked thoughtful. 'What's his story? Why did he become a monk?'

Godwyn's apprehension began to ease. It seemed she was not going to berate him for inaction. 'Thomas just says he always hankered for the sanctified life and, when he came here to get a sword wound attended to, he resolved never to leave.'

'I remember that. It was ten years ago. But I never did hear how he got the wound.'

'Nor I. He doesn't like to talk about his violent past.'

'Who paid for his admission to the priory?'

'Oddly enough, I don't know.' Godwyn often marvelled at his mother's ability to ask the revealing question. She might be tyrannical, but he had to admire her. 'It might have been Bishop Richard – I recall him promising the usual gift. But he wouldn't have had the resources personally – he wasn't a bishop, then, just a priest. Perhaps he was speaking for Earl Roland.'

'Find out.'

Godwyn hesitated. He would have to look through all the charters in the priory's library. The librarian, Brother Augustine, would not presume to question the sacrist, but someone else might. Then Godwyn would have the awkwardness of inventing a plausible story to explain what he was doing. If the gift had been cash, rather than land or other property – unusual, but possible – he would have to go through the account rolls...

'What's the matter?' his mother said sharply.

'Nothing. You're right.' He reminded himself that her domineering attitude was a sign of her love for him, perhaps the only way she knew how to express it. 'There must be a record. Come to think of it...'

'What?'

'A gift like that is usually trumpeted. The prior announces it in church, and calls down blessings on the head of the donor, then preaches a sermon on how people who give lands to the priory are rewarded in heaven. But I don't remember anything like that happening at the time Thomas came to us.'

'All the more reason to seek out the charter. I think Thomas is a man with a secret. And a secret is always a weakness.'

'I'll look into it. What do you think I should say to people who want me to stand for election?'

Petranilla smiled slyly. 'I think you should tell them you're not going to be a candidate.'

＊

BREAKFAST WAS OVER by the time Godwyn left his mother. Latecomers were not allowed to eat, by a longstanding rule. But the kitchener, Brother Reynard, could always find a morsel for someone he liked. Godwyn went to the kitchen and got a slice of cheese and a heel of bread. He ate it standing up, while around him the priory servants brought the breakfast bowls back from the refectory and scrubbed out the iron pot in which the porridge had been cooked.

As he ate he mulled over his mother's advice. The more he thought about it, the cleverer it seemed. Once he had announced he would not stand for election, everything else he said would carry the authority of a disinterested commentator. He could manipulate the election without being suspected of selfish motives. Then he could make his move at the last moment. He felt a warm glow of loving gratitude for the shrewdness of his mother's restless brain, and the loyalty of her indomitable heart.

Brother Theodoric found him there. Theodoric's fair complexion was flushed with indignation. 'Brother Simeon spoke to us at breakfast about Carlus becoming prior,' he said. 'It was all about continuing the wise traditions of Anthony. He's not going to change anything!'

That was sly, Godwyn thought. Simeon had taken advantage of Godwyn's absence to say, with authority, things that Godwyn would have challenged if he had been present. He said sympathetically: 'That's disgraceful.'

'I asked whether the other candidates would be permitted to address the monks at breakfast in the same way.'

Godwyn grinned. 'Good for you!'

'Simeon said there was no need for other candidates. "We're not holding an archery contest," he said. In his view, the decision has already been made: Prior Anthony chose Carlus as his successor by making him sub-prior.'

'That's complete rubbish.'

'Exactly. The monks are furious.'

This was very good, Godwyn thought. Carlus had offended even his supporters by trying to take away their right to vote. He was undermining his own candidacy.

Theodoric went on: 'I think we should press Carlus to withdraw himself from the contest.'

Godwyn wanted to say: Are you mad? He bit his tongue and tried to look as if he were mulling over what Theodoric had said. 'Is that the best way to deal with it?' he asked, as if genuinely unsure.

Theodoric was surprised by the question. 'What do you mean?'

'You say the brothers are all furious with Carlus and Simeon. If this goes on, they won't vote for Carlus. But if Carlus withdraws, the old guard will come up with another candidate. They could make a better choice the second time. It might be someone popular – Brother Joseph, for example.'

Theodoric was thunderstruck. 'I never thought of it that way.'

'Perhaps we should hope that Carlus remains the choice of the old guard. Everyone knows he's against any kind of change. The reason he's a monk is that he likes to know that every day will be the same: he'll walk the same paths, sit in the same seats, eat and pray and sleep in the same places. Perhaps it's because of his blindness, though I suspect he might have been like that anyway. The cause doesn't matter. He believes that nothing here needs changing. Now, there aren't many monks who are *that* contented – which makes Carlus relatively easy to beat. A candidate who represented the old guard but advocated a few minor reforms would be much more likely to win.' Godwyn realized he had forgotten to seem tentative and had started laying down the law. Backtracking quickly, he added: 'I don't know – what do you think?'

'I think you're a genius,' said Theodoric.

I'm not a genius, Godwyn thought, but I learn fast.

He went to the hospital, where he found Philemon sweeping out the private guest rooms upstairs. Lord William was still here, watching over his father, waiting for him to wake up or die. Lady Philippa was with him. Bishop Richard had returned to his palace in Shiring, but was expected back today for the big funeral service.

Godwyn took Philemon to the library. Philemon could barely read, but he would be useful for getting out the charters.

The priory had more than a hundred charters. Most were deeds to landholdings, the majority near Kingsbridge, some scattered around far parts of England and Wales. Other charters entitled the monks to establish their priory, to build a church, to take stone from a quarry on the earl of Shiring's land without payment, to parcel the land around the priory into house plots and rent them out, to hold courts, to have a weekly market, to charge a toll for crossing the bridge, to have an annual Fleece Fair, and to ship goods by river to Melcombe without paying taxes to the lords of any of the lands through which the river passed.

The documents were written with pen and ink on parchment, thin leather painstakingly cleaned and scraped and bleached and stretched to form a writing surface. Longer ones were rolled up and tied with a fine leather thong. They were kept in an ironbound chest. The chest was locked, but the key was in the library, in a small carved box.

Godwyn frowned with disapproval when he opened the chest. The charters were not lined up in neat stacks, but tumbled in the box in no apparent order. Some had small rips and frayed edges, and all were covered with dust. They should be kept in date sequence, he thought, each one numbered, and the numbered list fixed to the inside of the lid, so that any particular charter could be quickly located. If I become prior...

Philemon took the charters out one by one, blew off the dust, and laid them on a table for Godwyn. Most people disliked Philemon. One or two of the older monks mistrusted him, but Godwyn did not: it was hard to mistrust someone who treated you like a god. Most of the monks were just used to him – he had been around for so long. Godwyn remembered him as a boy, tall and awkward, always hanging around the priory, asking the monks which saint was best to pray to, and had they ever witnessed a miracle.

Most of the charters had originally been written out twice on a single sheet. The word 'chirograph' had been written in large letters between the two copies, then the sheet had been cut in half with a zigzag line through the word. Each of the parties kept half the sheet, and the match between the zigzags was taken as proof that both documents were genuine.

Some of the sheets had holes, probably where the living sheep had been bitten by an insect. Others appeared to have been nibbled, at some point in their history, presumably by mice.

They were written in Latin, of course. The more recent ones were easier to read, but the older style of handwriting was sometimes hard for Godwyn to decipher. He scanned each until he came to a date. He was looking for something written soon after All Hallows' Day ten years ago.

He examined every sheet and found nothing.

The nearest was a deed dated some weeks later in which Earl Roland gave permission to Sir Gerald to transfer his lands to the ownership of the priory, in exchange for which the priory would forgive Gerald's debts and support him and his wife for the rest of their lives.

Godwyn was not really disappointed. Rather the contrary. Either Thomas had been admitted without the usual gift – which would in itself be curious – or the charter was kept somewhere else, away from prying eyes. Either way, it seemed increasingly likely that Petranilla's instinct was right, and Thomas had a secret.

There were not many private places in a monastery. Monks were supposed to have no personal property and no secrets. Although some wealthy monasteries had built private cells for the senior monks, at Kingsbridge they slept in one big room – all except the prior himself. Almost certainly, the charter that had secured Thomas's admission was in the prior's house.

Which was now occupied by Carlus.

That made things difficult. Carlus would not let Godwyn search the place. Searching might hardly be necessary: there was probably a box or satchel somewhere in plain sight containing the late Prior Anthony's personal documents: a notebook from his novice days, a friendly letter from the archbishop, some sermons.

Carlus had probably had the contents examined after Anthony died. But he had no reason to permit Godwyn to do the same.

Godwyn frowned, thinking. Could someone else search? Edmund or Petranilla might ask to see their late brother's possessions, and it would be hard for Carlus to deny such a request. But he might remove any priory documents beforehand. No, the search had to be clandestine.

The bell rang for Terce, the morning office. Godwyn realized that the only time he could be certain Carlus would not be in the prior's house was during a service in the cathedral.

He would have to skip Terce. He could think up a plausible excuse. It would not be easy – he was the sacrist, the one person who should never skip services. But there was no alternative.

'I want you to come to me in the church,' he said to Philemon.

'All right,' said Philemon, though he looked worried: priory employees were not supposed to enter the chancel during worship.

'Come right after the verse. Whisper in my ear. It doesn't matter what you say. Take no notice of my reaction, just continue.'

Philemon frowned anxiously, but he nodded assent. He would do anything for Godwyn.

Godwyn left the library and joined the procession into the church. There was only a handful of people standing in the nave: most of the town would come later in the day to attend the mass for the victims of the bridge collapse. The monks took their places in the chancel, and the ritual began. 'O God, incline unto mine aid,' Godwyn said along with the rest.

They finished the verse and began the first hymn, and Philemon appeared. All the monks stared at him, as people always did stare at anything out of the ordinary that occurred during a familiar rite. Brother Simeon frowned disapprovingly. Carlus, conducting the singing, sensed a disturbance and looked puzzled. Philemon came to Godwyn's seat and bent over. 'Blessed is the man that walketh not in the counsel of the ungodly,' he whispered.

Godwyn pretended to be surprised, and continued to listen while Philemon recited psalm number one. After a few moments he shook his head vigorously, as if denying a request. Then he listened some more. He was going to have to think up an elaborate story to account for this pantomime. Perhaps he would say that his mother had insisted on speaking to him immediately about the funeral of her brother, Prior Anthony, and that she was threatening to come into the chancel herself unless Philemon took a message to Godwyn. Petranilla's overbearing personality, combined with family grief, made the story just about credible. As Philemon finished the psalm, Godwyn made a resigned face, and got up and followed Philemon out of the chancel.

They hurried around the cathedral to the prior's house. A young employee was sweeping the floor. He would not dare to question a monk. He might tell Carlus that Godwyn and Philemon had been here – but it would be too late then.

Godwyn thought the prior's house was a disgrace. It was smaller than Uncle Edmund's home in the main street. A prior should have a palace befitting his station, as the bishop did. There was nothing glorious about this building. A few tapestries covered the walls, depicting biblical scenes and keeping out the draughts, but overall the décor was dull and unimaginative – rather like the late Anthony.

They searched the place quickly and soon found what they were looking for. Upstairs in the bedroom, in a chest beside the prie-dieu, was a large wallet. It was made of soft ginger-brown goatskin and beautifully sewn with scarlet thread: Godwyn felt sure it had been a pious gift from one of the town's leather workers.

Watched intently by Philemon, he opened it.

Inside were about thirty sheets of parchment, laid flat and interleaved with protective linen cloths. Godwyn examined them quickly.

Several bore study notes on the Psalms: Anthony must at some time have contemplated writing a book of commentaries, but the work appeared to have been abandoned. The most surprising was a love poem, in Latin. Headed *Virent Oculi*, it was addressed to a man with green eyes. Uncle Anthony had green eyes flecked with gold, like all his family.

Godwyn wondered who had written it. Not many women

could write Latin well enough to compose a poem. Had a nun loved Anthony? Or was the poem from a man? The parchment was old and yellowing: the love affair, if such it was, had happened in Anthony's youth. But he had kept the poem. Perhaps he had not been quite as dull as Godwyn had imagined.

Philemon said: 'What is it?'

Godwyn felt guilty. He had peeped into a deeply private corner of his uncle's life, and he wished he had not. 'Nothing,' he said. 'Just a poem.' He picked up the next sheet – and struck gold.

It was a charter dated Christmas ten years ago. It concerned a landholding of five hundred acres near Lynn, in Norfolk. The lord had recently died. The deed assigned the vacant lordship to Kingsbridge Priory, and specified the annual dues – grain, fleeces, calves and chickens – payable to the priory by the serfs and tenants who farmed the land. It nominated one of the peasants to be a bailiff with the responsibility of delivering the produce to the priory annually. It also assigned money payments that could be offered instead of the actual produce – a practice that was now predominant, especially where the land was many miles from the residence of the lord.

It was a typical charter. Every year, after the harvest, representatives of dozens of similar communities made the pilgrimage to the priory to deliver what they owed. Those from nearby showed up early in the autumn; others came at intervals through the winter, with a few from long distances not arriving until after Christmas.

The deed also specified that the gift was given in consideration of the priory's accepting Sir Thomas Langley as a monk. That, too, was routine.

But one feature of this document was not commonplace. It was signed by Queen Isabella.

That was interesting. Isabella was the unfaithful wife of King Edward II. She had rebelled against her royal husband and installed, in his place, their fourteen-year-old son. Shortly afterwards the deposed king had died, and Prior Anthony had been present at his burial in Gloucester. Thomas had come to Kingsbridge at around the same time.

For a few years the queen and her lover, Roger Mortimer,

had ruled England; but, before long, Edward III had asserted his authority, despite his youth. The new king was now twenty-four and firmly in control. Mortimer was dead and Isabella, now forty-two, lived in opulent retirement at Castle Rising in Norfolk, not far from Lynn.

'This is it!' Godwyn said to Philemon. 'It was Queen Isabella who arranged for Thomas to become a monk.'

Philemon frowned. 'But why?'

Though uneducated, Philemon was shrewd. 'Why indeed?' Godwyn answered. 'Presumably she wanted to reward him, or silence him, or perhaps both. And this happened in the year of her coup.'

'He must have performed some service for her.'

Godwyn nodded. 'He carried a message, or opened the gates of a castle, or betrayed the king's plans to her, or secured for her the support of some important baron. But why is it a secret?'

'It's not,' said Philemon. 'The treasurer must know about it. And everyone in Lynn. The bailiff must talk to a few people when he comes here.'

'But no one knows that the whole arrangement was made for the benefit of Thomas – unless they have seen this charter.'

'So that's the secret – that Queen Isabella made this gift for Thomas's sake.'

'Exactly.' Godwyn packed up the documents, carefully interleaving the sheets of parchment with linen cloths, and replaced the wallet in the chest.

Philemon asked: 'But why is it a secret? There's nothing dishonest or shameful about such an arrangement – it happens all the time.'

'I don't know why it's a secret, and perhaps we don't need to know. The fact that people want to keep it hidden may be sufficient for our purpose. Let's get out of this house.'

Godwyn felt satisfied. Thomas had a secret and Godwyn knew about it. That gave Godwyn power. Now he felt confident enough to risk putting Thomas forward as a candidate for prior. He also felt apprehensive: Thomas was no fool.

They returned to the cathedral. The office of Terce ended a few moments later, and Godwyn began to prepare the church for the big funeral service. On his instructions, six monks lifted Anthony's coffin and placed it on a stand in front of the altar, then surrounded it with candles. Townspeople began to gather in the nave. Godwyn nodded to his cousin Caris, who had covered her everyday headgear in black silk. Then he spotted Thomas, carrying in a large, ornate chair, with the help of a novice. This was the bishop's throne, or cathedra, that gave the church its special cathedral status.

Godwyn touched Thomas's arm. 'Let Philemon do that.'

Thomas bristled, thinking that Godwyn was offering help because of his missing arm. 'I can manage.'

'I know you can. I want a word.'

Thomas was older – he was thirty-four, Godwyn thirty-one – but Godwyn was his superior in the monastic hierarchy. All the same, Godwyn was always a little afraid of Thomas. The matricularius usually showed the appropriate deference to the sacrist, but all the same Godwyn felt he was getting just as much respect as Thomas thought he merited, and no more. Though Thomas conformed in every way to the discipline of St Benedict's Rule, nevertheless he seemed to have brought into the priory with him a quality of independence and self-sufficiency that he never lost.

It would not be easy to deceive Thomas – but that was exactly what Godwyn planned to do.

Thomas allowed Philemon to take his side of the throne, and Godwyn drew him into the aisle. 'They're talking about you as possibly the next prior,' Godwyn said.

'They're saying the same about you,' Thomas rejoined.

'I shall refuse to stand.'

Thomas raised his eyebrows. 'You surprise me, brother.'

'Two reasons,' Godwyn said. 'One, I think you would do a better job.'

Thomas looked more surprised. He probably had not suspected Godwyn of such modesty. He was right: Godwyn was lying.

'Two,' Godwyn continued, 'you're more likely to win.' Now Godwyn was telling the truth. 'The youngsters like me, but you're popular across the range of all ages.'

Thomas's handsome face looked quizzical. He was waiting for the catch.

'I want to help you,' Godwyn said. 'I believe the only important thing is to have a prior who will reform the monastery and improve its finances.'

'I think I could do that. But what do you want in return for your support?'

Godwyn knew better than to ask for nothing. Thomas would not believe that. He invented a plausible lie. 'I'd like to be your sub-prior.'

Thomas nodded, but did not immediately consent. 'How would you help me?'

'First, by gaining you the support of the townspeople.'

'Just because Edmund Wooler is your uncle?'

'It's not that simple. The townspeople are worried about the bridge. Carlus won't say when he'll begin building, if ever. They're desperate to stop him becoming prior. If I tell Edmund that you'll start work on the bridge as soon as you're elected, you'll have the whole town behind you.'

'That won't win me the votes of many monks.'

'Don't be so sure. Remember, the monks' choice has to be ratified by the bishop. Most bishops are prudent enough to consult local opinion – and Richard is as keen as anyone to avoid trouble. If the townspeople come out for you, it will make a difference.'

Godwyn could see that Thomas did not trust him. The matricularius studied him, and Godwyn felt a bead of sweat trickle down his spine as he fought to remain expressionless under that keen gaze. But Thomas was listening to his arguments. 'There's no doubt we need a new bridge,' he said. 'Carlus is foolish to prevaricate.'

'So you would be promising something you intend to do anyway.'

'You're very persuasive.'

Godwyn held up his hands in a defensive gesture. 'I don't mean to be. You must do what you feel is God's will.'

Thomas looked sceptical. He did not believe that Godwyn

was so dispassionate. But he said: 'All right.' Then he added: 'I'll pray about it.'

Godwyn sensed he would get no stronger commitment out of Thomas today, and it might be counterproductive to push any harder. 'So will I,' he said, and he turned away.

Thomas would do exactly what he had promised, and pray about it. He had little in the way of personal desires. If he thought it was God's will he would stand as prior and, if not, not. Godwyn could do no more with him, for the moment.

There was now a blaze of candles around Anthony's coffin. The nave was filling with townspeople and peasants from the surrounding villages. Godwyn raked the crowd for the face of Caris, which he had spotted a few minutes earlier. He located her in the south transept, looking at Merthin's scaffolding in the aisle. He had affectionate memories of Caris as a child, when he had been her all-knowing grown-up cousin.

She had been looking glum since the bridge collapse, he had noticed, but today she seemed cheerful. He was glad: he had a soft spot for her. He touched her elbow. 'You look happy.'

'I am.' She smiled. 'A romantic knot just came untangled. But you wouldn't understand.'

'Of course not.' You have no idea, he thought, how many romantic tangles there are among monks. But he said nothing: lay people were best left in ignorance of sins that took place in the priory. He said: 'Your father should speak to Bishop Richard about rebuilding the bridge.'

'Really?' she said sceptically. As a child she had hero-worshipped him, but nowadays she was less in awe. 'What's the point? It's not his bridge.'

'The monks' choice for prior has to be approved by the bishop. Richard could let it be known that he won't approve anyone who refuses to rebuild the bridge. Some monks might be defiant, but others will say there's no point in voting for someone who isn't going to be ratified.'

'I see. You really think my father could help?'

'Absolutely.'

'Then I'll suggest it.'

'Thank you.'

The bell rang. Godwyn slipped out of the church and again joined the procession forming up in the cloisters. It was midday.

He had done a good morning's work.

16

WULFRIC AND GWENDA left Kingsbridge early on Monday morning to walk the long road back to their village of Wigleigh.

Caris and Merthin watched them cross the river on Merthin's new ferry. Merthin was pleased by how well it was working. The wooden gears would wear out quite quickly, he knew. Iron gears would be better, but—

Caris had other thoughts. 'Gwenda is so much in love,' she sighed.

'She has no chance with Wulfric,' Merthin said.

'You never know. She's a determined girl. Look how she escaped from Sim Chapman.'

'But Wulfric's engaged to that Annet – who is much prettier.'

'Good looks aren't everything in a romance.'

'For which I thank God every day.'

She laughed. 'I love your funny face.'

'But Wulfric fought my brother over Annet. He must love her.'

'Gwenda's got a love potion.'

Merthin gave her a disapproving look. 'So you think it's all right for a girl to manoeuvre a man into marrying her when he loves someone else?'

She was struck silent for a moment. The soft skin of her throat turned pink. 'I never thought of it that way,' she said. 'Is it really the same thing?'

'It's similar.'

'But she's not coercing him – she just wants to make him love her.'

'She should try to do that without a potion.'

'Now I feel ashamed of helping her.'

'Too late.' Wulfric and Gwenda were getting off the ferry on the far side. They turned to wave, then headed along the road through the suburbs with Skip, the dog, at their heels.

Merthin and Caris walked back up the main street. Caris said: 'You haven't spoken to Griselda yet.'

'I'm going to do it now. I don't know whether I'm looking forward to it or dreading it.'

'You've got nothing to fear. She's the one who lied.'

'That's true.' He touched his face. The bruise had almost healed. 'I just hope her father doesn't get violent again.'

'Do you want me to come with you?'

He would have been glad of her support, but he shook his head. 'I made this mess, and I have to straighten it out.'

They stopped outside Elfric's house. Caris said: 'Good luck.'

'Thanks.' Merthin kissed her lips briefly, resisted the temptation to kiss her again, and walked in.

Elfric was sitting at the table eating bread and cheese. A cup of ale stood in front of him. Beyond him, Merthin could see Alice and the maid in the kitchen. There was no sign of Griselda.

Elfric said: 'Where have you been?'

Merthin decided that if he had nothing to fear he had better act fearlessly. He ignored Elfric's question. 'Where's Griselda?'

'Still in bed.'

Merthin shouted up the stairs: 'Griselda! I want to talk to you.'

Elfric said: 'No time for that. We've got work to do.'

Again Merthin ignored him. 'Griselda! You'd better get up now.'

'Hey!' Elfric said. 'Who do you think you are, to give orders?'

'You want me to marry her, don't you?'

'So what?'

'So she'd better get used to doing what her husband tells her.' He raised his voice again. 'Get down here now, or you'll just have to hear what I've got to say from someone else.'

She appeared at the top of the stairs. 'I'm coming!' she said irritably. 'What's all the fuss about?'

Merthin waited for her to come down, then said: 'I've found out who the father of the baby is.'

Fear flashed in her eyes. 'Don't be stupid, it's you.'

'No, it's Thurstan.'

'I never lay with Thurstan!' She looked at her father. 'Honestly I didn't.'

Elfric said: 'She doesn't lie.'

Alice came out of the kitchen. 'That's right,' she said.

Merthin said: 'I lay with Griselda on the Sunday of Fleece Fair week – fifteen days ago. Griselda is three months pregnant.'

'I'm not!'

Merthin looked hard at Alice. 'You knew, didn't you?' Alice looked away. Merthin went on: 'And yet you lied – even to Caris, your own sister.'

Elfric said: 'You don't know how long pregnant she is.'

'Look at her,' Merthin replied. 'You can see the bulge in her belly. Not much, but it's there.'

'What do you know of such things? You're just a boy.'

'Yes – you were all relying on my ignorance, weren't you? And it almost worked.'

Elfric wagged his finger. 'You lay with Griselda, and now you'll marry Griselda.'

'Oh no I won't. She doesn't love me. She lay with me to get a father for her baby, after Thurstan ran away. I know I did wrong, but I'm not going to punish myself for the rest of my life by marrying her.'

Elfric stood up. 'You are, you know.'

'No.'

'You've got to.'

'No.'

Elfric's face turned red, and he shouted: 'You will marry her!'

Merthin said: 'How long do you want me to keep on saying no?'

Elfric realized he was serious. 'In that case, you're dismissed,' he said. 'Get out of my house and never come back.'

Merthin had been expecting this, and it came as a relief. It meant the argument was over. 'All right.' He tried to step past Elfric.

Elfric blocked his way. 'Where do you think you're going?'

'To the kitchen, to get my things.'

'Your tools, you mean.'

'Yes.'

'They're not yours. I paid for them.'

'An apprentice is always given his tools at the end of his...' Merthin tailed off.

'You haven't finished your apprenticeship, so you don't get your tools.'

Merthin had not expected this. 'I've done six and a half years!'

'You're supposed to do seven.'

Without tools Merthin could not earn his living. 'That's unfair. I'll appeal to the carpenters' guild.'

'I look forward to it,' Elfric said smugly. 'It will be interesting to hear you argue that an apprentice who is sacked for lying with his master's daughter should be rewarded with a free set of tools. The carpenters in the guild have all got apprentices, and most of them have daughters. They'll throw you out on your arse.'

Merthin realized he was right.

Alice said: 'There you are, you're in real trouble now, aren't you?'

'Yes,' Merthin said. 'But whatever happens, it won't be as bad as life with Griselda and her family.'

*

LATER THAT MORNING, Merthin went to St Mark's church for the funeral of Howell Tyler. He attended because he hoped someone there would give him a job.

Looking up at the timber ceiling – the church did not have a stone vault – Merthin could see a man-shaped hole in the painted wood, grim testament to the manner of Howell's death. Everything up there was rotten, the builders at the funeral said knowingly; but they said it after the accident, their sagacity coming too late to save Howell. It was now clear that the roof was too weak to be repaired, but must be demolished completely and rebuilt from scratch. That meant closing the church.

St Mark's was a poor church. It had a pitiful endowment, a single farm ten miles away that was kept by the priest's brother and just about managed to feed the family. The priest, Father Joffroi, had to get his income from the eight or nine hundred citizens of his parish in the poorer north end of town. Those who were not actually destitute generally pretended to be, so their tithes brought in only a modest sum. He made his living by christening, marrying and burying them, charging a lot less than the monks at the cathedral. His parishioners married early, had many children and died young, so there was plenty of work for him, and in the end he did well enough. But if he closed the church his income would dry up – and he would not be able to pay the builders.

Consequently the work on the roof had stopped.

All the town's builders came to the funeral, including Elfric. Merthin tried to look unashamed as he stood in the church, but it was difficult: most of them knew he had been dismissed. He had been unjustly treated but, unfortunately, he was not completely innocent.

Howell had had a young wife who was friendly with Caris, and now Caris walked in with the widow and the bereaved family. Merthin moved next to Caris and told her what had happened with Elfric.

Father Joffroi conducted the service dressed in an old robe. Merthin thought about the roof. It seemed to him there must be a way to dismantle it without closing the church. The standard approach, when repairs had been postponed too long and the timbers were too badly rotted to bear the weight of workmen, was to build scaffolding around the church and knock the timbers down into the nave. The building was then open to the elements until the new roof was finished and tiled. But it should be possible to build a swivelling hoist, supported by the thick side wall of the church, which would lift the roof timbers up one by one, instead of pushing them down, and swing them across the wall and down into the graveyard. That way, the wooden ceiling could be left intact, and replaced only after the roof had been rebuilt.

At the graveside, he looked at the men one by one, wondering which of them was most likely to employ him. He decided to approach Bill Watkin, the town's second largest builder and no admirer of Elfric's. Bill had a bald dome with a fringe of black hair, a natural version of the monkish tonsure. He did most of the house building in Kingsbridge. Like Elfric, he employed a stonemason and a carpenter, a handful of labourers and one or two apprentices.

Howell had not been prosperous, and his body was lowered into the grave in a shroud, without a coffin.

When Father Joffroi had departed, Merthin approached Bill Watkin. 'Good day, Master Watkin,' he said formally.

Bill's response was not warm. 'Well, young Merthin?'

'I've parted company with Elfric.'

'I know that,' said Bill. 'And I know why.'

'You've heard Elfric's side of the story.'

'I've heard all I need to hear.'

Elfric had been talking to people before and during the service, Merthin realized. He was sure Elfric had left out of his account the fact that Griselda had tried to make Merthin the substitute father for Thurstan's baby. But he felt he would do himself no good by making excuses. Better to admit his fault. 'I realize I did wrong, and I'm sorry, but I'm still a good carpenter.'

Bill nodded agreement. 'The new ferry testifies to that.'

Merthin was encouraged. 'Will you hire me?'

'As what?'

'As a carpenter. You said I was a good one.'

'But where are your tools?'

'Elfric wouldn't give them to me.'

'And he was right – because you haven't finished your apprenticeship.'

'Then take me on as an apprentice for six months.'

'And give you a new set of tools for nothing at the end of it? I can't afford that kind of generosity.' Tools were expensive because iron and steel were costly.

'I'll work as a labourer, and save up to buy my own tools.' It would take a long time, but he was desperate.

'No.'

'Why not?'

'Because I've got a daughter too.'

This was outrageous. 'I'm not a menace to maidens, you know.'

'You're an example to apprentices. If you get away with this, what's to stop the others trying their luck?'

'That is so unjust!'

Bill shrugged. 'You might think so. But ask any other master carpenter in town. I think you'll find they feel as I do.'

'But what am I to do?'

'I don't know. You should have thought of that before you shagged her.'

'You don't care about losing a good carpenter?'

Bill shrugged again. 'All the more work for the rest of us.'

Merthin turned away. That was the trouble with guilds, he thought bitterly: it was in their interest to exclude people, for good or bad reasons. A shortage of carpenters would just drive up their wages. They had no incentive to be fair.

Howell's widow left, accompanied by her mother. Caris, liberated from her duty of commiseration, came over to Merthin. 'Why do you look unhappy?' she said. 'You hardly knew Howell.'

'I may have to leave Kingsbridge,' he said.

She went pale. 'Why on earth would you do that?'

He told her what Bill Watkin had said. 'So, you see, no one in Kingsbridge will hire me, and I can't work on my own account for I've no tools. I could live with my parents, but I can't take the food from their mouths. So I'll have to seek work some place where no one knows about Griselda. In time, perhaps I can save up enough money to buy a hammer and chisel and then move to another town and try to gain admittance to the carpenters' guild.'

As he explained this to Caris, he began to appreciate the full misery of the situation. He saw her familiar features as if for the first time, and he was enchanted again by her sparkling green eyes, her small, neat nose and the determined set of her jaw. Her mouth, he realized, did not quite fit the rest of her face: it was too wide, and the lips were too full. It unbalanced the regularity of her physiognomy the way her sensual nature subverted her tidy mind. It was a mouth made for sex, and the thought that he might have to go away and never kiss it again filled him with despair.

Caris was furious. 'This is iniquitous! They have no right.'

'That's what I think. But there seems to be nothing I can do about it. I just have to accept it.'

'Wait a minute. Let's think about this. You can live with your parents, and have your dinner at my house.'

'I don't want to become a dependant, like my father.'

'Nor should you. You can buy Howell Tyler's tools – his widow was just telling me she's asking a pound for them.'

'I haven't any money.'

'Ask my father for a loan. He's always liked you, I'm sure he'll do it.'

'But it's against the rules for anyone to employ a carpenter who isn't in the guild.'

'Rules can be broken. There must be someone in town desperate enough to defy the guild.'

Merthin realized he had allowed the old men to quench his spirit, and he was grateful to Caris for refusing to accept defeat. She was right, of course: he should stay in Kingsbridge and fight this unjust ruling. And he knew someone who was in desperate need of his talents. 'Father Joffroi,' he said.

'Is he desperate? Why?'

Merthin explained about the roof.

'Let's go and see him,' Caris said.

The priest lived in a small house next to the church. They found him preparing a dinner of salt fish in a stew with spring greens. Joffroi was in his thirties, built like a soldier, tall with broad shoulders. His manner was brusque, but he had a reputation for sticking up for the poor.

Merthin said: 'I can repair your roof without closing your church.'

Joffroi looked wary. 'You're an answer to prayer if you can.'

'I'll build a hoist that will lift the roof timbers and deposit them in the graveyard.'

'Elfric sacked you.' The priest shot an embarrassed look in Caris's direction.

She said: 'I know what happened, Father.'

Merthin said: 'He dismissed me because I would not marry his daughter. But the child she is bearing is not mine.'

Joffroi nodded. 'Some say you were treated unjustly. I can believe it. I have no great love for the guilds – their decisions are rarely unselfish. All the same, you haven't completed your apprenticeship.'

'Can any member of the carpenters' guild repair your roof without closing your church?'

'I heard you haven't even got any tools.'

'Leave that problem to me to solve.'

Joffroi looked thoughtful. 'How much do you want to be paid?'

Merthin stuck his neck out. 'Four pence a day, plus the cost of materials.'

'That's a journeyman carpenter's wage.'

'If I don't have the skill of a qualified carpenter, you shouldn't hire me.'

'You're cocky.'

'I'm just saying what I can do.'

'Arrogance is not the worst sin in the world. And I can afford four pence a day if I can keep my church open. How long will it take you to build your hoist?'

'Two weeks at the most.'

'I'm not going to pay you until I can be sure it will work.'

Merthin breathed in. He would be penniless, but he could cope with that. He could live with his parents and eat at Edmund Wooler's table. He would get by. 'Pay for the materials, and save my wages up until the first roof timber is removed and safely brought to ground.'

Joffroi hesitated. 'I'll be unpopular ... but I have no choice.' He held out his hand.

Merthin shook it.

17

ALL THE WAY FROM KINGSBRIDGE to Wigleigh – a distance of twenty miles, a full day's walk – Gwenda was hoping for a chance to use the love potion; but she was disappointed.

It was not that Wulfric was wary. On the contrary, he was open and friendly. He talked about his family, and told her how he wept every morning when he woke up and realized their deaths were not a dream. He was considerate, asking whether she was tired and needed to rest. He told her that he felt land was a trust, something a man held for a lifetime then passed to his heirs, and that when he improved his land – by weeding fields, fencing sheepfolds or clearing stones from pasture – he was fulfilling his destiny.

He even patted Skip.

By the end of the day she was more in love with him than ever. Unfortunately, he showed no sign of feeling anything for her more than a kind of camaraderie, caring but not passionate. In the forest with Sim Chapman, she had wished with all her heart that men were not so much like wild beasts; but now she wanted Wulfric to have a bit more of the beast in him. All day she did little things to arouse his interest. As if by accident, she let him see her legs, which were firm and shapely. When the terrain was hilly, she made it an excuse to take deep breaths and stick out her chest. At every opportunity she brushed against him, touched his arm or put a hand on his shoulder. None of it had the least effect. She was not pretty, she knew, but there was something about her that often made men look hard at her and breathe through their mouths – but it was not working on Wulfric.

They stopped for a rest at noon, and ate the bread and cheese they carried with them; but they drank water from a clear stream, using their hands as cups, and she had no opportunity to give him the potion.

All the same, she was happy. She had him all to herself for a whole day. She could look at him, talk to him, make him laugh, sympathize with him, and occasionally touch him. She pretended to herself that she could kiss him any time she liked, but that at the moment she was not so disposed. It was almost like being married. And it was over too soon.

They arrived in Wigleigh early in the evening. The village stood on a rise, its fields sloping away to all sides, and it was always windy. After two weeks in the bustle of Kingsbridge, the familiar place seemed small and quiet, just a scatter of rough dwellings along the road that led to the manor house and the church. The manor was as large as a Kingsbridge merchant's home, with bedrooms on an upper floor. The priest's house was also a fine dwelling, and a few of the peasant houses were substantial. But most of the homes were two-room hovels, one room normally being occupied by livestock and the other serving as kitchen and bedroom for all the family. Only the church was built of stone.

The first of the more substantial houses belonged to Wulfric's family. Its doors and shutters were closed, giving it a desolate look. He walked past it to the second big house, which was where Annet lived with her parents. He gave Gwenda a casual wave of farewell and went inside, smiling in anticipation.

She felt the sharp tug of loss, as if she had just woken out of a delightful dream. She swallowed her discontent and set out across the fields. The early-June rain had been good for the crops, and the wheat and barley were green, but now they needed sunshine to ripen them. Village women were moving along the rows of grain, bent double, pulling up weeds. Some waved to her.

As she approached her home, Gwenda felt a mixture of apprehension and anger. She had not seen her parents since the day her father had sold her to Sim Chapman for a cow. Almost certainly, Pa thought she was still with Sim. Her appearance would come as a shock. What would he say when he saw her? And what was she going to say to the father who had betrayed her trust?

She felt sure her mother knew nothing of the sale. Pa had probably told Ma some story about Gwenda running off with a boy. Ma was going to fly into a fearsome rage.

She felt happy at the prospect of seeing the little ones – Cath, Joanie and Eric. She realized now how much she had missed them.

On the far side of the hundred-acre field, half hidden in the trees at the edge of the forest, was her home. It was even smaller than the peasants' hovels, having only one room, which was shared with the cow at night. It was made of wattle-and-daub: tree branches stuck upright in the ground, with twigs interwoven basket-fashion, the gaps plugged with a sticky mixture of mud, straw and cow dung. There was a hole in the thatched roof to let out the smoke of the fire in the middle of the earth floor. Such houses lasted only a few years then had to be rebuilt. It now seemed meaner than ever to Gwenda. She was determined not to spend her life in such a place, having babies every year or two, most of whom died for lack of food. She would not live like her mother. She would rather die.

When she was still a hundred yards from the house, she saw her father coming towards her. He was carrying a jug, probably going to buy ale from Peg Perkins, Annet's mother, who was the village brewster. Pa always had money at this time of year, for there was plenty of work to be had in the fields.

At first he did not see her.

She studied his thin figure as he walked along the narrow gap between two field strips. He wore a long smock that came to his knees, a battered cap and home-made sandals tied to his feet with straw. His gait managed to be both furtive and jaunty: he always looked like a nervous foreigner defiantly pretending to be at home. His eyes were set closely either side of a big nose, and he had a wide jaw with a knob of a chin, so that his face looked like a lumpy triangle: Gwenda knew that she resembled him in that. He glanced sidelong at the women he passed in the field, as if he did not want them to know he was observing them.

As he came close, he threw her one of his sneaky looks, up from under his lowered eyelids. He looked down instantly, then looked up again. She lifted her chin and stared back at him haughtily.

Astonishment spread across his face. 'You!' he said. 'What happened?'

'Sim Chapman wasn't a tinker, he was an outlaw.'

'And where is he now?'

'He's in hell, Pa. You'll meet him there.'

'Did you kill him?'

'No.' She had long ago decided to lie about this. 'God killed him. The bridge at Kingsbridge collapsed while Sim was crossing it. God punished him for his sin. Has he punished you yet?'

'God forgives good Christians.'

'Is that all you have to say to me? That God forgives good Christians?'

'How did you escape?'

'I used my wits.'

A crafty look came over his face. 'You're a good girl,' he said.

She stared at him suspiciously. 'What mischief are you planning now?'

'You're a good girl,' he repeated. 'Go in to your mother now. You shall have a cup of ale with your supper.' He walked on.

Gwenda frowned. Pa did not seem afraid of what Ma would say when she learned the truth. Perhaps he thought Gwenda would not tell her, out of shame. Well, he was wrong.

Cath and Joanie were outside the house, playing in the dirt. When they saw Gwenda they jumped up and ran to her. Skip barked hysterically. Gwenda hugged her sisters, remembering how she had thought she would never see them again; and at that moment she was fiercely glad she had stuck a long knife into Alwyn's head.

She went inside. Ma was sitting on a stool, giving little Eric some milk, helping him hold the cup steady so that he did not spill any. She gave a cry of joy when she saw Gwenda. She put down the cup, stood up and embraced her. Gwenda began to weep.

Once she had started crying it was hard to stop. She cried because Sim had led her out of town on a rope, and because she

KEN FOLLETT

had let Alwyn fuck her, and for all the people who had died when the bridge collapsed, and because Wulfric loved Annet.

When her sobs subsided enough for her to speak again, she said: 'Pa sold me, Ma. He sold me for a cow, and I had to go with outlaws.'

'That was wrong,' her mother said.

'It was worse than wrong! He's wicked, evil – he's a devil.'

Ma withdrew from the embrace. 'Don't say such things.'

'They're true!'

'He's your father.'

'A father doesn't sell his children like livestock. I have no father.'

'He's fed you for eighteen years.'

Gwenda stared uncomprehendingly. 'How can you be so hard? He sold me to outlaws!'

'And he got us a cow. So there's milk for Eric, even though my breasts have dried up. And you're here, aren't you?'

Gwenda was shocked. 'You're defending him!'

'He's all I've got, Gwenda. He's not a prince. He's not even a peasant. He's a landless labourer. But he's done everything he can for this family for almost twenty-five years. He worked when he could and thieved when he had to. He kept you alive, and your brother, and with a fair wind he'll do the same for Cath and Joanie and Eric. Whatever his faults, we'd be worse off without him. So don't you call him a devil.'

Gwenda was struck dumb. She had hardly got used to the idea that her father had betrayed her. Now she had to face the fact that her mother was as bad. She felt disoriented. It was like when the bridge had moved under her feet: she could hardly understand what was happening to her.

Her father came into the house carrying the jug of ale. He seemed not to notice the atmosphere. He took three wooden cups from the shelf over the fireplace. 'Now, then,' he said cheerfully. 'Let's drink to the return of our big girl.'

Gwenda was hungry and thirsty after walking all day. She took the cup and drank deeply. But she knew her father in this mood. 'What are you planning?' she said.

'Well, now,' he said. 'It's the Shiring Fair next week, isn't it?'

'So what?'

'Well ... we could do it again.'

She could hardly believe what she was hearing. 'Do what again?'

'I sell you, you go with the buyer, then you escape and come home. You're none the worse.'

'None the worse?'

'And we've got a cow worth twelve shillings! Why, it takes me near half a year of labouring to earn twelve shillings.'

'And after that? What then?'

'Well, there's other fairs – Winchester, Gloucester, I don't know how many.' He refilled her cup from the ale jug. 'Why – this could be better than the year you stole Sir Gerald's purse!'

She did not drink. There was a bitter taste in her mouth, as if she had eaten something corrupt. She thought of arguing with him. Harsh words came to her lips, angry accusations, curses – but she did not speak them. The way she felt was beyond rage. What was the point of having a row? She could never trust her father again. And, because Ma refused to be disloyal to him, Gwenda could not trust her either.

'What am I to do?' she said aloud, but she did not want an answer from anyone in the room: the question was to herself. In this family she had become a commodity, to be sold at city fairs. If she was not prepared to accept that, what could she do?

She could leave.

She realized with a shock that this house was no longer a home to her. The blow shook the foundations of her existence. She had lived here since before she could remember. Now she did not feel safe here. She had to get out.

Not next week, she realized; not even tomorrow morning – she had to go now.

She had nowhere to go, but that made no difference. To stay here, and eat the bread her father put on the table, would be to yield to his authority. She would be accepting his evaluation of her, as a commodity to be sold. She was sorry she had drunk the first cup of ale. Her only chance was to reject him immediately and get out from under his roof.

Gwenda looked at her mother. 'You're wrong,' she said. 'He is a devil. And the old stories are right: when you make a bargain with the devil, you end up paying more than you thought.'

Ma looked away.

Gwenda stood up. The refilled cup was still in her hand. She tipped it, pouring the ale on the floor. Skip immediately started to lick it up.

Her father said angrily: 'I paid a farthing for this jug of ale!'

'Goodbye,' said Gwenda, and she walked out.

18

ON THE FOLLOWING SUNDAY, Gwenda attended the court hearing that would decide the fate of the man she loved.

The manorial court was held in the church after the service. It was the forum in which the village took collective action. Some of the questions it addressed were disputes – arguments over field boundaries, accusations of theft or rape, quarrels about debts – but more often it made pragmatic decisions, such as when to begin ploughing with the communal eight-ox team.

In theory, the lord of the manor sat in judgement over his serfs. But Norman law – brought to England by invaders from France almost three centuries earlier – compelled lords to follow the customs of their predecessors; and, in order to find out what those customs were, they had to formally consult twelve men of good standing in the village – a jury. So, in practice, the proceedings often became a negotiation between lord and villagers.

On this particular Sunday, Wigleigh had no lord. Sir Stephen had been killed in the collapse of the bridge. Gwenda had brought this news to the village. She also reported that Earl Roland, who had the task of appointing Stephen's replacement, had been gravely injured. On the day before she left Kingsbridge, the earl had recovered consciousness for the first time – but he had woken into a fever so violent that he was unable to speak a coherent sentence. So there was no prospect of a new lord of Wigleigh yet.

This was not an unusual circumstance. Lords were frequently away: at war, in Parliament, fighting lawsuits, or just attending on their earl or the king. Earl Roland always appointed a deputy, usually one of his sons – but, in this case, he had not been able to do so. In the absence of an overlord, the bailiff had to manage the landholding as best he could.

The job of a bailiff or reeve was, in theory, to carry out the lord's decisions, but this inevitably gave him a degree of power over his fellows. Exactly how much power depended on the lord's personal preference: some held tight control, others were lax. Sir Stephen had kept a loose rein, but Earl Roland was notoriously strict.

Nate Reeve had been bailiff to Sir Stephen and to Sir Henry before him, and would presumably be bailiff to whoever came next. He was a hunchback, a small, bent figure, thin and energetic. He was shrewd and greedy, careful to make the most of his limited power by demanding bribes from the villagers at every opportunity.

Gwenda disliked Nate. It was not his greed she objected to: all bailiffs had that vice. But Nate was a man twisted by resentment as much as by his physical defect. His father had been bailiff to the earl of Shiring, but Nate had not inherited that grand position, and he blamed his hump for the fact that he had ended up in the small village of Wigleigh. He seemed to hate all young, strong, handsome people. In his leisure hours he liked to drink wine with Perkin, Annet's father – who always paid for the liquor.

The question before the court today was what to do about Wulfric's family's land.

It was a large holding. Peasants were not all equal, and they did not have equal lands. The standard was a virgate, which was thirty acres in this part of England. In theory a virgate was the area of land one man could farm, and normally yielded enough to feed one family. However, most Wigleigh peasants had a half-virgate, fifteen acres, or thereabouts. They were obliged to find additional means of support for their families: netting birds in the woods, trapping fish in the stream that ran through Brookfield, making belts or sandals from cheap leather offcuts, weaving cloth from yarn for Kingsbridge merchants, or poaching the king's deer in the forest. A few had more than a virgate. Perkin had a hundred acres, and Wulfric's father, Samuel, had had ninety. Such wealthy peasants needed help to farm their land, either from their sons and other relatives, or from hired labourers such as Gwenda's father.

When a serf died, his land might be inherited by his widow,

his sons or a married daughter. In any event, the handover had to be licensed by the lord, and a stiff tax, called a heriot, was due. In normal circumstances Samuel's land would automatically have been inherited by his two sons, and there would have been no need for a court hearing. They would have clubbed together to pay the heriot, then either divided up the land or farmed it together, and made some arrangement for their mother. But one of Samuel's sons had died with him, which complicated matters.

Every adult in the village attended the court, in general. Gwenda had a particular interest today. Wulfric's future would be decided, and the fact that he planned to spend that future with another woman did not dampen Gwenda's concern. Perhaps she should have wished him a miserable life with Annet, she sometimes thought; but she could not. She wanted him to be happy.

When the service was over, a large wooden chair and two benches were brought in from the manor house. Nate took the chair and the jurymen sat on the benches. Everyone else stood.

Wulfric spoke simply. 'My father held ninety acres of the lord of Wigleigh,' he said. 'Fifty acres were held by his father before him, and forty by his uncle who died ten years ago. As my mother is dead, and so is my brother, and I have no sisters, I am the sole heir.'

'How old are you?' said Nate.

'Sixteen years.'

'You can't even call yourself a man, yet.'

It seemed Nate was going to make things difficult. Gwenda knew why. He wanted a bribe. But Wulfric had no money.

'Years aren't everything,' Wulfric said. 'I'm taller and stronger than most grown men.'

Aaron Appletree, one of the jurors, said: 'David Johns inherited from his father when he was eighteen.'

Nate said: 'Eighteen isn't sixteen. I don't recall an instance where a sixteen-year-old was allowed to inherit.'

David Johns was not a juror, and he was standing next to Gwenda. 'I didn't have no ninety acres, neither,' he said, and there was a ripple of laughter. David had a half-virgate, like most of them.

Another juror spoke. 'Ninety acres is too much for one man, let alone a boy. Why, it was farmed by three until now.' The speaker was Billy Howard, a man in his middle twenties who had wooed Annet unsuccessfully – which might be why he wanted to side with Nate in putting obstacles in Wulfric's way. 'I've got forty acres, and I have to hire labourers at harvest time.'

Several of the men nodded agreement. Gwenda began to feel pessimistic. It was not going Wulfric's way.

'I can get help,' Wulfric said.

Nate said: 'Have you got money to pay labourers?'

Wulfric looked a bit desperate, and Gwenda's heart went out to him. 'My father's purse was lost when the bridge collapsed, and I spent what money I had on the funeral,' he said. 'But I can offer my labourers a share of the harvest.'

Nate shook his head. 'Everyone in the village is already working full time on their own lands, and those who have no land are already employed. And no one is likely to give up a job that pays cash for one that offers a share of an uncertain crop.'

'I will get the harvest in,' Wulfric said with passionate determination. 'I can work day and night, if I have to. I'll prove to you all that I can handle it.'

There was so much yearning on his handsome face that Gwenda wanted to jump up and shout her support for him. But the men were shaking their heads. Everyone knew that one man could not harvest ninety acres on his own.

Nate turned to Perkin. 'He's engaged to your daughter. Can't you do something for him?'

Perkin looked thoughtful. 'Perhaps you should transfer the land to me, for the time being. I could pay the heriot. Then, when he marries Annet, he could take over his land.'

'No!' Wulfric said immediately.

Gwenda knew why he was so against the idea. Perkin was nothing if not sly. He would spend every waking minute between now and the wedding trying to figure out a way of keeping Wulfric's land for himself.

Nate said to Wulfric: 'If you have no money, how will you pay the heriot?'

'I'll have money when I get the harvest in.'

'If you get the harvest in. And then it may not be enough. Your father paid three pounds for his father's lands and two pounds for his uncle's.'

Gwenda gasped. Five pounds was a fortune. It seemed impossible that Wulfric could raise so much money. It would probably have taken all his family's savings.

Nate went on: 'Besides, the heriot is normally paid before the inheritor takes possession – not after the harvest.'

Aaron Appletree said: 'In the circumstances, Nate, you might show leniency on that point.'

'Might I? A lord may show leniency, for he holds sway over his own possessions. But if a bailiff shows leniency, he's giving away someone else's gold.'

'But we will only be making a recommendation, in any case. Nothing will be final until approved by the new lord of Wigleigh, whoever he may be.'

That was true, strictly speaking, Gwenda thought; but in practice it was unlikely a new lord would overturn an inheritance from father to son.

Wulfric said: 'Sir, my father's heriot was not so much as five pounds.'

'We must check the rolls.' Nate's response was so quick that Gwenda guessed he had been waiting for Wulfric to challenge the amount. Nate often engineered a pause of some kind in the middle of a hearing, she reflected. She presumed it was to give the parties an opportunity to offer him a bribe. Perhaps he thought Wulfric was concealing some money.

Two jurors brought from the vestry the chest containing the manorial rolls, the record of the manor court's decisions, written on long strips of parchment rolled into cylinders. Nate could read and write – a bailiff had to be literate, in order to compile accounts for the lord. He searched through the box for the right one.

Gwenda felt that Wulfric was doing badly. His plain speaking and evident honesty were not enough. Nate wanted above all else to make sure he collected the lord's heriot. Perkin was manoeuvring to get the land for himself. Billy Howard wanted to do Wulfric down out of sheer malice. And Wulfric had no money for a bribe.

He was also guileless. He believed that if he stated his case he would get justice. He had no sense of managing the situation.

Perhaps she could help him. A child of Joby's could not grow up without learning something about guile.

Wulfric had not appealed to the villagers' self-interest in his arguments. She would do so for him. She turned to David Johns, standing beside her. 'I'm surprised you men aren't more worried about this,' she said.

He gave her a shrewd look. 'What are you getting at, lass?'

'Despite the sudden deaths, this is an inheritance from father to son. If you let Nate quibble about this one, he'll question them all. He can always dream up some reason for arguing about a legacy. Aren't you afraid he'll interfere with your own sons' rights?'

David looked worried. 'You might have a point, there, girl,' he said, and he turned to talk to his neighbour on the other side.

Gwenda also felt it was a mistake for Wulfric to demand a final ruling today. Better to ask for a temporary judgement, which the jurymen would grant more readily. She went to speak to Wulfric. He was arguing with Perkin and Annet. When Gwenda appeared Perkin looked suspicious, and Annet put her nose in the air, but Wulfric was as courteous as ever. 'Hello, my travelling companion,' he said. 'I heard you left your father's house.'

'He threatened to sell me.'

'A second time?'

'As many times as I could escape. He thinks he's found a bottomless purse.'

'Where are you living?'

'Widow Huberts took me in. And I've been working for the bailiff, on the lord's lands. A penny a day, sunrise to sunset – Nate likes his labourers to go home tired. Do you think he'll give you what you want?'

Wulfric made a face. 'He seems reluctant.'

'A woman would handle it so differently.'

He looked surprised. 'How so?'

Annet glared at her, but Gwenda ignored the look. 'A woman would not demand a ruling, especially when everyone knows that today's decision isn't final. She would not risk a No for the chance of a Maybe.'

Wulfric looked thoughtful. 'What would she do?'

'She would just ask to be allowed to continue working the land, for now. She would let the binding decision wait until the new lord is appointed. She would know that in the interim everyone would get used to her being in possession, so that when the new lord showed up his approval would seem like a formality. She would gain her objective without giving people much chance to argue about it.'

Wulfric was not sure. 'Well...'

'It's not what you want, but it's the most you can get today. And how can Nate refuse you, when he has no one else to bring in the harvest?'

Wulfric nodded. He was working out the possibilities. 'People would see me reaping the crop, and become accustomed to the idea. After that, it would seem unjust to deny me the inheritance. And I'd be able to pay the heriot, or some of it.'

'You'd be a lot closer to your goal than you are now.'

'Thank you. You're very wise.' He touched her arm, then turned back to Annet. She said something sharp to him in an undertone. Her father looked annoyed.

Gwenda turned away. Don't tell me I'm wise, she thought. Tell me I'm ... what? Beautiful? Never. The love of your life? That's Annet. A true friend? To hell with that. So what do I want? Why am I desperate to help you?

She had no answer.

She noticed David Johns speaking emphatically to one of the jurors, Aaron Appletree.

Nate flourished the manor roll. 'Wulfric's father, Samuel, paid thirty shillings to inherit from his father, and a pound to inherit from his uncle.' A shilling was twelve pennies. There was no shilling coin, but everyone talked about shillings just the same. Twenty shillings made a pound. The sum Nate had announced was exactly half what he had originally said.

David Johns spoke up. 'A man's lands should go to his son,'

he said. 'We don't want to give our new lord, whoever he may be, the impression that he can pick and choose who shall inherit.'

There was a murmur of agreement.

Wulfric stepped forward. 'Bailiff, I know you can't make a final decision today, and I'm content to wait until the new lord is appointed. All I ask is that I should be allowed to continue to work the land. I will bring in the harvest, I swear it. But nothing is lost to you if I fail. And nothing is promised to me if I succeed. When the new lord comes, I will throw myself on his mercy.'

Nate looked cornered. Gwenda felt sure he had been hoping for some way of making money out of this. Perhaps he had expected a bribe from Perkin, Wulfric's prospective father-in-law. She watched Nate's face as he tried to think of a way to refuse Wulfric's more modest request. As he hesitated, one or two villagers began to mutter, and he realized he was doing himself no good by revealing his reluctance. 'Very well,' he said with a show of grace that was not very convincing. 'What does the jury say?'

Aaron Appletree conferred briefly with his fellow jurors, then said: 'Wulfric's request is modest and reasonable. He should occupy the lands of his father until the new lord of Wigleigh is appointed.'

Gwenda sighed with relief.

Nate said: 'Thank you, jurymen.'

The court broke up and people began to head home for dinner. Most of the villagers could afford to eat meat once a week, and Sunday was the usual day they chose. Even Joby and Ethna could generally manage a stew of squirrel or hedgehog, and at this time of year there were plenty of young rabbits to be caught. Widow Huberts had a neck of mutton in a pot on the fire.

Gwenda caught Wulfric's eye as they were leaving the church. 'Well done,' she said as they strolled out together. 'He couldn't refuse you, though he seemed to want to.'

'It was your idea,' he said admiringly. 'You knew exactly what I needed to say. I don't know how to thank you.'

She resisted the temptation to tell him. They walked through the graveyard. She said: 'How will you manage the harvest?'

'I don't know.'

'Why don't you let me come and labour for you?'

'I've no money.'

'I don't care, I'll work for food.'

He stopped at the gate, turned and gave her a candid look. 'No, Gwenda. I don't think that would be a good plan. Annet wouldn't like it and, to be frank, she'd be right.'

Gwenda found herself blushing. There was no doubt what he meant. If he had wanted to reject her because she might be too weak, or something, there would have been no need for the direct look, nor for the mention of his fiancée's name. He knew, she realized with mortification, that she was in love with him, and he was refusing her offer of help because he did not want to encourage her hopeless passion. 'All right,' she whispered, looking down. 'Whatever you say.'

He smiled warmly. 'But thank you for the offer.'

She made no reply and, after a moment, he turned and walked away.

19

GWENDA GOT UP while it was still dark.

She slept in the straw on the floor of Widow Huberts's house. Somehow her sleeping mind knew the time, and woke her just before dawn. The widow, lying next to her, did not stir when Gwenda unwrapped her blanket and stood up. Finding her way by touch, she opened the back door and stepped into the yard. Skip followed her, shaking himself.

She stood still for a moment. There was a fresh breeze, as always in Wigleigh. The night was not totally black, and she could make out vague shapes: the duck house, the privy, the pear tree. She could not see the neighbouring house, which was Wulfric's; but she heard a low growl from his dog, tethered outside the small sheepfold, and she murmured a quiet phrase so that it would recognize her voice and be reassured.

It was a peaceful time – but nowadays there were too many such moments in her day. All her life she had lived in a tiny house full of babies and children, and at any instant at least one of them was clamouring for food, crying because of a minor hurt, shouting a protest or screaming with helpless infantile rage. She would never have guessed she might miss that. But she did, living with the quiet widow, who chatted amiably enough but was equally comfortable with silence. Sometimes Gwenda longed to hear a child cry, just so that she could pick it up and comfort it.

She found the old wooden bucket and washed her hands and face, then went back inside. She located the table in the dark, opened the bread box and cut a thick slice from the week-old loaf. Then she set out, eating the bread as she walked.

The village was silent: she was the first up. Peasants worked from sunup to sundown, and at this time of year it was a long, weary day. They treasured every moment of rest. Only Gwenda also used the hour between dawn and sunrise, and the hour of twilight at the end of the day.

Dawn broke as she left the houses behind and set out across the fields. Wigleigh had three great fields: Hundredacre, Brookfield and Longfield. Different crops were grown on each in a three-year cycle. Wheat and rye, the most valuable grains, were sown in the first year; then lesser crops such as oats, barley, peas and beans in the second year; and in the third year the field was left fallow. This year, Hundredacre was in wheat and rye, Brookfield in various secondary crops, and Longfield was fallow. Each field was divided into strips of about one acre; and each serf's land consisted of a number of strips scattered across all three fields.

Gwenda went to Hundredacre and began weeding one of Wulfric's strips, pulling up the persistent new growth of dockweed, marigolds and dogfennel from between his stalks of wheat. She was happy working on his land, helping him, whether he knew about it or not. Every time she bent down, she was saving his back the same effort; every time she pulled a weed she made his crop greater. It was like giving him presents. As she worked she thought of him, picturing his face when he laughed, hearing his voice, the deep voice of a man yet with the eagerness of a boy. She touched the green shoots of his wheat and imagined she was stroking his hair.

She weeded until sunrise then moved to the demesne lands – those strips farmed by the lord, or his labourers – and worked for pay. Although Sir Stephen was dead, his crops still had to be reaped, and his successor would demand a strict account of what had been done with the proceeds. At sundown, having earned her daily bread, Gwenda would move to another part of Wulfric's holding and work there until dark – longer, if there was a moon.

She had said nothing to Wulfric. But, in a village of only two hundred people, few things remained secret for long. Widow Huberts had asked her, with gentle curiosity, what she hoped to achieve. 'He's going to marry Perkin's girl, you know – you can't prevent that.'

'I just want him to succeed,' Gwenda had replied. 'He deserves it. He's an honest man with a good heart, and he's willing to work until he drops. I want him to be happy, even if he does marry that bitch.'

Today the demesne workers were in Brookfield, harvesting the lord's early peas and beans, and Wulfric was nearby, digging a drainage ditch: the land was swampy after the heavy rain of early June. Gwenda watched him working, wearing only his drawers and boots, his broad back bending over the spade. He moved as tirelessly as a millwheel. Only the sweat glistening on his skin betrayed the effort he was making. At midday Annet came to him, looking pretty with a green ribbon in her hair, carrying a jug of ale and some bread and cheese wrapped in a piece of sacking.

Nate Reeve rang a bell, and everyone stopped work and retreated to the fringe of trees at the north end of the field. Nate gave out cider, bread and onions to the demesne workers: dinner was included in their remuneration. Gwenda sat with her back against a hornbeam tree and studied Wulfric and Annet with the fascination of a condemned man watching the carpenter build the gallows.

At first, Annet was her usual flirtatious self, tilting her head, batting her eyelids, playfully striking Wulfric in mock punishment for something he said. Then she became serious, speaking to him insistently while he seemed to protest innocence. They both looked at Gwenda, and she guessed they were talking about her. She presumed Annet had found out about her working on Wulfric's strips in the mornings and evenings. Eventually Annet left, looking petulant, and Wulfric finished his dinner in thoughtful solitude.

After eating, everyone rested for the remainder of the dinner hour. The older people lay full length on the ground and dozed while the youngsters chatted. Wulfric came to where Gwenda sat and crouched beside her. 'You've been weeding my strips,' he said.

Gwenda was not going to apologize. 'I suppose Annet scolded you.'

'She doesn't want you working for me.'

'What would she like me to do, put the weeds back in the earth?'

He glanced around and lowered his voice, not wanting others

to hear – although everyone could surely guess what he and Gwenda were saying to one another. 'I know you mean well, and I'm grateful, but it's causing trouble.'

She enjoyed being this close to him. He smelled of earth and sweat. 'You need help,' she said. 'And Annet isn't much use.'

'Please don't criticize her. In fact, don't speak of her at all.'

'All right, but you can't get the harvest in alone.'

He sighed. 'If only the sun would shine.' Automatically, he looked up at the sky, a peasant reflex. There was thick cloud from horizon to horizon. All the grain crops were struggling in the cool, damp weather.

'Let me work for you,' Gwenda begged. 'Tell Annet you need me. A man is supposed to be master of his wife, not the other way around.'

'I'll think about it,' he said.

But the next day he hired a labourer.

He was a travelling man who showed up at the end of the afternoon. The villagers gathered around him in the twilight to hear his story. His name was Gram and he came from Salisbury. He said his wife and children had been killed when his house burned down. He was on his way to Kingsbridge, where he hoped to get employment, perhaps at the priory. His brother was a monk there.

Gwenda said: 'I probably know him. My brother, Philemon, has worked at the priory for years. What's your brother's name?'

'John.' There were two monks called John but, before Gwenda could ask which was Gram's brother, he went on: 'When I started out, I had a little money to buy food along the way. Then I was robbed by outlaws, and now I'm penniless.'

There was a lot of sympathy for the man. Wulfric invited him to sleep at his house. The next day, Saturday, he started to work for Wulfric, accepting board and lodging and a share of the harvest as his remuneration.

Gram worked hard all day Saturday. Wulfric was shallow-ploughing his fallow land in Longfield to destroy thistles. It was a two-man job: Gram led the horse, whipping it on when it flagged, while Wulfric guided the plough. On Sunday they rested.

In church on Sunday, Gwenda burst into tears when she saw

Cath, Joanie and Eric. She had not realized how badly she missed them. She held Eric through the service. Afterwards, her mother spoke harshly to her. 'You're breaking your heart for that Wulfric. Weeding his strips won't make him love you. He's cross-eyed for that worthless Annet.'

'I know,' Gwenda said. 'But I want to help him anyway.'

'You should leave the village. There's nothing for you here.'

She knew her mother was right. 'I will,' she said. 'I'll leave the day after their wedding.'

Ma lowered her voice. 'If you must stay, watch out for your father. He hasn't given up hope of another twelve shillings.'

'What do you mean?' Gwenda asked.

Ma just shook her head.

'He can't sell me now,' Gwenda said. 'I've left his house. He doesn't feed or shelter me. I work for the lord of Wigleigh. I'm not Pa's to dispose of any longer.'

'Just watch out,' said Ma, and she would say no more.

Outside the church the travelling man, Gram, talked to Gwenda, asking her questions about herself, and suggested they take a stroll together after dinner. She guessed what he meant by a 'stroll' and turned him down flat, but later she saw him with yellow-haired Joanna, the daughter of David Johns, who was only fifteen and stupid enough to fall for the blandishments of a travelling man.

On Monday, Gwenda was weeding Wulfric's wheat on Hundredacre in the half-light before sunrise when Wulfric came across the field towards her at a run. His face was grim with fury.

She had continued to defy his wishes, working on his lands every morning and evening, and it looked as if she had driven him too far. What would he do – beat her up? After the way she had provoked him, he could probably do violence to her with impunity – people would say she had asked for it, and she had no one to stick up for her now that she had left her parents' home. She felt scared. She had seen Wulfric break Ralph Fitzgerald's nose.

Then she told herself not to be foolish. Although he had been in many fights, she had never known him to strike a woman or a child. All the same, his anger made her tremble.

But it was nothing like that. As soon as he got within hailing distance he shouted: 'Have you seen Gram?'

'No, why?'

He came closer and stopped, breathing hard. 'How long have you been here?'

'I got up before dawn.'

Wulfric's shoulders slumped. 'Then, if he came this way, he's out of reach by now.'

'What's happened?'

'He's disappeared – and so has my horse.'

That explained Wulfric's rage. A horse was a valuable asset – only wealthy peasants such as his father could afford one. Gwenda recalled how quickly Gram had changed the subject when she said she might know his brother. He did not have a brother at the priory, of course, nor had he lost his wife and child in a fire. He was a liar who had wormed his way into the confidence of the villagers with the intention of stealing. 'What fools we were to listen to his story,' she said.

'And I the biggest fool of all, to take him into my house,' Wulfric said bitterly. 'He stayed just long enough for the animals to get to know him, so that the horse was willing to go with him, and the dog didn't bark when he left.'

Gwenda's heart ached for Wulfric, losing the horse at a time when he needed it most. 'I don't think he came this way,' she said thoughtfully. 'He can't have left before me – the night was too dark. And if he had followed me I would have seen him.' There was only one road into and out of the village, and it dead-ended at the manor house. But there were numerous pathways across the fields. 'He probably took the lane between Brookfield and Longfield – it's the quickest way into the forest.'

'The horse can't move very fast in the woods. I might catch him yet.' Wulfric turned and ran back the way he had come.

'Good luck,' Gwenda called after him, and he waved acknowledgement without turning his head.

However, he did not have good luck.

Late that afternoon, as Gwenda was carrying a sack of peas from Brookfield to the lord's barn, she walked past Longfield and saw Wulfric again. He was digging over his fallow land with a spade. Obviously he had not caught up with Gram, nor retrieved his horse.

She put down the sack and crossed the field to speak to him. 'You can't do this,' she said. 'You've got thirty acres here, and you've ploughed, what, ten? No man can dig over twenty acres.'

He did not meet her eye. He carried on digging, his face set. 'I can't plough,' he said. 'I've no horse.'

'Put yourself in harness,' she said. 'You're strong, and it's a light plough – you're only killing thistles.'

'I've no one to guide the plough.'

'Yes, you have.'

He stared at her.

'I'll do it,' she said.

He shook his head.

She said: 'You've lost your family, and now you've lost your horse. You can't manage on your own. You have no choice. You have to let me help you.'

He looked away, across the fields, towards the village, and she knew he was thinking about Annet.

'I'll be ready first thing tomorrow morning,' Gwenda said.

His gaze returned to her. His face worked with emotion. He was torn between love of the land and a desire to please Annet.

'I'll knock on your door,' Gwenda said. 'We'll plough the rest together.' She turned and walked away, then stopped and looked back.

He did not say Yes.

But he did not say No.

*

THEY PLOUGHED FOR two days, then made hay, then picked spring vegetables.

Now that Gwenda was no longer earning money to pay Widow Huberts for bed and board, she needed somewhere else to sleep, so she moved into Wulfric's cowshed. She explained the reason, and he made no objection.

After the first day, Annet ceased to bring Wulfric's dinner at midday, so Gwenda would prepare food for them both from his cupboard: bread, ale in a jug, boiled eggs or cold bacon, and spring onions or beets. Once again, Wulfric accepted the change without comment.

She still had the love potion. The little pottery vial was in a tiny leather bag attached to a thong around her neck. It hung between her breasts, hidden from view. She could have dosed his ale at any dinner time, but she would not be able to take advantage of its effects out in the fields in the middle of the day.

Every evening he went to Perkin's house and had supper with Annet and her family, so Gwenda sat alone in his kitchen. When he returned he often looked grim, but he said nothing to Gwenda, so she assumed he must have overruled Annet's objections. He went to bed without taking anything more to eat or drink, so she was not able to use the potion.

On the Saturday after Gram ran off, Gwenda made herself a supper of greens boiled with salt pork. Wulfric's house was stocked with food for four adults, so there was plenty to eat. The evenings were cool, even though it was now July, and after she had eaten she put another log on the kitchen fire and sat watching it catch alight, thinking of the simple, predictable life she had led until a few short weeks ago, marvelling at how that life had collapsed as completely as the bridge at Kingsbridge.

When the door opened, she thought it was Wulfric coming home. She always retired to the cowshed when he came back, but she enjoyed the few friendly words they exchanged before going to bed. She looked up eagerly, expecting to see his handsome face; but she suffered an unpleasant shock.

It was not Wulfric, but her father.

With him was a rough-looking stranger.

She leaped to her feet, full of fear. 'What do you want?'

Skip gave a hostile bark, but retreated from Joby in fear.

Joby said: 'Now, then, my little girl, no need to be afraid, I'm your pa.'

She recalled, with dismay, her mother's vague warning in church. 'Who is he?' she said, pointing at the stranger.

'This here is Jonah from Abingdon, a dealer in hides.'

Jonah might once have been a merchant, Gwenda thought grimly, and he might even come from Abingdon, but his boots were worn, his clothes were filthy, and his matted hair and straggly beard showed that he had not visited a city barber for some years.

Showing more courage than she felt, Gwenda said: 'Get away from me.'

'I told you she was feisty,' Joby said to Jonah. 'But she's a good girl, and strong.'

Jonah spoke for the first time. 'Not to worry,' he said. He licked his lips as he studied Gwenda, and she wished she were wearing more than her light wool dress. 'I've broken in a few fillies in my time,' he added.

Gwenda had no doubt that her father had carried out his threat and sold her again. She had thought that leaving his house would make her safe. Surely the villagers would not permit the abduction of a labourer employed by one of their number? But it was dark, now, and she might be far away before anyone realized what had happened.

There was no one to help her.

All the same, she was not going without a fight.

She looked around desperately, searching for a weapon. The log she had put on a few minutes ago was blazing at one end, but it was about eighteen inches long, and the other end stuck out invitingly. She bent quickly and snatched it up.

'Now, then, no need for that sort of thing,' said Joby. 'You don't want to hurt your old pa, do you?' He stepped closer.

A rush of rage overwhelmed her. How dare he speak of himself as her old pa when he was trying to sell her? Suddenly she did want to hurt him. She leaped at him, screaming with rage, thrusting the burning log at his face.

He jumped back, but she kept coming, mad with fury. Skip yapped frantically. Joby lifted his arms to protect himself, trying to knock the brand away, but she was strong, too. His flailing arms failed to stop her rush, and she pushed the red-hot end of the log into his face. He screamed in pain as it scorched his cheek. His dirty beard caught fire, and there was a sickening smell of roasting flesh.

Then Gwenda was grabbed from behind. Jonah's arms encircled her, pinning her own arms to her side. She dropped the burning log. Flames leaped up immediately from the straw on the floor. Skip, terrified of fire, ran out of the house. Gwenda struggled, wriggling in Jonah's grasp, throwing herself from side to side, but he was surprisingly strong. He lifted her off her feet.

A tall figure appeared in the doorway. Gwenda saw only the shape, then it disappeared again. Gwenda felt herself thrown to the ground. For a moment she was stunned. When she came to her senses, Jonah was kneeling on her, tying her hands with a rope.

The tall figure reappeared, and Gwenda recognized Wulfric. This time he was carrying a big oak bucket. Swiftly, he emptied the bucket on to the burning straw, putting out the flames. Then he changed his grip, swung the bucket and hit the kneeling Jonah a mighty blow on top of the head.

Jonah's grip on Gwenda relaxed. She pulled her wrists apart and felt the rope loosen. Wulfric swung the bucket and hit Jonah a second time, even harder. Jonah's eyes closed and he slumped to the floor.

Joby put out the flames of his burning beard by pressing his sleeve against it, then sank to his knees, moaning in agony.

Wulfric picked up the unconscious Jonah by his tunic front. 'Who on earth is this?'

'His name is Jonah. My father wanted to sell me to him.'

Wulfric lifted the man by the belt, carried him to the front door, and threw him out into the road.

Joby groaned. 'Help me, my face is burned.'

'Help you?' said Wulfric. 'You've set fire to my house and attacked my labourer, and you want me to help you? Get out!'

Joby got to his feet, moaning piteously, and staggered to the front door. Gwenda searched her heart and found no compassion. What little love she might have had left for him had been destroyed tonight. As he went out through the door, she hoped he would never speak to her again.

Perkin came to the back door, carrying a rush light. 'What happened?' he said. 'I thought I heard a scream.' Gwenda saw Annet hovering behind him.

Wulfric answered the question. 'Joby came here with another ruffian. They tried to take Gwenda away.'

Perkin grunted. 'You seem to have dealt with the problem.'

'Without difficulty.' Wulfric realized he still had the bucket in his hand and he put it down.

Annet said: 'Are you hurt?'

'Not in the least.'

'Do you need anything?'

'I just want to go to sleep.'

Perkin and Annet took the hint and went away. No one else seemed to have heard the commotion. Wulfric closed the doors.

He looked at Gwenda in the firelight. 'How do you feel?'

'Shaky.' She sat on the bench and leaned her elbows on the kitchen table.

He went to the cupboard. 'Drink a little wine to steady yourself.' He took out a small barrel, put it on the table and got two cups off the shelf.

Gwenda was suddenly alert. Could this be her chance? She tried to pull herself together. She would have to act quickly.

Wulfric poured wine into the cups, then returned the barrel to the cupboard.

Gwenda had only a second or two. While his back was turned, she reached into her bosom and pulled out the bag that hung around her neck on its leather thong. She fumbled the vial from the bag. With a trembling hand she unstoppered it and emptied it into his cup.

He turned around as she was pushing the bag back into her neckline. She patted herself as if she had merely been straightening her clothing. Typical man, he noticed nothing amiss, and sat opposite her at the table.

She picked up her cup and raised it in a toast. 'You saved me,' she said. 'Thank you.'

'Your hand is shaking,' he said. 'You've had a nasty shock.'

They both drank.

Gwenda wondered how long the potion would take to have its effect.

Wulfric said: 'You saved me, by helping me in the fields. Thank you.'

They drank again.

'I don't know what's worse,' Gwenda said. 'To have a father like mine, or to be like you and have no father at all.'

'I feel sorry for you,' Wulfric said thoughtfully. 'At least I have good memories of my parents.' He emptied his cup. 'I don't usually drink wine – I don't like that woozy feeling – but this is great.'

She watched him carefully. Mattie Wise had said that he would become amorous. Gwenda looked for the signs. Sure enough, he soon began to stare as if seeing her for the first time. After a while he said: 'You know, you've got such a nice face. There's a lot of kindness in it.'

Now she was supposed to use her feminine wiles to seduce him. But, she realized with a panicky feeling, she had had no practice at this. Women such as Annet did it all the time. However, when she thought of the things Annet did – smiling coyly, touching her hair, fluttering her eyelashes – she could not bring herself even to try. She would just feel stupid.

'You're kind,' she said, talking to gain time. 'But your face shows something else.'

'What?'

'Strength. The kind that comes, not from big muscles, but from determination.'

'I feel strong tonight.' He grinned. 'You said no man could dig over twenty acres – but I feel as if I could, right now.'

She put her hand over his on the table. 'Enjoy your rest,' she said. 'There's plenty of time for digging.'

He looked at her small hand on his large one. 'We've got different colour skin,' he said, as if discovering an amazing fact. 'Look: yours is brown, mine's pink.'

'Different skin, different hair, different eyes. I wonder what our babies would be like?'

He smiled at the thought. Then his expression changed as he realized something was wrong with what she had said. Abruptly, his face became grave. The change might have been comical if she had not cared so much about his feelings for her. He said solemnly: 'We're not going to have babies.' He took his hand away.

'Let's not think about that,' she said desperately.

'Don't you sometimes wish . . .' He tailed off.

'What?'

'Don't you sometimes wish the world could be different from the way it is?'

She got up, walked around the table and sat close to him. 'Don't wish,' she said. 'We're alone, and it's night. You can do anything you want.' She looked directly into his eyes. 'Anything.'

He stared back at her. She saw the yearning in his face, and realized with a thrill of triumph that he desired her. It had required a potion to bring it out, but it was unmistakably genuine. Right now he wanted nothing in the world other than to make love to her.

Still he made no move.

She took his hand. He did not resist as she drew it to her lips. She held the big, rough fingers, then pressed the palm to her mouth. She kissed it, then licked it with the tip of her tongue. Then she pressed his hand to one breast.

His hand closed over it, making it seem very small. His mouth opened a fraction, and she could see that he was breathing hard. She tilted her head back, ready to be kissed, but he did nothing.

She stood up and quickly pulled her dress up over her head and threw it to the floor. She stood naked in front of him in the firelight. He gazed at her, eyes wide, mouth open, as if he were witnessing a miracle.

She took his hand again. This time, she touched it to the soft place between her thighs. It covered the triangle of hair there. She was so wet that his finger slipped inside her, and she gave an involuntary groan of pleasure.

But he did nothing of his own volition, and she understood that he was paralysed by indecision. He wanted her, but he had not forgotten Annet. Gwenda could move him like a puppet all night, perhaps even have sex with his inert body, but that would change nothing. She needed him to take the initiative.

She leaned forward, still holding his hand against her groin. 'Kiss me,' she said. She moved her face closer to his. 'Please,' she said. She was an inch away from his mouth. She would not get nearer: he had to close the gap.

Suddenly, he moved.

He withdrew his hand, turned away from her and stood up. 'This is wrong,' he said.

And she knew that she had lost.

Tears came to her eyes. She picked up her dress from the floor and held it in front of her, covering her nakedness.

'I'm sorry,' he said. 'I shouldn't have done any of those things. I misled you. I've been cruel.'

No, you haven't, she thought. I've been cruel. I've misled you. But you were too strong. You're too loyal, too faithful. You're too good for me.

But she said nothing.

He kept his gaze steadfastly away from her. 'You must go to the cowshed,' he said. 'Go to sleep. We'll feel differently in the morning. It might be all right then.'

She ran out through the back door, not bothering to get dressed. It was moonlight, but there was no one to see her, and she would not have cared anyway. She was inside the cowshed in seconds.

At one end of the wooden building was a raised loft where clean straw was kept. That was where she made her bed each night. She climbed the ladder and threw herself down, too miserable to care about the sharp prickle of straw on her bare skin. She wept with disappointment and shame.

When eventually she calmed down, she stood up and put her dress on, then wrapped a blanket around her. As she did so, she thought she heard a step outside. She looked through a gap in the rough wattle-and-daub of the wall.

The moon was almost full, and she could see clearly. Wulfric was outside. He walked towards the door of the cowshed. Gwenda's heart leaped. Perhaps it was not all over yet. But he hesitated at the door, then walked away. He returned to the house, turned at the kitchen door, came back to the cowshed and turned again.

She watched him pace up and down, her heart thudding, but she did not move. She had done all she could to encourage him. He had to take the last step himself.

He stopped at the kitchen door. His body was profiled by the moonlight, a silver line running from his forelock to his boots. She saw clearly as he reached into his drawers. She knew what he was going to do: she had seen her older brother do the same thing. She heard Wulfric groan as he began to rub himself with the motion that caricatured lovemaking. She stared at him, beautiful in the moonlight, wasting his desire, and she felt as if her heart would break.

20

GODWYN MOVED AGAINST Blind Carlus on the Sunday before the birthday of St Adolphus.

On that Sunday every year, a special service was held in Kingsbridge Cathedral. The bones of the saint were carried around the church by the prior, followed by the monks in procession; and they prayed for good harvest weather.

As always, it was Godwyn's job to prepare the church for the service – placing candles, getting incense ready and moving furniture – helped by novices and employees such as Philemon. The Feast of St Adolphus required a secondary altar, an elaborately carved wooden table set on a platform that could be moved about the church as required. Godwyn placed this altar on the eastern edge of the crossing and put on it a pair of silver-gilt candlesticks. As he did so he anxiously mulled over his position.

Now that he had persuaded Thomas to stand for election as prior, his next step was to eliminate the opposition. Carlus ought to be an easy target – but in a way that was a disadvantage, for Godwyn did not want to appear callous.

He placed in the centre of the altar a reliquary cross, a bejewelled gold crucifix with a core of wood from the True Cross. This, the actual timber upon which Christ was killed, had been miraculously found a thousand years ago by Helena, the mother of Constantine the Great, and pieces of it had found their way to churches all over Europe.

As Godwyn was arranging the ornaments on the altar he saw Mother Cecilia nearby, and broke off from his work to speak to her. 'I understand that Earl Roland has recovered his mind,' he said. 'Praise God.'

'Amen,' she said. 'The fever was on him so long that we feared for his life. Some evil humour must have entered his brain after his skull was fractured. Nothing he said made sense. Then, this morning, he woke up and spoke normally.'

'You cured him.'

'God cured him.'

'Still, he should be grateful to you.'

She smiled. 'You're young, Brother Godwyn. You'll learn that men of power never show gratitude. Whatever we give them, they accept as their right.'

Her condescension annoyed Godwyn, but he concealed his irritation. 'At any rate, we can now hold the election for prior, at last.'

'Who will win?'

'Ten monks have promised firmly to vote for Carlus, and only seven for Thomas. With the candidates' own votes, that makes the score eleven to eight, with six uncommitted.'

'So it could go either way.'

'But Carlus is in the lead. Thomas could do with your support, Mother Cecilia.'

'I don't have a vote.'

'But you have influence. If you were to say that the monastery needs stricter control and a measure of reform, and you felt Thomas was more likely to deliver such a programme, it would sway some of the waverers.'

'I ought not to take sides.'

'Perhaps not, but you could say that you will not continue to subsidize the monks unless they manage their money better. What could be wrong with that?'

Her bright eyes glittered with amusement: she was not so easily persuaded. 'That would be a coded message of support for Thomas.'

'Yes.'

'I am strictly neutral. I will happily work with whomever the monks choose. And that's my last word, brother.'

He bowed his head deferentially. 'I respect your decision, of course.'

She nodded and moved away.

Godwyn was pleased. He had never expected her to endorse

Thomas. She was conservative. Everyone assumed she favoured Carlus. But Godwyn could now spread the word that she would be content with either candidate. In effect, he had undermined her implicit support for Carlus. She might even be cross when she heard what use he was making of her words, but she would not withdraw her statement of neutrality.

I am so clever, he thought; I really deserve to be prior.

Neutralizing Cecilia was helpful, but it would not be enough to crush Carlus. Godwyn needed to give the monks a vivid demonstration of how incompetent Carlus was to lead them. He was hoping anxiously for such an opportunity today.

Carlus and Simeon were in the church now, rehearsing the service. Carlus was the acting prior, so he had to lead the procession, carrying the ivory-and-gold reliquary that contained the bones of the saint. Simeon, the treasurer and Carlus's crony, was walking him through it, and Godwyn could see Carlus counting his paces, so that he would be able to do it on his own. The congregation was impressed when Carlus moved around confidently despite his blindness: it seemed like a minor miracle.

The procession always began at the east end of the church, where the relics were stored under the high altar. The prior would unlock the cupboard and remove the reliquary. He would carry it along the north aisle of the chancel, around the north transept, down the north aisle of the nave, across the west end, and back up the centre of the nave and into the crossing. There he would climb two steps to place it on the second altar that Godwyn had put in position ready. The holy relics would remain there, for the congregation to stare at, throughout the service.

Looking around the church, Godwyn's eye fell on the repairs in the south aisle of the chancel, and he stepped closer to see how they were coming along. Merthin was no longer involved, having been sacked by Elfric, but his startlingly simple method was still being operated. Instead of expensive wooden formwork supporting the new masonry while the mortar set, each stone was held in place by a simple rope, draped over the long edge of the stone and weighted with a rock. The system could not be used to build the ribs of the vault, which were composed of long, slender stones laid end to end, so formwork had to be made for those elements; but, all the same, Merthin had saved the priory a small fortune in carpentry.

Godwyn recognized Merthin's genius, but still felt uneasy with him, and preferred to work with Elfric. Elfric could be trusted always to be a willing tool, never to make trouble; whereas Merthin was all too likely to walk his own road.

Carlus and Simeon left. The church was ready for the service. Godwyn sent away the men who had been helping him, all but Philemon, who was sweeping the floor of the crossing.

For a moment, the great cathedral was empty but for the two of them.

This was Godwyn's chance. The plan he had half formulated now appeared complete in his mind. He hesitated, for it was dreadfully risky. But he decided to gamble.

He beckoned to Philemon. 'Now,' he said. 'Quickly – move the platform forward a yard.'

*

MUCH OF THE TIME, the cathedral was no more than a place of work to Godwyn. It was a space to be used, a building to be repaired, a source of income and at the same time a financial burden. But, on an occasion such as this, its majesty was renewed. The candle flames flickered, their reflections glinting on the gold of the candlesticks; the robed monks and nuns glided between the ancient stone pillars; and the voices of the choir soared to the high vault. No wonder the crowd of hundreds of townspeople were hushed as they stood watching.

Carlus led the procession. As the monks and nuns sang, he opened the compartment under the high altar – working by touch – and took out the ivory-and-gold reliquary. Holding it high, he began to process around the church. He was the picture of a holy innocent, with his white beard and unseeing eyes.

Would he fall into Godwyn's trap? It was so simple – it seemed too easy. Godwyn, following a few paces behind Carlus, bit his lip and tried to remain calm.

The congregation was awestruck. Godwyn never failed to marvel at how willing they were to be manipulated. They could not see the bones and, if they had, they could not have distinguished them from any other human remains. But, because of the costly extravagance of the box, the eerie beauty of the singing, the uniform robes of the monks and nuns, and the towering architecture that dwarfed them all, they felt the presence of something holy.

Godwyn watched Carlus carefully. As he reached the precise midpoint of the westernmost bay of the north aisle, he turned sharply left. Simeon stood ready to correct him if he misjudged, but it was not necessary. Good: the more confident Carlus was, the more likely he was to stumble at the crucial moment.

Counting his paces, Carlus marched to the exact centre of the nave then turned again, heading straight for the altar. On cue, the singing stopped, and the procession carried on in a reverent hush.

It must be a bit like finding your way to the latrine in the middle of the night, Godwyn thought. Carlus had followed this route several times a year for most of his life. He was now doing it as leader of the procession, which must make him tense; but he appeared calm, only the slight movement of his lips betraying the fact that he was counting. But Godwyn had ensured that his count would be wrong. Would he make a fool of himself? Or would he somehow recover?

The congregation fell back fearfully as the sacred bones went by. Touching the casket could work miracles, they knew, but they also believed that any disrespect shown to the relics would have disastrous consequences. The spirits of the dead were ever present, watching over their remains while they waited for the day of judgement; and those who had led holy lives enjoyed almost unlimited powers to reward or punish the living.

The thought crossed Godwyn's mind that St Adolphus might be displeased with him for what was about to happen in Kingsbridge Cathedral. He shivered with momentary terror. Then he reassured himself that he was acting for the good of the priory that housed the sacred bones, and that the all-wise saint, who could see into men's hearts, would understand that this was for the best.

Carlus slowed as he approached the altar, but his paces were the same measured length. Godwyn stopped breathing. Carlus seemed to hesitate as he took the step that should, by his own calculations, bring him just short of the platform on which the altar stood. Godwyn watched helplessly, dreading some last-moment change of routine.

Then, confidently, Carlus walked on.

His foot struck the edge of the platform a yard sooner than expected. In the silence, the sound of his sandal on the hollow wood resounded loudly. He let out a cry of shock and fear. His momentum carried him forward.

Godwyn's heart was lifted by a surge of triumph – but it lasted only an instant, then disaster struck.

Simeon reached out to grab Carlus's arm, but he was too late. The casket flew from Carlus's hands. The congregation gave a collective gasp of horror. The precious box hit the stone floor and burst open, scattering the bones of the saint. Carlus crashed into the heavy carved-wood altar, pushing it back off the platform, sending its ornaments and candles tumbling to the floor.

Godwyn was horrified. This was much worse than he had intended.

The skull of the saint rolled across the floor and came to rest at Godwyn's feet.

His plan had worked – but too well. He had wanted Carlus to fall, and appear helpless, but he had not intended the holy remains to be desecrated. He stared, horrified, at the skull on the ground, and its empty eyes seemed to look back at him accusingly. What dreadful punishment would befall him?

Could he ever make restitution for such a crime?

Because he had been expecting an incident, he was slightly less shocked than everyone else, and he regained his composure first. Standing over the bones, he raised both arms in the air and shouted over the hubbub: 'Everyone – on your knees! We must pray!'

Those at the front knelt down, and the rest quickly followed suit. Godwyn began a familiar prayer, and the monks and nuns joined in. As the chanting filled the church, he righted the reliquary, which seemed undamaged. Then, moving with theatrical slowness, he picked up the skull in both hands. He was shaking with superstitious dread, but he managed to hold it. Speaking the Latin words of the prayer, he carried the skull to the casket and placed it inside.

He saw that Carlus was struggling to his feet. He pointed at two nuns. 'Help the sub-prior to the hospital,' he said. 'Brother Simeon, Mother Cecilia, will you go with him?'

He picked up another bone. He was frightened, knowing that he more than Carlus was to blame for what had happened; but his intentions had been pure, and he still hoped to mollify the saint. At the same time, he was aware that his actions must look good in the eyes of everyone present: he was taking charge in a crisis, like a true leader.

However, this moment of awe and horror could not be allowed to last too long. He needed to gather up the bones more quickly. 'Brother Thomas,' he said. 'Brother Theodoric. Come and help me.' Philemon stepped forward, but Godwyn waved him back: he was not a monk, and only men of God should touch the bones.

Carlus limped out of the church, helped by Simeon and Cecilia, leaving Godwyn the undisputed master of the occasion.

Godwyn beckoned Philemon and another employee, Otho, and told them to right the altar. They set it straight on the platform. Otho picked up the candlesticks and Philemon the jewelled crucifix. They placed them reverently on the altar then retrieved the scattered candles.

All the bones were picked up. Godwyn tried to close the lid of the reliquary, but it had buckled and did not quite fit. Making the best of it, he ceremoniously placed the casket on the altar.

Godwyn remembered, just in time, that he was seeking to show Thomas, not himself, in the light of leader of the priory – for the present. He picked up the book Simeon had been carrying and handed it to Thomas. Thomas did not need to be told what to do. He opened the book, found the correct page and read the verse. The monks and nuns formed lines either side of the altar, then Thomas led them in singing the psalm.

Somehow, they got through the service.

*

GODWYN BEGAN TO tremble again as soon as he got out of the church. It had been a near-disaster, but he seemed to have got away with it.

The monks burst into excited chatter as the procession reached the cloisters and broke up. Godwyn leaned against a pillar, struggling to regain his composure. He listened to the comments of the monks. Some felt the desecration of the relics was a sign that God did not want Carlus to be prior – the reaction Godwyn had intended. But, to his dismay, most expressed compassion for Carlus. That was not what Godwyn wanted. He realized he might have given Carlus the benefit of a sympathetic backlash.

He pulled himself together and hurried to the hospital. He needed to get to Carlus while the man was still demoralized, and before he got wind of the monks' understanding.

The sub-prior was sitting up in bed with one arm in a sling and a bandage around his head. He was pale and looked shaken, and every few moments his face would twitch nervously. Simeon was sitting beside him.

Simeon gave Godwyn a filthy look. 'I suppose you're pleased,' he said.

Godwyn ignored him. 'Brother Carlus, you'll be glad to know that the relics of the saint have been restored to their usual place with hymns and prayers. The saint will surely forgive us all for this tragic accident.'

Carlus shook his head. 'There are no accidents,' he said. 'Everything is ordained by God.'

Godwyn's hopes lifted. This was promising.

Simeon's thoughts followed the same lines, and he tried to restrain Carlus. 'Don't say anything hasty, brother.'

'It's a sign,' Carlus said. 'God is telling us he does not want me to be prior.'

This was what Godwyn had been hoping for.

Simeon said: 'Nonsense.' He picked up a cup from a table beside the bed. Godwyn guessed it contained warm wine and honey, Mother Cecilia's prescription for most ills. Simeon put the cup into Carlus's hand. 'Drink.'

Carlus drank, but he was not to be diverted from his theme. 'It would be a sin to ignore such a portent.'

'Portents are not so easily interpreted,' Simeon protested.

'Perhaps not. But even if you're right, will the brothers vote for a prior who can't carry the relics of the saint without falling over?'

Godwyn said: 'Some of them might, in fact, be drawn to you in commiseration, rather than repelled.'

Simeon shot him a puzzled look, wondering what he was up to.

Simeon was right to be suspicious. Godwyn was playing devil's advocate because he wanted more than vague expressions of doubt from Carlus. Could he possibly extract a definite withdrawal?

As he hoped, Carlus argued with him. 'A man should be made prior because the brothers respect him and believe he can lead them wisely – not out of pity.' He spoke with the bitter conviction of a lifetime of disability.

'I suppose that's true,' Godwyn said with feigned reluctance, as if the admission had been wrung from him against his will. Taking a risk, he added: 'But perhaps Simeon is right, and you should postpone any final decision until you feel more yourself.'

'I'm as well as I'm ever going to be,' Carlus retorted, refusing to admit to weakness in front of young Godwyn. 'Nothing is going to change. I'll feel tomorrow the way I feel today. I will not stand for election as prior.'

Those were the words Godwyn had been waiting for. He stood up abruptly and bowed his head as if in acknowledgement, hiding his face for fear he might reveal his sense of triumph. 'You are as clear as always, Brother Carlus,' he said. 'I will convey your wishes to the rest of the monks.'

Simeon opened his mouth to protest, but he was forestalled by Mother Cecilia, coming into the room from the stairwell. She looked flustered. 'Earl Roland is demanding to see the sub-prior,' she said. 'He's threatening to get out of bed, but he must not move, for his skull may not yet be fully healed. But Brother Carlus should not move either.'

Godwyn looked at Simeon. 'We'll go,' he said.

They went together up the stairs.

Godwyn was feeling good. Carlus did not even know that he had been routed. Of his own accord, he had withdrawn himself from the contest, leaving only Thomas. And Godwyn could eliminate Thomas any time he liked.

The plan had been astonishingly successful – so far.

Earl Roland was lying on his back, and his head was thickly bandaged, but all the same he managed to look like a man in power. The barber must have visited him, for his face was shaved and his black hair – as much of it as was not covered by the bandage – had been neatly trimmed. He wore a short purple tunic and new hose, the two legs fashionably dyed different colours, one red and one yellow. Despite lying in bed he wore a belt with a dagger and short leather boots. His elder son, William, and William's wife, Philippa, stood by the bed. His young secretary, Father Jerome, in priestly robes, sat at a nearby writing desk with pens and sealing wax ready.

The message was clear: the earl was back in charge.

'Is the sub-prior there?' he said in a clear, strong voice.

Godwyn was quicker-thinking than Simeon, and he replied first. 'Sub-prior Carlus has suffered a fall and is himself lying here in this hospital, lord,' he said. 'I am the sacrist, Godwyn, and with me is the treasurer, Simeon. We thank God for your miraculous recovery, for He guided the hands of the physician-monks who have been attending you.'

'It was the barber who mended my broken head,' said Roland. 'Thank him.'

Because the earl was lying on his back, looking up at the ceiling, Godwyn could not see his face well; but he had the impression that the earl's expression was curiously blank, and he wondered whether the injury had done some permanent damage. He said: 'Do you have everything you need to make you comfortable?'

'If I don't, you'll soon know. Now, listen. My niece, Margery, is to marry Monmouth's younger son, Roger. I presume you know this.'

'Yes.' Godwyn had a sudden flash of memory: Margery lying

on her back in this very room, her white legs in the air, fornicating with her cousin Richard, the bishop of Kingsbridge.

'The wedding has been unduly delayed by my injuries.'

That was not true, Godwyn reflected. The collapse of the bridge had taken place only a month ago. The truth was probably that the earl needed to prove that the injury had not diminished him, and he was still a power worthy of an alliance with the earl of Monmouth.

Roland went on: 'The wedding will take place in Kingsbridge Cathedral three weeks from today.'

Strictly speaking the earl should have made a request, not issued a command, and an elected prior might have bristled at his high-handedness; but, of course, there was no prior. Anyway, Godwyn could think of no reason why Roland should not have his wish. 'Very well, my lord,' he said. 'I will make the necessary preparations.'

'I want the new prior installed in time for the service,' Roland went on.

Simeon grunted in surprise.

Godwyn quickly calculated that haste would suit his plans remarkably well. 'Very good,' he replied. 'There were two candidates, but today sub-prior Carlus withdrew his name, leaving only Brother Thomas, the matricularius. We can hold the election as soon as you like.' He could hardly believe his luck.

Simeon knew he was looking defeat in the face. 'Wait a minute,' he said.

But Roland was not listening. 'I don't want Thomas,' he said.

Godwyn had not been expecting that.

Simeon grinned, pleased at this last-minute reprieve.

Shocked, Godwyn said: 'But, my lord—'

Roland did not permit him to interrupt. 'Summon my nephew, Saul Whitehead, from St-John-in-the-Forest,' he said.

Godwyn's heart filled with foreboding. Saul was his contemporary. As novices, they had been friends. They had gone to Oxford together – but there they had grown apart, Saul becoming more devout and Godwyn more worldly. Saul was now the competent prior of the remote cell of St John. He took very seriously the monastic virtue of humility, and he would never have put forward his own name. But he was bright, devout, and liked by everyone.

'Get him here as soon as possible,' said Roland. 'I shall nominate him as the next prior of Kingsbridge.'

21

MERTHIN SAT ON THE ROOF of St Mark's church, at the north end of Kingsbridge. From here he could see the whole town. To the south-east, a bend in the river cradled the priory in the crook of its elbow. A quarter of the town was taken up by the priory buildings and the grounds around them – cemetery, market place, orchard and vegetable garden – with the cathedral rising from its surroundings like an oak in a field of nettles. He could see priory employees picking vegetables in the garden, mucking out a stable and unloading barrels from a cart.

The centre of town was the wealthy neighbourhood, especially the main street, climbing the slope from the river as the first monks must have climbed it hundreds of years ago. Several wealthy merchants, identifiable by the glowing colours of their fine wool coats, walked purposefully along the street: merchants were always busy. Another wide thoroughfare, the high street, ran west to east through the middle of the town, bisecting the main street at right angles near the north-west corner of the priory. On the same corner he could see the broad roof of the guild hall, the largest building in town outside the priory.

On the main street next to the Bell were the priory gates, with Caris's house opposite, taller than most of the other buildings. Outside the Bell Merthin could see a crowd gathered around Friar Murdo. The friar, who did not seem to be attached to any particular fraternal order, had stayed in Kingsbridge after the bridge collapse. Shocked and bereaved people were particularly susceptible to his emotional roadside sermons, and he was raking in the silver halfpennies and farthings. Merthin thought he was a fraud, his holy anger faked and his tears a cover for cynicism and greed – but Merthin was in a minority.

At the bottom of the main street, the stumps of the bridge still stuck up out of the water, and next to them Merthin's ferry was crossing the water bearing a cart loaded with tree trunks. To the south-west was the industrial sector, where large houses on broad plots encompassed abattoirs, tanneries, breweries, bakeries and workshops of all kinds – too smelly and dirty for the town's leading citizens, but nevertheless a district where plenty of money was made. The river widened there, dividing into two channels either side of Leper Island. Merthin could see Ian Boatman rowing his small craft to the island, his passenger a monk, probably carrying food to the one remaining leper. The south bank of the river was lined with wharves and warehouses, and rafts and barges were being unloaded at several of them. Beyond was the suburb of Newtown, where rows of poor houses ran between orchards, pastures and gardens in which priory employees produced food for the monks and nuns.

The north end of town, where St Mark's stood, was the poor quarter, and the church was surrounded by the huddled homes of labourers, widows, the unsuccessful and the old. It was a poor church – luckily for Merthin.

Four weeks ago, a desperate Father Joffroi had hired Merthin to build a hoist and repair his roof. Caris had persuaded Edmund to lend Merthin the money to buy tools. Merthin had hired a fourteen-year-old boy, Jimmie, to labour for a halfpenny a day. And today the hoist was finished.

Somehow, word had got around that Merthin was about to try out a new machine. Everyone had been impressed by his ferry, and people were fascinated to see what he had come up with now. Down in the graveyard a small crowd had gathered, mostly idlers but including Father Joffroi, Edmund and Caris, and some of the town's builders, notably Elfric. If Merthin failed today, he would fail in front of his friends and enemies.

That was not the worst of it. This job had saved him from the need to leave town in search of work. But such a fate still hung over him. If the hoist went wrong, people would conclude that hiring Merthin brought bad luck. They would say that the spirits did not want him in town. He would be under greater pressure to leave. He would have to say goodbye to Kingsbridge – and to Caris.

Over the last four weeks, as he had shaped the wood and joined the pieces of his hoist, he had for the first time seriously thought about losing her; and it dismayed him. He had realized that she was all the joy in his world. If the weather was fine, he wanted to walk in the sunshine with her; if he saw something beautiful, he wanted to show it to her; if he heard something funny, his first thought was to tell her, and see her smile. His work gave him pleasure, especially when he came up with clever solutions to intractable problems; but it was a cold, cerebral satisfaction, and he knew that his life would be a long winter without Caris.

He stood up. It was time to put his skill to the test.

He had built a normal hoist with one innovative feature. Like all hoists, it had a rope that ran through a series of pulleys. On top of the church wall, at the edge of the roof, Merthin had built a timber structure like a gallows, with an arm that reached across the roof. The rope ran out to the end of the arm. At the other end of the rope, on the ground in the graveyard, was a treadwheel, which wound up the rope when operated by the boy, Jimmie. All this was standard. The innovation was that the gallows incorporated a swivel, so that the arm could swing.

To save himself from the fate of Howell Tyler, Merthin had a belt under his arms that was tied to a sturdy stone pinnacle: if he fell, he would not fall far. So protected, he had removed the slates from a section of the roof then tied the rope of the hoist to a timber. Now he called down to Jimmie: 'Turn the wheel!'

Then he held his breath. He was sure it would work – it had to – but, all the same, this was a moment of high anxiety.

Jimmie, inside the great treadmill on the ground, began to walk. The wheel could move only one way. It had a brake pressing on its asymmetric teeth: one side of each tooth was gently angled, so that the brake moved gradually along the slope; but the other side was vertical, so that any reverse movement was immediately arrested.

As the wheel turned, the roof timber rose.

When the timber was clear of the roof structure, Merthin shouted: 'Whoa!'

Jimmie stopped, the brake engaged, and the timber hung in the air, swinging gently. So far, so good. The next part was where things might go wrong.

Merthin turned the hoist, so that its arm began to swing. He watched it, holding his breath. New strains were brought to bear on the structure as the weight of the load moved its position. The wood of the hoist creaked. The arm swung through half a circle, bringing the timber from its original location over the roof to a new point over the graveyard. There was a collective murmur of wonder from the crowd: they had never seen a hoist that could swivel.

'Let it down!' Merthin called.

Jimmie operated the brake, allowing the load to fall jerkily, a foot at a time, as the wheel turned and the rope unwound.

Everyone watched in silence. When the timber touched the ground there was a round of applause.

Jimmie detached the timber from the rope.

Merthin permitted himself a moment of triumph. It had worked.

He climbed down the ladder. The crowd cheered. Caris kissed him. Father Joffroi shook his hand. 'It's a marvel,' the priest said. 'I've never seen anything like it.'

'No one has,' Merthin said proudly. 'I invented it.'

Several more men congratulated him. Everyone was pleased to have been among the first to witness the phenomenon – all but Elfric, looking cross at the back of the crowd.

Merthin ignored him. He said to Father Joffroi: 'Our agreement was that you would pay me if it worked.'

'Gladly,' said Joffroi. 'I owe you eight shillings so far, and the sooner I have to pay you for removing the rest of the timbers and rebuilding the roof, the happier I'll be.' He opened the wallet at his waist and took out some coins tied up in a rag.

Elfric said loudly: 'Wait a moment!'

Everyone looked at him.

'You can't pay this boy, Father Joffroi,' he said. 'He's not a qualified carpenter.'

Surely this could not happen, Merthin thought. He had done the work – it was too late now to deny him the wages. But Elfric cared nothing for fairness.

'Nonsense!' said Joffroi. 'He's done what no other carpenter in town could do.'

'All the same, he's not in the guild.'

'I wanted to join,' Merthin put in. 'You would not admit me.'

'That's the prerogative of the guild.'

Joffroi said: 'I say that's unjust – and many people in town would agree. He's done six and a half years of his apprenticeship, with no wages but his food and a bed on the kitchen floor, and everyone knows he's been doing the work of a qualified carpenter for years. You should not have turned him out without his tools.'

There was a murmur of assent from the men gathered around. Elfric was generally thought to have gone a bit too far.

Elfric said: 'With due respect to your reverence, that is for the guild to decide, not you.'

'All right.' Joffroi folded his arms. 'You tell me not to pay Merthin – even though he is the only man in town who can repair my church without closing it. I defy you.' He handed the coins to Merthin. 'Now you can take the case to court.'

'The prior's court.' Elfric's face twisted in spite. 'When a man has a grievance against a priest, is he likely to get a fair hearing in a court run by monks?'

There was some sympathy in the crowd for this. They knew of too many instances where the prior's court had unjustly favoured the clergy.

But Joffroi shot back: 'Can an apprentice get a fair hearing in a guild run by masters?'

The crowd laughed at that: they appreciated clever arguments.

Elfric looked crushed. Whatever the court, he could win a dispute between himself and Merthin, but he could not so easily prevail against a priest. Resentfully, he said: 'It's a bad day for the town when apprentices defy their masters and priests support the boys.' But he sensed he had lost, and he turned away.

Merthin felt the weight of the coins in his hand: eight shillings, ninety-six silver pennies, two-fifths of a pound. He knew he should count them, but he was too happy to bother. He had earned his first wages.

He turned to Edmund. 'This is your money,' he said.

'Pay me five shillings now, the rest later,' Edmund said generously. 'Keep some money for yourself – you deserve it.'

Merthin smiled. That would leave him three shillings to spend – more money than he had ever had in his life. He did not know what to do with it. Perhaps he would buy his mother a chicken.

It was midday, and the crowd began to disperse, heading home for dinner. Merthin went with Caris and Edmund. He felt his future was secure. He had proved himself as a carpenter, and few people would hesitate to employ him now that Father Joffroi had set the precedent. He could earn a living. He could have a house of his own.

He could get married.

Petranilla was waiting for them. As Merthin counted out five shillings for Edmund, she put on the table a fragrant dish of fish baked with herbs. In celebration of Merthin's triumph, Edmund poured sweet Rhenish wine into cups for all of them.

But Edmund was not a man to linger over the past. 'We must get on with the new bridge,' he said impatiently. 'Five weeks have gone by and nothing has been done!'

Petranilla said: 'I hear the earl's health is rapidly returning to normal, so perhaps the monks will hold the election soon. I must ask Godwyn – but I haven't seen him since yesterday, when Blind Carlus fell over during the service.'

'I'd like to have a bridge design ready,' Edmund said. 'Then work could begin as soon as the new prior is elected.'

Merthin's ears pricked up. 'What have you got in mind?'

'We know it has to be a stone bridge. I want it wide enough for two carts to pass.'

Merthin nodded. 'And it should be ramped at both ends, so that people will step off the bridge on to dry ground, not a muddy beach.'

'Yes – excellent.'

Caris said: 'But how do you build stone walls in the middle of a river?'

Edmund said: 'I've no idea, but it must be possible. There are lots of stone bridges.'

Merthin said: 'I've heard men talk about this. You have to build a special structure called a coffer dam to keep the water out of the area where you're building. It's quite simple, but they say you have to be very careful to make sure it's watertight.'

Godwyn came in, looking anxious. He was not supposed to make social calls in the town – in theory, he could leave the priory only on a specific errand. Merthin wondered what had happened.

'Carlus withdrew his name from the election,' he said.

'Good news!' Edmund said. 'Have a cup of this wine.'

'Don't celebrate yet,' Godwyn said.

'Why not? That leaves Thomas as the only candidate – and Thomas wants to build the new bridge. Our problem is solved.'

'Thomas is no longer the only candidate. The earl is nominating Saul Whitehead.'

'Oh.' Edmund was thoughtful. 'Is that necessarily bad?'

'Yes. Saul is well liked and has shown himself a competent prior of St-John-in-the-Forest. If he accepts the nomination, he's likely to get the votes of former supporters of Carlus – which means he could win. Then, as the earl's nominee, and his cousin too, Saul is likely to do his sponsor's bidding – and the earl may oppose the building of the new bridge, on the grounds that it might take business away from Shiring market.'

Edmund looked worried. 'Is there anything we can do?'

'I hope so. Someone has to go to St John to tell Saul the news and bring him to Kingsbridge. I've volunteered for that job, and I'm hoping there's some way I can persuade him to refuse.'

Petranilla spoke. 'That may not solve the problem,' she said. Merthin listened carefully to her: he did not like her, but she was clever. She went on: 'The earl might nominate another candidate. Any nominee of his could oppose the bridge.'

Godwyn nodded agreement. 'So, assuming I can keep Saul out of the contest, we must make sure the earl's second choice is someone who can't possibly get elected.'

'Who do you have in mind?' his mother asked.

'Friar Murdo.'

'Excellent.'

Caris said: 'But he's awful!'

'Exactly,' Godwyn said. 'Greedy, drunken, a sponger, a self-righteous rabble-rouser. The monks will never vote for him. That's why we want him to be the earl's candidate.'

Godwyn was like his mother, Merthin realized, in having a talent for this kind of plotting.

Petranilla said: 'How shall we proceed?'

'First, we need to persuade Murdo to put his name forward.'

'That won't be hard. Just tell him he's in with a chance. He'd love to be prior.'

'Agreed. But I can't do it. Murdo would immediately suspect my motives. Everyone knows I'm backing Thomas.'

'I'll speak to him,' said Petranilla. 'I'll tell him you and I are at odds, and I don't want Thomas. I'll say the earl is looking for someone to nominate, and Murdo could be the right man. He's popular in the town, especially among the poor and ignorant, who labour under the delusion that he's one of them. All he needs to do, to get the nomination, is make it clear that he's willing to be the earl's pawn.'

'Good.' Godwyn stood up. 'I'll try to be present when Murdo speaks to Earl Roland.' He kissed his mother's cheek and went out.

The fish was all gone. Merthin ate his bread trencher, rich with juices. Edmund offered him more wine, but he declined: he was afraid he might fall off the roof of St Mark's this afternoon if he drank too much. Petranilla went into the kitchen and Edmund retired to the parlour to sleep. Merthin and Caris were left alone.

He moved to sit on the bench next to her, and kissed her.

She said: 'I'm so proud of you.'

He glowed. He was proud of himself. He kissed her again, this time with a long, moist kiss that gave him an erection. He touched her breast through the linen of her robe, squeezing her nipple gently with his fingertips.

She touched his erection and giggled. 'Do you want me to bring you off?' she whispered.

She did that sometimes late in the evening, when her father and Petranilla were asleep, and Merthin and she were alone on the ground floor of the house. But this was broad daylight, and someone could walk in at any moment. 'No!' he said.

'I could do it quickly.' She tightened her grasp.

'I'm too embarrassed.' He stood up and moved to the other side of the table.

'I'm sorry.'

'Well, maybe we won't have to do this much longer.'

'Do what?'

'Hide, and worry about people walking in.'

She looked hurt. 'Don't you like it?'

'Of course I do! But it would be nicer for us to be alone. I could take a house, now that I'm getting paid.'

'You've only been paid once.'

'That's true ... but you seem very pessimistic all of a sudden. Have I said something wrong?'

'No, but ... why do you want to change the way things are?'

He was baffled by this question. 'I just want more of the same, in private.'

She looked defiant. 'I'm happy now.'

'Well, so am I ... but nothing goes on for ever.'

'Why not?'

He felt as if he were explaining something to a child. 'Because we can't spend the rest of our lives living with our parents and stealing kisses when no one's looking. We have to get a home of our own, and live as man and wife, and sleep together every night, and have real sex instead of bringing each other off, and raise a family.'

'Why?' she said.

'I don't know why,' he said in exasperation. 'That's the way it is, and I'm not going to try to explain any more, because I think you're determined not to understand; or, at least, to pretend you don't understand.'

'All right.'

'And besides, I have to go back to work.'

'Go on, then.'

This was incomprehensible. He had been frustrated, during the last half year, by not being able to marry Caris, and he had assumed she felt the same. Now it seemed she did not. Indeed, she resented his assumption. But did she really believe that they could continue this adolescent relationship indefinitely?

He looked at her, trying to read her face, and saw only a sulky obstinacy there. He turned away and went out through the door.

He hesitated on the street outside. Perhaps he should go back in and make her say what was on her mind. But, remembering the look on her face, he knew this was not the moment to try to make her do anything. So he walked on, heading for St Mark's, thinking: How did such a wonderful day turn so bad?

22

GODWYN WAS PREPARING Kingsbridge Cathedral for the big wedding. The church had to look its best. In addition to the earl of Monmouth and the earl of Shiring, there would be several barons and hundreds of knights in attendance. Broken flagstones had to be replaced, chipped masonry repaired, crumbling mouldings carved anew, walls whitewashed, pillars painted and everything scrubbed clean.

'And I want the repairs to the south aisle of the chancel finished,' Godwyn said to Elfric as they walked through the church.

'I'm not sure that's possible—'

'It must be done. We can't have scaffolding in the chancel during a wedding of this importance.' He saw Philemon waving urgently at him from the south transept door. 'Excuse me.'

'I haven't got the men!' Elfric called after him.

'You shouldn't be so quick to sack them,' Godwyn said over his shoulder.

Philemon was looking excited. 'Friar Murdo is asking to see the earl,' he said.

'Good!' Petranilla had spoken to the friar last night, and this morning Godwyn had instructed Philemon to lurk near the hospital and watch out for Murdo. He had been expecting an early visit.

He hurried to the hospital, with Philemon in tow. He was relieved to see that Murdo was still waiting in the big room on the ground floor. The fat friar had smartened up his appearance: his face and hands were clean, the fringe of hair around his tonsure was combed, and he had sponged the worst of the stains off his robe. He did not look like a prior, but he almost looked like a monk.

Godwyn ignored him and went up the stairs. Standing guard outside the earl's room he saw Merthin's brother, Ralph, who was one of the earl's squires. Ralph was handsome, except for a broken nose, a recent injury. Squires were always breaking bones. 'Hello, Ralph,' Godwyn said amiably. 'What happened to your nose?'

'I had a fight with a peasant bastard.'

'You should have got it set properly. Did that friar come up here?'

'Yes. They asked him to wait.'

'Who's with the earl?'

'Lady Philippa and the clerk, Father Jerome.'

'Ask if they'll see me.'

'Lady Philippa says the earl must not see anyone.'

Godwyn gave Ralph a man-to-man grin. 'But she's only a woman.'

Ralph grinned back, then opened the door and put his head inside. 'Brother Godwyn, the sacrist?' he said.

There was a pause, and then Lady Philippa stepped out and closed the door behind her. 'I told you no visitors,' she said angrily. 'Earl Roland is not getting the rest he needs.'

Ralph said: 'I know, my lady, but Brother Godwyn wouldn't bother the earl unnecessarily.'

Something in Ralph's tone made Godwyn look at him. Although Ralph's words were mundane, the expression on his face was adoring. Godwyn noticed, then, how voluptuous Philippa was. She wore a dark-red dress belted at the waist, and the fine wool clung to her breasts and hips. She looked like a statue representing Temptation, Godwyn thought, and he wished, yet again, that he could find a way to ban women from the priory. It was bad enough if a squire fell in love with a married woman, but for a monk to do the same would be a catastrophe.

'I regret the need to trouble the earl,' Godwyn said. 'But there's a friar waiting downstairs to see him.'

'I know – Murdo. Is his business so urgent?'

'On the contrary. But I need to forewarn the earl what to expect.'

'So you know what the friar is going to say?'

'I believe I do.'

'Well, I think it's best if the two of you see the earl together.'

Godwyn said: 'But—' then pretended to stifle a protest.

Philippa looked at Ralph. 'Get the friar up here, please.'

Ralph summoned Murdo, and Philippa ushered him and Godwyn into the room. Earl Roland was on the bed, fully dressed as before, but this time he was sitting up, his bandaged head cushioned with feather pillows. 'What's this?' he said with his usual bad temper. 'A meeting of the chapter? What do you monks want?'

Looking at his visage directly for the first time since the bridge collapse, Godwyn was shocked to see that the entire right side of his face was paralysed: the eyelid drooped, the cheek hardly moved and the mouth was slack. What made it so startling was that the left side was animated. When Roland spoke the left side of his forehead frowned, his left eye opened wide and seemed to blaze with authority, and he spoke vehemently out of the left side of his mouth. The doctor in Godwyn was fascinated. He knew that head injuries could have unpredictable effects, but he had never heard of this particular manifestation.

'Don't gawk at me,' the earl said impatiently. 'You look like a pair of cows staring over a hedge. State your business.'

Godwyn pulled himself together. He had to tread carefully over the next few minutes. He knew that Roland would reject Murdo's application to be nominated as prior. All the same, he wanted to plant in Roland's mind the idea of Murdo as a possible alternative to Saul Whitehead. Therefore Godwyn's job was to strengthen Murdo's application. He would do this, paradoxically, by objecting to Murdo, thereby showing Roland that Murdo would owe no allegiance to the monks – for Roland wanted a prior who served him alone. But, on the other hand, Godwyn must not protest too strongly, for he did not want the earl to realize what a truly hopeless candidate Murdo actually was. It was a tortuous path to walk.

Murdo spoke first, in his sonorous pulpit voice. 'My lord, I come to ask you to consider me for the position of prior of Kingsbridge. I believe—'

'Not so loud, for the love of the saints,' Roland protested.

Murdo lowered his voice. 'My lord, I believe that I—'

'Why do you want to be prior?' Roland said, interrupting him again. 'I thought a friar was a monk without a church – by definition.' This point of view was old-fashioned. Friars originally were travellers who held no property, but nowadays some of the fraternal orders were as wealthy as traditional monks. Roland knew this, and was just being provocative.

Murdo gave the standard answer. 'I believe that God accepts both forms of sacrifice.'

'So you're willing to turn your coat.'

'I have come to think that the talents he gave me could be put to better use in a priory, so yes, I would be happy to embrace the Rule of St Benedict.'

'But why should I consider you?'

'I am also an ordained priest.'

'No shortage of those.'

'And I have a following in Kingsbridge and the surrounding countryside such that, if I may be allowed to boast, I must be the most influential man of God in the area.'

Father Jerome spoke for the first time. He was a confident young man with an intelligent face, and Godwyn sensed that he was ambitious. 'It's true,' he said. 'The friar is extraordinarily popular.'

He was not popular with the monks, of course – but neither Roland nor Jerome knew that, and Godwyn was not about to enlighten them.

Nor was Murdo. He bowed his head and said unctuously: 'I thank you from my heart, Father Jerome.'

Godwyn said: 'He is popular with the ignorant multitude.'

'As was our Saviour,' Murdo shot back.

'Monks should lead lives of poverty and self-denial,' Godwyn said.

Roland put in: 'The friar's clothes look poor enough. And as for self-denial, it seems to me that Kingsbridge monks eat better than many peasants.'

'Friar Murdo has been seen drunk in taverns!' Godwyn protested.

Murdo said: 'St Benedict's Rule permits monks to drink wine.'

'Only if they are sick, or labouring in the fields.'

'I preach in the fields.'

Murdo was a formidable opponent in an argument, Godwyn noted. He was glad that he did not actually want to win this one. He turned to Roland. 'All I can say is that as the sacrist here I strongly counsel your lordship against nominating Murdo as prior of Kingsbridge.'

'Noted,' Roland said coldly.

Philippa gave Godwyn a look of mild surprise, and he realized he had yielded a little too easily. But Roland had not noticed: he did not deal in nuances.

Murdo had not finished. 'The prior of Kingsbridge must serve God, of course; but, in all things temporal, he should be guided by the king, and the king's earls and barons.'

That was about as plain as could be, Godwyn thought. Murdo might as well have said: 'I will be your man.' It was an outrageous declaration. The monks would be horrified. It would wipe out any support there might have been among them for Murdo's candidacy.

Godwyn made no comment, but Roland looked inquiringly at him. 'Anything to say to that, sacrist?'

'I'm sure the friar did not mean to say that the priory of Kingsbridge should be in subjection to the earl of Shiring in any matter, temporal or otherwise – did you, Murdo?'

'I have said what I have said,' Murdo replied in his pulpit voice.

'Enough,' said Roland, bored now with the game. 'You're wasting your time, both of you. I shall nominate Saul Whitehead. Off you go.'

*

St-John-in-the-Forest was a miniature version of Kingsbridge Priory. The church was small, as were the stone-built cloisters and dormitory; the rest of the buildings were simple wood-frame structures. There were eight monks and no nuns. In addition to their lives of prayer and meditation, they grew most of their own food and made a goat's cheese that was famous throughout south-west England.

Godwyn and Philemon had been riding for two days, and it

was early evening when the road emerged from the forest and they saw a wide acreage of cleared land with the church in the middle. Godwyn knew at once that his fears were true, and reports that Saul Whitehead was doing a good job as prior of this cell were, if anything, understated. There was a look of order and neatness about everything: the hedges trimmed, the ditches straight, the trees planted at measured intervals in the orchard, the fields of ripening grain free of weeds. He felt sure he would find that the services were held at the correct times and conducted reverently. He had to hope that Saul's evident fitness for leadership had not made him ambitious.

As they rode along the path through the fields, Philemon said: 'Why is the earl so keen to make his cousin prior of Kingsbridge?'

'For the same reason that he had his younger son made bishop of Kingsbridge,' Godwyn replied. 'Bishops and priors are powerful. The earl wants to make sure that any influential man in his neighbourhood is an ally, not an enemy.'

'What might they quarrel about?'

Godwyn was interested to see that young Philemon was beginning to be intrigued by the chess game of power politics. 'Land, taxes, rights, privileges ... for example, the prior might want to build a new bridge at Kingsbridge, to bring more business to the Fleece Fair; and the earl might oppose such a scheme, on the grounds that it would take business away from his own fair at Shiring.'

'But I don't really see how the prior could fight against the earl. A prior has no soldiers...'

'A clergyman can influence the mass of the people. If he preaches a sermon against the earl, or calls upon the saints to bring misfortune to the earl, people will begin to believe that the earl is cursed. Then they will discount his power, mistrust him, and expect all his projects to be doomed. It can be very hard for a nobleman to oppose a truly determined cleric. Look what happened to King Henry II after the murder of Thomas Becket.'

They rode into the farmyard and dismounted. The horses immediately drank from the trough. There was no one about but a monk with his robe hitched up mucking out a pigsty behind the stables. He was sure to be a youngster, doing a job like that. Godwyn called to him. 'Hey, you, lad! Come and help us with our horses.'

'Righto!' the monk called back. He finished cleaning out the sty with a few more passes of his rake, then leaned the tool up against the stable wall and walked towards the newcomers. Godwyn was about to tell him to get a move on when he recognized the blond fringe of Saul.

Godwyn disapproved. A prior should not muck out a pigsty. Ostentatious humility was, after all, ostentation. However, in this case Saul's meekness might suit Godwyn's purpose.

He gave Saul a friendly smile. 'Hello, brother. I didn't mean to order the prior to unsaddle my horse.'

'Why not?' said Saul. 'Someone must do it, and you've been travelling all day.' Saul led the horses into the stable. 'The brothers are in the fields,' he called out. 'But they'll be back soon for Evensong.' He re-emerged. 'Come into the kitchen.'

They had never been close. Godwyn could not help feeling criticized by Saul's piety. Saul was never unfriendly, but with quiet determination he simply did things differently. Godwyn had to take care not to become irritated. He felt stressed enough already.

Godwyn and Philemon followed Saul across the farmyard and into a one-storey building with a high roof. Although made of wood, it had a stone fireplace and chimney. They sat gratefully on a rough bench at a scrubbed table. Saul drew two generous cups of ale from a large barrel.

He sat opposite them. Philemon drank thirstily, but Godwyn just sipped. Saul offered no food, and Godwyn guessed they would get nothing more until after Evensong. He felt too tense to eat, anyway.

This was another delicate moment, he reflected anxiously. He had had to protest against Murdo's nomination in such a way as not to dissuade Roland. Now he had to invite Saul to stand in a way that he could not possibly accept. He knew what he was going to say, but he had to say it right. If he made a false step, Saul would become suspicious, and then anything could happen.

Saul gave him no time for further worry. 'What brings you here, brother?' he said.

'Earl Roland has recovered his wits.'

'I thank God.'

'This means we can hold the election for prior.'

'Good. We should not go too long without one.'

'But who should it be?'

Saul sidestepped the question. 'Have any names been put forward?'

'Brother Thomas, the matricularius.'

'He'd be a good manager. No one else?'

Godwyn told a half-truth. 'Not formally.'

'What about Carlus? When I came to Kingsbridge for Prior Anthony's funeral, the sub-prior was the leading candidate.'

'He feels he is not capable of the job.'

'Because of his blindness?'

'Perhaps.' Saul did not know about Carlus falling over during the service for St Adolphus's birthday. Godwyn decided not to tell him. 'At any rate, he has thought and prayed about it, and made his decision.'

'Has the earl not made a nomination?'

'He's thinking about it.' Godwyn hesitated. 'That's why we're here. The earl is ... considering nominating you.' This was not really a lie, Godwyn told himself; just a misleading emphasis.

'I'm honoured.'

Godwyn studied him. 'But not completely surprised, perhaps?'

Saul flushed. 'Forgive me. The great Philip was in charge here at St John and then became prior of Kingsbridge, and others have followed the same route. That is not to say that I'm worthy as they were, of course. But the thought had crossed my mind, I confess.'

'Nothing to be ashamed of. How would you feel about being nominated?'

'How would I feel?' Saul seemed mystified. 'Why ask that? If the earl wishes, he will nominate me; and if my brethren want me, they'll vote for me; and I will consider myself called by God. It makes no difference how I feel about it.'

This was not the answer Godwyn wanted. He needed Saul to make up his own mind. Talk of God's will was counterproductive. 'It's not quite so simple,' he said. 'You don't have to accept the nomination. That's why the earl sent me here.'

'It's not like Roland to ask where he might command.'

Godwyn almost winced. Never forget how shrewd Saul is, he told himself. He backpedalled hastily. 'No, indeed. However, if you think you might refuse, he needs to know as soon as possible, so that he can nominate someone else.' That was probably true, though Roland had not said it.

'I didn't realize it was done this way.'

It was not done this way, Godwyn thought. But he said: 'Last time it happened, when Prior Anthony was elected, you and I were both novices, so we didn't know what went on.'

'True.'

'Do you feel you have the ability to fill the role of prior of Kingsbridge?'

'Certainly not.'

'Ah.' Godwyn pretended disappointment, though he had been relying on Saul's humility to produce that answer.

'However...'

'What?'

'With God's help, who knows what might be accomplished?'

'How true.' Godwyn concealed his annoyance. The humble answer had just been a formality. The truth was that Saul thought he could do the job. 'Of course, you should reflect and pray about it tonight.'

'I'm sure I'll think of little else.' They heard distant voices. 'The brothers are returning from their work.'

'We can talk again in the morning,' Godwyn said. 'If you decide to be a candidate, you must come back to Kingsbridge with us.'

'Very well.'

There was a serious danger of Saul's accepting, Godwyn feared. But he had one more arrow to shoot. 'Something else you might bear in mind in your prayers,' he said. 'A nobleman never offers a free gift.'

Saul looked worried. 'What do you mean?'

'Earls and barons dispense titles, land, positions, monopolies – but these things always have a price.'

'And in this case?'

'If you are elected, Roland will expect you to make recompense. You are his cousin, anyway; and you'll owe your position to him. You will be his voice in chapter, making sure the priory's actions don't interfere with his interests.'

'Will he make that an explicit condition of the nomination?'

'Explicit? No. But, when you return with me to Kingsbridge, he will question you, and the questions will be designed to reveal your intentions. If you insist that you will be an independent prior, showing no special favour to your cousin and sponsor, he will nominate someone else.'

'I had not thought of that.'

'Of course, you may simply give him the answers he wants to hear and then change your mind after the election.'

'But that would be dishonest.'

'Some would think so.'

'God would think so.'

'That's something for you to pray about tonight.'

A group of young monks came into the kitchen, muddy from the fields, talking loudly; Saul got up to serve them ale, but the worried look remained on his face. It stayed there when they went into the little church, with its wall painting of the Day of Judgement over the altar, for Evensong. It was still there when at last the evening meal was served and Godwyn's hunger was assuaged by the delicious cheese the monks made.

Godwyn lay awake that night, although he ached from two days on horseback. He had confronted Saul with an ethical dilemma. Most monks would have been willing to shade their position while talking to Roland, and speak words which promised a degree of subservience to the earl much greater than they really intended. But not Saul. He was driven by moral imperatives. Would he find a way through the dilemma, and accept the nomination? Godwyn did not see how he could.

Saul still wore the worried look when the monks got up, at first light, for the service of Lauds.

After breakfast, he told Godwyn he could not accept the nomination.

*

GODWYN COULD NOT get used to Earl Roland's face. It was the strangest thing to look at. The earl was now wearing a hat to cover the bandages on his head; but, by making his appearance more normal, the hat emphasized the paralysis of the right side of his face. Roland also seemed even more bad-tempered than usual, and Godwyn guessed he was still suffering severe headaches.

'Where is my cousin Saul?' he said as soon as Godwyn walked into the room.

'Still at St John, my lord. I gave him your message—'

'Message? It was a command!'

Lady Philippa, standing beside the bed, said softly: 'Don't excite yourself, lord – you know it makes you feel ill.'

Godwyn said: 'Brother Saul simply said that he cannot accept the nomination.'

'Why the devil not?'

'He thought and prayed—'

'Of course he prayed, that's what monks do. What reason did he give for defying me?'

'He does not feel himself capable of such a challenging role.'

'Nonsense. What challenge? He's not being asked to lead a thousand knights into battle – just make sure a handful of monks sing their hymns at the right times of day.'

That was rubbish, so Godwyn bowed his head and said nothing.

The earl's tone changed suddenly. 'I've just realized who you are. You're the son of Petranilla, aren't you?'

'Yes, lord.' That Petranilla whom you jilted, Godwyn thought.

'She was sly, and I'll bet you are too. How do I know you didn't talk Saul out of accepting? You want Thomas Langley to be prior, don't you?'

My plan is a lot more devious than that, you fool, Godwyn thought. He said: 'Saul did ask me what you might want in return for nominating him.'

'Ah, now we come to it. What did you tell him?'

'That you would expect him to listen to one who was his cousin, his sponsor and his earl.'

'And he was too pig-headed to accept that, I suppose. Right. That settles it. I shall nominate that fat friar. Now get out of my sight.'

Godwyn had to hide his elation as he bowed out of the room. The penultimate stage of his plan had worked perfectly. Earl Roland had not the least suspicion of how he had been nudged into nominating the most hopeless candidate Godwyn could think of.

Now for the final step.

He left the hospital and entered the cloisters. It was the hour of study before the midday service of Sext, and most of the monks were standing or sitting around reading, being read to or meditating. Godwyn spotted Theodoric, his young ally, and summoned him with a jerk of the head.

In a low voice, he said: 'Earl Roland has nominated Friar Murdo as prior.'

Theodoric said loudly: 'What?'

'Hush.'

'It's impossible!'

'Of course it is.'

'No one will vote for him.'

'That's why I'm pleased.'

Understanding dawned on Theodoric's face. 'Oh ... I see. So it's good for us, really.'

Godwyn wondered why he always had to explain these things, even to intelligent men. No one saw below the surface, except him and his mother. 'Go around telling everyone – quietly. No need to show your outrage. They'll get angry enough without encouragement.'

'Should I say that this is good for Thomas?'

'Absolutely not.'

'Right,' said Theodoric. 'I understand.'

He evidently did not, but Godwyn felt he could be trusted to follow instructions.

Godwyn left him and went in search of Philemon. He found

him sweeping out the refectory. 'Do you know where Murdo is?' he asked.

'Probably in the kitchen.'

'Find him and ask him to meet you in the prior's house when all the monks are in church for Sext. I don't want anyone to see you there with him.'

'All right. What do I tell him?'

'First of all, you say: "Brother Murdo, no one must ever know that I told you this." Is that clear?'

'No one must ever know that I told you this. All right.'

'Then show him the charter we found. You remember where it is – in the bedroom beside the prie-dieu, there's a chest with a ginger-coloured leather wallet inside.'

'Is that all?'

'Point out that the land Thomas brought to the priory belonged originally to Queen Isabella, and that this fact has been kept secret for ten years.'

Philemon looked puzzled. 'But we don't know what Thomas is trying to hide.'

'No. But there's always a reason for a secret.'

'Don't you think Murdo will try to use this information against Thomas?'

'Of course.'

'What will Murdo do?'

'I don't know but, whatever it is, it's sure to be bad for Thomas.'

Philemon frowned. 'I thought we were supposed to be helping Thomas.'

Godwyn smiled. 'That's what everyone thinks.'

The bell rang for Sext.

Philemon went off in search of Murdo, and Godwyn joined the rest of the monks in church. In unison with the others he said: 'O God, incline unto mine aid.' On this occasion he prayed with unusual earnestness. Despite the confidence he had shown Philemon, he knew he was gambling. He had staked everything on Thomas's secret, but he did not know what the face of the card would show when he turned it up.

However, it was clear he had succeeded in stirring up the

monks. They were restless and talkative, and Carlus had to call for quiet twice during the psalms. They disliked friars in general, for taking an attitude of moral superiority on the question of earthly possessions while, at the same time, sponging off those they condemned. And they disliked Murdo in particular for being pompous, greedy and drunk. They would have anyone rather than him.

As they left the church after the service, Simeon spoke to Godwyn. 'We cannot have the friar,' he said.

'I agree.'

'Carlus and I will not be putting forward another name. If the monks appear divided, the earl will be able to present his candidate as a necessary compromise. We must sink our differences and rally round Thomas. If we show the world a united front, it will be difficult for the earl to oppose us.'

Godwyn stopped and faced Simeon. 'Thank you, brother,' he said, forcing himself to look humble and hide the exultation he felt.

'We're doing it for the good of the priory.'

'I know. But I appreciate your generosity of spirit.'

Simeon nodded and walked away.

Godwyn smelled victory.

The monks went into the refectory for dinner. Murdo joined them. He missed services, but not meals. All monasteries had a general rule that any monk or friar was welcome at the table – though few people exploited the practice as thoroughly as Murdo. Godwyn studied his face. The friar looked excited, as if he had news he was bursting to share. However, he contained himself while dinner was served, and remained silent throughout the meal, listening to a novice read.

The passage chosen was the story of Susanna and the Elders. Godwyn disapproved: the story was too sexy to be read aloud in a celibate community. But today even the attempts of two lascivious old men to blackmail a woman into having sex with them failed to capture the monks' attention. They kept whispering among themselves, looking sidelong at Murdo.

When the food was finished, and the prophet Daniel had saved Susanna from execution by interrogating the elders separately and showing that they told inconsistent stories, the monks got ready to leave. At that moment, Murdo spoke to Thomas.

'When you came here, Brother Thomas, you had a sword wound, I believe.'

He spoke loudly enough for everyone to hear, and the other monks stopped to listen.

Thomas looked at him stonily. 'Yes.'

'The wound that eventually caused you to lose your left arm. I wonder, did you receive that wound in the service of Queen Isabella?'

Thomas turned pale. 'I've been a monk of Kingsbridge for ten years. My previous life is forgotten.'

Murdo carried on unperturbed. 'I ask because of the parcel of land that you brought with you when you joined the priory. A very productive little village in Norfolk. Five hundred acres. Near Lynn – where the queen lives.'

Godwyn interrupted, pretending to be indignant. 'What does an outsider know of our property?'

'Oh, I've read the charter,' Murdo said. 'These things aren't secret.'

Godwyn looked at Carlus and Simeon, sitting side by side. Both men looked startled. As sub-prior and treasurer, they knew already. They must be wondering how Murdo had got sight of the deed. Simeon opened his mouth to speak.

Murdo said: 'Or, at least, they're not supposed to be secret.'

Simeon closed his mouth again. If he demanded to know how Murdo had found out, he would himself face questions about why he had kept the secret.

Murdo went on: 'And the farm at Lynn was donated to the priory by...' He paused for dramatic effect. 'Queen Isabella,' he finished.

Godwyn looked around. There was consternation among the monks, all but Carlus and Simeon, who both looked stone-faced.

Friar Murdo leaned across the table. Green herbs from the dinnertime stew adhered to his teeth. 'I ask you again,' he said aggressively. 'Did you receive your wound in the service of Queen Isabella?'

Thomas said: 'Everyone knows what I did before I was a monk. I was a knight, I fought battles, I killed men. I have confessed and received absolution.'

'A monk may put his past behind him – but the prior of Kingsbridge carries a heavier burden. He may be asked who he killed, and why, and – most importantly – what reward he received.'

Thomas stared back at Murdo without speaking. Godwyn tried to read Thomas's face. It was rigidly set in an expression of some strong emotion – but what? There was no sign of guilt, or even embarrassment: whatever the secret was, Thomas did not feel he had done something shameful. The look was not rage, either. Murdo's sneering tone might have provoked many men to violence, but Thomas did not look as if he were about to lash out. No, what Thomas seemed to be feeling was something different, colder than embarrassment, quieter than rage. It was, Godwyn realized at last, fear. Thomas was afraid. Of Murdo? Hardly. No, he feared something that might happen because of Murdo, some consequence of Murdo's having discovered the secret.

Murdo continued like a dog with a bone. 'If you don't answer the question here in this room, it will be asked elsewhere.'

Godwyn's calculations called for Thomas to give up at this point. But it was not a certainty. Thomas was tough. For ten years he had shown himself to be quiet, patient and resilient. When approached by Godwyn to stand as prior, he must have decided that the past could be buried. He must now realize he had been wrong. But how would he react to that realization? Would he see his mistake and back away? Or would he grit his teeth and see it through? Godwyn bit his lip and waited.

Thomas spoke at last. 'I think you may be right about the question being asked elsewhere,' he said. 'Or, at least, I think you will do everything in your power, no matter how unbrotherly or dangerous, to make your forecast come true.'

'I don't know if you're implying—'

'You need say no more!' Thomas said, rising abruptly to his feet. Murdo recoiled. Thomas's height and soldierly physique, combined with a sharp rise in his voice, achieved the rare result of silencing the friar.

'I have never answered questions about my past,' Thomas said. His voice was quiet again, and every monk in the room was still and silent, straining to hear. 'I never will.' He pointed at Murdo. 'But this ... slug ... makes me realize that, if I became your prior, such questions would never cease. A monk may keep his past to himself, but a prior is different, I now see. A prior may have enemies, and any mystery is a weakness. And then, of course, by the leader's vulnerability the institution itself is threatened. My brain should have led me where Friar Murdo's malice led him – to the conclusion that a man who does not want to answer questions about his past cannot be a prior. Therefore—'

Young Theodoric said: 'No!'

'Therefore I now withdraw my candidacy in the coming election.'

Godwyn breathed a long sigh of satisfaction. He had achieved his object.

Thomas sat down; Murdo looked smug; and everyone else tried to speak at the same time.

Carlus banged the table, and slowly they quietened down. He said: 'Friar Murdo, as you don't have a vote in this election, I must ask you to leave us now.'

Murdo slowly walked out, looking triumphant.

When he had gone, Carlus said: 'This is a catastrophe – Murdo the only candidate!'

Theodoric said: 'Thomas cannot be allowed to withdraw.'

'But he has!'

Simeon said: 'There must be another candidate.'

'Yes,' said Carlus. 'And I propose Simeon.'

'No!' said Theodoric.

'Let me speak,' said Simeon. 'We must choose the one among us who is most certain to unite the brethren against Murdo. That is not myself. I know I don't have enough backing among the youngsters. I think we all know who would gather most support from all sections.'

He turned and looked at Godwyn.

'Yes!' Theodoric said. 'Godwyn!'

The younger monks cheered, and the older ones looked resigned. Godwyn shook his head, as if reluctant even to respond to them. They began to bang the tables and chant his name: 'God-wyn! God-wyn!'

At last he stood up. His heart was full of elation, but he kept his face straight. He held up his hands for quiet. Then, when the room was silent, he said in a low, modest voice: 'I shall obey the will of my brethren.'

The room erupted in cheering.

23

GODWYN DELAYED THE ELECTION. Earl Roland was going to be angry at the result, and Godwyn wanted to give him as little time as possible to fight the decision before the wedding.

The truth was that Godwyn was frightened. He was going up against one of the most powerful men in the kingdom. There were only thirteen earls. Together with about forty lesser barons, twenty-one bishops and a handful of others, they governed England. When the king summoned Parliament, they were the Lords, the aristocratic group, by contrast with the Commons, who were knights, gentry and merchants. The earl of Shiring was one of the more powerful and prominent men of his class. And yet Brother Godwyn, age thirty-one, son of the widow Petranilla, who had risen no higher than sacrist of Kingsbridge Priory, was in conflict with the earl – and, what was even more dangerous, he was winning.

So he dithered – but, six days before the wedding, Roland put his foot down and said: 'Tomorrow!'

Guests were already arriving for the nuptials. The earl of Monmouth had moved into the hospital, using the private room next to Roland's. Lord William and Lady Philippa had had to remove to the Bell inn. Bishop Richard was sharing the prior's house with Carlus. Lesser barons and knights filled the taverns, along with their wives and children, squires and servants and horses. The town enjoyed a surge of spending, much needed after the disappointing profits from the rain-drenched Fleece Fair.

On the morning of the election, Godwyn and Simeon went to the treasury, a small windowless room behind a heavy oak door off the library. The precious ornaments used for special services were there, locked in an ironbound chest. Simeon as treasurer held the keys.

The election was a foregone conclusion, or so thought everyone except Earl Roland. No one suspected Godwyn's hidden hand. He had suffered one tense moment, when Thomas had wondered aloud how Friar Murdo got to know about the Isabella charter. 'He can't have discovered it accidentally – he's never been seen reading in the library, and anyway that deed isn't kept with the others,' Thomas had said to Godwyn. 'Someone must have told him about it. But who? Only Carlus and Simeon knew of it. Why would they have let the secret out? They didn't want to help Murdo.' Godwyn had said nothing, and Thomas had remained baffled.

Godwyn and Simeon dragged the treasure chest into the light of the library. The cathedral jewels were wrapped in blue cloth and cushioned in protective sheets of leather. As they sorted through the box, Simeon unwrapped some of the items, admiring them and checking that they were undamaged. There was a plaque a few inches wide made of ivory, delicately carved, showing the crucifixion of St Adolphus, at which the saint had asked God to grant good health and long life to all those who venerated his memory. There were numerous candlesticks and crucifixes, all of gold or silver, most decorated with precious stones. In the strong light from the tall library windows the gems glittered and the gold glowed. These things had been given to the priory, over the centuries, by devout worshippers. Their combined value was awesome: there was more wealth here than most people ever saw in one place.

Godwyn had come for a ceremonial crosier, or shepherd's crook, made of wood encased in gold, with an elaborately jewelled handle. This was ritually handed to the new prior at the end of the election process. The crook was at the bottom of the chest, not having been used for thirteen years. As Godwyn drew it out, Simeon let out an exclamation.

Godwyn looked up sharply. Simeon was holding a large crucifix on a stand, intended to be placed on an altar. 'What's the matter?' Godwyn said.

Simeon showed him the back of the cross and pointed to a shallow cup-shaped indentation just below the crosspiece.

Godwyn immediately saw that a ruby was missing. 'It must have fallen out,' he said. He glanced around the library: they were alone.

They were both worried. As treasurer and sacrist they shared responsibility. They would be blamed for any loss.

Together they examined every item in the chest. They unwrapped each one and shook out every blue cloth. They looked at all the leather sheets. Frantically, they scrutinized the empty box and the floor all around. The ruby was nowhere to be seen.

Simeon said: 'When was the crucifix last used?'

'At the feast of St Adolphus, when Carlus fell. He knocked it off the table.'

'Perhaps the ruby fell out then. But how is it possible that no one noticed?'

'The stone was on the back of the cross. But surely someone would have seen it on the floor?'

'Who picked up the crucifix?'

'I don't remember,' Godwyn said quickly. 'The situation was confused.' In fact he remembered perfectly well.

It was Philemon.

Godwyn could picture the scene. Philemon and Otho together had righted the altar, setting it squarely on its platform. Then Otho had picked up the candlesticks and Philemon the cross.

With a growing feeling of dismay, Godwyn recalled the disappearance of Lady Philippa's bracelet. Had Philemon stolen again? He trembled to think how it might affect him. Everyone knew that Philemon was Godwyn's unofficial acolyte. Such a dreadful sin – stealing a jewel from a sacred ornament – would bring shame on everyone associated with the perpetrator. It could easily upset the election.

Simeon obviously did not recollect the scene exactly, and he accepted without question Godwyn's feigned inability to remember who had picked up the cross. But others among the monks would surely recall seeing it in Philemon's hands. Godwyn had to put this right quickly, before suspicion could fall on Philemon. But first he had to get Simeon out of the way.

'We must search for the ruby in the church,' Simeon said.

'But the service was two weeks ago,' Godwyn protested. 'A ruby can't have lain on the floor unnoticed for that length of time.'

'It's unlikely, but we must check.'

Godwyn saw that he had to go with Simeon, and wait for an opportunity to get away from him and seek out Philemon. 'Of course,' he said.

They put the ornaments away and locked the treasury door. As they left the library, Godwyn said: 'I suggest we say nothing about this until we're sure the jewel has been lost. No point in bringing blame on our heads prematurely.'

'Agreed.'

They hurried around the cloisters and entered the church. They stood in the centre of the crossing and scanned the ground all around them. A month ago, the idea that a ruby could lie hidden somewhere on the church floor would have been more plausible; but recently the flagstones had been repaired, and the cracks and chips had disappeared. A ruby would have stood out.

Simeon said: 'Now that I come to think of it, wasn't it Philemon who picked up the crucifix?'

Godwyn looked at Simeon's face. Was there accusation in the expression? He could not tell. 'It may have been Philemon,' Godwyn said. Then he saw a chance to get away. 'I'll go and fetch him,' he suggested. 'Perhaps he will be able to recall exactly where he was standing at the time.'

'Good idea. I'll wait here.' Simeon got down on his knees and began to pat the floor with his hands, as if the ruby might be found by touch more easily than by sight.

Godwyn hurried out. He went first to the dormitory. The blanket cupboard was in the same place. He pulled it away from the wall, found the loose stone, and removed it. He put his hand into the hidey-hole where Philemon had stashed Lady Philippa's bracelet.

He found nothing there.

He cursed. It was not going to be that easy.

I'll have to dismiss Philemon from the monastery, he thought as he strode through the priory buildings looking for him. If he has stolen this ruby, I can't cover up for him again. He's out.

Then he realized, with a shock of dismay, that he could not dismiss Philemon – not now, perhaps not ever. It was Philemon who had told Friar Murdo about the Isabella charter. If dismissed, Philemon could confess what he had done, and reveal that he had done it at Godwyn's instigation. And he would be believed. Godwyn recalled Thomas's puzzling over who had told Murdo the secret, and why. Philemon's revelation would gain conviction by answering that question.

There would be an outcry at such underhand work. Even if the disclosure were made after the election, it would undermine Godwyn's authority and cripple his ability to lead the monks. The ominous truth dawned on him that he now had to protect Philemon in order to protect himself.

He found Philemon sweeping the hospital floor. He beckoned him outside and led him around to the back of the kitchen, where it was unlikely that anyone would see them.

He looked Philemon in the eye and said: 'There's a ruby missing.'

Philemon looked away. 'How terrible.'

'It's from the altar crucifix that was knocked to the floor when Carlus fell over.'

Philemon pretended innocence. 'How could it have gone missing?'

'The ruby may have become dislodged when the crucifix hit the floor. But it's not on the floor now – I've just looked. Someone found it – and kept it.'

'Surely not.'

Godwyn felt angered by Philemon's false air of innocence. 'You fool, everyone saw you pick up that crucifix!'

Philemon's voice rose to a higher pitch. 'I know nothing about it!'

'Don't waste time lying to me! We have to put this right. I could lose the election on your account.' Godwyn pushed Philemon up against the wall of the bakehouse. 'Where is it?'

To his astonishment, Philemon began to cry.

'For the love of the saints,' Godwyn said disgustedly. 'Stop this nonsense – you're a grown man!'

Philemon continued to sob. 'I'm sorry,' he said. 'I'm sorry.'

'If you don't stop that—' Godwyn checked himself. Nothing was to be gained by berating Philemon. The man was truly pathetic. Speaking more gently, he said: 'Try to pull yourself together. Where is the ruby?'

'I hid it.'

'Yes...'

'In the refectory chimney.'

Godwyn immediately turned away, heading for the refectory. 'Mary save us, it could fall into the fire!'

Philemon followed, his tears drying. 'There's no fire in August. I would have moved it before the cold weather.'

They entered the refectory. At one end of the long room was a wide fireplace. Philemon put his arm up the chimney and fumbled for a moment. Then he produced a ruby the size of a sparrow's egg, covered with soot. He wiped it clean on his sleeve.

Godwyn took it. 'Now come with me,' he said.

'What are we going to do?'

'Simeon is going to find this.'

They went to the church. Simeon was still searching on hands and knees. 'Now,' Godwyn said to Philemon. 'Try to remember exactly where you were when you picked up the crucifix.'

Simeon looked at Philemon and, seeing signs of emotion on his face, spoke kindly to him. 'Don't be afraid, lad, you've done nothing wrong.'

Philemon positioned himself on the east side of the crossing, close to the steps leading up to the chancel. 'I think it was here,' he said.

Godwyn climbed the two steps and looked under the choir stalls, pretending to search. Surreptitiously, he placed the ruby under one of the rows of seats, close to the near end, where it was not visible to a casual glance. Then, as if changing his mind about the likeliest place to look, he moved to the south side of the chancel. 'Come and search under here, Philemon,' he said.

As he had hoped, Simeon then moved to the north side and got down on his knees to look under the stalls, murmuring a prayer as he did so.

Godwyn expected Simeon to see the ruby immediately. He pretended to search the south aisle, waiting for Simeon to find it. He began to think there must be something wrong with Simeon's eyesight. He might have to go over there and 'find' it himself. Then at last Simeon called out: 'Oh! Here!'

Godwyn pretended to be excited. 'Have you found it?'

'Yes! Hallelujah!'

'Where was it?'

'Here – under the choir stalls!'

'Praise be to God,' said Godwyn.

*

GODWYN TOLD HIMSELF not to be frightened of Earl Roland. As he climbed the stone stairs of the hospital to the guest rooms, he asked himself what the earl could do to him. Even if Roland had been capable of getting out of his bed and drawing a sword, he would not be foolish enough to attack a monk within the precincts of a monastery – even a king would hardly get away with that.

Ralph Fitzgerald announced him, and he went into the room.

The earl's sons stood either side of the bed: tall William, in soldierly brown hose and muddy boots, his hair already receding from his forehead; and Richard, in bishop's purple, his growing roundness of figure evidence of a sybaritic nature and the means to indulge it. William was thirty, a year younger than Godwyn; he had his father's strength of will, but it was sometimes softened by the influence of his wife, Philippa. Richard was twenty-eight, and presumably took after his late mother, for he had little of the earl's imposing bearing and forcefulness.

'Well, monk?' said the earl, speaking out of the left side of his mouth. 'Have you held your little election?'

Godwyn suffered a moment of resentment for this discourteous form of address. One day, he vowed silently, Roland would call him Father Prior. Indignation gave him the courage he needed to tell the earl the news. 'We have, lord,' he said. 'I have the honour to tell you that the monks of Kingsbridge have chosen me as their prior.'

'What?' the earl bellowed. 'You?'

Godwyn bowed his head in an affectation of humility. 'No one could be more surprised than I.'

'You're nothing but a boy!'

The insult stung Godwyn into a rejoinder. 'I'm older than your son, the bishop of Kingsbridge.'

'How many votes did you get?'

'Twenty-five.'

'And how many for Friar Murdo?'

'None. The monks were unanimous—'

'None?' Roland roared. 'There must have been a conspiracy – this is treason!'

'The election was held in strict accordance with the rules.'

'I don't care a pig's prick for your rules. I won't be ignored by a bunch of effeminate monks.'

'I am the choice of my brothers, my lord. The inauguration ceremony will be held this coming Sunday, before the wedding.'

'The monks' choice must be ratified by the bishop of Kingsbridge. And I can tell you he will not ratify you. Rerun the election, and this time bring me the result I want.'

'Very good, Earl Roland.' Godwyn went to the door. He had several more cards in his hand, but he was not going to lay them on the table all at once. He turned and addressed Richard. 'My lord bishop, when you wish to speak to me about this, you will find me in the prior's house.'

He stepped outside. 'You're not the prior!' Roland shouted as he shut the door.

Godwyn was trembling. Roland was formidable, especially when angry, and he was often angry. But Godwyn had stood his ground. Petranilla would be proud of him.

He went down the stairs on shaky legs and made his way to the prior's house. Carlus had already moved out. For the first time in fifteen years, Godwyn would have a bedroom to himself. His pleasure was only slightly damped by having to share the place with the bishop, who traditionally stayed there while visiting. The bishop was, technically, the abbot of Kingsbridge *ex officio* and, though his power was limited, his status was above that of the prior. Richard was rarely in the house during the day, but returned every night to sleep in the best bedroom.

Godwyn entered the ground-floor hall and sat in the big chair, waiting. It would not be long before Bishop Richard appeared, his ears burning with his father's scorching instructions. Richard was a rich and powerful man, but not frightening in the way the earl was. All the same, it was a bold monk who defied his bishop. However, Godwyn had an advantage in this confrontation, for he knew something shameful about Richard, and that was as good as a knife up his sleeve.

Richard bustled in a few minutes later, showing a confidence that Godwyn knew to be faked. 'I've struck a bargain for you,' he said without preamble. 'You can be sub-prior under Murdo. You'll be in charge of day-to-day management of the priory. Murdo doesn't want to be an administrator, anyway – he just wants the prestige. You'll have all the power, but my father will be satisfied.'

'Let me get this straight,' said Godwyn. 'Murdo agrees to make me his sub-prior. Then we tell the rest of the monks that he is the only one you'll ratify. And you think they will accept that.'

'They have no choice!'

'I have an alternative suggestion. Tell the earl that the monks will not have anyone but me – and that I must be ratified before the wedding, otherwise the monks will not take part in the nuptials. The nuns, too, will refuse.' Godwyn did not know whether the monks would go along with this – let alone Mother Cecilia and the nuns – but he was too far gone for caution.

'They wouldn't dare!'

'I'm afraid they would.'

Richard looked panicky. 'My father won't be bullied!'

Godwyn laughed. 'Small chance of that. But I hope he may be made to see reason.'

'He'll say the wedding must go ahead anyway. I'm the bishop, I can marry the couple, I don't need monks to help me.'

'Of course. But there will be no singing, no candles, no psalms, no incense – just you and Archdeacon Lloyd.'

'They will still be married.'

'How will the earl of Monmouth feel about such a mean wedding for his son?'

'He'll be furious, but he'll accept it. The alliance is the important thing.'

That was probably right, Godwyn thought, and he felt the cold draught of imminent failure.

It was time to draw his concealed knife.

'You owe me a kindness,' he said.

At first, Richard pretended not to know what he was talking about. 'Do I?'

'I concealed a sin you committed. Don't pretend to have forgotten, it was only a couple of months ago.'

'Ah, yes, that was generous of you.'

'I saw, with my own eyes, you and Margery on the bed in the guest room.'

'Hush, for pity's sake!'

'Now is your chance to repay me that kindness. Intercede with your father. Tell him to give in. Argue that the wedding is more important. Insist on ratifying me.'

Richard's face showed desperation. He looked crushed by opposing forces. 'I can't!' he said, and there was panic in his voice. 'My father won't be defied. You know what he's like.'

'Try.'

'I've already tried! I forced him to concede that you could be sub-prior.'

Godwyn doubted that Roland had conceded any such thing. Richard had almost certainly made it up, knowing that such a promise could easily be broken. All the same, Godwyn said: 'I thank you for that.' Then he added: 'But it's not enough.'

'Just think about it,' Richard pleaded. 'That's all I ask.'

'I will. And I suggest you ask your father to do the same.'

'Oh, God,' Richard groaned. 'This is going to be a catastrophe.'

*

THE WEDDING WAS scheduled for Sunday. On the Saturday, in place of the service of Sext, Godwyn ordered a rehearsal, beginning with the ceremony of inauguration of the new prior and continuing with the marriage service. Outside it was another sunless day, the sky full of low grey cloud heavy with rain, and the inside of the cathedral was gloomy. After the rehearsal, as the monks and nuns headed off for dinner and the novices began to tidy up the church, Godwyn was approached by Carlus and Simeon, both looking solemn.

'I think that went very smoothly, don't you?' Godwyn said brightly.

Simeon said: 'Is there actually going to be an inauguration for you?'

'Absolutely.'

'We hear the earl has ordered the election to be rerun.'

'Do you think he has the right to do that?'

'Indeed not,' said Simeon. 'He has the power of nomination, that's all. But he says Bishop Richard will not ratify you as prior.'

'Has Richard told you that?'

'Not himself, no.'

'I thought not. Trust me, the bishop will ratify me.' Godwyn heard his own voice sounding sincere and confident, and wished his feelings matched it.

Carlus said anxiously, 'Did you tell Richard the monks would refuse to take part in the wedding?'

'I did.'

'That's very hazardous. We're not here to oppose the will of noblemen.'

Godwyn could have predicted that Carlus would weaken at the first sign of serious opposition. Fortunately, he was not planning to test the monks' resolve. 'We won't have to do it, don't worry. It's just an empty threat. But don't tell the bishop I said so.'

'So you're not planning to ask the monks to boycott the wedding?'

'No.'

Simeon said: 'You're playing a dangerous game.'

'Perhaps – but I trust no one is in danger except me.'

'You did not even want to be prior. You would not allow your name to be put forward. You only accepted when all else failed.'

'I don't want to be prior,' Godwyn lied. 'But the earl of Shiring must not be allowed to choose for us, and that's more important than my personal feelings.'

Simeon looked at him with respect. 'You're being very honourable.'

'Like you, brother, I'm just trying to do the will of God.'

'May He bless your efforts.'

The two old monks left him. He felt a twinge of conscience for allowing them to believe that he was acting unselfishly. They saw him as some kind of martyr. But it was true, he told himself, that he was only trying to do the will of God.

He looked around: the church was back to normal. He was about to go to the prior's house for dinner when his cousin Caris appeared, her blue dress a startling splash of colour in the dim grey church. 'Are you going to be inaugurated tomorrow?' she said.

He smiled. 'Everyone's asking the same question. The answer is yes.'

'We hear the earl is putting up a fight.'

'He's going to lose it.'

Her shrewd green eyes gave him a penetrating stare. 'I've known you since you were a child, and I can tell when you're lying.'

'I'm not lying.'

'You're pretending to be more certain than you actually feel.'

'That's not a sin.'

'My father is worried about the bridge. Friar Murdo is even more likely to obey the earl's will than Saul Whitehead was.'

'Murdo is not going to be prior of Kingsbridge.'

'There you go again.'

Godwyn was annoyed by her perspicacity. 'I don't know what to say to you,' he snapped. 'I've been elected, and I mean to take the post. Earl Roland would like to stop me, but he doesn't have the right, and I'm fighting him with all the means at my disposal. Am I scared? Yes. But I still intend to beat him.'

She grinned. 'That's what I wanted to hear.' She punched his shoulder. 'Go and see your mother. She's in your house, waiting for you. That's what I came to tell you.' With that she turned and left.

Godwyn went out through the north transept. Caris was clever, he thought with a mixture of admiration and irritation. She had cajoled him into giving her an assessment of the situation more candid than anything he had said to anyone else.

But he was glad of the chance to talk to his mother. Everyone else doubted his power to win this fight. She would have confidence – and perhaps some strategic ideas.

He found Petranilla in the hall, sitting at the table, which was laid for two with bread, ale and a platter of salted fish. He kissed her forehead, said grace and sat down to eat. He allowed himself a moment of triumphant pleasure. 'Well,' he said. 'I'm the prior-elect, at least, and here we are having dinner in the prior's house.'

'But Roland is still fighting you,' she said.

'Harder than I expected. After all, he has the right of nomination, not selection. It's inherent in his position that his choice will not always be elected.'

'Most earls would accept that, but not him,' Petranilla said. 'He's felt superior to everyone he's ever met.' There was a bitterness in her tone which, Godwyn guessed, sprang from memories of their aborted engagement more than thirty years ago. She smiled vengefully. 'Soon he will realize how badly he's underestimated us.'

'He knows I'm your son.'

'Then that will be a factor. You probably remind him of the dishonourable way he behaved to me. That's enough to make him hate you.'

'It's a shame.' Godwyn lowered his voice in case a servant might be listening outside the door. 'Until this point, your plan has worked perfectly. Withdrawing myself from the contest, then discrediting everyone else, was brilliant.'

'Perhaps. But we may be about to lose everything. Have you said any more to the bishop?'

'No. I've reminded him that we know about Margery. He was scared, but not scared enough to defy his father, it seems.'

'He should be. If this comes out, he won't be forgiven. He

could end up a lowly knight on the level of Sir Gerald, wasting his days as a pensioner. Doesn't he realize that?'

'Perhaps he thinks I don't have the courage to reveal what I know.'

'Then you'll have to go to the earl with the information.'

'Heavens! He'll explode!'

'Steel your nerve.'

She always said this kind of thing. It was why he looked forward with such apprehension to meetings with her. She always wanted him to be a little more daring, and take greater risks, than was his inclination. But he could never refuse her.

She went on: 'If it came out that Margery's not a virgin, the marriage would be called off. Roland doesn't want that. He'll accept the lesser evil of you as prior.'

'But he'll be my enemy for the rest of his life.'

'He'll be that whatever happens.'

Small consolation, Godwyn thought; but he did not argue, for he could see that his mother was right.

There was a tap at the door, and Lady Philippa walked in. Godwyn and Petranilla stood up.

'I need to talk to you,' Philippa said to Godwyn.

He said: 'May I present my mother, Petranilla?'

Petranilla curtsied, then said: 'I'd better leave. You're obviously here to broker a deal, my lady.'

Philippa gave her an amused look. 'If you know that much, you know everything of importance. Perhaps you should stay.'

As the two women stood facing one another, Godwyn noticed that they were similar: same height, same statuesque build and the same imperious air. Philippa was younger, of course, by something like twenty years; and she had a relaxed authority, and a touch of humour, that contrasted with Petranilla's tight-wound determination – perhaps because Philippa had a husband and Petranilla had lost hers. But Philippa was a strong-willed woman who exercised power through a man – Lord William – and, Godwyn now realized, Petranilla also wielded influence through a man – himself.

'Let's sit down,' Philippa said.

Petranilla said: 'Has the earl approved whatever you're about to propose?'

'No.' Philippa made a helpless gesture with her hands. 'Roland is too proud to agree in advance to something that might then be rejected by the other side. If I can get Godwyn's agreement to what I'm about to suggest, then I've got a chance of persuading Roland to compromise.'

'I thought as much.'

Godwyn said: 'Would you like something to eat, my lady?'

Philippa dismissed the offer with an impatient wave. 'As things stand, everyone is going to lose,' she began. 'The wedding will take place, but without the proper pomp and ceremony; so that Roland's alliance with the earl of Monmouth will be blighted from the start. The bishop will refuse to ratify you as prior, Godwyn, so the archbishop will be called in to resolve the dispute; and he will dismiss both you and Murdo, and nominate someone new, probably a member of his staff whom he wants to be rid of. No one will get what they want. Am I right?'

She directed the question at Petranilla, who made a noncommittal sound.

'So why not anticipate the archbishop's compromise?' Philippa went on. 'Bring forward the third candidate now. Only –' she pointed a finger at Godwyn – 'the candidate is chosen by you – and he promises to make you sub-prior.'

Godwyn considered. This would relieve him of the need to confront the earl eyeball-to-eyeball and threaten him with the revelation of his son's behaviour. But the compromise would doom him to be sub-prior for an indefinite period – and then, when the new prior died, he would have to fight the battle all over again. He was inclined to refuse, despite his apprehension.

He glanced at his mother. She gave an almost imperceptible shake of the head. She did not like it either.

'I'm sorry,' Godwyn said to Philippa. 'The monks have held an election, and the result must stand.'

Philippa stood up. 'In that case, I must give you the message that is my official reason for coming here. Tomorrow morning the earl will rise from his sick bed. He wishes to inspect the cathedral and make sure all is ready in plenty of time for the wedding. You are to meet him in the church at eight o'clock. All the monks and nuns must be robed ready, and the church dressed with the usual ornaments.'

Godwyn bowed his head in acknowledgement, and she went out.

*

AT THE APPOINTED HOUR Godwyn stood in a bare, silent church.

He was alone: there were no monks or nuns with him. No furniture was to be seen, except for the fixed choir stalls. There were no candles, no crucifixes, no chalices, no flowers. The watery sun that had shone fitfully through rain clouds much of this summer now cast a weak, cold light into the nave. Godwyn held his hands tightly together behind his back to keep them from shaking.

On time, the earl walked in.

With him were Lord William, Lady Philippa, Bishop Richard, Richard's assistant Archdeacon Lloyd, and the earl's clerk Father Jerome. Godwyn would have liked to surround himself with an entourage, but none of the monks knew quite how risky his scheme was, and if they had known they might not have had the nerve to back him up; so he had decided to face the earl alone.

The bandages had been removed from Roland's head. He walked slowly but steadily. He must surely feel shaky after so many weeks in bed, Godwyn thought, but he seemed determined not to show it. He looked normal apart from the paralysis of half his face. His message to the world today would be that he was fully recovered and back in charge. And Godwyn was threatening to spoil that design.

The others looked with incredulity at the empty church, but the earl showed no surprise. 'You're an arrogant monk,' he said to Godwyn, speaking as always out of the left side of his mouth.

Godwyn was risking everything, and had nothing further to lose by being defiant, so he said: 'You're an obstinate earl.'

Roland put his hand on the hilt of his sword. 'I ought to run you through for that.'

'Go ahead.' Godwyn held his arms out sideways, ready to be crucified. 'Murder the prior of Kingsbridge, here in the cathedral, just as King Henry's knights murdered Archbishop Thomas Becket in Canterbury. Send me to heaven and yourself to eternal damnation.'

Philippa gasped with shock at Godwyn's disrespect. William moved as if to silence Godwyn. Roland restrained him with a gesture, and said to Godwyn: 'Your bishop orders you to ready the church for the wedding. Don't monks take a vow of obedience?'

'The lady Margery cannot be married here.'

'Why not – because you want to be prior?'

'Because she is not a virgin.'

Philippa's hand flew to her mouth. Richard groaned. William drew his sword. Roland said: 'This is treason!'

Godwyn said: 'Put away your sword, Lord William – you can't restore her maidenhead with that.'

Roland said: 'What do you know of such things, monk?'

'Two men of this priory witnessed the act, which took place in a private room of the hospital, the very room where you, my lord, are staying.'

'I don't believe you.'

'The earl of Monmouth will.'

'You would not dare to tell him.'

'I must explain to him why his son cannot marry Margery in Kingsbridge Cathedral – at least until she has confessed her sin and received absolution.'

'You have no proof of this slander.'

'I have two witnesses. But ask the girl. I believe she will confess. I imagine she favours the lover who took her virginity over the political match chosen by her uncle.' Once again Godwyn was going out on a limb. But he had seen Margery's face when Richard was kissing her, and at that moment he had felt sure she was in love. Having to marry the earl's son must be breaking her heart. It would be very difficult for such a young woman to lie convincingly if her emotions were as turbulent as Godwyn guessed.

The animated half of Roland's face was working with fury. 'And who is this man who you claim committed this crime? For, if you can prove what you allege, the villain will hang, I swear. And, if not, you will. So let him be sent for, and we'll see what he has to say.'

'He's already here.'

Roland looked with incredulity at the four men with him – his two sons, William and Richard, plus two priests, Lloyd and Jerome.

Godwyn stared at Richard.

Roland followed the direction of Godwyn's stare. In a moment, they were all looking at Richard.

Godwyn held his breath. What would Richard say? Would he bluster? Would he accuse Godwyn of lying? Would he fly into a rage and attack his accuser?

But his face showed defeat, not anger, and after a moment he bowed his head and said: 'It's no good. The damned monk is right – she will not withstand interrogation.'

Earl Roland went white. 'You did this?' he said. For once he was not shouting, but that seemed to make him more terrifying. 'The girl I betrothed to an earl's son – you fucked her?'

Richard made no reply, but looked down at the ground.

'You fool,' the earl said. 'You traitor. You—'

Philippa interrupted him. 'Who else knows?'

That stopped the tirade. They all looked at her.

'Perhaps the wedding may still take place,' she said. 'Thank God, the earl of Monmouth isn't here.' She looked at Godwyn. 'Who knows about this, other than the people here now, and the two men of the priory who witnessed the act?'

Godwyn tried to calm his thudding heart. He was so close to success that he seemed to taste it. 'No one else knows, my lady,' he said.

'All of us on the earl's side can keep the secret,' she said. 'What about your men?'

'They will obey their elected prior,' he said, with the slightest emphasis on the word 'elected'.

Philippa turned to Roland. 'Then the wedding can take place.'

Godwyn added: 'Provided the inauguration ceremony is held first.'

Everyone looked at the earl.

He took a step forward and suddenly hit Richard in the face. It was a powerful blow struck by a soldier who knew how to put all his weight into it. Although he used his open hand, Richard was knocked to the ground.

Richard lay still, looking terrified, blood trickling from his mouth.

Earl Roland's face was white and sweating: the blow had used up all his reserves, and he now looked shaky. Several silent seconds passed. At last he seemed to recover his strength. With a contemptuous glance at the purple-robed figure cowering on the floor, he turned on his heel and walked, slowly but steadily, out of the church.

24

CARIS STOOD ON THE GREEN in front of Kingsbridge Cathedral, along with at least half the population of the town, waiting for the bride and groom to emerge from the great west door of the church.

Caris was not sure why she was here. She had been feeling negative about marriage ever since the day Merthin had finished his hoist and they had had an abrasive conversation about their future. She felt angry with him, even though everything he had said made perfect sense. Of course he wanted to have his own house and live with her in it; of course he wanted to sleep with her every night and have children. That was what everyone wanted – everyone, it seemed, except Caris.

And in fact she wanted all those things too, in a way. She would have liked to lie down beside him every evening, and put her arms around his slim body any time she wanted, and feel his clever hands on her skin when she woke up in the morning, and give birth to a miniature version of him that they could both love and care for. But she did not want the things that went with marriage. She wanted a lover, not a master; she wanted to live with him, not dedicate her life to him. And she was angry with Merthin for forcing her to face up to the dilemma. Why could they not go on just as they were?

For three weeks she had hardly spoken to him. She pretended to have a summer cold, and in fact she developed a painful sore on her lip that gave her an excuse not to kiss him. He still took his meals at her house, and talked amiably with her father; but he did not linger after Edmund and Petranilla went to bed.

Now Caris's sore had healed and her anger had cooled. She still did not want to become Merthin's property, but she wished he would start kissing her again. However, he was not with her now. He was in the crowd, some distance away, talking to Bessie Bell, daughter of the landlord of the Bell inn. She was a small girl with a curvy body and the kind of grin that men called saucy and women called tarty. Merthin was making her laugh. Caris looked away.

The big wooden church door opened. A cheer went up from the crowd, and the bride emerged. Margery was a pretty girl of sixteen, dressed in white, with flowers in her hair. The groom followed her out, a tall, serious-looking man about ten years older than she.

They both looked completely miserable.

They hardly knew each other. Until this week, they had met only once, six months ago, when the two earls had arranged the marriage. There was a rumour that Margery loved someone else, but of course there was no question of her disobeying Earl Roland. And her new husband had a studious air, as if he would prefer to be in a library somewhere, reading a book about geometry. What would their life together be like? It was hard to imagine their developing the kind of passion for one another that Caris and Merthin enjoyed.

She saw Merthin coming towards her through the crowd, and suddenly she was struck by the thought that she was ungrateful. How lucky she was not to be the niece of an earl! No one was going to force her into an arranged marriage. She was free to marry the man she loved – and all she could do was find reasons not to.

She greeted him with a hug and a kiss on the lips. He looked surprised, but made no comment. Some men would have been unnerved by her change of mood, but Merthin had a bedrock equanimity that was hard to shake.

They stood together and watched as Earl Roland came out of the church, followed by the earl and countess of Monmouth, then Bishop Richard and Prior Godwyn. Caris noticed that her cousin Godwyn looked both pleased and apprehensive – almost as if he were the groom. The reason, no doubt, was that he had just been inaugurated as prior.

An escort of knights formed up, the Shiring men in Roland's red-and-black livery, the Monmouth men in yellow and green.

The procession moved off, heading for the guild hall. There Earl Roland was giving a banquet for the wedding guests. Edmund was going, but Caris had managed to get out of it, and Petranilla was to accompany him.

As the bridal party left the precincts, a light shower of rain began to fall. Caris and Merthin took shelter in the cathedral porch. 'Come with me to the chancel,' Merthin said. 'I want to look at Elfric's repairs.'

The wedding guests were still leaving the church. Moving against the flow, Merthin and Caris pushed through the crowd in the nave and went to the south aisle of the chancel. This part of the church was reserved for the clergy, and they would have disapproved of Caris's being there, but the monks and nuns had already left. Caris glanced around, but there was no one to see her except one unfamiliar woman, a well-dressed redhead of about thirty, presumably a wedding guest, apparently waiting for someone.

Merthin craned his neck to look up at the vaulted ceiling over the aisle. The repairs were not quite finished: a small section of the vault was still open, and a sheet of canvas, painted white, was stretched across the gap, so that the ceiling looked complete to a casual glance.

'He's doing a decent job,' Merthin said. 'I wonder how long it will last?'

'Why wouldn't it last indefinitely?' Caris asked.

'Because we don't know why the vault crumbled. These things don't happen for no reason – they're not acts of God, regardless of what the priests may say. Whatever caused the stonework to collapse once will, presumably, do so again.'

'Is it possible to discover the cause?'

'It's not easy. Elfric certainly can't do it. I might.'

'But you've been sacked.'

'Exactly.' He stood there for a few moments, head tilted back, then said: 'I want to see this from above. I'm going into the loft.'

'I'll come with you.'

They both looked around, but there was no one nearby except for the red-haired wedding guest, who was still loitering in the south transept. Merthin led Caris to a small door that opened on a narrow spiral staircase. She followed him up, wondering what the monks would think if they knew a woman was exploring their secret passageways. The staircase emerged into an attic over the south aisle.

Caris was intrigued to see the vault from the other side. 'What you're looking at is called the extrados,' Merthin said. She liked the casual way he gave her architectural information, assuming she would be interested and knowing she would understand. He never made stupid jokes about women not grasping technicalities.

He moved along the narrow walkway then lay down to examine the new stonework closely. Mischievously, she lay beside him and put her arm around him, as if they were in bed. Merthin touched the mortar between the new stones then put his finger on his tongue. 'It's drying out quite quickly,' he said.

'I'm sure it's very dangerous if there's moisture in the cleft.'

He looked at her. 'I'll give you moisture in the cleft.'

'You already have.'

He kissed her. She closed her eyes to enjoy it more.

After a minute she said: 'Let's go to my house. We'll have it to ourselves – my father and my aunt are both at the wedding banquet.'

They were about to get up when they heard voices. A man and a woman had come into the south aisle, immediately below the repair work. What they said was only a little muffled by the canvas sheet covering the hole in the ceiling. 'Your son is thirteen now,' the woman said. 'He wants to be a knight.'

'All boys do,' came the reply.

Merthin whispered: 'Don't move – they'll hear us.'

Caris presumed the female voice to be that of the wedding guest. The male voice was familiar, and she had the feeling the speaker was a monk – but a monk could not have a son.

'And your daughter is twelve. She's going to be beautiful.'

'Like her mother.'

'A little.' There was a pause, then the woman went on: 'I can't stay long – the countess may look for me.'

So she was in the entourage of the countess of Monmouth.

She might be a lady-in-waiting, Caris guessed. She seemed to be giving news of children to a father who had not seen them for years. Who could it be?

He said: 'Why did you want to meet me, Loreen?'

'Just to look at you. I'm sorry you lost your arm.'

Caris gasped, then covered her mouth, hoping she had not been heard. There was only one monk who had lost an arm: Thomas. Now that the name had come into her mind, she knew that the voice was his. Could it be that he had a wife? And two children? Caris looked at Merthin and saw that his face was a mask of incredulity.

'What do you tell the children of me?' Thomas asked.

'That their father is dead,' Loreen replied harshly. Then she began to cry. 'Why did you do it?'

'I had no choice. If I had not come here, I would have been killed. Even now, I almost never leave the precincts.'

'Why would anyone want to kill you?'

'To protect a secret.'

'I'd be better off if you'd died. As a widow, I could find a husband, someone to be a father to my children. But this way I have all the burdens of a wife and mother but no one to help me ... no one to put his arms around me in the night.'

'I'm sorry I'm still alive.'

'Oh, I didn't mean that. I don't wish you dead. I loved you once.'

'And I loved you as much as a man of my kind can love a woman.'

Caris frowned. What did he mean by 'a man of my kind'? Was he one of those men who loved other men? Monks often were.

Whatever he meant, Loreen seemed to understand, for she said gently: 'I know you did.'

There was a long silence. Caris knew she and Merthin should not be eavesdropping on such an intimate conversation – but it was now too late to reveal themselves.

Loreen said: 'Are you happy?'

'Yes. I was not made to be a husband, or a knight. I pray for my children every day – and for you. I ask God to wash from my hands the blood of all the men I killed. This is the life I always wanted.'

'In that case, I wish you well.'

'You're very generous.'

'You'll probably never see me again.'

'I know.'

'Kiss me, and say goodbye.'

There was a long silence, then light footsteps receded. Caris lay still, hardly daring to breathe. After another pause, she heard Thomas crying. His sobs were muffled, but seemed to come from deep inside. Tears came to her own eyes as she listened.

Eventually Thomas got himself under control. He sniffed, coughed, and muttered something that might have been a prayer; then she heard his steps as he walked away.

At last she and Merthin could move. They stood up and walked back along the loft and down the spiral stairs. Neither spoke as they went down the nave of the great church. Caris felt as if she had been staring at a painting of high tragedy, the figures frozen in their dramatic attitudes of the moment, their past and future only to be guessed at.

Like a painting, the scene aroused different emotions in different people, and Merthin's reaction was not the same as hers. As they emerged into a damp summer afternoon, he said: 'What a sad story.'

'It makes me angry,' Caris said. 'That woman has been ruined by Thomas.'

'You can hardly blame him. He had to save his life.'

'And now her life is over. She has no husband, but she can't marry again. She's forced to raise two children alone. At least Thomas has the monastery.'

'She has the court of the countess.'

'How can you compare the two?' Caris said irritably. 'She's probably a distant relation, kept on as an act of charity, asked to perform menial tasks, helping the countess dress her hair and choose her clothes. She's got no choice – she's trapped.'

'So is he. You heard him say he can't leave the precincts.'

'But Thomas has a role, he's the matricularius, he makes decisions, he does something.'

'Loreen has her children.'

'Exactly! The man takes care of the most important building for miles around, and the woman is stuck with her children.'

'Queen Isabella had four children, and for a while she was one of the most powerful people in Europe.'

'But she had to get rid of her husband first.'

They went on in silence, walking out of the priory grounds into the main street, and stopped in front of Caris's house. She realized that this was another quarrel, and it was on the same subject as last time: marriage.

Merthin said: 'I'm going to the Bell for dinner.'

That was Bessie's father's inn. 'All right,' Caris said despondently.

As Merthin walked away, she called after him: 'Loreen would be better off if she'd never married.'

He spoke over his shoulder. 'What else would she do?'

That was the problem, Caris thought resentfully as she entered her house. What else was a woman to do?

The place was empty. Edmund and Petranilla were at the banquet, and the servants had the afternoon off. Only Scrap the dog was there to welcome Caris with a lazy wag of her tail. Caris patted her black head absent-mindedly, then sat at the table in the hall, brooding.

Every other young woman in Christendom wanted nothing more than to marry the man she loved – why was Caris so horrified by the prospect? From where had she got such unconventional feelings? Certainly not from her own mother. Rose had wanted only to be a good wife to Edmund. She had believed what men said about the inferiority of women. Her subordination had embarrassed Caris and, though Edmund never complained, Caris suspected that he had been bored by it. Caris had more respect for her forceful, unlovable Aunt Petranilla than for her compliant mother.

Even Petranilla had allowed her life to be shaped by men. For years she had worked to manoeuvre her father up the social ladder until he became alderman of Kingsbridge. Her strongest emotion was resentment: towards Earl Roland because he had jilted her, and towards her husband because he had died. As a widow she had dedicated herself to Godwyn's career.

Queen Isabella had been similar. She had deposed her husband, King Edward II; but the result had been that her lover, Roger Mortimer, had effectively ruled England until her son grew old enough and confident enough to oust him.

Was that what Caris should do – live her life through men? Her father wanted her to work with him in the wool business. Or she could manage Merthin's career, helping him secure contracts to construct churches and bridges, expanding his business until he was the richest and most important builder in England.

She was roused from her thoughts by a tap at the door, and the bird-like figure of Mother Cecilia walked briskly in.

'Good afternoon!' Caris said in surprise. 'I was just asking myself whether all women are doomed to live their lives through men – and here you are, an obvious counter-example.'

'You're not quite right,' Cecilia said with a friendly smile. 'I live through Jesus Christ, who was a man, though he is God too.'

Caris was not sure whether that counted. She opened the cupboard and took out a small barrel of the best wine. 'Would you like a cup of my father's Rhenish?'

'Just a little, mixed with water.'

Caris half filled two cups with wine then topped up the drinks with water from a jug. 'You know that my father and aunt are at the banquet.'

'Yes. I came to see you.'

Caris had guessed as much. The prioress did not wander around the town making social calls without a purpose.

Cecilia sipped, then went on: 'I've been thinking about you, and the way you acted on the day the bridge collapsed.'

'Did I do something wrong?'

'On the contrary. You did everything perfectly. You were gentle but firm with the injured, and you obeyed my orders but at the same time used your initiative. I was impressed.'

'Thank you.'

'And you seemed ... not to enjoy it, exactly, but at least to find satisfaction in the work.'

'People were in distress, and we brought them relief – what could be more satisfying?'

'That's how I feel, and it's why I'm a nun.'

Caris saw where this was going. 'I couldn't spend my life in the priory.'

'The natural aptitude you showed for looking after the sick is only part of what I noticed. When people first started to walk into the cathedral carrying the injured and dead, I asked who had told them what to do. The answer was Caris Wooler.'

'It was obvious what should be done.'

'Yes – to you.' Cecilia leaned forward earnestly. 'The talent for organization is given to few people. I know – I have it, and I recognize it in others. When everyone around us is baffled, or panicked, or terrified, you and I take charge.'

Caris felt this was true. 'I suppose so,' she said reluctantly.

'I've watched you for ten years – since the day your mother died.'

'You brought her relief in her distress.'

'I knew then, just by talking to you, that you were going to grow up into an exceptional woman. My feeling was confirmed when you attended the nuns' school. You're twenty now. You must be thinking about what to do with your life. I believe that God has work for you.'

'How do you know what God thinks?'

Cecilia bristled. 'If anyone else in town asked me that question, I'd order them down on their knees to pray for forgiveness. But you're sincere, so I'll answer. I know what God thinks because I accept the teachings of His church. And I'm convinced he wants you to be a nun.'

'I like men too much.'

'Always a problem for me, as a youngster – but, I can assure you, a problem that diminishes with every passing year.'

'I can't be told how to live.'

'Don't be a Beguine.'

'What's that?'

'Beguines are nuns who accept no rules and consider their vows to be temporary. They live together, cultivate their lands and graze their cattle, and refuse to be governed by men.'

Caris was always intrigued to hear of women who defied the rules. 'Where are they to be found?'

'Mostly in the Netherlands. They had a leader, Marguerite Porete, who wrote a book called The Mirror of Simple Souls.'

'I'd like to read it.'

'Out of the question. The Beguines have been condemned by the Church for the heresy of the Free Spirit – the belief that we can attain spiritual perfection here on earth.'

'Spiritual perfection? What does that mean? It's just a phrase.'

'If you're determined to close your mind to God, you'll never understand it.'

'I'm sorry, Mother Cecilia, but every time I'm told something about God by a mere human, I think: "But humans are fallible, so the truth might be different."'

'How could the church be wrong?'

'Well, the Muslims have different beliefs.'

'They're heathens!'

'They call us infidels – it's the same thing. And Buonaventura Caroli says there are more Muslims than Christians in the world. So somebody's church is wrong.'

'Be careful,' Cecilia said severely. 'Don't allow your passion for argument to lead you into blasphemy.'

'Sorry, mother.' Caris knew that Cecilia enjoyed sparring with her, but there always came a moment when the prioress stopped arguing and started preaching, and Caris had to back down. It left her feeling slightly cheated.

Cecilia stood up. 'I know I can't persuade you against your will, but I wanted you to know the tendency of my thoughts. You could do nothing better than to join our nunnery and dedicate your life to the sacrament of healing. Thank you for the wine.'

As Cecilia was leaving, Caris said: 'What happened to Marguerite Porete? Is she still alive?'

'No,' said the prioress. 'She was burned at the stake.' She went out into the street, shutting the door behind her.

Caris stared at the closed door. A woman's life was a house of closed doors: she could not be an apprentice, she could not study at the university, she could not be a priest or a physician, nor shoot a bow nor fight with a sword, and she could not marry without submitting herself to the tyranny of her husband.

She wondered what Merthin was doing now. Was Bessie sitting at his table at the Bell inn, watching him drink her father's best ale, giving him that inviting smile, pulling the front of her dress tight to make sure he could see what nice breasts she had? Was he being charming and amusing to her, making her laugh? Was she parting her lips to show him her even teeth, and throwing back her head so that he could appreciate the soft skin of her white throat? Was he talking to her father, Paul Bell, asking respectful and interested questions about his business, so that later Paul would tell his daughter that Merthin was a good sort, a fine young man? Would Merthin get drunk and put his arm around Bessie's waist, resting his hand on her hip then slyly inching his fingertips towards that sensitive place between her thighs that was already itching for his touch – just as he once had with Caris?

Tears came to her eyes. She felt she was a fool. She had the best man in town and here she was handing him over to a barmaid. Why did she do these things to herself?

At that moment he walked in.

She looked at him through a mist of tears. Her vision was so blurred that she could not read his expression. Had he come to make friends again – or to berate her, venting his anger with the courage of several tankards of ale?

She stood up. For a moment she was held in suspense, as he closed the door behind him and came slowly to stand in front of her. Then he said: 'No matter what you do or say, I still love you.'

She threw her arms around him and burst out crying.

He stroked her hair and said nothing, which was just right.

After a while they started to kiss. She felt the familiar hunger, but stronger than ever: she wanted his hands all over her, his tongue in her mouth, his fingers inside her. She felt differently and she wanted their love to find a new expression. 'Let's take off all our clothes,' she said. They had never done that before.

He smiled with pleasure. 'All right, but what if someone comes in?'

'They'll be at the banquet for hours. And anyway we can go upstairs.'

They went to her bedroom. She kicked off her shoes. Suddenly she felt shy. What would he think when he saw her naked? She knew he loved her body bit by bit: her breasts, her legs, her throat, her cunt – he always told her how beautiful they were as he kissed and caressed them. But would he now notice that her hips were too wide, her legs a little short, her breasts quite small?

He seemed to have no such inhibitions. He threw off his shirt, pulled down his underdrawers, and stood unselfconsciously before her. His body was slight but strong, and he seemed full of pent-up energy, like a young deer. She noticed for the first time that the hair at his groin was the colour of autumn leaves. His cock stood up eagerly. Desire overcame her shyness, and she pulled her dress quickly over her head.

He stared at her bare body, but she no longer felt embarrassed – his look inflamed her like an intimate caress. 'You're beautiful,' he said.

'So are you.'

They lay side by side on the straw-filled palliasse that was her bed. As they kissed and touched one another, she realized that today she was not going to be satisfied with the games they usually played. 'I want to do it properly,' she said.

'You mean go the whole way?'

The thought of pregnancy surfaced in her mind, but she pushed it back down. She was too heated to think of consequences. 'Yes,' she whispered.

'So do I.'

He lay on top of her. Half her life she had wondered what this moment would be like. She looked up at his face. It wore the concentrated expression that she loved so much, the look he had when he was working, his small hands shaping wood with tenderness and skill. His fingertips softly spread the petals of her sex. She was slippery and yearning for him.

He said: 'Are you sure?'

Once again she suppressed the thought of pregnancy. 'I'm sure.'

She felt a moment of fear when he entered her. She tightened involuntarily, and he hesitated, feeling her body resisting him. 'It's all right,' she said. 'You can push harder. You won't hurt me.' She was wrong about that, and there was a sudden sharp pain as he thrust. She could not help crying out.

'I'm sorry,' he whispered.

'Just wait a minute,' she said.

They lay still. He kissed her eyelids and her forehead and the tip of her nose. She stroked his face and looked into his golden-brown eyes. Then the pain was gone and the desire came back, and she began to move, rejoicing in the feeling of having the man she loved deep inside her body for the first time. She thrilled to see the intensity of his pleasure. He stared at her, a faint smile on his lips, a deep hunger in his eyes, as they moved faster.

'I can't stop,' he said breathlessly.

'Don't stop, don't stop.'

She watched him intently. In a few moments he was overwhelmed by pleasure, his eyes shut tight and his mouth open and his whole body as taut as a bowstring. She felt his spasms inside her, and the jet of his ejaculation, and she thought that nothing in life had prepared her for such happiness. A moment later she herself was convulsed with ecstasy. She had had this sensation before, but not so powerfully, and she closed her eyes and gave herself up to it, pulling his body hard against her own as she shook like a tree in the wind.

When it was over they lay still for a long while. He buried his face in her neck, and she felt his panting breath on her skin. She stroked his back. His skin was damp with perspiration. Gradually her heartbeat slowed, and a deep contentment stole over her like twilight on a summer evening.

'So,' she said after a while, 'that's what all the fuss is about.'

25

THE DAY AFTER GODWYN WAS confirmed as prior of Kingsbridge, Edmund Wooler came to Merthin's parents' house early in the morning.

Merthin tended to forget what an important personage Edmund was, for Edmund treated him as a member of the family; but Gerald and Maud acted as if receiving an unexpected royal visitation. They were embarrassed that Edmund should see how poor their house was. There was only one room. Merthin and his parents slept on straw mattresses on the floor. There was a fireplace and a table and a small yard at the back.

Fortunately, the family had been up since sunrise, and had washed and dressed and tidied the place. All the same, when Edmund came stomping into the house with his uneven gait, Merthin's mother dusted a stool, patted her hair, closed the back door then opened it again, and put a log on the fire. His father bowed several times, put on a surcoat and offered Edmund a cup of ale.

'No, thank you, Sir Gerald,' said Edmund, no doubt knowing that the family had none to spare. 'However, I'll take a small bowl of your pottage, Lady Maud, if I may.' Every family kept a pot of oats on the fire to which they added bones, apple cores, pea pods and other scraps, to be slow-cooked for days. Flavoured with salt and herbs, the result was a soup that never tasted the same twice. It was the cheapest food.

Pleased, Maud ladled some pottage into a bowl and put it on the table with a spoon and a plate of bread.

Merthin was still feeling the euphoria of the previous afternoon. It was like being slightly drunk. He had gone to sleep thinking of Caris's naked body and woken up smiling. But he was suddenly reminded of his confrontation with Elfric over Griselda.

A false instinct told him that Edmund was going to scream 'You defiled my daughter!' and hit him across the face with a length of timber.

It was only a momentary vision, and it vanished as Edmund sat at the table. He picked up the spoon but, before he began to eat, he said to Merthin: 'Now that we've got a prior, I want to start work on the new bridge as soon as possible.'

'Good,' said Merthin.

Edmund swallowed a spoonful and smacked his lips. 'This is the best pottage I've ever tasted, Lady Maud.' Merthin's mother looked pleased.

Merthin was grateful to Edmund for being charming to his parents. They felt the humiliation of their reduced status, and it was balm to the wound to have the town's alderman eating at their table and calling them Sir Gerald and Lady Maud.

Now his father said: 'I almost didn't marry her, Edmund – did you know that?'

Merthin was sure Edmund had heard the story before, but he replied: 'Good lord, no – how did that happen?'

'I saw her in church on Easter Sunday, and fell in love with her instantly. There must have been a thousand people in Kingsbridge Cathedral, and she was the most beautiful woman there.'

'Now, Gerald, no need to exaggerate,' Maud said crisply.

'Then she disappeared into the crowd, and I couldn't find her! I didn't know her name. I asked people who was the pretty girl with the fair hair, and they said all the girls were pretty and fair.'

Maud said: 'I hurried away after the service. We were staying at the Holly Bush inn, and my mother was unwell, so I went back to take care of her.'

Gerald said: 'I looked all over town, but I couldn't find her. After Easter, everyone went home. I was living in Shiring, and she in Casterham, though I didn't know that. I thought I'd never see her again. I imagined she might have been an angel, come to earth to make sure everyone was attending the service.'

She said: 'Gerald, please.'

'But my heart was lost. I took no interest in other women. I expected to spend my life longing for the Angel of Kingsbridge.

This went on for two years. Then I saw her at a tournament in Winchester.'

She said: 'This complete stranger came up to me and said: "It's you – after all this time! You must marry me before you disappear again." I thought he was mad.'

'Amazing,' said Edmund.

Merthin thought Edmund's goodwill had been stretched far enough. 'Anyway,' he said, 'I've drawn some designs on the tracing floor in the mason's loft at the cathedral.'

Edmund nodded. 'A stone bridge wide enough for two carts?'

'As you specified – and ramped at both ends. And I've found a way to reduce the price by about a third.'

'That's astonishing! How?'

'I'll show you, as soon as you've finished eating.'

Edmund spooned up the last of the pottage and stood. 'I'm done. Let's go.' He turned to Gerald and inclined his head in a slight bow. 'Thank you for your hospitality.'

'It's a pleasure to have you here, alderman.'

Merthin and Edmund stepped out into a light drizzle. Instead of heading for the cathedral, Merthin led Edmund towards the river. Edmund's lopsided stride was instantly recognizable, and every second person on the street greeted him with a friendly word or a respectful bow.

Merthin suddenly felt nervous. He had been thinking about the bridge design for months. While he worked at St Mark's, supervising the carpenters who were constructing the new roof as the old was demolished, he mulled over the greater challenge of the bridge. Now for the first time his ideas would come under scrutiny by someone else.

As yet, Edmund had no idea how radical Merthin's plan was.

The muddy street wound downhill through houses and workshops. The city ramparts had fallen into disrepair during two centuries of civil peace, and in some places all that remained were humps of earth that now formed parts of garden walls. At the river's edge were industries that used large quantities of water, especially wool dyers and leather tanners.

Merthin and Edmund emerged on to the muddy foreshore between a slaughterhouse that gave off a strong smell of blood and a smithy where hammers clanged on iron. Directly in front of them, across a narrow stretch of water, was Leper Island. Edmund said: 'Why are we here? The bridge is a quarter of a mile upstream.'

'It was,' said Merthin. He took a breath and said: 'I think we should build the new one here.'

'A bridge to the island?'

'And another from the island to the far shore. Two small bridges instead of one big one. Much cheaper.'

'But people will have to walk across the island from one bridge to the other.'

'Why not?'

'Because it's a leper colony!'

'There's only one leper left. He can be moved elsewhere. The disease seems to be dying out.'

Edmund looked thoughtful. 'So everyone who comes to Kingsbridge will arrive at this spot, where we're standing.'

'We'll have to build a new street, and knock down some of these buildings – but the cost will be small by comparison with the money saved on the bridge.'

'And on the other side . . .'

'A pasture that belongs to the priory. I can see the whole layout when I'm on the roof of St Mark's. That's how come I thought of it.'

Edmund was impressed. 'That's very clever. I wonder why the bridge wasn't put here originally.'

'The first bridge was erected hundreds of years ago. The river probably had a different shape then. River banks must move their position as the centuries go by. The channel between the island and the pasture could have been wider at one time. Then there would have been no advantage in building here.'

Edmund peered across the water, and Merthin followed his gaze. The leper colony was a scatter of tumbledown wooden buildings spread over three or four acres. The island was too rocky for cultivation, but there were some trees and scrubby grass. The place was infested with rabbits, which the townspeople would not eat because of a superstition that they were the souls of dead lepers. At one time the ostracized inhabitants had kept their own chickens and pigs. Now, however, it was simpler for the priory to supply food to the last remaining inhabitant. 'You're right,' Edmund said. 'There hasn't been a new case of leprosy in the town for at least ten years.'

'I've never seen a leper,' Merthin said. 'As a child, I thought people were saying "leopard". I imagined that island to be occupied by spotted lions.'

Edmund laughed. Turning his back on the river, he looked at the buildings around. 'There will be some political work to do,' he mused. 'The people whose homes must be demolished will have to be convinced that they're the lucky ones, being moved to new and better houses while their neighbours missed out. And the island may have to be cleansed with holy water to convince people that it's safe. But we can handle all that.'

'I've drawn both bridges with pointed arches, like the cathedral,' Merthin said. 'They will be beautiful.'

'Show me.'

They left the riverside and walked uphill through the town to the priory. The cathedral dripped with rain under a layer of low cloud like smoke from a damp fire. Merthin was looking forward to seeing his drawings again – he had not been to the loft for a week or so – and to explaining them to Edmund. He had thought a great deal about the way the current had undermined the old bridge, and how he could protect the new one from the same fate.

He led Edmund through the north porch and up the spiral staircase. His wet shoes slipped on the worn stone steps. Edmund energetically hauled his withered leg up behind him.

Several lamps were burning in the mason's loft. At first Merthin was pleased, for that meant they would be able to see his drawings more clearly. Then he saw Elfric working on the tracing floor.

He felt momentarily frustrated. The enmity between himself and his former master was as great as ever. Elfric had failed to prevent townspeople from employing Merthin, but he continued to block Merthin's application to join the carpenters' guild – leaving Merthin in an anomalous position, illegitimate but accepted. Elfric's attitude was pointless, but spiteful.

Elfric's presence here would put a damper on Merthin's conversation with Edmund. He told himself not to be so sensitive. Why should it not be Elfric who was made uncomfortable?

He held the door for Edmund, and together they crossed the room to the tracing floor. Then he suffered a shock.

Elfric was bent over the tracing floor, drawing with a pair of compasses – on a fresh layer of plaster. He had re-covered the floor, totally obliterating Merthin's drawings.

Merthin said incredulously: 'What have you done?'

Elfric looked contemptuously at him and went on with his drawing, saying nothing.

'He's wiped out my work,' Merthin said to Edmund.

'What's your explanation, man?' Edmund demanded.

Elfric could not ignore his father-in-law. 'There's nothing to explain,' he said. 'A tracing floor has to be renewed at intervals.'

'But you've covered over important designs!'

'Have I? The prior has not commissioned this boy to make any drawings, and the boy has not asked permission to use the tracing floor.'

Edmund was never slow to anger, and Elfric's cool insolence was getting under his skin. 'Don't act stupid,' he said. 'I asked Merthin to prepare drawings for the new bridge.'

'I'm sorry, but only the prior has authority to do that.'

'Damn it, the guild is providing the money.'

'A loan, to be repaid.'

'It still gives us the right to a say on the design.'

'Does it? You'll have to speak to the prior about that. I don't think he'll be impressed by your choice of an inexperienced apprentice as your designer, though.'

Merthin was looking at the drawings Elfric had scratched in the new plaster. 'I suppose this is your bridge design,' he said.

'Prior Godwyn has commissioned me to build it,' Elfric said.

Edmund was shocked. 'Without asking us?'

Elfric said resentfully: 'What's the matter – don't you want the work to go to your own daughter's husband?'

'Round arches,' Merthin said, still studying Elfric's drawing. 'And narrow openings. How many piers will you have?'

Elfric was reluctant to answer, but Edmund was staring expectantly at him. 'Seven,' he said.

'The wooden bridge only had five!' Merthin said. 'Why are they so thick, and the openings so narrow?'

'To bear the weight of a stone-paved roadway.'

'You don't need thick piers for that. Look at this cathedral – its columns bear the entire weight of the roof, but they're slim and widely spaced.'

Elfric sneered. 'No one's going to drive a cart across the roof of a church.'

'That's true, but—' Merthin stopped. The rain on the cathedral's vast expanse of roof probably weighed more than an ox-cart loaded with stone, but why should he explain this to Elfric? It was not his role to educate an incompetent builder. Elfric's design was poor, but Merthin did not want to improve it, he wanted to replace it with his own, so he shut up.

Edmund also realized he was wasting his breath. 'This decision is not going to be made by you two,' he said, and he stomped off.

*

JOHN CONSTABLE's baby daughter was christened in the cathedral by Prior Godwyn. This honour was granted because he was an important employee of the priory. All the leading townspeople attended. Although John was neither wealthy nor well connected – his father had worked in the priory stables – Petranilla said that respectable people should take care to show friendship towards him and support for him. Caris thought they condescended to John because they needed him to protect their property.

It was raining again, and the people grouped around the font were wetter than the infant who was sprinkled with holy water. Strange feelings stirred in Caris as she looked at the tiny, helpless child. Since lying with Merthin she had simply refused to let herself think about pregnancy but, all the same, she felt a warm surge of protective emotion when she saw the baby.

She was named Jesca, after Abraham's niece.

Caris's cousin Godwyn had never been comfortable with babies and, as soon as the brief rite was over, he turned to leave. But Petranilla grabbed the sleeve of his Benedictine robe. 'What about this bridge?' she said.

She spoke in a low voice, but Caris heard, and made up her mind to listen to the rest.

Godwyn said: 'I've asked Elfric to prepare drawings and estimates.'

'Good. We should keep it in the family.'

'Elfric is the priory's builder.'

'Other people may want to horn in.'

'I shall decide who builds the bridge.'

Caris was annoyed enough to intervene. 'How dare you?' she said to Petranilla.

'I was not speaking to you,' her aunt said.

Caris ignored that. 'Why should Merthin's design not be considered?'

'Because he isn't family.'

'He practically lives with us!'

'But you're not married to him. If you were, it might be different.'

Caris knew she was at a disadvantage there, so she shifted her ground. 'You've always been prejudiced against Merthin,' she said. 'But everyone knows he's a better builder than Elfric.'

Her sister Alice heard that and joined in the argument. 'Elfric taught Merthin everything, and now Merthin pretends he knows better!'

That was dishonest, Caris knew, and she felt angry. 'Who built the ferry?' she said, raising her voice. 'Who repaired the roof of St Mark's?'

'Merthin was working with Elfric when he built the ferry. And no one asked Elfric about St Mark's.'

'Because they knew he wouldn't be able to solve the problem!'

Godwyn interrupted. 'Please!' he said, with his hands raised in front of himself protectively. 'I know you're my family, but I'm the prior and this is the cathedral. I can't be harangued by womenfolk in public.'

Edmund joined the circle. 'Just what I was going to say. Keep your voices down.'

Alice said accusingly: 'You should be supporting your son-in-law.'

It occurred to Caris that Alice was getting more like Petranilla. Although she was only twenty-one, and Petranilla was more than twice that age, Alice had the same purse-mouthed look of disapproval. She was also becoming more stout, her bosom filling out the front of her dress like wind in a sail.

Edmund looked sternly at Alice. 'This decision will not be made on the basis of family relationships,' he said. 'The fact that Elfric is married to my daughter won't help his bridge stay upright.'

He had strong views on this subject, Caris knew. He believed you should always do business with the most reliable supplier, always hire the best man for the job, regardless of friendship or family ties. Any man who needs to surround himself with loyal acolytes doesn't really believe in himself, he would say – and if he doesn't believe in himself, why should I?

Petranilla said: 'So how will the choice be made?' She gave him a shrewd look. 'You've obviously got a plan.'

'The priory and the guild will consider Elfric's design and Merthin's – and any others that may be put forward,' Edmund said decisively. 'All designs must be drawn and costed. The costing must be independently checked by other builders.'

Alice muttered: 'I've never heard of such goings-on. It's like an archery contest. Elfric is the priory's builder, he should do the job.'

Her father ignored her. 'Finally, the designers will be questioned by the leading citizens of the town at a meeting of the parish guild. And then –' he looked at Godwyn, who was pretending not to be bewildered by the way the decision process had been taken out of his hands – 'and then Prior Godwyn will make his choice.'

*

THE MEETING TOOK PLACE in the guild hall on the main street. It had a stone undercroft below and a timber superstructure, topped by a tiled roof and two stone chimneys. In the basement were the large kitchen that prepared food for the banquets, a jail and an office for the constable. The main floor was as spacious as a church, a hundred feet long and thirty feet wide. At one end was a chapel. Because it was so wide, and because timbers long enough to span a thirty-foot roof were rare and expensive, the main room was divided by a row of wooden pillars supporting the joists.

It appeared an unpretentious building, made of the materials used in the humblest dwellings, glorifying nobody. But, as Edmund often said, the money made by the people here paid for the limestone-and-stained-glass majesty of the cathedral. And the guild hall was comfortable in its unostentatious way. There were tapestries on the walls and glass in the windows, and two huge fireplaces kept it warm in winter. When business was booming, the food served here was fit for royalty.

The parish guild had been formed hundreds of years ago, when Kingsbridge was a small town. A few merchants had got together to raise money to buy ornaments for the cathedral. But when wealthy men eat and drink in a group they inevitably discuss their common concerns, and fund-raising soon became secondary to politics. From the start the guild was dominated by wool merchants, which was why a huge pair of scales and a standard weight for a woolsack – 364 pounds – stood at one end of the hall. As Kingsbridge grew, other guilds had been formed, representing crafts – carpenters, masons, brewers, goldsmiths – but their leading members also belonged to the parish guild, which retained its primacy. It was a less powerful version of the guild merchant that ruled most English towns, but was prohibited here by the town's landlord, Kingsbridge Priory.

Merthin had never attended a meeting or banquet here, but he had been inside several times on more mundane business. He liked to crane back his neck and study the complex geometry of the roof timbers, a lesson in how the weight of a broad expanse of roof could be funnelled down to a few slender wooden pillars. Most of the elements made sense, but one or two pieces of wood seemed to him to be superfluous, or even detrimental, transferring weight to weaker zones. That was because no one really knew what made buildings stand up. Builders went by instinct and experience, and sometimes got it wrong.

This evening Merthin was in a state of high anxiety, too nervous to really appreciate the woodwork. The guild was about to pass judgement on his bridge design. It was far superior to Elfric's – but would they see that?

Elfric had had the benefit of the tracing floor. Merthin might have asked Godwyn for permission to use it, but he had been afraid of further sabotage by Elfric, so he had devised an alternative. He had stretched a large piece of parchment across a wooden frame, and had drawn his design on the skin with a pen and ink. Tonight this might work to his advantage, for he had brought his design with him to the guild hall, so that members would have it in front of them, whereas Elfric's would only be in their memories.

He placed his framed drawing at the front of the hall on a three-legged stand he had devised for the purpose. Everyone came and looked at it as they arrived, although they had all seen it at least once over the last few days. They had also climbed the spiral staircase to the loft and looked at Elfric's drawings. Merthin thought most people preferred his design, but some were wary of backing a youngster against an experienced man. Many had kept their opinions to themselves.

The noise level rose as the hall filled up with men and a few women. They dressed up for the guild, as they did for church, the men in expensive wool coats despite the mild summer weather, the women in elaborate headdresses. Although everyone paid lip service to the untrustworthiness and general inferiority of women, in practice several of the town's wealthiest and most important citizens were female. There was Mother Cecilia, sitting now at the front with her personal assistant, the nun known as Old Julie. Caris was here – everyone acknowledged that she was Edmund's right hand. Merthin experienced a jolt of desire as she sat on the bench next to him, her thigh warm against his own. Anyone carrying on a trade in the town had to belong to a guild – outsiders could do business only on market days. Even monks and priests were compelled to join if they wanted to trade, which they often did. When a man died, it was common for his widow to continue his enterprise. Betty Baxter was the town's most prosperous baker; Sarah Taverner kept the Holly Bush inn. It would have been difficult and cruel to prevent such women earning a living. Much easier to include them in the guild.

Edmund normally chaired these meetings, sitting on a big wooden throne on a raised platform at the front. Today, however, there were two chairs on the platform. Edmund sat in one and, when Prior Godwyn arrived, Edmund invited him to take the other. Godwyn was accompanied by all the senior monks, and Merthin was pleased to see Thomas among them. Philemon was also in the entourage, lanky and awkward, and Merthin wondered briefly what on earth Godwyn had brought him for.

Godwyn was looking pained. Opening the proceedings, Edmund was careful to acknowledge that the prior was in charge of the bridge, and the choice of design was ultimately his. But everyone knew that, in fact, Edmund had taken the decision out of Godwyn's hands by calling this meeting. Provided there was a clear consensus tonight, Godwyn would have great difficulty in going against the expressed will of the merchants in a matter of commerce rather than religion. Edmund asked Godwyn to begin with a prayer, and Godwyn obliged, but he knew he had been outmanoeuvred, and that was why he looked as if there was a bad smell.

Edmund stood up and said: 'These two designs have been costed by Elfric and Merthin, who have used the same methods of calculation.'

Elfric interjected: 'Of course we have – he learned them from me.' There was a ripple of laughter from the older men.

It was true. There were formulae for calculating costs per square foot of wall, per cubic yard of infill, per foot of a roof span, and for more intricate work such as arches and vaulting. All builders used the same methods, though with their individual variations. The bridge calculations had been complex, but easier than for a building such as a church.

Edmund went on: 'Each man has checked the other's calculations, so there is no room for dispute.'

Edward Butcher called out: 'Yes – all builders overcharge by the same amount!' That got a big laugh. Edward was popular with the men for his quick wit, and with the women for his good looks and brown bedroom eyes. He was not so popular with his wife, who knew about his infidelities, and had recently attacked him with one of his own heavy knives: he still had a bandage on his left arm.

'Elfric's bridge will cost two hundred and eighty-five pounds,' Edmund said as the laughter died away. 'Merthin's comes out at three hundred and seven. The difference is twenty-two pounds, as most of you will have worked out faster than me.' There was a quiet chuckle at that: Edmund was often teased for having his daughter do his arithmetic for him. He still used the old Latin numerals, because he could not get used to the new Arabic digits that made calculation so much easier.

A new voice said: 'Twenty-two pounds is a lot of money.' It was Bill Watkin, the builder who had refused to hire Merthin, looking like one of the monks with his bald dome.

Dick Brewer said: 'Yes, but Merthin's bridge is twice as wide. It ought to cost twice as much – but it doesn't, because it's a cleverer design.' Dick was fond of his own product, ale, and in consequence had a protruding round belly like a pregnant woman.

Bill rejoined: 'How many days a year do we need a bridge wide enough for two carts?'

'Every market day and all of Fleece Fair week.'

'Not so,' said Bill. 'It's only for an hour in the morning and another in the afternoon.'

'I've waited two hours with a cartload of barley before now.'

'You should have the sense to bring your barley in on quiet days.'

'I bring barley in every day.' Dick was the largest brewer in the county. He owned a huge copper kettle that held five hundred gallons, in consequence of which his tavern was called the Copper.

Edmund interrupted this spat. 'There are other problems caused by delays on the bridge,' he said. 'Some traders go to Shiring, where there's no bridge and no queue. Others do their business while waiting in line, then go home without ever entering the town, and save themselves the bridge toll and the market taxes. It's forestalling, and it's illegal, but we've never succeeded in stopping it. And then there's the question of how people think of Kingsbridge. Right now we're the town whose bridge collapsed. If we're going to attract back all the business we're losing, we need to change that. I'd like us to become known as the town with the best bridge in England.'

Edmund was hugely influential, and Merthin began to scent victory.

Betty Baxter, an enormously fat woman in her forties, stood up and pointed to something on Merthin's drawing. 'What's this, here in the middle of the bridge parapet, over the pier?' she said. 'There's a little pointed bit that sticks out over the water, like a viewing platform. What is it for, fishing?' The others laughed.

'It's a pedestrian refuge,' Merthin answered. 'If you're walking over the bridge, and suddenly the earl of Shiring rides across with twenty mounted knights, you can step out of their way.'

Edward Butcher said: 'I hope it's big enough to fit Betty in.'

Everyone laughed, but Betty persisted with her questioning. 'Why is the pier underneath it pointed like that all the way down to the water? Elfric's piers aren't pointed.'

'To deflect debris. Look at any river bridge – you'll see the piers are chipped and cracked. What do you think causes that damage? It must be the large pieces of wood – tree trunks, or timbers from demolished buildings – that you see floating downstream and crashing into piers.'

'Or Ian Boatman when he's drunk,' said Edward.

'Boats or debris, they will cause less damage to my pointed piers. Elfric's will suffer the full impact.'

Elfric said: 'My walls are too strong to be knocked down by bits of wood.'

'On the contrary,' said Merthin. 'Your arches are narrower than mine, therefore the water will be drawn through them faster, and the debris will strike the piers with greater force, causing more damage.'

He could see from Elfric's face that the older man had not even thought of that. But the audience were not builders – how could they judge what was right?

Around the base of each pier, Merthin had drawn a pile of

rough stones, known to builders as riprap. This would prevent the current undermining his piers the way it had those of the old wooden bridge. But no one asked him about the riprap, so he did not explain it.

Betty had more questions. 'Why is your bridge so long? Elfric's begins at the water's edge. Yours starts several yards inland. Isn't that unnecessary expense?'

'My bridge is ramped at both ends,' Merthin explained. 'That's so that you step off the bridge on to dry land, instead of a swamp. No more ox-carts getting bogged down on the beach and blocking the bridge for an hour.'

'Cheaper to put down a paved road,' said Elfric.

Elfric was beginning to sound desperate. Then Bill Watkin stood up. 'I'm having trouble deciding who's right and who's wrong,' he said. 'When these two argue, it's difficult to make up your mind. And I'm a builder – it must be worse for those who aren't.' There was a murmur of agreement. Bill went on: 'So I think we should look at the men, not the designs.'

Merthin had been afraid of this. He listened with increasing despair.

'Which of the two do you know best?' said Bill. 'Which can you rely on? Elfric has been a builder in this town, man and boy, for twenty years. We can look at houses he's put up and see they're still standing. We can see the repairs he's done on the cathedral. On the other hand, here's Merthin – a clever lad, we know, but a bit of a tearaway, and never finished his apprenticeship. There's not a lot to indicate that he's capable of taking charge of the largest building project Kingsbridge has seen since the construction of the cathedral. I know which one I trust.' He sat down.

Several men voiced their approval. They would not judge the designs – they would decide on personalities. It was maddeningly unfair.

Then Brother Thomas spoke up. 'Has anyone in Kingsbridge ever been involved in a project that involved building below water level?'

Merthin knew the answer was No. He felt a surge of hope. This could rescue it for him.

Thomas went on: 'I would like to know how both men would handle that problem.'

Merthin was ready with his solution – but he was afraid that if he spoke first Elfric would simply echo him. He compressed his lips, hoping that Thomas – who usually helped him – would get the message.

Thomas caught Merthin's eye, and said: 'Elfric, what would you do?'

'The answer is simpler than you think,' Elfric said. 'You just have to drop loose rubble into the river at the point where your pier will stand. The rubble rests on the river bottom. You put more and more in until the pile is visible above water level. Then you build your pier on that foundation.'

As Merthin had expected, Elfric had come up with the crudest solution to the problem. Now Merthin said: 'There are two snags with Elfric's method. One is that a pile of rubble is no more stable under water than on land. Over time, it will shift and drop, and when that happens the bridge will subside. If you want a bridge to last only a few years, fine. But I think we should build for the long term.'

He heard a quiet rumble of concurrence.

'The second problem is the shape of the pile. It will naturally slope outwards below the water line, restricting the passage of boats, especially when the river is low. And Elfric's arches are already narrow.'

Elfric said irritably: 'What would you do instead?'

Merthin suppressed a smile. That was what he had wanted to hear – Elfric admitting that he did not know a better answer. 'I'll tell you,' he said. And I'll show everyone that I know better than the idiot who chopped my door to pieces, he thought. He looked around. They were all listening. Their decision hung on what he would say next.

He took a deep breath. 'First, I would take a pointed wooden stake and piledrive it into the river bed. Then I would bang in another next to it, touching; then another. In that way I would build a ring of stakes around the place in the river where I want to put my pier.'

'A ring of stakes?' Elfric jeered. 'That will never keep the water out.'

Brother Thomas, who had asked the question, said: 'Listen to him, please. He listened to you.'

Merthin said: 'Next, I would build a second ring inside the first, with a gap between them of half a foot.' He sensed that he had his audience's attention now.

'It still won't be waterproof,' said Elfric.

Edmund said: 'Shut up, Elfric, this is interesting.'

Merthin went on: 'Then I would pour a clay mortar into the gap between the two rings. The mixture would displace the water, being heavier. And it would plug any chinks between the wood stakes, making the ring watertight. This is called a coffer dam.'

The room was quiet.

'Finally, I would remove the water from inside by bucket, exposing the river bed, and build a mortared stone foundation.'

Elfric was dumbstruck. Both Edmund and Godwyn were staring at Merthin.

Thomas said: 'Thank you both. Speaking for myself, that makes the decision an easy one.'

'Yes,' said Edmund. 'I rather think it does.'

*

CARIS WAS SURPRISED that Godwyn had wanted Elfric to design the bridge. She understood that Elfric would seem a safer choice – but Godwyn was a reformer, not a conservative, and she had expected him to be enthusiastic about Merthin's clever, radical design. Instead he had timidly favoured the cautious option.

Fortunately, Edmund had been able to outmanoeuvre Godwyn, and now Kingsbridge would have a well-built, beautiful bridge that would allow two carts to cross at the same time. But Godwyn's eagerness to appoint the unimaginative sycophant rather than the bold man of talent was an ominous sign for the future.

And Godwyn had never been a good loser. When he was a boy Petranilla had taught him to play chess, letting him win to encourage him, and he had challenged his uncle Edmund; but after being beaten twice he had sulked and refused to play again. He was in the same mood after the meeting in the guild hall, she could tell. It was probably not that he was particularly attracted to Elfric's design. But he undoubtedly resented having the decision taken out of his hands. Next day, when she and her father went to the prior's house, she anticipated trouble.

Godwyn greeted them coolly and did not offer any refreshment. As always, Edmund pretended not to notice slights. 'I want Merthin to start work on the bridge immediately,' he said as he sat down at the table in the hall. 'I have pledges of money for the full amount of Merthin's budget—'

'From whom?' Godwyn interrupted.

'The town's wealthiest traders.'

Godwyn continued to look inquiringly at Edmund.

Edmund shrugged and said: 'Fifty pounds from Betty Baxter, eighty from Dick Brewer, seventy from myself, and ten pounds each from eleven others.'

'I didn't know our citizens possessed such riches,' Godwyn said. He seemed both awestruck and envious. 'God has been kind.'

Edmund added: 'Kind enough to reward people for a lifetime's hard work and worry.'

'No doubt.'

'Which is why I need to give them reassurances about the return of their money. When the bridge is built, the tolls will come to the parish guild, which will use them to repay loans – but who will collect the pennies as the passengers cross the bridge? I think it has to be a servant of the guild.'

'I never agreed to this,' Godwyn said.

'I know, that's why I'm raising it now.'

'I mean, I never agreed to pay the tolls to the parish guild.'

'What?'

Caris stared at Godwyn, flabbergasted. Of course he had agreed to it – what was he talking about? He had spoken to her as well as to Edmund and assured them that Brother Thomas—

'Oh,' she said. 'You promised that Thomas would build the bridge, if he was elected prior. Then, when Thomas withdrew and you became the candidate, we assumed...'

'You assumed,' Godwyn said. A smirk of triumph played about his lips.

Edmund could barely contain himself. 'This is not square dealing, Godwyn!' he said in a choked voice. 'You knew what the understanding was!'

'I knew no such thing, and you should call me Father Prior.'

Edmund's voice got louder. 'Then we're back where we were with Prior Anthony three months ago! Except that now, instead of an inadequate bridge, we have no bridge at all. Don't imagine it will be built at no cost to you. Citizens may lend their life savings to the priory, on the security of income from the bridge tolls, but they will not give their money away … Father Prior.'

'Then they must manage without a bridge. I have only just become prior – how can I start by alienating a right that has belonged to my priory for hundreds of years?'

'But it's only temporary!' Edmund exploded. 'And if you don't do this no one will gain any money from bridge tolls because there will be no cursed bridge!'

Caris was furious, but she bit her tongue and tried to figure out what Godwyn was up to. He was getting his revenge for last night, but did he really mean it? 'What do you want?' she said to him.

Edmund looked surprised by the question, but he said nothing: the reason he brought Caris with him to meetings was that she often saw things he missed, and asked questions he had not thought of.

'I don't know what you mean,' Godwyn replied.

'You've pulled a surprise,' she said. 'You've caught us wrong-footed. Very well. We admit we made an assumption that may have been unwarranted. But what's your purpose? Just to make us feel stupid?'

'You asked for this meeting, not I.'

Edmund burst out: 'What kind of way is that to talk to your uncle and your cousin?'

'Just a minute, Papa,' Caris said. Godwyn did have a secret agenda, she felt sure, but he did not want to admit it. All right, she thought, I'll have to guess it. 'Give me a minute to think,' she said. Godwyn still wanted the bridge – he had to, nothing else made sense. The business about alienating the priory's ancient rights was rhetoric, the kind of pompous prating that all students were taught at Oxford. Did he want Edmund to break down and agree to Elfric's design? She did not think so. Godwyn clearly resented the way Edmund had appealed over his head to the citizenry, but he must see that Merthin was offering twice as much bridge for almost the same money. So what else could it be?

Perhaps he just wanted a better deal.

He had looked hard at the priory's finances, she guessed. Having railed comfortably against Anthony's inefficiency for many years he was now confronted with the reality of having to do the job better himself. Perhaps it was not going to be as easy as he had imagined. Perhaps he was not as clever about money and management as he had thought. In desperation, he wanted the bridge *and* the money from tolls. But how did he think that could happen?

She said: 'What could we offer you that would make you change your mind?'

'Build the bridge without keeping the tolls,' he said instantly.

So that was his agenda. You always were a bit sneaky, Godwyn, she thought.

A flash of inspiration struck her, and she said: 'How much money are we talking about?'

Godwyn looked suspicious. 'Why do you want to know that?'

Edmund said: 'We can work it out. Not counting citizens, who don't pay the toll, about a hundred people cross the bridge every market day, and carts pay two pence. It's much less now, with the ferry, of course.'

Caris said: 'Say a hundred and twenty pennies a week, or ten shillings, which comes to twenty-six pounds a year.'

Edmund said: 'Then, during Fleece Fair week, about a thousand on the first day, and another two hundred each subsequent day.'

'That's two thousand two hundred, plus carts, call it two thousand four hundred pennies, which is ten pounds. Total, thirty-six pounds a year.' Caris looked at Godwyn. 'Is that about right?'

'Yes,' he acknowledged grudgingly.

'So, what you want from us is thirty-six pounds a year.'

'Yes.'

'Impossible!' said Edmund.

'Not necessarily,' Caris said. 'Suppose the priory were to grant the parish guild a lease on the bridge.' Thinking on her feet, she added: 'Plus an acre of ground at either end, and the island in the middle – for thirty-six pounds a year, in perpetuity.' Once the bridge was built, that land would be priceless, she knew. 'Would that give you what you want, Father Prior?'

'Yes.'

Godwyn clearly thought he was getting thirty-six pounds a year for something worthless. He had no idea how much rent could be charged for a plot of land at the end of a bridge. The worst negotiator in the world is a man who believes he's clever, Caris thought.

Edmund said: 'But how would the guild recoup the cost of construction?'

'With Merthin's design, the number of people and carts crossing should rise. Theoretically it could double. Everything over thirty-six pounds is the guild's. Then we could put up buildings either side to service travellers – taverns, stables, cook shops. They should be profitable – we could charge a good rent.'

'I don't know,' said Edmund. 'It seems very risky to me.'

For a moment, Caris felt furious with her father. She had come up with a brilliant solution, and he seemed to be finding unnecessary fault with it. Then she realized he was faking. She could see the light of enthusiasm in his eyes, not quite concealed. He loved the idea, but he did not want Godwyn to know how keen he was. He was hiding his feelings, for fear the prior would try to negotiate a better bargain. It was a ploy father and daughter had used before, when bargaining over wool.

Having figured out what he was up to, Caris played along, pretending to share his misgivings. 'I know it's hazardous,' she said gloomily. 'We could lose everything. But what alternative do we have? We've got our backs to the wall. If we don't build the bridge we'll go out of business.'

Edmund shook his head dubiously. 'All the same, I can't agree to this on behalf of the guild. I'll have to talk to the people who are putting up the money. I can't say what their reply will be.' He looked Godwyn in the eye. 'But I'll do my best to persuade them, if this is your best offer.'

Godwyn had not actually made an offer, Caris reflected; but he had forgotten that. 'It is,' he said firmly.

Got you, Caris thought triumphantly.

*

'YOU'RE REALLY VERY SHREWD,' Merthin said.

He was lying between Caris's legs, his head on her thigh, toying with her pubic hair. They had just made love for the second time ever, and he had found it even more joyous than the first. As they dozed in the pleasant daydream of satisfied lovers, she had told him about her negotiation with Godwyn. He was impressed.

Caris said: 'The best of it is, he thinks he's driven a hard bargain. In fact, a perpetual lease on the bridge and the land around it is priceless.'

'All the same, it's a bit dismaying if he's going to be no better at managing the priory's money than your uncle Anthony was.'

They were in the forest, in a clearing hidden by brambles and shaded by a stand of tall beech trees, where a stream ran over rocks to form a pool. It had probably been used by lovers for hundreds of years. They had stripped naked and bathed in the pool before making love on the grassy bank. Anyone travelling clandestinely through the woods would skirt the thicket, so they were not likely to be discovered, unless by children picking blackberries – which was how Caris had originally discovered the glade, she told Merthin.

Now he said idly: 'Why did you ask for that island?'

'I'm not sure. It's obviously not as valuable as the land at either end of the bridge, and it's no good for cultivation, but it could still be developed. The truth is, I guessed he wouldn't object, so I just threw it in.'

'Will you take over your father's wool business one day?'

'No.'

'So definite? Why?'

'It's too easy for the king to tax the wool trade. He has just imposed an extra duty of a pound per sack of wool – that's on top of the existing tax of two-thirds of a pound. The price of wool is now so high that the Italians are looking for wool from other countries, such as Spain. The business is too much at the mercy of the monarch.'

'Still, it's a living. What else would you do?' Merthin was edging the conversation towards marriage, a subject she never raised.

'I don't know.' She smiled. 'When I was ten, I wanted to be a doctor. I thought that if I had known about medicine I could have saved my mother's life. They all laughed at me. I didn't realize only men could be physicians.'

'You could be a wise woman, like Mattie.'

'That would shock the family. Imagine what Petranilla would say! Mother Cecilia thinks it's my destiny to be a nun.'

He laughed. 'If she could see you now!' He kissed the soft inside of her thigh.

'She'd probably want to do what you're doing,' Caris said. 'You know what people say about nuns.'

'Why would she think you wanted to join the convent?'

'It's because of what we did after the bridge collapsed. I helped her take care of the injured. She said I had a natural gift for it.'

'You have. Even I could see it.'

'I just did what Cecilia said.'

'But people seemed to feel better as soon as you spoke to them. And then you always listened to what they had to say before telling them what they should do.'

She stroked his cheek. 'I couldn't be a nun. I'm too fond of you.'

Her triangle of hair was reddish-brown with golden lights. 'You've got a little mole,' he said. 'Right here, on the left, beside the cleft.'

'I know. It's been there since I was a little girl. I used to think it was ugly. I was so pleased when my hair grew, because I thought that meant my husband wouldn't see it. I never imagined anyone would look as closely as you.'

'Friar Murdo would call you a witch – you'd better not let him see it.'

'Not if he were the last man on earth.'

'This is the blemish that saves you from blasphemy.'

'What are you talking about?'

'In the Arab world, every work of art has a tiny flaw, so that it doesn't sacrilegiously compete with the perfection of God.'

'How do you know that?'

'One of the Florentines told me. Listen, do you think the parish guild will want the island?'

'Why do you ask?'

'Because I'd like to own it.'

'Four acres of rock and rabbits. Why?'

'I'd build a dock and a builder's yard. Stone and timber coming by river could be delivered directly to my dock. When the bridge is finished, I'd build a house on the island.'

'Nice idea. But they wouldn't give it to you free.'

'How about as part payment for building the bridge? I could take, say, half wages for two years.'

'You charge four pence a day … so the price of the island would be just over five pounds. I should think the guild would be pleased to get that much for barren land.'

'Do you think it's a good idea?'

'I think you could build houses there and rent them, as soon as the bridge is finished and people can travel to and from the island easily.'

'Yes,' said Merthin thoughtfully. 'I'd better talk to your father about it.'

26

RETURNING TO EARLSCASTLE at the end of a day's hunting, when all the men in Earl Roland's entourage were in a good mood, Ralph Fitzgerald was happy.

They crossed the drawbridge like an invading army, knights and squires and dogs. Rain was falling in a light drizzle, coolly welcome to the men and animals, who were hot and tired and content. They had taken several summer-fat hinds that would make good eating, plus a big old stag, too tough for anything but dog meat, killed for its magnificent antlers.

They dismounted in the outer compound, within the lower circle of the figure-eight moat. Ralph unsaddled Griff, murmured a few words of thanks in his ear, fed him a carrot and handed him to a groom to be rubbed down. Kitchen boys dragged away the bloody carcasses of the deer. The men were noisily recalling the day's incidents, boasting and jeering and laughing, remembering remarkable jumps and dangerous falls and hair's-breadth escapes. Ralph's nostrils filled with a smell he loved, a mixture of sweating horses, wet dogs, leather and blood.

Ralph found himself next to Lord William of Caster, the earl's elder son. 'A great day's sport,' he said.

'Tremendous,' William agreed. He pulled off his cap and scratched his balding head. 'I'm sorry to lose old Bruno, though.'

Bruno, the leader of the dog pack, had gone in for the kill a few moments too early. When the stag was too exhausted to run any farther and turned to face the hounds, its heaving shoulders covered with blood, Bruno had leaped for its throat – but, with a last burst of defiance, the deer had dipped its head and swung its muscular neck and impaled the soft belly of the dog on the points of its antlers. The effort finished the beast off, and a moment later the other dogs were tearing it apart; but, as it thrashed its life away, Bruno's guts unravelled across the antlers like a tangled rope, and William had had to put him out of his misery, slashing his throat with a long dagger. 'He was a brave dog,' Ralph said, and put a hand on William's shoulder in commiseration.

'Like a lion,' William agreed.

On the spur of the moment, Ralph decided to speak about his prospects. There would never be a better moment. He had been Roland's man for seven years; he was brave and strong; and he had saved his lord's life after the bridge collapsed – yet he had been given no promotion, and was still a squire. What more could be asked of him?

Yesterday he had met his brother, by chance, at a tavern on the road from Kingsbridge to Shiring. Merthin, on his way to the priory's quarry, had been full of news. He was going to build the most beautiful bridge in England. He would be rich and famous. Their parents were thrilled. It had made Ralph feel even more frustrated.

Now, speaking to Lord William, he could not think of a neat way to introduce the subject that was on his mind, so he just plunged in. 'It's three months since I saved your father's life at Kingsbridge.'

'Several people claim that honour,' William said. The harsh look that came over his face reminded Ralph strongly of Roland.

'I pulled him out of the water.'

'And Matthew Barber mended his head, and the nuns changed his bandages, and the monks prayed for him. God saved his life, though.'

'Amen,' Ralph said. 'All the same, I was hoping for some sign of favour.'

'My father's a hard man to please.'

William's brother, Richard, was standing nearby, red-faced and sweating, and he overheard the remark. 'That's as true as the Bible,' he said.

'Don't complain,' William said. 'Our father's hardness made us strong.'

'As I recall, it made us miserable.'

William turned away, probably not wanting to argue the point in front of an underling.

When the horses were stabled, the men drifted across the compound, past the kitchens and barracks and chapel, to a second drawbridge that led to a small inner compound, the top loop of the figure eight. Here the earl lived in a traditional keep, with ground-floor storerooms, a great hall above, and a small upper storey for the earl's private bedchamber. A colony of rooks inhabited the high trees around the keep, and strutted on the battlements like sergeants, cawing their dissatisfaction. Roland was in the great hall, having changed out of his dirty hunting clothes into a purple robe. Ralph stood near the earl, determined to raise the question of his promotion at the first opportunity.

Roland was arguing good-naturedly with William's wife, Lady Philippa – one of the few people who could contradict him and get away with it. They were talking about the castle. 'I don't think it's changed for a hundred years,' Philippa said.

'That's because it's such a good design,' Roland said, speaking out of the left side of his mouth. 'The enemy expends most of his strength getting into the lower compound, then he faces a whole new battle to reach the keep.'

'Exactly!' said Philippa. 'It was built for defence, not comfort. But when was the last time a castle in this part of England came under attack? Not in my lifetime.'

'Nor in mine.' He grinned with the mobile half of his face. 'Probably because our defences are so strong.'

'There was a bishop who scattered acorns on the road wherever he travelled, to protect him from lions,' Philippa said. 'When they told him there were no lions in all England, he said: "It's more effective than I thought."'

Roland laughed.

Philippa added: 'Most noble families nowadays live in more comfortable homes.'

Ralph did not care for luxury, but he cared for Philippa. He gazed at her voluptuous figure as she talked, unaware of him. He imagined her lying beneath him, twisting her naked body, crying out in pleasure, or pain, or both. If he were a knight he could have a woman like that.

'You should knock down this old keep and build a modern house,' she was saying to her father-in-law. 'One with big windows and lots of fireplaces. You could have the hall at ground level, with the family apartments at one end, so that we could all have somewhere private to sleep when we come to visit you; and the kitchens at the other end, so that the food is still hot when it reaches the table.'

Suddenly Ralph realized he could make a contribution to this conversation. 'I know who could design such a house for you,' he said.

They turned to him in surprise. What would a squire know of house design? 'Who?' said Philippa.

'My brother, Merthin.'

She looked thoughtful. 'The funny-faced boy who told me to buy green silk to match my eyes?'

'He meant no disrespect.'

'I'm not sure what he meant. Is he a builder?'

'He's the best,' Ralph said proudly. 'He devised the new ferry at Kingsbridge, then he figured out how to repair the roof of St Mark's when no one else could, and now he's been commissioned to build the most beautiful bridge in England.'

'Somehow I'm not surprised,' she said.

'What bridge?' said Roland.

'The new one at Kingsbridge. It will have pointed arches, like a church, and be wide enough for two carts!'

'I've heard nothing of this,' Roland said.

Ralph realized the earl was displeased. What had annoyed him? 'The bridge must be rebuilt, mustn't it?' Ralph said.

'I'm not so sure,' Roland replied. 'Nowadays there's hardly enough business for two markets as close together as Kingsbridge and Shiring. But, if we must accept the Kingsbridge market, that doesn't mean we have to countenance a blatant attempt by the priory to steal customers from Shiring.' Bishop Richard had come in, and now Roland rounded on him. 'You didn't tell me about the new bridge at Kingsbridge.'

'Because I don't know about it,' Richard answered.

'You ought to, you're the bishop.'

Richard flushed at the reproof. 'The bishop of Kingsbridge has lived in or near Shiring ever since the civil war between King

Stephen and the Empress Maud, two centuries ago. The monks prefer it that way, and so do most bishops.'

'That doesn't prevent you keeping your ear to the ground. You should have some idea of what's happening there.'

'Since I don't, perhaps you'd be kind enough to tell me what you've learned.'

That kind of cool insolence passed over Roland's head. 'It's going to be wide enough for two carts. It will take business away from my market at Shiring.'

'There's nothing I can do about it.'

'Why not? You're the abbot, *ex officio*. The monks are supposed to do what you say.'

'They don't, though.'

'Perhaps they will if we take away their builder. Ralph, can you persuade your brother to give up the project?'

'I can try.'

'Offer him a better prospect. Tell him I want him to build a new palace for me here at Earlscastle.'

Ralph was excited to get a special commission from the earl, but he was daunted too. He had never been able to talk Merthin into anything – it was always the other way around. 'All right,' he said.

'Will they be able to go ahead without him?'

'He got the job because no one else in Kingsbridge knew how to build under water.'

Richard said: 'He's not the only man in England who can design a bridge, obviously.'

William said: 'Still, taking away their builder would surely delay them. They probably couldn't start for another year.'

'Then it's worth doing,' Roland said decisively. A look of hatred came over the animated half of his face, and he added: 'That arrogant prior has to be put in his place.'

*

THINGS HAD CHANGED in the life of Gerald and Maud, Ralph discovered. His mother wore a new green dress to church, and his father had leather shoes. Back at home there was a goose stuffed with apples roasting over the fire, filling the little house with a mouth-watering smell, and a loaf of wheat bread, the most expensive kind, standing on the table.

The money came from Merthin, Ralph soon learned. 'He gets paid four pence a day every day he works on St Mark's,' Maud said proudly. 'And he's building a new house for Dick Brewer. That's as well as getting ready to build the new bridge.'

Merthin received a lower wage for working on the bridge, he explained while his father carved the goose, because he had been given Leper Island in part payment. The last remaining leper, old and bedridden, had been moved to a small house in the monks' orchard on the far side of the river.

Ralph found that his mother's evident happiness left a sour taste in his mouth. He had believed, since he was a boy, that the destiny of the family lay in his hands. He had been sent away, at the age of fourteen, to join the household of the earl of Shiring, and he had known even then that it was up to him to wipe out his father's humiliation by becoming a knight, perhaps a baron, even an earl. Merthin, by contrast, had been apprenticed to a carpenter, and set on a road that could only lead farther down the social hill. Builders were never made knights.

It was some consolation that their father was unimpressed by Merthin's success. He showed signs of impatience when Maud talked about building projects. 'My elder son seems to have inherited the blood of Jack Builder, my only low-born ancestor,' he said, and his tone was amazed rather than proud. 'But, Ralph, tell us how you're getting on at the court of Earl Roland.'

Unfortunately, Ralph had so far mysteriously failed to rise in the nobility, whereas Merthin was buying his parents new clothes and expensive dinners. Ralph knew he should just be grateful that one of them had won success, and that even if his parents remained humble they could at least be comfortable. But, though his mind told him to rejoice, his heart seethed with resentment.

And now he had to persuade his brother to give up the bridge. The trouble with Merthin was that he would never see anything simply. He was not like the knights and squires with whom Ralph had spent the last seven years. They were fighting men. In their world loyalties were clear, bravery was the virtue, and the issue was life or death. There was never much need for deep thought. But Merthin thought about everything. He could not play a game of chequers without suggesting a change in the rules.

He was explaining to their parents why he had accepted four acres of barren rock in part payment for his work on the bridge. 'Everyone thinks the land is worthless because it's an island,' he said. 'What they don't realize is that when the bridge is built the island will become part of the city. Townspeople will walk across the bridge just as they walk along the main street. And four acres of city land is very valuable. If I build houses on it, the rents will be worth a fortune.'

Gerald said: 'You've a few years to wait before then.'

'I'm getting some income from it already. Jake Chepstow is renting half an acre to use as a timber yard. He's bringing logs from Wales.'

'Why from Wales?' Gerald asked. 'The New Forest is nearer – their wood should be cheaper.'

'It should be, but the earl of Shaftesbury charges a toll or a tax at every river ford and bridge in his territory.'

It was a familiar gripe. Many lords found ways to tax goods that passed through their territories.

As they started to eat, Ralph said to Merthin: 'I bring you news of another opportunity. The earl wants to build a new palace at Earlscastle.'

Merthin looked suspicious. 'He sent you to ask me to design it?'

'I suggested you. Lady Philippa was berating him about how old-fashioned the keep is, and I said I knew the right person to talk to.'

Maud was thrilled. 'Isn't that wonderful?'

Merthin remained sceptical. 'And the earl said he wanted me?'

'Yes.'

'Amazing. A few months ago I couldn't get a job. Now I've got too much to do. And Earlscastle is two days away. I don't see how I could build a palace there and a bridge here at the same time.'

'Oh, you'll have to give up the bridge,' Ralph said.

'What?'

'Work for the earl has to take precedence over everything else, naturally.'

'I'm not sure that's right.'

'Take it from me.'

'Did he say that?'

'Yes, as a matter of fact, he did.'

Their father joined in. 'This is a marvellous opportunity, Merthin,' he said. 'To build a palace for an earl!'

'Of course it is,' Merthin replied. 'But a bridge for this town is at least as important.'

'Don't be stupid,' his father said.

'I do my best not to be,' Merthin said sarcastically.

'The earl of Shiring is one of the great men of the land. The prior of Kingsbridge is a nobody, by comparison.'

Ralph cut a slice of goose thigh and put it in his mouth, but he could hardly swallow. He had been afraid of this. Merthin was going to be difficult. He would not take orders from their father, either. He had never been obedient, even as a child.

Ralph felt desperate. 'Listen,' he said. 'The earl doesn't want the new bridge to be built. He thinks it will take business away from Shiring.'

'Aha,' said Gerald. 'You don't want to go up against the earl, Merthin.'

'Is that what's behind this, Ralph?' Merthin asked. 'Is Roland offering me this job just to prevent the building of the bridge?'

'Not just for that reason.'

'But it's a condition. If I want to build his palace, I must abandon the bridge.'

Gerald said with exasperation: 'You don't have a choice, Merthin! The earl doesn't request, he commands.'

Ralph could have told him that an argument based on authority was not the way to persuade Merthin.

Merthin said: 'I don't think he can command the prior of Kingsbridge, who has commissioned me to build this bridge.'

'But he can command you.'

'Can he? He's not my lord.'

'Don't be foolish, son. You can't win a fight with an earl.'

'I don't think Roland's quarrel is with me, Father. This is between the earl and the prior. Roland wants to use me, as a hunter uses a dog, but I think I'd do better to stay out of the fight.'

'I think you should do what the earl says. Don't forget, he's your kinsman, too.'

Merthin tried a different argument. 'Has it occurred to you what a betrayal this would be of Prior Godwyn?'

Gerald made a disgusted noise. 'What loyalty do we owe the priory? It was the monks who forced us into penury.'

'And your neighbours? The people of Kingsbridge, among whom you've lived for ten years? They need the bridge – it's their lifeline.'

'We are of the nobility,' his father said. 'We're not required to take into account the needs of mere merchants.'

Merthin nodded. 'You may feel that way, but as a mere carpenter I can't share your view.'

'This isn't just about you!' Ralph burst out. He had to come clean, he realized. 'The earl has given me a mission. If I succeed, he may make me a knight, or at least a minor lord. If I fail, I could remain a squire.'

Maud said: 'It's very important that we all try to please the earl.'

Merthin looked troubled. He was always willing to go head-to-head with their father, but he did not like to argue with Mother. 'I've agreed to build the bridge,' he said. 'The town is counting on me. I can't give it up.'

'Of course you can,' Maud said.

'I don't want to get a reputation for unreliability.'

'Everyone would understand if you gave the earl precedence.'

'They might understand, but they wouldn't respect me for it.'

'You should put your family first.'

'I fought for this bridge, Mother,' Merthin said stubbornly. 'I made a beautiful design, and I persuaded the whole town to have faith in me. No one else can build it – not the way it should be done.'

'If you defy the earl, it will affect Ralph's whole life!' she said. 'Don't you see that?'

'His whole life shouldn't depend on something like this.'

'But it does. Are you willing to sacrifice your brother, just for the sake of a bridge?'

Merthin said: 'I suppose it's a bit like my asking him to save men's lives by not going to war.'

Gerald said: 'Come, now, you can't compare a carpenter to a soldier.'

That was tactless, Ralph thought. It showed Gerald's preference for the younger son. Merthin felt the sting, Ralph could tell. His brother's faced reddened and he bit his lip as if to restrain himself from a combative reply.

After a pause, Merthin spoke in a quiet voice that Ralph knew to be a sign that he had made up his mind irrevocably. 'I didn't ask to be a carpenter,' he said. 'Like Ralph, I wanted to be a knight. A foolish aspiration for me, I know that now. All the same, it was your decision that I should be what I am. As things have turned out, I'm good at it. I'm going to make a success of what you forced me into. One day I'd like to build the tallest building in England. This is what you made me – so you'd better learn to live with it.'

*

BEFORE RALPH WENT BACK to Earlscastle with the bad news, he racked his brains for a way to turn defeat into victory. If he could not talk his brother into abandoning the bridge, was there some other way he could get the project cancelled or delayed?

There was no point talking to Prior Godwyn or Edmund Wooler, he was sure. They would be more committed to the bridge even than Merthin, and anyway they would not be persuaded by a mere squire. What could the earl do? He might send a troop of knights to kill the construction workers, but that could cause more problems than it solved.

It was Merthin who gave him the idea. He had said that Jake Chepstow, the timber merchant who was using Leper Island as a store yard, was buying trees from Wales to avoid the taxes charged by the earl of Shaftesbury.

'My brother feels he must accept the authority of the prior of Kingsbridge,' Ralph said to Earl Roland on his return. Before the earl had time to get angry, he added: 'But there may be a better way to delay the building of the bridge. The priory's quarry is in the heart of your earldom, between Shiring and Earlscastle.'

'But it belongs to the monks,' Roland growled. 'The king gave it to them centuries ago. We can't stop them taking stone.'

'You could tax them, though,' Ralph said. He felt guilty: he was sabotaging a project dear to his brother's heart. But it had to be done, and he quelled his conscience. 'They will be transporting their stone through your earldom. Their heavy carts will wear away your roads and churn up your river fords. They ought to pay.'

'They'll squeal like pigs. They'll go to the king.'

'Let them,' Ralph said, sounding more confident than he felt. 'It will take time. There are only two months left of this year's building season – they have to stop work before the first frost. With luck, you could delay the start of the bridge until next year.'

Roland gave Ralph a hard look. 'I may have underestimated you,' he said. 'Perhaps you're good for more than pulling drowning earls out of rivers.'

Ralph concealed a triumphant smile. 'Thank you, my lord.'

'But how shall we enforce this tax? Usually there's a crossroads, a ford in a river, some place every cart has to pass through.'

'Since we're only interested in blocks of stone, we could simply camp a troop of men outside the quarry.'

'Excellent,' said the earl. 'And you can lead them.'

Two days later Ralph was approaching the quarry with four men-at-arms on horseback and two boys leading a string of packhorses carrying tents and food for a week. He was pleased with himself, so far. He had been given an impossible task and turned it around. The earl thought he was good for more than river rescue work. Things were looking up.

He was deeply uncomfortable about what he was doing to Merthin. He had lain awake much of the night recalling their childhood together. He had always revered his clever older brother. They had often fought, and Ralph had felt worse when he won than when he lost. They had always made friends afterwards, in those days. But grown-up fights were harder to forget.

He was not very anxious about the coming confrontation with the monks' quarrymen. It should not prove too challenging for a group of military men. He had no knights with him – such work was beneath their dignity – but he had Joseph Woodstock, whom he knew to be a hard man, and three others. All the same, he would be glad when it was over and he had achieved his aim.

It was just after dawn. They had camped the night before in the forest a few miles from the quarry. Ralph planned to get there in time to challenge the first cart that attempted to leave this morning.

The horses stepped daintily along a road muddied by the hooves of oxen and deeply rutted by the wheels of heavy carts. The sun rose into a sky of rain clouds broken by scraps of blue. Ralph's group were in a good mood, looking forward to exercising their power over unarmed men, with no serious risk to themselves.

Ralph smelled wood burning, then saw the smoke of several fires rising over the trees. A few moments later, the road widened into a muddy clearing in front of the largest hole in the ground he had ever seen. It was a hundred yards wide and stretched for at least a quarter of a mile. A mud ramp led down to the tents and wooden huts of the quarrymen, who were clustered around their fires cooking breakfast. A few were already at work, farther along the site, and Ralph could hear the dull thud of hammers driving wedges into cracks in the rock, splitting great slabs from the mass of stone.

The quarry was a day's journey from Kingsbridge, so most carters arrived in the evening and left the following morning. Ralph could see several carts dotted about the quarry, some being loaded with stone, and one already making its slow way along the track through the diggings towards the exit ramp.

The men in the quarry looked up, alerted by the sound of horses, but no one approached. Workers were never in a hurry to converse with men-at-arms. Ralph waited patiently. There appeared to be only one way out of the quarry, the long slope of mud that led to where he was.

The first cart lumbered slowly up the ramp, the carter urging the ox on with a long-tailed whip, the ox putting one foot in front of the other with mute resentment. Four huge stones were piled on its flatbed, rough-hewn and incised with the mark of the man who had quarried them. Each man's output was counted once at the quarry and again at the building site, and he was paid per stone.

As the cart came closer, Ralph saw that the carter was a Kingsbridge man, Ben Wheeler. He looked a bit like his ox, with a thick neck and massive shoulders. His face wore a similar expression of dull hostility. He might try to make trouble, Ralph guessed. However, he could be subdued.

Ben drove his ox towards the line of horses blocking the road. Instead of halting at a distance, he let the beast come closer and closer. The horses were not combat-trained destriers but everyday hacks, and they snorted nervously and backed. The ox stopped of its own accord.

Ben's attitude angered Ralph, who called out: 'You're a cocksure oaf.'

Ben said: 'Why do you stand in my way?'

'To collect the tax.'

'There's no tax.'

'To carry stone across the territory of the earl of Shiring, you must pay a penny per cartload.'

'I have no money.'

'Then you must get some.'

'Do you bar my passage?'

The fool was not as scared as he should have been, which infuriated Ralph. 'Don't presume to question me,' Ralph said. 'The stone stays here until someone has paid tax for it.'

Ben glared back at him for a long moment, and Ralph had the strongest feeling that the man was wondering whether to knock him off his horse. 'But I have no money,' he said eventually.

Ralph wanted to run him through with his sword, but he reined in his temper. 'Don't pretend to be even more stupid than you are,' he said contemptuously. 'Just go to the master quarryman and tell him the earl's men will not let you leave.'

Ben stared at him a little longer, mulling this over; then, without speaking, he turned and walked back down the ramp, leaving his cart.

Ralph waited, fuming, staring at the ox.

Ben entered a wooden hut half way along the quarry. He emerged a few minutes later accompanied by a slight man in a brown tunic. At first, Ralph presumed the second man was the quarrymaster. However, the figure looked familiar and, as the two came closer, Ralph recognized his brother, Merthin.

'Oh, no,' he said aloud.

He was not prepared for this. He felt tortured by shame as he watched Merthin walk up the long ramp. He knew he was here to betray his brother, but he had not expected Merthin to be here to see it.

'Hello, Ralph,' said Merthin as he came closer. 'Ben says you won't let him pass.'

Merthin had always been able to overcome him in an argument, Ralph recalled dismally. He decided to be formal. It would hide his emotions, and he could hardly get into trouble if he simply repeated his instructions. He said stiffly: 'The earl has decided to exercise his right to collect taxes from consignments of stone using his roads.'

Merthin ignored that. 'Aren't you going to get down off your horse to talk to your brother?'

Ralph would have preferred to stay mounted, but he did not want to refuse what seemed like some kind of challenge, so he got down. Then he felt as if he had already been bested.

'There's no tax on stone from here,' Merthin said.

'There is now.'

'The monks have been working this quarry for hundreds of years. Kingsbridge Cathedral is build of this stone. It has never been taxed.'

'Perhaps the earl forgave the tax for the sake of the church,' Ralph said, improvising. 'But he won't do it for a bridge.'

'He just doesn't want the town to have a new bridge. That's the reason for this. First he sends you to bribe me, then when that fails he invents a new tax.' Merthin looked thoughtfully at Ralph. 'This was your idea, wasn't it?'

Ralph was mortified. How had he guessed? 'No!' he said, but he felt himself redden.

'I can see from your face that it was. I gave you the notion, I'm sure, when I spoke of Jake Chepstow importing logs from Wales to avoid the earl of Shaftesbury's tax.'

Ralph was feeling more foolish and angry with every moment. 'There's no connection,' he said stubbornly.

'You berated me for putting my bridge before my brother, but you're happy to wreck my hopes for the sake of your earl.'

'It doesn't matter whose idea it was, the earl has decided to tax the stone.'

'But he doesn't have the right.'

Ben Wheeler was following the conversation intently, standing beside Merthin with his legs apart and his hands on his hips. Now he said to Merthin: 'Are you saying these men don't have the right to stop me?'

'That's exactly what I'm saying,' said Merthin.

Ralph could have told Merthin it was a mistake to treat such a man as if he was intelligent. Ben now took Merthin's words for permission to leave. He flicked his whip over his ox's shoulders. The beast leaned into its wooden collar and took the strain.

Ralph shouted angrily: 'Halt!'

Ben whipped the ox again and called: 'Hup!'

The ox pulled harder and the cart started forward with a jerk that startled the horses. Joseph Woodstock's mount whinnied and reared up, eyes rolling.

Joseph sawed at the reins and got the horse under control. Then he pulled from his saddlebag a long wooden club. 'You keep still when you're told,' he said to Ben. He urged his horse forward and lashed out with the club.

Ben dodged the blow, grabbed the club and pulled.

Joseph was already leaning out from his saddle. The sudden jerk unbalanced him, and he fell off his horse.

Merthin cried: 'Oh, no!'

Ralph knew why Merthin was dismayed. A man-at-arms could not overlook such humiliation. There was no avoiding violence now. But Ralph himself was not sorry. His brother had failed to treat the earl's men with the deference they merited, and now he would see the consequences.

Ben was holding Joseph's club in a two-handed grip. Joseph leaped to his feet. Seeing Ben brandishing the club, he reached for his dagger. But Ben was quicker – the carter must have fought in battle at some time, Ralph realized. Ben swung the club and landed a mighty blow on the top of Joseph's head. Joseph fell to the ground and lay motionless.

Ralph roared with rage. He drew his sword and ran at the carter.

Merthin shouted: 'No!'

Ralph stabbed Ben in the chest, thrusting the sword between his ribs as forcefully as he could. It passed through Ben's thick body and came out the other side. Ben fell back and Ralph pulled the sword out. Blood spurted from the carter in a fountain. Ralph felt a jolt of triumphant satisfaction. There would be no more insolence from Ben Wheeler.

He knelt beside Joseph. The man's eyes stared sightlessly. There was no heartbeat. He was dead.

In a way that was good. It simplified the explanations. Ben Wheeler had murdered one of the earl's men, and had died for it. No one would see any injustice in that – least of all Earl Roland, who had no mercy for those who defied his authority.

Merthin did not see it the same way. His face was twisted as if in pain. 'What have you done?' he said incredulously. 'Ben Wheeler has a two-year-old son! They call him Bennie!'

'The widow had better look for another husband, then,' said Ralph. 'This time, she should choose a man who knows his place.'

27

IT WAS A POOR HARVEST. There was so little sunshine in August that the grain had barely ripened by September. In the village of Wigleigh, spirits were low. There was none of the usual euphoria of harvest time: the dances, the drinking, the sudden romances. Wet crops were liable to rot. Many villagers would go hungry before spring.

Wulfric reaped his barley in the driving rain, scything the wet stalks while Gwenda followed behind binding the sheaves. On the first sunny day of September they started to harvest the wheat, the most valuable crop, in the hope that the fine weather would last long enough to dry it.

At some point Gwenda realized that Wulfric was powered by fury. The sudden loss of his entire family had enraged him. He would have blamed someone for his bereavement, if he could; but the collapse of the bridge seemed a random event, an act of evil spirits or a punishment by God; so he had no outlet for his passion except work. She herself was driven by love, which was just as potent.

They were in the fields before the crack of dawn, and they did not stop until it was too dark to see. Gwenda went to sleep with an aching back every night and woke when she heard Wulfric bang the kitchen door before dawn. Still they lagged behind everyone else.

Gradually, she sensed a change in the attitude of the village towards her and Wulfric. All her life, she had been looked down upon as the daughter of the disreputable Joby; and the women had disapproved of her even more when they realized she wanted to snatch Wulfric away from Annet. Wulfric was hard to dislike, but some felt that his desire to inherit such a big landholding was greedy and impractical. However, people could hardly fail to be impressed by their efforts to get the harvest in. A boy and a girl were trying to do the work of three men, and they were getting on better than anyone had expected. Men began to look at Wulfric with admiration, and women at Gwenda with sympathy.

In the end the villagers rallied around to help them. The priest, Father Gaspard, turned a blind eye to their working on Sundays. When Annet's family had got their harvest in, her father, Perkin, and her brother, Rob, joined Gwenda on Wulfric's land. Even Gwenda's mother, Ethna, showed up. As they carted the last of the sheaves to Wulfric's barn, there was a hint of the traditional harvest spirit, with everyone singing the old songs as they walked home behind the cart.

Annet was there, in violation of the saying that you should first follow the plough if you want to dance the harvest jig. She walked by Wulfric's side, as was her right, being his acknowledged fiancée. Gwenda watched her from behind, noting sourly how she swayed her hips, tossed her head and laughed prettily at everything he said. How could he be so stupid as to fall for that? Had he not noticed that Annet had done no work on his land?

No day had yet been fixed for the wedding. Perkin was nothing if not shrewd, and he would not let his daughter commit herself until the question of the inheritance was settled.

Wulfric had proved his ability to farm the land. No one would question that now. His age had come to seem irrelevant. The only remaining obstacle was the heriot. Would he be able to raise the money to pay the inheritance tax? It would depend how much he got for his cash crops. The harvest was poor but, if the bad weather had been widespread, the price of wheat would probably be high. In normal circumstances, a prosperous peasant family would have money saved up for the heriot; but Wulfric's family's savings were at the bottom of the river in Kingsbridge. So nothing was settled. And Gwenda could continue to dream that Wulfric would inherit the land and, somehow, transfer his affections to her. Anything was possible.

As they were unloading the cart into the barn, Nathan Reeve arrived. The hunchbacked bailiff was in a state of high excitement.

'Come to the church, quickly,' he said. 'Everybody! Stop what you're doing.'

Wulfric said: 'I'm not leaving my crops out in the open – it might rain.'

Gwenda said: 'We'll just drag the cart inside. What's the emergency, Nate?'

The bailiff was already hurrying to the next house. 'The new lord is arriving!' he said.

'Wait!' Wulfric ran after him. 'Will you recommend that I inherit?'

Everyone stood still, watching, waiting for the answer.

Nathan turned reluctantly and faced Wulfric. He had to look up, for Wulfric was taller by a foot. 'I don't know,' he said slowly.

'I've proved I can farm the land – you can see that. Just look in the barn!'

'You've done well, no question. But can you pay the heriot?'

'It depends on the price of wheat.'

Annet spoke. 'Father?' she said.

Gwenda wondered what was coming.

Perkin looked hesitant.

Annet prompted him again. 'You remember what you promised me.'

'Yes, I remember,' Perkin said at last.

'Tell Nate, then.'

Perkin turned to the bailiff. 'I'll guarantee the heriot, if the lord will let Wulfric inherit.'

Gwenda's hand flew to her mouth.

Nathan said: 'You'll pay it for him? It's two pounds and ten shillings.'

'If he's short, I'll lend him what he needs. Of course, they'll have to be married first.'

Nathan lowered his voice. 'And, in addition...?'

Perkin said something so quietly that Gwenda could not hear it, but she could guess what it was. Perkin was offering Nathan a bribe, probably a tenth of the tax, which would be five shillings.

'Very well,' Nathan said. 'I'll make the recommendation. Now get yourselves to the church, quickly!' He ran off.

Wulfric smiled broadly and kissed Annet. Everyone shook his hand.

Gwenda was heartsick. Her hopes were dashed. Annet had been too clever. She had persuaded her father to lend Wulfric the money he needed. He would inherit his land – and he would marry Annet.

Gwenda forced herself to help push the cart into the barn. Then she followed the happy couple as they walked through the village to the church. It was all over. A new lord, not knowing the village or the people, was unlikely to go against his bailiff's advice on a question such as this. The fact that Nathan had gone to the trouble of negotiating a bribe indicated his confidence.

It was partly her fault, of course. She had broken her back to make sure Wulfric got his harvest in, in the vain hope that somehow he would realize how much better a wife she would make than Annet. All summer long she had been digging her own grave, she thought as she walked through the cemetery to the church door. But she would do the same again. She could not have borne to see him struggle alone. Whatever happens, she thought, he'll always know I was the one who stuck it out with him. It was small consolation.

Most of the villagers were already in the church. They had not needed much urging from Nathan. They were eager to be among the first to pay their respects to their new lord, and curious to see what he was like: young or old, ugly or handsome, cheerful or dyspeptic, clever or stupid, and – most important of all – cruel or kind. Everything about him would affect their lives for as long as he remained lord, which might be years or decades. If he were reasonable, he could do a lot to make Wigleigh a happy and prosperous village. If he were a fool, they would have unwise decisions and unjust rulings, oppressive taxes and harsh punishments. And one of his first decisions would be whether to let Wulfric inherit.

The rumble of conversation died away, and a jingle of harness was heard. Gwenda heard Nathan's voice, low and obsequious, then the authoritative tone of a lord – a big man, she thought, confident, but young. Everyone looked at the church door. It flew open.

Gwenda gasped with shock.

The man who strode in was no more than twenty. He was well dressed in an expensive wool surcoat, and armed with sword and dagger. He was tall, and his expression was proud. He seemed pleased to be lord of Wigleigh, though there was a hint of insecurity in the haughty look. He had wavy dark hair and a handsome face disfigured by a broken nose.

He was Ralph Fitzgerald.

*

RALPH'S FIRST MANORIAL COURT was held the following Sunday.

In the interim, Wulfric was depressed. Gwenda wanted to weep every time she looked at him. He walked around with his eyes cast down, his broad shoulders slumped. All summer he had seemed tireless, working in the fields with the uncomplaining dependability of a plough horse; but now he looked weary. He had done all a man could do, but his fate had been given into the hands of one who hated him.

She would have liked to say something hopeful, in an attempt to cheer him up, but the truth was that she shared his pessimism. Lords were often petty and vindictive, and nothing about Ralph encouraged her to believe that he would be magnanimous. As a child, he had been stupid and brutal. She would never forget the day he had killed her dog with Merthin's bow and arrow.

There was no sign that he had improved since then. He had moved into the manor house with his sidekick, a beefy young squire called Alan Fernhill, and the two of them were drinking the best wine, eating the chickens and squeezing the breasts of the female servants with the carelessness typical of their class.

Nathan Reeve's attitude confirmed her fears. The bailiff was not bothering to negotiate an increased bribe – a sure sign that he expected failure.

Annet, too, seemed to have a poor view of Wulfric's prospects. Gwenda saw an unmistakable change in her. She did not toss her hair so gaily, nor walk with that swish of her hips, and the waterfall tinkle of her laughter was not heard so often. Gwenda hoped Wulfric would not see the difference in Annet: he had enough to be gloomy about. But it seemed to her that he did not stay so late at Perkin's house in the evenings, and when he returned home he was taciturn.

She was surprised to learn, on Sunday morning, that Wulfric still harboured the ghost of a hope. When the service ended, and Father Gaspard gave place to Lord Ralph, she saw that Wulfric's eyes were closed and his lips were moving, presumably in a prayer to his favourite saint, the Virgin Mary.

All the villagers were in church, of course, including Joby and Ethna. Gwenda did not stand with her parents. She talked to her mother sometimes, but only when her father was not around. Joby had an angry red patch on his cheek where she had burned him with the blazing log. He never met her eye. She was still afraid of him, but she sensed that he was now also afraid of her.

Ralph sat on the big wooden chair, staring at his serfs with the appraising look of a buyer at a cattle market. The court proceedings on this day consisted of a series of announcements. Nathan proclaimed the arrangements for getting the harvest in from the lord's fields, stating on which days of the coming week different villagers would be required to perform their customary duty on the lord's lands. No discussion was invited. Clearly Ralph did not intend to govern by consensus.

There were other details of the kind Nathan dealt with every week: gleaning should be completed in Hundredacre by Monday night so that livestock could graze the stubble from Tuesday morning, and autumn ploughing of Long Field would begin on Wednesday. Normally there would have been minor disputes about these plans, with the more argumentative villagers finding reasons to propose different arrangements, but today they were all quiet, waiting to get the measure of the new lord.

When the decision came, it seemed curiously low-key. As if he were simply stating another schedule of work, Nathan said: 'Wulfric will not be permitted to inherit his father's landholding, because he is only sixteen.'

Gwenda looked at Ralph. He was trying to smother a triumphant grin. His hand went to his face – unconsciously, she thought – and he touched his broken nose.

Nathan went on: 'Lord Ralph will consider what to do with the lands and give his judgement later.'

Wulfric groaned loud enough for everyone to hear. It was the decision he had been expecting, but its confirmation was bitter. She watched as he turned his back on the crowd in the church, hiding his face, and leaned against the wall as if to stop himself falling.

'That's all for today,' said Nathan.

Ralph stood up. He walked down the aisle slowly, his eyes continually turning to the distraught Wulfric. What kind of lord would he be, Gwenda thought, if his first instinct was to use his power for revenge? Nathan followed Ralph, looking at the floor: he knew that an injustice had been done. As they left the church, a buzz of comment arose. Gwenda spoke to no one, but watched Wulfric.

He turned from the wall, his face a picture of misery. His eyes raked the crowd and found Annet. She looked furious. Gwenda waited for her to meet Wulfric's eye, but she seemed determined not to look at him. Gwenda wondered what was going through her mind.

Annet walked towards the door, head held high. Her father, Perkin, and the family followed. Would she not even speak to Wulfric?

The same thought must have occurred to him, for he went after her. 'Annet!' he said. 'Wait.'

The place went quiet.

Annet turned. Wulfric stood before her. 'We'll still get married, won't we?' he said. Gwenda winced to hear the undignified note of pleading in his voice. Annet stared at him, apparently about to speak, but she said nothing for a long moment, and Wulfric spoke again. 'Lords need good serfs to farm the land. Perhaps Ralph will give me a smaller holding—'

'You broke his nose,' she said harshly. 'He will never give you anything.'

Gwenda recalled how pleased Annet had been, at the time, to have two men fighting over her.

Wulfric said: 'Then I'll be a labourer. I'm strong, I'll never lack for work.'

'But you'll be poor all your life. Is that what you're offering me?'

'We'll be together – just as we dreamed, that day in the forest, when you told me you loved me, don't you remember?'

'And what would life be like for me, married to a landless labourer?' Annet demanded angrily. 'I'll tell you.' She lifted her arm and pointed at Gwenda's mother, Ethna, standing with Joby and the three little ones. 'I would be like her – grim-faced with worry and as thin as a broom handle.'

Joby was stung by this. He waved the stump of his severed hand at Annet. 'You watch your mouth, you haughty minx.'

Perkin stepped in front of his daughter and made a patting gesture with both hands. 'Forgive her, Joby, she's overwrought, she means no harm.'

Wulfric said: 'No disrespect to Joby, but I'm not like him, Annet.'

'But you are!' she said. 'You've got no land. It's why he's poor, and it's why you'll be poor, and your children will be hungry and your wife will be drab.'

It was true. In hard times the landless were the first to suffer. Dismissing your employees was the quickest way to save money. All the same, Gwenda found it hard to believe that a woman would turn down the chance of spending her life with Wulfric.

Yet that seemed to be what Annet was doing.

Wulfric thought so, too. Plaintively, he said: 'Don't you love me any more?'

He had lost all his dignity and he looked pathetic; yet, at that moment, Gwenda felt more passion for him than ever before.

'I can't eat love,' Annet said, and she walked out of the church.

*

Two weeks later, she married Billy Howard.

Gwenda went to the wedding, as did everyone in the village except Wulfric. Despite the poor harvest, there was a good feast. By this marriage two large landholdings were united: Perkin's hundred acres with Billy's forty. Furthermore, Perkin had asked Ralph to give him Wulfric's family's lands. If Ralph agreed, Annet's children could be heirs to almost half the village. But

Ralph had gone to Kingsbridge, promising a decision as soon as he returned.

Perkin broached a barrel of his wife's strongest ale and slaughtered a cow. Gwenda ate and drank heartily. Her future was too uncertain for her to turn down good food.

She played with her little sisters, Cath and Joanie, throwing and catching a wooden ball; then she took baby Eric on her knee and sang to him. After a while her mother sat beside her and said: 'What will you do now?'

In her heart Gwenda was not completely reconciled with Ethna. They talked, and Ma asked concerned questions. Gwenda still resented her mother for forgiving Joby, but she answered the questions. 'I'll live in Wulfric's barn as long as I can,' she said. 'Perhaps I can stay there indefinitely.'

'And if Wulfric moves out – leaves the village, say?'

'I don't know.'

For now, Wulfric was still working in the fields, ploughing in the stubble and harrowing the fallow on the land that had been his family's, and Gwenda was helping him. They were paid the daily labourer's rate by Nathan, as they would have no part of the next harvest. Nathan was keen for them to stay, otherwise the land would deteriorate rapidly. They would continue until Ralph announced who the new tenant would be. At that point, they would have to offer themselves for hire.

'Where is Wulfric now?' Ethna asked.

'I assume he's not disposed to celebrate this wedding.'

'How does he feel about you?'

Gwenda gave her mother a candid look. 'He tells me I'm the best friend he's ever had.'

'What does that mean?'

'I don't know. But it doesn't mean "I love you," does it?'

'No,' said her mother. 'No, it doesn't mean that.'

Gwenda heard music. Aaron Appletree was playing a bagpipe, running up and down the scale in preparation for a tune. She saw Perkin coming out of his house with a pair of small drums attached to his belt. The dancing was about to begin.

She was in no mood to dance. She could have talked to the old women, but they would only ask the same questions as her mother, and she did not want to spend the rest of the day explaining her predicament. She recalled the last village wedding, and Wulfric slightly drunk, dancing around with great leaps, embracing all the women, though still favouring Annet. Without him there was no festival for Gwenda. She gave Eric back to her mother and drifted away. Her dog, Skip, stayed behind, knowing that such parties provided a banquet of dropped food and discarded scraps.

She went into Wulfric's house, half hoping he might be there, but the place was empty. It was a sturdy timber house, of post-and-beam construction, but with no chimney – such luxuries were for the rich. She looked in both ground-floor rooms and the upstairs bedroom. The place was as tidy and clean as it had been when his mother was alive, but that was because he used only one room. He ate and slept in the kitchen. The place was cold and unhomely. It was a family house with no family.

She went to the barn. It was full of bundled hay, for winter fodder, and sheaves of barley and wheat waiting to be threshed. She climbed the ladder to the loft and lay down in the hay. After a while she fell asleep.

When she woke up it was dark. She had no idea what time it was. She stepped outside to look at the sky. There was a low moon behind streaks of cloud, and she calculated that it was only an hour or two after nightfall. As she stood by the barn door, still half asleep, she heard weeping.

She knew instantly that it was Wulfric. She had heard him cry once before, when he saw the bodies of his parents and his brother lying on the floor of Kingsbridge Cathedral. He cried with great sobs that seemed torn from the depths of his chest. Tears came to her own eyes as she listened to his grief.

After a while, she went into the house.

She could see him by the light of the moon. He lay face down in the straw, his back heaving as he sobbed. He must have heard her lift the latch, but he was too distraught to care, and he did not look up.

Gwenda knelt beside him and tentatively touched his mane of hair. He made no response. She rarely touched him, and to stroke his hair was an unknown delight. Her caress seemed to soothe him, for his weeping subsided.

After a while, she dared to lie down beside him. She expected him to push her away, but he did not. He turned his face to her, eyes closed. She dabbed at his cheeks with her sleeve, wiping away the tears. She was thrilled to be this close to him, and to be permitted these small intimacies. She longed to kiss his closed eyelids, but she was afraid that would be a step too far, and she restrained herself.

A few moments later, she realized he was asleep.

She was pleased. It was a sign of how comfortable he felt with her, and it meant she could stay with him, at least until he woke up.

It was autumn, and the night was cold. As Wulfric's breathing became slower and steadier, she got up stealthily and took his blanket from its hook on the wall. She draped it over him. He slept on undisturbed.

Despite the chill in the air, she slipped her dress over her head and lay beside him naked, arranging the blanket so that it covered them both.

She moved close to him and laid her cheek against his chest. She could hear his heartbeat and feel the breeze of his breath on the top of her head. The heat of his big body warmed her. In time, the moon went down, and the room became pitch dark. She felt she could have stayed like this for ever.

She did not sleep. She had no intention of wasting any of this precious time. She savoured every moment, knowing it might never happen again. She touched him cautiously, careful not to wake him. Through his light wool shift, her fingertips explored the muscles of his chest and back, the bones of his ribs and hips, the turn of his shoulder and the knob of his elbow.

He moved in his sleep several times. He turned and lay flat on his back, whereupon she put her head on his shoulder and her arm across his flat belly. Later he turned away, and then she moved really close, fitting herself into the S-shape of his body, pressing her breasts against his broad back, her hips into his, her knees into the backs of his knees. Then he turned back to her, flinging one arm across her shoulders and one leg over her thighs. His leg was painfully heavy, but she relished the ache as proof that she was not dreaming.

He dreamed, though. In the middle of the night he suddenly kissed her, thrusting his tongue roughly into her mouth, grasping her breast with one big hand. She felt his erection as he rubbed up against her clumsily. For a moment she was bewildered. He could have her whatever way he wanted, but it was unlike him to be anything but gentle. She put her hand to his groin and grasped his penis, which was sticking out through the slit in his underdrawers. Then, just as suddenly, he turned away and lay on his back, breathing rhythmically, and she realized that he had never woken up, but had touched her in a dream. He was undoubtedly dreaming of Annet, she realized ruefully.

She did not sleep, but she daydreamed. She imagined him introducing her to a stranger, saying: 'This is my wife, Gwenda.' She saw herself pregnant, but still working in the fields, and fainting in the middle of the day; and in her fantasy he picked her up and carried her home, and bathed her face with cold water. She saw him as an old man, playing with their grandchildren, indulging them, giving them apples and honeycombs.

Grandchildren? she thought wryly. It was a big edifice to build on the strength of his allowing her to put her arm around him while he cried himself to sleep.

When she was thinking that it must be almost dawn, and her stay in paradise might soon be over, he begin to stir. His breathing changed. He rolled on to his back. Her arm fell across his chest and she left it there, tucking her hand under his arm. After a few moments she sensed that he was awake, thinking. She lay still, afraid that if she spoke or moved she would break the spell.

Eventually he rolled back towards her. He put his arm around her, and she felt his hand on the bare skin of her back. He stroked her there, but she did not know what the caress meant: he seemed to be exploring, surprised to find that she was naked. His hand went up to her neck and all the way down to the curve of her hip.

At last he spoke. As if afraid of being overheard, he whispered: 'She married him.'

Gwenda whispered back: 'Yes.'

'Her love is weak.'

'True love is never weak.'

His hand remained on her hip, maddeningly close to the places where she wanted him to touch her.

He said: 'Will I ever stop loving her?'

Gwenda took his hand and moved it. 'She has two breasts, like these,' she said, still whispering. She did not know why she did it: intuition was guiding her, and she followed it for good or ill.

He groaned, and she felt his hand close gently over one, then the other.

'And she has hair down here, like this,' she said, moving his hand again. His breathing became faster. Leaving his hand there, she explored his body beneath his wool shift, and found that he had an erection. She grasped it and said: 'Her hand feels just like this.' He began to move his hips rhythmically.

She suddenly felt afraid that the act would be over before it was fully consummated. She did not want that. It was all or nothing now. She pushed him gently on to his back, then quickly raised herself and straddled him. 'Inside, she's hot and wet,' she said, and she lowered herself on to him. Although she had done it before, it had not been anything like this; she felt filled up and yet she wanted more. She moved down against the thrust of his hips, then up as he withdrew. She lowered her face to his and kissed his bearded mouth.

He held her head in his hands and kissed her back.

'She loves you,' Gwenda whispered to him. 'She loves you so much.'

He cried out with passion, and she was rocked up and down, riding his hips like a wild pony, until at last she felt him come inside her, and he gave one last cry, then said: 'Oh, I love you too! I love you, Annet!'

28

WULFRIC WENT BACK TO SLEEP, but Gwenda lay awake. She was too excited to sleep. She had won his love – she knew it. It hardly mattered that she had had to half pretend to be Annet. He had made love to her with such hunger, and had kissed her afterwards with such tenderness and gratitude, that she felt he was hers for ever.

When her heart stopped racing and her mind calmed down, she thought about his inheritance. She was not willing to give up on it, especially now. As dawn broke outside, she racked her brains for some way to save it. When Wulfric woke up, she said: 'I'm going to Kingsbridge.'

He was startled. 'Why?'

'To find out whether there's some way you can still inherit.'

'How?'

'I don't know. But Ralph hasn't given the land to anyone else yet, so there's still a chance. And you deserve it – you've worked so hard and suffered so much.'

'What will you do?'

'I'll see my brother Philemon. He understands these things better than we do. He'll know what we need to do.'

Wulfric looked at her strangely.

She said: 'What is it?'

He said: 'You really love me, don't you?'

She smiled, full of happiness, and said: 'Let's do it again, shall we?'

On the following morning she was at Kingsbridge Priory, sitting on the stone bench by the vegetable garden, waiting for Philemon. During the long walk from Wigleigh she had gone over every second of Sunday night in her mind, relishing the physical pleasures, puzzling over the words spoken. Wulfric still had not said that he loved her, but he had said: 'You really love me.' And he had seemed pleased that she loved him, albeit a bit bewildered by the strength of her passion.

She longed to win back his birthright. She yearned for it almost as much as she had yearned for him. She wanted it for both of them. Even if he were a landless labourer like her father she would marry him, given the chance; but she wanted better for them both, and she was determined to get it.

When Philemon came out of the priory into the garden to greet her, she saw immediately that he was wearing the robes of a novice monk. 'Holger!' she said, using his real name in her shock. 'You're a novice – what you've always wanted!'

He smiled proudly, and benignly overlooked the use of his old name. 'It was one of Godwyn's first acts as prior,' he said. 'He is a wonderful man. It's such an honour to serve him.' He sat beside her on the bench. It was a mild autumn day, cloudy but dry.

'And how are you getting on with your lessons?'

'Slowly. It's hard to learn to read and write when you're grown up.' He grimaced. 'The small boys progress faster than I do. But I can copy out the Lord's Prayer in Latin.'

She envied him. She could not even write her name. 'That's wonderful!' she said. Her brother was on his way to achieving his life's dream, and becoming a monk. Perhaps the status of novice might ameliorate the feelings of worthlessness that, she felt sure, accounted for his sometimes being sly and deceitful.

'But what about you?' he said. 'Why have you come to Kingsbridge?'

'Did you know that Ralph Fitzgerald has become lord of Wigleigh?'

'Yes. He's here in town, staying at the Bell, living it up.'

'He has refused to let Wulfric inherit his father's land.' She told Philemon the story. 'I want to know whether the decision can be contested.'

Philemon shook his head. 'The short answer is No. Wulfric could appeal to the earl of Shiring, of course, asking him to overturn Ralph's decision, but the earl won't intervene unless he has a personal stake. Even if he thinks the decision unjust – which it obviously is – he won't undermine the authority of a new appointee. But what's your interest? I thought Wulfric was going to marry Annet.'

'When Ralph announced his decision, Annet jilted Wulfric and married Billy Howard.'

'And now you have a chance with Wulfric.'

'I think so.' She felt herself blush.

'How do you know?' he asked shrewdly.

'I took advantage of him,' she confessed. 'When he was distraught over the wedding, I went to his bed.'

'Don't worry. We who are born poor have to use cunning to get what we want. Scruples are for the privileged.'

She did not really like to hear him talk that way. Sometimes he seemed to think that any behaviour could be excused by their difficult childhood. But she was too disappointed to worry about that. 'Is there really nothing I can do?'

'Oh, I didn't say that. It can't be contested, I said. But Ralph might be talked round.'

'Not by me, I'm sure.'

'I don't know. Why don't you go and see Godwyn's cousin Caris? You've been friends with her since you were girls. She'll help you if she can. And she's close to Ralph's brother, Merthin. Perhaps he can think of something.'

Any hope was better than none. Gwenda stood up to go. 'I'll see her right away.' She leaned forward to kiss her brother goodbye, then realized that he was forbidden such contact now. Instead, she clasped his hand, which seemed peculiar.

'I'll pray for you,' he said.

Caris's house was opposite the priory gates. When Gwenda went in, there was no one in the dining hall, but she heard voices in the parlour, where Edmund usually did business. The cook, Tutty, told her Caris was with her father. Gwenda sat down to wait, tapping her foot impatiently, but after a few minutes the door opened.

Edmund came out accompanied by a man she did not recognize. He was tall, and had flared nostrils that gave his face a supercilious look. He wore the black robe of a priest, but no cross or other sacred symbol. Edmund nodded amiably to Gwenda and said to the stranger: 'I'll walk you back to the priory.'

Caris followed the two men out of the parlour and embraced Gwenda. 'Who was that man?' Gwenda asked as soon as he had left.

'His name is Gregory Longfellow. He's the lawyer hired by Prior Godwyn.'

'Hired for what?'

'Earl Roland has stopped the priory taking stone from its quarry. He's trying to charge a penny a cartload. Godwyn is going to appeal to the king.'

'Are you involved?'

'Gregory thinks we must argue that the town will be unable to pay its taxes without a bridge. That's the best way to persuade the king, he says. So my father will go with Godwyn to testify at the royal court.'

'Will you go too?'

'Yes. But tell me why you're here?'

'I lay with Wulfric.'

Caris smiled. 'Really? At last! How was it?'

'It was wonderful. I lay beside him all night while he slept, then when he woke up I ... persuaded him.'

'Tell me more, I want all the details.'

Gwenda told Caris the story. At the end, even though she was impatient to get on to the real purpose of her visit, she said: 'But something tells me you have news of the same kind.'

Caris nodded. 'I lay with Merthin. I told him I didn't want to get married, and he went off to see that fat sow Bessie Bell, and I got upset at the thought of her sticking out her big tits at him – then he came back, and I was so pleased I just had to do it with him.'

'Did you like it?'

'I loved it. It's the best thing ever. And it gets better. We do it whenever we get the chance.'

'What if you get pregnant?'

'I'm not even thinking about that. I don't care if I die. One time –' she lowered her voice – 'one time, we bathed in a pool in the forest, and afterwards he licked me ... down there.'

'Oh, disgusting! What was it like?'

'Nice. He liked it, too.'

'You didn't do the same to him.'

'Yes.'

'But did he...?'

Caris nodded. 'In my mouth.'

'Wasn't it foul?'

Caris shrugged. 'It tastes funny ... but it's so exciting to feel that happen. And he enjoyed it so much.'

Gwenda was shocked but intrigued. Perhaps she should do that to Wulfric. She knew a place where they could bathe, a stream in the forest far from any roads...

Caris said: 'But you didn't come all this way just to tell me about Wulfric.'

'No. It's about his inheritance.' Gwenda explained Ralph's decision. 'Philemon thought perhaps Merthin could persuade Ralph to change his mind.'

Caris shook her head pessimistically. 'I doubt it. They've quarrelled.'

'Oh, no!'

'It was Ralph who stopped the carts leaving the quarry. Unfortunately, Merthin was there at the time. There was a fight. Ben Wheeler killed one of the earl's ruffians, and Ralph killed Ben.'

Gwenda gasped. 'But Lib Wheeler has a two-year-old!'

'And now little Bennie has no father.'

Gwenda was dismayed for herself as well as for Lib. 'So a brother's influence won't help.'

'Let's go and see Merthin anyway. He's working on Leper Island today.'

They left the house and walked down the main street to the riverside. Gwenda was discouraged. Everyone believed her chances were slender. It was so unfair.

They got Ian Boatman to row them across to the island. Caris explained that the old bridge was to be replaced by two new ones which would use the island as a stepping stone.

They found Merthin with his boy assistant, fourteen-year-old Jimmie, laying out the abutments of the new bridge. His measuring stick was an iron pole more than twice the height of a man, and he was hammering pointed stakes into the rocky ground to mark where the foundations must be dug.

Gwenda watched the way Caris and Merthin kissed. It was different. There was a cosy relish in one another's bodies that seemed new. It matched how Gwenda herself felt about Wulfric. His body was not just desirable, it was hers to enjoy. It seemed to belong to her the way her own body did.

She and Caris watched while Merthin finished what he was doing, tying a length of twine between two stakes. Then he told Jimmie to pack up the tools.

Gwenda said: 'I suppose there's not much you can do without stone.'

'There are some preparations we can make. But I've sent all the masons to the quarry. They're dressing the stones there, instead of here on site. We're building a stockpile.'

'So, if you win your case in the royal court, you can start building right away.'

'I hope so. It depends on how long the case takes – and the weather. We can't build in deepest winter, in case the frost freezes the mortar. It's October already. We normally stop around the middle of November.' He looked up at the sky. 'We might have a bit longer, this year – rain clouds keep the earth warm.'

Gwenda told him what she wanted.

'I wish I could help you,' Merthin said. 'Wulfric is a decent man, and that fight was entirely Ralph's fault. But I've quarrelled with my brother. Before asking him a favour, I'd have to make friends. And I can't forgive him for killing Ben Wheeler.'

It was the third negative response in a row, Gwenda thought glumly. Perhaps this was a foolish errand.

Caris said: 'You may have to do this on your own.'

'Yes, I will,' Gwenda said decisively. It was time to stop asking for other people's help, and start relying on herself – the way she had all her life. 'Ralph is here in town, isn't he?'

'Yes,' Merthin said. 'He came to tell our parents the good news about his promotion. They're the only people in the county who are celebrating.'

'But he's not staying with them.'

'He's too grand for that, now. He's at the Bell.'

'What would be the best way to persuade him?'

Merthin thought for a few moments. 'Ralph feels our father's humiliation – a knight reduced to the status of a pensioner of the priory. He'll do anything that seems to enhance his social position.'

Gwenda thought about that as Ian Boatman rowed them all back to the city. How could she present her request as a way for Ralph to raise his standing? It was midday as she walked up the main street with the others. Merthin was going to Caris's house for dinner, and Caris invited Gwenda to join them, but she was impatient to see Ralph, and she went on to the Bell.

A potboy told her Ralph was upstairs in the best room. Most lodgers slept in a communal dormitory: Ralph was emphasizing his new position by taking an entire room – paid for, Gwenda thought sourly, out of the meagre harvests of Wigleigh peasants.

She knocked at the door and went in.

Ralph was there with his squire, Alan Fernhill, a boy of about eighteen with big shoulders and a small head. On the table between them stood a jug of ale, a loaf and a joint of hot beef with a wisp of steam coming from it. They were finishing their dinner, and looked thoroughly contented with their lot in life, Gwenda thought. She hoped they were not too drunk: men in that state could not talk to women, all they could do was make ribald remarks and laugh helplessly at each other's wit.

Ralph peered at her: the room was not well lit. 'You're one of my serfs, aren't you?'

'No, my lord, but I'd like to be. I'm Gwenda, and my father is Joby, a landless labourer.'

'And what are you doing so far from the village? It's not market day.'

She moved a step farther into the room so that she could see his face more clearly. 'Sir, I come to plead for Wulfric, son of the late Samuel. I know that he behaved disrespectfully to you once but, since then, he has suffered the torments of Job. His parents and brother were killed when the bridge collapsed, all the family's money was lost, and now his fiancée has married someone else. I hope you might feel that God has punished him harshly for the wrong he did you, and it is time for you to show mercy.' Remembering what Merthin had advised, she added: 'The mercy characteristic of the true nobleman.'

He belched fruitily and sighed. 'What do you care whether Wulfric inherits?'

'I love him, my lord. Now that he has been rejected by Annet, I hope he may marry me – with your gracious permission, of course.'

'Come closer,' he said.

She moved into the centre of the room and stood in front of him.

His eyes roamed all over her body. 'You're not a pretty girl,' he said. 'But there's something about you. Are you a virgin?'

'Lord – I – I—'

'Obviously not,' he laughed. 'Have you lain with Wulfric yet?'

'No!'

'Liar.' He grinned, enjoying himself. 'Well, now, what if I let Wulfric have his father's lands after all? Perhaps I should. What then?'

'You would be called a true nobleman by Wigleigh and all the world.'

'The world won't care. But will you be grateful to me?'

Gwenda had a horrible feeling that she knew where this was leading. 'Of course, deeply grateful.'

'And how would you show it?'

She backed towards the door. 'Any way I could without shame.'

'Would you take off your dress?'

Her heart sank. 'No, lord.'

'Ah. Not so grateful, then.'

She reached the door and touched the handle, but she did not go out. 'What ... what are you asking me, lord?'

'I want to see you naked. Then I'll decide.'

'Here?'

'Yes.'

She looked at Alan. 'In front of him?'

'Yes.'

It did not seem much, to show herself to these two men –

not by comparison with the prize, winning Wulfric's inheritance back.

Swiftly, she undid her belt and pulled her dress over her head. She held the dress in her hand, keeping the other hand on the doorknob, and stared defiantly at Ralph. He looked greedily at her body, then glanced over at his companion with a grin of triumph; and Gwenda saw that this was about showing his power as much as anything else.

Ralph said: 'An ugly cow, but nice udders – eh, Alan?'

Alan replied: 'I wouldn't climb over you to get at her.'

Ralph laughed.

Gwenda said: 'Now will you grant my petition?'

Ralph put his hand to his crotch and began to stroke himself. 'Lie with me,' he said. 'On that bed.'

'No.'

'Come on – you've already done it with Wulfric, you're no virgin.'

'No.'

'Think of the lands – ninety acres, all that his father had.'

She thought. If she agreed, Wulfric would have his heart's desire – and the two of them could look forward to a life of plenty. If she continued to refuse, Wulfric would be a landless labourer, like Joby, struggling all his life to make enough to feed his children, and often failing.

Still the thought revolted her. Ralph was an unpleasant man, petty and vengeful, a bully – so different from his brother. His being tall and handsome made little difference. It would be disgusting to lie with someone she disliked so much.

The fact that she had done it with Wulfric only yesterday made the prospect of sex with Ralph even more repellent. After her night of happy intimacy with Wulfric, it would be a terrible betrayal to do the same with another man.

Don't be a fool, she told herself. For the sake of five minutes of unpleasantness, will you condemn yourself to a life of hardship? She thought of her mother, and the babies that had died. She remembered the stealing she and Philemon had been forced to do. Was it not better to prostitute herself to Ralph one time, for just a few moments, than to condemn her unborn children to a life of poverty?

Ralph remained quiet while she vacillated. He was wise: any words from him would only have strengthened her revulsion. Silence served him better.

'Please,' Gwenda said at last. 'Don't make me do this.'

'Ah,' he said. 'That tells me you're willing.'

'It's a sin,' she said desperately. She did not often talk about sin, but she thought there was a chance it might move him. 'A sin for you to ask, and a sin for me to agree.'

'Sins can be forgiven.'

'What would your brother think of you?'

That gave him pause. For a moment he seemed to hesitate.

'Please,' she said. 'Just let Wulfric inherit.'

His face hardened again. 'I've made my decision. I'm not going to reverse it – unless you can persuade me. And just saying please won't work.' His eyes glistened with desire, and he was breathing a little faster, his mouth open, his lips moist behind his beard.

She dropped her dress to the floor and walked to the bed.

'Kneel on the mattress,' Ralph said. 'No, facing away from me.'

She did as he said.

'Better view from this side,' he said, and Alan laughed loudly. Gwenda wondered if Alan was going to stay to watch, but then Ralph said: 'Leave us alone.' A moment later the door slammed.

Ralph knelt on the bed behind Gwenda. She closed her eyes and prayed for forgiveness. She felt his thick fingers exploring her. She heard him spit, then he rubbed a wet hand on her. A moment later he entered her. She groaned with shame.

Ralph misinterpreted the sound and said: 'You like that, eh?'

She wondered how long this would take. He began to move rhythmically. To ease the discomfort she moved with him, and he laughed triumphantly, thinking he had excited her lust. Her greatest fear was that this would sour her entire experience of lovemaking. In future, when she lay with Wulfric, would she think of this moment?

And then, to her horror, a warm flush of pleasure began to

spread through her loins. She felt her face redden in shame. Despite her profound repugnance, her body betrayed her, and moisture flooded inside her, easing the friction of his thrusts. He sensed the change and moved faster. Disgusted with herself, she ceased to match his rhythm; but he grabbed her hips, pushing and pulling alternately, and she was helpless to resist. She remembered with dismay that her body had undermined her in the same way with Alwyn in the forest. Then as now, she had wanted her body to be a wooden statue, numb and impassive; both times, it had responded against her will.

She had killed Alwyn with his own knife.

She could not do the same to Ralph, even if she had wanted to, because he was behind her. She could not see him, and she had little control over her body. She was in his hands. She was glad when she sensed that he was approaching the climax. Soon it would be over. She felt an answering pressure in her own loins. She tried to make her body limp and her mind blank: it would be too humiliating if she, too, reached a climax. She felt Ralph ejaculate inside her, and she shuddered, not with pleasure but with loathing.

He sighed with satisfaction, withdrew from her and lay flat on the bed.

She got up and quickly pulled on her dress.

'That was better than I expected,' Ralph said, as if he were paying her some kind of polite compliment.

She went out and slammed the door behind her.

*

On the following Sunday, before church, Nathan Reeve came to Wulfric's house.

Gwenda and Wulfric were sitting in the kitchen. They had had breakfast and swept the room, and now Wulfric was sewing a pair of leather trousers while Gwenda wove a belt from cords. They sat close to the window, for better light – it was raining again.

Gwenda was pretending to live in the barn, so that Father Gaspard would not be offended, but she spent every night with Wulfric. He had not mentioned marriage, which disappointed her. However, they were living more or less as man and wife, in the way that people often did when they intended to marry as soon as they got around to the formalities. The nobility and the gentry were permitted no such laxity, but it was routinely overlooked among the peasantry.

As she had feared, she felt strange making love to him. The more she tried to put Ralph out of her mind, the more he intruded. Fortunately, Wulfric never noticed her mood. He made love to her with such enthusiasm and joy that it almost swamped her guilty conscience – but not quite.

And she had the consolation of knowing that he would inherit his family's lands after all. That made up for everything. She could not tell him this, of course, for then she would have needed to explain what had changed Ralph's mind. She had told him about her conversations with Philemon, Caris and Merthin, and had given him a partial version of her encounter with Ralph, saying only that he had promised to reconsider. So Wulfric was hopeful, rather than triumphant.

'Come to the manor house, right away, both of you,' Nathan said, putting his wet head around the door.

Gwenda said: 'What does the Lord Ralph want?'

'Will you refuse to go if the proposed topic of discussion fails to interest you?' Nathan said sarcastically. 'Don't ask stupid questions, just come.'

She put a blanket over her head to walk to the big house. She still did not have a cloak. Wulfric had money, from the sale of his crops, and could have bought her a cloak, but he was saving for the heriot.

They hurried through the rain to the manor house. It was a small version of a nobleman's castle, having a great hall with a long dining table, plus a small upper storey, called the solar, for the lord's private chamber. Now it bore the signs of a house occupied by men without wives: the walls were bare of tapestries, the straw on the floor gave up a pungent smell, the dogs snarled at the newcomers and a mouse nibbled a crust on the sideboard.

Ralph sat at the head of the table. On his right was Alan, who gave Gwenda a smirk she did her best to ignore. A minute later, Nathan came in. Behind him followed fat, sly Perkin, rubbing his hands and bowing obsequiously, his hair so oily it looked like a leather skullcap. With Perkin was his new son-in-law, Billy Howard. Billy shot a triumphant glance at Wulfric: I've got your girl, he was thinking, and now I'm going to get your land. He had a shock coming.

Nathan sat on Ralph's left. The rest of them remained standing.

Gwenda had been looking forward to this moment. It was the reward for her sacrifice. She eagerly anticipated the expression on Wulfric's face when he learned that he had inherited after all. He would be overjoyed – and she would too. Their future would be secure, or at least as secure as was possible in a world of unpredictable weather and oscillating grain prices.

Ralph said: 'Three weeks ago, I said that Wulfric, son of Samuel, could not inherit his father's land because he's too young.' He spoke slowly and ponderously. He loves this, Gwenda thought: sitting at the head of the table, pronouncing judgement, everyone hanging on his words. 'Wulfric has been working the land since then, while I have considered who should succeed old Samuel.' He paused, then said: 'But I've come to doubt my rejection of Wulfric.'

Perkin started. He had been confident of success, and this shocked him.

Billy Howard said: 'What's this? I thought Nate—' Then Perkin nudged him, and he shut up.

Gwenda could not restrain a smile of triumph.

Ralph said: 'Despite his youth, Wulfric has shown himself capable.'

Perkin glared at Nathan. Gwenda guessed that Nathan had promised the land to Perkin. Perhaps the bribe had already been paid.

Nathan was just as shocked as Perkin. He stared open-mouthed at Ralph for a moment, turned to Perkin with a baffled expression, then looked suspiciously at Gwenda.

Ralph added: 'In this he has been well supported by Gwenda, whose strength and loyalty have impressed me.'

Nathan stared at her speculatively. She could tell what he was thinking. He realized she had intervened, and he was wondering how she had managed to change Ralph's mind. He might even be guessing the truth. She did not care if he did, so long as Wulfric remained ignorant.

Suddenly Nathan seemed to make a decision. He stood up and leaned his twisted torso across the table. He spoke to Ralph quietly. Gwenda could not hear what he said.

'Really?' Ralph said in a normal voice. 'How much?'

Nathan turned to Perkin and murmured something to him.

Gwenda said: 'Wait a minute! What's all this whispering?'

Perkin looked angry, but said reluctantly: 'Yes, all right.'

'All right to what?' Gwenda said fearfully.

'Double?' said Nathan.

Perkin nodded.

Gwenda had a feeling of dread.

Nathan said aloud: 'Perkin offers to pay double the normal heriot, which would be five pounds.'

Ralph said: 'That makes a difference.'

Gwenda cried: 'No!'

Wulfric spoke for the first time. 'The heriot is laid down by custom, recorded in the manor rolls,' he said in his slow, boy-man voice. 'It's not for negotiation.'

Nathan said quickly: 'Heriots can change, though. They're not in the Domesday Book.'

Ralph said: 'Are you two lawyers? If not, shut up. The heriot is two pounds and ten shillings. Any other money that changes hands is none of your business.'

Gwenda realized with horror that Ralph was on the point of reneging on their deal. She spoke in a low, accusing voice, slow but clear. 'You made me a promise.'

'Why would I do something like that?' Ralph said.

It was the one question she could not answer. 'Because I pleaded with you,' she replied feebly.

'And I said I would think again. But I made no promise.'

She was powerless to make him keep his word. She wanted to kill him. 'Yes, you did!' she said.

'Lords don't bargain with peasants.'

She stared at him, lost for words. It had all been for nothing: the long walk to Kingsbridge, the humiliation of appearing naked in front of him and Alan, the shameful act she had performed on Ralph's bed. She had betrayed Wulfric, and he still would not inherit. She pointed a finger at Ralph and said bitterly: 'God damn you to hell, Ralph Fitzgerald.'

He went pale. The curse of a genuinely wronged woman was known to be powerful. 'Watch what you say,' he replied. 'We have a punishment for a witch who casts spells.'

Gwenda drew back. No woman could take such a threat lightly. The accusation of witchcraft was easy to make and hard to refute. Still she could not resist saying: 'Those who escape justice in this life will find it in the next.'

Ralph ignored that and turned to Perkin. 'Where is the money?'

Perkin had not got rich by telling people where he kept his cash. 'I'll fetch it right away, lord,' he said.

Wulfric said: 'Come on, Gwenda. There's no mercy for us here.'

Gwenda fought back tears. Anger had been replaced by grief. They had lost the battle, after all they had done. She turned away, head lowered to hide her emotions.

Perkin said: 'Wait, Wulfric. You need employment – and I need help. Work for me. I'll pay you a penny a day.'

Wulfric flushed with the shame of being offered a job as a labourer on lands his family had owned.

Perkin added: 'Gwenda, too. You're both young and willing.'

He did not intend to be malicious, Gwenda saw. He was single-minded in the pursuit of his own interests, and he was eager to hire two strong young labourers to help him farm his amalgamated holding. He did not care, or perhaps did not even know, that for Wulfric this was the final humiliation.

Perkin said: 'That's a shilling a week between you. You'll have plenty.'

Wulfric looked bitter. 'Work for a wage, on lands that my family has owned for decades?' he said. 'Never.' He turned away and left the house.

Gwenda followed, thinking: What are we going to do now?

29

WESTMINSTER HALL WAS HUGE, bigger than the inside of some cathedrals. It was dauntingly long and wide, and its distant ceiling was supported by a double row of tall pillars. It was the most important room in the Palace of Westminster.

Earl Roland was perfectly at home here, Godwyn thought resentfully. The earl and his son William swaggered about in their fashionable clothes, with one leg of their hose red and the other black. Every earl knew all the others, and most of the barons too, and they clapped their friends on the shoulders, mocked each other facetiously and hooted with laughter at their own humour. Godwyn wanted to remind them that the courts held in this room had the power to sentence any one of them to death, even if they were the nobility.

He and his entourage were quiet, speaking only to one another, and then in hushed tones. This was not out of reverence, he had to admit, but nervousness. Godwyn, Edmund and Caris were ill at ease here. None of them had been to London before. The only person they knew was Buonaventura Caroli, and he was out of town. They did not know their way around, their clothes looked old-fashioned, and the money they had brought – which they had thought would be plenty – was running out.

Edmund was not cowed by anything, and Caris seemed distracted – as if she had something more important on her mind, though it hardly seemed possible – but Godwyn was tormented by anxiety. He was a newly elected prior, challenging one of the greatest noblemen in the land. The issue was the future of the town. Without the bridge, Kingsbridge would die. The priory, currently the beating heart of one of England's great cities, would dwindle to a lonely outpost in a small village, where a few monks did their devotions in the echoing emptiness of a crumbling cathedral. Godwyn had not fought to be prior only to see his prize turn to dust.

With so much at stake, he wanted to be in control of events, confident that he was cleverer than almost everyone else, as he was in Kingsbridge. But here he felt the opposite, and the insecurity drove him to distraction.

His consolation was Gregory Longfellow. A friend of Godwyn's from university days, Gregory had a devious mind well suited to the law. The royal court was familiar to him. Aggressive and cocksure, he had guided Godwyn through the legal maze. He had presented the priory's petition to Parliament, as he had presented many petitions before. It was not debated by Parliament, of course, but passed to the king's council, which was overseen by the chancellor. The chancellor's team of lawyers – all of them friends or acquaintances of Gregory's – might have referred the matter to the king's bench, the court that dealt with disputes in which the king had an interest; but, again as Gregory had foreseen, they had decided this was too petty to bother the king with, and had instead sent the case to the common bench, or court of common pleas.

All this had taken a full six weeks. It was late November, and the weather was getting colder. The building season was nearly over.

Today at last they stood before Sir Wilbert Wheatfield, an experienced judge who was said to be liked by the king. Sir Wilbert was the younger son of a northern baron. His elder brother had inherited the title and the estate, and Wilbert had trained as a priest, studied law, come to London and found favour at the royal court. His inclination would be to side with an earl against a monk, Gregory warned; but he would put the king's interests ahead of all else.

The judge sat on a raised bench against the east wall of the palace, between windows that looked out on to the Green Yard and the River Thames. In front of him were two clerks at a long table. There were no seats for the litigants.

'Sir, the earl of Shiring has sent armed men to blockade the quarry owned by Kingsbridge Priory,' Gregory said as soon as Sir Wilbert looked at him. His voice quivered with simulated indignation. 'The quarry, which is within the earldom, was granted to the priory by King Henry I some two hundred years ago. A copy of the charter has been lodged with the court.'

Sir Wilbert had a pink face and white hair, and looked handsome until he spoke, when he showed rotten teeth. 'I have the charter before me,' he said.

Earl Roland spoke without waiting to be invited. 'The monks were given the quarry so that they could build their cathedral,' he said, speaking in a bored-sounding drawl.

Gregory said quickly: 'But the charter does not restrict their use of it to any one purpose.'

'Now they want to build a bridge,' Roland said.

'To replace the bridge that collapsed at Whitsun – a bridge that itself was built, many hundreds of years ago, with timber that was a gift of the king!' Gregory spoke as if he was outraged by the earl's every word.

'They don't need permission to rebuild a pre-existing bridge,' Sir Wilbert said briskly. 'And the charter does say that the king wishes to encourage the building of the cathedral, but it does not say they have to relinquish their rights when the church is finished, nor that they are forbidden to use the stone for any other purpose.'

Godwyn was heartened. The judge seemed to have seen the priory's side of the argument immediately.

Gregory made a spreading gesture with his hands, palms up, as if the judge had said something blindingly obvious. 'And, indeed, sir, that has been the understanding of priors of Kingsbridge and earls of Shiring for three centuries.'

That was not quite right, Godwyn knew. There had been disputes about the charter in the time of Prior Philip. But Sir Wilbert did not know that, nor did Earl Roland.

Roland's attitude was haughty, as if it was beneath his dignity to squabble with lawyers, but this was deceptive: he had a firm grip on the argument. 'The charter does not say the priory may escape tax.'

Gregory said: 'Why, then, has the earl never imposed such a tax until now?'

Roland had his answer ready. 'Former earls forgave the tax, as their contribution to the cathedral. It was a pious act. But no piety compels me to subsidize a bridge. Yet the monks refuse to pay.'

Suddenly the argument had swung the other way. How fast it moved, Godwyn thought; not like arguments in the monks' chapter house, which could go on for hours.

Gregory said: 'And the earl's men prevent movement of stones from the quarry, and have killed a poor carter.'

Sir Wilbert said: 'Then the dispute had better be resolved as soon as possible. What does the priory say to the argument that the earl has the right to tax consignments passing through his earldom, using roads and bridges and fords that belong to him, regardless of whether he has actually enforced this right in the past or not?'

'That since the stones are not passing through his lands, but originate there, the tax is tantamount to charging the monks for the stones, contrary to the charter of Henry I.'

Godwyn saw with dismay that the judge seemed unimpressed by this.

However, Gregory had not finished. 'And that the kings who gave Kingsbridge a bridge and a quarry did so for a good reason: they wanted the priory and the town to prosper. And the town's alderman is here to testify that Kingsbridge cannot prosper without a bridge.'

Edmund stepped forward. With his unkempt hair and provincial clothes he looked like a country bumpkin, by contrast with the gorgeously robed noblemen around; but, unlike Godwyn, he did not appear intimidated. 'I'm a wool merchant, sir,' he said. 'Without the bridge, there's no trade. And without trade, Kingsbridge will pay no taxes to the king.'

Sir Wilbert leaned forward. 'How much did the town yield in the last tenth?'

He was speaking of the tax, imposed by Parliament from time to time, of one-tenth or one-fifteenth of each individual's movable property. No one ever paid a tenth, of course – everyone understated their wealth – so the amount payable by each town or county had become fixed, and the burden was shared out more or less fairly, with poor men and lowly peasants paying nothing at all.

Edmund had been expecting this question, and he replied promptly: 'One thousand and eleven pounds, sir.'

'And the effect of the loss of the bridge?'

'Today, I estimate that a tenth would raise less than three hundred pounds. But our citizens are continuing to trade in the hope that the bridge will be rebuilt. If that hope were to be dashed in this court today, the annual Fleece Fair and the weekly market would almost disappear, and the yield from a tenth would fall below fifty pounds.'

'Next to nothing, in the scale of the king's needs,' the judge said. He did not say what they all knew: that the king was in dire need of money because in the last few weeks he had declared war on France.

Roland was needled. 'Is this hearing about the king's finances?' he said scornfully.

Sir Wilbert was not to be browbeaten, even by an earl. 'This is the king's court,' he said mildly. 'What would you expect?'

'Justice,' Roland replied.

'And you shall have it.' The judge implied, but did not say: Whether you like it or not. 'Edmund Wooler, where is the nearest alternative market?'

'Shiring.'

'Ah. So the business you lose will move to the earl's town.'

'No, sir. Some will move, but much will vanish. Many Kingsbridge traders will be unable to get to Shiring.'

The judge turned to Roland. 'How much does a tenth yield from Shiring?'

Roland conferred briefly with his secretary, Father Jerome, then said: 'Six hundred and twenty pounds.'

'And with the increased trade at Shiring market, could you pay one thousand six hundred and twenty pounds?'

'Of course not,' the earl said angrily.

The judge continued in his mild tone. 'Then your opposition to this bridge would cost the king dear.'

'I have my rights,' Roland said sulkily.

'And the king has his. Is there any way you could compensate the royal treasury for the loss of a thousand pounds every year or so?'

'By fighting alongside him in France – which wool merchants and monks will never do!'

'Indeed,' said Sir Wilbert. 'But your knights will require payment.'

'This is outrageous,' said Roland. He knew he was losing the argument. Godwyn tried not to look triumphant.

The judge did not like his proceedings being called outrageous. He fixed Roland with a look. 'When you sent your men-at-arms to blockade the priory's quarry, I feel sure you did not intend to damage the king's interests.' He paused expectantly.

Roland sensed a trap, but there was only one answer he could give. 'Certainly not.'

'Now that it has been made clear to the court, and to you, how the building of the new bridge serves the king's purposes, as well as those of Kingsbridge Priory and the town, I imagine you will agree to the reopening of the quarry.'

Godwyn realized Sir Wilbert was being clever. He was forcing Roland to consent to his ruling, making it difficult for him to appeal personally to the king later.

After a long pause, Roland said: 'Yes.'

'And to the transport of stones through your territory without tax.'

Roland knew he had lost. There was fury in his voice as he said again: 'Yes.'

'So ordered,' the judge said. 'Next case.'

*

IT WAS A GREAT VICTORY, but it had probably come too late.

November had turned into December. Building normally stopped about now. Because of the rainy weather, the frosts would come late this year but, even so, there were at most a couple of weeks left. Merthin had hundreds of stones stockpiled at the quarry, cut and shaped and ready to be laid. However, it would take months to cart them all to Kingsbridge. Although Earl

Roland had lost the court case, he had almost certainly succeeded in delaying the building of the bridge by a year.

Caris returned to Kingsbridge, with Edmund and Godwyn, in sombre mood. Reining in on the suburban side of the river, she saw that Merthin had already constructed his coffer dams. In each of the channels that ran either side of Leper Island, the ends of wooden boards stuck a couple of feet above the surface in a big circle. She recalled Merthin explaining, in the guild hall, how he planned to drive stakes into the river bed in a double ring then fill the gap between the rings with clay mortar to make a watertight seal. The water inside the coffer could then be taken out so that the builders could lay a foundation on the river bed.

One of Merthin's workmen, Harold Mason, was on the ferry as they crossed the river, and Caris asked him if the coffer dams had been drained. 'Not yet,' he said. 'The master wants to leave it until we're ready to start building.'

Caris noticed with pleasure that Merthin was now called the master, despite his youth. 'But why?' she said. 'I thought we wanted everything ready for a quick start.'

'He says the force of the river puts more strain on the dam when there's no water inside.'

Caris wondered how Merthin knew such things. He had learned the basics from his first master, Joachim, Elfric's father. He always talked a lot to strangers who came to town, especially men who had seen tall buildings in Florence and Rome. And he had read all about the construction of the cathedral in Timothy's Book. But he seemed also to have remarkable intuition about these matters. She would never have guessed that an empty dam would be weaker than a full one.

Although they were subdued as they entered the town, they wanted to tell Merthin the good news right away and find out what, if anything, he could get done before the end of the season. Pausing only to entrust their horses to stable boys, they went in search of him. They found him in the mason's loft, high in the north-west tower of the cathedral, working by the light of several oil lamps, scratching a design for a parapet on the tracing floor.

He looked up from his drawing, saw their faces and grinned widely. 'We won?' he said.

'We won,' said Edmund.

'Thanks to Gregory Longfellow,' Godwyn added. 'He cost a lot of money, but he was worth it.'

Merthin embraced both men – his quarrel with Godwyn forgotten, at least for now. He kissed Caris tenderly. 'I missed you,' he murmured. 'It's been eight weeks! I felt as if you were never coming back.'

She made no reply. She had something momentous to say to him, but she wanted privacy.

Her father did not notice her reticence. 'Well, Merthin, you can start building right away.'

'Good.'

Godwyn said: 'You can begin carting stones from the quarry tomorrow – but I suppose it's too late to get much building done before the winter frosts.'

'I've been thinking about that,' Merthin said. He glanced at the windows. It was mid-afternoon, the December day already darkening to evening. 'There might be a way to do it.'

Edmund was immediately enthusiastic. 'Well, out with it, lad! What's your idea?'

Merthin turned to the prior. 'Would you grant an indulgence to volunteers who bring stones from the quarry?' An indulgence was a special act of forgiveness of sins. Like a gift of money, it could either pay for past debts or stand in credit for future liabilities.

'I could,' Godwyn said. 'What have you got in mind?'

Merthin turned to Edmund. 'How many people in Kingsbridge own a cart?'

'Let me think,' Edmund said, frowning. 'Every substantial trader has one ... so it must come to a couple of hundred, at least.'

'Suppose we were to go around the town tonight and ask every one of them to drive to the quarry tomorrow and pick up stones.'

Edmund stared at Merthin, and a grin slowly spread across his face. 'Now,' he said delightedly, 'that's an idea!'

'We'll tell each one that everybody else is going,' Merthin went on. 'It will be like a holiday. Their families can go along, and they can take food and beer. If each one brings back a cartload of stone or rubble, in two days' time we'll have enough to build the piers of the bridge.'

That was brilliant, Caris thought wonderingly. It was typical of him, to think of something no one else could have imagined. But would it work?

'What about the weather?' said Godwyn.

'The rain has been a curse for the peasants, but it's held off the deep cold. We've a week or two yet, I think.'

Edmund was excited, stomping up and down the loft with his lopsided gait. 'But if you can build the piers in the next few days...'

'By the end of next year we can finish the bulk of the work.'

'Could we use the bridge the following year?'

'No ... but wait. We could put a temporary wooden roadbed on top in time for the Fleece Fair.'

'So we would have a usable bridge by the year after next – and miss only one Fleece Fair!'

'We'd have to finish the stone roadbed after the Fleece Fair, then it would harden in time to be used normally in the third year.'

'Damn it, we've got to do it!' Edmund said excitedly.

Godwyn said cautiously: 'You have yet to empty the water out of the coffer dams.'

Merthin nodded. 'That's hard work. In my original plan I allowed two weeks for it. But I've got an idea about that, too. However, let's get the carts organized first.'

They all moved to the door, animated with enthusiasm. As Godwyn and Edmund started down the narrow spiral staircase, Caris caught Merthin by the sleeve and held him back. He thought she wanted to kiss, and he put his arms around her, but she pushed him away. 'I've got some news,' she said.

'More?'

'I'm pregnant.'

She watched his face. He was startled at first, and his red-brown eyebrows rose. Then he blinked, tilted his head to one side and shrugged, as if to say: Nothing surprising about that. He grinned, at first ruefully, then with unmixed happiness. At the end he was beaming. 'That's wonderful!' he said.

She hated him momentarily for his stupidity. 'No, it's not!'

'Why not?'

'Because I don't want to spend my life as a slave to anyone, even if it is my own child.'

'A slave? Is every mother a slave?'

'Yes! How could you possibly not know that I feel that way?'

He looked baffled and hurt, and a part of her wanted to back off, but she had been nursing her anger too long. 'I did know, I suppose,' he said. 'But then you lay with me, so I thought...' He hesitated. 'You must have known it might happen – would happen, sooner or later.'

'Of course I knew, but I acted as if I didn't.'

'Yes, I can understand that.'

'Oh, stop being so understanding. You're such a weakling.'

His face froze. After a long pause he said: 'All right, then, I'll stop being so understanding. Just give me the information. What's your plan?'

'I don't have a plan, you fool. I just know I don't want to have a baby.'

'So you don't have a plan, and I'm a fool and a weakling. Do you want anything from me?'

'No!'

'Then what are you doing here?'

'Don't be so logical!'

He sighed. 'I'm going to stop trying to be what you tell me to be, because you make no sense.' He went around the room putting out the lamps. 'I'm glad we're having a baby, and I'd like us to be married and look after the child together – assuming this mood you're in is only temporary.' He put his drawing implements in a leather bag and slung it over his shoulder. 'But for now, you're so cantankerous that I'd rather not speak to you at all. And besides, I have work to do.' He went to the door, then paused. 'On the other hand, we could kiss and make up.'

'Go away!' she yelled.

He ducked through the low door and disappeared into the stairwell.

Caris began to cry.

*

MERTHIN HAD NO IDEA whether the people of Kingsbridge would rally to the cause. They all had work and worries of their own: would they see the communal effort to build the bridge as being more important? He was not sure. He knew, from his reading of Timothy's Book, that at moments of crisis Prior Philip had often prevailed by calling on the ordinary people to make a massive effort. But Merthin was not Philip. He had no right to lead people. He was just a carpenter.

They made a list of cart owners and divided it up by streets. Edmund rounded up ten leading citizens and Godwyn picked ten senior monks, and they went around in pairs. Merthin was teamed with Brother Thomas.

The first door they knocked on was Lib Wheeler's. She was continuing Ben's business with hired labour. 'You can have both my carts,' she said. 'And the men to drive them. Anything to give that damned earl a poke in the eye.'

But their second call brought a refusal. 'I'm not well,' said Peter Dyer, who had a cart for delivering the bales of woollen cloth he dyed yellow and green and pink. 'I can't travel.'

He looked perfectly all right, Merthin thought; he was probably scared of a confrontation with the earl's men. There would be no fight, Merthin felt sure; but he could understand the fear. What if all the citizens felt that way?

Their third call was on Harold Mason, a young builder who was hoping for several years of work building the bridge. He agreed immediately. 'Jake Chepstow will come, too,' he said. 'I'll make sure of that.' Harold and Jake were pals.

After that, almost everybody said yes.

They did not need to be told how important the bridge was – everyone who had a cart was a trader, obviously – and they had the additional incentive of a pardon for their sins. But the most important factor seemed to be the promise of an unexpected holiday. Most people said: 'Is so-and-so going?' When they heard that their friends and neighbours had volunteered, they did not want to be left out.

When they had made all their calls, Merthin left Thomas and went down to the ferry. They had to take the carts across overnight, to be ready to leave at sunrise. The ferry carried only one cart at a time – two hundred carts would take several hours. That was why they needed a bridge, of course.

An ox was revolving the great wheel, and carts were already crossing the river. On the other side, the owners turned their beasts out to graze in the pasture, then came back on the ferry and went to bed. Edmund had got John Constable and half a dozen of his deputies to spend the night in Newtown, guarding carts and beasts.

The ferry was still working when Merthin went to bed an hour or so after midnight. He lay thinking about Caris for a while. Her quirkiness and unpredictability were part of what he loved, but sometimes she was impossible. She was the cleverest individual in Kingsbridge, but also hopelessly irrational at times.

Most of all, though, he hated to be called weak. He was not sure he would ever forgive Caris for that jibe. Earl Roland had humiliated him, ten years ago, by saying he could not be a squire, and was fit only to be apprenticed to a carpenter. But he was not weak. He had defied Elfric's tyranny, he had routed Prior Godwyn over the bridge design, and he was about to save the entire town. I might be small, he thought, but by God I'm strong.

Still he did not know what to do about Caris, and he fell asleep worrying.

Edmund woke him at first light. By then almost every cart in Kingsbridge was on the far side of the river, in a straggly line that led through the suburb of Newtown and half a mile into the forest. It took a couple more hours to ferry the people over. The excitement of organizing what was effectively a pilgrimage diverted Merthin's mind from the problem of Caris and her pregnancy. Soon the pasture on the far side was a scene of good-natured chaos, as dozens of people caught their horses and oxen, led them to their carts and backed them into the traces. Dick Brewer brought over a huge barrel of ale and gave it away – 'To encourage the expedition,' he said – with mixed results: some people were so encouraged they had to lie down.

A crowd of spectators gathered on the city side of the river, watching. As the line of carts at last began to move off, a great cheer went up.

But stones were only half the problem.

Merthin turned his attention to the next challenge. If he was to begin laying stones as soon as they arrived from the quarry, he had to empty the coffer dams in two days instead of two weeks. As the cheering died down, he raised his voice and addressed the crowd. This was the moment to catch their interest, when the excitement was fading and they were beginning to wonder what to do next.

'I need the strongest men left in town!' he shouted. They went quiet, intrigued. 'Are there any strong men in Kingsbridge?' This was partly a come-on: the work would be heavy, but asking only for strong people also threw down a challenge that the young men would find hard to resist. 'Before the carts get back from the quarry tomorrow night, we have to empty the water out of the coffer dams. It will be the hardest work you've ever done – so no weaklings, please.' As he said this, he looked at Caris in the crowd and caught her eye, and he saw her flinch: she remembered using that word, and she knew she had insulted him. 'Any woman who thinks she is the equal of the men can join in,' he went on. 'I need you to find a bucket and meet me on the shore opposite Leper Island as soon as possible. Remember – only the strongest!'

He was not sure whether he had won them over. As he finished, he spotted the tall figure of Mark Webber, and pushed through the throng to him. 'Mark, will you encourage them?' he said anxiously.

Mark was a gentle giant, much liked in the town. Even though he was poor he had influence, especially among adolescents. 'I'll make sure the lads join in,' he said.

'Thank you.'

Next, Merthin found Ian Boatman. 'I'm going to need you all day, I hope,' he said. 'Ferrying people out to the coffer dams and back. You can work for pay or an indulgence – your choice.' Ian was excessively fond of his wife's younger sister, and would probably prefer the indulgence, either for a past sin or for one he was hoping to commit soon.

Merthin made his way through the streets to the shore where he was preparing to build the bridge. Could the coffer dams be emptied in two days? He really had no idea. He wondered how many gallons of water were in each. Thousands? Hundreds of thousands? There must be a way of calculating. The Greek philosophers had probably worked out a method but, if they had, it had not been taught at the priory school. To find out, he would probably have to go to Oxford, where there were mathematicians famous all over the world, according to Godwyn.

He waited at the river's edge, wondering if anyone would come.

The first to arrive was Megg Robbins, the strapping daughter of a corn dealer, with muscles enlarged by years of lifting sacks of grain. 'I can outdo most of the men in this town,' she said, and Merthin did not doubt it.

A group of young men came next, then three novice monks.

As soon as Merthin had ten people with buckets, he got Ian to row them and him to the nearer of the two dams.

Inside the rim of the dam he had built a ledge just above water level, strong enough for men to stand on. From the ledge four ladders reached all the way down to the river bed. In the centre of the dam, floating on the surface, was a large raft. Between the raft and the ledge there was a gap of about two feet, and the raft was held in a central position by protruding wooden spokes that reached almost to the wall and prevented movement of more than a few inches in any direction.

'You work in pairs,' he told them. 'One on the raft, one on the ledge. The one on the raft fills his bucket and passes it to the one on the ledge, who tosses the water over the edge into the river. As the empty bucket is passed back, another full one is passed forward.'

Megg Robbins said: 'What happens when the water level inside falls, and we can't reach one another?'

'Good thinking, Megg, you'd better be my forewoman in

charge here. When you can no longer reach, you work in threes, with one on a ladder.'

She caught on fast. 'And then fours, with two on a ladder...'

'Yes. Though by then we'll need to rest the men and bring in fresh ones.'

'Right.'

'Get started. I'll bring over another ten – you've got plenty of room still.'

Megg turned away. 'Pick your partners, everyone!' she called.

The volunteers started to dip their buckets. He heard Megg say: 'Let's keep a rhythm going. Dip, lift, pass, chuck! One, two, three, four. How about a song to give us the swing of it?' She raised her voice in a lusty contralto. 'Oh, *there* was *once* a *comely knight*...'

They knew the song, and all joined in the next line: 'His *blade* was *straight* and *true, oh!*'

Merthin watched. Everyone was soaking wet in a few minutes. He could see no apparent fall in the level of the water. It was going to be a long job.

He climbed over the side and into Ian's boat.

By the time he reached the bank there were thirty more volunteers with buckets.

He got the second coffer dam started, with Mark Webber as foreman, then doubled the numbers in both locations, then started replacing tired workers with fresh ones. Ian Boatman became exhausted and handed the oars over to his son. The water inside the dams fell inch by wearisome inch. As the level fell, the work went ever more slowly, for the buckets had to be lifted greater and greater distances to the rim.

Megg was the first to discover that a person cannot hold a full bucket in one hand and an empty one in the other and still keep balance on a ladder. She devised a one-way bucket chain, with full buckets going up one ladder and empty ones down another. Mark instituted the same system in his dam.

The volunteers worked an hour and rested an hour, but Merthin did not stop. He was organizing the teams, supervising the transport of volunteers to and from the dams, replacing buckets that broke. Most of the men drank ale during their rest periods, and in consequence there were several accidents during the afternoon, with people dropping buckets and falling off ladders. Mother Cecilia came to take care of the injured, with the help of Mattie Wise and Caris.

Too soon, the light began to fail, and they had to stop. But both coffers were more than half empty. Merthin asked everyone to come back in the morning, then went home. After a few spoonfuls of his mother's soup he fell asleep at the table, waking only long enough to wrap a blanket around himself and lie down in the straw. When he woke the next morning, his first thought was to wonder whether any of the volunteers would show up for the second day.

He hurried down to the river at first light with an anxious heart. Both Mark Webber and Megg Robbins were there already, Mark eating his way through a doorstep of bread and Megg lacing a pair of high boots in the hope of keeping her feet dry. No one else showed up for the next half hour, and Merthin began to wonder what he would do with no volunteers. Then some of the young men arrived, carrying their breakfast with them, followed by the novice monks, then a whole crowd.

Ian Boatman turned up, and Merthin got him to row Megg out with some volunteers, and they began again.

The work was harder today. Everyone was aching from yesterday's efforts. Every bucket had to be lifted ten feet or more. But the end was in sight. The levels continued to drop, and the volunteers began to glimpse the river bed.

In the middle of the afternoon, the first of the carts arrived back from the quarry. Merthin directed the owner to unload his stone in the pasture and ferry his cart back across the river to the town. A short while later, in Megg's coffer, the raft bumped the river bed.

There was more to be done. When the last of the water was lifted out, the raft itself had to be dismantled and raised, plank by plank, up the ladders and out. Then dozens of fish were revealed, flapping in muddy pools on the bottom, and they had to be netted and shared out among the volunteers. But, when that was finished, Merthin stood on the ledge, weary but jubilant, and looked down a twenty-foot hole at the flat mud of the river bed.

Tomorrow he would drop several tons of rubble into each hole, and drench the rubble with mortar, forming a massive, immovable foundation.

Then he would start building the bridge.

*

WULFRIC WAS in a depression.

He ate almost nothing and forgot to wash himself. He got up automatically at daybreak and lay down again when it got dark, but he did not work, and he did not make love to Gwenda in the night. When she asked him what was the matter, he would say: 'I don't know, really.' He answered all questions with such uninformative replies, or just with grunts.

There was little to do in the fields anyway. This was the season when villagers sat by their fires, sewing leather shoes and carving oak shovels, eating salt pork and soft apples and cabbage preserved in vinegar. Gwenda was not worried about how they were going to feed themselves: Wulfric still had money from the sale of his crops. But she was desperately anxious about him.

Wulfric had always lived for his work. Some villagers grumbled constantly and were happy only on rest days, but he was not like that. The fields, the crops, the beasts and the weather were what he cared about. On Sundays he had always been restless until he found some occupation that was not forbidden, and on holidays he had done all he could to circumvent the rules.

She knew she had to get him to return to his normal state of mind. Otherwise he might fall sick with some physical illness. And his money would not last for ever. Sooner or later they must both work.

However, she did not give him her news until two full moons had passed, and she was sure.

Then, one morning in December, she said: 'I have something to tell you.'

He grunted. He was sitting at the kitchen table, whittling a stick, and he did not look up from this idle occupation.

She reached across the table and held his wrists, stopping the whittling. 'Wulfric, would you please look at me?'

He did so with a surly expression on his face, resentful at being ordered but too lethargic to defy her.

'It's important,' she said.

He looked at her in silence.

'I'm going to have a baby,' she said.

His expression did not change, but he dropped the knife and stick.

She looked back at him for a long moment. 'Do you understand me?' she said.

He nodded. 'A baby,' he said.

'Yes. We will have a child.'

'When?'

She smiled. It was the first question he had asked for two months. 'Next summer, before the harvest.'

'The child must be cared for,' he said. 'You, too.'

'Yes.'

'I must work.' He looked depressed again.

She held her breath. What was coming?

He sighed, then set his jaw. 'I'll go and see Perkin,' he said. 'He'll need help with his winter ploughing.'

'And manuring,' she said happily. 'I'll come with you. He offered to hire us both.'

'All right.' He was still staring at her. 'A child,' he said, as if it were a marvel. 'Boy or girl, I wonder?'

She got up and walked around the table to sit on the bench next to him. 'Which would you prefer?'

'A little girl. It was all boys in my family.'

'I want a boy, a miniature version of you.'

'We might have twins.'

'One of each.'

He put his arm around her. 'We should get Father Gaspard to marry us properly.'

Gwenda sighed contentedly and leaned her head on his shoulder. 'Yes,' she said. 'Perhaps we should.'

*

MERTHIN MOVED OUT OF his parents' house just before Christmas. He had built a one-room house for himself on Leper Island, which was now his land. He said he needed to guard the growing stockpile of valuable building materials he was keeping on the island – timber, stones, lime, ropes and iron tools.

At the same time, he stopped coming to Caris's house for meals.

On the last but one day of December, she went to see Mattie Wise.

'No need to tell me why you're here,' said Mattie. 'Three months gone?'

Caris nodded and avoided her eye. She looked around the little kitchen, with its bottles and jars. Mattie was heating something in a small iron pot, and it gave off an acrid smell that made Caris want to sneeze.

'I don't want to have a baby,' Caris said.

'I wish I had a chicken for every time I've heard that said.'

'Am I wicked?'

Mattie shrugged. 'I make potions, not judgements. People know the difference between right and wrong – and if they don't, that's what priests are for.'

Caris was disappointed. She had been hoping for sympathy. More coolly, she said: 'Do you have a potion to get rid of this pregnancy?'

'I do…' Mattie looked uneasy.

'Is there a snag?'

'The way to get rid of a pregnancy is to poison yourself. Some girls drink a gallon of strong wine. I make up a dose with several toxic herbs. Sometimes it works, sometimes it doesn't. But it always makes you feel dreadful.'

'Is it dangerous? Could I die?'

'Yes, though it's not as risky as childbirth.'

'I'll take it.'

Mattie took her pot off the fire and put it on a stone slab to cool. Turning to her scarred old workbench, she took a small pottery bowl from a cupboard and poured into it small quantities of different powders.

Caris said: 'What's the matter? You say you don't make judgements, but you look disapproving.'

Mattie nodded. 'You're right. I do make judgements, of course; everyone does.'

'And you're judging me.'

'I'm thinking that Merthin is a good man and you love him, but you don't seem able to find happiness with him. That makes me sad.'

'You think I should be like other women, and throw myself at the feet of some man.'

'It seems to make them happy. But I chose a different way of life. And so will you, I suppose.'

'Are you happy?'

'I wasn't born to be happy. But I help people, I make a living, and I'm free.' She poured her mixture into a cup, added some wine and stirred, dissolving the powders. 'Have you had breakfast?'

'Just some milk.'

She dripped a little honey into the cup. 'Drink this, and don't bother to eat dinner – you'll only throw it up.'

Caris took the cup, hesitated, then swallowed the draught. 'Thank you.' It had a vilely bitter taste that was only partly masked by the sweetness of the honey.

'It should be all over by tomorrow morning – one way or the other.'

Caris paid her and left. Walking home, she felt an odd mixture of elation and sadness. Her spirits were lifted by having made a decision, after all the weeks of worry; but she also felt a tug of loss, as if she were saying goodbye to someone – Merthin, perhaps. She wondered if their separation would be permanent. She could contemplate the prospect calmly, because she still felt angry with him, but she knew she would miss him terribly. He would find another lover eventually – Bessie Bell, perhaps – but Caris felt sure she would not do the same. She would never love anyone as she had loved Merthin.

When she got home, the smell of roasting pork in the house nauseated her, and she went out again. She did not want to gossip with other women in the main street or talk business with the men at the guild hall, so she drifted into the priory grounds, her heavy wool cloak wrapped around her for warmth, and sat on a tombstone in the graveyard, looking at the north wall of the cathedral, marvelling at the perfection of its carved mouldings and the grace of its flying buttresses.

It was not long before she felt ill.

She puked on a grave, but her stomach was empty, and nothing came up except a sour fluid. Her head began to ache. She wanted to lie down, but she was reluctant to go home because of the kitchen smell. She decided to go to the priory hospital. The nuns would let her lie down for a minute. She left the graveyard, crossed the green in front of the cathedral and entered the hospital. Suddenly she was terribly thirsty.

She was greeted by the kindly, podgy face of Old Julie. 'Oh, Sister Juliana,' Caris said gratefully. 'Would you bring me a cup of water?' The priory had water piped from upstream, cool and clear and safe to drink.

'Are you ill, child?' said Old Julie anxiously.

'A little nauseated. If I may, I'll just lie down for a moment.'

'Of course. I'll fetch Mother Cecilia.'

Caris lay down on one of the straw mattresses lined up neatly on the floor. For a few moments she felt better, then the headache became worse. Julie returned with a jug and a cup, and Mother Cecilia. Caris drank some water, threw up, and drank some more.

Cecilia asked her some questions then said: 'You've eaten something corrupt. You need to be purged.'

Caris hurt so much she could make no response. Cecilia left and returned moments later with a bottle and a spoon. She gave Caris a spoonful of treacly medicine that tasted of cloves.

Caris lay back with her eyes closed and longed for the pain to go away. After a while, she was afflicted with stomach cramps, followed by uncontrollable diarrhoea. She assumed vaguely that it had been brought on by the treacle. After an hour it went away. Julie undressed her, washed her, gave her a nun's robe instead of her own soiled dress, and put her on a clean mattress. She lay down and closed her eyes, exhausted.

Prior Godwyn came to see her and said she must be bled. Another monk came to do the job. He made her sit up and stretch out her arm with her elbow over a large bowl. Then he took a sharp knife and opened the vein in the crook of her arm. She hardly noticed the pain of the cut or the slow throb of the bleeding. After a while the monk put a dressing on the cut and told her to hold it there firmly. He took away the bowl of blood.

She was vaguely conscious of people coming to see her: her father, Petranilla, Merthin. Old Julie put a cup to her lips from time to time and she always drank, for she was insatiably thirsty. At some point she noticed candles, and realized it must be night. Eventually she fell into a troubled sleep, and had terrifying dreams about blood. Every time she woke, Julie gave her water.

At last she woke to daylight. The pain had receded, leaving only a dull headache. The next thing she realized was that someone was washing her thighs. She raised herself on her elbow.

A novice nun with the face of an angel crouched beside the mattress. Caris's dress was up around her waist, and the nun was bathing her with a cloth dipped in warm water. After a moment, she remembered the girl's name. 'Mair,' she said.

'Yes,' the novice answered with a smile.

As she squeezed out the cloth into a bowl, Caris was frightened to see that it was red. 'Blood!' she said fearfully.

'Don't worry,' said Mair. 'It's just your monthly cycle. Heavy, but normal.'

Caris saw that her dress and the mattress were soaked with blood.

She lay back, looking up at the ceiling. Tears came to her eyes, but she did not know whether she was crying out of relief or sadness.

She was no longer pregnant.

Part Four

June 1338 to May 1339

Part Four

30

THE JUNE OF 1338 WAS dry and sunny, but the Fleece Fair was a catastrophe – for Kingsbridge in general, and for Edmund Wooler in particular. By the middle of the week, Caris knew that her father was bankrupt.

The townspeople had expected that it would be difficult, and had done all they could to prepare. They commissioned Merthin to build three large rafts that could be poled across the river, to supplement the ferry and Ian's boat. He could have built more, but there was no room to land them on the banks. The priory's grounds were opened a day early, and the ferry operated all night, by torchlight. They persuaded Godwyn to give permission for Kingsbridge shopkeepers to cross to the suburban side and sell to the queue, in the hope that Dick Brewer's ale and Betty Baxter's buns would mollify the people waiting.

It was not enough.

Fewer people than usual came to the fair, but the queues were worse than ever. The extra rafts were insufficient but, even so, the shore on both sides became so swampy that carts were constantly getting stuck in the mud and having to be towed out by teams of oxen. Worse, the rafts were difficult to steer, and on two occasions there were collisions that threw passengers into the water, though fortunately no one drowned.

Some traders anticipated these problems and stayed away. Others turned back when they saw the length of the queue. Of those willing to wait half a day to get into the city, some then did such paltry business that they left after a day or two. By Wednesday the ferry was taking more people away than it was bringing in.

That morning, Caris and Edmund made a tour of the bridge works with Guillaume of London. Guillaume was not as big a customer as Buonaventura Caroli, but he was the best they had this year, and they were making a fuss of him. He was a tall, beefy man in a cloak of expensive Italian cloth, bright red.

They borrowed Merthin's raft, which had a raised deck and a built-in hoist for transporting building materials. His young assistant, Jimmie, poled them out into the river.

The midstream piers that Merthin had constructed in such a rush last December were still surrounded by their coffer dams. He had explained to Edmund and Caris that he would leave the dams in place until the bridge was almost finished to protect the stonework from accidental damage by his own workmen. When he demolished them he would put in their place a pile of loose large stones, the riprap, which he said would prevent the current undermining the piers.

The massive stone columns had now grown, like trees, spreading their arches sideways towards smaller piers built in the shallower water near the banks. These in turn were growing arches, on one side towards the central piers and on the other towards abutments on the bank. A dozen or more masons were busy on the elaborate scaffolding that clung to the stonework like gulls' nests on a cliff.

They landed on Leper Island and found Merthin with Brother Thomas, supervising the masons building the abutment from which the bridge would spring across the northern branch of the river. The priory still owned and controlled the bridge, even though the land was leased to the parish guild and the construction was financed by loans from individual townspeople. Thomas was often on site. Prior Godwyn took a proprietorial interest in the work, and especially in how the bridge would look, evidently feeling it was going to be some kind of monument to him.

Merthin looked up at the visitors with his golden-brown eyes, and Caris's heart seemed to beat faster. She hardly saw him, these days, and when they spoke it was always about business; but she still felt strange in his presence. She had to make an effort to breathe normally, to meet his eye with feigned indifference, and to slow her speech to a moderate speed.

They had never patched up their quarrel. She had not told

him about her abortion, so he did not know whether her pregnancy had terminated spontaneously or otherwise. Neither of them had ever referred to it. On two occasions since then he had come to talk to her, solemnly, and had begged her to make a fresh start with him. Both times, she had told him that she would never love another man, but she was not going to spend her life as someone's wife and someone else's mother. 'How *will* you spend your life, then?' he had asked, and she had replied simply that she did not know.

Merthin was not as impish as he used to be. His hair and beard were neatly trimmed – he was now a regular customer of Matthew Barber. He was dressed in a russet tunic, like the masons, but he wore a yellow cape trimmed with fur, a sign of his status as a master, and a cap with a feather in it, which made him look a bit taller.

Elfric, whose enmity continued, had objected to Merthin dressing like a master, on the grounds that he was not a member of any guild. Merthin's reply was that he was a master, and the solution to the problem was for him to be admitted to a guild. And there the matter remained, unresolved.

Merthin was still only twenty-one, and Guillaume looked at him and said: 'He's young!'

Caris said defensively: 'He's been the best builder in town since he was about seventeen.'

Merthin said a few more words to Thomas then came over. 'The abutments of a bridge need to be heavy, with deep foundations,' he said, explaining the massive bulwark of stone he was constructing.

Guillaume said: 'Why is that, young man?'

Merthin was used to being condescended to, and he took it lightly. With a small smile, he said: 'Let me show you. Stand with your feet as far apart as you can, like this.' Merthin demonstrated, and Guillaume – after a moment's hesitation – imitated him. 'Your feet feel as if they might slide farther apart, don't they?'

'Yes.'

'And the ends of a bridge tend to spread, like your feet. This puts a strain on the bridge, just as you're now feeling the tension in your groin.' Merthin stood upright and placed his own booted foot firmly up against Guillaume's soft leather shoe. 'Now your foot can't move, and the strain on your groin has eased, hasn't it?'

'Yes.'

'The abutment has the same effect as my foot, in bracing your foot and relieving the strain.'

'Very interesting,' Guillaume said thoughtfully as he straightened up, and Caris knew he was telling himself not to underestimate Merthin.

'Let me show you around,' Merthin said.

The island had changed completely in the last six months. All signs of the old leper colony had gone. Much of the rocky land was now taken up with stores: neat piles of stone, barrels of lime, stacks of timber and coils of rope. The place was still infested with rabbits, but they were now competing for space with the builders. There was a smithy, where a blacksmith was repairing old tools and forging new ones; several masons' lodges; and Merthin's new house, small but carefully built and beautifully proportioned. Carpenters, stone carvers and mortar makers were labouring to keep the men on the scaffolding supplied with materials.

'There seem to be more people at work than usual,' Caris murmured in Merthin's ear.

He grinned. 'I've put as many as possible in highly visible positions,' he replied quietly. 'I want every visitor to notice how fast we're working to build the new bridge. I want them to believe the fair will be back to normal next year.'

At the west end of the island, away from the twin bridges, were storage yards and warehouses on plots of land Merthin had rented to Kingsbridge merchants. Although his rents were lower than what tenants would have to pay within the city walls, Merthin was already earning a good deal more than the token sum he paid every year for the lease.

He was also seeing a lot of Elizabeth Clerk. Caris thought she was a cold bitch, but she was the only other woman in town with the brains to challenge Merthin. She had a small box of books she had inherited from her father, the bishop, and Merthin spent evenings at her house, reading. Whether anything else went on, Caris did not know.

When the tour was over, Edmund took Guillaume back across the water, but Caris stayed behind to talk to Merthin. 'Good customer?' he asked as they watched the raft being poled away.

'We've just sold him two sacks of cheap wool for less than we paid.' A sack was 364 pounds' weight of wool, washed clean and dried. This year, the cheap wool was selling for thirty-six shillings a sack, the good quality for about double that.

'Why?'

'When prices are falling, it's better to have cash than wool.'

'But surely you anticipated a poor fair.'

'We didn't expect it to be this bad.'

'I'm surprised. In the past, your father has always had a supernatural ability to foresee trends.'

Caris hesitated. 'It's the combination of slack demand and the lack of a bridge.' In truth, she was surprised too. She had watched her father buy fleeces in the same quantity as usual, despite the poor prospects, and had wondered why he did not play safe by reducing his purchases.

'I suppose you'll try to sell your surplus at the Shiring Fair,' Merthin said.

'It's what Earl Roland wants everyone to do. The trouble is, we're not regulars there. The locals will cream off the best of the business. It's what happens in Kingsbridge: my father and two or three others strike large deals with the biggest buyers, leaving smaller operators and outsiders to scrabble for the leftovers. I'm sure the Shiring merchants do the same. We might sell a few sacks there, but there's no real chance we can get rid of it all.'

'What will you do?'

'That's why I've come to talk to you. We may have to stop work on the bridge.'

He stared at her. 'No,' he said quietly.

'I'm very sorry, but my father doesn't have the money. He's put it all into fleeces that he can't sell.'

Merthin looked as if he had been slapped. After a moment he said: 'We have to find another way!'

Her heart went out to him, but she could think of nothing hopeful to say. 'My father pledged seventy pounds to the bridge.

He's paid out half already. The rest, I'm afraid, is in woolsacks at his warehouse.'

'He can't be completely penniless.'

'Very nearly. And the same applies to several other citizens who promised money for the bridge.'

'I could slow down,' Merthin said desperately. 'Lay off some craftsmen, and run down the stocks of materials.'

'Then you wouldn't have a bridge ready by next year's fair, and we'd be in worse trouble.'

'Better than giving up altogether.'

'Yes, it would be,' she said. 'But don't do anything yet. When the Fleece Fair is over, we'll think again. I just wanted you to know the situation.'

Merthin still looked pale. 'I appreciate it.'

The raft came back, and Jimmie waited to take her to the shore. As she walked on board, she said casually: 'And how is Elizabeth Clerk?'

Merthin pretended to be a little surprised by the question. 'She's fine, I think,' he said.

'You seem to be seeing a lot of her.'

'Not especially. We've always been friends.'

'Yes, of course,' Caris said, though it was not really true. Merthin had completely ignored Elizabeth for most of last year, when he and Caris were spending so much time together. But it would have been undignified to contradict him, so she said no more.

She waved goodbye and Jimmie pushed the raft off. Merthin was trying to give the impression that his relationship with Elizabeth was not a romance. Perhaps that was true. Or perhaps he was embarrassed to admit to Caris that he was in love with someone else. She could not tell. One thing she felt sure of: it was a romance on Elizabeth's side. Caris could tell, just by the way Elizabeth looked at him. Elizabeth might be an ice maiden, but she was hot for Merthin.

The raft bumped against the opposite bank. Caris stepped off and walked up the hill into the centre of the city.

Merthin had been deeply shaken by her news. Caris felt like crying when she recalled the shock and dismay on his face. That was how he had looked when she had refused to rekindle their love affair.

She still did not know how she was going to spend her life. She had always assumed that, whatever she did, she would live in a comfortable house paid for by a profitable business. Now even that ground was moving under her feet. She racked her brains for some way out of the mess. Her father was oddly serene, as if he had not yet grasped the scale of his losses; but she knew that something had to be done.

Walking up the main street she passed Elfric's daughter, Griselda, carrying her six-month-old baby. It was a boy, and she had named him Merthin, a permanent reproach to the original Merthin for not marrying her. Griselda was still maintaining a pretence of injured innocence. Everyone else now accepted that Merthin was not the father, though some townspeople still thought he should have married her anyway, as he had lain with her.

As Caris came to her own house, her father came out. She stared at him in astonishment. He was dressed only in his underwear: a long undershirt, drawers and hose. 'Where are your clothes?' she said.

He looked down at himself and made a disgusted sound. 'I'm getting absent-minded,' he said, and he went back indoors.

He must have taken his coat off to go to the privy, she thought, then forgotten to put it on again. Was that just his age? He was only forty-eight, and besides, it seemed worse than mere forgetfulness. She felt unnerved.

He returned normally dressed, and they crossed the main street together and entered the priory grounds. Edmund said: 'Did you tell Merthin about the money?'

'Yes. He was terribly shocked.'

'What did he say?'

'That he could spend less by slowing the pace.'

'But then we wouldn't have a bridge in time for next year.'

'But, as he said, that would be better than abandoning the bridge half built.'

They came to the stall of Perkin Wigleigh, selling laying hens. His flirtatious daughter, Annet, had a tray of eggs held up by a strap around her neck. Behind the counter Caris saw her friend Gwenda, who was now working for Perkin. Eight months pregnant, with heavy breasts and a swollen belly, Gwenda stood with one hand on her hip, stretching in the classic pose of the expectant mother with an aching back.

Caris calculated that she, too, would now be eight months pregnant, if she had not taken Mattie's potion. After the abortion her breasts had leaked milk, and she could not help feeling that this was her body's reproach for what she had done. She suffered pangs of regret but, whenever she thought about it logically, she knew that if she had her time over again she would do the same.

Gwenda caught Caris's eye and smiled. Against all the odds, Gwenda had got what she wanted: Wulfric for her husband. He was there now, strong as a horse and twice as handsome, lifting a stack of wooden crates on to the flatbed of a cart. Caris was thrilled for Gwenda. 'How do you feel today?' she said.

'My back's been hurting all morning.'

'Not long, now.'

'A couple of weeks, I think.'

Edmund said: 'Who's this, my dear?'

'Don't you remember Gwenda?' said Caris. 'She's been a guest at your house at least once a year for the past ten years!'

Edmund smiled. 'I didn't recognize you, Gwenda – it must be the pregnancy. You look well, though.'

They moved on. Wulfric had not been given his inheritance, Caris knew: Gwenda had failed in that task. Caris was not sure exactly what had gone on, last September, when Gwenda had gone to plead with Ralph, but it seemed Ralph had made some kind of promise then reneged. Anyway, Gwenda now hated Ralph with a passion that was almost frightening.

Nearby was a line of stalls at which local cloth merchants were selling brown burel, the loosely woven fabric that was bought by all but the rich for their home-made clothing. They seemed to be doing good business, unlike the wool merchants. Raw wool was a wholesale business – the absence of a few big buyers could ruin the market. But cloth was retail. Everyone needed it, everyone bought it. A bit less, perhaps, when times were hard, but they still needed clothes.

A vague thought formed in the back of Caris's mind. When merchants could not sell their wool, they sometimes had it woven and tried to sell it as cloth. But it was a lot of work, and there was not much profit in brown burel. Everyone bought the cheapest, and sellers had to keep the price down.

She looked at the cloth stalls with new eyes. 'I wonder what fetches the most money?' she said. The burel was twelve pence per yard. You had to pay half as much again for cloth that had been fulled – thickened by pounding in water – and still more for colours other than the natural dull brown. Peter Dyer's stall featured green, yellow and pink cloth at two shillings – twenty-four pence – per yard, even though the colours were not very bright.

She turned to her father, to tell him the notion that was forming in her mind; but, before she could speak, something happened to distract her.

*

BEING AT THE Fleece Fair reminded Ralph unpleasantly of the same event a year ago, and he touched his misshapen nose. How had that occurred? It had started with him harmlessly teasing the peasant girl, Annet, then teaching her oafish paramour a lesson in respect; but somehow it had ended up in humiliation for Ralph.

As he approached Perkin's stall, he consoled himself by reflecting on what had happened since. He had saved Earl Roland's life after the collapse of the bridge; he had pleased the earl by his decisive behaviour at the quarry; and he had at last been made a lord, albeit over nothing more than the little village of Wigleigh. He had killed a man, Ben Wheeler – a carter, so there was no honour in it, but all the same he had proved to himself that he could do it.

He had even made up his quarrel with his brother. Their mother had forced the issue, inviting them both to dinner on Christmas Day, insisting that they shake hands. It was a misfortune, their father had said, that they served masters who were rivals, but each had a duty to do his best, like soldiers who found themselves on opposing sides in a civil war. Ralph was pleased, and he thought Merthin felt the same.

He had been able to take a satisfying revenge on Wulfric, by denying him his inheritance and, at the same time, his girl. The eye-catching Annet was now married to Billy Howard, and Wulfric had to content himself with the ugly, though passionate, Gwenda.

It was a pity Wulfric did not look more crushed. He seemed to walk tall and proud around the village, as if he, not Ralph, owned the place. All his neighbours liked him and his pregnant wife worshipped him. Despite the defeats Ralph had inflicted, Wulfric somehow emerged as the hero. Perhaps it was because his wife was so lusty.

Ralph would have liked to tell Wulfric about Gwenda's visit to him at the Bell. 'I lay with your wife,' he wanted to say. 'And she liked it.' That would wipe the proud look off Wulfric's face. But then Wulfric would also know that Ralph had made a promise and, shamefully, broken it – which would just make Wulfric feel superior all over again. Ralph shuddered when he thought of the contempt Wulfric and others would feel for him if they ever found out about that betrayal. His brother Merthin in particular, would despise him for it. No, his tumble with Gwenda would have to remain a secret.

They were all at the stall. Perkin was the first to see Ralph approaching, and greeted his lord as obsequiously as ever. 'Good day, Lord Ralph,' he said, bowing; and his wife, Peg, curtseyed behind him. Gwenda was there, rubbing her back as if it hurt. Then Ralph saw Annet with her tray of eggs, and he remembered touching her small breast, round and firm like the eggs on the tray. She saw him looking, and dropped her eyes demurely. He wanted to touch her breast again. Why not? he thought – I'm her lord. Then he saw Wulfric, at the back of the stall. The boy had been loading crates on to a cart, but now he stood still, looking at Ralph. His face was carefully expressionless, but his gaze was level and steady. His look could not be called insolent, but for Ralph there was no mistaking the threat. It could not have been clearer if Wulfric had said: Touch her and I'll kill you.

Perhaps I should do it, Ralph thought. Let him attack me. I'll run him through with my sword. I will be completely in the right, a lord defending himself against a peasant maddened with hatred. Holding Wulfric's gaze, he lifted his hand to fondle Annet's breast – and then Gwenda let out a sharp cry of pain and distress, and all eyes turned to her.

31

CARIS HEARD A CRY OF PAIN, and recognized the voice of Gwenda. She felt a throb of fear. Something was wrong. In a few hurried steps she was at Perkin's stall.

Gwenda was sitting on a stool, looking pale, her face twisted in a grimace of pain, her hand on her hip again. Her dress was wet.

Perkin's wife, Peg, said briskly: 'Her waters have broken. Her labour is beginning.'

'It's early,' Caris said anxiously.

'The baby is coming anyway.'

'This is dangerous.' Caris made a decision. 'Let's take her to the hospital.' Women did not normally go to the hospital to give birth, but they would admit Gwenda if Caris insisted. An early baby could be vulnerable, everyone knew that.

Wulfric appeared. Caris was struck by how young he looked. He was seventeen and about to become a father.

Gwenda said: 'I feel a bit wobbly. I'll be all right in a minute.'

'I'll carry you,' Wulfric said, and he picked her up effortlessly.

'Follow me,' said Caris. She walked ahead of him through the stalls, calling: 'Stand aside, please – stand aside!' In a minute they were at the hospital.

The door was wide open. Overnight visitors had been tipped out hours ago, and their straw mattresses were now piled high against one wall. Several employees and novices were energetically washing the floor with mops and buckets. Caris addressed the nearest cleaner, a middle-aged woman with bare feet. 'Fetch Old Julie, quickly – tell her Caris sent you.'

Caris found a reasonably clean mattress and spread it on the floor near the altar. She was not sure how effective altars were at helping sick people, but she followed the convention. Wulfric put Gwenda down on the bed as carefully as if she had been made of glass. She lay with her knees up and her legs parted.

A few moments later Old Julie arrived, and Caris thought how often in her life she had been comforted by this nun, who was probably not much past forty but seemed ancient. 'This is Gwenda Wigleigh,' said Caris. 'She may be fine, but the baby is coming several weeks early, and I thought it a sensible precaution to bring her here. We were just outside, anyway.'

'Very wise,' said Julie, gently pushing Caris aside to kneel by the bed. 'How do you feel, my dear?' she said to Gwenda.

While Julie talked to Gwenda in a low voice, Caris looked at Wulfric. His handsome young face was contorted with anxiety. Caris knew that he had never intended to marry Gwenda – he had always wanted Annet. However, he now seemed as concerned for her as if he had loved her for years.

Gwenda cried out in pain. 'There, there,' said Julie. She knelt between Gwenda's feet and looked up her dress. 'Baby's coming quite soon,' she said.

Another nun appeared, and Caris recognized Mair, the novice with the angel face. She said: 'Shall I get Mother Cecilia?'

'No need to bother her,' said Julie. 'Just go to the storeroom and fetch me the wooden box with "Birth" written on the top.'

Mair hurried away.

Gwenda said: 'Oh, God, it hurts.'

'Keep pushing,' said Julie.

Wulfric said: 'What's wrong, for God's sake?'

'Nothing's wrong,' said Julie. 'This is normal. This is how women give birth. You must be the youngest of your family, otherwise you would have seen your mother like this.'

Caris, too, was the young sibling in her family. She knew that childbirth was painful, but she had never actually watched it, and she was shocked by how bad it was.

Mair returned and placed a wooden box on the floor next to Julie.

Gwenda stopped groaning. Her eyes closed, and she looked almost as if she might have been asleep. Then, a few minutes later, she cried out again.

Julie said to Wulfric: 'Sit beside her and hold her hand.' He obeyed immediately.

Julie was still looking up Gwenda's dress. 'Stop pushing now,' she said after a while. 'Take lots of short breaths.' She panted to show Gwenda what she meant. Gwenda complied and it seemed to ease her distress for a few minutes. Then she cried out again.

Caris could hardly stand it. If this was normal, what was childbirth like when there were difficulties? She lost her sense of time: everything was happening very quickly, but Gwenda's torment seemed endless. Caris had the powerless feeling that she hated so much, the feeling that had overwhelmed her when her mother died. She wanted to help, but she did not know what to do, and it made her so anxious that she bit her lip until she tasted blood.

Julie said: 'Here comes baby.' She reached between Gwenda's legs. The dress fell away, and suddenly Caris could clearly see the baby's head, face down, covered in wet hair, emerging from an opening that seemed impossibly stretched. 'God help us, no wonder it hurts!' she said in horror.

Julie supported the head with her left hand. The baby slowly turned sideways, then its tiny shoulders came out. Its skin was slippery with blood and some other fluid. 'Just relax, now,' Julie said. 'It's nearly over. Baby looks beautiful.'

Beautiful? Caris thought. To her it looked horrible.

The baby's torso came out with a fat, pulsing blue cord attached to its navel. Then its legs and feet came all in a rush. Julie picked up the baby in both hands. It was tiny, its head not much bigger than the palm of Julie's hand.

Something seemed wrong. Caris realized the baby was not breathing.

Julie brought the baby's face close to her own and blew into its miniature nostrils.

The baby suddenly opened its mouth, gasped air, and cried.

'Praise God,' said Julie.

She wiped the baby's face with the sleeve of her robe, tenderly cleaning around the ears, eyes, nose and mouth. Then she pressed the newborn to her bosom, closing her eyes; in that instant Caris saw a lifetime of self-denial. The moment passed, and Julie laid the baby on Gwenda's chest.

Gwenda looked down. 'Is it a boy or a girl?'

Caris realized that none of them had looked. Julie leaned over and parted the baby's knees. 'A boy,' she said.

The blue cord stopped pulsing and shrivelled, turning white. Julie took from the box two short lengths of string, and tied off the umbilical cord. Then she took out a small, sharp knife and cut the cord between the two knots.

Mair took the knife from her and handed her a tiny blanket from the box. Julie took the baby from Gwenda, wrapped him in the blanket, and gave him back. Mair found some pillows and propped Gwenda up. Gwenda pushed down the neck of her shift and took out a swollen breast. She gave the baby the nipple, and he began to suck. After a minute, he seemed to sleep.

The other end of the cord was still hanging out of Gwenda. A few minutes later it moved, and a shapeless red mass slipped out: the afterbirth. Blood soaked the mattress. Julie lifted the mass, handed it to Mair and said: 'Burn this.'

Julie scrutinized Gwenda's pelvic area and frowned. Caris followed her gaze, and saw that the blood was still flowing. Julie wiped the stains away from Gwenda's body, but the red streaks reappeared immediately.

When Mair came back, Julie said: 'Fetch Mother Cecilia, please, right away.'

Wulfric said: 'Is something wrong?'

'The bleeding should have stopped by now,' Julie answered.

Suddenly there was tension in the air. Wulfric looked frightened. The baby cried, and Gwenda gave him the nipple again. He suckled briefly and slept again. Julie kept looking at the doorway.

At last Cecilia appeared. She looked at Gwenda and said: 'Has the afterbirth come out?'

'A few minutes ago.'

'Did you put the baby to the breast?'

'As soon as we had cut the cord.'

'I'll get a physician.' Cecilia walked quickly away.

She was gone some minutes. When she returned she was carrying a small glass vessel containing a yellowish fluid. 'Prior Godwyn has prescribed this,' she said.

Caris was indignant. 'Doesn't he want to examine Gwenda?'

'Certainly not,' Cecilia said crisply. 'He's a priest as well as a monk. Such men don't look upon women's private parts.'

'*Podex*,' Caris said contemptuously. It was the Latin for arsehole.

Cecilia pretended not to hear. She knelt beside Gwenda. 'Drink this, my dear.'

Gwenda drank the potion, but she continued to bleed. She was pale, and looked weaker than she had done immediately after the birth. The baby slept contentedly on her breast, but everyone else was scared. Wulfric kept standing up and sitting down again. Julie wiped the blood off Gwenda's thighs and looked as if she might cry. Gwenda asked for something to drink, and Mair brought a cup of ale.

Caris took Julie aside and said in a whisper: 'She's bleeding to death!'

'We've done what we can,' Julie said.

'Have you seen cases like this before?'

'Yes, three.'

'How did they end?'

'The women died.'

Caris gave a low groan of despair. 'There must be something we can do!'

'She's in God's hands, now. You could pray.'

'That's not what I meant by doing something.'

'You be careful what you say.'

Caris immediately felt guilty. She did not want to quarrel with someone as kindly as Julie. 'I'm sorry, sister. I didn't mean to deny the power of prayer.'

'I should hope not.'

'But I'm not yet ready to leave Gwenda in the hands of God.'

'What else is there to do?'

'You'll see.' Caris hurried out of the hospital.

She pushed impatiently through the customers strolling around the fair. It seemed amazing to her that people could still be buying and selling when a drama of life and death was going on a few yards away. But there had been many occasions when she had heard that a mother-to-be had gone into labour, and she had never stopped what she was doing, just wished the woman well then carried on.

She emerged from the priory grounds and ran through the streets of the town to Mattie Wise's house. She knocked on the door and opened it. To her relief, Mattie was at home.

'Gwenda's just had her baby,' she said.

'What's gone wrong?' Mattie said immediately.

'The baby's all right, but Gwenda's still bleeding.'

'Has the afterbirth come out?'

'Yes.'

'The bleeding should have stopped.'

'Can you help her?'

'Perhaps. I'll try.'

'Hurry, please!'

Mattie took a pot off the fire and put on her shoes, then the two of them left, Mattie locking her door behind her.

Caris said vehemently: 'I'm never going to have a baby, I swear.'

They rushed to the priory and went into the hospital. Caris noticed the strong smell of blood.

Mattie was careful to acknowledge Old Julie. 'Good afternoon, Sister Juliana.'

'Hello, Mattie.' Julie looked disapproving. 'Do you believe you can help this woman, when the holy prior's remedies have not been blessed with success?'

'If you pray for me and for the patient, sister, who knows what may happen?'

It was a diplomatic answer, and Julie was mollified.

Mattie knelt beside mother and child. Gwenda was becoming paler. Her eyes were closed. The baby sought blindly for the nipple, but Gwenda seemed too tired to help him.

Mattie said: 'She must keep drinking – but not strong liquor. Please bring her a jug of warm water with a small glass of wine mixed into it. Then ask the kitchener if he has a clear soup, warm but not hot.'

Mair looked questioningly at Julie, who hesitated, then said: 'Go – but don't tell anyone that you're doing Mattie's bidding.' The novice hurried off.

Mattie pushed Gwenda's dress up as high as it would go, exposing all of her abdomen. The skin that had been stretched so taut, a few hours ago, was now flabby and folded. Mattie grasped the loose flesh, digging her fingers gently but firmly into Gwenda's belly. Gwenda grunted, but it was a sound of discomfort rather than pain.

Mattie said: 'The womb is soft. It has failed to contract. That's why she's bleeding.'

Wulfric, who seemed close to tears, said: 'Can you do anything for her?'

'I don't know.' Mattie began to massage, her fingers apparently pressing Gwenda's womb through the skin and flesh of her belly. 'Sometimes this provokes the womb to shrink,' she said.

Everyone watched in silence. Caris was almost afraid to breathe.

Mair came back with the water-and-wine mixture. 'Give her some, please,' Mattie said without pausing in her massage. Mair held a cup to Gwenda's lips and she drank thirstily. 'Not too much,' Mattie warned. Mair took the cup away.

Mattie continued to massage, glancing from time to time at Gwenda's pelvis. Julie's lips moved in silent prayer. The blood flowed without let-up.

Looking worried, Mattie changed her position. She put her left hand on Gwenda's belly just below the navel, then her right hand over the left. She pressed down, slowly putting on more pressure. Caris was afraid it must hurt the patient, but Gwenda seemed only half conscious. Mattie leaned farther over Gwenda until she seemed to be putting all her weight on to her hands.

Julie said: 'She's stopped bleeding!'

Mattie did not change her position. 'Can anyone here count to five hundred?'

'Yes,' Caris said.

'Slowly, please.'

Caris began to count aloud. Julie wiped the blood off Gwenda again, and this time the streaks did not reappear. She began to pray aloud. 'Holy Mary, Mother of the Lord Jesus Christ...'

Everyone was still, like a group of statuary: the mother and baby on the bed, the wise woman pressing down on the mother's belly; the husband, the praying nun and Caris counting: 'A hundred and eleven, a hundred and twelve...'

As well as her own voice and Julie's, Caris could hear the sound of the fair outside, the roar of hundreds of people all speaking at once. The strain of pressing down began to show on Mattie's face, but she did not move. Wulfric was crying silently, tears streaming down his sunburned cheeks.

When Caris reached five hundred, Mattie slowly eased her weight off Gwenda's abdomen. Everyone looked at her vagina, dreading the gush of blood.

It did not come.

Mattie breathed a long sigh of relief. Wulfric smiled. Julie said: 'Praise God!'

Mattie said: 'Give her another drink, please.'

Once again, Mair put a full cup to Gwenda's lips. Gwenda opened her eyes and drank it all.

'You're going to be all right now,' Mattie said.

Gwenda whispered: 'Thank you.' Then she closed her eyes.

Mattie looked at Mair. 'Perhaps you should go and see about that soup,' she said. 'The woman must rebuild her strength, otherwise her milk will dry up.'

Mair nodded and left.

The baby cried. Gwenda seemed to revive. She moved the baby to her other breast and helped him find the nipple. Then she looked up at Wulfric and smiled.

Julie said: 'What a beautiful little boy.'

Caris looked at the baby again. For the first time, she saw him as an individual. What would he be like – strong and true like Wulfric, or weak and dishonest like his grandfather Joby? He did not resemble either, she thought. 'Who does he look like?' she said.

Julie said: 'He has his mother's colouring.'

That was right, Caris thought. The baby had dark hair and

beige skin, where Wulfric had fair skin and a mane of dark-blond hair. The baby's face reminded her of someone, and after a moment she realized it was Merthin. A foolish thought crossed her mind, and she dismissed it immediately. All the same, the resemblance was there. 'You know who he reminds me of?' she said.

Suddenly she caught a look from Gwenda. Her eyes widened, an expression of panic crossed her face, and she gave a barely perceptible shake of her head. It was gone in an instant, but the message was unmistakable: Shut up! Caris clamped her teeth together.

'Who?' said Julie innocently.

Caris hesitated, desperately thinking of something to say. At last she was inspired. 'Philemon, Gwenda's brother,' she said.

'Of course,' said Julie. 'Someone should tell him to come and see his new nephew.'

Caris was bewildered. So the baby was not Wulfric's? Then whose? It could not be Merthin's. He might have lain with Gwenda – he was certainly vulnerable to temptation – but he could never have kept it secret from Caris afterwards. If not Merthin...

Caris was struck by a dreadful thought. What *had* gone on that day when Gwenda went to plead with Ralph for Wulfric's inheritance? Could the baby be *Ralph's*? It was too grim to contemplate.

She looked at Gwenda, then at the baby, then at Wulfric. Wulfric was smiling with joy, though his face was still wet with tears. He had no suspicions.

Julie said: 'Have you thought about the baby's name?'

'Oh, yes,' said Wulfric. 'I want to name him Samuel.'

Gwenda nodded, looking down at the baby's face. 'Samuel,' she said. 'Sammy. Sam.'

'After my father,' Wulfric said happily.

32

ONE YEAR AFTER THE DEATH of Anthony, Kingsbridge Priory was a different place, Godwyn thought, with satisfaction, as he stood in the cathedral on the Sunday after the Fleece Fair.

The main difference was the separation of monks and nuns. They no longer mingled in the cloisters, the library or the scriptorium. Even here in the church, a new carved-oak screen running down the centre of the choir prevented them from looking at one another during the services. Only in the hospital were they sometimes forced to mix.

In his sermon, Prior Godwyn said the collapse of the bridge a year ago had been God's punishment for laxity in the monks and nuns, and for sin among the townspeople. The new spirit of rigour and purity at the priory, and piety and submission in the town, would lead to a better life for all, in this world and the hereafter. He felt it went down quite well.

Afterwards he had dinner with Brother Simeon, the treasurer, in the prior's house. Philemon served them stewed eel and cider. 'I want to build a new prior's house,' Godwyn said.

Simeon's long, thin face seemed to get longer. 'Any particular reason?'

'I'm sure I am the only prior in Christendom who lives in a house like a leather tanner's. Think of the people who have been guests here in the last twelve months – the earl of Shiring, the bishop of Kingsbridge, the earl of Monmouth – this building isn't appropriate for such folk. It gives a poor impression of us and of our order. We need a magnificent building to reflect the prestige of Kingsbridge Priory.'

'You want a palace,' said Simeon.

Godwyn detected a disapproving note in Simeon's tone of voice, as if Godwyn's aim was to glorify himself rather than the priory. 'Call it a palace, if you wish,' he said stiffly. 'Why not? Bishops and priors live in palaces. It's not for their own comfort, but for that of their guests, and for the reputation of the institution they represent.'

'Of course,' said Simeon, giving up that line of argument. 'But you can't afford it.'

Godwyn frowned. In theory, his senior monks were encouraged to debate with him, but the truth was that he hated to be opposed. 'That's ridiculous,' he said. 'Kingsbridge is one of the richest monasteries in the land.'

'So it is always said. And we do own vast resources. But the price of wool has fallen this year, for the fifth year in succession. Our income is shrinking.'

Philemon suddenly interjected: 'They say the Italian merchants are buying fleeces in Spain.'

Philemon was changing. Since achieving his ambition, and becoming a novice monk, he had lost the awkward-boy look, and had grown in confidence to the point where he could join in a conversation between prior and treasurer – and make an interesting contribution.

'Could be,' said Simeon. 'Also, the Fleece Fair was smaller, because there's no bridge, so we earned a lot less in duty and tolls than we usually do.'

Godwyn said: 'But we hold thousands of acres of farmland.'

'In this part of the country, where most of our lands are, there was a poor harvest last year, after all that rain. Many of our serfs struggled to stay alive. It's hard to force them to pay their rents when they're hungry—'

'They must pay, all the same,' Godwyn said. 'Monks get hungry too.'

Philemon spoke again. 'If the bailiff of a village says that a serf has defaulted on his rent, or that part of the land is untenanted therefore no rent is due, you haven't really got any way of checking that he's telling the truth. Bailiffs can be bribed by serfs.'

Godwyn felt frustrated. He had had numerous conversations like this in the past year. He had been determined to tighten up control of the priory's finances, but every time he tried to change

things he ran into barriers. 'Have you got a suggestion?' he said
irritably to Philemon.

'Send an inspector on a tour of the villages. Let him speak to
bailiffs, look at the land, go into the cottages of serfs who are said
to be starving.'

'If the bailiff can be bribed, so can the inspector.'

'Not if he's a monk. What use have we for money?'

Godwyn recalled Philemon's old inclination to stealing. It was
true that monks had no use for personal money, at least in theory,
but that did not mean they were incorruptible. However, a visit
from the prior's inspector would certainly put bailiffs on their
toes. 'It's a good idea,' Godwyn said. 'Would you like to be the
inspector?'

'I'd be honoured.'

'Then it's settled.' Godwyn turned back to Simeon. 'All the
same, we still have a huge income.'

'And huge costs,' Simeon replied. 'We pay a subvention to
our bishop. We feed, clothe and house twenty-five monks, seven
novices and nineteen pensioners of the priory. We employ thirty
people as cleaners, cooks, stable boys and so on. We spend a
fortune on candles. Monks' robes—'

'All right, I've grasped your point,' Godwyn said impatiently.
'But I still want to build a palace.'

'Where will you go for the money, then?'

Godwyn sighed. 'Where we always go, in the end. I'll ask
Mother Cecilia.'

He saw her a few minutes later. Normally he would have
asked her to come to him, as a sign of the superiority of the male
within the church; but on this occasion he thought it best to
flatter her.

The prioress's house was an exact copy of the prior's, but it
had a different feel. There were cushions and rugs, flowers in a
bowl on the table, embroidered samplers on the wall illustrating
Bible stories and texts, and a cat asleep in front of the fireplace.
Cecilia was finishing a dinner of roast lamb and dark-red wine.
She put on a veil when Godwyn arrived, in accordance with a
rule Godwyn had introduced, for occasions when monks had to
talk to nuns.

He found Cecilia difficult to read, veiled or not. She had formally welcomed his election as prior, and had gone along unprotestingly with his stricter rules about separation of monks and nuns, making only the occasional practical point about the efficient running of the hospital. She had never opposed him, and yet he felt she was not really on his side. It seemed he was no longer able to charm her. When he was younger he had been able to make her laugh like a girl. Now she was no longer susceptible – or perhaps he had lost the knack.

Small talk was difficult with a woman in a veil, so he plunged straight into his topic. 'I think we should build two new houses for entertaining noble and high-ranking guests,' he said. 'One for men, one for women. They would be called the prior's house and the prioress's house, but their main purpose would be to accommodate visitors in the style to which they're accustomed.'

'That's an interesting idea,' Cecilia said. As ever, she was compliant without being enthusiastic.

'We should have impressive stone buildings,' Godwyn went on. 'After all, you have been prioress here for more than a decade – you are one of the most senior nuns in the kingdom.'

'We want the guests to be impressed, not by our wealth, but by the holiness of the priory and the piety of the monks and nuns, of course,' she said.

'Indeed – but the buildings should symbolize that, as the cathedral symbolizes the majesty of God.'

'Where do you think the new buildings should be sited?'

This was good, Godwyn thought – she was already getting down to details. 'Close to where the old houses are now.'

'So, yours near the east end of the church, next to the chapter house, and mine down here by the fishpond.'

It crossed Godwyn's mind that she might be mocking him. He could not see her expression. Imposing a veil on women had its disadvantages, he reflected. 'You might prefer a new location,' he said.

'Yes, I might.'

There was a short silence. Godwyn was finding it hard to broach the subject of money. He was going to have to change the rule about veils – make an exception for the prioress, perhaps. It was just too difficult to negotiate like this.

He was forced to plunge again. 'Unfortunately, I would not be able to make any contribution to the building costs. The monastery is very poor.'

'To the cost of the prioress's house, you mean?' she said. 'I wouldn't expect it.'

'No, actually, I meant the cost of the prior's house.'

'Oh. So you want the nunnery to pay for your new house as well as mine.'

'I'm afraid I would have to ask you that, yes. I hope you don't mind.'

'Well, if it's for the prestige of Kingsbridge Priory...'

'I knew you would see it that way.'

'Let me see ... Right now I'm building new cloisters for the nuns, as we no longer share with the monks.'

Godwyn made no comment. He was irritated that Cecilia had employed Merthin to design the cloisters, rather than the cheaper Elfric, which was a wasteful extravagance; but this was not the moment to say so.

Cecilia went on: 'And when that's done, I need to build a nuns' library and buy some books for it, as we can't use your library any more.'

Godwyn tapped his foot impatiently. This seemed irrelevant.

'And then we need a covered walkway to the church, as we now take a different route to that used by the monks, and we have no protection in bad weather.'

'Very reasonable,' Godwyn commented, though he wanted to say: Stop dithering!

'So,' she said with an air of finality, 'I think we could consider this proposal in three years' time.'

'Three years? I want to start now!'

'Oh, I don't think we can contemplate that.'

'Why not?'

'We have a budget for building, you see.'

'But isn't this more important?'

'We must stick to our budget.'

'Why?'

'So that we remain financially strong and independent,' she said; then she added pointedly: 'I wouldn't like to go begging.'

Godwyn did not know what to say. Worse, he had a ghastly feeling that she was laughing at him behind the veil. He could not stand to be laughed at. He stood up abruptly. 'Thank you, Mother Cecilia,' he said coldly. 'We'll talk about this again.'

'Yes,' she said, 'in three years' time. I look forward to it.'

Now he was sure she was laughing. He turned away and left as quickly as he could.

Back in his own house, he threw himself in a chair, fuming. 'I hate that woman,' he said to Philemon, who was still there.

'She said no?'

'She said she would consider it in three years' time.'

'That's worse than a no,' said Philemon. 'It's a three-year no.'

'We're always in her power, because she has money.'

'I listen to the talk of the older men,' Philemon said, apparently irrelevantly. 'It's surprising how much you learn.'

'What are you getting at?'

'When the priory first built mills and dug fishponds and fenced off rabbit warrens, the priors made a law that townspeople had to use the monks' facilities, and pay for them. They weren't allowed to grind their corn at home, or full cloth by treading it, nor could they have their own ponds and warrens – they had to buy from us. The law ensured that the priory got back its costs.'

'But the law fell out of use?'

'It changed. Instead of a prohibition, people were allowed their own facilities if they paid a fine. Then *that* fell out of use, in Prior Anthony's time.'

'And now there's a hand mill in every house.'

'And all the fishmongers have ponds, there are half a dozen warrens, and dyers full their own cloth by making their wives and children tread it, instead of bringing it to the priory's fulling mill.'

Godwyn was excited. 'If all those people paid a fine for the privilege of having their own facilities...'

'It could be quite a lot of money.'

'They would squeal like pigs.' Godwyn frowned. 'Can we prove what we say?'

'There are plenty of people who remember the fines. But it's bound to be written in the priory records somewhere – probably in Timothy's Book.'

'You'd better find out exactly how much the fines were. If we're resting on the ground of precedent, we'd better get it right.'

'If I may make a suggestion...'

'Of course.'

'You could announce the new regime from the pulpit of the cathedral on Sunday morning. That would serve to emphasize that it's the will of God.'

'Good idea,' said Godwyn. 'That's exactly what I'll do.'

33

'I'VE GOT THE SOLUTION,' Caris said to her father.

He sat back in the big wooden seat at the head of the table, a slight smile on his face. She knew that look. It was sceptical, but willing to listen. 'Go on,' he said.

She was a little nervous. She felt sure her idea would work – saving her father's fortune and Merthin's bridge – but could she convince Edmund? 'We take our surplus wool and have it woven into cloth and dyed,' she said simply. She held her breath, waiting for his reaction.

'Wool merchants often try that in hard times,' he said. 'But tell me why you think it would work. What would it cost?'

'For cleaning, spinning and weaving, four shillings per sack.'

'And how much cloth would that make?'

'A sack of poor-quality wool, that you bought for thirty-six shillings and wove for four more shillings, would make forty-eight yards of cloth.'

'Which you would sell for...?'

'Undyed, brown burel sells for a shilling a yard, so forty-eight shillings – eight more than we would have paid out.'

'It's not much, considering the work we would have put in.'

'But that's not the best of it.'

'Keep going.'

'Weavers sell their brown burel because they're in a hurry to get the money. But if you spend another twenty shillings fulling the cloth, then dyeing and finishing it, you can get double the price – two shillings a yard, ninety-six shillings for the whole lot – thirty-six shillings more than you paid!'

Edmund looked dubious. 'If it's so easy, why don't more people do it?'

'Because they don't have the money to lay out.'

'Nor do I!'

'You've got three pounds from Guillaume of London.'

'Am I to have nothing with which to buy wool next year?'

'At these prices, you're better off out of the business.'

He laughed. 'By the saints, you're right. Very well, try it out with some cheap stuff. I've got five sacks of coarse Devon wool that the Italians never want. I'll give you a sack of that, and see if you can do what you say.'

*

TWO WEEKS LATER, Caris found Mark Webber smashing up his hand mill.

She was shocked to see a poor man destroying a valuable piece of equipment – so much so that, for a moment, she forgot her own troubles.

The hand mill consisted of two stone discs, each slightly roughened on one face. The smaller sat on the larger, fitting perfectly into a shallow indentation, rough side to rough. A protruding wooden handle enabled the upper stone to be turned while the lower remained still. Ears of grain placed between the two stones would be rapidly ground to flour.

Most Kingsbridge people of the lower class had a hand mill. The very poor could not afford one, and the affluent did not need one – they could buy flour already ground by a miller. But for families such as the Webbers, who needed every penny they earned to feed their children, a hand mill was a money-saving godsend.

Mark had laid his on the ground in front of his small house. He had borrowed from somewhere a long-handled sledgehammer with an iron head. Two of his children were watching, a thin girl in a ragged dress and a naked toddler. He lifted the hammer over his head and swung it in a long arc. It was a sight to see: he was the biggest man in Kingsbridge, with shoulders like a carthorse. The stone crazed like an eggshell and fell into pieces.

Caris said: 'What on earth are you doing?'

'We must grind corn at the prior's watermills, and forfeit one sack in twenty-four as a fee,' Mark replied.

He seemed phlegmatic about it, but she was horrified. 'I

thought the new rules applied only to unlicensed windmills and watermills.'

'Tomorrow I have to go around with John Constable, searching people's homes, breaking up illicit hand mills. I can't have them saying I've got one of my own. That's why I'm doing this in the street, where everyone can see.'

'I didn't realize Godwyn intended to take the bread out of the mouths of the poor,' Caris said grimly.

'Luckily for us, we've got some weaving to do – thanks to you.'

Caris turned her mind to her own business. 'How are you getting on?'

'Finished.'

'That was quick!'

'It takes longer in winter. But in summer, with sixteen hours of daylight, I can weave six yards in a day, with Madge helping.'

'Wonderful!'

'Come inside and I'll show you.'

His wife, Madge, was standing over the cooking fire at the back of the one-room house, with a baby on one arm and a shy boy at her side. Madge was shorter than her husband by more than a foot, but her build was chunky. She had a large bust and a jutting behind, and she made Caris think of a plump pigeon. Her protruding jaw gave her an aggressive air that was not entirely misleading. Although combative, she was good-hearted, and Caris liked her. She offered her visitor a cup of cider, which Caris refused, knowing the family could not afford it.

Mark's loom was a wooden frame, more than a yard square, on a stand. It took up most of the living space. Behind it, close to the back door, was a table with two benches. Obviously they all slept on the floor around the loom.

'I make narrow dozens,' Mark explained. 'A narrow dozen is a cloth a yard wide and twelve yards long. I can't make broadcloth, because I haven't room for such a wide loom.' Four rolls of brown burel were stacked against the wall. 'One sack of wool makes four narrow dozens,' he said.

Caris had brought him the raw fleeces in a standard woolsack. Madge had arranged for the wool to be cleaned, sorted and spun into yarn. The spinning was done by the poor women of the town, and the cleaning and sorting by their children.

Caris felt the cloth. She was excited: she had completed the first stage of her plan. 'Why is it so loosely woven?' she asked.

Mark bristled. 'Loose? My burel is the tightest weave in Kingsbridge!'

'I know – I didn't mean to sound critical. But Italian cloth feels so different – yet they make it from our wool.'

'Partly it depends on the weaver's strength, and how hard he can press down the batten to pack the wool.'

'I don't think the Italian weavers are all stronger than you.'

'Then it's their machines. The better the loom, the closer the weave.'

'I was afraid of that.' The implication was that Caris could not compete with high-quality Italian wool unless she bought Italian looms, which seemed impossible.

One problem at a time, she told herself. She paid Mark, counting out four shillings, of which he would have to give about half to the women who had done the spinning. Caris had made eight shillings profit, theoretically. Eight shillings would not pay for much work on the bridge. And at this rate it would take years to weave all her father's surplus wool. 'Is there any way we can produce cloth faster?' she said to Mark.

Madge answered. 'There are other weavers in Kingsbridge, but most of them are committed to work for existing cloth merchants. I can find you more outside the town, though. The larger villages often have a weaver with a loom. He usually makes cloth for the villagers from their own yarn. Such men can easily switch to another job, if the money's good.'

Caris concealed her anxiety. 'All right,' she said. 'I'll let you know. Meanwhile, will you deliver these cloths to Peter Dyer for me?'

'Of course. I'll take them now.'

Caris went home for dinner, deep in thought. To make any real difference, she would have to spend most of what money her father had left. If things went wrong, they would be even worse off. But what was the alternative? Her plan was risky, but no one else had any kind of plan at all.

When she arrived home, Petranilla was serving a mutton stew. Edmund sat at the head of the table. The financial setback of the Fleece Fair seemed to have affected him more severely than Caris would have expected. His normal exuberance was subdued, and he often appeared thoughtful, not to say distracted. Caris was worried about him.

'I saw Mark Webber smashing up his hand mill,' she said as she sat down. 'Where's the sense in that?'

Petranilla put her nose in the air. 'Godwyn is entirely within his rights,' she said.

'Those rights are out of date – they haven't been enforced for years. Where else does a priory do such things?'

'In St Albans,' Petranilla said triumphantly.

Edmund said: 'I've heard of St Albans. The townspeople periodically riot against the monastery.'

'Kingsbridge Priory is entitled to recoup the money it spent building mills,' Petranilla argued. 'Just as you, Edmund, want to get back the money you're putting into the bridge. How would you feel if someone built a second bridge?'

Edmund did not answer her, so Caris did. 'It would depend entirely on how soon it happened,' she said. 'The priory's mills were built hundreds of years ago, as were the warrens and fishponds. No one has the right to hold back the development of the town for ever.'

'The prior has a right to collect his dues,' she said stubbornly.

'Well, if he carries on like this, there will be no one to collect dues from. People will go and live in Shiring. They're allowed hand mills there.'

'Don't you understand that the needs of the priory are sacred?' Petranilla said angrily. 'The monks serve God! By comparison with that, the lives of the townspeople are insignificant.'

'Is that what your son Godwyn believes?'

'Of course.'

'I was afraid of that.'

'Don't you believe the prior's work is sacred?'

Caris had no answer to that, so she just shrugged, and Petranilla looked triumphant.

The dinner was good, but Caris was too tense to eat much. As soon as the others had finished, she said: 'I have to go and see Peter Dyer.'

Petranilla protested: 'Are you going to spend more? You've already given Mark Webber four shillings of your father's money.'

'Yes – and the cloth is worth twelve shillings more than the wool was, so I've made eight shillings.'

'No, you haven't,' Petranilla said. 'You haven't sold the cloth yet.'

Petranilla was expressing doubts that Caris shared, in her more pessimistic moments, but she was stung into denial. 'I will sell it, though – especially if it's dyed red.'

'And what will Peter charge for dyeing and fulling four narrow dozens?'

'Twenty shillings – but the red cloth will be worth double the brown burel, so we'll make another twenty-eight shillings.'

'If you sell it. And if you don't?'

'I'll sell it.'

Her father intervened. 'Let her be,' he said to Petranilla. 'I've told her she can give this a try.'

*

SHIRING CASTLE STOOD on top of a hill. It was the home of the county sheriff. At the foot of the hill stood the gallows. Whenever there was a hanging, the prisoner was brought down from the castle on a cart, to be hanged in front of the church.

The square in which the gallows stood was also the market place. The Shiring Fair was held here, between the guild hall and a large timber building that was the wool exchange. The bishop's palace and numerous taverns also stood around the square.

This year, because of the troubles at Kingsbridge, there were more stalls than ever, and the fair spilled into the streets off the market place. Edmund had brought forty sacks of wool on ten carts, and could get more brought from Kingsbridge before the end of the week, if necessary.

To Caris's dismay, it was not necessary. He sold ten sacks on the first day, then nothing until the end of the fair, when he sold another ten by reducing the price below what he had paid. She could not remember seeing him so down.

She put her four lengths of dull brownish-red cloth on his stall and, over the week, yard by yard, she sold three of the four. 'Look at it this way,' she said to her father on the last day of the fair. 'Before, you had a sack of unsaleable wool and four shillings. Now, you've got thirty-six shillings and a length of cloth.'

But her cheerfulness was only for his benefit. She was deeply depressed. She had boasted bravely that she could sell cloth. The result was not a complete failure, but it was no triumph. If she could not sell the cloth for more than it cost, then she did not have the solution to the problem. What was she going to do? She left the stall and went to survey other cloth sellers.

The best cloth came from Italy, as always. Caris stopped at the stall of Loro Fiorentino. Cloth merchants such as Loro were not wool buyers, though they often worked closely with buyers. Caris knew that Loro gave his English takings to Buonaventura, who used it to pay English merchants for their raw wool. Then, when the wool reached Florence, Buonaventura's family would sell it, and with the proceeds pay back Loro's family. That way, they all avoided the hazards of transporting barrels of gold and silver coins across Europe.

Loro had on his stall only two rolls of cloth, but the colours were much brighter than anything the local people could produce. 'Is this all you brought?' Caris asked him.

'Of course not. I've sold the rest.'

She was surprised. 'Everyone else is having a bad fair.'

He shrugged. 'The finest cloth always sells.'

An idea was taking shape in Caris's head. 'How much is the scarlet?'

'Only seven shillings per yard, mistress.'

That was seven times the price of burel. 'But who can afford it?'

'The bishop took a lot of my red, Lady Philippa some blue and green, a few daughters of the brewers and bakers in town, some lords and ladies from the villages round about ... Even when times are hard, someone is prospering. This vermilion will be so beautiful on you.' With a swift motion, he unrolled the bale and draped a length over Caris's shoulder. 'Marvellous. See how everyone is looking at you already.'

She smiled. 'I can see why you sell so much.' She handled the cloth. It was closely woven. She already had a cloak of Italian scarlet, the one that she had inherited from her mother. It was her favourite garment. 'What dye do they use to get this red?'

'Madder, the same as everyone.'

'But how do they make it so bright?'

'It's no secret. They use alum. It brightens the colour and also fixes it, so it won't fade. A cloak in this colour, for you, would be wonderful, a joy for ever.'

'Alum,' she repeated. 'Why don't English dyers use it?'

'It's very expensive. It comes from Turkey. Such luxury is only for special women.'

'And the blue?'

'Like your eyes.'

Her eyes were green, but she did not correct him. 'It's such a deep colour.'

'English dyers use woad, but we get indigo from Bengal. Moorish traders bring it from India to Egypt, and then our Italian merchants buy it in Alexandria.' He smiled. 'Think how far it has travelled – to complement your outstanding beauty.'

'Yes,' said Caris. 'Just think of that.'

*

THE RIVERSIDE WORKSHOP of Peter Dyer was a house as big as Edmund's, but built of stone, and with no interior walls or floors – just a shell. Two iron cauldrons stood over great fires. Beside each was a hoist, like the ones Merthin made for building work. These were used to lift huge sacks of wool or cloth and lower them into the vats. The floors were permanently wet and the air was thick with steam. The apprentices worked barefoot, in their underdrawers because of the heat, their faces running with sweat, their hair gleaming with damp. There was an acrid smell that bit at the back of Caris's throat.

She showed Peter her unsold length of cloth. 'I want the bright scarlet that the Italian cloths have,' she said. 'That's what sells best.'

Peter was a lugubrious man who always looked injured, no matter what you said to him. Now he nodded glumly, as if acknowledging a justified criticism. 'We'll dye it again with madder.'

'And with alum, to fix the colour and make it brighter.'

'We don't use alum. Never have. I don't know anyone who does.'

Caris cursed inwardly. She had not thought to check this. She had assumed a dyer would know everything about dyes. 'Can't you try it?'

'I haven't got any.'

Caris sighed. Peter seemed to be one of those craftsmen for whom everything is impossible unless they have done it before. 'Suppose I could get you some?'

'Where from?'

'Winchester, I suppose, or London. Or perhaps from Melcombe.' That was the nearest big port. Ships came from all over Europe to Melcombe.

'If I had some, I wouldn't know how to use it.'

'Can't you find out?'

'Who from?'

'I'll try to find out, then.'

He shook his head pessimistically. 'I don't know...'

She did not want to quarrel with him: he was the only large-scale dyer in town. 'We'll cross that bridge when we come to it,' she said in a conciliatory tone. 'I won't take up any more of your time discussing it now. First I'll see if I can get some alum.'

She left him. Who in town might know about alum? She wished now that she had asked Loro Fiorentino more questions. The monks ought to know about things like this, but they were no longer allowed to talk to women. She decided to see Mattie Wise. Mattie was forever mixing strange ingredients – maybe alum was one of them. More importantly, if she did not know she would admit her ignorance, unlike a monk or an apothecary who might make something up for fear of being thought foolish.

Mattie's first words were: 'How is your father?'

'He seems a bit shaken by the failure of the Fleece Fair,' Caris said. It was typical of Mattie to know what she was worried about. 'He's becoming forgetful. He seems older.'

'Take care of him,' said Mattie. 'He's a good man.'

'I know.' Caris was not sure what Mattie was getting at.

'Petranilla is a self-centred cow.'

'I know that, too.'

Mattie was grinding something with a mortar and pestle. She pushed the bowl towards Caris. 'If you do this for me, I'll pour you a cup of wine.'

'Thank you.' Caris began to grind.

Mattie poured yellow wine from a stone jug into two wooden cups. 'Why are you here? You're not ill.'

'Do you know what alum is?'

'Yes. In small quantities, we use it as an astringent, to close wounds. It can also stop diarrhoea. But in large quantities it's poisonous. Like most poisons, it makes you vomit. There was alum in the potion I gave you last year.'

'What is it, a herb?'

'No, it's an earth. The Moors mine it in Turkey and Africa. Tanners employ it in the preparation of leather, sometimes. I suppose you want to use it to dye cloth.'

'Yes.' As always, Mattie's guesswork seemed supernaturally accurate.

'It acts as a mordant – it helps the dye to bite the wool.'

'And where do you get it?'

'I buy it in Melcombe,' said Mattie.

✳

CARIS MADE THE two-day journey to Melcombe, where she had been several times before, accompanied by one of her father's employees as a bodyguard. At the quayside she found a merchant who dealt in spices, cage birds, musical instruments and all kinds of curiosities from remote parts of the world. He sold her both the red dye made from the root of the madder plant, cultivated in France, and a type of alum known as Spiralum that he said came from Ethiopia. He charged her seven shillings for a small barrel of madder and a pound for a sack of alum, and she had no idea whether she was paying fair prices or not. He sold her his entire stock, and promised to get more from the next Italian ship to come into port. She asked him what quantities of dye and alum she should use, but he did not know.

When she got home, she began to dye pieces of her unsold cloth in a cooking pot. Petranilla objected to the smell, so Caris built a fire in the back yard. She knew that she had to put the cloth in a solution of dye and boil it, and Peter Dyer told her the correct strength of the dye solution. However, no one knew how much alum she needed or how she should use it.

She began a frustrating process of trial and error. She tried soaking the cloth in alum before dyeing it; putting the alum in at the same time as the dye; and boiling the dyed cloth in a solution of alum afterwards. She tried using the same quantity of alum as dye, then more, then less. At Mattie's suggestion she experimented with other ingredients: oak galls, chalk, lime water, vinegar, urine.

She was short of time. In all towns, no one could sell cloth but members of the guild – except during a fair, when the normal rules were relaxed. And all fairs were held in summer. The last was St Giles's Fair, which took place on the downs to the east of Winchester on St Giles's Day, 12 September. It was now mid-July, so she had eight weeks.

She started early in the morning and worked until long after dark. Agitating the cloth continuously and lifting it in and out of the pot made her back ache. Her hands became red and sore from constant dipping in the harsh chemicals, and her hair began to smell. But, despite the frustration, she occasionally felt happy, and sometimes she hummed or even sang as she worked, old tunes whose words she could barely remember from childhood. Neighbours in their own back yards watched her curiously across the fences.

Now and again there came into her mind the thought: Is this my fate? More than once she had said that she did not know what to do with her life. But she might not have a free choice. She was not to be allowed to be a physician; becoming a wool merchant looked like a bad idea; she did not want to enslave herself to a husband and children – but she had never dreamed that she might end up as a dyer. When she thought about it, she knew that this was not what she wanted to do. Having started it, she was determined to succeed – but it was not going to be her destiny.

At first she could only get the cloth to turn brownish red or pale pink. When she began to approach the right shade of scarlet she found, maddeningly, that it faded when she dried it in the sun, or came out when washed. She tried double-dyeing, but the effect proved temporary. Peter told her, rather late, that the material would soak up dye more completely if she worked with the yarn before it was woven, or even with raw fleeces; and that improved the shade, but not the fastness.

'There's only one way to learn dyeing, and that's from a master,' Peter said several times. They all thought that way, Caris realized. Prior Godwyn learned medicine by reading books that were hundreds of years old, and prescribed medicines without even looking at his patient. Elfric had punished Merthin for carving the parable of the virgins in a new way. Peter had never even tried to dye cloth scarlet. Only Mattie based her decisions on what she could see for herself, rather than on some venerated authority.

Caris's sister, Alice, stood watching her late one evening, with folded arms and pursed lips. As darkness gathered in the corners of the yard, the light of Caris's fire reddened Alice's disapproving face. 'How much of our father's money have you spent on this foolishness?' she said.

Caris added it up. 'Seven shillings for the madder, a pound for the alum, twelve shillings for the cloth – thirty-nine shillings.'

'God save us!' Alice was horrified.

Caris herself was daunted. It was more than a year's wages for most people in Kingsbridge. 'It is a lot, but I'll make more,' she said.

Alice was angry. 'You have no right to spend his money like this.'

'No right?' Caris said. 'I have his permission – what more do I need?'

'He's showing signs of age. His judgement is not what it was.'

Caris pretended not to know this. 'His judgement is fine, and a lot better than yours.'

'You're spending our inheritance!'

'Is *that* what's bothering you? Don't worry, I'm making you money.'

'I don't want to take the risk.'

'You're not taking the risk, he is.'

'He shouldn't throw away money that should come to us!'

'Tell him that.'

Alice went away defeated, but Caris was not as confident as she pretended. She might never get it just right. And then what would she and her father do?

When finally she found the right formula, it was remarkably simple: an ounce of madder and two ounces of alum for every three ounces of wool. She boiled the wool in the alum first, then added the madder to the pot without re-boiling the liquid. The extra ingredient was lime water. She could hardly believe the result. It was more successful than she could have hoped. The red was bright, almost like the Italian red. She felt sure it would fade and give her another disappointment; but the colour remained the same through drying, re-washing and fulling.

She gave Peter the formula and, under her close supervision, he used all her remaining alum to dye twelve yards of best-quality wool cloth in one of his giant vats. When it had been fulled, Caris paid a finisher to draw off the loose threads with a teasel, the prickly head of a wild flower, and to repair small blemishes.

She went to St Giles's Fair with a bale of perfect bright red cloth.

As she was unrolling it, she was addressed by a man with a London accent. 'How much is that?' he said.

She looked at him. His clothes were expensive without being ostentatious, and she guessed he was wealthy but not noble. Trying to mask the trembling in her voice, she said: 'Seven shillings a yard. It's the best—'

'No, I meant how much for the whole cloth.'

'It's twelve yards, so that would be eighty-four shillings.'

He rubbed the cloth between finger and thumb. 'It's not as close-woven as Italian cloth, but it's not bad. I'll give you twenty-seven gold florins.'

The gold coin of Florence was in common use, because England had no gold currency of its own. It was worth about three shillings, thirty-six English silver pennies. The Londoner was offering to buy her entire cloth for only three shillings less than she would get selling it yard by yard. But she sensed that he was not very serious about haggling – otherwise he would have started lower. 'No,' she said, marvelling at her own temerity. 'I want the full price.'

'All right,' he said immediately, confirming her instinct. She watched, thrilled, as he took out his purse. A moment later she held in her hand twenty-eight gold florins.

She examined one carefully. It was a bit larger than a silver penny. On one side was St John the Baptist, the patron saint of Florence, and on the other the flower of Florence. She placed it on a balance to compare its weight with that of a new-minted florin her father kept for the purpose. The coin was good.

'Thank you,' she said, hardly believing her success.

'I'm Harry Mercer of Cheapside, London,' he said. 'My father is the largest cloth merchant in England. When you've got more of this scarlet, come to London. We'll buy as much as you can bring us.'

*

'LET'S WEAVE IT ALL!' she said to her father when she returned home. 'You've got forty sacks of wool left. We'll turn it all into red cloth.'

'It's a big enterprise,' he said thoughtfully.

Caris was sure her scheme would work. 'There are plenty of weavers, and they're all poor. Peter isn't the only dyer in Kingsbridge, we can teach the others to use the alum.'

'Others will copy you, once the secret gets out.'

She knew he was right to think of snags, but all the same she felt impatient. 'Let them copy,' she said. 'They can make money too.'

He was not going to be pushed into anything. 'The price will come down if there's a lot of cloth for sale.'

'It will have to fall a long way before the business becomes unprofitable.'

He nodded. 'That's true. But can you sell that much in Kingsbridge and Shiring? There aren't that many rich people.'

'Then I'll take it to London.'

'All right.' He smiled. 'You're so determined. It's a good plan – but even if it were a bad one, you'd probably make it work.'

She went immediately to Mark Webber's house and arranged for him to begin work on another sack of wool. She also arranged for Madge to take one of Edmund's ox-carts and four sacks of wool, and go around neighbouring villages looking for weavers.

But the rest of Caris's family were not happy. Next day, Alice came to dinner. As they sat down, Petranilla said to Edmund: 'Alice and I think you should reconsider your cloth-making project.'

Caris wanted him to tell her that the decision was made and it was too late to go back. But instead he said mildly: 'Really? Tell me why.'

'You'll be risking just about every penny you've got, that's why!'

'Most of it's at risk now,' he said. 'I've got a warehouse full of wool that I can't sell.'

'But you could make a bad situation worse.'

'I've decided to take that chance.'

Alice broke in: 'It's not fair on me!'

'Why not?'

'Caris is spending my inheritance!'

His face darkened. 'I'm not dead yet,' he said.

Petranilla clamped her mouth shut, recognizing the undertone in his low voice; but Alice did not notice how angry he was, and ploughed on. 'We have to think about the future,' she said. 'Why should Caris be allowed to spend my birthright?'

'Because it's not yours yet, and perhaps it never will be.'

'You can't just throw away money that should come to me.'

'I won't be told what to do with my money – especially by my children,' he said, and his voice was so taut with anger that even Alice noticed.

More quietly, she said: 'I didn't intend to annoy you.'

He grunted. It was not much of an apology, but he could never remain grumpy for long. 'Let's have dinner and say no more about it,' he said; and Caris knew that her project had survived another day.

After dinner she went to see Peter Dyer, to warn him of the large quantity of work coming his way. 'It can't be done,' he said.

That took her by surprise. He always looked gloomy, but he normally did what she wanted. 'Don't worry, you won't have to dye it all,' she said. 'I'll give some of the work to others.'

'It's not the dyeing,' he said. 'It's the fulling.'

'Why?'

'We're not allowed to full the cloth ourselves. Prior Godwyn has issued a new edict. We have to use the priory's fulling mill.'

'Well, then, we'll use it.'

'It's too slow. The machinery is old, and keeps breaking down. It's been repaired again and again, so the wood is a mixture of new and old, which never sorts well. It's no faster than a man treading in a bath of water. But there's only one mill. It will barely cope with the normal work of Kingsbridge weavers and dyers.'

This was maddening. Surely her whole scheme could not fail because of a stupid ruling by her cousin Godwyn? She said indignantly: 'But if the mill can't do the work, the prior must permit us to tread the cloth by foot!'

Peter shrugged. 'Tell him that.'

'I will!'

She marched off towards the priory but, before she got there, she thought again. The hall of the prior's house was used for his meetings with townspeople, but all the same it would be unusual for a woman to go in alone without an appointment, and Godwyn was increasingly touchy about such things. Moreover, a straight confrontation might not be the best way to change his mind. She realized she would do better to think this through. She returned to her house and sat down with her father in the parlour.

'Young Godwyn is on weak ground here,' Edmund said immediately. 'There never was a charge for using the fulling mill. According to legend, it was built by a townsman, Jack Builder, for the great Prior Philip; and, when Jack died, Philip gave the town the right to use the mill in perpetuity.'

'Why did people stop using it?'

'It fell into disrepair, and I think there was an argument about who should pay for its upkeep. The argument was never resolved, and people went back to treading cloth themselves.'

'Why, then, he has no right to charge a fee, nor to force people to use it!'

'No, indeed.'

Edmund sent a message to the priory asking when it might be convenient for Godwyn to see him, and the reply came back saying he was free right away, so Edmund and Caris crossed the street and went to the prior's house.

Godwyn had changed a lot in a year, Caris thought. There was no boyish eagerness left. He seemed wary, as if he expected them to be aggressive. She was beginning to wonder whether he had the strength of character to be prior.

Philemon was with him, pathetically eager as ever to fetch chairs and pour drinks, but with a new touch of assurance in his manner, the look of someone who knew he belonged here.

'So, Philemon, you're an uncle now,' Caris said. 'What do you think of your new nephew, Sam?'

'I'm a novice monk,' he said prissily. 'We give up all worldly relations.'

Caris shrugged. She knew he was fond of his sister Gwenda but, if he wanted to pretend otherwise, she was not going to argue.

Edmund laid out the problem starkly for Godwyn. 'Work on the bridge will have to stop if the wool merchants of Kingsbridge can't improve their fortunes. Happily, we have come up with a new source of income. Caris has discovered how to produce high-quality scarlet cloth. Only one thing stands in the way of the success of this new enterprise: the fulling mill.'

'Why?' said Godwyn. 'The scarlet cloth can be fulled at the mill.'

'Apparently not. It's old and inefficient. It can barely handle the existing production of cloth. It has no capacity for extra. Either you build a new fulling mill—'

'Out of the question,' Godwyn interrupted. 'I have no spare cash for that sort of thing.'

'Very well, then,' said Edmund. 'You'll have to permit people to full cloth in the old way, by putting it in a bath of water and stamping on it with their bare feet.'

The look that came over Godwyn's face was familiar to Caris. It was compounded of resentment, injured pride and mulish obstinacy. In childhood he had looked like that whenever he was opposed. It meant he would try to bully the other children into submission or, failing that, stamp his foot and go home. Wanting his own way was only part of it. He seemed, Caris thought, to feel humiliated by disagreement, as if the idea that someone might think him wrong was too wounding to be borne. Whatever the explanation, she knew as soon as she saw the look that he was not going to be reasonable.

'I knew you would oppose me,' he said petulantly to Edmund. 'You seem to think the priory exists for the benefit of Kingsbridge. You'll just have to realize that it's the other way around.'

Edmund rapidly became exasperated. 'Don't you see that we depend on one another? We thought you understood that interrelationship – that's why we helped you get elected.'

'I was elected by the monks, not the merchants. The town may depend on the priory, but there was a priory here before there was a town, and we can exist without you.'

'You can exist, perhaps, but as an isolated outpost, rather than as the throbbing heart of a bustling city.'

Caris put in: 'You must want Kingsbridge to prosper, Godwyn – why else would you have gone to London to oppose Earl Roland?'

'I went to the royal court to defend the ancient rights of the priory – as I am trying to do here and now.'

Edmund said indignantly: 'This is treachery! We supported you as prior because you led us to believe you would build a bridge!'

'I owe you nothing,' Godwyn replied. 'My mother sold her house to send me to the university – where was my rich uncle then?'

Caris was amazed that Godwyn was still resentful over what had happened ten years ago.

Edmund's expression became coldly hostile. 'I don't think you have the right to force people to use the fulling mill,' he said.

A glance passed between Godwyn and Philemon, and Caris realized they knew this. Godwyn said: 'There may have been times when the prior generously allowed the townspeople to use the mill without charge.'

'It was the gift of Prior Philip to the town.'

'I know nothing of that.'

'There must be a document in your records.'

Godwyn became angry. 'The townspeople have allowed the mill to fall into disrepair, so that the priory has to pay to put it right. That is enough to annul any gift.'

Edmund was right, Caris realized: Godwyn was on weak ground. He knew about Prior Philip's gift, but he intended to ignore it.

Edmund tried again. 'Surely we can settle this between us?'

'I will not back down from my edict,' Godwyn said. 'It would make me appear weak.'

That was what really bothered him, Caris realized. He was frightened that the townspeople would disrespect him if he changed his mind. His obstinacy came, paradoxically, from a kind of timidity.

Edmund said: 'Neither of us wants the trouble and expense of another visit to the royal court.'

Godwyn bristled. 'Are you threatening me with the royal court?'

'I'm trying to avoid it. But . . .'

Caris closed her eyes, praying that the two men would not push their argument to the brink. Her prayer was not answered.

'But what?' said Godwyn challengingly.

Edmund sighed. 'But yes, if you force the townspeople to use the fulling mill, and prohibit home fulling, I will appeal to the king.'

'So be it,' said Godwyn.

34

THE DEER WAS A YOUNG FEMALE, a year or two old, sleek across the haunches, well muscled under a soft leather skin. She was on the far side of a clearing, pushing her long neck through the branches of a bush to reach a patch of scrubby grass. Ralph Fitzgerald and Alan Fernhill were on horseback, the hooves of their mounts muffled by the carpet of wet autumn leaves, and their dogs were trained to silence. Because of this, and perhaps because she was concentrating on straining to reach her fodder, the deer did not hear their approach until it was too late.

Ralph saw her first, and pointed across the clearing. Alan was carrying his longbow, grasping it and the reins in his left hand. With the speed of long practice, he fitted an arrow to the string in a heartbeat, and shot.

The dogs were slower. Only when they heard the thrum of the bowstring, and the whistle of the arrow as it flew through the air, did they react. Barley, the bitch, froze in place, head up, ears erect; and Blade, her puppy, now grown larger than his mother, uttered a low, startled woof.

The arrow was a yard long, flighted with swan feathers. Its tip was two inches of solid iron with a socket into which the shaft fitted tightly. It was a hunting arrow, with a sharp point: a battle arrow would have had a square head, so that it would punch through armour without being deflected.

Alan's shot was good, but not perfect. It struck the deer low in the neck. She jumped with all four feet – shocked, presumably, by the sudden, agonizing stab. Her head came up out of the bush. For an instant, Ralph thought she was going to fall down dead, but a moment later she bounded away. The arrow was still buried in her neck, but the blood was oozing rather than spurting from the wound, so it must have lodged in her muscles, missing the major blood vessels.

The dogs leaped forward as if they, too, had been shot from bows; and the two horses followed without urging. Ralph was on Griff, his favourite hunter. He felt the rush of excitement that was what he mainly lived for. It was a tingling in the nerves, a constriction in the neck, an irresistible impulse to yell at the top of his voice; a thrill so like sexual excitement that he could hardly have said what the difference was.

Men such as Ralph existed to fight. The king and his barons made them lords and knights, and gave them villages and lands to rule over, for a reason: so that they would be able to provide themselves with horses, squires, weapons and armour whenever the king needed an army. But there was not a war every year. Sometimes two or three years would go by without so much as a minor police action on the borders of rebellious Wales or barbarian Scotland. Knights needed something to do in the interim. They had to keep fit and maintain their horsemanship and – perhaps most important of all – their blood lust. Soldiers had to kill, and they did it better when they longed for it.

Hunting was the answer. All noblemen, from the king down to minor lords such as Ralph, hunted whenever they got the chance, often several times a week. They enjoyed it, and it ensured they were fit for battle whenever called upon. Ralph hunted with Earl Roland on his frequent visits to Earlscastle, and often joined Lord William's hunt at Casterham. When he was at his own village of Wigleigh, he went out with his squire, Alan, in the forests round about. They usually killed boar – there was not much meat on the wild pigs, but they were exciting to hunt because they put up a good fight. Ralph also went after foxes and the occasional, rare, wolf. But a deer was best: agile, fast, and a hundred pounds of good meat to take home.

Now Ralph thrilled to the feel of Griff beneath him, the horse's weight and strength, the powerful action of its muscles and the drumbeat of its tread. The deer disappeared into the vegetation, but Barley knew where it had gone, and the horses followed the dogs. Ralph carried a spear ready in his right hand, a long shaft of ash with a fire-hardened point. As Griff swerved and jumped, Ralph ducked under overhanging branches and swayed with the horse, his boots firmly in the stirrups, keeping his seat effortlessly by the pressure of his knees.

In the undergrowth the horses were not as nimble as the deer, and they fell behind; but the dogs had the advantage, and Ralph heard frantic barking as they closed in. Then there was a lull, and in a few moments Ralph found out why: the deer had broken out of the vegetation on to a pathway, and was leaving the dogs behind. Here, however, the horses had the advantage, and they quickly passed the dogs and began to gain on the deer.

Ralph could see that the beast was weakening. He saw blood on its rump, and deduced that one of the dogs had got a bite. Its gait became irregular as it struggled to get away. It was a sprinter, made for the sudden quick dash, and it could not keep up its initial pace for long.

His blood raced as he closed on his prey. He tightened his grip on the lance. It took a great deal of strength to force a wooden point into the tough body of a big animal: the skin was leathery, the muscles dense, the bones hard. The neck was the softest target, if you could contrive to miss the vertebrae and hit the jugular vein. You had to choose the exact moment, then thrust quickly with all your might.

Seeing the horses almost upon it, the deer made a desperate turn into the bushes. This gave it a few seconds' respite. The horses slowed as they crashed through undergrowth over which the deer had bounded without pause. But the dogs caught up again, and Ralph saw that the deer could not go much farther.

The usual pattern was that the dogs would inflict more and more wounds, slowing the deer until the horses could catch it and the hunter could deliver the death blow. But, on this occasion, there was an accident.

When the dogs and the horses were almost upon the deer, she dodged sideways. Blade, the younger dog, went after her with more enthusiasm than sense, and swerved in front of Griff. The horse was going too fast to stop or even avoid the dog, and kicked him with a mighty foreleg. The dog was a mastiff, weighing seventy or eighty pounds, and the impact caused the horse to stumble.

Ralph was thrown. He let go of his spear as he flew through the air. His greatest fear, in that instant, was that his horse would fall on him. But he saw, in the moment before he landed, that Griff had somehow regained his balance.

Ralph fell into a thorn bush. His hands and face were scratched painfully, but the branches broke his fall. All the same, he was enraged.

Alan reined in. Barley went after the deer but returned in a few moments: the beast had obviously got away. Ralph struggled to his feet, cursing. Alan caught Griff then dismounted, holding both horses.

Blade lay motionless on the dead leaves, blood dripping from his mouth. He had been struck on the head by Griff's iron horseshoe. Barley went up to him, sniffed, nudged him with her nose and licked the blood on his face, then turned away, looking bewildered. Alan prodded the dog with the toe of his boot. There was no response. Blade was not breathing. 'Dead,' Alan said.

'Damn fool dog deserved to die,' Ralph said.

They walked the horses through the woods, looking for a place to rest. After a while Ralph heard running water. Following the sound, he came to a fast-flowing stream. He recognized the stretch of water: they were only a little way beyond the fields of Wigleigh. 'Let's have some refreshment,' he said. Alan tied up the horses then took from his saddlebag a stoppered jug, two wooden cups and a canvas sack of food.

Barley went to the stream and lapped the cold water thirstily. Ralph sat on the bank, resting his back against a tree. Alan sat beside him and handed him a cup of ale and a wedge of cheese. Ralph took the drink and refused the food.

Alan knew his boss in a bad mood, and said nothing while Ralph drank, wordlessly refilling Ralph's cup from the jug. In the silence they both heard female voices. Alan looked at Ralph with a raised eyebrow. Barley growled. Ralph stood up, shushing the dog, and walked softly in the direction of the sound. Alan followed.

A few yards downstream Ralph stopped, looking through the vegetation. A small group of village women were doing laundry on the near bank of the stream, where the water flowed fast over an outcrop of rocks. It was a damp October day, cool but not cold, and they wore their sleeves rolled up and the skirts of their shifts raised to thigh level to keep them dry.

Ralph studied them one by one. There was Gwenda, all muscular forearms and calves, with her baby – now four months old – strapped to her back. He identified Peg, the wife of Perkin, scrubbing her husband's underdrawers with a stone. His own housemaid, Vira, was there, a hard-faced woman of about thirty who had looked so stonily at him when he patted her arse that he never touched her again. The voice that he had heard belonged to the widow Huberts, a great talker, no doubt because she lived alone. The widow was standing in midstream, calling out to the others, carrying on a gossipy conversation at a distance.

And there was Annet.

She stood on a rock, washing some small garment, bending to dip it in the stream then standing upright to scrub it. She had long, white legs that disappeared enchantingly into her rucked-up dress. Every time she bent over, her neckline fell open to reveal the pale fruit of her small breasts hanging like temptation on a tree. Her fair hair was wet at the ends, and there was a petulant look on her pretty face, as if she felt she had not been born for this kind of work.

They had been there for some time, Ralph guessed, and their presence might have remained unknown to him, had not Widow Huberts raised her voice to call out. He lowered himself to the ground and knelt behind a bush, peering through the leafless twigs. Alan squatted beside him.

Ralph liked spying on women. He had often done it as an adolescent. They scratched themselves, sprawled on the ground with their legs apart, and talked about things they would never speak of if they knew a man was listening. In fact they acted like men.

He feasted his eyes on the unsuspecting women of his village, and strained to hear what they were saying. He watched Gwenda, looking at her small, strong body, remembering her naked, kneeling on the bed, and reliving how it had felt to hold her hips and pull her to him. He recalled how her attitude had changed. At first she had been coldly passive, struggling to conceal her resentment and distaste for the act she was performing; then he had seen a slow alteration. The skin on her neck had flushed, her chest had betrayed her excited breathing, and she had bent her head and closed her eyes in what seemed to him to be a mixture of shame and pleasure. The memory made him breathe faster and brought out a film of perspiration on his brow, despite the chill October air. He wondered if he would get another chance to lie with Gwenda.

Too soon, the women prepared to depart. They folded the damp washing and packed it into baskets, or wrapped it in bundles to be balanced on their heads, and then began to move away along the pathway beside the stream. Then an argument began between Annet and her mother. Annet had done only half the laundry she had brought. She was proposing to take the dirty half home, and it seemed Peg thought she should stay and finish it. In the end Peg stomped off and Annet stayed, looking sulky.

Ralph could hardly believe his luck.

In a low voice he said to Alan: 'We'll have some fun with her. Sneak around and cut off her retreat.'

Alan disappeared.

Ralph watched as Annet dipped the remaining laundry perfunctorily in the stream, then sat on the bank staring at the water grumpily. When he judged that the other women were out of earshot and Alan must be in place, he stood up and walked forward.

She heard him pushing through the undergrowth and looked up, startled. He enjoyed seeing the expression on her face change from surprise and curiosity to fear as she realized she was alone with him in the forest. She leaped to her feet, but by that time he was next to her, holding her arm in a light but firm grip. 'Hello, Annet,' he said. 'What are you doing here ... all alone?'

She looked over his shoulder – hoping, he guessed, that he might be accompanied by others who would restrain him, and her face registered dismay when she saw only Barley. 'I'm going home,' she said. 'My mother's just left.'

'Don't rush,' he said. 'You look so attractive like this, with your hair damp and your knees bare.'

She tried hastily to push the skirt of her dress down. With

his free hand, he held the point of her chin and made her look at him. 'How about a smile?' he said. 'Don't look so worried. I wouldn't harm you – I'm your lord.'

She attempted a smile. 'I'm just a bit flustered,' she said. 'You startled me.' She mustered a trace of her habitual coquetry. 'Perhaps you would escort me home,' she said with a simper. 'A girl needs protection in the forest.'

'Oh, I'll protect you. I'll look after you much better than that fool Wulfric, or your husband.' He took his hand from her chin and grasped her breast. It was as he remembered, small and firm. He released her arm so that he could use both hands, one on each breast.

But as soon as he let go of her, she fled. He laughed as she ran along the path and into the trees. A moment later he heard her give a cry of shock. He stayed where he was, and Alan brought her to him, her arm twisted behind her back so that her chest stuck out invitingly.

Ralph drew his knife, a sharp dagger with a blade a foot long. 'Take off your dress,' he said.

Alan let her go, but she did not immediately comply. 'Please, lord,' she said. 'I've always shown you respect—'

'Take off your dress, or I'll cut your cheeks and scar you for ever.'

It was a well-chosen threat for a vain woman, and she gave in immediately. She began to cry as she lifted the plain brown wool shift over her head. At first she held the crumpled garment in front of her, covering her nakedness, but Alan snatched it from her and threw it aside.

Ralph stared at her naked body. She stood with her eyes down, tears on her face. She had slim hips with a prominent bush of dark-blonde hair. 'Wulfric never saw you like this, did he?' Ralph said.

She shook her head in negation without raising her eyes.

He thrust his hand between her legs. 'Did he ever touch you here?'

She said: 'Please, lord, I'm a married woman—'

'All the better – you've no virginity to lose, nothing to worry about. Lie down.'

She tried to back away from him, and bumped into Alan, who expertly tripped her, so that she fell on her back. Ralph grabbed her ankles, so that she could not get up, but she wriggled desperately. 'Hold her down,' Ralph said to Alan.

Alan forced her head down then put his knees on her upper arms and his hands on her shoulders.

Ralph got his cock out and rubbed it to make it harder. Then he knelt between Annet's thighs.

She began to scream, but no one heard her.

35

FORTUNATELY, GWENDA WAS one of the first people to see Annet after the incident.

Gwenda and Peg brought home the laundry and hung it to dry around the fire in the kitchen of Perkin's house. Gwenda was still working as a labourer for Perkin but now, in autumn, when there was less to do in the fields, she helped Peg with her domestic chores. When they had dealt with the laundry they began to prepare the midday meal for Perkin, Rob, Billy Howard and Wulfric. After an hour Peg said: 'What can have happened to Annet?'

'I'll go and see.' Gwenda first checked on her baby. Sammy was lying in a basketwork crib, wrapped in an old bit of brown blanket, his alert dark eyes watching the smoke from the fire gathering in curls under the ceiling. Gwenda kissed his forehead then went to look for Annet.

She retraced her steps across the windy fields. Lord Ralph and Alan Fernhill galloped past her, heading up to the village, their day's hunting apparently cut short. Gwenda entered the forest and followed the short path that led to the spot where the woman did laundry. Before she got there she met Annet coming the other way.

'Are you all right?' Gwenda said. 'Your mother is worried.'

'I'm fine,' Annet replied.

Gwenda could tell something was wrong. 'What has happened?'

'Nothing.' Annet would not meet her eye. 'Nothing happened, leave me alone.'

Gwenda stood squarely in front of Annet and looked her up and down. Her face told Gwenda unmistakably that there had been some calamity. At first glance she did not appear to be physically hurt – though most of her body was covered by the long wool shift – but then Gwenda saw dark smears on her dress that looked like bloodstains.

Gwenda recalled Ralph and Alan galloping past. 'Did Lord Ralph do something to you?'

'I'm going home.' Annet tried to push past Gwenda. Gwenda grabbed her arm to stop her. She did not squeeze hard, but nevertheless Annet cried out in pain, her hand flying to her upper arm.

'You're hurt!' Gwenda exclaimed.

Annet burst into tears.

Gwenda put her arm around Annet's shoulders. 'Come home,' she said. 'Tell your mother about it.'

Annet shook her head. 'I'm not telling anyone,' she said.

Too late for that, Gwenda thought.

Walking Annet back to Perkin's house, Gwenda ran over the possibilities in her mind. Clearly Annet had suffered some kind of assault. She might have been attacked by one or more travellers, though there was no road nearby. Outlaws were always a possibility, but it was a long time since any had been seen near Wigleigh. No, the likeliest suspects were Ralph and Alan.

Peg was brisk. She sat Annet down on a stool and pulled her dress down over her shoulders. Both upper arms showed swollen red bruises. 'Someone held you down,' Peg said angrily.

Annet made no reply.

Peg persisted. 'Am I right? Answer me, child, or you'll be in worse trouble. Did someone hold you down?'

Annet nodded.

'How many men? Come on, out with it.'

Annet did not speak, but held up two fingers.'

Peg reddened with fury. 'Did they fuck you?'

Annet nodded.

'Who were they?'

Annet shook her head.

Gwenda knew why she did not want to say. It was dangerous for a serf to accuse a lord of a crime. She said to Peg: 'I saw Ralph and Alan riding away.'

Peg said to Annet: 'Was it them – Ralph and Alan?'

Annet nodded.

Peg's voice fell almost to a whisper. 'I suppose Alan held you down while Ralph did it.'

Annet nodded again.

Peg softened, now that she had got the truth. She put her arms around her daughter and hugged her. 'You poor child,' she said. 'My poor baby.'

Annet began to sob.

Gwenda left the house.

The men would be home soon for their midday dinner, and they would quickly find out that Ralph had raped Annet. Annet's father, her brother, her husband and her former lover would be mad with rage. Perkin was too old to do anything foolish, Rob would do what Perkin told him and Billy Howard probably was not brave enough to make trouble – but Wulfric would be incandescent. He would kill Ralph.

And then he would be hanged.

Gwenda had to turn the course of events, otherwise she would lose her husband. She hurried through the village, speaking to no one, and went to the manor house. There, she hoped to be told that Ralph and Alan had finished their dinner and gone out again; but it was a little too early and, to her dismay, they were still at home.

She found them in the stable behind the house, looking at a horse with an infected hoof. Normally she was uncomfortable in the presence of Ralph or Alan, for she felt sure that whenever they looked at her they remembered the sight of her kneeling naked on the bed at the Bell in Kingsbridge. But today the thought hardly entered her head. Somehow she had to make them leave the village – now, before Wulfric found out what they had done. What was she going to say?

For a moment she was struck dumb. Then in desperation she said: 'Lord, there was a messenger here from Earl Roland.'

Ralph was surprised. 'When was this?'

'An hour ago.'

Ralph looked at the groom who was holding the horse's foot up for inspection. The man said: 'No one came here.'

Naturally, a messenger would have come to the manor house

and spoken to the lord's servants. Ralph said to Gwenda: 'Why did he give this message to *you*?'

She improvised desperately. 'I met him on the road just outside the village. He asked for Lord Ralph, and I told him you were out hunting and you would be back for dinner – but he wouldn't stay.'

This was unusual behaviour for a messenger, who would normally stop to eat and drink and rest his horse. Ralph said: 'Why was he in such a hurry?'

Inventing excuses extempore, Gwenda said: 'He had to get to Cowford by sundown ... I didn't make so bold as to question him.'

Ralph grunted. The last part was plausible: a messenger from Earl Roland was not likely to subject himself to cross-examination by a peasant woman. 'Why didn't you tell me this earlier?'

'I came across the fields to meet you, but you didn't see me and galloped past.'

'Oh. I think I did see you. No matter – what's the message?'

'Earl Roland summons you to Earlscastle as soon as possible.' She took a breath and added another layer of implausibility. 'The messenger said to tell you not to wait to eat your dinner, but take fresh horses and leave at once.' It was barely credible, but she had to get Ralph away before Wulfric showed up.

'Really? Did he say why he needs me in such a terrible hurry?'

'No.'

'Hm.' Ralph looked thoughtful and said nothing for a few moments.

Gwenda said anxiously: 'So, will you go now?'

He glared at her. 'That's no concern of yours.'

'It's just that I wouldn't want it to be said that I hadn't made the urgency clear enough.'

'Oh, wouldn't you? Well, I don't care what you would or wouldn't want. Be off.'

Gwenda had to go.

She returned to Perkin's house. She arrived just as the men were coming in from the fields. Sam was quiet and happy in his crib. Annet was sitting in the same place, with her dress pulled down to show the bruises on her arms. Peg said accusingly: 'Where have you been?'

Gwenda did not answer, and Peg was distracted by Perkin coming in and saying: 'What's this? What's the matter with Annet?'

Peg said: 'She had the misfortune to meet Ralph and Alan when she was alone in the forest.'

Perkin's face darkened with anger. 'Why was she alone?'

'It's my fault,' Peg said, and she began to cry. 'Only she was so lazy about the laundry, as she always is, and I made her stay back and finish it, after the other women went home, and that's when those two animals must have come along.'

'We saw them a while ago, riding across Brookfield,' Perkin said. 'They must have just come from the place.' He looked frightened. 'This is very dangerous,' he said. 'It's the kind of thing that can ruin a family.'

'But *we've* done nothing wrong!' Peg protested.

'Ralph's guilt will make him hate us for our innocence.'

That was probably true, Gwenda realized. Perkin was shrewd, beneath his obsequious manner.

Annet's husband, Billy Howard, came in, wiping his muddy hands on his shirt. Her brother, Rob, was close behind. Billy looked at his wife's bruises and said: 'What happened to you?'

Peg answered for her. 'It was Ralph and Alan.'

Billy stared at his wife. 'What did they do to you?'

Annet lowered her eyes and said nothing.

'I'll kill them both,' Billy said furiously, but it was obviously an idle threat: Billy was a mild-mannered man, slim built, and had never been known to fight, even when drunk.

Wulfric was the last to come through the door. Too late, Gwenda realized how attractive Annet was looking. She had a long neck and pretty shoulders, and the tops of her breasts were showing. The ugly bruises only emphasized her other charms. Wulfric stared at her with undisguised admiration – he never could hide his feelings. Then, after a moment, he registered the angry bruises, and he frowned.

Billy said: 'Did they rape you?'

Gwenda was watching Wulfric. As he grasped the significance of the scene, his expression registered shock and dismay, and his fair skin flushed with emotion.

Billy said: 'Did they, woman?'

Gwenda felt a surge of compassion for the unlovable Annet. Why did everyone feel they had the right to ask her bullying questions?

At last, Annet answered Billy's question with a silent nod.

Wulfric's face was suffused with black rage. 'Who?' he growled.

Billy said: 'This is none of your business, Wulfric. Go home.'

Perkin said tremulously: 'I don't want trouble. We mustn't let this destroy us.'

Billy looked angrily at his father-in-law. 'What are you saying? That we should do nothing?'

'If we make an enemy of Lord Ralph, we could suffer for the rest of our lives.'

'But he's raped Annet!'

Wulfric said incredulously: 'Ralph did this?'

Perkin said: 'God will punish him.'

'So will I, by Christ,' said Wulfric.

Gwenda said: 'Please, Wulfric, no!'

Wulfric made for the door.

Gwenda went to him, frantic with fright, and grabbed his arm. Only a few minutes had gone by since she had given Ralph the fake message. Even if he believed it, she did not know how seriously he would take the urgency. There was a good chance he had not left the village yet. 'Don't go to the manor house,' she pleaded with Wulfric. 'Please.'

He shook her off roughly. 'Get away from me,' he said.

'Look at your baby!' she cried, pointing at Sammy in the crib. 'Are you going to leave him without a father?'

Wulfric went out.

Gwenda followed, and the other men came after. Wulfric marched through the village like the angel of death, fists clenched at his sides, staring straight ahead, his face twisted into a rictus of fury. Other villagers, on their way home for the midday meal, spoke to him but got no reply. Some followed him. In the few minutes it took to walk to the manor house he gathered a small crowd. Nathan Reeve came out of his house and asked Gwenda what was happening, but all she could say was: 'Stop him, someone, please!' It was useless: none of them could have restrained Wulfric even if they had dared to try.

He threw open the front door of the manor house and marched in. Gwenda was right behind him, and the crowd pushed through after them. The housekeeper, Vira, said indignantly: 'You're supposed to knock!'

'Where is your master?' said Wulfric.

Vira saw the expression on Wulfric's face and looked scared. 'He went to the stable,' she said. 'He's about to leave for Earlscastle.'

Wulfric pushed past her and went through the kitchen. As he and Gwenda stepped out of the back door, they saw Ralph and Alan mounting up. Gwenda could have screamed – they were just seconds too early!

Wulfric jumped forward. With desperate inspiration, Gwenda stuck out her foot and hooked it around Wulfric's ankle.

Wulfric fell flat on his face in the mud.

Ralph did not see either of them. He kicked his horse and it trotted out of the yard. Alan saw them, read the situation, decided to avoid trouble and followed Ralph. As they left the yard Alan urged his horse into a canter, passing Ralph, whereupon Ralph's horse eagerly increased its pace.

Wulfric leaped to his feet, cursing, and chased them. Gwenda ran after him. Wulfric could not catch the horses, but Gwenda was terrified that Ralph would look behind and rein in to see what the fuss was about.

But the two men were enjoying the lively energy of fresh horses, and without a backward glance they raced away along the track that led out of the village. In seconds they disappeared.

Wulfric slumped on his knees in the mud.

Gwenda caught up with him and took his arm to help him to his feet. He pushed her aside so forcefully that she staggered and almost fell. She was shocked: it was completely out of character for him to be rough with her.

'You tripped me up,' he said as he got to his feet unaided.

'I saved your life,' she said.

He stared at her with hatred in his eyes and said: 'I will never forgive you.'

*

WHEN RALPH REACHED Earlscastle he was told that Roland had not sent for him at all, never mind urgently. The rooks on the battlements laughed mockingly at him.

Alan conjectured an explanation. 'It's to do with Annet,' he said. 'Just as we left, I saw Wulfric coming out of the back door of the manor house. I thought nothing of it at the time, but maybe he was intending to confront you.'

'I'll bet he was,' Ralph said. He touched the long dagger at his belt. 'You should have told me – I'd welcome an excuse to stick my knife in his belly.'

'And no doubt Gwenda knows that, so perhaps she invented the message to get you away from her murderous husband.'

'Of course,' said Ralph. 'That would explain why no one else saw this messenger – he never existed. Crafty bitch.'

She should be punished, but it might be difficult. She would probably say she did it for the best, and Ralph could hardly argue that she had been wrong to prevent her husband attacking the lord of the manor. Worse, if he made a fuss about her deception he would call attention to the fact that she had outwitted him. No, there would be no formal penalty – though he might find unofficial ways to chastise her.

As he was at Earlscastle, he took the opportunity to go hunting with the earl and his entourage, and he forgot about Annet – until the end of the second day, when Roland called him into his private chamber. Only the earl's clerk, Father Jerome, was with him. Roland did not ask Ralph to sit down. 'The priest of Wigleigh is here,' he said.

Ralph was surprised. 'Father Gaspard? At Earlscastle?'

Roland did not bother to answer these rhetorical questions. 'He complains that you raped a woman called Annet, the wife of Billy Howard, one of your serfs.'

Ralph's heart missed a beat. He had not imagined the peasants would have the nerve to complain to the earl. It was very difficult for a serf to accuse a lord in a court of law. But they could be sly, and someone in Wigleigh had cleverly persuaded the priest to make the complaint.

Ralph put on an expression of carelessness. 'Rubbish,' he said. 'All right, I lay with her, but she was willing.' He gave Roland a man-to-man grin. 'More than willing.'

An expression of distaste came over Roland's face, and he turned to Father Jerome with an inquiring look.

Jerome was an educated, ambitious young man, a type Ralph particularly disliked. He had a snooty look as he said: 'The girl is here. Woman, I should say, though she is only nineteen. She has massive bruises on her arms and a bloodstained dress. She says you encountered her in the forest, and your squire knelt on her to hold her down. And a man called Wulfric is here to say that you were seen riding away from the scene.'

Ralph guessed it was Wulfric who had persuaded Father Gaspard to come here to Earlscastle. 'It's not true,' he said, trying to put a note of indignation into his voice.

Jerome looked sceptical. 'Why would she lie?'

'Maybe someone saw us and told her husband. He gave her the bruises, I expect. She cried rape to stop him beating her. Then she stained her dress with chicken blood.'

Roland sighed. 'It's a bit oafish, isn't it, Ralph?'

Ralph was not sure what he meant. Did he expect his men to behave like damned monks?

Roland went on: 'I was warned you'd be like this. My daughter-in-law always said you'd give me problems.'

'Philippa?'

'Lady Philippa, to you.'

Enlightenment dawned on Ralph, and he said incredulously: 'Is that why you didn't promote me after I saved your life – because a *woman* was against me? What sort of an army will you have if you let girls pick your men?'

'You're right, of course, and that's why I went against her judgement in the end. What women never realize is that a man without some bile in him is good for nothing but tilling the land. We can't take milksops into battle. But she was right when she warned me that you would cause trouble. I don't want to be bothered, in peacetime, with damned priests whining about serfs' wives being raped. Don't do it again. I don't care if you lie with the peasant women. If it comes to that, I don't care if you lie with the men. But if you take a man's wife, willing or otherwise, be prepared to compensate the husband in some way. Most peasants can be bought. Just don't let it become my problem.'

'Yes, lord.'

Jerome said: 'What am I to do with this Gaspard?'

'Let me see,' Roland said thoughtfully. 'Wigleigh is on the edge of my territory, not far from my son William's landholding, is it not?'

'Yes,' Ralph said.

'How far were you from the border when you met this girl?'

'A mile. We were only just outside Wigleigh.'

'No matter.' He turned to Jerome. 'Everyone will know this is just an excuse, but tell Father Gaspard that the incident took place in Lord William's territory, so I can't adjudicate.'

'Very good, my lord.'

Ralph said: 'What if they go to William?'

'I doubt that they will. But, if they persist, you'll have to come to some arrangement with William. The peasants will tire of complaining eventually.'

Ralph nodded, relieved. For a moment, he had suffered the dread thought that he had made a terrible error of judgement, and that after all he might be made to pay the price for raping Annet. But, in the end, he had got away with it, as he had expected to.

'Thank you, my lord,' he said.

He wondered what his brother would say about this. The thought filled him with shame. But perhaps Merthin would never find out.

*

'WE MUST COMPLAIN to Lord William,' said Wulfric when they got back to Wigleigh.

The entire village had gathered in the church to discuss the matter. Father Gaspard and Nathan Reeve were there but, somehow, Wulfric seemed to be the leader, despite his youth. He had gone to the front, leaving Gwenda and baby Sammy in the crowd.

Gwenda was praying that they would decide to drop the matter. It was not that she wanted Ralph to go unpunished – on the contrary, she would have liked to see him boiled alive. She herself had killed two men for merely threatening her with rape, something she remembered, every now and again during the discussion, with a shudder. But she did not like Wulfric taking the leading role. It was partly because he was driven by the unquenched flame of his feeling for Annet, which hurt and saddened Gwenda. But, more importantly, she feared for him. The enmity between him and Ralph had already cost Wulfric his inheritance. What other vengeance would Ralph take?

Perkin said: 'I'm the father of the victim, and I don't want any more trouble over this. It's very dangerous to complain of the actions of a lord. He always finds a way to punish the complainers, right or wrong. Let's drop it.'

'Too late for that,' said Wulfric. 'We've already complained, or at least our priest has. There's nothing to be gained by backing down now.'

'We've gone far enough,' Perkin argued. 'Ralph has been embarrassed in front of his earl. He knows now that he can't do just whatever he pleases.'

'On the contrary,' said Wulfric. 'He thinks he's got away with it. I'm afraid he'll do it again. No woman in the village will be safe.'

Gwenda herself had said to Wulfric all the things Perkin was saying. Wulfric had not answered her. He had hardly spoken to her since she tripped him up at the back door of the manor house. At first, she had told herself that he was merely sulking because he had felt foolish. She had expected him to have forgotten about it by the time he returned from Earlscastle. But she had been wrong. He had not touched her, in bed or out of it, for a week; he rarely met her eye; and he talked to her in monosyllables and grunts. It was beginning to depress her.

Nathan Reeve said: 'You'll never win against Ralph. Serfs never overcome lords.'

'I'm not so sure,' Wulfric said. 'Everyone has enemies. We

might not be the only people who would like to see Ralph reined in. Perhaps we will never see him convicted in court – but we must inflict the maximum of trouble and embarrassment on him if we want him to hesitate before doing this sort of thing again.'

Several villagers nodded agreement, but no one spoke in support of Wulfric, and Gwenda began to hope that he would lose the argument. However, her husband was nothing if not determined, and he now turned to the priest. 'What do you think, Father Gaspard?'

Gaspard was young, poor and earnest. He had no fear of the nobility. He was not ambitious – he did not want to become a bishop and join the ruling class – so he felt no need to please aristocrats. He said: 'Annet has been cruelly violated, the peace of our village has been criminally broken, and Lord Ralph has committed a wicked, vile sin which he must confess and repent. For the sake of the victim, for our own self-respect, and to save Lord Ralph from the flames of hell, we must go to Lord William.'

There was a rumble of assent.

Wulfric looked at Billy Howard and Annet, sitting side by side. In the end, Gwenda thought, people would probably do what Annet and Billy wanted. 'I don't want trouble,' Billy said. 'But we should finish what we've started, for the sake of all the women in the village.'

Annet did not raise her eyes from the floor, but she nodded assent, and Gwenda realized with dismay that Wulfric had won.

'Well, you got what you wanted,' she said to him as they left the church.

He grunted.

She persisted: 'So, I suppose you will continue to risk your life for the honour of Billy Howard's wife, while refusing to speak to your own wife.'

He said nothing. Sammy sensed the hostility and began to cry.

Gwenda felt desperate. She had moved heaven and earth to get the man she loved, she had married him and had his baby, and now he was treating her like an enemy. Her father had never behaved this way to her mother – not that Joby's behaviour was a model for anyone. But she had no idea how to deal with him.

She had tried using Sammy, holding him in one arm while touching Wulfric with the other hand, in an attempt to win back his affection by associating herself with the baby boy he loved; but he just moved away, rejecting them both. She had even tried sex, pressing her breasts against his back at night, brushing her hand across his belly, touching his penis, but it did not work – as she might have known, remembering how resistant he had been last summer, before Annet married Billy.

Now, in frustration, she cried out: 'What is wrong with you? I only tried to save your life!'

'You should not have done it,' he said.

'If I'd let you kill Ralph, you'd have been hanged!'

'You had no right.'

'What does it matter if I had the right or not?'

'That's your father's philosophy, isn't it?'

She was startled. 'What do you mean?'

'Your father believes it doesn't matter whether or not he has the right to do something. If it's for the best, he does it. Like selling you to feed his family.'

'They sold me to be raped! I tripped you up to save you from the gallows. That's completely different.'

'As long as you go on telling yourself that, you'll never understand him or me.'

She realized she was not going to win back his affection by trying to prove him wrong. 'Well ... I don't understand, then.'

'You took away my power to make my own decisions. You treated me the way your father treated you, as a thing to be controlled, not as a person. It doesn't matter whether I was right or wrong. What matters is that it was up to me to decide, not you. But you can't see that, just as your father can't see what he took away from you when he sold you.'

She still thought the two things were completely different, but she did not argue the point, because she was beginning to see what had made him angry. He was passionate about his independence – something she could empathize with, for she felt the same way. And she had robbed him of that. She said falteringly: 'I ... I think I understand.'

'Do you?'

'At any rate, I'll try not to do anything of that kind again.'

'Good.'

She only half believed she had been wrong, but she was desperate to end the war between them, so she said: 'I'm very sorry.'

'All right.'

He wasn't saying much, but she sensed he might be softening. 'You know that I don't want you to complain to Lord William about Ralph — but, if you're determined to, I won't try to stop you.'

'I'm glad.'

'In fact,' she said, 'I might be able to help you.'

'Oh?' he said. 'How?'

36

THE HOME OF LORD WILLIAM and Lady Philippa, at Casterham, had once been a castle. There was still a round stone keep with battlements, though it was in ruins and used as a cowshed. The wall around the courtyard was intact, but the moat had dried up, and the ground in the slight remaining dip was used to grow vegetables and fruit trees. Where once there had been a drawbridge, a simple ramp now led up to the gatehouse.

Gwenda, carrying Sammy, passed under the arch of the gatehouse with Father Gaspard, Billy Howard, Annet and Wulfric. A young man-at-arms was lolling on a bench, presumably on guard, but he saw the priest's robe and did not challenge them. The relaxed atmosphere encouraged Gwenda. She was hoping to get a private audience with Lady Philippa.

They entered the house by the main door and found themselves in a traditional great hall, with high windows like those of a church. It seemed to take up about half the total space of the house. The rest, presumably, would be personal chambers, in the modern fashion, which emphasized the privacy of the noble family and played down military defences.

A middle-aged man in a leather tunic was sitting at a table counting notches on a tally stick. He glanced up at them, finished his count, made a note on a slate, then said: 'Good day to you, strangers.'

'Good day, Master Bailiff,' said Gaspard, deducing the man's occupation. 'We've come to see Lord William.'

'He's expected back by suppertime, father,' the bailiff said politely. 'What's your business with him, may I ask?'

Gaspard began to explain, and Gwenda slipped back outside.

She went around the house to the domestic end. There was a wooden extension that she guessed was the kitchen. A maid sat on a stool by the kitchen door with a sack of cabbages, washing the mud off in a big bowl of water. The maid was young, and looked fondly at the baby. 'How old is he?' she said.

'Four months, nearly five. His name is Samuel. We call him Sammy, or Sam.'

The baby smiled at the girl, and she said: 'Ah.'

Gwenda said: 'I'm just an ordinary woman, like you, but I need to speak to the Lady Philippa.'

The girl frowned and looked troubled. 'I'm only the kitchen maid,' she said.

'But you must see her sometimes. You could speak to her for me.'

She glanced behind her, as if worried about being overheard. 'I don't like to.'

Gwenda realized this might be more difficult than she had anticipated. 'Couldn't you just give her a message for me?' she said.

The maid shook her head.

Then a voice came from inside: 'Who wants to send me a message?'

Gwenda tensed, wondering if she was in trouble. She looked towards the kitchen door.

A moment later, Lady Philippa stepped out.

She was not quite beautiful, and certainly not pretty, but she was good-looking. She had a straight nose and a strong jaw, and her green eyes were large and clear. She was not smiling, in fact she wore a slight frown, but nevertheless there was something friendly and understanding about her face.

Gwenda answered her question. 'I'm Gwenda from Wigleigh, my lady.'

'Wigleigh.' Philippa's frown deepened. 'And what do you have to say to me?'

'It's about Lord Ralph.'

'I was afraid it might be. Well, come inside and let's warm that baby by the kitchen fire.'

Many noble ladies would have refused to speak to someone as lowly as Gwenda, but she had guessed that Philippa had a big heart underneath that rather formidable exterior. She followed

Philippa inside. Sammy began to grizzle, and Gwenda gave him the breast.

'You can sit down,' Philippa said.

That was even more unusual. A serf would normally remain standing when talking to a lady. Philippa was being kind because of the baby, Gwenda guessed.

'All right, out with it,' Philippa said. 'What has Ralph done?'

'You may remember, lady, a fight at the Fleece Fair in Kingsbridge last year.'

'I certainly do. Ralph groped a peasant girl, and her handsome young fiancé broke his nose. The boy shouldn't have done it, of course, but Ralph is a brute.'

'Indeed he is. Last week he came across the same girl, Annet, in the woods. His squire held her down while Ralph raped her.'

'Oh, God save us.' Philippa looked distressed. 'Ralph is an animal, a pig, a wild boar. I knew he should never have been made a lord. I told my father-in-law not to promote him.'

'A pity the earl didn't follow your advice.'

'And I suppose the fiancé wants justice.'

Gwenda hesitated. She was not sure how much of the complicated story to tell. But she sensed it would be a mistake to hold anything back. 'Annet is married, lady, but to a different man.'

'So what lucky girl got Mr Handsome?'

'As it happens, Wulfric married me.'

'Congratulations.'

'Though Wulfric is here, with Annet's husband, to bear witness.'

Philippa gave Gwenda a sharp look, and seemed about to comment, then changed her mind. 'So why have you come here? Wigleigh is not in my husband's territory.'

'The incident happened in the forest, and the earl says it was on Lord William's land, so he can't adjudicate.'

'That's an excuse. Roland adjudicates anything he likes. He just doesn't want to punish a man he's recently elevated.'

'Anyway, our village priest is here to tell Lord William what happened.'

'And what do you want me to do?'

515

'You're a woman, you understand. You know how men make excuses for rape. They say the girl must have been flirting, or doing something provocative.'

'Yes.'

'If Ralph gets away with this, he might do it again – perhaps to me.'

'Or me,' said Philippa. 'You should see the way he stares at me – like a dog looking at a goose on the pond.'

That was encouraging. 'Perhaps you can make Lord William understand how important it is that Ralph should not get away with this.'

Philippa nodded. 'I think I can.'

Sammy had stopped sucking and gone to sleep. Gwenda stood up. 'Thank you, lady.'

'I'm glad you came to me,' said Philippa.

*

LORD WILLIAM SUMMONED them the next morning. They met with him in the great hall. Gwenda was glad to see Lady Philippa sitting beside him. She gave Gwenda a friendly look, and Gwenda hoped that meant she had spoken to her husband.

William was tall and black-haired, like his father the earl, but he was going bald, and the dome above the dark beard and eyebrows suggested a more thoughtful kind of authority, matching his reputation. He examined the bloodstained dress and looked at Annet's bruises, which were blue now, rather than the original angry red. All the same, they brought a look of fury to Lady Philippa's face. Gwenda guessed it was not so much the severity of the injuries as the grim picture they conjured up of a brawny squire kneeling on a girl's arms to hold her down while another man raped her.

'Well, you've done everything correctly so far,' William said to Annet. 'You went immediately to the nearest village, you showed your injuries to men of good reputation there, and you named your attacker. Now you have to offer a bill to a justice of the peace in the Shiring County Court.'

She looked anxious. 'What does that mean?'

'A bill is an accusation, written in Latin.'

'I can't write English, lord, let alone Latin.'

'Father Gaspard can do it for you. The justice will put the bill before an indicting jury, and you will tell them what happened. Can you do that? They may ask for embarrassing details.'

Annet nodded determinedly.

'If they believe you, they will order the sheriff to summon Lord Ralph to the court a month later to be tried. Then you will need two sureties, people who will pledge a sum of money to guarantee that you will appear at the trial.'

'But who will be my sureties?'

'Father Gaspard can be one, and I will be the other. I'll put up the money.'

'Thank you, lord!'

'Thank my wife, who has persuaded me that I can't allow the king's peace to be breached on my territory by an act of rape.'

Annet shot a grateful look at Philippa.

Gwenda looked at Wulfric. She had told her husband about her conversation with the lord's wife. Now he met her eye and gave an almost imperceptible nod of acknowledgement. He knew she had made this happen.

William went on: 'At the trial, you will tell your story again. Your friends will all have to be witnesses: Gwenda will say she saw you coming from the forest in your bloodstained dress, Father Gaspard will say you told him what happened, Wulfric will say he saw Ralph and Alan riding away from the scene.'

They all nodded solemnly.

'One more thing. Having started something like this, you can't stop it. Withdrawing an appeal is an offence, and you would be severely punished – to say nothing of what revenge Ralph might take on you.'

Annet said: 'I won't change my mind. But what will happen to Ralph? How will he be punished?'

'Oh, there's only one penalty for rape,' said Lord William. 'He'll be hanged.'

*

THEY ALL SLEPT in the great hall of the castle, with William's servants and squires and dogs, wrapping their cloaks around them and nestling into the carpet of rushes on the floor. As the light from the embers in the huge fireplace dimmed to a glow, Gwenda hesitantly reached for her husband, putting a tentative hand on his arm, stroking the wool of his cloak. They had not made love since the rape, and she was unsure whether he wanted her or not. She had angered him grievously by tripping him up: would he feel that her intervention with Lady Philippa made up for that?

He responded immediately, drawing her to him and kissing her lips. She relaxed gratefully into his arms. They toyed with each other for a while. Gwenda was so happy she wanted to weep.

She waited for him to roll on top of her, but he did not do so. She could tell he wanted to, for he was being very affectionate, and his penis was hard in her hand; but perhaps he hesitated to do it in the company of so many others. People did have sex in halls like this, of course; it was normal, and no one took any notice. But perhaps Wulfric felt shy.

However, Gwenda was determined to seal the repair of their love, and after a while she climbed on to him, drawing her cloak over them both. As they began to move together, she saw an adolescent boy watching them, wide-eyed, a few yards away. Adults would politely look the other way, of course, but he was at the age where sex was a captivating mystery, and he obviously could not tear his gaze away. Gwenda was feeling so happy that she hardly cared. She met his eye, then smiled at him, without ceasing to move. His mouth fell open in shock, and he was struck by agonizing embarrassment. Looking mortified, he rolled over and covered his eyes with his arm.

Gwenda pulled her cloak up over her head and Wulfric's, buried her face in his neck and gave herself up to pleasure.

37

CARIS FELT CONFIDENT the second time she went to the royal court. The vast interior of Westminster Hall no longer intimidated her, nor did the mass of wealthy and powerful people crowding around the judges' benches. She had been here before, she knew the ropes; everything that had seemed so strange a year ago was now familiar. She even had a dress in the London fashion, green on the right side and blue on the left. She enjoyed studying those around her and reading their lives in their faces: cocksure or desperate, bewildered or sly. She could spot people who were new to the capital by their wide-eyed gaze and their air of uncertainty, and she felt pleasantly knowledgeable and superior.

If she had any misgivings they centred on her lawyer, Francis Bookman. He was young and well informed and – like most lawyers, she thought – he seemed very sure of himself. A small man with sandy hair, quick in his movements and always ready for an argument, he made her think of a cheeky bird on a window ledge, pecking crumbs and aggressively chasing away rivals. He had told them that their case was incontrovertible.

Godwyn had Gregory Longfellow, of course. Gregory had won the case against Earl Roland, and Godwyn had naturally asked him to represent the priory again. He had proved his ability, whereas Bookman was an unknown. However, Caris had a weapon up her sleeve, something that would come as a shock to Godwyn.

Godwyn showed no awareness that he had betrayed Caris, her father and the entire city of Kingsbridge. He had always presented himself as a reformer, impatient of stick-in-the-mud Prior Anthony, sympathetic with the needs of the town, eager for the prosperity of monks and merchants alike. Then, within a year of becoming prior, he had turned to face the opposite way, and become even more of a traditionalist than Anthony. Yet he appeared to feel no shame. Caris flushed with anger every time she thought of it.

He had no right to force the townspeople to use the fulling mill. His other impositions – the ban on hand mills, the fines for private fishponds and warrens – were technically correct, albeit outrageously harsh. But the fulling mill should be free, and Godwyn knew it. Caris wondered whether he believed that any deceit was pardonable provided it was done for the sake of God's work. Surely men of God should be *more* scrupulous about honesty than laymen, not less?

She put the point to her father, as they hung around the court, waiting for their case to come up. He said: 'I never trust anyone who proclaims his morality from the pulpit. That high-minded type can always find an excuse for breaking his own rules. I'd rather do business with an everyday sinner who thinks it's probably to his advantage, in the long run, to tell the truth and keep his promises. He's not likely to change his mind about that.'

In moments such as that, when Papa was his old self, Caris realized how much he had changed. Nowadays he was not often shrewd and quick-witted. More usually, he was forgetful and distracted. Caris suspected the decline had begun some months before she had noticed, and it probably accounted for his disastrous failure to anticipate the collapse of the wool market.

After several days' wait, they were called before Sir Wilbert Wheatfield, the pink-faced judge with rotten teeth who had ruled for the priory against Earl Roland a year ago. Caris's confidence began to ebb away as the judge took his seat on the bench against the east wall. It was frightening that a mere mortal should have such power. If he made the wrong decision, Caris's new cloth-manufacturing enterprise would be blighted, her father would be ruined, and no one would be able to pay for the new bridge.

Then, as her lawyer began to speak, she started to feel better. Francis commenced with the history of the fulling mill, saying how it had been invented by the legendary Jack Builder, who built the first one, and how Prior Philip had given the townspeople the right to use it free.

He then dealt with Godwyn's counter-arguments, disarming the prior in advance. 'It is true that the mill is in bad repair, slow, and prone to frequent breakdowns,' he said. 'But how can the prior argue that the people have lost the right to it? The mill is the priory's property, and it is for the priory to keep it in good repair. The fact that he has failed in this duty makes no difference. The people have no right to repair the mill, and they certainly have no obligation so to do. Prior Philip's grant was not conditional.'

At this point, Francis produced his secret weapon. 'In case the prior should attempt to claim that the grant *was* conditional, I invite the court to read this copy of Prior Philip's will.'

Godwyn was astonished. He had tried to pretend that the will had been lost. But Thomas Langley had agreed to look for it, as a favour to Merthin, and he had sneaked it out of the library for a day: time enough for Edmund to have it copied.

Caris could not help enjoying the look of shock and outrage on Godwyn's face when he found that his deception had been foiled. He stepped forward and said indignantly: 'How was this obtained?'

The question was revealing. He did not ask: 'Where was it found?' – which would have been the logical inquiry if it had really been lost.

Gregory Longfellow looked annoyed, and waved at him with a hushing gesture; and Godwyn closed his mouth and stepped back, realizing he had given himself away – but it was surely too late, Caris thought. The judge must see that the only reason for Godwyn to be angry was that he knew the document favoured the townspeople, and had attempted to suppress it.

Francis wound up quickly after that – a good decision, Caris thought, for Godwyn's duplicity would be fresh in the judge's mind while Gregory made the case for the defence.

But Gregory's approach took them all completely by surprise.

He stepped forward and said to the judge: 'Sir, Kingsbridge is not a chartered borough.' He stopped there, as if that was all he had to say.

It was true, technically. Most towns had a royal charter giving them the freedom to trade and hold markets without obligations to the local earl or baron. Their citizens were free men, owing allegiance to no one but the king. However, a few towns such as Kingsbridge remained the property of an overlord, usually a bishop or a prior: St Albans and Bury St Edmunds were examples. Their status was less clear.

The judge said: 'That makes a difference. Only free men can appeal to the royal court. What do you have to say to that, Francis Bookman? Are your clients serfs?'

Francis turned to Edmund. In a low, urgent voice he said: 'Have the townspeople appealed to the royal court before?'

'No. The prior has—'

'But not the parish guild? Even before your time?'

'There's no record of it—'

'So we can't argue from precedent. Damn.' Francis turned back to the judge. His face changed from worried to confident in a flash, and he spoke as if condescending to deal with something trivial. 'Sir, the townspeople are free. They enjoy burgess tenure.'

Gregory said quickly: 'There is no universal pattern of burgess tenure. It means different things in different places.'

The judge said: 'Is there a written statement of customs?'

Francis looked at Edmund, who shook his head. 'No prior would ever agree to such things being written down,' he muttered.

Francis turned back to the judge. 'There is no written statement, sir, but clearly—'

'Then this court must decide whether or not you are free men,' the judge said.

Edmund spoke directly to the judge. 'Sir, the citizens have the freedom to buy and sell their homes.' This was an important right not granted to serfs, who needed their lord's permission.

Gregory said: 'But you have feudal obligations. You must use the prior's mills and fishponds.'

Sir Wilbert said: 'Forget fishponds. The key factor is the citizens' relationship to the system of royal justice. Does the town freely admit the king's sheriff?'

Gregory answered that. 'No, he must ask permission to enter the town.'

Edmund said indignantly: 'That is the prior's decision, not ours!'

Sir Wilbert said: 'Very well. Do the citizens serve on royal juries, or claim exemption?'

Edmund hesitated. Godwyn looked exultant. Serving on juries was a time-consuming chore that everyone avoided if they could. After a pause, Edmund said: 'We claim exemption.'

'Then that settles the matter,' the judge said. 'If you refuse that duty on the grounds that you are serfs, you cannot appeal over the head of your landlord to the king's justice.'

Gregory said triumphantly: 'In the light of that, I beg you to dismiss the townspeople's application.'

'So ruled,' said the judge.

Francis appeared outraged. 'Sir, may I speak?'

'Certainly not,' said the judge.

'But, sir—'

'Another word and I'll hold you in contempt.'

Francis closed his mouth and bowed his head.

Sir Wilbert said: 'Next case.'

Another lawyer began to speak.

Caris was dazed.

Francis addressed her and her father in tones of protest. 'You should have told me you were serfs!'

'We're not.'

'The judge has just ruled that you are. I can't win cases on partial information.'

She decided not to squabble with him. He was the type of young man who cannot admit a mistake.

Godwyn was so pleased with himself that he looked as if he might burst. As he left, he could not resist a parting shot. He wagged a finger at Edmund and Caris. 'I hope that, in future, you'll see the wisdom of submitting to the will of God,' he said solemnly.

Caris said: 'Oh, piss off,' and turned her back.

She spoke to her father. 'This makes us completely powerless! We proved we had the right to use the fulling mill free, but Godwyn can still withhold that right!'

'So it seems,' he said.

She turned to Francis. 'There must be *something* we can do,' she said angrily.

'Well,' he said, 'you could get Kingsbridge made into a proper borough, with a royal charter setting out your rights and freedoms. Then you would have access to the royal court.'

Caris saw a glimmer of hope. 'How do we go about that?'

'You apply to the king.'

'Would he grant it?'

'If you argued that you need this to be able to pay your taxes, he would certainly listen.'

'Then we must try.'

Edmund warned: 'Godwyn will be furious.'

'Let him,' Caris said grimly.

'Don't underestimate the challenge,' her father persisted. 'You know how ruthless he is, even over small disputes. Something like this will lead to total war.'

'So be it,' said Caris bleakly. 'Total war.'

*

'OH, RALPH, how could you do it?' said his mother.

Merthin studied his brother's face in the dim light of their parents' home. Ralph appeared torn between outright denial and self-justification.

In the end, Ralph said: 'She led me on.'

Maud was distressed more than angry. 'But, Ralph, she is another man's wife!'

'A peasant's wife.'

'Even so.'

'Don't worry, Mother, they'll never convict a lord on the word of a serf.'

Merthin was not so sure. Ralph was a minor lord, and it seemed he had incurred the enmity of William of Caster. There was no telling how the trial would come out.

Their father said sternly: 'Even if they don't convict you – which I pray for – just think of the shame of it! You're the son of a knight – how could you forget that?'

Merthin was horrified and upset, but not surprised. That

streak of violence had always been in Ralph's nature. In their boyhood he had ever been ready for a fight, and Merthin had often steered him away from fisticuffs, deflating a confrontation with a conciliatory word or a joke. Had anyone other than his brother committed this horrible rape, Merthin would have been hoping to see the man hang.

Ralph kept glancing at Merthin. He was worried about Merthin's disapproval – perhaps more so than his mother's. He had always looked up to his older brother. Merthin just wished there was some way Ralph could be shackled to prevent his attacking people, now that he no longer had Merthin nearby to keep him out of trouble.

The discussion with their distraught parents was set to go on for some time, but there was a knock at the door of the modest house and Caris came in. She smiled at Gerald and Maud, though her face changed when she saw Ralph.

Merthin guessed she wanted him. He stood up. 'I didn't know you were back from London,' he said.

'Just arrived,' she replied. 'Can we have a few words?'

He pulled a cloak around his shoulders and stepped outside with her into the dim grey light of a cold December day. It was a year since she had terminated their love affair. He knew that her pregnancy had ended in the hospital, and he guessed she had somehow brought on the abortion deliberately. Twice in the following few weeks he had asked her to come back to him, but she had refused. It was bewildering: he sensed that she still loved him, but she was adamant. He had given up hope, and assumed that in time he would cease to grieve. So far, that had not happened. His heart still beat faster when he saw her, and he was happier talking to her than doing anything else in the world.

They walked to the main street and turned into the Bell. In the late afternoon the tavern was quiet. They ordered hot spiced wine.

'We lost the case,' Caris said.

Merthin was shocked. 'How is that possible? You had Prior Philip's will—'

'It made no difference.' She was bitterly disappointed, Merthin could see. She explained: 'Godwyn's smart lawyer argued that Kingsbridge people are serfs of the prior, and serfs have no right to appeal to the royal court. The judge dismissed the case.'

Merthin felt angry. 'But that's stupid. It means the prior can do anything he likes, regardless of laws and charters—'

'I know.'

Merthin realized she was impatient because he was saying things she had said to herself many times. He suppressed his indignation and tried to be practical. 'What are you going to do?'

'Apply for a borough charter. That would free the town from the control of the prior. Our lawyer thinks we have a strong case. Mind you, he thought we would win against the fulling mill. However, the king is desperate for money for this war against France. He needs prosperous towns to pay his taxes.'

'How long would it take to get a charter?'

'That's the bad news – at least a year, perhaps more.'

'And in that time, you can't manufacture scarlet cloth.'

'Not with the old fulling mill.'

'So we'll have to stop work on the bridge.'

'I can't see any way out of it.'

'Damn.' It seemed so unreasonable. Here they had at their fingertips the means to restore the town's prosperity, and one man's stubbornness was preventing them. 'How we all misjudged Godwyn,' Merthin said.

'Don't remind me.'

'We've got to escape from his control.'

'I know.'

'But sooner than a year from now.'

'I wish there was a way.'

Merthin racked his brains. At the same time, he was studying Caris. She was a wearing a new dress from London, particoloured in the current fashion, which gave her a playful look, even though she was solemn and anxious. The colours, deep green and mid-blue, seemed to make her eyes sparkle and her skin glow. This happened every so often. He would be deep in conversation with her over some problem to do with the bridge – they rarely talked of anything else – then suddenly he would realize how lovely she was.

Even while he was thinking about that, the problem-solving part of his mind came up with a proposal. 'We should build our own fulling mill.'

Caris shook her head. 'It would be illegal. Godwyn would order John Constable to pull it down.'

'What if it were outside the town?'

'In the forest, you mean? That's illegal too. You'd have the king's verderers on your back.' Verderers enforced the laws of the forest.

'Not in the forest, then. Somewhere else.'

'Wherever you went, you'd need the permission of some lord.'

'My brother's a lord.'

A look of distaste crossed Caris's face at the mention of Ralph, then her expression changed as she thought through what Merthin was saying. 'Build a fulling mill at Wigleigh?'

'Why not?'

'Is there a fast-flowing stream to turn the mill wheel?'

'I believe so – but if not it can be driven by an ox like the ferry.'

'Would Ralph let you?'

'Of course. He's my brother. If I ask him, he'll say yes.'

'Godwyn will go mad with rage.'

'Ralph doesn't care about Godwyn.'

Caris was pleased and excited, Merthin could see; but what were her feelings towards him? She was glad they had a solution to their problem, and eager to outwit Godwyn, but beyond that he could not read her mind.

'Let's think this through before we rejoice,' she said. 'Godwyn will make a rule saying cloth can't be taken out of Kingsbridge to be fulled. Lots of towns have laws like that.'

'Very hard for him to enforce such a rule without the cooperation of a guild. And, if he does, you can get around it. Most of the cloth is being woven in the villages anyway, isn't it?'

'Yes.'

'Then don't bring it into the city. Send it from the weavers to Wigleigh. Dye it there, full it in the new mill, then take it to London. Godwyn will have no jurisdiction.'

'How long would it take to build a mill?'

Merthin considered. 'The timber building can be put up in a couple of days. The machinery will be wooden, too, but it will take longer, as it has to be precisely measured. Getting the men and materials there will take the most time. I could have it finished a week after Christmas.'

'That's wonderful,' she said. 'We'll do it.'

*

ELIZABETH ROLLED THE dice and moved her last counter into the home position on the board. 'I win!' she said. 'That's three out of three. Pay up.'

Merthin handed her a silver penny. Only two people ever beat him at tabula: Elizabeth and Caris. He did not mind losing. He was grateful for a worthy opponent.

He sat back and sipped his pear wine. It was a cold Saturday afternoon in January, and already dark. Elizabeth's mother was asleep in a chair near the fire, snoring gently with her mouth open. She worked at the Bell, but she was always at home when Merthin visited her daughter. He preferred it that way. It meant he never had to decide whether to kiss Elizabeth or not. It was a question he did not want to confront. He would have liked to kiss her, of course. He remembered the touch of her cool lips and the firmness of her flat breasts. But it would mean admitting that his love affair with Caris was over for ever, and he was not yet ready for that.

'How is the new mill at Wigleigh?' Elizabeth asked.

'Finished, and rolling,' Merthin said proudly. 'Caris has been fulling cloth there for a week.'

Elizabeth raised her eyebrows. 'Herself?'

'No, that was a figure of speech. As a matter of fact, Mark Webber is running the mill, though he is training some of the village men to take over.'

'It will be good for Mark if he becomes Caris's second-in-command. He's been poor all his life – this is a big opportunity.'

'Caris's new enterprise will be good for us all. It will mean I can finish the bridge.'

'She's a clever girl,' Elizabeth said in a level voice. 'But what does Godwyn have to say?'

'Nothing. I'm not sure he knows about it yet.'

'He will, though.'

'I don't believe there's anything he can do.'

'He's a prideful man. If you've outwitted him, he'll never forgive you.'

'I can live with that.'

'And what about the bridge?'

'Despite all the problems, the work is only a couple of weeks behind schedule. I've had to spend money to catch up, but we will be able to use the bridge – with a temporary wooden roadbed – for the next Fleece Fair.'

'You and Caris between you have saved the town.'

'Not yet – but we will.'

There was a knock at the door, and Elizabeth's mother woke up with a start. 'Now who could that be?' she said. 'It's dark out.'

It was one of Edmund's apprentice boys. 'Master Merthin is wanted at the parish guild meeting,' he said.

'What for?' Merthin asked him.

'Master Edmund said to tell you, you're wanted at the parish guild meeting,' the boy said. He had obviously learned the message off by heart and knew nothing more.

'Something about the bridge, I expect,' Merthin said to Elizabeth. 'They're worried about the cost.' He picked up his cloak. 'Thank you for the wine – and the game.'

'I'll play you any time you like,' she said.

He walked beside the apprentice to the guild hall on the high street. The guild was holding a business meeting, not a banquet. The twenty or so most important people in Kingsbridge were sitting at a long trestle table, some drinking ale or wine, talking in low voices. Merthin sensed tension and anger, and he became apprehensive.

Edmund was at the head of the table. Prior Godwyn sat next to him. The prior was not a member of the guild: his presence suggested that Merthin's surmise had been right, and the meeting was about the bridge. However, Thomas the matricularius was not present, although Philemon was. That was odd.

Merthin had recently had a small dispute with Godwyn. His contract had been for a year at two pence a day plus the lease on

Leper Island. It was due for renewal, and Godwyn had proposed to continue paying him two pence a day. Merthin had insisted on four pence, and in the end Godwyn had conceded the point. Had he complained about this to the guild?

Edmund spoke with characteristic abruptness. 'We've called you here because Prior Godwyn wishes to dismiss you as master builder in charge of the bridge.'

Merthin felt as if he had been punched in the face. He was not expecting anything like this. 'What?' he said. 'But Godwyn appointed me!'

Godwyn said: 'And therefore I have the right to dismiss you.'

'But why?

'The work is behind schedule and over budget.'

'It's behind schedule because the earl closed the quarry – and it's over budget because I had to spend money to catch up.'

'Excuses.'

'Am I inventing the death of a carter?'

Godwyn shot back: 'Killed by your own brother!'

'What has that to do with anything?'

Godwyn ignored the question. 'A man who is accused of rape!' he added.

'You can't dismiss a master builder because of his brother's behaviour.'

'Who are you to say what I can do?'

'I'm the builder of your bridge!' Then it occurred to Merthin that much of his work as master builder was complete. He had designed all the most complicated parts, and made wooden templates to guide the stonemasons. He had built the coffer dams, which no one else knew how to do. And he had constructed the floating cranes and hoists needed to move the heavy stones into position in midstream. Any builder could now finish the job, he realized with dismay.

'There is no guarantee of renewal of your contract,' Godwyn said.

It was true. Merthin looked around the room for support. No one would meet his eye. They had already argued this out with Godwyn, he deduced. Despair overwhelmed him. Why had this happened? It was not because the bridge was behind schedule and over budget – the delay was not Merthin's fault, and anyway he was catching up. What was the real reason? As soon as he had asked the question, the answer came into his mind. 'This is because of the fulling mill at Wigleigh!' he said.

Godwyn said primly: 'The two things are not necessarily connected.'

Edmund said quietly but distinctly: 'Lying monk.'

Philemon spoke for the first time. 'Take care, alderman!' he said.

Edmund was undeterred. 'Merthin and Caris outwitted you, didn't they, Godwyn? Their mill at Wigleigh is entirely legitimate. You brought defeat on yourself by your greed and obstinacy. And this is your revenge.'

Edmund was right. No one was as capable a builder as Merthin. Godwyn must know that, but clearly he did not care. 'Who will you hire instead of me?' Merthin asked. Then he answered the question himself. 'Elfric, I suppose.'

'That has to be decided.'

Edmund said: 'Another lie.'

Philemon spoke again, his voice more shrill. 'You can be brought before the ecclesiastical court for talk like that!'

Merthin wondered if this might be no more than a move in the game, a way for Godwyn to renegotiate his contract. He said to Edmund: 'Is the parish guild in agreement with the prior on this?'

Godwyn said: 'It is not for them to agree or disagree!'

Merthin ignored him and looked expectantly at Edmund.

Edmund was shamefaced. 'It cannot be denied that the prior has the right. The guildsmen are financing the bridge by loans, but the prior is overlord of the town. This was agreed from the start.'

Merthin turned to Godwyn. 'Do you have anything else to say to me, lord prior?' He waited, hoping in his heart that Godwyn would come out with his real demands.

But Godwyn said stonily: 'No.'

'Goodnight, then.'

He waited a second longer. No one spoke. The silence told him it was all over.

He left the room.

Outside the building, he took a deep breath of the cold night air. He could hardly believe what had happened. He was no longer master of the bridge.

He walked through the dark streets. It was a clear night, and he could find his way by starlight. He walked past Elizabeth's house: he did not want to talk to her. He hesitated outside Caris's, but passed that too and went down to the waterside. His small rowing-boat was tied up opposite Leper Island. He got in and rowed himself across.

When he reached his house, he paused outside and looked up at the stars, fighting back tears. The truth was that in the end he had *not* outwitted Godwyn – rather the reverse. He had underestimated the lengths to which the prior would go to punish those who opposed him. Merthin had thought himself clever, but Godwyn had been cleverer, or at least more ruthless. He was prepared to damage the town and the priory, if necessary, to avenge a wound to his pride. And that had given him victory.

Merthin went inside and lay down, alone and beaten.

38

RALPH LAY AWAKE all through the night before his trial.

He had seen many people die by hanging. Every year, twenty or thirty men and a few women rode the sheriff's cart from the prison in Shiring Castle down the hill to the market square where the gallows stood waiting. It was a common occurrence, but those people had remained in Ralph's memory, and on this night they returned to torment him.

Some died fast, their necks snapped by the drop; but not many. Most strangled slowly. They kicked and struggled and opened their mouths wide in silent breathless screaming. They pissed and shat themselves. He recalled an old woman convicted of witchcraft: when she dropped she bit right through her tongue and spat it out, and the crowd around the gallows had backed away in fright from the bloody lump of flesh as it flew through the air and fell on the dusty ground.

Everyone told Ralph he was not going to be hanged, but he could not get the thought out of his mind. People said that Earl Roland could not allow one of his lords to be executed on the word of a serf. However, so far the earl had done nothing to intervene.

The preliminary jury had returned an indictment against Ralph to the justice of the peace in Shiring. Like all such juries, it had consisted mainly of knights of the county owing allegiance to Earl Roland – but, despite this, they had acted on the evidence of the Wigleigh peasants. The men – jurors were never women, of course – had not flinched from indicting one of their own. In fact the jurors had shown, by their questions, some distaste for what Ralph had done, and several had refused to shake his hand afterwards.

Ralph had planned to prevent Annet testifying again, at the trial proper, by imprisoning her in Wigleigh before she could leave for Shiring. However, when he went to her house to seize her he found she had already departed. She must have anticipated his move and left earlier to foil him.

Today another jury would hear the case but, to Ralph's dismay, at least four of the men had been on the preliminary jury too. Since the evidence on both sides was likely to be exactly the same, he could not see how this group could return a different verdict, unless some kind of pressure was put on the jurors – and it was getting very late for that.

He got up at first light and went downstairs to the ground floor of the Courthouse inn on the market square of Shiring. He found a shivering boy breaking the ice on the well in the back yard and told him to fetch bread and ale. Then he went to the communal dormitory and woke his brother, Merthin.

They sat together in the cold parlour, with the stale smell of last night's ale and wine, and Ralph said: 'I'm afraid they'll hang me.'

'So am I,' said Merthin.

'I don't know what to do.' The boy brought two tankards and half a loaf. Ralph picked up his ale in a shaking hand and took a long draught.

Merthin ate some bread automatically, frowning and looking upwards out of the corners of his eyes in the way he always did when he was racking his brains. 'The only thing I can think of is to try to persuade Annet to drop the charge and come to a settlement. You'll have to offer her compensation.'

Ralph shook his head. 'She can't back out – it's not allowed. They'll punish her if she does.'

'I know. But she could deliberately give weak evidence, making room for doubt. That's how it's usually done, I believe.'

Hope sparked in Ralph's heart. 'I wonder if she would consent.'

The potboy brought in an armful of logs and knelt before the fireplace to start a fire.

Merthin said thoughtfully: 'How much money could you offer Annet?'

'I've got twenty florins.' That was worth three pounds of English silver pennies.

Merthin ran a hand through his untidy red hair. 'It's not much.'

'It's a lot to a peasant girl. On the other hand, her family are rich, for peasants.'

'Doesn't Wigleigh yield you much money?'

'I've had to buy armour. When you're a lord you need to be ready to go to war.'

'I could lend you money.'

'How much have you got?'

'Thirteen pounds.'

Ralph was so astonished that for a moment he forgot his troubles. 'Where did you get all that?'

Merthin looked faintly resentful. 'I work hard and I'm paid well.'

'But you were sacked as master builder of the bridge.'

'There's plenty more work. And I rent out land on Leper Island.'

Ralph was indignant. 'So a carpenter is richer than a lord!'

'Luckily for you, as it happens. How much do you think Annet will want?'

Ralph thought of a snag, and his spirits fell again. 'It's not her, it's Wulfric. He's the ringleader in this.'

'Of course.' Merthin had spent a lot of time in Wigleigh while building the fulling mill, and he knew that Wulfric had married Gwenda only after being jilted by Annet. 'Then let's talk to him.'

Ralph did not think it would do any good, but he had nothing to lose.

They went out into the bleak grey daylight, pulling their cloaks around their shoulders against a cold February wind. They crossed the market place and entered the Bull, where the Wigleigh folk were staying – paid for, Ralph presumed, by Lord William, without whose help they would not have begun this process. But Ralph had no doubt that his real enemy was William's voluptuous, malevolent wife, Philippa, who seemed to hate Ralph, even though – or perhaps because – he found her fascinating and alluring.

Wulfric was up, and they found him eating porridge with

bacon. When he saw Ralph his face turned thunderous and he rose from his seat.

Ralph put his hand on his sword, ready to fight there and then, but Merthin hastily stepped forward, holding his hands open in front of him in a conciliatory gesture. 'I come as a friend, Wulfric,' he said. 'Don't get angry, or you'll end up on trial instead of my brother.'

Wulfric remained standing with his hands at his sides. Ralph was disappointed: the agony of his suspense would have been eased by a fight.

Wulfric spat a piece of bacon rind on the floor and swallowed, then said: 'What do you want, if not trouble?'

'To make a settlement. Ralph is willing to pay Annet ten pounds by way of recompense for what he did.'

Ralph was startled by the amount. Merthin would have to pay most of it – but he showed no hesitation.

Wulfric said: 'Annet can't withdraw the charge – it's not allowed.'

'But she can alter her evidence. If she says that at first she consented, then changed her mind when it was too late, the jury wouldn't convict Ralph.'

Ralph watched Wulfric's face eagerly for a sign of willingness, but his expression remained stony, and he said: 'So you're offering her a bribe to commit perjury?'

Ralph began to despair. He could see that Wulfric did not want Annet to be paid money. Revenge was his aim, not compensation. He wanted a hanging.

Merthin said reasonably: 'I'm offering her a different kind of justice.'

'You're trying to get your brother off the hook.'

'Wouldn't you do the same? You had a brother once.' Ralph recalled that Wulfric's brother had been killed, along with his parents, when the bridge collapsed. Merthin went on: 'Wouldn't you try to save his life – even if he had done wrong?'

Wulfric appeared startled by this appeal to family feeling. Clearly it had never occurred to him to think of Ralph as someone with kinfolk who loved him. But he recovered after a moment and said: 'My brother David would never have done what Ralph did.'

'Of course,' Merthin said soothingly. 'All the same, you can't blame me for wanting to find a way to save Ralph, especially if it can be managed without doing an injustice to Annet.'

Ralph admired his brother's smooth way of talking. He could charm a bird out of a tree, he thought.

But Wulfric was not easily persuaded. 'The villagers want to see the back of Ralph. They're afraid he might do the same thing again.'

Merthin sidestepped that. 'Perhaps you should put our offer to Annet. It should be her decision, surely.'

Wulfric looked thoughtful. 'How could we be certain you would pay the money?'

Ralph's heart leaped. Wulfric was softening.

Merthin replied: 'We'll give the cash to Caris Wooler before the trial. She will pay Annet after Ralph is declared innocent. You trust Caris, and we do too.'

Wulfric nodded. 'As you say, it's not my decision. I'll put it to her.' He went upstairs.

Merthin let out his breath in a long sigh. 'By heaven, there's an angry man.'

'You talked him round, though,' Ralph said admiringly.

'He's only agreed to pass on a message.'

They sat at the table Wulfric had vacated. A potboy asked them if they wanted breakfast, but they both refused. The parlour was full of guests calling for ham and cheese and ale. The inns were crowded with people attending the court. Unless they had a good excuse, all the knights of the shire were obliged to come, as were most other prominent men of the county: senior clergymen, wealthy merchants, and anyone with an income over forty pounds a year. Lord William, Prior Godwyn and Edmund Wooler were all included. Ralph and Merthin's father, Sir Gerald, had been a regular attender before his fall from grace. They had to offer themselves as jurors and transact other business, such as paying their taxes or electing their Members of Parliament. In addition there was a host of accused men, victims, witnesses and sureties. A court brought a lot of business to the inns of a town.

Wulfric kept them waiting. Ralph said: 'What do you think they're talking about, up there?'

Merthin said: 'Annet may be inclined to take the money. Her father would support her in that, and perhaps her husband, Billy Howard, too. But Wulfric is the type who thinks telling the truth is more important than money. His wife, Gwenda, will support him out of loyalty, and Father Gaspard will do the same on principle. Most importantly, they'll have to consult Lord William; and he'll do what Lady Philippa wants. She hates you, for some reason. On the other hand, a woman is more likely to choose reconciliation over confrontation.'

'So it could go either way.'

'Exactly.'

The patrons of the inn finished their breakfasts and began to drift out, heading across the square to the Courthouse inn, where the session would be held. Soon it would be too late.

At last Wulfric reappeared. 'She says no,' he said abruptly, and he turned away.

'Just a minute!' Merthin said.

Wulfric took no notice, and disappeared again up the stairs.

Ralph cursed. For a while he had hoped for a reprieve. Now he was in the hands of the jury.

He heard the sound of a handbell being rung vigorously outside. A sheriff's deputy was summoning all concerned to the court. Merthin stood up. Reluctantly, Ralph followed suit.

They walked back to the Courthouse and went into the large back room. At the far end, the justice's bench stood on a raised dais. Although always called a bench, it was in fact a carved wooden chair like a throne. The justice was not seated, but his clerk was at a table in front of the dais, reading a scroll. Two long benches for the jurymen stood to one side. There were no other seats in the room: everyone else would stand wherever he wished. Order was maintained by the power of the justice to sentence instantly anyone who misbehaved: no trial was necessary for a crime that the judge had himself witnessed. Ralph spotted Alan Fernhill, looking terrified, and stood beside him without speaking.

Ralph began to think he should never have come here. He could have made an excuse: sickness, a misunderstanding about dates, a horse lamed on the road. But that would only have brought him a postponement. Eventually the sheriff would come, with armed deputies, to arrest him; and if he evaded them he would be declared an outlaw.

However, that was better than hanging. He wondered if he should flee now. He could probably fight his way out of the tavern. But he would not get far on foot. He would be chased by half the town, and if they did not catch him the sheriff's deputies would follow on horseback. And his flight would be seen as an admission of guilt. As things stood, he still had a chance of acquittal. Annet might be too intimidated to give her evidence clearly. Perhaps key witnesses would fail to show up. There could be some last-minute intervention by Earl Roland.

The courtroom filled up: Annet, the villagers, Lord William and Lady Philippa, Edmund Wooler and Caris, Prior Godwyn and his slimy assistant Philemon. The clerk banged on his table for quiet, and the justice came through a side door. It was Sir Guy de Bois, a large landholder. He had a bald head and a fat belly. He was an old comrade-in-arms of the earl's, which might stand in Ralph's favour; but, on the other side of the balance, he was Lady Philippa's uncle, and she might have whispered malice in his ear. He had the flushed look of a man who has breakfasted on salt beef and strong ale. He sat down, farted loudly, sighed with satisfaction and said: 'All right, let's get on with it.'

Earl Roland was not present.

Ralph's case came first: it was the one that most interested everybody, including the justice. The indictment was read, and Annet was called to give her evidence.

Ralph found it strangely difficult to concentrate. He had heard it all before, of course, but he should have been listening hard for any discrepancy in the story Annet told today, any sign of uncertainty, any hesitation or faltering. But he felt fatalistic. His enemies were out in full force. His one powerful friend, Earl Roland, was absent. Only his brother stood beside him, and Merthin had already tried his best to help, and failed. Ralph was doomed.

The witnesses followed: Gwenda, Wulfric, Peg, Gaspard. Ralph had thought he had absolute power over these people, but somehow they had conquered him. The foreman of the jury, Sir Herbert Montain, was one of those who had refused to shake

Ralph's hand, and he asked questions that seemed designed to emphasize the horror of the crime: How bad was the pain? How much blood? Was she weeping?

When it was Ralph's turn to speak, he told the story that had been disbelieved by the jury of indictment, and he told it in a low voice, stumbling over his words. Alan Fernhill did better, saying firmly that Annet had been eager to lie with Ralph, and that the two lovers had asked him to make himself scarce while they enjoyed one another's favours beside the stream. But the jury did not believe him: Ralph could tell by their faces. He began to feel almost bored by the proceedings, wishing they would be over, and his fate sealed.

As Alan stepped back, Ralph was conscious of a new figure at his shoulder, and a low voice said: 'Listen to me.'

Ralph glanced behind and saw Father Jerome, the earl's clerk, and the thought crossed his mind that a court such as this had no power over priests, even if they committed crimes.

The justice turned to the jury and asked for their verdict.

Father Jerome murmured: 'Your horses stand outside, saddled and ready to go.'

Ralph froze. Was he hearing correctly? He turned and said: 'What?'

'Run for it.'

Ralph looked behind him. A hundred men barred his way to the door, many of them armed. 'It's not possible.'

'Use the side door,' Jerome said, indicating with a slight inclination of his head the entrance through which the justice had come. Ralph saw immediately that only the Wigleigh people stood between him and the side door.

The foreman of the jury, Sir Herbert, stood up, looking self-important.

Ralph caught the eye of Alan Fernhill, standing beside him. Alan had heard everything and looked expectant.

'Go now!' whispered Jerome.

Ralph put his hand on his sword.

'We find Lord Ralph of Wigleigh guilty of rape,' said the foreman.

Ralph drew his sword. Waving it in the air, he dashed for the door.

There was a second of stunned silence, then everyone shouted at once. But Ralph was the one man in the room with a weapon in his hand, and he knew it would take the others a moment to draw.

Only Wulfric tried to stop him, stepping into his path heedlessly, not even looking scared, just determined. Ralph raised his sword and brought it down, as hard as he could, aiming at the middle of Wulfric's skull, intending to cleave it in two. But Wulfric stepped nimbly back and to the side. Nevertheless, the point of the sword sliced through the left side of his face, cutting it open from the temple to the jaw. Wulfric cried out in sudden agony, and his hands flew to his cheek; and then Ralph was past him.

He flung open the door, stepped through and turned. Alan Fernhill dashed past him. The foreman of the jury was close behind Alan, sword drawn and raised. Ralph experienced a moment of pure elation. This was how things should be settled – by a fight, not a discussion. Win or lose, he preferred it this way.

With a yell of exhilaration he thrust at Sir Herbert. The point of his sword touched the foreman's chest, ripping through his leather tunic; but the man was too distant for the blow to penetrate the ribs, and it merely cut his skin then glanced off the bones. All the same, Herbert cried out – more in fear than pain – and stumbled back, colliding with those behind him. Ralph slammed the door on them.

He found himself in a passage that ran the length of the house, with a door to the market square at one end and another to the stable yard at the other. Where were the horses? Jerome had said only that they were outside. Alan was already running for the back door, so Ralph followed. As they burst into the yard, a hubbub behind them told him that the courtroom door had been opened and the crowd was after him.

There was no sign of their horses in the yard.

Ralph ran under the arch that led to the front.

There stood the most welcome sight in the world: his hunter,

Griff, saddled and pawing the ground, with Alan's two-year-old Fletch beside him, both held by a barefoot stable boy with his mouth full of bread.

Ralph seized the reins and jumped on his horse. Alan did the same. They kicked their beasts just as the mob from the courtroom came through the arch. The stable boy threw himself out of the way, terrified. The horses surged forward and away.

Someone in the crowd threw a knife. It stuck a quarter of an inch into Griff's flank, then fell away, serving only to spur the horse on.

They galloped flat out through the streets, scattering townspeople before them, careless of men, women, children and livestock. They charged through a gate in the old wall and passed into a suburb of houses interspersed with gardens and orchards. Ralph looked behind. No pursuers were in sight.

The sheriff's men would come after them, of course, but they had first to fetch horses and saddle them. Ralph and Alan were already a mile from the market square, and their mounts showed no signs of tiring. Ralph was filled with glee. Five minutes ago he had reconciled himself to being hanged. Now he was free!

The road forked. Choosing at random, Ralph turned left. A mile away across the fields he could see woodland. Once there, he would turn off the track, and disappear.

But what would he do then?

39

'EARL ROLAND WAS CLEVER,' Merthin said to Elizabeth Clerk. 'He allowed justice to take its course almost to the end. He didn't bribe the judge or influence the jury or intimidate the witnesses, and he avoided a quarrel with his son, Lord William. But he escaped the humiliation of seeing one of his men hanged.'

'Where is your brother now?' she said.

'No idea. I haven't spoken to him or even seen him since that day.'

They were sitting in Elizabeth's kitchen on Sunday afternoon. She had made dinner for him: boiled ham with stewed apples and winter greens, and a small jug of wine that her mother had bought, or perhaps stolen, from the inn where she worked.

Elizabeth said: 'What will happen now?'

'The sentence of death still hangs over him. He can't return to Wigleigh, or come here to Kingsbridge, without getting arrested. In effect, he's declared himself an outlaw.'

'Is there nothing he can do?'

'He could get a pardon from the king – but that costs a fortune, far more money than he or I could raise.'

'And how do you feel about him?'

Merthin winced. 'Well, he deserves punishment for what he did, of course. All the same, I can't wish it on him. I just hope he's all right, wherever he is.'

He had told the story of Ralph's trial many times in the last few days, but Elizabeth had asked the most astute questions. She was intelligent and sympathetic. The thought crossed his mind that it would be no hardship to spend every Sunday afternoon this way.

Her mother, Sairy, was dozing by the fire, as usual, but now she opened her eyes and said: 'My soul! I've forgotten the pie.'

She stood up, patting her mussed grey hair. 'I promised to ask Betty Baxter to make a pie with ham and eggs for the leather-tanners' guild. They're holding their last-before-Lent dinner at the Bell tomorrow.' She draped a blanket around her shoulders and went out.

It was unusual for them to be left alone together, and Merthin felt slightly awkward, but Elizabeth seemed relaxed enough. She said: 'What are you doing with yourself, now that you no longer work on the bridge?'

'I'm building a house for Dick Brewer, among other things. Dick's ready to retire and hand over to his son, but he says he'll never stop work while he's living at the Copper, so he wants a house with a garden outside the old city walls.'

'Oh – is that the building site beyond Lovers' Field?'

'Yes. It will be the biggest house in Kingsbridge.'

'A brewer is never short of money.'

'Would you like to see it?'

'The site?'

'The house. It's not finished, but it's got four walls and a roof.'

'Now?'

'There's still an hour of daylight.'

She hesitated, as if she might have had another plan; but then she said: 'I'd love to.'

They put on heavy cloaks with hoods and went out. It was the first day of March. Flurries of snow chased them down the main street. They took the ferry to the suburban side.

Despite the ups and downs of the wool trade, the town seemed to grow a little every year, and the priory turned more and more of its pasture and orchards into house plots for rent. Merthin guessed there must be fifty dwellings that had not been here when he first came to Kingsbridge, as a boy, twelve years ago.

Dick Brewer's new home was a two-storey structure set back from the road. As yet it had no window shutters or doors, so the gaps in the walls had been temporarily covered with hurdles, wood frames filled in with woven reeds. The front entrance was thus blocked, but Merthin took Elizabeth to the back, where there was a temporary wooden door with a lock.

Merthin's assistant, Jimmie, now sixteen, was in the kitchen, guarding the place from thieves. He was a superstitious boy, always crossing himself and throwing salt over his shoulder. He was sitting on a bench in front of a big fire, but he looked anxious. 'Hello, master,' he said. 'Now that you're here, may I go and get my dinner? Lol Turner was supposed to bring it, but he hasn't come.'

'Make sure you're back before it gets dark.'

'Thank you.' He hurried off.

Merthin stepped through the doorway to the interior of the house. 'Four rooms downstairs,' he said, showing her.

She was incredulous. 'What will they use them all for?'

'Kitchen, parlour, dining room and hall.' There was no staircase yet, but Merthin climbed a ladder to the upper floor, and Elizabeth followed. 'Four bedrooms,' he said as she reached the top.

'Who will live here?'

'Dick and his wife, his son Danny and *his* wife, and his daughter, who probably won't remain single for ever.'

Most Kingsbridge families lived in one room, and all slept side by side on the floor: parents, children, grandparents and in-laws. Elizabeth said: 'This place has more rooms than a palace!'

It was true. A nobleman with a big entourage might still live in two rooms: a bedchamber for himself and his wife, and a great hall for everyone else. But Merthin had now designed several houses for wealthy Kingsbridge merchants, and the luxury they all craved was privacy. It was a new trend, he thought.

'I suppose there will be glass in the windows,' Elizabeth said.

'Yes.' That was another trend. Merthin could remember the time when there was no glazier in Kingsbridge, just an itinerant who called every year or two. Now the city had a resident glazier.

They returned to the ground floor. Elizabeth sat on Jimmie's bench in front of the fire and warmed her hands. Merthin sat beside her. 'I'll build a house like this for myself, one day,' he said. 'In a big garden with fruit trees.'

To his surprise, she leaned her head on his shoulder. 'What a nice dream,' she said.

They both stared into the fire. Her hair tickled Merthin's

cheek. After a moment, she laid a hand on his knee. In the silence, he could hear her breathing, and his own, and the crackle of burning logs.

'In your dream, who's in the house?' she said.

'I don't know.'

'Just like a man. I can't see my house, but I know who's in it: a husband, some babies, my mother, an elderly parent-in-law and three servants.'

'Men and women have different dreams.'

She lifted her head, looked at him and touched his face. 'And when you put them together, you have a life.' She kissed his mouth.

He closed his eyes. He remembered the soft touch of her lips from years ago. Her mouth lingered on his for just a moment, then she drew back.

He felt oddly detached, as if he were watching himself from a corner of the room. He did not know how he felt. He looked at her and saw again how lovely she was. He asked himself what was so striking about her, and realized immediately that everything was in harmony, like the parts of a beautiful church. Her mouth, her chin, her cheekbones and her forehead were just as he would have drawn them if he had been God creating a woman.

She looked back at him with calm blue eyes. 'Touch me,' she said. She opened her cloak.

He took her breast gently in his hand. He remembered doing this, too. Her breasts were firm and flat against her chest. Her nipple hardened immediately to his touch, betraying her calm demeanour.

'I want to be in your dream house,' she said, and she kissed him again.

She was not acting on the spur of the moment; Elizabeth never did. She had been thinking about this. While he had been casually visiting her, enjoying her company without thinking any farther, she had been imagining their life together. Perhaps she had even planned this scene. That would explain why her mother had left them with an excuse about a pie. He had almost spoiled her plan by proposing to show her Dick Brewer's house, but she had improvised.

There was nothing wrong with such an unemotional approach. She was a reasoning person. It was one of the things he liked about her. He knew that passions burned nonetheless beneath the surface.

What seemed wrong was his own lack of feeling. It was not his way to be coolly rational about women – quite the reverse. When he had felt love, it had taken him over, making him feel rage and resentment as well as lust and tenderness. Now he felt interested, flattered and titillated, but he was not out of control.

She sensed that his kiss was lukewarm, and drew back. He saw the ghost of an emotion on her face, fiercely suppressed, but he knew there was fear behind the mask. She was so poised, by nature, that it must have cost her a lot to be so forward, and she dreaded rejection.

She drew away from him, stood up and lifted the skirt of her dress. She had long, shapely legs covered with nearly invisible fine blonde hair. Although she was tall and slim, her body widened just below the hips in a delightfully womanly way. His gaze homed in helplessly on the delta of her sex. Her hair was so fair that he could see through it, to the pale swelling of the lips and the delicate line between them.

He looked up to her face and read desperation there. She had tried everything, and she saw that it had not worked.

Merthin said: 'I'm sorry.'

She dropped her skirts.

'Listen,' he said. 'I think—'

She interrupted him. 'Don't speak.' Her desire was turning to anger. 'Whatever you say now will be a lie.'

She was right. He had been trying to formulate some soothing half-truth: he was not feeling well, or Jimmie might be back at any moment. But she did not want to be mollified. She had been rebuffed, and feeble excuses would only make her feel patronized as well.

She stared at him, grief struggling with rage on the battleground of her beautiful face. Tears of frustration came to her eyes. 'Why not?' she cried; but when he opened his mouth to reply she said: 'Don't answer! It won't be the truth'; and again she was right.

She turned to go, then came back. 'It's Caris,' she said, her face working with emotion. 'That witch has cast a spell on you. She won't marry you, but no one else can have you. She's evil!'

At last she walked away. She flung open the door and stepped out. He heard her sob once, then she was gone.

Merthin stared into the fire. 'Oh, hell,' he said.

*

'THERE'S SOMETHING I need to explain to you,' Merthin said to Edmund a week later, as they were leaving the cathedral.

Edmund's face took on a look of mild amusement that was familiar to Merthin. I'm thirty years older than you, the look said, and you should be listening to me, not giving me lessons; but I enjoy youthful enthusiasm. Besides, I'm not yet too old to learn something. 'All right,' he said. 'But explain it in the Bell. I want a cup of wine.'

They went into the tavern and sat close to the fire. Elizabeth's mother brought their wine, but she stuck her nose in the air and did not talk to them. Edmund said: 'Is Sairy angry with you or me?'

'Never mind that,' said Merthin. 'Have you ever stood at the edge of the ocean, with your bare feet on the sand, and felt the sea wash over your toes?'

'Of course. All children play in water. Even I was a boy once.'

'Do you remember how the action of the waves, flowing in and out, seems to scour the sand from under the edges of your feet, making a little channel?'

'Yes. It's a long time ago, but I think I know what you mean.'

'That's what happened to the old wooden bridge. The flowing river scoured the earth from under the central pier.'

'How do you know?'

'By the pattern of cracks in the woodwork just before the collapse.'

'What's your point?'

'The river hasn't changed. It will undermine the new bridge just as surely as it did the old – unless we prevent it.'

'How?'

'In my drawing, I showed a pile of large, loose stones surrounding each of the piers of the new bridge. They will break up the current and enfeeble its effect. It's the difference between being tickled by loose thread and being flogged with a tightly woven rope.'

'How do you know?'

'I asked Buonaventura about it, immediately after the bridge collapsed, before he went back to London. He said he had seen such piles of stones around the piers of bridges in Italy, and he had often wondered what they were for.'

'Fascinating. Are you telling me this for general enlightenment, or is there some more specific purpose?'

'People like Godwyn and Elfric don't understand this, and wouldn't listen if I told them. Just in case Elfric takes it into his fool head not to follow my design exactly, I want to be sure that at least one person in town knows the reason for the pile of stones.'

'But one person does – you.'

'I'm leaving Kingsbridge.'

That shocked him. 'Leaving?' he said. 'You?'

At that moment, Caris appeared. 'Don't stay here too long,' she said to her father. 'Aunt Petranilla is preparing dinner. Do you want to join us, Merthin?'

Edmund said: 'Merthin's leaving Kingsbridge.'

Caris paled.

Seeing her reaction, Merthin felt a jolt of satisfaction. She had rejected him, but she was dismayed to hear that he was leaving town. He immediately felt ashamed of such an unworthy emotion. He was too fond of her to want her to suffer. All the same, he would have felt worse if she had received the news with equanimity.

'Why?' she said.

'There's nothing for me here. What am I going to build? I can't work on the bridge. The town already has a cathedral. I don't want to do nothing but merchants' houses for the rest of my life.'

In a quiet voice, she said: 'Where will you go?'

'Florence. I've always wanted to see the buildings of Italy. I'll ask Buonaventura Caroli for letters of introduction. I might even be able to travel with one of his consignments.'

'But you own property here in Kingsbridge.'

'I wanted to speak to you about that. Would you manage it for me? You could collect my rents, take a commission and give the balance to Buonaventura. He can transfer money to Florence by letter.'

'I don't want a damn commission,' she said huffily.

Merthin shrugged. 'It's work, you should be paid.'

'How can you be so cold about it?' she said. Her voice was shrill, and around the parlour of the Bell several people looked up. She took no notice. 'You'll be leaving all your friends!'

'I'm not cold about it. Friends are great. But I'd like to get married.'

Edmund put in: 'Plenty of girls in Kingsbridge would marry you. You're not handsome, but you're prosperous, and that's worth more than good looks.'

Merthin smiled wryly. Edmund could be disarmingly blunt. Caris had inherited the trait. 'For a while I thought I might marry Elizabeth Clerk,' he said.

Edmund said: 'So did I.'

Caris said: 'She's a cold fish.'

'No, she's not. But when she asked me, I backed off.'

Caris said: 'Oh – so that's why she's so bad-tempered lately.'

Edmund said: 'And why her mother won't look at Merthin.'

'Why did you refuse her?' Caris asked.

'There's only one woman in Kingsbridge I could marry – and she doesn't want to be anyone's wife.'

'But she doesn't want to lose you.'

Merthin became angry. 'What should I do?' he said. His voice was loud, and people around them stopped their conversations to listen. 'Godwyn has fired me, you've rejected me and my brother is an outlaw. In God's name, why should I stay here?'

'I don't want you to go,' she said.

'That's not enough!' he shouted.

The room was silent now. Everyone there knew them: the landlord, Paul Bell, and his curvy daughter Bessie; the grey-haired barmaid Sairy, Elizabeth's mother; Bill Watkin, who had refused to employ Merthin; Edward Butcher, the notorious adulterer; Jake Chepstow, Merthin's tenant; Friar Murdo, Matthew Barber and Mark Webber. They all knew the history of Merthin and Caris, and they were fascinated by the quarrel.

Merthin did not care. Let them listen. He said furiously: 'I'm not going to spend my life hanging around you, like your dog Scrap, waiting for your attention. I'll be your husband, but I won't be your pet.'

'All right, then,' she said in a small voice.

Her sudden change of tone surprised him, and he was not sure what she meant. 'All right, what?'

'All right, I'll marry you.'

For a moment, he was too shocked to speak. Then he said suspiciously: 'Do you mean it?'

She looked up at him at last and smiled shyly. 'Yes, I mean it,' she said. 'Just ask me.'

'All right.' He took a deep breath. 'Will you marry me?'

'Yes, I will,' she said.

Edmund shouted: 'Hoorah!'

Everyone in the tavern cheered and clapped.

Merthin and Caris started laughing. 'Will you, really?' he said. 'Yes.'

They kissed, then he put his arms around her and squeezed as hard as he could. When he let her go, he saw that she was crying.

'Some wine for my betrothed,' he called out. 'A barrel, in fact – give everyone a cup, so they can all drink our health!'

'Coming right up,' said the landlord, and they all cheered again.

*

A WEEK LATER, Elizabeth Clerk became a novice nun.

40

RALPH AND ALAN WERE MISERABLE. They were living on venison and cold water, and Ralph found himself dreaming about food he would normally scorn: onions, apples, eggs, milk. They slept in a different place every night, always lighting a fire. They each had a good cloak, but it was not enough out in the open, and they woke shivering every dawn. They robbed any vulnerable people they met on the road, but most of the loot was either paltry or useless: ragged clothes, animal fodder, and money, which would buy nothing in the forest.

Once they stole a big barrel of wine. They rolled it a hundred yards into the woods, drank as much as they could and fell asleep. When they woke up, hung over and ill-tempered, they realized they could not take the three-quarters-full barrel with them, so they just left it there.

Ralph thought nostalgically of his former life: the manor house, the roaring fires, the servants, the dinners. But, in his realistic moments, he knew he did not want that life either. It was too dull. That was probably why he had raped the girl. He needed excitement.

After a month in the forest, Ralph decided they had to get organized. They needed a base where they could build some kind of shelter and store food. And they had to plan their robberies so that they stole items that would be really valuable to them, such as warm clothing and fresh food.

Around the time he was coming to this realization, their wanderings brought them to a range of hills a few miles from Kingsbridge. Ralph recalled that the hillsides, bleak and bare in winter, were used for summer grazing by shepherds, who had built rough stone shelters in the folds of the landscape. As adolescents he and Merthin had discovered these crude buildings while out hunting, and had lit fires and cooked the rabbits and partridges they shot with their bows. Even in those days, he recalled, he had craved the thrill of the hunt: chasing and shooting a terrified creature, finishing it off with a knife or club – the ecstatic sense of power that came from taking a life.

No one would come here until the new season's grass was thick. The traditional day was Whit Sunday, also the opening day of the Fleece Fair, still two months away. Ralph selected a hut that looked sturdy and they made it their home. There were no doors or windows, just a low entrance, but there was a hole in the roof to let smoke out, and they lit a fire and slept warm for the first time in a month.

Proximity to Kingsbridge gave Ralph another bright idea. The time to rob people, he realized, was when they were on their way to market. They were carrying cheeses, flagons of cider, honey, oatcakes: all the things that were produced by villagers and needed by townspeople – and by outlaws.

Kingsbridge market was on a Sunday. Ralph had lost track of the days of the week, but he found out by asking a travelling friar, before robbing him of three shillings and a goose. On the following Saturday, he and Alan made camp not far from the road to Kingsbridge, and stayed awake all night by their fire. At dawn they made their way to the road and lay in wait.

The first group to come along were carting fodder. Kingsbridge had hundreds of horses and very little grass, so the town constantly needed supplies of hay. However, it was no use to Ralph: Griff and Fletch had no end of grazing in the forest.

Ralph was not bored waiting. Preparing an ambush was like watching a woman get undressed. The longer the anticipation, the more intense the thrill.

Soon afterwards they heard singing. The hairs on the back of Ralph's neck stood up: it sounded like angels. The morning was hazy, and when he first saw the singers they seemed to have haloes. Alan, obviously thinking the same as Ralph, even gave a sob of fear. But it was only the weak winter sun lighting the mist behind the travellers. They were peasant women, each carrying a basket of eggs – hardly worth robbing. Ralph let them go by without revealing himself.

The sun rose a little higher. Ralph began to worry that soon the road would become sufficiently crowded with market-goers to make robbery difficult. Then along came a family: a man and woman in their thirties with two adolescent children, a boy and a girl. They were vaguely familiar: no doubt he had seen them at Kingsbridge market during the years he lived there. They carried an assortment of goods. The husband had a heavy basket of vegetables on his back; the wife balanced on her shoulder a long pole bearing several live chickens, trussed; the boy had a heavy ham on his shoulder, and the girl a crock that probably contained salted butter. Ralph's mouth watered at the thought of ham.

The excitement rose in his guts, and he gave Alan a nod.

As the family drew level, Ralph and Alan came out of the bushes at a run.

The woman screamed and the boy gave a shout of fear.

The man tried to shrug off his basket but, before it fell from his shoulders, Ralph ran him through, his sword piercing the man's abdomen under the ribs and then rising up. The man's scream of agony was cut off abruptly as the point of the sword penetrated his heart.

Alan swung at the woman and cut through most of her neck, so that blood spurted from her severed throat in a sudden red jet.

Exhilarated, Ralph turned to the son. The lad was quick to react: he had already dropped his ham and drawn a knife. While Ralph's weapon was still on the upswing, the boy darted close and stabbed him. It was an unprofessional blow, too wild to do much damage. The knife completely missed Ralph's chest, but the point caught in the flesh of his upper right arm, and the sudden agonizing pain made him drop his sword. The boy turned and ran away, going in the direction of Kingsbridge.

Ralph looked at Alan. Before turning to the girl, Alan finished off the mother, and the delay almost cost him his life. Ralph saw the girl throw her crock of butter at Alan. Either accurate or lucky, she hit him square on the back of the head, and Alan fell to the ground as if poleaxed.

Then she ran after her brother.

Ralph stooped, picked up his sword in his left hand and gave chase.

They were young and fleet, but he had long legs and he soon gained on them. The boy looked over his shoulder and saw Ralph coming close. To Ralph's astonishment the lad stopped, turned and came running back at him, screaming, knife raised in his fist.

Ralph stopped running and lifted his sword. The boy ran at him – then stopped outside his reach. Ralph stepped forward and lunged, but it was a feint. The boy dodged the blow, then, thinking to catch Ralph off balance, tried to step inside his guard and stab him at close quarters. But that was exactly what Ralph was expecting. He stepped nimbly back, stood on the balls of his feet and thrust his sword precisely into the boy's throat, pushing it through until the point came out of the back of his neck.

The boy fell dead, and Ralph withdrew his sword, pleased with the accuracy and efficiency of the death blow.

He looked up to see the girl disappearing into the distance. He saw immediately that he could not catch her on foot; and by the time he fetched his horse she would be in Kingsbridge.

He turned and looked back. To his surprise, Alan was struggling to his feet. 'I thought she'd killed you,' Ralph said. He wiped his sword on the dead boy's tunic, sheathed his blade and clamped his left hand over the wound in his right arm, trying to stop the bleeding.

'My head hurts like Satan,' Alan replied. 'Did you kill them all?'

'The girl got away.'

'Do you think she knew us?'

'She might know me. I've seen this family before.'

'In that case, we're now branded as murderers.'

Ralph shrugged. 'Better to hang than starve.' He looked at the three bodies. 'All the same, let's get these peasants off the road before someone comes along.'

With his left hand he dragged the man to the edge of the road. Alan picked up the body and threw it into the bushes. They did the same with the woman and the boy. Ralph made sure the corpses were not visible to passers-by. The blood on the road was already darkening to the colour of the mud into which it was soaking.

Ralph cut a strip off the woman's dress and tied it around the cut in his arm. It still hurt, but the flow of blood was less. He felt the slight depression that always followed a fight, like the sadness after sex.

Alan began to collect up the loot. 'A nice haul,' he said. 'Ham, chickens, butter –' he looked into the basket the man had been carrying – 'and onions! Last year's, of course, but still good.'

'Old onions taste better than no onions. My mother says that.'

As Ralph bent to pick up the butter crock that had felled Alan, he felt a sharp iron point stick into his arse. Alan was in front of him, dealing with the trussed chickens. Ralph said: 'Who...?'

A harsh voice said: 'Don't move.'

Ralph never obeyed such instructions. He sprang forward, away from the voice, and spun round. Six or seven men had materialized from nowhere. He was bewildered, but he managed, left-handed, to draw his sword. The man nearest him – who presumably had prodded him – raised his sword to fight, but the others were grabbing the loot, snatching chickens and fighting over the ham. Alan's sword flashed in defence of his chickens as Ralph engaged with his antagonist. He realized that another group of outlaws was trying to rob him. He was filled with indignation: he had killed people for this stuff, and now they wanted to take it from him! He felt no fear, only anger. He attacked his opponent with the energy of outrage, despite being forced to fight left-handed. Then an authoritative voice said loudly: 'Put away your blades, you fools.'

All the newcomers stood still. Ralph held his sword at the ready, suspicious of a trick, and looked towards the voice. He saw a handsome man in his twenties with something of the nobility about him. He wore clothes that looked expensive but were filthy dirty: a cloak of Italian scarlet covered with leaves and twigs, a rich brocade coat marked with what appeared to be food stains, and hose of a rich chestnut leather, scratched and muddy.

'It amuses me to steal from thieves,' the newcomer said. 'It's not a crime, you see.'

Ralph knew he was in a tight spot but, all the same, he was intrigued. 'Are you the one they call Tam Hiding?' he said.

'There were stories of Tam Hiding when I was a child,' the

man replied. 'But every now and again someone comes along to act the part, like a monk impersonating Lucifer in a mystery play.'

'You're not a common type of outlaw.'

'Nor are you. I'm guessing that you're Ralph Fitzgerald.'

Ralph nodded.

'I heard about your escape, and I've been wondering when I'd run into you.' Tam looked up and down the road. 'We happened upon you by accident. What made you choose this spot?'

'I picked the day and time, first. It's Sunday, and at this hour the peasants are taking their produce to market in Kingsbridge, which is on this road.'

'Well, well. Ten years I've been living outside the law, and I never thought of doing that. Perhaps we should team up. Are you going to put your weapon away?'

Ralph hesitated, but Tam was unarmed, so he could not see the disadvantage. Anyway, he and Alan were so heavily outnumbered that it would be best to avoid a fight. Slowly, he sheathed his sword.

'That's better.' Tam put an arm around Ralph's shoulders, and Ralph realized they were the same height. Not many people were as tall as Ralph. Tam walked him into the woods, saying: 'The others will bring the loot. Come this way. We've got a lot to talk about, you and I.'

*

EDMUND RAPPED ON the table. 'I've called this emergency meeting of the parish guild to discuss the outlaw problem,' he said. 'But, as I'm getting old and lazy, I've asked my daughter to summarize the situation.'

Caris was a member of the parish guild now, by virtue of her success as a manufacturer of scarlet cloth. The new business had rescued her father's fortunes. Numerous other Kingsbridge people were prospering because of it, notably the Webber family. Her father had been able to fulfil his pledge to lend money for the building of the bridge, and in the general upturn several other merchants had done the same. Bridge building continued apace – supervised now by Elfric, not Merthin, unfortunately.

Her father took little initiative, these days. The moments

when he was his sharp-witted former self were becoming rarer. She was worried about him, but there was nothing she could do. She felt the rage that had possessed her during her mother's illness. Why was there no help for him? Nobody understood what was wrong; no one could even put a name to his malady. They said it was old age, but he was not yet fifty!

She prayed he would live to see her wedding. She was going to marry Merthin in Kingsbridge Cathedral on the Sunday after the Fleece Fair, now just a month away. The wedding of the daughter of the town's alderman would be a big event. There would be a banquet in the guild hall for the leading citizens, and a picnic in Lovers' Field for several hundred more guests. Some days her father would spend hours planning the menus and the entertainment, only to forget everything he had said and start again from scratch the next day.

She put that out of her mind, and turned her attention to a problem she hoped would be more tractable. 'In the last month there has been a big increase in attacks by outlaws,' she said. 'They take place mainly on Sundays, and the victims are invariably people bringing produce to Kingsbridge.'

She was interrupted by Elfric. 'It's your fiancé's brother that's doing it!' he said. 'Talk to Merthin, not us.'

Caris suppressed a flash of exasperation. Her sister's husband never missed a chance to snipe at her. She was painfully aware of Ralph's likely involvement. It was a cause of agony to Merthin. Elfric relished that.

Dick Brewer said: 'I think it's Tam Hiding.'

'Perhaps it's both,' Caris said. 'I believe that Ralph Fitzgerald, who has some military training, may have joined forces with an existing band of outlaws and simply made them more organized and effective.'

Fat Betty Baxter, the town's most successful baker, said: 'Whoever it is, they'll be the ruination of this town. No one comes to market any more!'

That was an exaggeration, but attendance at the weekly market was down drastically, and the effects were felt by just about every enterprise in town, from bakeries to brothels. 'That's not the worst of it, though,' Caris said. 'In four weeks' time we've got the Fleece Fair. Several people here have invested enormous sums of money in the new bridge, which should be ready for use, with a temporary timber roadbed, in time for the opening. Most of us depend on the annual fair for our prosperity. I personally have a warehouse full of costly scarlet cloth to sell. If it gets around that people coming to Kingsbridge are likely to be robbed by outlaws, we may have no customers.'

She was even more worried than she let herself appear. Neither she nor her father had any cash left. Everything they had was either invested in the bridge or tied up in raw wool and scarlet cloth. The Fleece Fair was their chance to get their money back. If attendance was poor, they would be in deep trouble. Among other things, who would pay for the wedding?

She was not the only worried citizen. Rick Silvers, the head of the jewellers' guild, said: 'That would be the third bad year in succession.' He was a prim, fussy man, always immaculately dressed. 'It would finish some of my people,' he went on. 'We do half our year's business at the Fleece Fair.'

Edmund said: 'It would finish this town. We can't let it happen.'

Several others joined in. Caris, who was unofficially presiding, let them grumble. A heightened sense of urgency would predispose them to accept the radical solution she was going to propose.

Elfric said: 'The Sheriff of Shiring ought to do something about it. What's he paid for, if not to keep the peace?'

Caris said: 'He can't search the entire forest. He doesn't have enough men.'

'Earl Roland has.'

This was wishful thinking, but again Caris let the discussion run, so that when she proposed her solution they would be aware that there were no real alternatives.

Edmund said to Elfric: 'The earl won't help us – I've already asked him.'

Caris, who had in fact written Edmund's letter to Roland, said: 'Ralph was the earl's man, and still is. You notice the outlaws don't attack people going to Shiring market.'

Elfric said indignantly: 'Those Wigleigh peasants should never have made a complaint against a squire of the earl's – who do they think they are?'

Caris was about to respond indignantly but Betty Baxter beat her to it. 'Oh, so you think lords should be allowed to rape anyone they like?'

Edmund intervened. 'That's a different question,' he said briskly, showing some of his old authority. 'It's happened, and Ralph is preying on us, so what are we going to do? The sheriff can't help us and the earl won't.'

Rick Silvers said: 'What about Lord William? He took the side of the Wigleigh people – it's his fault that Ralph's an outlaw.'

'I asked him, too,' Edmund said. 'He said we're not in his territory.'

Rick said: 'That's the trouble with having the priory as your landlord – what use is a prior when you need protection?'

Caris said: 'Another reason why we are applying to the king for a borough charter. We'd be under royal protection then.'

Elfric said: 'We've got our own constable, what's he doing?'

Mark Webber spoke. He was one of the constable's deputies. 'We're ready to do whatever's necessary,' he said. 'Just give us the word.'

Caris said: 'No one doubts your bravery. But your role is to deal with troublemakers within the town. John Constable doesn't have the expertise to hunt down outlaws.'

Mark, who was close to Caris because he ran her fulling mill at Wigleigh, was mildly indignant. 'Well, who does, then?'

Caris had been leading the discussion towards this question. 'As a matter of fact, there is an experienced soldier who is willing to help us,' she said. 'I took the liberty of asking him to come here tonight, and he's waiting in the chapel.' She raised her voice. 'Thomas, will you join us?'

Thomas Langley came out of the little chapel at the end of the hall.

Rick Silvers said sceptically: 'A monk?'

'Before he was a monk, he was a soldier,' Caris explained. 'That's how he lost his arm.'

Elfric said grumpily: 'Guild members' permission should have been sought before he was invited.' No one took any notice, Caris was pleased to see: they were too interested to hear what Thomas would have to say.

'You need to form a militia,' Thomas began. 'By all accounts there are twenty or thirty outlaws in the troop. That's not many. Most townsmen can use a longbow effectively, thanks to the Sunday-morning practice sessions. A hundred of you, well prepared and intelligently led, could overcome the outlaws easily.'

'That's all very well,' said Rick Silvers. 'But we have to find them.'

'Of course,' said Thomas. 'But I feel sure there is someone in Kingsbridge who knows where they are.'

*

MERTHIN HAD ASKED the timber merchant, Jake Chepstow, to bring him a piece of slate from Wales – the largest piece he could find. Jake had come back from his next logging expedition with a thin sheet of grey Welsh slate about four feet square. Merthin had encased it in a wooden frame, and he used it for sketching plans.

This evening, while Caris was at the parish guild, Merthin was at his own house on Leper Island, working on a map of the island. Renting parts of it for wharves and warehouses was the least of his ambitions. He foresaw an entire street of inns and shops crossing the island from one bridge to the other. He would construct the buildings himself and rent them to enterprising Kingsbridge traders. It excited him to look into the future of the town and imagine the buildings and streets it was going to need. This was the kind of thing the priory would have done, if it had had better leadership.

Included in the plan was a new house for him and Caris. This little place would be cosy when they were first married, but they would need more room eventually, especially if they had children. He had marked out a site on the southern shore, where they would get fresh air off the river. Most of the island was rocky, but the patch he had in mind featured a small area of cultivable soil where he might be able to grow some fruit trees. As he planned the house, he relished the vision of the two of them living side by side, day by day, always.

His dream was interrupted by a knock at the door. He was startled. Normally no one came to the island at night – except Caris, and she would not knock. 'Who is it?' he called nervously.

Thomas Langley came in.

'Monks are supposed to be asleep at this time,' Merthin said.

'Godwyn doesn't know I'm here.' Thomas looked at the slate. 'You draw left-handed?'

'Left or right, it makes no difference. Would you like a cup of wine?'

'No, thanks. I'll have to be up for Matins in a few hours, so I don't want to get sleepy.'

Merthin liked Thomas. There had been a bond between them ever since that day, twelve years ago, when he had promised that if Thomas should die he would take a priest to the place where the letter was buried. Later, when they had worked together on cathedral repairs, Thomas had always been clear in his instructions and gracious to apprentices. He managed to be sincere about his religious calling without becoming prideful: all men of God should be like that, Merthin thought.

He waved Thomas to a chair by the fire. 'What can I do for you?'

'It's about your brother. He has to be stopped.'

Merthin winced, as if at a sudden stab of pain. 'If I could do anything, I would. But I haven't seen him and, when I do, I'm not sure he will listen to me. There was a time when he looked to me for guidance, but I think those days are over.'

'I've just come from a meeting of the parish guild. They asked me to organize a militia.'

'Don't expect me to be part of it.'

'No, I didn't come for that purpose.' Thomas gave a wry smile. 'Your many amazing talents don't actually include military skills.'

Merthin nodded ruefully. 'Thanks.'

'But there is something you could do to help me, if you would.'

Merthin felt uneasy. 'Well, ask me.'

'The outlaws must have a hideout somewhere not far from Kingsbridge. I want you to think about where your brother might be. It's probably a place you both know – a cave, perhaps, or an abandoned verderer's hut in the forest.'

Merthin hesitated.

Thomas said: 'I know you'd hate to betray him. But think of that first family he attacked: a decent, hard-working peasant, his pretty wife, a lad of fourteen and a little girl. Now three of them are dead and the little girl has no parents. Even though you love your brother, you have to help us catch him.'

'I know.'

'Can you think where he might be?'

Merthin was not yet ready to answer the question. 'Will you take him alive?'

'If I can.'

Merthin shook his head. 'Not good enough. I need a guarantee.'

Thomas was silent for a few moments. At last he said: 'All right. I'll take him alive. I don't know how, but I'll find a way. I promise.'

'Thank you.' Merthin paused. He knew he had to do this, but his heart rebelled. After a moment, he forced himself to speak. 'When I was about thirteen we used to go hunting, often with older boys. We would stay out all day and cook whatever we shot. Sometimes we used to go as far as the chalk hills and meet the families who spend the summer up there grazing sheep. Shepherdesses tend to be quite free and easy – some would let you kiss them.' He smiled briefly. 'In winter, when they weren't there, we used their huts for shelter. That might be where Ralph is hiding out.'

'Thank you,' said Thomas. He stood up.

'Remember your promise.'

'I will.'

'You trusted me with a secret twelve years ago.'

'I know.'

'I never betrayed you.'

'I realize that.'

'Now I'm trusting you.' Merthin knew that his words could be interpreted two ways: either as a plea for reciprocity, or as a veiled threat. That was all right. Let Thomas take it how he wished.

Thomas put out his one hand, and Merthin clasped it. 'I'll keep my word,' Thomas said. Then he went out.

*

RALPH AND TAM rode side by side up the hill, followed by Alan Fernhill on his horse and the rest of the outlaws on foot. Ralph was feeling good: it had been another successful Sunday morning's work. Spring had arrived, and the peasants were beginning to bring the new season's produce to market. The members of the gang were carrying half a dozen lambs, a jar of honey, a stoppered jug of cream and several leather bottles of wine. As usual, the outlaws had suffered only minor injuries, a few cuts and bruises inflicted by the more foolhardy of their victims.

Ralph's partnership with Tam had been extraordinarily successful. A couple of hours' easy fighting brought them all they needed for a week of living in luxury. They spent the rest of their time hunting in the day and drinking in the evenings. There were no clodhopping serfs to badger them about boundary disputes or cheat them of rent. All they lacked were women, and today they had remedied that, by kidnapping two plump girls, sisters of about thirteen and fourteen years.

His only regret was that he had never fought for the king. It had been his ambition since boyhood, and he still felt the tug. Being an outlaw was too easy. He could not feel very proud of killing unarmed serfs. The boy in him longed yet for glory. He had never proved, to himself and others, that he had in him the soul of a true knight.

However, he would not allow that thought to lower his spirits. As he breasted the rise that hid the upland pasture where their hideout was, he looked forward to a feast tonight. They would roast a lamb on a spit and drink cream with honey. And the girls ... Ralph decided he would make them lie side by side, so that each would see her sister being violated by one man after another. The thought made his heart beat faster.

They came within sight of the stone shelters. They would not be able to use these much longer, Ralph reflected. The grass was growing and the shepherds would be here soon. Easter had been early this year, so Whitsun would come soon after May Day. The outlaws would have to find another base.

When he was fifty yards from the nearest hut, he was shocked to see someone walk out of it.

He and Tam both reined in, and the outlaws gathered around them, hands on their weapons.

The man approached them, and Ralph saw that it was a monk. Tam, beside Ralph, said: 'What in the name of heaven...?'

One sleeve of the monk's robe flapped empty, and Ralph recognized him as Brother Thomas from Kingsbridge. Thomas walked up to them as if meeting them by chance on the main street. 'Hello, Ralph,' he said. 'Remember me?'

Tam said to Ralph: 'Do you know this man?'

Thomas came up on the right side of Ralph's horse and extended his good right arm to shake hands. What the hell was he doing here? On the other hand, what harm could there be in a one-armed monk? Baffled, Ralph reached down and took the proffered hand. Thomas slipped his hand up Ralph's arm and grasped his elbow.

Out of the corner of his eye, Ralph saw movement near the stone huts. Glancing up, he saw a man step out through the doorway of the nearest building, closely followed by a second man, then three more; then he saw that they were pouring out of all the huts – and fitting arrows to the tall longbows they carried. He realized that he and his band had been ambushed – but, in that moment, the grip on his elbow tightened and, with a sudden strong heave, he was pulled off his horse.

A shout went up from the outlaws. Ralph crashed to the ground, landing on his back. His horse, Griff, skittered sideways, frightened. As Ralph tried to get up, Thomas fell on him like a tree, flattening him to the ground, and lay on top of him like a lover. 'Lie still and you won't get killed,' he said in Ralph's ear.

Then Ralph heard the sound of dozens of arrows being shot simultaneously from longbows, a deadly swish that was unmistakable, like the sudden wind of a flash thunderstorm. The noise was tremendous – there must have been a hundred archers, he thought. They had obviously crammed themselves into the shelters. Thomas's grasping Ralph's arm must have been the signal for them to come out and shoot.

He considered fighting Thomas off, and thought better of it. He could hear the cries of the outlaws as the arrows struck home. From ground level he could not see much, but some of his men were drawing their swords. However, they were too far from the archers: if they ran at their enemy, they would be shot down before they could engage. It was a massacre, not a battle. Hooves drummed the earth, and Ralph wondered whether Tam was charging the archers or riding away.

Confusion reigned, but not for long. Within moments he could tell that the outlaws were in full retreat.

Thomas got off him, pulled a long dagger from under his Benedictine robe, and said: 'Don't even think about drawing your sword.'

Ralph stood up. He looked at the archers, and recognized many of them: fat Dick Brewer, randy Edward Butcher, convivial Paul Bell, grumpy Bill Watkin – timid, law-abiding citizens of Kingsbridge, every one. He had been captured by tradesmen. But that was not the most surprising thing.

He looked curiously at Thomas. 'You saved my life, monk,' he said.

'Only because your brother asked me to,' Thomas replied crisply. 'If it had been up to me, you would have been dead before you hit the ground.'

*

THE KINGSBRIDGE JAIL was in the basement of the guild hall. The pen had stone walls, a dirt floor and no windows. There was no fire either, and prisoners occasionally died of cold in the winter; but this was May, and Ralph had a wool cloak to keep him warm at night. He also had a few items of furniture – a chair, a bench and a small table – rented from John Constable and paid for by Merthin. On the other side of the barred oak door was John Constable's office. On market days and during the fair, he and his deputies sat there waiting to be summoned to deal with trouble.

Alan Fernhill was in the cell with Ralph. A Kingsbridge archer had brought him down with an arrow in the thigh, and although the wound was not serious he had been unable to run. However, Tam Hiding had got away.

Today was their last here. The sheriff was due at midday to take them to Shiring. They had already been sentenced to death, in their absence, for the rape of Annet, and for the crimes they had committed in that court under the judge's eye: wounding the foreman of the jury, wounding Wulfric and escaping. When they got to Shiring they would be hanged.

An hour before noon, Ralph's parents brought them dinner: hot ham, new bread and a jug of strong ale. Merthin came with them, and Ralph surmised that this was goodbye.

His father confirmed it. 'We'll not follow you to Shiring,' he said.

His mother added: 'We don't want to see you—' She broke down, but he knew what she was going to say. They would not journey to Shiring to see him hang.

Ralph drank the ale but found it difficult to eat. He was going to the gallows, and food seemed pointless. Anyway, he had no appetite. Alan tucked in: he seemed to have no sense of the doom that awaited him.

The family sat in an awkward silence. Although these were their last minutes together, no one knew what to say. Maud wept quietly, Gerald looked thunderous and Merthin sat with his head in his hands. Alan Fernhill just looked bored.

Ralph had a question for his brother. Part of him did not want to ask it, but now he realized that this was his last chance. 'When Brother Thomas pulled me off my horse, protecting me from the arrows, I thanked him for saving my life,' he said. Looking at his brother, he went on: 'Thomas said he did it for you, Merthin.'

Merthin just nodded.

'Did you ask him to?'

'Yes.'

'So you knew what was going to happen.'

'Yes.'

'So ... how did Thomas know where to find me?'

Merthin did not answer.

Ralph said: 'You told him, didn't you?'

Their father was shocked. 'Merthin!' he said. 'How could you?'

Alan Fernhill said: 'You treacherous swine.'

Merthin said to Ralph: 'You were murdering people! Innocent peasants and their wives and children! You had to be stopped!'

Ralph did not feel angry, somewhat to his surprise. He felt a choking sensation. He swallowed, then said: 'But why did you ask Thomas to spare my life? Was it because you preferred that I should hang?'

Maud said: 'Ralph, don't,' and sobbed.

'I don't know,' Merthin said. 'Perhaps I just wanted you to live a little longer.'

'But you did betray me.' Ralph found that he was on the verge of breaking down. Tears seemed to gather behind his eyes, and he felt the pressure in his head. 'You betrayed me,' he repeated.

Merthin stood up and said angrily: 'By God, you deserved it!'

Maud said: 'Don't fight.'

Ralph shook his head sadly. 'We're not going to fight,' he said. 'Those days are over.'

The door opened and John Constable stepped in. 'The sheriff is outside,' he announced.

Maud put her arms around Ralph and clung to him, weeping. After a few moments, Gerald gently pulled her away.

John walked out and Ralph followed him. He was surprised not to be tied up or chained. He had escaped once before – were they not afraid he would do the same again? He walked through the constable's office and out into the open air. His family came behind.

It must have been raining earlier, for now bright sunshine reflected off the wet street and Ralph had to screw up his eyes against the glare. As he adjusted to the light he recognized his own horse, Griff, saddled ready. The sight gladdened his heart. He took the reins and spoke into the horse's ear. 'You never betrayed me, boy, did you, eh?' The horse blew through its nostrils and stamped, pleased to have its master back.

The sheriff and several deputies were waiting, mounted and armed to the teeth: they were going to let Ralph ride to Shiring, but they were not taking any risks with him. There would be no escape this time, he realized.

Then he looked again. The sheriff was here, but the other armed riders were not his deputies. They were Earl Roland's men. And there was the earl himself, black-haired and black-bearded, mounted on a grey charger. What was he doing here?

Without dismounting, the earl leaned down and handed a rolled sheet of parchment to John Constable. 'Read that, if you can,' Roland said, speaking as always out of one side of his mouth. 'It is a writ from the king. All the prisoners in the county are pardoned and freed – on condition they come with me to join the king's army.'

Gerald shouted: 'Hoorah!' Maud burst into tears. Merthin looked over the constable's shoulder and read the writ.

Ralph looked at Alan, who said: 'What does it mean?'

'It means we're free!' Ralph said.

John Constable said: 'It does, if I read it aright.' He looked at the sheriff. 'Do you confirm this?'

'I do,' said the sheriff.

'Then there is no more to be said. These men are free to go with the earl.' The constable rolled up the parchment.

Ralph looked at his brother. Merthin was weeping. Were they tears of joy, or frustration?

He was given no more time to wonder. 'Come on,' said Roland impatiently. 'We've completed the formalities, let's get on the road. The king is in France – we've a long way to go!' He wheeled his horse and rode down the main street.

Ralph kicked Griff's sides, and the horse eagerly broke into a trot and followed the earl.

41

'YOU CAN'T WIN,' Gregory Longfellow said to Prior Godwyn, sitting in the large chair in the hall of the prior's house. 'The king is going to grant a borough charter to Kingsbridge.'

Godwyn stared at him. This was the lawyer who had won two cases for him at the royal court, one against the earl and the other against the alderman. If such a champion declared himself beaten then, surely, defeat must be inevitable.

It was not to be borne. If Kingsbridge became a royal borough, the priory would be sidelined. For hundreds of years, the prior had ruled the town. In Godwyn's eyes, the town existed only to serve the priory, which served God. Now the priory would become just part of a town ruled by merchants, serving the god of Money. And the Book of Life would show that the prior who let this happen was Godwyn.

Dismayed, he said: 'Are you quite certain?'

'I'm always quite certain,' said Gregory.

Godwyn was aggravated. Gregory's cocksure attitude was all very well when he was sneering at your opponents, but when he turned it on you it became infuriating. Angrily, Godwyn said: 'You came all the way to Kingsbridge to tell me you can't do what I asked for?'

'And to collect my fee,' Gregory said blithely.

Godwyn wished he could have him thrown into the fishpond in his London clothes.

It was the Saturday of Whitsun weekend, the day before the opening of the Fleece Fair. Outside, on the green to the west of the cathedral, hundreds of traders were setting up their stalls, and their conversations and cries to one another combined to make a roar that could be heard here in the hall of the prior's house, where Godwyn and Gregory sat at either end of the dining table.

Philemon, sitting on the bench at the side, said to Gregory: 'Perhaps you could explain to the lord prior how you have reached this pessimistic conclusion?' He was developing a tone of voice that sounded half obsequious and half contemptuous. Godwyn was not sure he liked it.

Gregory did not react to the tone. 'Of course,' he said. 'The king is in France.'

Godwyn said: 'He has been there for almost a year, but nothing much has happened.'

'You will hear of action this winter.'

'Why?'

'You must have heard of the French raids on our southern ports.'

'I have,' Philemon said. 'They say the French sailors raped nuns at Canterbury.'

'We always claim the enemy has raped nuns,' Gregory said with condescension. 'It encourages the common people to support the war. But they did burn Portsmouth. And there has been serious disruption to shipping. You may have noticed a fall in the price you get for your wool.'

'We certainly have.'

'That's partly due to the difficulty of shipping it to Flanders. And the price you're paying for wine from Bordeaux is up for the same reason.'

We couldn't afford wine at the old prices, Godwyn thought; but he did not say so.

Gregory went on: 'These raids appear to be no more than preliminaries. The French are assembling an invasion fleet. Our spies say they already have more than two hundred vessels anchored in the mouth of the Zwyn river.'

Godwyn noted that Gregory talked of 'our spies' as if he were part of the government. In reality he was only retailing gossip. All the same, it sounded convincing. 'But what does the French war have to do with whether or not Kingsbridge becomes a borough?'

'Taxes. The king needs money. The parish guild has argued that the town will be more prosperous, and therefore will pay more tax, if the merchants are freed from the control of the priory.'

'And the king believes this?'

'It has proved true before. That's why kings create boroughs. Boroughs generate trade, and trade produces tax revenue.'

Money again, Godwyn thought with disgust. 'Is there nothing we can do?'

'Not in London. I advise you to concentrate on the Kingsbridge end. Can you persuade the parish guild to withdraw the application? What's the old alderman like? Can he be bribed?'

'My uncle Edmund? He's in poor health, and fading fast. But his daughter, my cousin Caris, is the real driving force behind this.'

'Ah, yes, I remember her at the trial. Rather arrogant, I felt.'

There was a case of the pot calling the kettle black, Godwyn thought sourly. 'She's a witch,' he said.

'Is she, now? That might help.'

'I didn't mean literally.'

Philemon said: 'As a matter of fact, lord prior, there have been rumours.'

Gregory raised his eyebrows. 'Interesting!'

Philemon went on: 'She is a great friend of a wise woman called Mattie, who mixes potions for gullible townspeople.'

Godwyn was about to pour scorn on the witchcraft idea, then he decided to shut up. Any weapon that might shoot down the notion of a borough charter must surely have been sent by God. Perhaps Caris does use witchcraft, he thought; who knows?

Gregory said: 'I see you hesitate. Of course, if you are fond of your cousin...'

'I was when we were younger,' Godwyn said, and he felt a pang of regret for the old simplicities. 'But I regret to say she has not grown into a God-fearing woman.'

'In that case...'

'I must investigate this,' Godwyn said.

Gregory said: 'If I might make a suggestion?'

Godwyn had had enough of Gregory's suggestions, but he did not quite have the nerve to say so. 'Of course,' he said with slightly exaggerated politeness.

'Heresy investigations can be ... mucky. You shouldn't get your own hands soiled. And people may be nervous about talking to a prior. Delegate the task to someone less intimidating. This young novice, for example.' He indicated Philemon, who glowed with pleasure. 'His attitude strikes me as ... sensible.'

Godwyn recalled that it was Philemon who had discovered Bishop Richard's weakness – his affair with Margery. He was certainly the man for any dirty work. 'All right,' he said. 'See what you can find out, Philemon.'

'Thank you, lord prior,' said Philemon. 'Nothing would give me more pleasure.'

*

ON SUNDAY MORNING, people were still pouring into Kingsbridge. Caris stood and watched them streaming over Merthin's two wide bridges on foot, on horseback, or driving two-wheeled and four-wheeled horse-carts and ox-carts laden with goods for the fair. The sight gladdened her heart. There had been no grand opening ceremony – the bridge was not really finished, but was usable thanks to a temporary timber roadbed – but, all the same, word had got around that it was open, and that the roads were safe from outlaws. Even Buonaventura Caroli was here.

Merthin had suggested a different way of collecting the tolls, which the parish guild had adopted eagerly. Instead of a single booth at the end of the bridge, creating a bottleneck, they had stationed ten men on Leper Island in temporary booths spread across the road between the two bridges. Most people handed over their penny without breaking stride. 'There isn't even a queue,' Caris said aloud, talking to herself.

And the weather was sunny and mild with no sign of rain. The fair was going to be a triumph.

Then, a week from today, she would marry Merthin.

She still had misgivings. The idea of losing her independence, and becoming someone's property, had not ceased to terrify her, even though she knew Merthin was not the kind of man to take advantage by bullying his wife. On the rare occasions when she had confessed this feeling – to Gwenda, for example, or to Mattie Wise – she had been told that she thought like a man. Well, so be it, that was how she felt.

But the prospect of losing him had seemed even more bleak. What would she have left, except for a cloth-manufacturing business that did not inspire her? When he finally announced his intention of leaving town, the future had suddenly seemed empty. And she had realized that the only thing worse than being married to him might be not being married to him.

At least, that was what she told herself in her more positive moments. Then, sometimes, when she lay awake in the middle of the night, she saw herself backing out at the last minute, often in the middle of the wedding, refusing to take the vows and rushing out of the church, to the consternation of the entire congregation.

That was nonsense, she felt now in the light of day, with everything going so well. She would marry Merthin and be happy.

She left the river bank and walked through the town to the cathedral, already crowded with worshippers waiting for the morning service. She remembered Merthin feeling her up behind a pillar. She felt nostalgic for the thoughtless passion of their early relationship; the long, intense conversations and the stolen kisses.

She found him near the front of the congregation, studying the south aisle of the choir, the part of the church that had collapsed in front of their eyes two years ago. She recalled going up into the space over the vaulting with Merthin, and overhearing that dreadful interaction between Brother Thomas and his estranged wife, the conversation that had crystallized all her fears and made her turn Merthin down. She put the thought out of her mind. 'The repairs seem to be holding,' she said, guessing what he was thinking about.

He looked dubious. 'Two years is a short time in the life of a cathedral.'

'There's no sign of deterioration.'

'That's what makes it difficult. An invisible weakness can work away for years, unsuspected, until something comes tumbling down.'

'Perhaps there is no weakness.'

'There must be,' he said with a touch of impatience. 'There was a reason why that collapse took place two years ago. We never found out what it was, so we haven't put it right. If it hasn't been put right, it's still a weakness.'

'It might have corrected itself spontaneously.'

She was just being argumentative, but he took her seriously. 'Buildings don't usually repair themselves – but you're right, it's possible. There might have been some seepage of water, for example from a blocked gargoyle, which somehow became diverted to a less harmful route.'

The monks began to enter in procession, singing, and the congregation went quiet. The nuns appeared from their separate entrance. One of the novice nuns looked up, a beautiful pale face in the line of hooded heads. It was Elizabeth Clerk. She saw Merthin and Caris together, and the sudden malice in her eyes made Caris shudder. Then Elizabeth bowed her head and disappeared back into her anonymous uniform.

'She hates you,' Merthin said.

'She thinks I stopped you marrying her.'

'She's right.'

'No, she's not – you could have married anyone you wanted!'

'But I only wanted you.'

'You toyed with Elizabeth.'

'It must have seemed that way to her,' Merthin said regretfully. 'But I just liked talking to her. Especially after you turned to ice.'

She felt uncomfortable. 'I know. But Elizabeth feels cheated. The way she looks at me makes me nervous.'

'Don't be afraid. She's a nun, now. She can't do you any harm.'

They were quiet for a while, standing side by side, their shoulders touching intimately, watching the ritual. Bishop Richard sat on the throne at the east end, presiding over the service. Merthin liked this sort of thing, Caris knew. He always felt better afterwards, and he said that was what going to church was supposed to do for you. Caris went because people noticed if she stayed away, but she had doubts about the whole business. She believed in God, but she was not sure He revealed His wishes exclusively to men such as her cousin Godwyn. Why would a God want praise, for example? Kings and earls required worship, and the more petty their rank the more deference they demanded. It seemed to her that an almighty God would not care one way or another whether the people of Kingsbridge sang His praises, any more than she cared whether the deer in the forest feared her. She occasionally gave voice to these ideas, but no one took her seriously.

Her thoughts drifted to the future. The signs were good that the king would grant Kingsbridge a borough charter. Her father would probably be the first mayor, if his health recovered. Her cloth business would continue to grow. Mark Webber would be rich. With increased prosperity, the parish guild could build a wool exchange, so that everyone could do business comfortably even in bad weather. Merthin could design the building. Even the priory was going to be better off, though Godwyn would not thank her.

The service came to an end, and the monks and nuns began to process out. A novice monk broke out of line and entered the congregation. It was Philemon. To Caris's surprise, he approached her. 'May I have a word?' he said.

She repressed a shudder. There was something loathsome about Gwenda's brother. 'What about?' she replied, barely politely.

'I want to ask your advice, really,' he said, with an attempt at a charming smile. 'You know Mattie Wise.'

'Yes.'

'What do you think of her methods?'

She gave him a hard look. Where was this going? She decided she had better defend Mattie anyway. 'She has never studied the texts of the ancients, of course. Despite that, her remedies work – sometimes better than those of the monks. I think it's because she bases her treatments on what has worked previously, rather than on a theory about the humours.'

People standing nearby were listening with curiosity, and some of them now joined in uninvited.

'She gave our Nora a potion that brought her fever down,' said Madge Webber.

John Constable said: 'When I broke my arm, her medicine took the pain away while Matthew Barber set the bone.'

Philemon said: 'And what kind of spells does she pronounce when she's making her mixtures?'

'No spells!' Caris said indignantly. 'She tells people to pray when they take their medicines, because only God can heal – she says.'

'Could she be a witch?'

'No! It's a ridiculous idea.'

'Only there has been a complaint to the ecclesiastical court.'

A chill gripped Caris. 'From whom?'

'I can't say. But I've been asked to investigate.'

Caris was mystified. Who could Mattie's enemy be? She said to Philemon: 'Well, you of all people know Mattie's worth – she saved the life of your sister when she gave birth to Sam. Gwenda would have bled to death if not for Mattie.'

'So it seems.'

'Seems? Gwenda's alive, isn't she?'

'Yes, of course. So you feel sure Mattie does not call on the devil?'

Caris noticed that he asked the question in a slightly raised voice, as if he wanted to make sure the listeners around heard it. She was puzzled, but she had no doubt of her answer. 'Of course I'm sure! I'll swear an oath if you want.'

'Not necessary,' Philemon said smoothly. 'Thank you for your advice.' He inclined his head in a sort of bow, and slithered away.

Caris and Merthin walked towards the exit. 'What rubbish!' Caris said. 'Mattie a witch!'

Merthin looked troubled. 'You would expect Philemon to want evidence against her, wouldn't you?'

'Yes.'

'So why did he come to you? He could have guessed that you, of all people, would deny the charge. Why would he be keen to clear her name?'

'I don't know.'

They passed through the great west doorway and out on to the green. The sun was shining on hundreds of stalls loaded with colourful goods. 'It doesn't make sense,' Merthin said. 'And that troubles me.'

'Why?'

'It's like the cause of weakness in the south aisle. If you can't see it, it may be working away invisibly to undermine you – and you won't know it until everything comes crashing down all around.'

*

THE SCARLET CLOTH on Caris's market stall was not as good as that sold by Loro Fiorentino, although you had to have a sharp eye for wool to see the difference. The weave was not so close, because the Italian looms were somehow superior. The colour was just as bright, but it was not perfectly even over the length of the bale, no doubt because Italian dyers were more skilled. In consequence, she charged one-tenth less than Loro.

All the same, it was easily the best English scarlet that had ever been seen at Kingsbridge, and business was brisk. Mark and Madge sold it retail by the yard, measuring and cutting for individual customers, and Caris dealt with wholesale buyers, negotiating reductions for one bale or six with drapers from Winchester, Gloucester and even London. By midday on Monday she knew she would sell out before the end of the week.

When business slowed down for the dinner break she strolled around the fair. She felt a profound sense of satisfaction. She had triumphed over adversity, and so had Merthin. She stopped at Perkin's stall to talk to the Wigleigh folk. Even Gwenda had triumphed. Here she was, married to Wulfric – something that had seemed impossible – and there was her baby, Sammy, a year old, sitting on the ground, fat and happy. Annet was selling eggs from a tray, as always. And Ralph had gone to France to fight for the king, and might never come back.

Farther on she saw Joby, Gwenda's father, selling his squirrel furs. There was a wicked man. But he seemed to have lost his power to hurt Gwenda.

Caris stopped at her own father's stall. She had persuaded him to buy fleece in smaller quantities this year. The international wool market could not possibly thrive when the French and English were raiding one another's ports and burning ships. 'How is business?' she asked him.

'Steady,' he said. 'I think I've judged it about right.' He forgot that it had been her judgement, not his, that had counselled caution. But that was all right.

Their cook, Tutty, appeared with Edmund's dinner: mutton stew in a pot, a loaf of bread and a jug of ale. It was important to look prosperous, but not overly so. Edmund had explained to Caris, many years ago, that although customers needed to believe they were buying from a successful business, they would resent contributing to the wealth of someone who appeared to be rolling in money.

'Are you hungry?' he asked her.

'Starving.'

He stood up to reach for the stew pot. Then he staggered, made an odd sound half way between a grunt and a cry, and fell to the ground.

The cook screamed.

Caris cried: 'Father!' But she knew he would not respond. She could tell he was unconscious by the way he hit the earth, inertly heavy, like a sack of onions. She fought down the urge to scream. She knelt beside him. He was alive, and breathing hoarsely. She grasped his wrist and felt his pulse: it was strong, but slow. His face seemed flushed. It was always reddish, but now it seemed more so than usual.

Tutty said: 'What is it? What is it?'

Caris forced herself to speak calmly. 'He's had a fit,' she said. 'Fetch Mark Webber. He can carry Father into the hospital.'

The cook ran off. People from the neighbouring stalls gathered around. Dick Brewer appeared and said: 'Poor Edmund – what can I do?'

Dick was too old and fat to lift Edmund. Caris said: 'Mark's coming to take him to the hospital.' She began to cry. 'I hope he'll be all right,' she said.

Mark appeared. He lifted Edmund easily, cradling him gently in his strong arms, and walked towards the hospital, negotiating his way through the crowds, calling: 'Mind out, there! Out of the way, please! Injured man, injured man.'

Caris followed, distraught. She could hardly see through her tears, so she stayed close to Mark's broad back. They reached the hospital building and went inside. Caris was grateful to see the familiar knobbly face of Old Julie. 'Fetch Mother Cecilia, as quick as you can!' Caris said to her. The old nun hurried away, and Mark laid Edmund on a pallet near the altar.

Edmund was still unconscious, eyes closed, breathing hoarsely. Caris felt his forehead: he was neither hot nor cold. What had caused this? It had been so sudden. One moment he had been talking normally, the next he fell down unconscious. How could such a thing happen?

Mother Cecilia came. Her bustling efficiency was reassuring. She knelt beside the pallet and felt Edmund's heart, then his pulse. She listened to his breathing and touched his face. 'Get him a pillow and a blanket,' she said to Julie. 'Then fetch one of the monk-physicians.'

She stood up and looked at Caris. 'He's had a fit,' she said. 'He may recover. All we can do is make him comfortable. The physician may recommend bleeding, but apart from that the only treatment is prayer.'

That was not good enough for Caris. 'I'm going for Mattie,' she said.

She ran out of the building and dodged through the fair, remembering that she had done exactly the same thing a year ago, rushing to fetch Mattie when Gwenda was bleeding to death. This time it was her father, and she felt a different kind of panic. She had been desperately worried about Gwenda, but now it was as if the world was falling apart. The fear that her father might die gave her the dreadful feeling she sometimes got in dreams, when she found herself on the roof of Kingsbridge Cathedral with no way down but to jump.

The physical effort of running through the streets calmed her a little, and she was in control of her emotions by the time she came to Mattie's house. Mattie would know what to do. She would say: I've seen this before, I know what will happen next, here's the treatment that helps.

Caris banged on the door. Hearing no immediate answer, she impatiently tried the latch and found it open. She dashed inside, saying: 'Mattie, you have to come to the hospital right away, it's my father!'

The front room was empty. Caris pulled aside the curtain that screened off the kitchen. Mattie was not there, either. Caris said aloud: 'Oh, why would you be out of the house at this very moment?' She looked around for some clue as to where Mattie might have gone. Then she noticed how stripped the room appeared. All the little jars and bottles had gone, leaving the shelves bare. There were none of the mortars and pestles Mattie used for grinding ingredients, none of her small pots for melting and boiling, no knives for chopping herbs. Caris returned to the front half of the house and saw that Mattie's personal possessions had also disappeared: her sewing box, her polished wood cups for wine, the embroidered shawl she had hung on the wall for decoration, the carved bone comb she treasured.

Mattie had packed up and gone.

And Caris could guess why. Mattie must have heard about Philemon's questions in church yesterday. Traditionally, the ecclesiastical court held a session on the Saturday of Fleece Fair week. Only two years ago the monks had used the occasion for the trial of Crazy Nell on the absurd charge of heresy.

Mattie was no heretic, of course, but it was difficult to prove that, as many old women had learned. She had calculated her chances of surviving a trial, and found the answer frightening. Without telling anyone, she had packed up her possessions and left town. Probably she had found a peasant returning home after selling his produce, and persuaded him to take her on his ox-cart. Caris imagined her leaving at first light, her box beside her on the cart, the hood of her cloak pulled forward to hide her face. No one could even guess where she had gone.

'What am I going to do?' Caris said to the empty room. Mattie knew better than anyone else in Kingsbridge how to help sick people. This was the worst possible moment for her to disappear, just when Edmund lay unconscious in the hospital. Caris felt despair.

She sat down on Mattie's chair, still panting from the effort of running. She wanted to run back to the hospital, but there was no point. She would not be able to help her father. Nobody could.

The town must have a healer, she thought; one who does not rely on prayers and holy water, or bleeding, but uses simple treatments that have been shown to work. And as she sat in Mattie's empty house, she realized that there was one person who could fill the role, someone who knew Mattie's methods and believed in her practical philosophy. That person was Caris herself.

The thought burst on her with the blinding light of a revelation, and she sat dead still, bewildered by the implications. She knew the recipes for Mattie's main potions: one for easing pain, one to cause vomiting, one for washing wounds, one to bring down a fever. She knew the uses of all the common herbs: dill for indigestion, fennel for fever, rue for flatulence, watercress for infertility. She knew the treatments Mattie *never* prescribed: poultices made with dung, medicines containing gold and silver, verses written on vellum and bound to the ailing part of the body.

And she had an instinct for it. Mother Cecilia had said so, had practically pleaded with Caris to become a nun. Well, she was not going to enter the priory, but she might perhaps take Mattie's place. Why not? The cloth business could be run by Mark Webber – he was doing most of the work anyway.

She would seek out other wise women – in Shiring, in Winchester, perhaps in London – and question them about their methods, what succeeded and what failed. Men were secretive about their craft skills – their 'mysteries' as they called them, as if there were something supernatural about tanning leather or making horseshoes – but women were usually willing to share knowledge with other women.

She would even read some of the monks' ancient texts. There might be some truth in them. Perhaps the instinct that Cecilia attributed to her would help her winnow the seeds of practical treatment from the chaff of priestly mumbo-jumbo.

She stood up and left the house. She walked slowly back, dreading what she would find at the hospital. She felt fatalistic now. Her father would either be all right, or he would not. All she could do was carry out her resolution so that in future, when the people she loved were sick, she would know she was doing everything possible to help them.

She fought back tears as she made her way through the fair

to the priory buildings. When she entered the hospital, she hardly dared look at her father. She approached the bed, which was surrounded by people: Mother Cecilia, Old Julie, Brother Joseph, Mark Webber, Petranilla, Alice, Elfric.

What must be, must be, she thought. She touched the shoulder of her sister, Alice, who moved aside, making room. At last Caris looked at her father.

He was alive and conscious, though he looked pale and tired. His eyes were open, and he looked straight at her and tried a weak smile. 'I'm afraid I gave you a scare,' he said. 'I'm sorry, my dear.'

'Oh, thank God,' said Caris, and she began to cry.

*

ON WEDNESDAY MORNING Merthin came to Caris's stall in consternation. 'Betty Baxter just asked me a strange question,' he said. 'She wanted to know who was going to stand against Elfric in the election for alderman.'

'What election?' Caris said. 'My father is alderman ... oh.' She realized what must be going on. Elfric was telling people that Edmund was too old and sick to fulfil the role, and the town needed someone new. And he was presenting himself as a candidate. 'We must tell my father right away.'

Caris and Merthin left the fairground and crossed the main street to the house. Edmund had left the priory hospital yesterday, saying – correctly – that there was nothing the monks could do for him but bleed him, which made him feel worse. He had been carried home, and a bed had been made up for him in the parlour on the ground floor.

This morning he was reclining on a stack of pillows in his improvised bed. He looked so weak that Caris hesitated to bother him with the news, but Merthin sat down beside him and laid out the facts starkly.

'Elfric is right,' Edmund said when Merthin had finished. 'Look at me. I can hardly sit upright. The parish guild needs strong leadership. It's no job for a sick man.'

'But you'll be better soon!' Caris exclaimed.

'Perhaps. But I'm getting old. You must have noticed how

absent-minded I've become. I forget things. And I was fatally slow to react to the downturn in the market for raw wool – I lost a lot of money last year. Thank God, we've rebuilt our fortune with the scarlet cloth – but you did that, Caris, not me.'

She knew all that, of course, but still she felt indignant. 'Are you just going to let Elfric take over?'

'Certainly not. He would be a disaster. He's too much in thrall to Godwyn. Even after we become a borough, we'll need an alderman who can stand up to the priory.'

'Who else could do the job?'

'Talk to Dick Brewer. He's one of the richest men in town, and the alderman must be rich, to have the respect of the other merchants. Dick's not afraid of Godwyn or any of the monks. He'd be a good leader.'

Caris found herself reluctant to do as he said. It seemed like accepting that he was going to die. She could not remember a time when her father had not been alderman. She did not want her world to change.

Merthin understood her reluctance, but urged her on. 'We have to accept this,' he said. 'If we ignore what's happening, we could end up with Elfric in charge. He would be a disaster – he might even withdraw the application for the borough charter.'

That decided her. 'You're right,' she said. 'Let's find Dick.'

Dick Brewer had several carts in different locations in the fairground. Each bore a huge barrel. His children, grandchildren and in-laws were selling ale from the barrels as fast as they could pour it. Caris and Merthin found him setting an example by drinking a large pot of his own brew while he watched his family making money for him. They took him aside and explained what was going on.

Dick said to Caris: 'When your father dies, I suppose his fortune will be divided equally between you and your sister?'

'Yes.' Edmund had already told Caris that this was in his will.

'When Alice's inheritance is added to Elfric's existing wealth, he will be very rich.'

Caris realized that half the money she was making from her scarlet cloth might go to her sister. She had not thought of this before, because she had not thought about her father dying. It came as a shock. Money itself was not important to her, but she did not want to help Elfric become alderman. 'It's not just a question of who is the richest man,' she said. 'We need someone who will stand up for the merchants.'

'Then you must put up a rival candidate,' Dick said.

'Will you stand?' she asked him directly.

He shook his head. 'Don't bother trying to persuade me. At the end of this week I'm handing over to my eldest son. I'm planning to spend the rest of my days drinking beer instead of brewing it.' He took a long draught from his tankard and belched contentedly.

Caris felt she had to accept that: he seemed quite sure. She said: 'Who do you think we might approach?'

'There's only one real possibility,' he said. 'You.'

Caris was astonished. 'Me! Why?'

'You're the driving force behind the campaign for a borough charter. Your fiancé's bridge has saved the Fleece Fair, and your cloth business has pretty much rescued the town's prosperity after the wool slump. You're the child of the existing alderman and, although it's not an inherited office, people think leaders breed leaders. And they're right. You've actually been acting as alderman for almost a year, ever since your father's powers started to fail.'

'Has the town ever had a woman alderman?'

'Not as far as I know. Nor one as young as you. Both these things will count heavily against you. I'm not saying you're going to win. I'm telling you no one else has a better chance of beating Elfric.'

Caris had a faintly dizzy feeling. Was it possible? Could she do the job? What about her vow to become a healer? Were there not many other people in town who would be better than she as alderman? 'What about Mark Webber?' she said.

'He'd be good, especially with that shrewd wife of his at his side. But people in this town still think of Mark as a poor weaver.'

'He's prosperous now.'

'Thanks to your scarlet cloth. But people are suspicious of new money. They would just say Mark is a jumped-up weaver. They want an alderman from a well-established family – someone whose father was rich, and preferably grandfather too.'

Caris wanted to beat Elfric, but she did not feel sure of her ability. She thought of her father's patience and shrewdness, his hearty conviviality, his inexhaustible energy. Did she have any such qualities? She looked at Merthin.

He said: 'You would be the best alderman the town has ever had.'

His unhesitating confidence decided her. 'All right,' she said. 'I'll do it.'

*

GODWYN INVITED ELFRIC to dine with him on the Friday of the fair. He ordered an expensive dinner: swan cooked with ginger and honey. Philemon served them, and sat down to eat with them.

The citizens had decided to elect a new alderman and, in a remarkably short time, two candidates had emerged as the principal contestants: Elfric and Caris.

Godwyn did not like Elfric, but he was useful. He was not a particularly good builder, but he had successfully ingratiated himself with Prior Anthony, and thereby gained the contract for cathedral repairs. When Godwyn took office he had seen in Elfric a servile toady and had kept him on. Elfric was not well liked, but he either employed or subcontracted most of the building craftsmen and suppliers in town, and they in their turn courted him in the hope of work. Having won his confidence, they all wanted him to continue in a position where he could grant them favours. And that gave him a power base.

'I don't like uncertainty,' Godwyn said.

Elfric tasted the swan and grunted appreciatively. 'In what context?'

'The election of a new alderman.'

'By its nature, an election is uncertain – unless there is only one candidate.'

'Which would be my preference.'

'Mine, too, provided that candidate was me.'

'That's what I'm suggesting.'

Elfric looked up from his dinner. 'Really?'

'Tell me, Elfric – how badly do you want to be alderman?'

Elfric swallowed his mouthful. 'I want it,' he said. His voice sounded a little hoarse, and he slurped some wine. 'I deserve it,' he went on, a note of indignation creeping into his tone. 'I'm as good as any of them, am I not? Why should I not be alderman?'

'Would you proceed with the application for a borough charter?'

Elfric stared at him. Thoughtfully, he said: 'Are you asking me to withdraw it?'

'If you're elected alderman, yes.'

'Are you offering to help me get elected?'

'Yes.'

'But how?'

'By eliminating the rival candidate.'

Elfric looked sceptical. 'I don't see how you could achieve that.'

Godwyn nodded to Philemon, who said: 'I believe Caris is a heretic.'

Elfric dropped his knife. 'You're going to try Caris as a witch?'

'You must not tell anyone about this,' Philemon said. 'If she hears about it beforehand, she may flee.'

'As Mattie Wise did.'

'I have let some townspeople believe that Mattie has been captured, and it is she who will be tried on Saturday at the ecclesiastical court. But, at the last minute, a different person will be accused.'

Elfric nodded. 'And, as it's an ecclesiastical court, there is conveniently no need for indictments or juries.' He turned to Godwyn. 'And you will be judge.'

'Unfortunately, no,' Godwyn said. 'Bishop Richard will preside. So we must prove our point.'

'Have you any evidence?' Elfric said sceptically.

Godwyn replied: 'Some, but we'd like more. What we already have would be plenty if the accused were some old woman with no family or friends, like Crazy Nell. But Caris is well known and comes from a wealthy and influential family, as I need hardly tell you.'

Philemon put in: 'It's extremely fortunate for us that her father is too ill to leave his bed – God has ordained it so that he will not be able to defend her.'

Godwyn nodded. 'Nevertheless, she has many friends. So our evidence must be strong.'

'What have you got in mind?' said Elfric.

Philemon answered. 'It would be helpful if a member of her family were to come forward and say that she had called upon the devil, or turned a crucifix upside down, or spoken to some presence in an empty room.'

For a moment, Elfric looked as if he did not understand; then enlightenment dawned. 'Oh!' he said. 'You mean me?'

'Think very carefully before you answer.'

'You're asking me to help send my sister-in-law to Gallows Cross.'

Godwyn said: 'Your sister-in-law; my cousin. Yes.'

'All right, I'm thinking.'

Godwyn saw on Elfric's face ambition, greed and vainglory, and he marvelled at the way God used even men's weaknesses to His holy purpose. He could guess what Elfric was thinking. The position of alderman was a burdensome task for an unselfish man such as Edmund, who exercised his power for the benefit of the town's merchants; but for someone with his eye on the main chance it offered endless opportunities for profit and self-aggrandizement.

Philemon continued in a smooth, assured voice. 'If you have never witnessed anything suspicious, then of course that is the end of the matter. But I beg you to search your memory carefully.'

Godwyn noticed again how much Philemon had learned in the last two years. The awkward priory servant had vanished. He talked like an archdeacon.

'There may have been incidents that seemed at the time perfectly harmless, but which take on a sinister cast in the light of what you have been told today. On mature reflection, you may feel that these events were not as innocent as they at first appeared.'

'I get your meaning, brother,' Elfric said.

There was a long silence. None of them ate. Godwyn waited patiently for Elfric's decision.

Philemon said: 'And, of course, if Caris were dead, then Edmund's entire fortune would come to the other sister, Alice ... your wife.'

'Yes,' Elfric said. 'I'd thought of that.'

'Well?' said Philemon. 'Is there anything you can think of that might help us?'

'Oh, yes,' Elfric said at last. 'I can think of quite a lot.'

42

CARIS WAS UNABLE TO find out the truth about Mattie Wise. Some people said she had been captured and was locked in a cell in the priory. Others thought she would be tried in her absence. A third strand of opinion claimed that someone else entirely would stand trial for heresy. Godwyn refused to answer Caris's questions, and the rest of the monks said they knew nothing.

Caris went to the cathedral on Saturday morning determined to defend Mattie whether she was present or not, and to stand up for any other poor old woman who suffered this absurd accusation. Why did monks and priests hate women so? They worshipped their Blessed Virgin, but treated every other female as an incarnation of the devil. What was the matter with them?

In a secular court there would have been a jury of indictment and a preliminary hearing, and Caris would have been able to find out in advance what the evidence against Mattie might be. But the church made its own rules.

Whatever they alleged, Caris would say loud and clear that Mattie was a genuine healer who used herbs and drugs and told people to pray to God to make them well. Some of the many townspeople who had been helped by Mattie would surely speak up for her.

Caris stood with Merthin in the north transept and remembered the Saturday two years ago when Crazy Nell had been tried. Caris had told the court Nell was mad but harmless. It had done no good.

Today, as then, there was a big crowd of townspeople and visitors in the cathedral, hoping for drama: accusations, counter-accusations, quarrels, hysterics, curses, and the spectacle of a woman being flogged through the streets and then hanged at Gallows Cross. Friar Murdo was present. He always showed up for sensational trials. They provided an opportunity for him to do what he did best, whip up hysteria in a congregation.

While they were waiting for the clergy, Caris's mind wandered. Tomorrow, in this church, she would marry Merthin. Betty Baxter and her four daughters were already busy making the bread and pastry for the feast. Tomorrow night, Caris and Merthin would sleep together in his house on Leper Island.

She had stopped worrying about the marriage. She had made her decision and she would take the consequences. In truth she felt very happy. Sometimes she wondered how she could have been so scared. Merthin could not make anyone his slave – it was not in his nature. He was even kind to his boy labourer, Jimmie.

Most of all she loved their sexual intimacy. It was the best thing that had ever happened to her. What she looked forward to most was having a home and a bed of their own, and being able to make love whenever they wanted to, on going to bed or on waking up, in the middle of the night or even the middle of the day.

At last the monks and nuns came in, led by Bishop Richard with his assistant, Archdeacon Lloyd. When they had taken their seats, Prior Godwyn stood up and said: 'We are here today to try the charge of heresy against Caris, daughter of Edmund Wooler.'

The crowd gasped.

Merthin shouted: 'No!'

Everyone turned to look at Caris. She felt sick with fear. She had had no suspicion of this. It hit her like a punch in the dark. Bewildered, she said: 'Why?' No one answered her.

She remembered her father warning her that Godwyn would have an extreme reaction to the threat of a borough charter. 'You know how ruthless he is, even over small disputes,' Edmund had said. 'Something like this will lead to total war.' Caris shuddered now to remember her reply: 'So be it – total war.'

Even so, Godwyn's chance of success would have been slender indeed if her father had been in good health. Edmund would have fought Godwyn to a standstill, and probably destroyed him. But Caris alone was a different matter. She did not have her father's power, authority or popular support – not yet. Without him, she had become vulnerable.

She noticed her Aunt Petranilla in the crowd. She was one of the few people *not* looking at Caris. How could she stand there in silence? Of course she supported her son, Godwyn, in general – but surely she would try to stop him condemning Caris to death? She had once said she wanted to be like a mother to Caris. Would she remember that? Somehow, Caris felt she would not. Her devotion to her son was too great. That was why she could not meet Caris's eye. She had already made up her mind not to stand in Godwyn's way.

Philemon stood up. 'My lord bishop,' he said, formally addressing the judge. But he immediately turned to the crowd. 'As everyone knows, the woman Mattie Wise has fled, too frightened and guilty to be tried. Caris has been a regular visitor to Mattie's house for some years. Only days ago she defended the woman, in front of witnesses, here in the cathedral.'

So that was why Philemon had questioned her about Mattie, Caris realized. She caught Merthin's eye. He had been worried because he could not figure out what Philemon was up to. He had been right to worry. Now they knew.

At the same time, part of her mind marvelled at the transformation of Philemon. That awkward, unhappy boy was now a confident, arrogant man, standing in front of the bishop, the prior and the townspeople, as full of spite as a snake about to strike.

Philemon said: 'She offered to swear on oath that Mattie is no witch. Why would she do that – unless to cover her own guilt?'

Merthin shouted out: 'Because she's innocent, and so is Mattie, you mendacious hypocrite!'

He might have been put in the stocks for that, but others were shouting at the same time, and his insult passed without comment.

Philemon went on: 'Recently, Caris has miraculously dyed wool the exact shade of Italian scarlet, something Kingsbridge dyers have never been able to do. How has this been achieved? By a magic spell!'

Caris heard the rumble of Mark Webber's bass voice: 'This is a lie!'

'She could not do this by daylight, of course. She lit a fire in her back yard at night, as was seen by people living nearby.'

Philemon had been assiduous, Caris noted with foreboding. He had interviewed her neighbours.

'And she chanted strange rhymes. Why?' Caris had sung to herself out of boredom, as she boiled up dyes and dipped the cloth, but Philemon had the ability to turn innocent trivia into evidence of evil. He dropped his voice to a thrilling stage whisper and said: 'Because she was calling for the secret aid of the Prince of Darkness –' he raised his voice to a shout – 'Lucifer!'

The crowd groaned with dread.

'That cloth is Satan's scarlet!'

Caris looked at Merthin. He was aghast. 'The fools are starting to believe him!' he said.

Caris's courage began to return. 'Don't despair,' she said. 'I haven't had my say yet.'

He took her hand.

'This is not the only spell she has used,' Philemon continued in a more normal voice. 'Mattie Wise also made love potions.' He looked accusingly around the crowd. 'There may even be wicked girls in this church now who have made use of Mattie's powers to bewitch a man.'

Including your own sister, Caris thought. Did Philemon know about that?

He said: 'This novice nun will testify.'

Elizabeth Clerk stood up. She spoke in a quiet voice, eyes lowered, the picture of nun-like modesty. 'I say this on my oath as I hope to be saved,' she began. 'I was betrothed to Merthin Builder.'

Merthin called out: 'Liar!'

'We were in love and very happy,' Elizabeth went on. 'Suddenly he changed. He seemed like a stranger to me. He became cold.'

Philemon asked her: 'Did you notice anything else unusual, sister?'

'Yes, brother. I saw him hold his knife in his left hand.'

The crowd gasped. This was an acknowledged sign of

bewitchment – although, as Caris knew, Merthin was ambidextrous.

Elizabeth said: 'Then he announced he was going to marry Caris.'

It was amazing, Caris thought, how the truth could be just a little skewed so that it sounded sinister. She knew what had really happened. Merthin and Elizabeth had been friends until Elizabeth made it clear she wanted to be more than a friend, at which point he had told her that he did not share her feelings, and they had parted. But a satanic spell made a much better story.

Elizabeth might have convinced herself that she was telling the truth. But Philemon knew this was a lie. And Philemon was Godwyn's tool. How could Godwyn reconcile his conscience with this level of wickedness? Was he telling himself that anything was justified in the service of the priory?

Elizabeth finished: 'I can never love another man. That is why I have decided to give my life to God.' She sat down.

It was powerful evidence, Caris realized, and her dismay darkened like a winter sky. The fact that Elizabeth had become a nun lent conviction to her testimony. She was operating a kind of sentimental blackmail: How can you disbelieve me when I have made such a sacrifice?

The townspeople were quieter now. This was not the hilarious spectacle of a mad old woman being condemned. They were watching a battle for the life of a fellow citizen.

Philemon said: 'Most damning of all, my lord bishop, is the final witness, a close member of the accused woman's own family: her brother-in-law, Elfric Builder.'

Caris gasped. She had been accused by her cousin, Godwyn; by her best friend's brother, Philemon; and by Elizabeth – but this was worse. For her sister's husband to speak against her was astonishing treachery. Surely no one would ever respect Elfric again?

Elfric stood up. The expression of defiance on his face told Caris he was ashamed of himself. 'I say this on my oath as I hope to be saved,' he began.

Caris looked around for her sister, Alice, but did not see her. If she had been here, she would surely have stopped Elfric. No doubt Elfric had ordered her to stay at home on some pretext. She probably knew nothing of this.

Elfric said: 'Caris speaks to unseen presences in empty rooms.'

'Spirits?' Philemon prompted.

'I fear so.'

A murmur of horror came from the crowd.

Caris was aware that she often talked aloud to herself. She had always thought of it as a harmless, if mildly embarrassing, habit. Her father said all imaginative people did it. Now it was being used to condemn her. She bit back a protest. It was better to let the prosecution run its course, then refute the accusations one by one.

'When does she do this?' Philemon asked Elfric.

'When she thinks she is alone.'

'And what does she say?'

'The words are difficult to make out. She might be speaking a foreign tongue.'

The crowded reacted to that, too: witches and their familiars were said to have their own language that no one else could understand.

'What does she seem to be saying?'

'To judge by her tone of voice, she is asking for help, pleading for good luck, cursing those who cause her misfortune, that sort of thing.'

Merthin shouted: 'This is not evidence!' Everyone looked at him, and he added: 'He has admitted he did not understand the words – he's just making this up!'

There was a rumble of support from the more level-headed citizens, but it was not as loud nor as indignant as Caris would have liked.

Bishop Richard spoke for the first time. 'Be quiet,' he said. 'Men who disrupt the proceedings will be put outside by the constable. Carry on, please, Brother Philemon, but do not invite witnesses to fabricate evidence when they have admitted they do not know the truth.'

That was at least even-handed, Caris thought. Richard and his family had no love for Godwyn after the quarrel over Margery's wedding. On the other hand, as a cleric Richard might not want the town to pass out of the priory's control. Perhaps he would at least be neutral in this. Her hopes rose a little.

Philemon said to Elfric: 'Do you think the familiars she speaks to help her in any way?'

'Most certainly,' Elfric replied. 'Caris's friends, those she favours, are lucky. Merthin has become a successful builder although he never even completed his apprenticeship as a carpenter. Mark Webber was a poor man, but now he is rich. Caris's friend Gwenda is married to Wulfric, even though Wulfric was betrothed to someone else. How are these things achieved, if not with unnatural help?'

'Thank you.'

Elfric sat down.

As Philemon summarized his evidence, Caris fought down a rising feeling of terror. She tried to put out of her mind the vision of Crazy Nell being flogged behind a cart. She struggled to concentrate on what she should say to defend herself. She could ridicule every statement made about her, but that might not be enough. She needed to explain why people had lied about her, and show what their motives were.

When Philemon was finished, Godwyn asked her if she had anything to say. In a loud voice that sounded more confident than she felt, she replied: 'Of course I do.' She made her way to the front of the crowd: she would not let her accusers monopolize the position of authority. She took her time, making them all wait for her. She walked up to the throne and looked Richard in the eye. 'My lord bishop, I say this on my oath as I hope to be saved –' she turned to the crowd and added – 'which I notice Philemon did not say.'

Godwyn interrupted: 'As a monk, he does not need to swear.'

Caris raised her voice. 'And a good thing for him, otherwise he would burn in hell for the lies he has told today!'

Score a point to me, she thought, and her hopes rose another notch.

She spoke to the crowd. Although the decision would be made by the bishop, he would be heavily influenced by the reaction of the townspeople. He was not a man of high principle.

'Mattie Wise healed many people in this town,' she began.

'On this day two years ago, when the old bridge collapsed, she was one of the foremost in tending to the injured, working alongside Mother Cecilia and the nuns. Looking around the church today I see many people who benefited from her care at that terrible time. Did anyone hear her invoke the devil on that day? If so, let him speak now.'

She paused to let the silence impress itself on her audience.

She pointed at Madge Webber. 'Mattie gave you a potion that brought down your child's fever. What did she say to you?'

Madge looked scared. No one was comfortable being called as a witness in the defence of a witch. But Madge owed a lot to Caris. She straightened her shoulders, looked defiant, and said: 'Mattie said to me: "Pray to God, for only He can heal."'

Caris pointed at the constable. 'John, she eased your pain while Matthew Barber set your broken bones. What did she say to you?'

John was used to being on the prosecuting side, and he, too, looked uneasy, but he told the truth in a strong voice. 'She said: "Pray to God, for only He can heal."'

Caris turned to the crowd. 'Everyone knows that Mattie was no witch. In that case, says Brother Philemon, why did she flee? Easy question. She was afraid that lies would be told about her – as they have been told about me. Which of you women, if falsely accused of heresy, would feel confident about proving your innocence to a court of priests and monks?' She looked around, letting her eyes rest on the prominent women of the town: Lib Wheeler, Sarah Taverner, Susanna Chepstow.

'Why did I mix dyes at night?' she resumed. 'Because the days were short! Like many of you, my father failed to sell all his fleeces last year, and I wanted to turn the raw wool into something I could market. It was very difficult to discover the formula, but I did it, by hard work, over many hours, day and night – but without the help of Satan.' She paused for breath.

When she began again, she used a different tone of voice, more playful. 'I am accused of bewitching Merthin. I have to admit that the case against me is strong. Look at Sister Elizabeth. Stand up, please, sister.'

Reluctantly, Elizabeth stood.

'She is beautiful, isn't she?' Caris said. 'She is also clever. And she is the daughter of a bishop. Oh, forgive me, my lord bishop, I meant no disrespect.'

The crowd chuckled at that cheeky stab. Godwyn looked outraged, but Bishop Richard smothered a smile.

'Sister Elizabeth cannot see why any man would prefer me to her. Nor can I. Unaccountably, Merthin loves me, plain as I am. I cannot explain it.' There was more giggling. 'I'm sorry Elizabeth is so angry. If we lived in Old Testament times, Merthin could have two wives and everyone would be happy.' They laughed loudly at that. She waited for the sound to subside, then said gravely: 'What I am most sorry about is that the commonplace jealousy of a disappointed woman should become the pretext, in the untrustworthy mouth of a novice monk, for a charge as serious as that of heresy.'

Philemon stood up to protest the charge of untrustworthiness, but Bishop Richard flapped a hand at him, saying: 'Let her speak, let her speak.'

Caris decided she had made her point about Elizabeth, and moved on. 'I confess that I sometimes use vulgar words when I am alone – especially if I stub my toe. But you may ask why my own brother-in-law would testify against me and tell you that my mutterings were invocations to evil spirits. I'm afraid I can answer that.' She paused, then spoke solemnly. 'My father is ill. If he dies, his fortune will be divided between me and my sister. But, if I die first, my sister will get it all. And my sister is Elfric's wife.'

She paused again, looking quizzically at the crowd. 'Are you shocked?' she said. 'So am I. But men kill for less money than that.'

She moved away, as if she had finished, and Philemon got up from his bench. Caris turned around and addressed him in Latin. '*Caput tuum in ano est.*'

The monks laughed loudly, and Philemon flushed.

Caris turned to Elfric. 'You didn't understand that, did you, Elfric?'

'No,' he said sulkily.

'Which is why you might have thought I was using some

sinister witchcraft tongue.' She turned back to Philemon. 'Brother, you know what language I was using, don't you?'

'Latin,' Philemon replied.

'Perhaps you would tell us what I just said to you.'

Philemon looked an appeal at the bishop. But Richard was amused, and just said: 'Answer the question.'

Looking furious, Philemon obeyed. 'She said: "You've got your head up your arse."'

The townspeople roared with laughter, and Caris walked back to her place.

When the noise died down, Philemon began to speak, but Richard interrupted him. 'I don't need to hear any further from you,' he said. 'You've made a strong case against her, and she has mounted a vigorous defence. Does anyone else have anything to say about this accusation?'

'I do, my lord bishop.' Friar Murdo came forward. Some of the townspeople cheered, others groaned: Murdo aroused contrary reactions. 'Heresy is an evil,' he began, his voice modulating into fruity preaching mode. 'It corrupts the souls of women and men—'

'Thank you, brother, but I know what heresy does,' said Richard. 'Do you have anything else to say? If not—'

'Just this,' Murdo replied. 'I agree with, and reiterate—'

'If it has been said before—'

'—your own comment that the case is strong, and the defence similar.'

'In which case—'

'I have a solution to propose.'

'All right, Brother Murdo, what is it? In the minimum number of words.'

'She must be examined for the Devil's Mark.'

Caris's heart seemed to stop.

'Of course,' said the bishop. 'I seem to remember you making the same suggestion at an earlier trial.'

'Indeed, lord, for the devil greedily sucks the hot blood of his acolytes through his own special nipple, as the newborn babe sucks the swollen breasts—'

'Yes, thank you, friar, no need for further details. Mother Cecilia, will you and two other nuns please take the accused woman to a place of examination?'

Caris looked at Merthin. He was pale with horror. They were both thinking the same.

Caris had a mole.

It was tiny, but the nuns would find it – in just the kind of place they thought the devil was most interested in: on the left side of her vulva, just beside the cleft. It was dark brown, and the red-gold hair around did not hide it. The first time Merthin had noticed it, he had joked: 'Friar Murdo would call you a witch – you'd better not let him see it.' And Caris had laughed and said: 'Not if he were the last man on earth.'

How could they have spoken of it in such a carefree way? Now she would be condemned to death for it.

She looked around desperately. She would have run, but she was surrounded by hundreds of people, some of whom would stop her. She saw Merthin's hand on the knife at his belt; but, even if the knife had been a sword and he had been a great fighter – which he was not – he could not have cut his way through such a crowd.

Mother Cecilia came to her and took her hand.

Caris decided she would escape as soon as she got outside the church. Crossing the cloisters she could easily break free.

Then Godwyn said: 'Constable, take one of your deputies and escort the woman to the place of examination, and stand outside the door until it is done.'

Cecilia could not have held Caris, but two men could.

John looked at Mark Webber, normally his first choice among the deputies. Caris felt a faint hope: Mark was a loyal friend to her. But the constable apparently had the same thought, for he turned from Mark and pointed to Christopher Blacksmith.

Cecilia tugged gently on Caris's hand.

As if sleepwalking, Caris allowed herself to be led out of the church. They left by the north door, Cecilia and Caris followed by Sister Mair and Old Julie, with John Constable and Christopher Blacksmith close behind. They crossed the cloisters, entered the nuns' quarters and made their way to the dormitory. The two men stayed outside.

Cecilia closed the door.

'No need to examine me,' Caris said dully. 'I've got a mark.'

'We know,' said Cecilia.

Caris frowned. 'How?'

'We have washed you.' She indicated Mair and Julie. 'All three of us. When you were in the hospital, two Christmases ago. You had eaten something that poisoned you.'

Cecilia did not know, or was pretending not to have guessed, that Caris had taken a potion to end her pregnancy.

She went on: 'You were puking and shitting all over the place, and bleeding down there. You had to be washed several times. We all saw the mole.'

Hopeless despair washed over Caris in an irresistible tide. She closed her eyes. 'So now you will condemn me to death,' she said in a voice so low it was almost a whisper.

'Not necessarily,' said Cecilia. 'There could be another way.'

*

MERTHIN WAS DISTRAUGHT. Caris was trapped. She would be condemned to death, and there was nothing he could do. He could not have rescued her even if he had been Ralph, with big shoulders and a sword and a relish for violence. He stared, horrified, at the door through which she had disappeared. He knew where Caris's mole was, and he felt sure the nuns would find it – that was just the kind of place where they would look most carefully.

All around him the noise of excited chatter rose from the crowd. People were arguing for or against Caris, rerunning the trial, but he seemed to be inside a bubble, and he could hardly follow what anyone said. In his ears, their talk sounded like the random beating of a hundred drums.

He found himself staring at Godwyn, wondering what he was thinking. Merthin could understand the others – Elizabeth was eaten up with jealousy, Elfric was possessed by greed and Philemon was pure malevolence – but the prior mystified him.

Godwyn had grown up with his cousin Caris, and he knew she was not a witch. Yet he was prepared to see her die. How could he do something so wicked? What excuse did he make to himself? Did he tell himself that this was all for the glory of God? Godwyn had once seemed to be a man of enlightenment and decency, the antidote to Prior Anthony's narrow conservatism. But he had turned out to be worse than Anthony: more ruthless in the pursuit of the same obsolete aims.

If Caris dies, Merthin thought, I'm going to kill Godwyn.

His parents came up to him. They had been in the cathedral throughout the trial. His father said something, but Merthin could not understand him. 'What?' he said.

Then the north door opened, and the crowd became silent. Mother Cecilia walked in alone and closed the door behind her. There was a murmur of curiosity. What now?

Cecilia walked up to the bishop's throne.

Richard said: 'Well, Mother Prioress? What do you have to report to the court?'

Cecilia said slowly: 'Caris has confessed—'

There was a roar of shock from the crowd.

Cecilia raised her voice. '...confessed her sins.'

They went quiet again. What did this mean?

'She has received absolution—'

'From whom?' Godwyn interrupted. 'A nun cannot give absolution!'

'From Father Joffroi.'

Merthin knew Joffroi. He was the priest at St Mark's, the church where Merthin had repaired the roof. Joffroi had no love for Godwyn.

But what was going on? Everyone waited for Cecilia to explain.

She said: 'Caris has applied to become a novice nun here at the priory—'

Once again she was interrupted by a shout of shock from the assembled townspeople.

She yelled over their voices: '– and I have accepted her!'

There was uproar. Merthin could see Godwyn yelling at the top of his voice, but his words were lost. Elizabeth was enraged;

Philemon stared at Cecilia with poisonous hatred; Elfric looked bewildered; Richard was amused. Merthin's own mind reeled with the implications. Would the bishop accept this? Did it mean the trial was over? Had Caris been saved from execution?

Eventually the tumult died down. As soon as he could be heard, Godwyn spoke, his face white with fury. 'Did she, or did she not, confess to heresy?'

'The confessional is a sacred trust,' Cecilia replied imperturbably. 'I don't know what she said to the priest, and if I did I could not tell you or anyone else.'

'Does she bear the mark of Satan?'

'We did not examine her.' This answer was evasive, Merthin realized, but Cecilia quickly added: 'It was not necessary once she had received absolution.'

'This is unacceptable!' Godwyn bellowed. He had dropped the pretence that Philemon was the prosecutor. 'The prioress cannot frustrate the proceedings of the court in this way!'

Bishop Richard said: 'Thank you, Father Prior—'

'The order of the court must be carried out!'

Richard raised his voice. 'That will do!'

Godwyn opened his mouth to protest further, then thought better of it.

Richard said: 'I don't need to hear any more argument. I have made my decision, and I will now announce my judgement.'

Silence fell.

'The proposal that Caris be permitted to enter the nunnery is an interesting one. If she is a witch, she will be unable to do any harm in the holiness of her surroundings. The devil cannot enter here. On the other hand, if she is not a witch, we will have been saved from the error of condemning an innocent woman. Perhaps the nunnery would not have been Caris's choice as a way of life, but her consolation will be an existence dedicated to serving God. On balance, then, I find this a satisfactory solution.'

Godwyn said: 'What if she should leave the nunnery?'

'Good point,' said the bishop. 'That is why I am formally sentencing her to death, but suspending the sentence for as long as she remains a nun. If she should renounce her vows, the sentence would be carried out.'

That's it, thought Merthin in despair: a life sentence; and he felt tears of rage and grief come to his eyes.

Richard stood up. Godwyn said: 'The court is adjourned!' The bishop left, followed by the monks and nuns in procession.

Merthin moved in a daze. His mother spoke to him in a consoling voice, but he ignored her. He let the crowd carry him to the great west door of the cathedral and out on to the green. The traders were packing up their leftover goods and dismantling their stalls: the Fleece Fair was over for another year. Godwyn had got what he wanted, he realized. With Edmund dying and Caris out of the way, Elfric would become alderman and the application for a borough charter would be withdrawn.

He looked at the grey stone walls of the priory buildings: Caris was in there somewhere. He turned that way, moving across the tide of the crowd, and headed for the hospital.

The place was empty. It had been swept clean, and the straw-filled palliasses used by the overnight visitors were stacked neatly against the walls. A candle burned on the altar at the eastern end. Merthin walked slowly the length of the room, not sure what to do next.

He recalled, from Timothy's Book, that his ancestor Jack Builder had briefly become a novice monk. The author had hinted that Jack had been a reluctant recruit, and had not taken easily to monastic discipline; at any rate, his novitiate had ended abruptly in circumstances over which Timothy drew a tactful veil.

But Bishop Richard had stated that if Caris ever left the nunnery she would be under sentence of death.

A young nun came in. When she recognized Merthin she looked scared. 'What do you want?' she said.

'I must speak to Caris.'

'I'll go and ask,' she said, and hurried out.

Merthin looked at the altar, and the crucifix, and the triptych on the wall showing Elizabeth of Hungary, the patron saint of hospitals. One panel showed the saint, who had been a princess, wearing a crown and feeding the poor; the second showed her building her hospital; and the third illustrated the miracle in which the food she carried beneath her cloak was turned into roses. What would Caris do in this place? She was a sceptic, doubtful of just about everything the church taught. She did not believe that a princess could turn bread into roses. 'How do they know that?' she would say to stories that everyone else accepted without question – Adam and Eve, Noah's ark, David and Goliath, even the Nativity. She would be a caged wildcat in here.

He had to talk to her, to find out what was in her mind. She must have some plan that he was not able to guess at. He waited impatiently for the nun to return. She did not come back, but Old Julie appeared. 'Thank heaven!' he said. 'Julie, I have to see Caris, quickly!'

'I'm sorry, young Merthin,' she said. 'Caris doesn't want to see you.'

'Don't be ridiculous,' he said. 'We're betrothed – we're supposed to get married tomorrow. She has to see me!'

'She's a novice nun, now. She won't be getting married.'

Merthin raised his voice. 'If that's true, don't you think she should tell me herself?'

'It's not for me to say. She knows you're here, and she won't see you.'

'I don't believe you.' Merthin pushed past the old nun and went through the door by which she had entered. He found himself in a small lobby. He had never been here before: few men had ever entered the nuns' area of the priory. He passed through another door and found himself in the nuns' cloisters. Several of them stood there, some reading, some walking around the square meditatively, some talking in quiet voices.

He ran along the arcade. A nun caught sight of him and screamed. He ignored her. Seeing a staircase, he ran up it and entered the first room. He found himself in a dormitory. There were two lines of mattresses, with neatly folded blankets on top. No one was there. He went a few steps along the corridor and tried another door. It was locked. 'Caris!' he shouted. 'Are you in there? Speak to me!' He banged on the door with his fist. He scraped the skin of his knuckles, which started to bleed, but he hardly felt the pain. 'Let me in!' he yelled. 'Let me in!'

A voice behind him said: 'I'll let you in.'

He spun round to see Mother Cecilia.

She took a key from her belt and calmly unlocked the door.

Merthin threw it open. Beyond it was a small room with a single window. All around the walls were shelves packed with folded clothes.

'This is where we keep our winter robes,' Cecilia said. 'It's a storeroom.'

'Where is she?' Merthin shouted.

'She's in a room that is locked by her own request. You won't find the room and, if you did, you couldn't get in. She will not see you.'

'How do I know she's not dead?' Merthin heard his voice crack with emotion, but he did not care.

'You know me,' Cecilia said. 'She's not dead.' She looked at his hand. 'You've hurt yourself,' she said sympathetically. 'Come with me and let me put some ointment on your cuts.'

He looked at his hand, and then at her. 'You're a devil,' he said.

He ran from her, back the way he had come, into the hospital, past a scared-looking Julie, out into the open. He made his way through the end-of-fair chaos in front of the cathedral and emerged on to the main street. He thought of speaking to Edmund, but decided against it: someone else could tell Caris's ailing father the terrible truth. Whom could he trust? He thought of Mark Webber.

Mark and his family had moved to a big house on the main street, with a large stone-built ground-floor storeroom for bales of cloth. There was no loom in their kitchen now: all the weaving was done by others whom they organized. Mark and Madge were sitting on a bench, looking solemn. When Merthin walked in, Mark jumped up. 'Have you seen her?' he cried.

'They won't let me.'

'That's outrageous!' Mark said. 'They don't have the right to stop her seeing the man she's supposed to marry!'

'The nuns say she doesn't want to see me.'

'I don't believe them.'

'Nor do I. I went in and looked for her, but I couldn't find her. There are a lot of locked doors.'

'She must be there somewhere.'

'I know. Will you come back with me, and bring a hammer, and help me break down every door until we find her?'

Mark looked uncomfortable. Strong as he was, he hated violence.

Merthin said: 'I have to find her – she might be dead!'

Before he could reply, Madge said: 'I've got a better idea.'

The two men looked at her.

'I'll go to the nunnery,' Madge said. 'The nuns won't be so nervous of a woman. Perhaps they will persuade Caris to see me.'

Mark nodded. 'At least then we'll know that she's alive.'

Merthin said: 'But ... I need more than that. What is she thinking? Is she going to wait until the fuss dies down, then escape? Should I try to break her out of there? Or should I just wait – and, if so, how long? A month? A year? Seven years?'

'I'll ask her, if they'll let me in.' Madge stood up. 'You wait here.'

'No, I'm coming with you,' Merthin said. 'I'll wait outside.'

'In that case, Mark, why don't you come, too, to keep Merthin company?'

To keep Merthin out of trouble, she meant, but he made no objection. He had asked for their help. And he was grateful to have two people he trusted on his side.

They hurried back to the priory close. Mark and Merthin waited outside the hospital while Madge went in. Merthin saw that Caris's old dog, Scrap, was sitting at the door, waiting for her to reappear.

After Madge had been gone for half an hour, Merthin said: 'I think they must have let her in, otherwise she'd be back by now.'

'We'll see,' said Mark.

They watched the last of the traders pack up and depart, leaving the cathedral green a sea of churned mud. Merthin paced up and down while Mark sat like a statue of Samson. One hour followed another. Despite his impatience, Merthin was glad of the delay, for almost certainly Madge was talking to Caris.

The sun was sinking over the west side of town when at last Madge emerged. Her expression was solemn and her face was wet with tears. 'Caris is alive,' she said. 'And there's nothing wrong with her, physically or mentally. She's in her right mind.'

'What did she say?' Merthin asked urgently.

'I'll tell you every word. Come, let's sit in the garden.'

They went to the vegetable patch and sat on the stone bench, looking at the sunset. Madge's equanimity gave Merthin a bad feeling. He would have preferred her to be spitting with rage. Her manner told him the news was bad. He felt hopeless. He said: 'Is it true that she doesn't want to see me?'

Madge sighed. 'Yes.'

'But why?'

'I asked her that. She said it would break her heart.'

Merthin began to cry.

Madge went on in a low, clear voice. 'Mother Cecilia left us alone, so that we could speak frankly, without being overheard. Caris believes that Godwyn and Philemon are determined to get rid of her, because of the application for a borough charter. She's safe in the nunnery, but if she ever leaves they will find her and kill her.'

'She could escape and I could take her to London!' Merthin said. 'Godwyn would never find us there!'

Madge nodded. 'I said that to her. We discussed it for a long time. She feels the two of you would be fugitives for the rest of your lives. She's not willing to condemn you to that. It's your destiny to be the greatest builder of your generation. You will be famous. But, if she is with you, you will always have to lie about your identity and hide from the light of day.'

'I don't care about that!'

'She told me you would say that. But she believes you do care about it, and what is more she thinks you should. Anyway, she cares about it. She will not take away your destiny, even if you ask her to.'

'She could say this to me herself!'

'She's afraid you would talk her round.'

Merthin knew Madge was telling the truth. Cecilia had been telling the truth, too. Caris did not want to see him. He felt choked with grief. He swallowed, wiped the tears from his face with his sleeve and struggled to speak. 'But what will she do?' he said.

'Make the best of it. Try to be a good nun.'

'She hates the church!'

'I know she has never been very respectful of the clergy. In this town, it's not surprising. But she believes she can find some kind of consolation in a life dedicated to healing her fellow women and men.'

Merthin thought about that. Mark and Madge watched him in silence. He could imagine Caris working in the hospital, taking care of sick people. But how would she feel about spending half the night singing and praying? 'She might kill herself,' he said after a long pause.

'I don't think so,' Madge said with conviction. 'She's terribly sad, but I don't see her taking that way out.'

'She might kill someone else.'

'That's more likely.'

'Then again,' Merthin said slowly and reluctantly, 'she might find a kind of happiness.'

Madge said nothing. Merthin looked hard at her. She nodded.

That was the terrible truth, he realized. Caris might be happy. She was losing her home, her freedom and her husband-to-be; but she might still be happy, in the end.

There was nothing more to say.

Merthin stood up. 'Thank you for being my friends,' he said. He began to walk away.

Mark said: 'Where are you going?'

Merthin stopped and turned back. There was a thought spinning in his head, and he waited for it to become clear. When it did, he was astonished. But he saw immediately that the idea was right. It was not merely right, it was perfect.

He wiped the tears from his face and looked at Mark and Madge in the red light of the dying sun.

'I'm going to Florence,' he said. 'Goodbye.'

Part Five

March 1346 to December 1348

Part Five

North Coast to December

She picked up the bowl of water that had been set for hand washing and used ... the length of the horse to calm it ... outside. A man ... she did not know was relieving himself ... the outside wall ... she guessed she was a traveller hoping for a bed. Next time use the stirrup behind the stable she snapped.

43

SISTER CARIS LEFT THE nuns' cloisters and walked briskly into the hospital. There were three patients lying in beds. Old Julie was now too infirm to attend services or climb the stairs to the nuns' dormitory. Bella Brewer, the wife of Dick Brewer's son Danny, was recovering from a complicated birth. And Rickie Silvers, aged thirteen, had a broken arm which Matthew Barber had set. Two other people sat on a bench to one side, talking: a novice nun called Nellie, and a priory servant, Bob.

Caris's experienced gaze swept the room. Beside each bed was a dirty dinner plate. The dinner hour was long over. 'Bob!' she said. He leaped to his feet. 'Take away these plates. This is a monastery, and cleanliness is a virtue. Jump to it!'

'Sorry, sister,' he said.

'Nellie, have you taken Old Julie to the latrine?'

'Not yet, sister.'

'She always needs to go after dinner. My mother was the same. Take her quick, before she has an accident.'

Nellie began to get the old nun up.

Caris was trying to develop the quality of patience, but after seven years as a nun she still had not succeeded, and she became frustrated by having to repeat instructions again and again. Bob knew he should clear away as soon as dinner was over – Caris had told him often. Nellie knew Julie's needs. Yet they sat on a bench gossiping until Caris surprised them with a lightning inspection.

She picked up the bowl of water that had been used for hand washing and walked the length of the room to throw it outside. A man she did not know was relieving himself against the outside wall. She guessed he was a traveller hoping for a bed. 'Next time, use the latrine behind the stable,' she snapped.

He leered at her, holding his penis in his hand. 'And who are you?' he said insolently.

'I'm in charge of this hospital, and if you want to stay here tonight you'll have to improve your manners.'

'Oh!' he said. 'The bossy type, eh?' He took his time shaking the drops off.

'Put away your pathetic prick, or you won't be allowed to spend a night in this town, let alone at the priory.' Caris threw the bowl of water at his middle. He jumped back, shocked, his hose soaked.

She went back inside and refilled the bowl at the fountain. There was an underground pipe running through the priory that brought clean water from upstream of the town and fed fountains in the cloisters, the kitchens and the hospital. A separate branch of the subterranean stream flushed the latrines. One day, Caris wanted to build a new latrine adjacent to the hospital, so that senile patients such as Julie would not have to go so far.

The stranger followed her in. 'Wash your hands,' she said, handing him the bowl.

He hesitated, then took the bowl from her.

She looked at him. He was about her own age, twenty-nine. 'Who are you?' she said.

'Gilbert of Hereford, a pilgrim,' he said. 'I've come to reverence the relics of St Adolphus.'

'In that case, you'll be welcome to stay a night here at the hospital, provided you speak respectfully to me – and to anyone else here, for that matter.'

'Yes, sister.'

Caris returned to the cloisters. It was a mild spring day, and the sun shone on the smooth old stones of the courtyard. Along the west walk, Sister Mair was teaching the girls' school a new hymn, and Caris paused to observe. People said that Mair looked like an angel: she had clear skin, bright eyes and a mouth shaped like a bow. The school was technically one of Caris's responsibilities – she was guest master, in charge of everyone who came into the nunnery from the outside world. She had attended this school herself, almost twenty years ago.

There were ten pupils, aged from nine to fifteen. Some were

the daughters of Kingsbridge merchants, others were noblemen's children. The hymn, on the theme that God is good, came to an end, and one of the girls asked: 'Sister Mair, if God is good, why did he let my parents die?'

It was the child's personal version of a classic question, one asked by all intelligent youngsters sooner or later: How can bad things happen? Caris had asked it herself. She looked with interest at the questioner. She was Tilly Shiring, twelve-year-old niece of Earl Roland, a girl with an impish look that Caris liked. Tilly's mother had bled to death after giving birth to her, and her father had broken his neck in a hunting accident not long afterwards, so she had been brought up in the earl's household.

Mair gave a bland answer about God's mysterious ways. Tilly clearly was not satisfied, but was unable to articulate her misgivings, and fell silent. The question would come up again, Caris felt sure.

Mair started them singing the hymn again, then stepped over to speak to Caris.

'A bright girl,' Caris said.

'The best in the class. In a year or two she'll be arguing with me fiercely.'

'She reminds me of someone,' Caris said, frowning. 'I'm trying to remember her mother...'

Mair touched Caris's arm lightly. Gestures of affection were prohibited between nuns, but Caris was not strict about such things. 'She reminds you of yourself,' Mair said.

Caris laughed. 'I was never that pretty.'

But Mair was right: even as a child, Caris had asked sceptical questions. Later, when she became a novice nun, she had started an argument at every theology class. Within a week, Mother Cecilia had been obliged to order her to be silent during lessons. Then Caris had begun breaking the nunnery rules, and responding to correction by questioning the rationale behind convent discipline. Once again she had been enjoined to silence.

Before long, Mother Cecilia had offered her a deal. Caris could spend most of her time in the hospital – a part of the nuns' work she did believe in – and skip services whenever necessary. In exchange, Caris had to stop flouting discipline and keep her theological ideas to herself. Caris had agreed, reluctantly and sulkily, but Cecilia was wise, and the arrangement had worked. It was still working, for Caris now spent most of her time supervising the hospital. She missed more than half the services, and rarely said or did anything openly subversive.

Mair smiled. 'You're pretty now,' she said. 'Especially when you laugh.'

Caris found herself momentarily spellbound by Mair's blue eyes. Then she heard a child scream.

She turned away. The scream had come, not from the group in the cloisters, but from the hospital. She hurried through the little lobby. Christopher Blacksmith was carrying a girl of about eight into the hospital. The child, whom Caris recognized as his daughter Minnie, was screaming in pain.

'Lay her on a mattress,' Caris said.

Christopher put the child down.

'What happened?'

Christopher was a strong man in a panic, and he spoke in a strangely high-pitched voice. 'She stumbled in my workshop and fell with her arm against a bar of red-hot iron. Do something for her, quickly, sister, she's in such agony!'

Caris touched the child's cheek. 'There, there, Minnie, we'll ease the pain very soon.' Poppy seed extract was too strong, she thought: it might kill such a small child. She needed a milder potion. 'Nellie, go to my pharmacy and fetch the jar marked "Hemp essence". Walk quickly, but don't run – if you should stumble and break the vial, it will take hours to make up a new batch.' Nellie hurried away.

Caris studied Minnie's arm. She had a nasty burn but, fortunately, it was restricted to the arm, nothing like as dangerous as the all-over burns people got in house fires. There were large angry blisters over most of the girl's forearm, and in the middle the skin was burned away to reveal charred flesh underneath.

She looked up for help and saw Mair. 'Go to the kitchen and get me half a pint of wine and the same quantity of olive oil, in two separate jugs, please. Both need to be warm but not hot.' Mair left.

Caris spoke to the child. 'Minnie, you must try to stop

screaming. I know it hurts, but you need to listen to me. I'm getting you some medicine. It will ease the pain.' The screaming abated somewhat, and began to turn into sobbing.

Nellie arrived with the hemp essence. Caris poured some on to a spoon, then thrust the spoon into Minnie's open mouth and held her nose. The child swallowed. She screamed again, but after a minute she began to calm down.

'Give me a clean towel,' Caris said to Nellie. They used a lot of towels in the hospital, and the cupboard behind the altar was always full of clean ones, by Caris's edict.

Mair came back from the kitchen with the oil and wine. Caris put a towel on the floor beside Minnie's mattress, and moved the burned arm over the towel. 'How do you feel?' she asked.

'It hurts,' Minnie wailed.

Caris nodded in satisfaction. Those were the first coherent words the patient had uttered. The worst was over.

Minnie began to look sleepy as the hemp took effect. Caris said: 'I'm going to put something on your arm to make it better. Try to keep still, will you?'

Minnie nodded.

Caris poured a little of the warm wine on to Minnie's wrist, where the burn was least bad. The child flinched, but did not try to snatch her arm away. Encouraged, Caris slowly moved the jug up the arm, pouring the wine over the worst of the burn to cleanse it. Then she did the same with the olive oil, which would soothe the place and protect the flesh from bad influences in the air. Finally she took a fresh towel and wrapped it lightly around the arm to keep the flies off.

Minnie was moaning, but half asleep. Caris looked anxiously at her complexion. Her face was flushed pink with strain. That was good – if she had been turning pale, it would have been a sign that the dose had been too strong.

Caris was always nervous about drugs. The strength varied from batch to batch, and she had no precise way of measuring it. When weak, the medicine was ineffectual; when strong, dangerous. She was especially frightened of overdosing children, though the parents always pressured her for powerful medicine because they were so distressed by their children's pain.

At that point Brother Joseph came in. He was old, now – somewhere in his late fifties – and all his teeth had fallen out, but he was still the priory's best monk-physician. Christopher Blacksmith immediately leaped to his feet. 'Oh, Brother Joseph, thank God you're here,' he said. 'My little girl has a terrible burn.'

'Let's have a look,' said Joseph.

Caris stood back, hiding her irritation. Everyone believed the monks were powerful doctors, able to work near-miracles, whereas the nuns just fed the patients and cleared up. Caris had long ago stopped fighting that attitude, but it still annoyed her.

Joseph took off the towel and looked at the patient's arm. He prodded the burnt flesh with his fingers. Minnie whimpered in her drugged sleep. 'A bad burn, but not fatal,' he said. He turned to Caris. 'Make up a poultice of three parts chicken fat, three parts goat dung and one part white lead, and cover the burn with it. That will bring forth the pus.'

'Yes, brother.' Caris was doubtful of the value of poultices. She had noticed that many injuries healed well without bringing forth the pus that monks thought such a healthy sign. In her experience, wounds sometimes became corrupt beneath such ointments. But the monks disagreed – except for Brother Thomas, who was convinced he had lost his arm because of the poultice prescribed by Prior Anthony almost twenty years ago. However, this was another battle Caris had given up. The monks' techniques had the authority of Hippocrates and Galen, the ancient writers on medicine, and everyone agreed they must be right.

Joseph left. Caris made sure that Minnie was comfortable and her father was reassured. 'When she wakes up, she will be thirsty. Make sure she gets plenty to drink – weak ale or watered wine.'

She was in no hurry to make the poultice. She would give God a few hours to work unaided before she began Joseph's treatment. The likelihood that the monk-physician would come back later to check on his patient was small. She sent Nellie out to collect goat dung from the green to the west of the cathedral; then she went to her pharmacy.

It was next to the monks' library. Unfortunately, she did not have large windows matching those in the library. The room was small and dark. However, it had a workbench, some shelves for her jars and vials, and a small fireplace for heating ingredients.

In a cupboard she kept a small notebook. Parchment was expensive, and a text block of identical sheets would be used only for holy scriptures. However, she had gathered a stack of odd-shaped offcuts and sewn them together. She kept a record of every patient with a serious complaint. She wrote down the date, the patient's name, the symptoms and the treatment given; then later she added the results, always noting exactly how many hours or days had passed before the patient got better or worse. She often looked back over past cases to refresh her memory on how effective different treatments had been.

When she wrote down Minnie's age, it occurred to her that her own child would have been eight this year, if she had not taken Mattie Wise's potion. For no good reason, she thought her baby would have been a girl. She wondered how she would have reacted if her own daughter had suffered an accident. Would she have been able to deal so coolly with the emergency? Or would she have been almost hysterical with fear, like Christopher Blacksmith?

She had just finished logging the case when the bell rang for evensong, and she went to the service. Afterwards it was time for the nuns' supper. Then they went to bed, to get some sleep before they had to rise for Matins at three o'clock in the morning.

Instead of going to bed, Caris went back to her pharmacy to make the poultice. She did not mind the goat's dung – anyone who worked in a hospital saw worse things. But she wondered how Joseph could imagine it was a good thing to put on burned flesh.

She would not be able to apply it until morning, now. Minnie was a healthy child: her recovery would be well advanced by then.

While she was working, Mair came in.

Caris looked at her curiously. 'What are you doing out of bed?'

Mair stood beside her at the work bench. 'I came to help you.'

'It doesn't take two people to make a poultice. What did Sister Natalie say?' Natalie was the sub-prioress, in charge of discipline, and no one could leave the dormitory at night without her permission.

'She's fast asleep. Do you really think you're not pretty?'

'Did you get out of bed to ask me that?'

'Merthin must have thought you were.'

Caris smiled. 'Yes, he did.'

'Do you miss him?'

Caris finished mixing the poultice and turned away to wash her hands in a bowl. 'I think about him every day,' she said. 'He is now the richest architect in Florence.'

'How do you know?'

'I get news of him every Fleece Fair from Buonaventura Caroli.'

'Does Merthin get news of you?'

'What news? There's nothing to tell. I'm a nun.'

'Do you long for him?'

Caris turned back and gave Mair a direct look. 'Nuns are forbidden to long for men.'

'But not for women,' Mair said, and she leaned forward and kissed Caris on the mouth.

Caris was so surprised that for a second she froze. Mair held the kiss. The touch of a woman's lips was soft, not like Merthin's. Caris was shocked, though not horrified. It was seven years since anyone had kissed her, and she realized suddenly how much she missed it.

In the silence, there was a loud noise from the library next door.

Mair jerked away guiltily. 'What was that?'

'It sounded like a box being dropped on the floor.'

'Who could it be?'

Caris frowned. 'There shouldn't be anyone in the library at this time of night. Monks and nuns are in bed.'

Mair looked scared. 'What should we do?'

'We'd better go and look.'

They left the pharmacy. Although the library was adjacent, they had to walk through the nuns' cloisters and into the monks' cloisters to reach the library door. It was a dark night, but they had both lived here for years, and they could find their way blindfold. When they reached their destination they saw a flickering light in the high windows. The door, normally locked at night, was ajar.

Caris pushed it open.

For a moment, she could not make out what she was looking at. She saw a closet door standing open, a box on a table, a candle next to it and a shadowy figure. After a moment, she realized that the closet was the treasury, where charters and other valuables were kept, and the box was the chest containing the jewelled gold and silver ornaments used in the cathedral for special services. The shadowy man was taking objects out of the box and putting them in some kind of bag.

The figure looked up, and Caris recognized the face. It was Gilbert of Hereford, the pilgrim who had arrived earlier today. Except that he was no pilgrim, and he probably was not even from Hereford. He was a thief.

They stared at each other for a moment, no one moving.

Then Mair screamed.

Gilbert put out the candle.

Caris pulled the door shut, to delay him a second longer. Then she dashed along the cloisters and darted into a recess, pulling Mair with her.

They were at the foot of the stairs that led to the monks' dorm. Mair's scream would have awakened the men, but they might be slow to react. 'Tell the monks what's happening!' Caris yelled at Mair. 'Go on, run!' Mair dashed up the stairs.

Caris heard a creak, and guessed that the library door was opening. She listened for the sound of footsteps on the flagstones of the cloisters, but Gilbert must have been a practised burglar, for he walked silently. She held her breath and listened for his. Then a commotion broke out upstairs.

The thief must have realized then that he had only a few seconds to escape, for he broke into a run, and Caris heard his tread.

She did not care greatly for the precious cathedral ornaments, believing that gold and jewels probably pleased the bishop and the prior more than they pleased God; but she had taken a dislike to Gilbert, and she hated the idea that he might get rich by robbing the priory. So she stepped out of her recess.

She could hardly see, but there was no mistaking the running steps hurtling towards her. She held her arms out to protect herself, and he cannoned into her. She was knocked off balance, but grasped his clothing, and they both fell to the ground. There was a clatter as his sack of crucifixes and chalices hit the paving stones.

The pain of the fall enraged Caris, and she let go of his clothes and reached for where she thought his face might be. She encountered skin and dragged her fingernails across it, digging deep. He roared with pain and she felt blood flow under her fingertips.

But he was stronger. He grappled with her and swung himself on top. A light appeared from the head of the monks' stairs, and suddenly she could see Gilbert – and he could see her. Kneeling astride her, he punched her face, first with his right fist, then with his left, then with the right again. She cried out in agony.

There was more light. The monks were stumbling down the stairs. Caris heard Mair scream: 'Leave her alone, you devil!' Gilbert leaped to his feet and scrabbled for his sack, but he was too late: suddenly Mair was flying at him with some kind of blunt instrument. He took a blow to the head, turned to retaliate, and fell beneath a tidal wave of monks.

Caris got to her feet. Mair came to her and they hugged.

Mair said: 'What did you do?'

'Tripped him up then scratched his face. What did you hit him with?'

'The wooden cross off the dormitory wall.'

'Well,' said Caris, 'so much for turning the other cheek.'

44

GILBERT HEREFORD WAS TRIED before the ecclesiastical court, found guilty and sentenced, by Prior Godwyn, to an appropriate punishment for those who robbed churches: he would be flayed alive. His skin would be cut off him, while he was fully conscious, and he would bleed to death.

On the day of the flaying, Godwyn had his weekly meeting with Mother Cecilia. Their deputies would also attend: sub-prior Philemon and sub-prioress Natalie. Waiting in the hall of the prior's house for the nuns to arrive, Godwyn said to Philemon: 'We must try to persuade them to build a new treasury. We can no longer keep our valuables in a box in the library.'

Philemon said thoughtfully: 'Would it be a shared building?'

'It would have to be. We can't afford to pay for it.'

Godwyn thought regretfully of the ambitions he had once had, as a young man, to reform the monastery's finances and make it rich again. This had not happened, and he still did not understand why. He had been tough, forcing the townspeople to use and pay for the priory's mills, fishponds and warrens, but they seemed to find ways around his rules – like building mills in neighbouring villages. He had imposed harsh sentences on men and women caught poaching or illegally cutting down trees in the priory's forests. And he had resisted the blandishments of those who would tempt him to spend the priory's money by building mills, or waste the priory's timber by licensing charcoal burners and iron smelters. He felt sure his approach was right, but it had not yet yielded the increased income he felt he deserved.

'So you will ask Cecilia for the money,' Philemon said thoughtfully. 'There might be advantages in keeping our wealth in the same place as the nuns'.'

Godwyn saw which way Philemon's devious mind was leading him. 'But we wouldn't say that to Cecilia.'

'Of course not.'

'All right, I'll propose it.'

'While we're waiting...'

'Yes?'

'There's a problem you need to know about in the village of Long Ham.'

Godwyn nodded. Long Ham was one of dozens of villages that paid homage – and feudal dues – to the priory.

Philemon explained: 'It has to do with the landholding of a widow, Mary-Lynn. When her husband died, she agreed to let a neighbour farm her land, a man called John Nott. Now the widow has remarried, and she wants the land back so that her new husband can farm it.'

Godwyn was puzzled. This was a typical peasant squabble, too trivial to require his intervention. 'What does the bailiff say?'

'That the land should revert to the widow, since the arrangement was always intended to be temporary.'

'Then that is what must happen.'

'There is a complication. Sister Elizabeth has a half-brother and two half-sisters in Long Ham.'

'Ah.' Godwyn might have guessed there would be a reason for Philemon's interest. Sister Elizabeth, formerly Elizabeth Clerk, was the nuns' matricularius, in charge of their buildings. She was young and bright, and would rise farther up the hierarchy. She could be a valuable ally.

'They are the only family she's got, apart from her mother, who works at the Bell,' Philemon went on. 'Elizabeth is fond of her peasant relatives, and they in turn revere her as the holy one of the family. When they come to Kingsbridge they bring gifts to the nunnery – fruit, honey, eggs, that sort of thing.'

'And...?'

'John Nott is the half-brother of Sister Elizabeth.'

'Has Elizabeth asked you to intervene?'

'Yes. And she also asked that I should not tell Mother Cecilia of the request.'

Godwyn knew that this was just the kind of thing Philemon

liked. He loved to be regarded as a powerful person who could use his influence to favour one side or the other in a dispute. Such things fed his ego, which was never satisfied. And he was drawn to anything clandestine. The fact that Elizabeth did not want her superior to know about this request delighted Philemon. It meant he knew her shameful secret. He would store the information away like miser's gold.

'What do you want to do?' Godwyn asked.

'It's for you to say, of course, but I suggest we let John Nott keep the land. Elizabeth would be in our debt, and that cannot fail to be useful at some point in the future.'

'That's hard on the widow,' Godwyn said uneasily.

'I agree. But that must be balanced against the interests of the priory.'

'And God's work is more important. Very well. Tell the bailiff.'

'The widow will receive her reward in the hereafter.'

'Indeed.' There had been a time when Godwyn had hesitated to authorize Philemon's underhand schemes, but that was long ago. Philemon had proved too useful – as Godwyn's mother, Petranilla, had forecast all those years ago.

There was a tap at the door, and Petranilla herself came in.

She now lived in a comfortable small house in Candle Court, just off the main street. Her brother Edmund had left her a generous bequest, enough to last her the rest of her life. She was fifty-eight years old, her tall figure was now stooped and frail, and she walked with a stick, but she still had a mind like a bear trap. As always, Godwyn was glad to see her but also apprehensive that he might have done something to displease her.

Petranilla was the head of the family now. Anthony had been killed in the bridge collapse and Edmund had died seven years ago, so she was the last survivor of her generation. She never hesitated to tell Godwyn what to do. She was the same with her niece Alice. Alice's husband, Elfric, was the alderman, but she gave him orders too. Her authority even extended to her step-granddaughter Griselda, and she terrorized Griselda's eight-year-old son, Little Merthin. Her judgement was as sound as ever, so they all obeyed her most of the time. If for some reason she did not take command, they would usually ask her opinion anyway. Godwyn was not sure how they would manage without her. And on the rare occasions when they did not do her bidding, they worked very hard to hide the fact. Only Caris stood up to her. 'Don't you dare tell me what to do,' she had said to Petranilla more than once. 'You would have let them kill me.'

Petranilla sat down and looked around the room. 'This is not good enough,' she said.

She was often abrupt, but all the same Godwyn became edgy when she spoke like this. 'What do you mean?'

'You should have a better house.'

'I know.' Eight years ago, Godwyn had tried to persuade Mother Cecilia to pay for a new palace. She had promised to give him the money three years later but, when the time came, she said she had changed her mind. He felt sure it was because of what he had done to Caris. After that heresy trial, his charm had ceased to work on Cecilia, and it had become difficult to get money out of her.

Petranilla said: 'You need a palace for entertaining bishops and archbishops, barons and earls.'

'We don't get many of those, nowadays. Earl Roland and Bishop Richard have been in France for much of the last few years.' King Edward had invaded north-east France in 1339 and spent all of 1340 there; then in 1342 he had taken his army to north-west France and fought in Brittany. In 1345 English troops had done battle in the south-western wine district of Gascony. Now Edward was back in England, but assembling another army of invasion.

'Roland and Richard aren't the only noblemen,' Petranilla said testily.

'The others never come here.'

Her voice hardened. 'Perhaps that's because you can't accommodate them in the style they expect. You need a banqueting hall, and a private chapel, and spacious bedchambers.'

She had been awake all night thinking about this, he guessed. That was her way: she brooded over things then shot off her ideas like arrows. He wondered what had brought on this particular complaint. 'It sounds very extravagant,' he said, playing for time.

'Don't you understand?' she snapped. 'The priory is not as influential as it might be, simply because you don't ever see the powerful men of the land. When you've got a palace with beautiful rooms for them, they will come.'

She was probably right. Wealthy monasteries such as Durham and St Albans even complained about the number of noble and royal visitors they were obliged to entertain.

She went on: 'Yesterday was the anniversary of my father's death.' So that's what brought this on, Godwyn thought: she's been remembering grandfather's glorious career. 'You've been prior here for almost nine years,' she said. 'I don't want you to get stuck. The archbishops and the king should be considering you for a bishopric, a major abbey such as Durham, or a mission to the pope.'

Godwyn had always assumed that Kingsbridge would be his springboard to higher things but, he realized now, he had let his ambition wane. It seemed only a little while ago that he had won the election for prior. He felt he had only just got on top of the job. But she was right, it was more than eight years.

'Why aren't they thinking of you for more important posts?' she asked rhetorically. 'Because they don't know you exist! You are prior of a great monastery, but you haven't told anyone about it. Display your magnificence! Build a palace. Invite the archbishop of Canterbury to be your first guest. Dedicate the chapel to his favourite saint. Tell the king you have built a royal bedchamber in the hope that he will visit.'

'Wait a moment, one thing at a time,' Godwyn protested. 'I'd love to build a palace, but I haven't got the money.'

'Then get it,' she said.

He wanted to ask her how, but at that moment the two leaders of the nunnery came into the room. Petranilla and Cecilia greeted one another with wary courtesy, then Petranilla took her leave.

Mother Cecilia and Sister Natalie sat down. Cecilia was fifty-one now, with grey in her hair and poor eyesight. She still darted about the place like a busy bird, poking her beak into every room, chirping her instructions to nuns, novices and servants; but she had mellowed with the years, and would go a long way to avoid a conflict.

Cecilia was carrying a scroll. 'The nunnery has received a legacy,' she said as she made herself comfortable. 'From a pious woman of Thornbury.'

Godwyn said: 'How much?'

'One hundred and fifty pounds in gold coins.'

Godwyn was startled. It was a huge sum. It was enough to build a modest palace. 'The nunnery has received it – or the priory?'

'The nunnery,' she said firmly. 'This scroll is our copy of her will.'

'Why did she leave you so much money?'

'Apparently we nursed her when she fell ill on her way home from London.'

Natalie spoke. She was a few years older than Cecilia, a round-faced woman with a mild disposition. 'Our problem is, where are we going to keep the money?'

Godwyn looked at Philemon. Natalie had given them an opening for the topic they had planned to raise. 'What do you do with your money at present?' he asked her.

'It's in the prioress's bedroom, which can be reached only by going through the dormitory.'

As though thinking of it for the first time, Godwyn said: 'Perhaps we should spend a little of the bequest on a new treasury.'

'I think that's necessary,' said Cecilia. 'A simple stone building with no windows and a stout oak door.'

'It won't take long to construct,' Godwyn said. 'And shouldn't cost more than five or ten pounds.'

'For safety, we think it should be part of the cathedral.'

'Ah.' That was why the nuns had to discuss the plan with Godwyn. They would not have needed to consult him about building within their own area of the priory, but the church was common to monks and nuns. He said: 'It could go up against the cathedral wall, in the corner formed by the north transept and the choir, but be entered from inside the church.'

'Yes – that's just the kind of thing I had in mind.'

'I'll speak to Elfric today, if you like, and ask him to give us an estimate.'

'Please do.'

Godwyn was happy to have extracted from Cecilia a fraction of her windfall, but he was not satisfied. After the conversation with his mother, he yearned to get his hands on more of it. He would have liked to grab it all. But how?

The cathedral bell tolled, and the four of them stood up and went out.

The condemned man was outside the west end of the church. He was naked, and tied tightly by his hands and feet to an upright wooden rectangle like a door frame. A hundred or so townspeople stood waiting to watch the execution. The ordinary monks and nuns had not been invited: it was considered improper for them to see bloodshed.

The executioner was Will Tanner, a man of about fifty whose skin was brown from his trade. He wore a clean canvas apron. He stood by a small table on which he had laid out his knives. He was sharpening one of them on a stone, and the scrape of steel on granite made Godwyn shudder.

Godwyn said several prayers, ending with an extempore plea in English that the death of the thief would serve God by deterring others from the same sin. Then he nodded to Will Tanner.

Will stood behind the tethered thief. He took a small knife with a sharp point and inserted it into the middle of Gilbert's neck, then drew it downwards in a long straight line to the base of the spine. Gilbert roared with pain, and blood welled out of the cut. Will made another slash across the man's shoulders, forming the shape of the letter T.

Will then changed his knife, selecting one with a long, thin blade. He inserted it carefully at the point where the two cuts met, and pulled away a corner of skin. Gilbert cried out again. Then, holding the corner in the fingers of his left hand, Will began carefully to cut the skin of Gilbert's back away from his body.

Gilbert began to scream.

Sister Natalie made a noise in her throat, turned away and ran back into the priory. Cecilia closed her eyes and began to pray. Godwyn felt nauseated. Someone in the crowd fell to the ground in a dead faint. Only Philemon seemed unmoved.

Will worked quickly, his sharp knife slicing through the subcutaneous fat to reveal the woven muscles below. Blood flowed copiously, and he stopped every few seconds to wipe his hands on his apron. Gilbert screamed in undiminished agony at every cut. Soon the skin of his back hung in two broad flaps.

Will knelt on the ground, his knees an inch deep in blood, and began to work on the legs.

The screaming stopped suddenly: Gilbert appeared to have passed out. Godwyn was relieved. He had intended the man to suffer agony for trying to rob a church – and he had wanted others to witness the thief's torment – but, all the same, he had found it hard to listen to that screaming.

Will continued his work phlegmatically, apparently unconcerned whether his victim was conscious or not, until all the back skin – body, arms and legs – was detached. Then he went around to the front. He cut around the ankles and wrists, then detached the skin so that it hung from the victim's shoulders and hips. He worked upwards from the pelvis, and Godwyn realized he was going to try to take the entire skin off in one piece. Soon there was no skin left attached except for the head.

Gilbert was still breathing.

Will made a careful series of cuts around the skull. Then he put down his knives and wiped his hands one more time. Finally he grasped Gilbert's skin at the shoulders and gave a sudden jerk upwards. The face and scalp were ripped off the head, yet remained attached to the rest of the skin.

Will held Gilbert's bloody hide up in the air like a hunting trophy, and the crowd cheered.

*

CARIS WAS UNEASY about sharing the new treasury with the monks. She pestered Beth with so many questions about the safety of their money that in the end Beth took her to inspect the place.

Godwyn and Philemon were in the cathedral at the time, as if by chance, and they saw the nuns and followed them.

They passed through a new arch in the south wall of the choir into a little lobby and halted in front of a formidable studded door. Sister Beth took out a big iron key. She was a humble, unassuming woman, like most nuns. 'This is ours,' she said to Caris. 'We can enter the treasury any time we like.'

'I should think so, since we paid for it,' said Caris crisply.

They entered a small square room. It contained a counting table with a stack of parchment rolls, a couple of stools and a big ironbound chest.

'The chest is too big to be taken out through the door,' Beth pointed out.

Caris said: 'So how did you it get in here?'

Godwyn answered: 'In pieces. It was put together by the carpenter here in the room.'

Caris gave Godwyn a cold look. This man had tried to kill her. Ever since the witchcraft trial she had looked at him with loathing and avoided speaking to him if at all possible. Now she said flatly: 'The nuns will need a key to the chest.'

'Not necessary,' Godwyn said quickly. 'It contains the jewelled cathedral ornaments, which are in the care of the sacrist, who is always a monk.'

Caris said: 'Show me.'

She could see that he was offended by her tone, and had half a mind to refuse her, but he wanted to appear open and guileless, so he conceded. He took a key from the wallet at his belt and opened the chest. As well as the cathedral ornaments, it contained dozens of scrolls, the priory's charters.

'Not just the ornaments, then,' Caris said, her suspicions vindicated.

'The records too.'

'Including the nuns' charters,' she persisted.

'Yes.'

'In which case we will have a key.'

'My idea is that we copy all our charters, and keep the copies in the library. Whenever we need to read a charter, we consult the library copy, so that the precious originals can remain under lock and key.'

Beth hated conflict, and intervened nervously. 'That sounds like quite a sensible idea, Sister Caris.'

Caris said grudgingly: 'So long as the nuns always have access to their documents in some form.' The charters were a secondary issue. Addressing Beth, rather than Godwyn, she said: 'More importantly, where do we keep the money?'

Beth said: 'In hidden vaults in the floor. There are four of them – two for the monks and two for the nuns. If you look carefully you can see the loose stones.'

Caris studied the floor, and after a moment said: 'I wouldn't have noticed if you hadn't told me, but I can see them now. Can they be locked?'

'I suppose they could,' said Godwyn. 'But then it would be obvious where they were, which would defeat the purpose of hiding them under flagstones.'

'But this way the monks and nuns have access to one another's money.'

Philemon spoke up. He looked accusingly at Caris and said: 'Why are you here? You're the guest master – nothing to do with the treasury.'

Caris's attitude to Philemon was simple loathing. She felt he was not fully human. He seemed to have no sense of right and wrong, no principles or scruples. Whereas she despised Godwyn as a wicked man who knew when he was doing evil, she felt that Philemon was more like a vicious animal, a mad dog or a wild boar. 'I have an eye for detail,' she told him.

'You're very mistrustful,' he said resentfully.

Caris gave a humourless laugh. 'Coming from you, Philemon, that's ironic.'

He pretended to be hurt. 'I don't know what you can mean.'

Beth spoke again, trying to keep the peace. 'I just wanted Caris to come and look because she asks questions I don't think of.'

Caris said: 'For example, how can we be sure that the monks don't take the nuns' money?'

'I'll show you,' said Beth. Hanging on a hook on the wall was a stout length of oak. Using it as a lever, she prised up a flagstone. Underneath was a hollow space containing an ironbound chest. 'We've had a locked casket made to fit each of these vaults,' she said. She reached inside and lifted out the chest.

Caris examined it. It seemed strongly made. The lid was hinged, and the clasp was secured by a barrel padlock made of iron. 'Where did we get the lock?' she asked.

'Christopher Blacksmith made it.'

That was good. Christopher was a well-established Kingsbridge citizen who would not risk his reputation by selling duplicate keys to thieves.

Caris was not able to fault the arrangements. Perhaps she had worried unnecessarily. She turned to go.

Elfric appeared, accompanied by an apprentice with a sack. 'Is it all right to put up the warning?' Elfric said.

Philemon replied: 'Yes, please, go ahead.'

Elfric's assistant took from his sack something that looked like a big piece of leather.

Beth said: 'What's that?'

'Wait,' said Philemon. 'You'll see.'

The apprentice held the object up against the door.

'I've been waiting for it to dry out,' Philemon said. 'It's Gilbert Hereford's skin.'

Beth gave a cry of horror.

Caris said: 'That's disgusting.'

The skin was turning yellow and the hair was falling out of the scalp, but you could still make out the face: the ears, two holes for the eyes, and a gash of a mouth that seemed to grin.

'That should scare thieves away,' Philemon said with satisfaction.

Elfric took out a hammer and began to nail the hide to the treasury door.

*

THE TWO NUNS LEFT. Godwyn and Philemon waited for Elfric to finish his gruesome task, then they went back inside the treasury.

Godwyn said: 'I think we're safe.'

Philemon nodded: 'Caris is a suspicious woman, but all her questions were answered satisfactorily.'

'In which case...'

Philemon closed the door and locked it. Then he lifted the stone slab over one of the nuns' two vaults and took out the chest.

'Sister Beth keeps a small amount of cash for everyday needs somewhere in the nuns' quarters,' he explained to Godwyn. 'She comes in here only to deposit or withdraw larger sums. She always goes to the other vault, which contains mostly silver pennies. She almost never opens this chest, which contains the bequest.'

He turned the box around and looked at the hinge at the back. It was fixed to the wood by four nails. He took from his pocket a thin steel chisel and a pair of pliers for gripping. Godwyn wondered where he had got the tools, but did not ask. Sometimes it was best not to know too many details.

Philemon slipped the sharp blade of the chisel under the edge of the iron hinge and pushed. The hinge came away from the wood slightly, and he pushed the blade in a little farther. He worked delicately and patiently, careful to make sure that the damage would not be visible to a casual glance. Gradually the flat plate of the hinge became detached, the nails coming out with it. When he had made enough room for the pliers to grip the nailheads, he pulled them out. Then he was able to detach the hinge and lift the lid.

'Here's the money from the pious woman of Thornbury,' he said.

Godwyn looked into the chest. The money was in Venetian ducats. These gold coins showed the Doge of Venice kneeling before St Mark on one side and, on the other, the Virgin Mary, surrounded by stars to indicate that she was in heaven. Ducats were intended to be interchangeable with florins from Florence, and were the same size, weight and purity of metal. They were worth three shillings, or thirty-six English silver pennies. England had its own gold coins now, an innovation of King Edward's – nobles, half-nobles and quarter-nobles – but these had been in circulation less than two years, and had not yet displaced foreign gold coins.

Godwyn took fifty ducats, worth seven pounds and ten shillings. Philemon closed the lid of the chest. He wrapped each of the nails in a thin strip of leather, to make them a tight fit, and reattached the hinge. He put the chest back in the vault and lowered the slab over the hole.

'Of course they will notice the loss, sooner or later,' he said.

'It may not be for years,' Godwyn said. 'We'll cross that bridge when we come to it.'

They went out, and Godwyn locked the door.

Godwyn said: 'Find Elfric, and meet me in the cemetery.'

Philemon left. Godwyn went to the eastern end of the graveyard, just beyond the existing prior's house. It was a blowy May day, and the fresh wind made his robe flap around his legs. A loose goat was grazing among the tombstones. Godwyn watched it meditatively.

He was risking a terrible row with the nuns, he knew. He did not think they would discover their loss for a year or more, but he could not be sure. When they did find out, there would be hell to pay. But what, exactly, could they do? He was not like Gilbert Hereford, stealing money for himself. He had taken the bequest of a pious woman to use for holy purposes.

He thrust his worries aside. His mother was right: he needed to glorify his role as prior of Kingsbridge if he was going to make further progress.

When Philemon returned with Elfric, Godwyn said: 'I want to build the prior's palace here, well to the east of the present building.'

Elfric nodded. 'A very good location, if I may say so, lord prior – close to the chapter house and the east end of the cathedral, but separated from the market place by the graveyard, so you'll have privacy and quiet.'

'I want a big dining hall downstairs for banquets,' Godwyn went on. 'About a hundred feet long. It must be a really prestigious, impressive room, for entertaining the nobility, perhaps even royalty.'

'Very good.'

'And a chapel at the east end of the ground floor.'

'But you'll be just a few steps from the cathedral.'

'Noble guests don't always want to expose themselves to the people. They must be able to worship in private if they wish.'

'And upstairs?'

'The prior's own chamber, of course, with room for an altar and a writing desk. And three large chambers for guests.'

'Splendid.'

'How much will it cost?'

'More than a hundred pounds – perhaps two hundred. I'll make a drawing then give you a more accurate estimate.'

'Don't let it go above a hundred and fifty pounds. That's all I can afford.'

If Elfric wondered where Godwyn had suddenly acquired a hundred and fifty pounds, he did not ask. 'I'd better start stockpiling the stone as soon as possible,' he said. 'Can you give me some money to begin with?'

'How much would you like – five pounds?'

'Ten would be better.'

'I'll give you seven pounds ten shillings, in ducats,' Godwyn said, and handed over the fifty gold coins he had taken from the nuns' reserves.

Three days later, as the monks and nuns were filing out of the cathedral after the dinnertime service of Nones, Sister Elizabeth spoke to Godwyn.

Nuns and monks were not supposed to talk to one another casually, so she had to contrive a pretext. As it happened, there was a dog in the nave, and it had barked during the service. Dogs were always getting into the church and making a minor nuisance of themselves, but they were generally ignored. However, on this occasion Elizabeth left the procession to shoo the dog out. She was obliged to cross the line of monks, and timed her move so that she walked in front of Godwyn. She smiled apologetically at him and said: 'I beg your pardon, Father Prior.' Then she lowered her voice and said: 'Meet me in the library, as if by accident.' She chased the dog out of the west door.

Intrigued, Godwyn made his way to the library and sat down to read the Rule of St Benedict. Shortly afterwards, Elizabeth appeared and took out the Gospel of St Matthew. The nuns had built their own library, after Godwyn took over as prior, in order to improve the separation between males and females; but when they removed all their books from the monks' library, the place had been denuded, and Godwyn had reversed his decision. The nuns' library building was now used as a schoolroom in cold weather.

Elizabeth sat with her back to Godwyn, so that anyone coming in would not get the impression that they were conspiring, but she was close enough for him to hear her clearly. 'Something I felt I should tell you,' she said. 'Sister Caris doesn't like the nuns' money being kept in the new treasury.'

'I knew that already,' Godwyn said.

'She has persuaded Sister Beth to count the money, to make sure it's all still there. I thought you might like to know that, just in case you have ... borrowed from them.'

Godwyn's heart missed a beat. An audit would find the reserves short by fifty ducats. And he was going to need the rest to build his palace. He had not been expecting this so soon. He cursed Caris. How had she guessed what he had done so secretly?

'When?' he said, and there was a catch in his voice.

'Today. I don't know at what hour – it could be any time. But Caris was most emphatic that you should have no advance warning.'

He was going to have to put the ducats back, and fast. 'Thank you very much,' he said. 'I appreciate your telling me this.'

'It's because you showed favour to my family in Long Ham,' she said; and she got up and went out.

Godwyn hurried after her. What luck that Elizabeth felt indebted to him! Philemon's instinct for intrigue was invaluable. As that thought crossed his mind, he saw Philemon in the cloisters. 'Get those tools and meet me in the treasury!' he whispered. Then he left the priory.

He hurried across the green and into the main street. Elfric's wife, Alice, had inherited the house of Edmund Wooler, one of the largest homes in town, along with all the money Caris had made dyeing cloth. Elfric now lived in great luxury.

Godwyn knocked on the door and entered the hall. Alice was sitting at the table amid the remains of dinner. With her was her stepdaughter, Griselda, and Griselda's son, Little Merthin. No one now believed that Merthin Fitzgerald was the little boy's father – he looked just like Griselda's runaway boyfriend Thurstan. Griselda had married one of her father's employees, Harold Mason. Polite people called the eight-year-old Merthin Haroldson, and the others called him Merthin Bastard.

Alice leaped up from her seat when she saw Godwyn. 'Well, Cousin Prior, what a pleasure to have you in our house! Will you take a little wine?'

Godwyn ignored her polite hospitality. 'Where's Elfric?'

'He's upstairs, taking a short nap before he goes back to work. Sit in the parlour, and I'll fetch him.'

'Right away, if you please.' Godwyn stepped into the next room. There were two comfortable-looking chairs, but he paced up and down.

Elfric came in rubbing his eyes. 'Sorry about this,' he said. 'I was just—'

'Those fifty ducats I gave you three days ago,' Godwyn said. 'I need them back.'

Elfric was startled. 'But the money was for stone.'

'I know what it was for! I have to have it right now.'

'I've spent some of it, paying carters to bring the stones from the quarry.'

'How much?'

'About half.'

'Well, you can make that up out of your own funds, can't you?'

'Don't you want a palace any more?'

'Of course I do, but I must have that money. Don't ask why, just give it to me.'

'What am I to do with the stones I've bought?'

'Just keep them. You'll get the money again, I just need it for a few days. Hurry!'

'All right. Wait here. If you will.'

'I'm not going anywhere.'

Elfric went out. Godwyn wondered where he kept his money. In the hearth, under the firestone was the usual place. Being a builder, Elfric might have a more cunning hidey-hole. Wherever it was, he was back in a few moments.

He counted fifty gold coins into Godwyn's hand.

Godwyn said: 'I gave you ducats – some of these are florins.' The florin was the same size, but stamped with different images: John the Baptist on one side and a flower on the other.

'I don't have the same coins! I told you I've spent some of them. They're all worth the same, aren't they?'

They were. Would the nuns notice the difference?

Godwyn thrust the money into the wallet at his belt and left without another word.

He hurried back to the cathedral and found Philemon in the treasury. 'The nuns are going to carry out an audit,' he explained breathlessly. 'I've got the money back from Elfric. Open that chest, quickly.'

Philemon opened the vault in the floor, took out the chest and removed the nails. He lifted the lid.

Godwyn sifted through the coins. They were all ducats.

It could not be helped. He dug down into the money and pushed his florins to the bottom. 'Close it up and put it back,' he said.

Philemon did so.

Godwyn felt a moment of relief. His crime was partly concealed. At least now it would not be glaringly obvious.

'I want to be here when she counts it,' he said to Philemon. 'I'm worried about whether she'll notice that she's now got some florins mixed in with her ducats.'

'Do you know when they intend to come?'

'No.'

'I'll put a novice to sweeping the choir. When Beth shows up, he can come and fetch us.' Philemon had a little coterie of admiring novice monks eager to do his bidding.

However, the novice was not needed. As they were about to leave the treasury, Sister Beth and Sister Caris arrived.

Godwyn pretended to be in the middle of a conversation about accounts. 'We'll have to look in an earlier account roll, brother,' he said to Philemon. 'Oh, good day, sisters.'

Caris opened both nuns' vaults and took out the two chests.

'Something I can help you with?' Godwyn said.

Caris ignored him.

Beth said: 'We're just checking something, thank you, Father Prior. We won't be long.'

'Go ahead, go ahead,' he said benevolently, though his heart was hammering in his chest.

Caris said irritably: 'There's no need to apologize for our being here, Sister Beth. It's our treasury and our money.'

Godwyn opened an account roll at random, and he and Philemon pretended to study it. Beth and Caris counted the silver in the first chest: farthings, halfpennies, pennies and a few Luxembourgs, forged pennies crudely made of adulterated silver and used as small change. There were a few assorted gold coins, too: florins, ducats and similar coins – the genovino from Genoa and the reale from Naples – plus some larger French moutons and new English nobles. Beth checked the totals against a small notebook. When they had finished she said: 'Exactly right.'

They replaced all the coins in the chest, locked it and put it back in its underfloor vault.

They began counting the gold coins in the other chest, putting them in piles of ten. When they got towards the bottom of the chest, Beth frowned and made a puzzled sound.

'What is it?' Caris said.

Godwyn felt a guilty dread.

Beth said: 'This chest contains only the bequest from the pious woman of Thornbury. I kept it separate.'

'And...?'

'Her husband traded with Venice. I was sure the entire amount was in ducats. But there are some florins here too.'

Godwyn and Philemon froze, listening.

'That's odd,' Caris said.

'Perhaps I made a mistake.'

'It's a bit suspicious.'

'Not really,' Beth said. 'Thieves don't put money into your treasury, do they?'

'You're right, they don't,' Caris said reluctantly.

They finished counting. They had one hundred stacks of ten coins, worth a hundred and fifty pounds. 'That's the exact figure in my book,' Beth said.

'So every pound and penny is correct,' Caris said.

Beth said: 'I told you so.'

45

CARIS SPENT MANY HOURS thinking about Sister Mair.

She had been startled by the kiss, but more surprised at her own reaction to it. She had found it exciting. Until now, she had not felt attracted to Mair or any other woman. In fact there was only one person who had ever made her yearn to be touched and kissed and penetrated, and that was Merthin. In the nunnery she had learned to live without physical contact. The only hand that touched her sexually was her own, in the darkness of the dormitory, when she remembered the days of her courtship, and buried her face in the pillow so that the other nuns would not hear her panting.

She did not feel for Mair the same happy lust that Merthin inspired in her. But Merthin was a thousand miles away and seven years in the past. And she was fond of Mair. It was something to do with her angelic face, something about her blue eyes, some response to her gentleness in the hospital and the school.

Mair always spoke sweetly to Caris and, when no one was looking, touched her arm, or her shoulder, and once her cheek. Caris did not rebuff her, but she held back from responding. It was not that she thought it would be a sin. She felt sure God was much too wise to make a rule against women harmlessly pleasuring themselves or each other. But she was afraid of disappointing Mair. Instinct told her that Mair's feelings were strong and definite, whereas her own were uncertain. She's in love with me, Caris thought, but I'm not in love with her. If I kiss her again, she may hope that the two of us will be soul mates for life, and I can't promise her that.

So she did nothing, until Fleece Fair week.

The Kingsbridge fair had recovered from the slump of 1338.

The trade in raw wool was still suffering from interference by the king, and the Italians came only every second year, but the new business of weaving and dyeing compensated. The town was still not as prosperous as it might have been, for Prior Godwyn's prohibition of private mills had driven the industry out of the city and into the surrounding villages; but most of the cloth was sold in the market, indeed it had become known as Kingsbridge Scarlet. Merthin's bridge had been finished by Elfric, and people poured across the wide double span with their packhorses and wagons.

So, on the Saturday night before the official opening of the fair, the hospital was full to bursting with visitors.

And one of them was ill.

His name was Maldwyn Cook, and his trade was to make salty little savouries with flour and scraps of meat or fish, cook them quickly in butter over a fire, and sell them six for a farthing. Soon after he arrived, he was afflicted with a sudden, savage belly ache, followed by vomiting and diarrhoea. There was nothing Caris could do for him other than give him a bed near the door.

She had long wanted to give the hospital its own latrine, so that she could supervise its cleanliness. But that was only one of the improvements she hoped for. She needed a new pharmacy, adjacent to the hospital, a spacious, well-lit room where she could prepare medicines and make her notes. And she was trying to figure out a way to give patients more privacy. At present everyone in the room could see a woman giving birth, a man having a fit, a child vomiting. People in distress should have small rooms of their own, she felt, like the side chapels in a large church. But she was not sure how to achieve this: the hospital was not big enough. She had had several discussions with Jeremiah Builder – who had been Merthin's apprentice, Jimmie, many years ago – but he had not come up with a satisfactory solution.

Next morning, three more people had the same symptoms as Maldwyn Cook.

Caris fed the visitors breakfast and tipped them out into the market. Only the sick were allowed to stay behind. The floor of the hospital was filthier than usual, and she had it swept and swabbed. Then she went to the service in the cathedral.

Bishop Richard was not present. He was with the king, preparing to invade France again – he had always regarded his bishopric mainly as a means of supporting his aristocratic lifestyle. In his absence the diocese was run by Archdeacon Lloyd, who collected the bishop's tithes and rents, baptized children and conducted services with dogged but unimaginative efficiency – a trait he illustrated by giving a tedious sermon on why God was more important than Money, an odd note on which to open one of England's great commercial fairs.

Nevertheless, everyone was in high spirits, as was usual on the first day. The Fleece Fair was the high point of the year for the townspeople and the peasants of the surrounding villages. People made money at the fair and lost it gambling in the inns. Strapping village girls allowed themselves to be seduced by slick city boys. Prosperous peasants paid the town's prostitutes for services they dared not ask their wives to perform. There was usually a murder, often several.

Caris spotted the heavy-set, richly dressed figure of Buonaventura Caroli in the congregation, and her heart faltered. He might have news of Merthin. She went through the service distractedly, mumbling the psalms. On the way out she managed to catch Buonaventura's eye. He smiled at her. She tried to indicate, with an inclination of her head, that she wanted him to meet her afterwards. She was not sure whether he got the message.

However, she went to the hospital – the only place in the priory where a nun could meet a man from outside – and Buonaventura came in not long afterwards. He wore a costly blue coat and pointed shoes. He said: 'Last time I saw you, you had just been consecrated a nun by Bishop Richard.'

'I'm guest master now,' she said.

'Congratulations! I never expected you to take so well to convent life.' Buonaventura had known her since she was a little girl.

'Nor did I,' she laughed.

'The priory seems to be doing well.'

'What makes you say that?'

'I see that Godwyn is building a new palace.'

'Yes.'

'He must be prospering.'

'I suppose he is. How about you? Is trade good?'

'We have some problems. The war between England and France has disrupted transport, and your King Edward's taxes make English wool more expensive than the Spanish. But it's also better quality.'

They always complained about taxes. Caris came to the subject that really interested her. 'Any news of Merthin?'

'As a matter of fact, there is,' Buonaventura said; and although his manner was as urbane as ever, she detected a hesitation. 'Merthin is married.'

Caris felt as if she had been punched. She had never expected this, never even thought of it. How could Merthin do this? He was ... they were ...

There was no reason at all why he should not get married, of course. She had rejected him more than once, and on the last occasion she had made her rejection final by entering the nunnery. It was only remarkable that he had waited so long. She had no right to feel hurt.

She forced a smile. 'How splendid!' she said. 'Please send him my congratulations. Who is the girl?'

Buonaventura pretended not to notice her distress. 'Her name is Silvia,' he said, as casually as if he were passing on harmless gossip. 'She's the younger daughter of one of the city's most prominent citizens, Alessandro Christi, a trader in oriental spices who owns several ships.'

'How old?'

He grinned. 'Alessandro? He must be about my age...'

'Don't tease me!' She was grateful to Buonaventura for lightening the tone. 'How old is Silvia?'

'Twenty-three.'

'Six years younger than me.'

'A beautiful girl...'

She sensed the unspoken qualification. 'But...?'

He tilted his head to one side apologetically. 'She has the

reputation of being sharp-tongued. Of course, people say all sorts of things ... but perhaps that is why she remained single so long – girls in Florence generally marry before the age of eighteen.'

'I'm sure it's true,' Caris said. 'The only girls Merthin liked in Kingsbridge were me and Elizabeth Clerk, and we're both shrews.'

Buonaventura laughed. 'Not so, not so.'

'When was the wedding?'

'Two years ago. Not long after I last saw you.'

Caris realized that Merthin had remained single until she had been consecrated as a nun. He would have heard, via Buonaventura, that she had taken the final step. She thought of him waiting and hoping, for more than four years, in a foreign country; and her brittle façade of good cheer began to crack.

Buonaventura said: 'And they have a child, a little baby girl called Lolla.'

That was too much. All the grief Caris had felt seven years ago – the pain she thought had gone for ever – came back in a rush. She had not truly lost him back then in 1339, she realized. He had remained loyal to her memory for years. But she had lost him now, finally, eternally.

She was shaken as if by a fit, and she knew she could not hold out much longer. Trembling, she said: 'It's such a pleasure to see you, and catch up with the news, but I must get back to my work.'

His face showed concern. 'I hope I haven't upset you too much. I thought you would prefer to know.'

'Don't be kind to me – I can't stand it.' She turned from him and hurried away.

She bent her head to hide her face as she walked from the hospital into the cloisters. Searching for somewhere to be alone, she ran up the stairs to the dormitory. There was no one there in the daytime. She began to sob as she walked the length of the bare room. At the far end was Mother Cecilia's bedroom. No one was allowed in there without an invitation, but Caris went in anyway, slamming the door behind her. She fell on Cecilia's bed, not caring that her nun's cap had fallen off. She buried her face in the straw mattress, and wept.

After a while she felt a hand on her head, stroking her short-cropped hair. She had not heard the person enter the room. She did not care who it was. All the same she was slowly, gradually soothed. Her sobs became less wrenching, her tears dried, and the storm of her emotions began to die down. She rolled over and looked up at her comforter. It was Mair.

Caris said: 'Merthin is married – he has a baby girl.' She began to cry again.

Mair lay down on the bed and cradled Caris's head in her arms. Caris pressed her face into Mair's soft breasts, letting the woollen robe soak up the tears. 'There, there,' said Mair.

After a while, Caris calmed down. She was too drained to feel any more sorrow. She thought of Merthin holding a dark-haired little Italian baby, and saw how happy he would be. She was glad that he was happy, and she drifted into an exhausted sleep.

*

THE ILLNESS THAT HAD started with Maldwyn Cook spread like a summer fire through the crowds at the Fleece Fair. On Monday it leaped from the hospital to the taverns, then on Tuesday from the visitors to the townspeople. Caris noted its characteristics in her book: it began with stomach pains, led quickly to vomiting and diarrhoea, and lasted between twenty-four and forty-eight hours. It left adults not much the worse, but killed old people and small babies.

On Wednesday, it struck the nuns and the children in the girls' school. Both Mair and Tilly were affected. Caris sought out Buonaventura, at the Bell, and worriedly asked him whether Italian doctors had any treatment for such diseases. 'There's no cure,' he said. 'None that works, anyway, though doctors nearly always prescribe something just to get more money out of people. But some Arab physicians believe you can retard the spread of such illnesses.'

'Oh, really?' Caris was interested. Traders said that Muslim doctors were superior to their Christian counterparts, although the priest-physicians denied this hotly. 'How?'

'They believe the disease is acquired when a sick person looks at you. Sight functions by beams that issue from the eyes and touch the things we see – rather like extending a finger to feel whether something is warm, or dry, or hard. But the beams may also project sickness. Therefore you can avoid the disease by never being in the same room as a sufferer.'

Caris did not think illness could be transmitted by looks. If that were true then, after an important service in the cathedral, everyone in the congregation would acquire any illness the bishop had. Whenever the king was ill, he would infect all the hundreds of people who saw him. And surely someone would have noticed that.

However, the notion that you should not share a room with someone who was ill did seem convincing. Here in the hospital, Maldwyn's illness seemed to spread from a sufferer to those nearby: the sick man's wife and family were the first to catch it, followed by people in neighbouring beds.

She had also observed that certain kinds of illness – stomach upsets, coughs and colds, and poxes of all sorts – seemed to flare up during fairs and markets; so it seemed obvious that they were passed from one person to another by some means.

On Wednesday night at supper, half the guests in the hospital were suffering from the illness; then by Thursday morning every one of them had it. Several priory servants also succumbed, so Caris was short of people to clean up.

Surveying the chaos at breakfast time, Mother Cecilia suggested closing the hospital.

Caris was ready to consider anything. She felt dismayed at her own powerlessness to combat the disease, and devastated by the filth of her hospital. 'But where would the people sleep?' she said.

'Send them to the taverns.'

'The taverns have the same problem. We could put them in the cathedral.'

Cecilia shook her head. 'Godwyn won't have peasants puking in the nave while services go on in the choir.'

'Wherever they sleep, we ought to separate the sick from the well. That's the way to retard the spread of the illness, according to Buonaventura.'

'It makes sense.'

Caris was struck by a new idea, something that suddenly

seemed very obvious, though she had not thought of it before. 'Perhaps we shouldn't just improve the hospital,' she said. 'Maybe we should build a new one, just for sick people, and keep the old one for pilgrims and other healthy visitors.'

Cecilia looked thoughtful. 'It would be costly.'

'We've got a hundred and fifty pounds.' Caris's imagination began to work. 'It could incorporate a new pharmacy. We could have private rooms for people who are chronically ill.'

'Find out what it would cost. You could ask Elfric.'

Caris hated Elfric. She had disliked him even before he had given evidence against her. She did not want him to build her new hospital. 'Elfric is busy building Godwyn's new palace,' she said. 'I'd rather consult Jeremiah.'

'By all means.'

Caris felt a rush of affection for Cecilia. Although she was a martinet, tough on discipline, she gave her deputies room to make their own decisions. She had always understood the conflicting passions that drove Caris. Instead of trying to suppress those passions, Cecilia had found ways to make use of them. She had given Caris work that engaged her, and provided outlets for her rebellious energy. Here I am, Caris thought, plainly incapable of dealing with the crisis in front of me, and my superior is calmly telling me to forge ahead with a new long-term project. 'Thank you, Mother Cecilia,' she said.

Later that day she walked around the priory grounds with Jeremiah and explained her aspirations. He was as superstitious as ever, seeing the work of saints and devils in the most trivial of everyday incidents. Nevertheless, he was an imaginative builder, open to new ideas: he had learned from Merthin. They quickly settled on the best location for the new hospital, immediately to the south of the existing kitchen block. It would be apart from the rest of the buildings, so that sick people would have less contact with the healthy, but food would not have to be carried far, and the new building could still be accessed conveniently from the nuns' cloisters. With the pharmacy, the new latrines and an upper floor with private rooms, Jeremiah thought it would cost about a hundred pounds – most of the legacy.

Caris discussed the site with Mother Cecilia. It was land that belonged neither to the monks nor the nuns, so they went to see Godwyn about it.

They found him on the site of his own building project, the new palace. The shell was up and the roof was on. Caris had not visited the site for some weeks, and she was surprised at its size – it was going to be as big as her new hospital. She saw why Buonaventura had called it impressive: the dining hall was larger than the nuns' refectory. The site was swarming with workmen, as if Godwyn was in a hurry to get it finished. Masons were laying a floor of coloured tiles in a geometric pattern, several carpenters were making doors, and a master glazier had set up a furnace to make the windows. Godwyn was spending a lot of money.

He and Philemon were showing the new building to Archdeacon Lloyd, the bishop's deputy. Godwyn broke off as the nuns approached. Cecilia said: 'Don't let us interrupt you – but, when you're finished, will you meet me outside the hospital? There's something I need to show you.'

'By all means,' said Godwyn.

Caris and Cecilia walked back through the market place in front of the cathedral. Friday was bargain day at the Fleece Fair, when traders sold their remaining stocks at reduced prices so that they would not have to carry the goods home. Caris saw Mark Webber, round-faced and round-bellied now, wearing a coat of his own bright scarlet. His four children were helping at his stall. Caris was especially fond of Dora, now fifteen, who had her mother's bustling confidence in a slimmer body.

'You're looking prosperous,' Caris said to Mark with a smile.

'The wealth should have come to you,' he replied. 'You invented the dye. I just did what you said. I almost feel as if I cheated you.'

'You've been rewarded for hard work,' she said. She did not mind that Mark and Madge had done so well out of her invention. Although she had always enjoyed the challenge of doing business, she had never lusted for money – perhaps because she had always taken it for granted, growing up in her father's wealthy household. Whatever the reason, she felt no pang of regret that the Webbers were making a fortune that might have been hers. The cashless life of the priory seemed to suit her well. And she was thrilled to see the Webber children healthy and well dressed. She remembered when all six of them had to find sleeping space on the floor of a single room, most of which was taken up by a loom.

She and Cecilia went to the south end of the priory grounds. The land around the stables looked like a farmyard. There were a few small buildings: a dovecote, a henhouse and a tool shed. Chickens scratched in the dirt, and pigs rooted in the kitchen garbage. Caris itched to tidy it up.

Godwyn and Philemon joined them soon, with Lloyd tagging along. Cecilia indicated the patch of land next to the kitchens, and said: 'I'm going to build a new hospital, and I want to put it there. What do you think?'

'A new hospital?' Godwyn said. 'Why?'

Caris thought he looked anxious, which puzzled her.

Cecilia said: 'We want a hospital for the sick and a separate guest house for healthy visitors.'

'What an extraordinary idea.'

'It's because of the stomach illness that started with Maldwyn Cook. This is a particularly virulent example, but diseases often flare up at markets, and part of the reason they spread so fast may be that we have the sick and the well eating and sleeping and going to the latrine together.'

Godwyn took umbrage. 'Oho!' he said. 'So the nuns are the physicians, now, are they?'

Caris frowned. This kind of sneering was not Godwyn's style. He used charm to get his way, especially with powerful people such as Cecilia. This fit of pique was covering something else.

'Of course not,' Cecilia said. 'But we all know that some illnesses spread from one sufferer to the next – that's obvious.'

Caris put in: 'The Muslim physicians believe illness is transmitted by looking at the sick person.'

'Oh, do they? How interesting!' Godwyn spoke with ponderous sarcasm. 'Those of us who have spent seven years studying medicine at the university are always glad to be lectured on illness by young nuns barely out of their novitiate.'

Caris was not intimidated. She felt no inclination to show

respect to a lying hypocrite who had tried to murder her. She said: 'If you don't believe in the transmission of illness, why don't you prove your sincerity by coming to the hospital tonight and sleeping alongside a hundred people suffering from nausea and diarrhoea?'

Cecilia said: 'Sister Caris! That will be enough.' She turned to Godwyn. 'Forgive her, Father Prior. It wasn't my intention to engage you in a discussion about disease with a mere nun. I just want to make sure you don't object to my choice of site.'

'You can't build it now, anyway,' Godwyn said. 'Elfric is too busy with the palace.'

Caris said: 'We don't want Elfric – we're using Jeremiah.'

Cecilia turned on her. 'Caris, be quiet! Remember your place. Don't interrupt my conversation with the lord prior again.'

Caris realized she was not helping Cecilia, and – against her inclination – she lowered her head and said: 'I'm sorry, Mother Prioress.'

Cecilia said to Godwyn: 'The question is not *when* we build, it's *where*.'

'I'm afraid I don't approve of this,' he said stiffly.

'Where would you prefer the new building to be sited?'

'I don't think you need a new hospital at all.'

'Forgive me, but I am in charge of the nunnery,' Cecilia said with asperity. 'You can't tell me how I should spend our money. However, we normally consult one another before putting up new buildings – although it has to be said that you forgot this little courtesy when planning your palace. Nevertheless, I am consulting you – merely on the question of the location of the building.' She looked at Lloyd. 'I'm sure the archdeacon will agree with me on this.'

'There must be agreement,' Lloyd said noncommittally.

Caris frowned, baffled. Why did Godwyn care? He was building his palace on the north side of the cathedral. It made no difference to him if the nuns put up a new building down here in the south, where most monks hardly ever came. What was he worried about?

Godwyn said: 'I'm telling you that I do not approve of the location nor of the building, so that is the end of the matter!'

Caris suddenly saw, in a flash of inspiration, the reason for Godwyn's behaviour. She was so shocked that she blurted it out. 'You stole our money!'

Cecilia said: 'Caris! I told you—'

'He's stolen the legacy of the woman of Thornbury!' Caris said, overriding Cecilia in her outrage. 'That's where he got the money for his palace, of course. And now he's trying to stop us building because he knows we'll go to the treasury and find that our money has vanished!' She felt so indignant she might burst.

Godwyn said: 'Don't be preposterous.'

As a response, it was so muted that Caris knew she must have touched a nerve. Confirmation made her even angrier. 'Prove it!' she yelled. She forced herself to speak more calmly. 'We'll go to the treasury now and check the vaults. You wouldn't object to that, would you, Father Prior?'

Philemon chipped in: 'It would be a completely undignified proceeding, and there is no question of the prior submitting himself to it.'

Caris ignored him. 'There should be one hundred and fifty pounds in gold in the nuns' reserves.'

'Out of the question,' said Godwyn.

Caris said: 'Well, clearly the nuns will have to check the vaults anyway, now that the accusation has been made.' She looked at Cecilia, who nodded in agreement. 'So, if the prior prefers not to be present, no doubt the archdeacon will be happy to attend as a witness.'

Lloyd looked as if he would have preferred not to get involved in this dispute, but it was hard for him to refuse to play the role of umpire, so he muttered: 'If I can help both sides, of course ...'

Caris's mind was racing on. 'How did you open the chest?' she said. 'Christopher Blacksmith made the lock, and he's too honest to give you a duplicate key and help you steal from us. You must have broken the box open, then repaired it somehow. What did you do, take off the hinge?' She saw Godwyn glance involuntarily at his sub-prior. 'Ah,' Caris said triumphantly, 'so *Philemon* took the hinge off. But the prior took the money, and gave it to Elfric.'

Cecilia said: 'Enough speculation. Let's settle the matter. We'll all go to the treasury and open the box, and that will be an end to it.'

Godwyn said: 'It wasn't stealing.'

Everyone stared at him. There was a shocked silence.

Cecilia said: 'You're admitting it!'

'It wasn't stealing,' Godwyn repeated. 'The money is being used for the benefit of the priory and the glory of God.'

Caris said: 'It makes no difference. It wasn't your money!'

'It's God's money,' Godwyn said stubbornly.

Cecilia said: 'It was left to the nunnery. You know that. You saw the will.'

'I know nothing of any will.'

'Of course you do. I gave it to you, to make a copy...' Cecilia tailed off.

Godwyn said again: 'I know nothing of any will.'

Caris said: 'He's destroyed it. He said he would make a copy, and put the original in the chest, in the treasury ... but he destroyed it.'

Cecilia was staring open-mouthed at Godwyn. 'I should have known,' she said. 'After what you tried to do to Caris – I should never have trusted you again. But I thought your soul might yet have been saved. I was so wrong.'

Caris said: 'It's a good thing we made our own copy of the will, before handing it over.' She was inventing this in desperation.

Godwyn said: 'A forgery, obviously.'

Caris said: 'If the money was yours in the first place, you will have had no need to break open the casket to get it. So let's go and look. That will settle it one way or another.'

Philemon said: 'The fact that the hinge has been tampered with proves nothing.'

'So I was right!' said Caris. 'But how do you know about the hinge? Sister Beth has not opened the vault since the audit, and the box was fine then. You must have removed it from the vault yourself, if you know that it has been interfered with.'

Philemon looked bewildered, and had no answer.

Cecilia turned to Lloyd. 'Archdeacon, you are the bishop's representative. I think it's your duty to order the prior to return this money to the nuns.'

Lloyd looked worried. He said to Godwyn: 'Have you got any of the money left?'

Caris said furiously: 'When you've caught a thief, you don't ask him whether he can afford to relinquish his ill-gotten gains!'

Godwyn said: 'More than half has already been spent on the palace.'

'Building must stop immediately,' Caris said. 'The men must be dismissed today, the building torn down and the materials sold. You have to return every penny. What you can't pay in cash, after the palace has been demolished, you must make up in land or other assets.'

'I refuse,' Godwyn said.

Cecilia addressed Lloyd again. 'Archdeacon, please do your duty. You cannot allow one of the bishop's subordinates to steal from another, no matter that they both do God's work.'

Lloyd said: 'I can't adjudicate a dispute such as this myself. It's too serious.'

Caris was speechless with fury and dismay at Lloyd's weakness.

Cecilia protested: 'But you must!'

He looked trapped, but he shook his head stubbornly. 'Accusations of theft, destruction of a will, a charge of forgery ... This must go to the bishop himself!'

Cecilia said: 'But Bishop Richard is on his way to France – and no one knows when he will be back. Meanwhile, Godwyn is spending the stolen money!'

'I can't help that, I'm afraid,' Lloyd said. 'You must appeal to Richard.'

'Very well, then,' said Caris. Something in her tone made them all look at her. 'In that case there's only one thing to do. We'll go and find our bishop.'

46

In July of 1346, King Edward III assembled the largest invasion fleet England had ever seen, almost a thousand ships, at Portsmouth. Contrary winds delayed the armada, but they finally set sail on 11 July, their destination a secret.

Caris and Mair arrived in Portsmouth two days later, just missing Bishop Richard, who had sailed with the king.

They decided to follow the army to France.

It had not been easy to get approval even for the trip to Portsmouth. Mother Cecilia had invited the nuns in chapter to discuss the proposal, and some had felt that Caris would be in moral and physical danger. But nuns did leave their convents, not just on pilgrimages, but on business errands to London, Canterbury and Rome. And the Kingsbridge sisters wanted their stolen money back.

However, Caris was not sure that she would have got permission to cross the Channel. Fortunately she was not able to ask.

She and Mair could not have followed the army immediately, even if they had known the king's destination, because every seaworthy vessel on the south coast of England had been commandeered for the invasion. So they fretted with impatience at a nunnery just outside Portsmouth and waited for news.

Caris learned later that King Edward and his army disembarked on a broad beach at St-Vaast-la-Hogue, on the north coast of France near Barfleur. However, the fleet did not return immediately. Instead, the ships followed the coast eastward for two weeks, tracking the invading army as far as Caen. There they loaded their holds with booty: jewellery, expensive cloth, and gold and silver plate looted by Edward's army from the prosperous burgesses of Normandy. Then they returned.

One of the first back was the *Grace*, which was a cog – a broad-built cargo ship with rounded prow and stern. Her captain, a leather-faced salt called Rollo, was full of praise for the king. He had been paid at scarcity rates for his ship and his men, and he had gained a good share of the plunder himself. 'Biggest army I've ever seen,' Rollo said with relish. He thought there were at least fifteen thousand men, about half of them archers, and probably five thousand horses. 'You'll have your work cut out to catch up with them,' he said. 'I'll take you to Caen, the last place I know them to have been, and you can pick up their trail there. Whatever direction they've taken, they'll be about a week ahead of you.'

Caris and Mair negotiated a price with Rollo then went aboard the *Grace* with two sturdy ponies, Blackie and Stamp. They could not travel any faster than the army's horses, but the army had to stop and fight every so often, Caris reasoned, and that should enable her to catch up.

When they reached the French side and sailed into the estuary of the Orne, early on a sunny August morning, Caris sniffed the breeze and noticed the unpleasant smell of old ashes. Studying the landscape on either side of the river, she saw that the farmland was black. It looked as if the crops had been burned in the fields. 'Standard practice,' Rollo said. 'What the army can't take must be destroyed, otherwise it could benefit the enemy.' As they neared the port of Caen they passed the hulks of several burned-out ships, presumably fired for the same reason.

'No one knows the king's plan,' Rollo told them. 'He may go south and advance on Paris, or swing north-east to Calais and hope to meet up there with his Flemish allies. But you'll be able to follow his trail. Just keep the blackened fields on either side of you.'

Before they disembarked, Rollo gave them a ham. 'Thank you, but we've got some smoked fish and hard cheese in our saddlebags,' Caris said to him. 'And we have money – we can buy anything else we need.'

'Money may not be much use to you,' the captain replied. 'There may be nothing to buy. An army is like a plague of locusts, it strips the country bare. Take the ham.'

'You're very kind. Goodbye.'

'Pray for me, if you would, sister. I've committed some heavy sins in my time.'

Caen was a city of several thousand houses. Like Kingsbridge, its two halves, Old Town and New Town, were divided by a river, the Odon, which was spanned by St Peter's Bridge. On the river bank near the bridge, a few fishermen were selling their catch. Caris asked the price of an eel. She found the answer difficult to understand: the fisherman spoke a dialect of French she had never heard. When at last she was able to make out what he was saying, the price took her breath away. Food was so scarce, she realized, that it was more precious than jewels. She was grateful for Rollo's generosity.

They had decided that if they were questioned they would say they were Irish nuns travelling to Rome. Now, however, as she and Mair rode away from the river, Caris wondered nervously whether local people would know from her accent that she was English.

There were not many local people to be seen. Broken-down doors and smashed shutters revealed empty houses. There was a ghostly hush – no vendors crying their wares, no children quarrelling, no church bells. The only work being done was burial. The battle had taken place more than a week ago, but small groups of grim-faced men were still bringing corpses out of buildings and loading them on to carts. It looked as if the English army had simply massacred men, women and children. They passed a church where a huge pit had been dug in the churchyard, and saw the bodies being tipped into a mass grave, without coffins or even shrouds, while a priest intoned a continuous burial service. The stench was unspeakable.

A well-dressed man bowed to them and asked if they needed assistance. His proprietorial manner suggested that he was a leading citizen concerned to make sure no harm came to religious visitors. Caris declined his offer of help, noting that his Norman French was no different from that of a nobleman in England. Perhaps, she thought, the lower orders all had their different local dialects, while the ruling class spoke with an international accent.

The two nuns took the road east out of town, glad to leave

the haunted streets behind. The countryside was deserted, too. The bitter taste of ash was always on Caris's tongue. Many of the fields and orchards on either side of the road had been fired. Every few miles they rode through a heap of charred ruins that had been a village. The peasants had either fled before the army or died in the conflagration, for there was little life: just the birds, the occasional pig or chicken overlooked by the army's foragers, and sometimes a dog, nosing through the debris in a bewildered way, trying to pick up the scent of its master in a pile of cold embers.

Their immediate destination was a nunnery half a day's ride from Caen. Whenever possible, they would spend the night at a religious house – nunnery, monastery or hospital – as they had on the way from Kingsbridge to Portsmouth. They knew the names and locations of fifty-one such institutions between Caen and Paris. If they could find them, as they hurried in the scorched footprints of King Edward, their accommodation and food would be free and they would be safe from thieves – and, Mother Cecilia would add, from fleshly temptations such as strong drink and male company.

Cecilia's instincts were sharp, but she had not sensed that a different kind of temptation was in the air between Caris and Mair. Because of that, Caris had at first refused Mair's request to come with her. She was focused on moving fast, and she did not want to complicate her mission by entering into a passionate entanglement – or by refusing so to do. On the other hand, she needed someone courageous and resourceful as her companion. Now she was glad of her choice: of all the nuns, Mair was the only one with the guts to go chasing the English army through France.

She had planned to have a frank talk before they left, saying that there should be no physical affection between them while they were away. Apart from anything else, they could get into terrible trouble if they were seen. But somehow she had never got around to the frank talk. So here they were in France with the issue still hanging unmentioned, like an invisible third traveller riding between them on a silent horse.

They stopped at midday by a stream on the edge of a wood,

where there was an unburned meadow for the ponies to graze. Caris cut slices from Rollo's ham, and Mair took from their baggage a loaf of stale bread from Portsmouth. They drank the water from the stream, though it had the taste of cinders.

Caris suppressed her eagerness to get going, and forced herself to let the horses rest for the hottest hour of the day. Then, as they were getting ready to leave, she was startled to see someone watching her. She froze, with the ham in one hand and her knife in the other.

Mair said: 'What is it?' Then she followed Caris's gaze, and understood.

Two men stood a few yards away, in the shade of the trees, staring at them. They looked quite young, but it was hard to be sure, for their faces were sooty and their clothing was filthy.

After a moment, Caris spoke to them in Norman French. 'God bless you, my children.'

They made no reply. Caris guessed they were unsure what to do. But what possibilities were they considering? Robbery? Rape? They had a predatory look.

She was scared, but she made herself think calmly. Whatever else they might want, they must be starving, she calculated. She said to Mair: 'Quickly, give me two trenchers of that bread.'

Mair cut two thick slices off the big loaf. Caris cut corresponding slabs from the ham. She put the ham on the bread, then said to Mair: 'Give them one each.'

Mair looked terrified, but she walked across the grass with an unhesitating step and offered the food to the men.

They both snatched it and began to wolf it down. Caris thanked her stars that she had guessed right.

She quickly put the ham in her saddlebag and the knife in her belt, then climbed on to Blackie. Mair followed suit, stowing the bread and mounting Stamp. Caris felt safer on horseback.

The taller of the two men came towards them, moving quickly. Caris was tempted to kick her pony and take off, but she did not quite have time; and then the man's hand was holding her bridle. He spoke through a mouthful of food. 'Thank you,' he said with the heavy local accent.

Caris said: 'Thank God, not me. He sent me to help you. He is watching over you. He sees everything.'

'You have more meat in your bag.'

'God will tell me who to give it to.'

There was a pause, while the man thought that over, then he said: 'Give me your blessing.'

Caris was reluctant to extend her right arm in the traditional gesture of blessing – it would take her hand too far away from the knife at her belt. It was only a short-bladed food knife of the kind carried by every man and woman, but it was enough to slash the back of the hand that held her bridle and cause the man to let go.

Then she was inspired. 'Very well,' she said. 'Kneel down.'

The man hesitated.

'You must kneel to receive my blessing,' she said in a slightly raised voice.

Slowly, the man knelt, still holding his food in his hand.

Caris turned her gaze on his companion. After a moment, the second man did the same.

Caris blessed them both, then kicked Blackie and quickly trotted away. After a moment she looked back. Mair was close behind her. The two starving men stood staring at them.

Caris mulled over the incident anxiously as they rode through the afternoon. The sun shone cheerfully, as on a fine day in hell. In some places, smoke was rising fitfully from a patch of woodland or a smouldering barn. But the countryside was not totally deserted, she realized gradually. She saw a pregnant woman harvesting beans in a field that had escaped the English torches; the scared faces of two children looking out from the blackened stones of a manor house; and several small groups of men, usually flitting through the fringes of woodland, moving with the alert purposefulness of scavengers. The men worried her. They looked hungry, and hungry men were dangerous. She wondered whether she should stop fretting about speed and worry instead about safety.

Finding their way to the religious houses where they planned to stop was also going to be more difficult than Caris had thought.

She had not anticipated that the English army would leave such devastation in its wake. She had assumed there would be peasants around to direct her. It could be hard enough in normal times to get such information from people who had never travelled farther than the nearest market town. Now her interlocutors would also be elusive, terrified or predatory.

She knew by the sun that she was heading east, and she thought, judging by the deep cartwheel ruts in the baked mud, that she was on the main road. Tonight's destination was a village named, after the nunnery at its centre, Hôpital-des-Soeurs. As the shadow in front of her grew longer, she looked about with increasing urgency for someone whom she could ask for directions.

Children fled from their approach in fear. Caris was not yet desperate enough to risk getting close to the hungry-looking men. She hoped to come across a woman. There were no young women anywhere, and Caris had a bleak suspicion about the fate they might have met at the hands of the marauding English. Occasionally she saw, in the far distance, a few lonely figures harvesting a field that had escaped burning; but she was reluctant to go too far from the road.

At last they found a wrinkled old woman sitting under an apple tree next to a substantial stone house. She was eating small apples wrenched from the tree long before they were ripe. She looked terrified. Caris dismounted, to seem less intimidating. The old woman tried to hide her poor meal in the folds of her dress, but she seemed not to have the strength to run away.

Caris addressed her politely. 'Good evening, mother. Will this road take us to Hôpital-des-Soeurs, may I ask?'

The woman seemed to pull herself together, and answered intelligently. Pointing in the direction in which they were heading, she said: 'Through the woods and over the hill.'

Caris saw that she had no teeth. It must have been almost impossible to eat unripe apples with your gums, she thought with pity. 'How far?' she asked.

'A long way.'

All distances were long at her age. 'Can we get there by nightfall?'

'On a horse, yes.'

'Thank you, mother.'

'I had a daughter,' said the old woman. 'And two grandsons. Fourteen years and sixteen. Fine boys.'

'I'm very sorry to hear that.'

'The English,' said the old woman. 'May they all burn in hell.'

Evidently it did not occur to her that Caris and Mair might be English. That answered Caris's question: local people could not tell the nationality of strangers. 'What were the boys' names, mother?'

'Giles and Jean.'

'I will pray for the souls of Giles and Jean.'

'Have you any bread?'

Caris looked around, to make sure there was no one else lurking nearby, ready to pounce, but they were alone. She nodded to Mair, who took from her saddlebag the remains of the loaf and offered it to the old woman.

The woman snatched it from her and began to gnaw it with her gums.

Caris and Mair rode away.

Mair said: 'If we keep giving our food away, we're going to starve.'

'I know,' said Caris. 'But how can you refuse?'

'We can't fulfil our mission if we're dead.'

'But we are nuns, after all,' Caris said with asperity. 'We must help the needy, and leave it to God to decide when it's time for us to die.'

Mair was startled. 'I've never heard you talk like that before.'

'My father hated people who preached about morality. We're all good when it suits us, he used to say: that doesn't count. It's when you want so badly to do something wrong – when you're about to make a fortune from a dishonest deal, or kiss the lovely lips of your neighbour's wife, or tell a lie to get yourself out of terrible trouble – that's when you need the rules. Your integrity is like a sword, he would say: you shouldn't wave it until you're about to put it to the test. Not that he knew anything about swords.'

Mair was silent for a while. She might have been mulling

over what Caris had said, or she might simply have given up the argument: Caris was not sure.

Talk of Edmund always made Caris realize how much she missed him. After her mother died he had become the cornerstone of her life. He had always been there, standing at her shoulder, as it were, ready when she needed sympathy and understanding, or shrewd advice, or just information: he had known so much about the world. Now, when she turned in that direction, there was just an empty space.

They passed through a patch of woodland then breasted a rise, as the old woman had forecast. Looking down on a shallow valley they saw another burned village, the same as all the rest but for a cluster of stone buildings that looked like a small convent. 'This must be Hôpital-des-Soeurs,' said Caris. 'Thank God.'

She realized, as she approached, how used to nunnery life she had become. As they rode down the hill she found herself looking forward to the ritual washing of hands, a meal taken in silence, bed time at nightfall, even the sleepy peacefulness of Matins at three o'clock in the morning. After what she had seen today, the security of those grey stone walls was alluring, and she kicked the tired Blackie into a trot.

There was no one moving about the place, but that was not really surprising: it was a small house in a village, and you would not expect the kind of hustle and bustle seen at a major priory such as Kingsbridge. Still, at this time of day there should have been a column of smoke from a kitchen fire as the evening meal was prepared. However, as she came closer she saw further ominous signs, and a sense of dismay slowly engulfed her. The nearest building, which looked like a church, appeared to have no roof. The windows were empty sockets, lacking shutters or glass. Some of the stone walls were blackened, as if by smoke.

The place was silent: no bells, no cries of ostlers or kitchen hands. It was deserted, Caris realized despondently as she reined in. And it had been fired, like every other building in the village. Most of the stone walls were still standing, but the timber roofs had fallen in, doors and other woodwork had burned, and glass windows had shattered in the heat.

Mair said unbelievingly: 'They set fire to a nunnery?'

Caris was equally shocked. She had believed that invading armies invariably left ecclesiastical buildings intact. It was an iron rule, people said. A commander would not hesitate to put to death a soldier who violated a holy place. She had accepted that without question. 'So much for chivalry,' she said.

They dismounted and walked, stepping cautiously around charred beams and scorched rubble, to the domestic quarters. As they approached the kitchen door, Mair gave a shriek and said: 'Oh, God, what's that?'

Caris knew the answer. 'It's a dead nun.' The corpse on the ground was naked, but had the cropped hair of a nun. The body had somehow survived the fire. The woman was about a week dead. The birds had already eaten her eyes, and parts of her face had been nibbled by some scavenging animal.

Also, her breasts had been cut off with a knife.

Mair said in amazement: 'Did the English do this?'

'Well, it wasn't the French.'

'Our soldiers have foreigners fighting alongside them, don't they? Welshmen and Germans and so on. Perhaps it was them.'

'They're all under the orders of our king,' Caris said with grim disapprobation. 'He brought them here. What they do is his responsibility.'

They stared at the hideous sight. As they looked, a mouse came out of the corpse's mouth. Mair screamed and turned away.

Caris hugged her. 'Calm down,' she said firmly, but she stroked Mair's back to comfort her. 'Come on,' she said after a moment. 'Let's get away from here.'

They returned to their horses. Caris resisted an impulse to bury the dead nun: if they delayed, they would still be here at nightfall. But where were they to go? They had planned to spend the night here. 'We'll go back to the old woman with the apple tree,' she said. 'Her house is the only intact building we've seen since we left Caen.' She glanced anxiously at the setting sun. 'If we push the horses, we can be there before it's full dark.'

They urged their tired ponies forward and headed back along the road. Directly ahead of them the sun sank all too quickly below the horizon. The last of the light was fading when they arrived back at the house by the apple tree.

The old woman was happy to see them, expecting them to share their food, which they did, eating in the dark. Her name was Jeanne. There was no fire, but the weather was mild, and the three women rolled up side by side in their blankets. Not fully trusting their hostess, Caris and Mair lay down clutching the saddlebags that contained their food.

Caris lay awake for a while. She was pleased to be on the move after such a long delay in Portsmouth, and they had made good progress in the last two days. If she could find Bishop Richard, she felt sure he would force Godwyn to repay the nuns' money. He was no paragon of integrity, but he was open-minded, and in his lackadaisical way he dispensed justice even-handedly. Godwyn had not had things all his own way even in the witchcraft trial. She felt sure she could persuade Richard to give her a letter ordering Godwyn to sell priory assets in order to give back the stolen cash.

But she was worried about her safety and Mair's. Her assumption that soldiers would leave nuns alone had been quite wrong: what they had seen at Hôpital-des-Soeurs had made that clear. She and Mair needed a disguise.

When she woke up at first light, she said to Jeanne: 'Your grandsons – do you still have their clothes?'

The old woman opened a wooden chest. 'Take what you want,' she said. 'I have no one to give them to.' She picked up a bucket and went off to fetch water.

Caris began to sort through the garments in the chest. Jeanne had not asked for payment. Clothes had little monetary value after so many people had died, she guessed.

Mair said: 'What are you up to?'

'Nuns aren't safe,' Caris said. 'We're going to become pages in the service of a minor lord – Pierre, Sieur of Longchamp in Brittany. Pierre is a common name and there must be lots of places called Longchamp. Our master has been captured by the English, and our mistress has sent us to find him and negotiate his ransom.'

'All right,' Mair said eagerly.

'Giles and Jean were fourteen and sixteen, so with luck their clothes will fit us.'

Caris picked out a tunic, leggings and a cape with a hood, all in the dull brown of undyed wool. Mair found a similar outfit in green, with short sleeves and an undershirt. Women did not usually wear underdrawers, but men did, and fortunately Jeanne had lovingly washed the linen garments of her dead family. Caris and Mair could keep their own shoes: the practical footwear of nuns was no different from what men wore.

'Shall we put them on?' said Mair.

They pulled off their nuns' robes. Caris had never seen Mair undressed, and she could not resist a peek. Her companion's naked body took her breath away. Mair's skin seemed to glow like a pink pearl. Her breasts were generous, with pale girlish nipples, and she had a luxuriant bush of fair pubic hair. Caris was suddenly conscious that her own body was not as beautiful. She looked away, and quickly began to put on the clothes she had chosen.

She pulled the tunic over her head. It was just like a woman's dress except that it stopped at the knee instead of the ankles. She pulled up the linen underdrawers and the leggings, then put her shoes and belt back on.

Mair said: 'How do I look?'

Caris studied her. Mair had put a boy's cap over her short blonde hair, and tilted it at an angle. She was grinning. 'You look so happy!' Caris said in surprise.

'I've always liked boys' clothes.' Mair swaggered up and down the small room. 'This is how they walk,' she said. 'Always taking more space than they need.' It was such an accurate imitation that Caris burst out laughing.

Caris was struck by a thought. 'Are we going to have to pee standing up?'

'I can do it, but not in undershorts – too inaccurate.'

Caris giggled. 'We can't leave off the drawers – a sudden flurry of wind could expose our ... pretences.'

Mair laughed. Then she began to stare at Caris in a way that was strange but not entirely unfamiliar, looking her up and down, meeting her eyes and holding her gaze.

'What are you doing?' said Caris.

'This is how men look at women, as if they own us. But be careful – if you do it to a man, he becomes aggressive.'

'This could be more difficult than I thought.'

'You're too beautiful,' Mair said. 'You need a dirty face.' She went to the fireplace and blackened her hand with soot. Then she smeared it on Caris's face. Her touch was like a caress. My face isn't beautiful, Caris thought; no one ever judged it so – except Merthin, of course...

'Too much,' Mair said after a minute, and wiped some off with her other hand. 'That's better.' She smeared Caris's hand and said: 'Now do me.'

Caris spread a faint smudge on Mair's jawline and throat, making it look as if she might have a light beard. It felt very intimate, to be looking so hard at her face, and touching her skin so softly. She dirtied Mair's forehead and cheeks. Mair looked like a pretty boy – but she did not look like a woman.

They studied one another. A smile played on the red bow of Mair's lips. Caris felt a sense of anticipation, as if something momentous was about to happen. Then a voice said: 'Where are the nuns?'

They both turned round guiltily. Jeanne stood in the doorway, holding a heavy bucket of fresh water, looking frightened. 'What have you done to the nuns?' she said.

Caris and Mair burst out laughing, and then Jeanne recognized them. 'How you have changed yourselves!' she exclaimed.

They drank some of the water, and Caris shared out the rest of the smoked fish for breakfast. It was a good sign, she thought as they ate, that Jeanne had not recognized them. If they were careful, perhaps they could get away with this.

They took their leave of Jeanne and rode off. As they breasted the rise before Hôpital-des-Soeurs, the sun came up directly ahead of them, casting a red light on the nunnery, making the ruins look as if they were still burning. Caris and Mair trotted quickly through the village, trying not to think about the mutilated corpse of the nun lying there in the debris, and rode on into the sunrise.

47

By Tuesday 22 August the English army was on the run.

Ralph Fitzgerald was not sure how it had happened. They had stormed across Normandy from west to east, looting and burning, and no one had been able to withstand them. Ralph had been in his element. On the march, a soldier could take anything he saw – food, jewellery, women – and kill any man who stood in his way. It was how life ought to be lived.

The king was a man after Ralph's own heart. Edward III loved to fight. When he was not at war he spent most of his time organizing elaborate tournaments, costly mock battles with armies of knights in specially designed uniforms. On the campaign, he was always ready to lead a sortie or raiding party, hazarding his life, never pausing to balance risks against benefits like a Kingsbridge merchant. The older knights and earls commented on his brutality, and had protested about incidents such as the systematic rape of the women of Caen, but Edward did not care. When he had heard that some of the Caen citizens had thrown stones at soldiers who were ransacking their homes, he had ordered that everyone in the town should be killed, and only relented after vigorous protests by Sir Godfrey de Harcourt and others.

Things had started to go wrong when they came to the river Seine. At Rouen they had found the bridge destroyed, and the town – on the far side of the water – heavily fortified. King Philippe VI of France was there in person, with a mighty army.

The English marched upstream, looking for a place to cross, but they found that Philippe had been there before them, and one bridge after another was either strongly defended or in ruins. They went as far as Poissy, only twenty miles from Paris, and Ralph thought they would surely attack the capital – but older men shook their heads sagely and said it was impossible. Paris was a city of fifty thousand men, and they must by now have heard the news from Caen, so they would be prepared to fight to the death, knowing they could expect no mercy.

If the king did not intend to attack Paris, Ralph asked, what was his plan? No one knew, and Ralph suspected that Edward had no plan other than to wreak havoc.

The town of Poissy had been evacuated, and the English engineers were able to rebuild its bridge – fighting off a French attack at the same time – so at last the army crossed the river.

By then it was clear that Philippe had assembled an army larger by far than the English, and Edward decided on a dash to the north, with the aim of joining up with an Anglo-Flemish force invading from the north-east.

Philippe gave chase.

Today the English were encamped south of another great river, the Somme, and the French were playing the same trick as they had at the Seine. Sorties and reconnaissance parties reported that every bridge had been destroyed, every riverside town heavily fortified. Even more ominously, an English detachment had seen, on the far bank, the flag of Philippe's most famous and frightening ally, John, the blind king of Bohemia.

Edward had started out with fifteen thousand men in total. In six weeks of campaigning many of those had fallen, and others had deserted, to find their way home with their saddlebags full of gold. He had about ten thousand left, Ralph calculated. Reports of spies suggested that in Amiens, a few miles upstream, Philippe now had sixty thousand foot soldiers and twelve thousand mounted knights, an overwhelming advantage in numbers. Ralph was more worried than he had been since he first set foot in Normandy. The English were in trouble.

Next day they marched downstream to Abbeville, location of the last bridge before the Somme widened into an estuary; but the burgesses of the town had spent money, over the years, strengthening the walls, and the English could see it was impregnable. So cocksure were the citizens that they sent out a large force of knights to attack the vanguard of the English army, and there was a fierce skirmish before the locals withdrew back inside their walled town.

When Philippe's army left Amiens, and started advancing from the south, Edward found himself trapped in the point of a triangle: on his right the estuary, on his left the sea, and behind him the French army, baying for the blood of the barbaric invaders.

That afternoon, Earl Roland came to see Ralph.

Ralph had been fighting in Roland's retinue for seven years. The earl no longer regarded him as an untried boy. Roland still gave the impression that he did not much like Ralph, but he certainly respected him, and would always use him to shore up a weak point in the line, lead a sally or organize a raid. Ralph had lost three fingers from his left hand, and had walked with a limp when tired ever since a Frenchman's pikestaff had cracked his shinbone outside Nantes in 1342. Nevertheless, the king had not yet knighted Ralph, an omission which caused Ralph bitter resentment. For all the loot he had garnered – most of it held for safekeeping by a London goldsmith – Ralph was unfulfilled. He knew that his father would be equally dissatisfied. Like Gerald, Ralph fought for honour, not money; but in all this time he had not climbed a single step up the staircase of nobility.

When Roland appeared, Ralph was sitting in a field of ripening wheat that had been trampled to shreds by the army. He was with Alan Fernhill and half a dozen comrades, eating a gloomy dinner, pea soup with onions: food was running out, and there was no meat left. Ralph felt as they did, tired from constant marching, dispirited by repeated encounters with broken bridges and well-defended towns, and scared of what would happen when the French army caught up with them.

Roland was now an old man, his hair and beard grey, but he still walked erect and spoke with authority. He had learned to keep his expression stonily impassive, so that people hardly noticed that the right side of his face was paralysed. He said: 'The estuary of the Somme is tidal. At low tide, the water may be shallow in places. But the bottom is thick mud, making it impassable.'

'So we can't cross,' said Ralph. But he knew Roland had not come just to give him bad news, and his spirits lifted optimistically.

'There may be a ford – a point where the bottom is firmer,' Roland went on. 'If there is, the French will know.'

'You want me to find out.'

'As quick as you like. There are some prisoners in the next field.'

Ralph shook his head. 'Soldiers might have come from anywhere in France, or even other countries. It's the local people who will have the information.'

'I don't care who you interrogate. Just come to the king's tent with the answer by nightfall.' Roland walked away.

Ralph drained his bowl and leaped to his feet, glad to have something aggressive to do. 'Saddle up, lads,' he said.

He still had Griff. Miraculously, his favourite horse had survived seven years of war. Griff was somewhat smaller than a warhorse, but had more spirit than the oversized destriers most knights preferred. He was now experienced in battle, and his iron-shod hooves gave Ralph an extra weapon in the melee. Ralph was more fond of him than of most of his human comrades. In fact the only living creature to whom he felt closer was his brother, Merthin, whom he had not seen for seven years – and might never see again, for Merthin had gone to Florence.

They headed north-east, towards the estuary. Every peasant living within half a day's walk would know of the ford if there was one, Ralph calculated. They would use it constantly, crossing the river to buy and sell livestock, to attend the weddings and funerals of relatives, to go to markets and fairs and religious festivals. They would be reluctant to give information to the invading English, of course – but he knew how to solve that problem.

They rode away from the army into territory that had not yet suffered from the arrival of thousands of men, where there were sheep in the pastures and crops ripening in the fields. They came to a village from which the estuary could be seen in the far distance. They kicked their horses into a canter along the grassy track that led into the village. The one-room and two-room hovels of the serfs reminded Ralph of Wigleigh. As he expected, the peasants fled in all directions, the women carrying babies and children, most of the men holding an axe or a sickle.

Ralph and his companions had played out this drama twenty or thirty times in the past few weeks. They were specialists in gathering intelligence. Usually, the army's leaders wanted to know where local people had hidden their stocks. When they heard the English were coming, the sly peasants drove their cattle and sheep into woods, stashed sacks of flour in holes in the ground, and hid bales of hay in the bell tower of the church. They knew they would probably starve to death if they revealed where their food was, but they always told sooner or later. On other occasions the army needed directions, perhaps to an important town, a strategic bridge, a fortified abbey. The peasants would usually answer such inquiries unhesitatingly, but it was necessary to make sure they were not lying, for the shrewder among them might try to deceive the invading army, knowing the soldiers were not able to return to punish them.

As Ralph and his men chased the fleeing peasants across gardens and fields, they ignored the men and concentrated on the women and children. Ralph knew that if he captured them, their husbands and fathers would come back.

He caught up with a girl of about thirteen. He rode alongside her for a few seconds, watching her terrified expression. She was dark-haired and dark-skinned, with plain, homely features, young but with a rounded woman's body – the type he liked. She reminded him of Gwenda. In slightly different circumstances he would have enjoyed her sexually, as he had several similar girls in the last few weeks.

But today he had other priorities. He turned Griff to cut her off. She tried to dodge him, tripped over her own feet and fell flat in a vegetable patch. Ralph leaped off his horse and grabbed her as she got up. She screamed and scratched his face, so he punched her in the stomach to quiet her, then he grabbed her long hair. Walking his horse, he began to drag her back to the village. She stumbled and fell, but he just kept going, dragging her along by the hair; and she struggled to her feet, crying in pain. After that, she did not fall again.

They gathered in the little wooden church. The eight English soldiers had captured four women, four children and two babies in arms. They made them sit on the floor in front of the altar. A few moments later a man ran in, babbling in the local French, begging and pleading. Four others followed.

Ralph was pleased.

He stood at the altar, which was only a wooden table painted white. 'Quiet!' he shouted. He waved his sword. They fell silent. He pointed at a young man. 'You,' he said. 'What are you?'

'A leather worker, lord. Please don't harm my wife and child, they've done you no wrong.'

He pointed to another man. 'You?'

The girl he had captured gasped, and Ralph concluded that they were related; father and daughter, he guessed.

'Just a poor cowherd, lord.'

'A cowherd?' That was good. 'And how often do you take cattle across the river?'

'Once or twice a year, lord, when I go to market.'

'And where is the ford?'

He hesitated. 'Ford? There is no ford. We have to cross the bridge at Abbeville.'

'Are you sure?'

'Yes, lord.'

He looked around. 'All of you – is this the truth?'

They nodded.

Ralph considered. They were scared – terrified – but they could still be lying. 'If I fetch the priest, and he brings a Bible, will you all swear on your immortal souls that there is no ford across the estuary?'

'Yes, lord.'

But that would take too long. Ralph looked at the girl he had captured. 'Come here.'

She took a step back.

The cowherd fell to his knees. 'Please, lord, don't harm an innocent child, she is only thirteen—'

Alan Fernhill picked up the girl as if she were a sack of onions and threw her to Ralph, who caught her and held her.

'You're lying to me, all of you. There is a ford, I'm sure there is. I just need to know exactly where it is.'

'All right,' said the cowherd. 'I'll tell you, but leave the child alone.'

'Where is the ford?'

'It's a mile downstream from Abbeville.'

'What's the name of the village?'

The cowherd was thrown by the question for a moment, then he said: 'There is no village, but you can see an inn on the far side.'

He was lying. He had never travelled, so he did not realize that there was always a village by a ford.

Ralph took the girl's hand and placed it on the altar. He drew his knife. With a swift movement, he cut off one of her fingers. His heavy blade easily split her small bones. The girl screamed in agony, and her blood spurted red over the white paint of the altar. All the peasants cried out with horror. The cowherd took an angry step forward, but was stopped by the point of Alan Fernhill's sword.

Ralph kept hold of the girl with one hand, and held up the severed finger on the point of his knife.

'You are the devil himself,' the cowherd said, shaking with shock.

'No, I'm not.' Ralph had heard that accusation before, but it still stung him. 'I'm saving the lives of thousands of men,' he said. 'And if I have to, I'll cut off the rest of her fingers, one by one.'

'No, no!'

'Then tell me where the ford really is.' He brandished the knife.

The cowherd shouted: 'The Blanchetaque, it's called the Blanchetaque, please leave her alone!'

'The Blanchetaque?' said Ralph. He was pretending scepticism, but in fact this was promising. It was an unfamiliar word, but it sounded as if it might mean a white platform, and it was not the kind of thing that a terrified man would invent on the spur of the moment.

'Yes, lord, they call it that because of the white stones on the river bottom that enable you to cross the mud.' He was panic-stricken, tears streaming down his face, so he was almost certainly telling the truth, Ralph thought with satisfaction. The cowherd babbled on: 'People say the stones were put there in olden times, by the Romans, please leave my little girl alone.'

'Where is it?'

'Ten miles downstream from Abbeville.'

'Not a mile?'

'I'm telling the truth this time, lord, as I hope to be saved!'

'And the name of the village?'

'Saigneville.'

'Is the ford always passable, or only at low tide?'

'Only at low tide, lord, especially with livestock or a cart.'

'But you know the tides.'

'Yes.'

'Now, I have only one more question for you, but it is a very important one. If I even suspect you may be lying to me, I will cut off her whole hand.' The girl screamed. Ralph said: 'You know I mean it, don't you?'

'Yes, lord, I'll tell you anything!'

'When is low tide tomorrow?'

A look of panic came over the cowherd. 'Ah – ah – let me work it out!' The man was so wrought up he could barely think.

The leather worker said: 'I'll tell you. My brother crossed yesterday, so I know. Low tide tomorrow will be in the middle of the morning, two hours before noon.'

'Yes!' said the cowherd. 'That's right! I was just trying to calculate. Mid-morning, or a little after. Then again in the evening.'

Ralph kept hold of the girl's bleeding hand. 'How sure are you?'

'Oh, lord, as sure as I am of my own name, I swear!'

The man probably did not know his own name right now, he was so distracted with terror. Ralph looked at the leather worker. There was no sign of deceit on his face, no defiance or eagerness to please in his expression: he just looked a bit ashamed of himself, as if he had been forced, against his will, to do something wrong. This is the truth, Ralph thought exultantly; I've done it.

He said: 'The Blanchetaque. Ten miles downstream from Abbeville, at the village of Saigneville. White stones on the river bottom. Low tide at mid-morning tomorrow.'

'Yes, lord.'

Ralph let go of the girl's wrist, and she ran sobbing to her father, who put his arms around her. Ralph looked down at the pool of blood on the white altar table. There was a lot of it, for a slip of a girl. 'All right, men,' he said. 'We're finished here.'

*

THE TRUMPETS WOKE Ralph at first light. There was no time to light a fire or eat breakfast: the army struck camp immediately. Ten thousand men had to travel six miles by mid-morning, most of them on foot.

The prince of Wales's division led the march off, followed by the king's division, then the baggage train, then the rearguard. Scouts were sent out to check how far away the French army was. Ralph was in the vanguard, with the sixteen-year-old prince, who had the same name as his father, Edward.

They hoped to surprise the French by crossing the Somme at the ford. Last night the king had said: 'Well done, Ralph Fitzgerald.' Ralph had long ago learned that such words meant nothing. He had performed numerous useful or brave tasks for King Edward, Earl Roland and other nobles, but he still had not been knighted. On this occasion he felt little resentment. His life was in as much danger today as it had ever been, and he was so glad to have found an escape route for himself that he hardly cared whether anyone gave him credit for saving the entire army.

As they marched, dozens of marshals and under-marshals patrolled constantly, heading the army in the right direction, keeping the formation together, maintaining the separation of divisions and rounding up stragglers. The marshals were all noblemen, for they had to have the authority to give orders. King Edward was fanatical about orderly marching.

They headed north. The land rose in a gentle slope to a ridge from which they could see the distant glint of the estuary. From there they descended through cornfields. As they passed through villages the marshals ensured there was no looting, because they did not want to carry extra baggage across the river. They also refrained from setting fire to the crops, for fear the smoke might betray their exact position to the enemy.

The sun was about to rise when the leaders reached Saigneville. The village stood on a bluff thirty feet above the river. From the lip of the bank, Ralph looked over a formidable obstacle: a mile and a half of water and marshland. He could see the whitish stones on the bottom marking the ford. On the other side of the estuary was a green hill. As the sun appeared on his right, he saw on the far slope a glint of metal and a flash of colour, and his heart filled with dismay.

The strengthening light confirmed his suspicion: the enemy was waiting for them. The French knew where the ford was, of course, and a wise commander had provided for the possibility that the English might discover its location. So much for surprise.

Ralph looked at the water. It was flowing west, showing that the tide was going out; but it was still too deep for a man to wade. They would have to wait.

The English army continued to build up at the shore, hundreds more men arriving every minute. If the king had tried now to turn the army round and go back, the confusion would have been nightmarish.

A scout returned, and Ralph listened as the news was related to the prince of Wales. King Philippe's army had left Abbeville and was approaching on this bank of the river.

The scout was sent to determine how fast the French army was moving.

There was no turning back, Ralph realized with fear in his heart: the English had to cross the water.

He studied the far side, trying to figure out how many French were on the north bank. More than a thousand, he thought. But the greater danger was the army of tens of thousands coming up from Abbeville. Ralph had learned, in many encounters with the French, that they were extraordinarily brave – foolhardy, sometimes – but they were also undisciplined. They marched in disarray, they disobeyed orders, and they sometimes attacked, to prove their valour, when they would have been wiser to wait. But if they could overcome their disorderly habits and get here in the next few hours, they would catch King Edward's army in midstream. With the enemy on both banks, the English could be wiped out.

After the devastation they had wrought in the last six weeks, they could expect no mercy.

Ralph thought about armour. He had a fine suit of plate armour that he had taken from a French corpse at Cambrai seven years ago, but it was on a wagon in the baggage train. Furthermore, he was not sure he could wade through a mile and a half of water and mud so encumbered. He was wearing a steel cap and a short cape of chain-mail, which was all he could manage on the march. It would have to do. The others had similar light protection. Most of the infantry carried their helmets hanging from their belts, and they would put them on before coming within range of the enemy; but no one marched in full armour.

The sun rose high in the east. The water level fell until it was just knee deep. The noblemen came from the king's entourage with orders to begin the crossing. Earl Roland's son, William of Caster, brought the instructions to Ralph's group. 'The archers go first, and begin firing as soon as they are near enough to the other side,' William told them. Ralph looked at him stonily. He had not forgotten that William had tried to have him hanged for doing what half the English army had done in the last six weeks. 'Then, when you get to the beach, the archers scatter left and right to let the knights and men-at-arms through.' It sounded simple, Ralph thought; orders always did. But it was going to be bloody. The enemy would be perfectly positioned, on the slope above the river, to pick off the English soldiers struggling unprotected through the water.

The men of Hugh Despenser led the advance, carrying his distinctive black-on-white banner. His archers waded in, holding their bows above the water line, and the knights and men-at-arms splashed along behind. Roland's men followed, and soon Ralph and Alan were riding through the water.

A mile and a half was not far to walk but, Ralph now realized, it was a long way to wade, even for a horse. The depth varied: in some places they walked on swampy ground above the surface, in others the water came up to the waists of the infantry. Men and animals tired quickly. The August sun beat down on their heads while their wet feet grew numb with cold. And all the time, as they looked ahead, they could see, more and more clearly, the enemy waiting for them on the north bank.

Ralph studied the opposing force with growing trepidation. The front line, along the shore, consisted of crossbowmen. He knew that these were not Frenchmen but Italian mercenaries, always called Genoese but in fact coming from various parts of Italy. The crossbow had a slower rate of fire than the longbow, but the Genoese were going to have plenty of time to reload while their targets lumbered through the shallows. Behind the archers, on the green rise, stood foot soldiers and mounted knights ready to charge.

Looking back, Ralph saw thousands of English crossing the river behind him. Once again, turning back was not an option; in fact, those behind were pressing forward, crowding the leaders.

Now he could see the enemy ranks clearly. Ranged along the shore were the heavy wooden shields, called pavises, used by the crossbowmen. As soon as the English came within range, the Genoese began to shoot.

At a distance of three hundred yards, their aim was inaccurate, and the bolts fell with diminished force. All the same, a handful of horses and men were hit. The injured fell and drifted downstream to drown. Wounded horses thrashed in the water, turning it bloody. Ralph's heart beat faster.

As the English came closer to the shore, the accuracy of the Genoese improved, and the bolts landed with greater power. The crossbow was slow, but it fired a steel-tipped iron bolt with terrible force. All around Ralph, men and horses fell. Some of those hit died instantly. There was nothing he could do to protect himself, he realized with an apprehension of doom: either he would be lucky, or he would die. The air filled with the awful noise of battle: the swish of deadly arrows, the curses of wounded men, the screams of horses in agony.

The archers at the front of the English column shot back. Their six-foot longbows dragged their ends in the water, so they had to hold them at an unfamiliar angle, and the river bottom beneath their feet was slippery, but they did their best.

Crossbow bolts could penetrate armour plate at close range, but none of the English was wearing any serious armour anyway. Apart from their helmets, they had little protection from the deadly hail.

Ralph would have turned and run if he could. However, behind him ten thousand men and half as many horses were pressing forward, and would have trampled him and drowned him if he had tried to go back. He had no alternative but to lower his head to Griff's neck and urge him on.

The survivors among the leading English archers at last reached shallow water and began to deploy their longbows more effectively. They shot in a trajectory, over the top of the pavises. Once they got started, English bowmen could shoot twelve arrows a minute. The shafts were made of wood – usually ash – but they had steel tips, and when they fell like rain they were terrifying. Suddenly the shooting from the enemy side lessened. Some of the shields fell. The Genoese were driven back, and the English began to reach the foreshore.

As soon as the archers got their feet on solid ground they dispersed left and right, leaving the shore clear for the knights, who charged out of the shallows at the enemy lines. Ralph, still wading across the river, had seen enough battles to know what the French tactics should be at this point: they needed to hold their line and let the crossbowmen continue to slaughter the English on the beach and in the water. But the chivalric code would not permit the French nobility to hide behind low-born archers, and they broke the line to ride forth and engage with the English knights – thereby throwing away much of the benefit of their position. Ralph felt a glimmer of hope.

The Genoese fell back, and the beach was a melee. Ralph's heart pounded with fear and excitement. The French still had the advantage of charging downhill, and they were fully armoured: they slaughtered Hugh Despenser's men wholesale. The vanguard of the charge splashed into the shallows, cutting down the men still in the water.

Earl Roland's archers reached the edge just ahead of Ralph and Alan. Those who survived gained the shore and divided. Ralph felt that the English were doomed, and he was sure to die, but there was nowhere to go except forward, and suddenly he was charging, head down by Griff's neck, sword in the air, straight at the French line. He ducked a scything sword and reached dry ground. He struck uselessly at a steel helmet, then Griff cannoned into another horse. The French horse was larger but younger, and it stumbled, throwing its rider to the mud. Ralph whirled Griff around, went back and prepared to charge again.

His sword was of limited use against plate armour, but he was a big man on a spirited horse, and his best hope was to knock enemy soldiers off their mounts. He charged again. At this point in a battle he felt no fear. Instead, he was possessed by an exhilarating rage that drove him to kill as many of the enemy as he could. When battle was joined, time stood still, and he fought from moment to moment. Later, when the action came to an end, if he was still alive, he would be astonished to see that the sun was setting and a whole day had gone by. Now he rode at the enemy again and again, dodging their swords, thrusting where he saw an opportunity; never slowing his pace, for that was fatal.

At some point — it might have been after a few minutes or a few hours — he realized, with incredulity, that the English were no longer being slaughtered. In fact, they seemed to be winning ground and gaining hope. He detached himself from the melee and paused, panting, to take stock.

The beach was carpeted with corpses, but there were as many French as English, and Ralph realized the folly of the French charge. As soon as the knights on both sides engaged, the Genoese crossbowmen had stopped firing, for fear of hitting their own side, so the enemy had no longer been able to pick off the English in the water like ducks on a pond. Ever since then the English had streamed out of the estuary in their hordes, all following the same orders, archers spreading left and right, knights and infantrymen pushing relentlessly forward, so that the French were inundated by sheer weight of numbers. Glancing back at the water, Ralph saw that the tide was now rising again, so those English still in the river were desperate to get out, regardless of the fate that might await them on the beach.

As he was catching his breath, the French lost their nerve. Forced off the beach, chased up the hill, overwhelmed by the army stampeding out of the rising water, they began to retreat. The English pressed forward, hardly able to believe their luck; and, as so often happened, it took remarkably little time for retreat to turn into flight, with every man for himself.

Ralph looked back over the estuary. The baggage train was in midstream, horses and oxen pulling the heavy carts across the ford, lashed by drivers frantic to beat the tide. There was scrappy fighting on the far bank, now. The vanguard of King Philippe's army must have arrived and engaged a few stragglers, and Ralph thought he recognized, in the sunlight, the colours of the Bohemian light cavalry. But they were too late.

He slumped in his saddle, suddenly weak with relief. The battle was over. Incredibly, against all expectations, the English had slipped out of the French trap.

For today, they were safe.

48

CARIS AND MAIR arrived in the vicinity of Abbeville on 25 August, and were dismayed to find the French army already there. Tens of thousands of foot soldiers and archers were camped in the fields around the town. On the road they heard, not just regional French accents, but the tongues of places farther afield: Flanders, Bohemia, Italy, Savoy, Majorca.

The French and their allies were chasing King Edward of England and his army – as were Caris and Mair. Caris wondered how she and Mair could ever get ahead in the race.

When they passed through the gates and entered the town, late in the afternoon, the streets were crowded with French noblemen. Caris had never seen such a display of costly clothing, fine weapons, magnificent horses and new shoes, not even in London. It seemed as if the entire aristocracy of France was here. The innkeepers, bakers, street entertainers and prostitutes of the town were working non-stop to fulfil the needs of their guests. Every tavern was full of counts and every house had knights sleeping on the floor.

The abbey of St Peter was on the list of religious houses where Caris and Mair had planned to take shelter. But even if they had still been dressed as nuns they would have had trouble getting into the guest quarters: the king of France was staying there, and his entourage took up all the available space. The two Kingsbridge nuns, disguised now as Christophe de Longchamp and Michel de Longchamp, were directed to the grand abbey church, where several hundred of the king's squires, grooms and other attendants were bedding down at night on the cold stone floor of the nave. However, the marshal in charge told them there was no room, and they would have to sleep in the fields like everyone else of low station.

The north transept was a hospital for the wounded. On the way out, Caris paused to watch a surgeon sewing up a deep cut on the cheek of a groaning man-at-arms. The surgeon was quick and skilful, and when he had finished Caris said admiringly: 'You did that very well.'

'Thank you,' he said. Glancing at her he added: 'But how would you know, laddie?'

She knew because she had watched Matthew Barber at work many times, but she had to make up a story quickly, so she said: 'Back in Longchamp, my father is surgeon to the sieur.'

'And are you with your sieur now?'

'He has been captured by the English, and my lady has sent me and my brother to negotiate his ransom.'

'Hmm. You might have done better to go straight to London. If he isn't there now, he soon will be. However, now that you're here, you can earn a bed for the night by helping me.'

'Gladly.'

'Have you seen your father wash wounds with warm wine?'

Caris could wash wounds in her sleep. In a few moments she and Mair were doing what they knew best, taking care of sick people. Most of the men had been hurt the previous day, in a battle at a ford over the river Somme. Injured noblemen had been attended to first, and now the surgeon was getting around to the common soldiers. They worked non-stop for several hours. The long summer evening turned to twilight and candles were brought. At last all the bones had been set, the crushed extremities amputated and the wounds sewn up; and the surgeon, Martin Chirurgien, took them to the refectory for supper.

They were treated as part of the king's entourage, and fed stewed mutton with onions. They had not tasted meat for a week. They even had good red wine. Mair drank with relish. Caris was glad they had the opportunity to build up their strength, but she was still anxious about catching up with the English.

A knight at their table said: 'Do you realize that in the abbot's dining room, next door, four kings and two archbishops are eating supper?' He counted on his fingers as he named them: 'The kings of France, Bohemia, Rome and Majorca, and the archbishops of Rouen and Sens.'

Caris decided she had to see. She went out of the room by the door that seemed to lead to the kitchen. She saw servants carrying laden platters into another room, and peeped through the door.

The men around the table were undoubtedly high-ranking – the board was loaded with roasted fowls, huge joints of beef and mutton, rich puddings and pyramids of sugared fruits. The man at the head was presumably King Philippe, fifty-three years old with a scatter of grey hairs in his blond beard. Beside him, a younger man who resembled him was holding forth. 'The English are not noblemen,' he said, red-faced with fury. 'They are like thieves, who steal in the night and then run away.'

Martin appeared at Caris's shoulder and murmured in her ear: 'That's my master – Charles, count of Alençon, the king's brother.'

A new voice said: 'I disagree.' Caris saw immediately that the speaker was blind, and concluded that he must be King Jean of Bohemia. 'The English cannot run much longer. They are low on food, and they're tired.'

Charles said: 'Edward wants to join forces with the Anglo-Flemish army that has invaded north-east France from Flanders.'

Jean shook his head. 'We learned today that that army has gone into retreat. I think Edward has to stand and fight. And, from his point of view, the sooner the better, for his men are only going to become more dispirited as the days go by.'

Charles said excitedly: 'Then we may catch them tomorrow. After what they have done to Normandy, every one of them should die – knights, noblemen, even Edward himself!'

King Philippe put a hand on Charles's arm, silencing him. 'Our brother's anger is understandable,' he said. 'The crimes of the English are disgusting. But remember: when we encounter the enemy, the most important thing is to put aside any differences there may be between us – forget our quarrels and grudges – and trust one another, at least for the course of the battle. We outnumber the English, and we should vanquish them easily – but we must fight together, as one army. Let us drink to unity.'

That was an interesting toast, Caris decided as she discreetly withdrew. Clearly the king could not take it for granted that his allies would act as a team. But what worried her about the conversation was the likelihood that there would be a battle soon, perhaps tomorrow. She and Mair would have to take care not to get mixed up in it.

As they returned to the refectory, Martin said quietly: 'Like the king, you have an unruly brother.'

Caris saw that Mair was getting drunk. She was overplaying her boyish role, sitting with her legs splayed and her elbows on the table. 'By the saints, that was a good stew, but it's making me fart like the devil,' said the sweet-faced nun in men's clothing. 'Sorry about the stink, lads.' She refilled her wine cup and drank deeply.

The men laughed at her indulgently, amused by the sight of a boy getting drunk for the first time, doubtless remembering embarrassing incidents in their own pasts.

Caris took her arm. 'Time you were in bed, baby brother,' she said. 'Off we go.'

Mair went willingly enough. 'My big brother acts like an old woman,' she said to the company. 'But he loves me – don't you, Christophe?'

'Yes, Michel, I love you,' Caris said, and the men laughed again.

Mair held on tightly to her. Caris walked her back to the church and found the spot in the nave where they had left their blankets. She made Mair lie down, and covered her with her blanket.

'Kiss me goodnight, Christophe,' said Mair.

Caris kissed her lips, then said: 'You're drunk. Go to sleep. We have to start early in the morning.'

Caris lay awake for some time, worrying. She felt she had had terribly bad luck. She and Mair had almost caught up with the English army and Bishop Richard – but at exactly the same moment the French had also caught up with them. She should keep well away from the battlefield. On the other hand, if she and Mair got stuck in the rear of the French army they might never catch the English.

On balance she thought she had better set off first thing in the morning, and try to get ahead of the French. An army this big could not move fast – it would take hours just to form up into marching order. If she and Mair were nimble they should be able to stay ahead. It was risky – but they had done nothing but take risks since leaving Portsmouth.

She drifted off to sleep, and woke when the bell rang for Matins soon after three o'clock in the morning. She roused Mair, and was unsympathetic when she complained of a headache. While the monks sang psalms in the church, Caris and Mair went to the stables and found their horses. The sky was clear, and they could see by starlight.

The town's bakers had been working all night, so they were able to buy loaves for their journey. But the city gates were still closed: they had to wait impatiently until dawn, shivering in the cool air, eating the new bread.

At about half past four they at last left Abbeville and headed north-west along the right bank of the Somme, the direction the English army was said to be taking.

They were only a quarter of a mile away when the trumpets sounded a reveille on the walls of the town. Like Caris, King Philippe had decided on an early start. In the fields, the soldiers and men-at-arms began to stir. The marshals must have got their orders last night, for they seemed to know what to do, and before long some of the army joined Caris and Mair on the road.

Caris still hoped to reach the English ahead of these troops. The French would obviously have to stop and regroup before joining battle. That ought to give Caris and Mair time to reach their countrymen and find some safe place beyond the battlefield. She did not want to get caught between the two sides. She was beginning to think she had been foolhardy to set out on this mission. Knowing nothing of war, she had not been able to imagine the difficulties and dangers. But it was too late now for regrets. And they had got this far without coming to harm.

The soldiers on the road were not French but Italian. They carried steel crossbows and sheaves of iron arrows. They were friendly, and Caris chatted to them in a mixture of Norman French, Latin, and the Italian she had picked up from Buonaventura Caroli. They told her that in battle they always formed the front line, and fired from behind their heavy wooden pavises, which at the moment were in wagons somewhere behind them. They grumbled about their hasty breakfast, disparaged French knights as impulsive and quarrelsome, and spoke with admiration of their leader, Ottone Doria, who could be seen a few yards ahead.

The sun climbed in the sky and everyone got hot. Because the crossbowmen knew they might do battle today, they were wearing heavy quilted coats and carrying iron helmets and knee guards as well as their bows and arrows. Towards noon, Mair declared that she would faint unless they stopped for a break. Caris, too, felt exhausted – they had been riding since dawn – and she knew their horses also needed rest. So, against her inclination, she was forced to stop while thousands of crossbowmen overtook them.

Caris and Mair watered their ponies in the Somme and ate some more bread. When they set off again, they found themselves marching with French knights and men-at-arms. Caris recognized Philippe's choleric brother Charles at the head of the group. She was in the thick of the French army, but there was nothing to do but keep moving and hope for a chance to get ahead.

Soon after midday an order came down the line. The English were not west of here, as previously believed, but north; and the French king had ordered that his army should swing in that direction – not in a column, but all at the same time. The men around Caris and Mair, led by Count Charles, turned off the riverside road down a narrow path through the fields. Caris followed with a sinking heart.

A familiar voice hailed her, and Martin Chirurgien came alongside. 'This is chaos,' he said grimly. 'The marching order has completely broken down.'

A small group of men on fast horses appeared across the fields and hailed Count Charles. 'Scouts,' said Martin, and he went forward to hear what they had to say. Caris and Mair's ponies went too, with the natural instinct of horses to stick together.

'The English have halted,' they heard. 'They've taken up a defensive position on a ridge near the town of Crécy.'

Martin said: 'That's Henri le Moine, an old comrade of the king of Bohemia.'

Charles was pleased by the news. 'Then we shall have battle today!' he said, and the knights around him gave a ragged cheer.

Henri raised a hand in caution. 'We're suggesting that all units stop and regroup,' he said.

'Stop now?' Charles roared. 'When the English are at last willing to stand and fight? Let's get at them!'

'Our men and horses need rest,' Henri said quietly. 'The king is far in the rear. Give him a chance to catch up and look at the battlefield. He can make his dispositions today for an attack tomorrow, when the men will be fresh.'

'To hell with dispositions. There are only a few thousand English. We'll just overrun them.'

Henri made a helpless gesture. 'It is not for me to command you, my lord. But I will ask your brother the king for his orders.'

'Ask him! Ask him!' said Charles, and he rode on.

Martin said to Caris: 'I don't know why my master is so intemperate.'

Caris said thoughtfully: 'I suppose he has to prove that he's brave enough to rule, even though by an accident of birth he's not the king.'

Martin shot her a sharp look. 'You're very wise, for a mere boy.'

Caris avoided his eye, and vowed to remember her false identity. There was no hostility in Martin's voice, but he was suspicious. As a surgeon, he would be familiar with the subtle differences in bone structure between men and women, and he might have noticed that Christophe and Michel de Longchamp were abnormal. Fortunately, he did not press the matter.

The sky began to cloud over, but the air was still warm and humid. Woodland appeared on the left, and Martin told Caris this was the Forest of Crécy. They could not be far from the English – but now Caris wondered how she was going to detach herself from the French and join the English without being killed by one side or the other.

The effect of the forest was to crowd the left flank of the marching army, so that the road on which Caris was riding became jam-packed with troops, the different divisions getting hopelessly mixed up.

Couriers came down the line with new orders from the king: the army was instructed to halt and make camp. Caris's hopes rose: now she would have a chance to get ahead of the French army. There was an altercation between Charles and a courier, and Martin went to Charles's side to listen. He came back looking incredulous. 'Count Charles is refusing to obey the orders!' he said.

'Why?' Caris asked in dismay.

'He thinks his brother is over-cautious. He, Charles, will not be so lily-livered as to halt before such a weak enemy.'

'I thought everyone had to obey the king in battle.'

'They should. But nothing is more important to French noblemen than their code of chivalry. They would die rather than do something cowardly.'

The army marched on in defiance of its orders. 'I'm glad you two are here,' Martin said. 'I'm going to need your help again. Win or lose, there will be a lot of wounded men by sundown.'

Caris realized she could not escape. But somehow she no longer wanted to get away. In fact she felt a strange eagerness. If these men were mad enough to maim one another with swords and arrows, she could at least come to the aid of the wounded.

Soon the crossbowmen's leader, Ottone Doria, came riding back through the crowd – not without difficulty, given the crush – to speak to Charles of Alençon. 'Halt your men!' he shouted at the count.

Charles took offence. 'How dare you give orders to me?'

'The orders come from the king! We are to halt – but my men can't stop, because of yours pushing from behind!'

'Then let them march on.'

'We are within sight of the enemy. If we go any farther we'll have to do battle.'

'So be it.'

'But the men have been marching all day. They're hungry and thirsty and tired. And my crossbowmen don't have their pavises.'

'Are they too cowardly to fight without shields?'

'Are you calling my men cowards?'

'If they won't fight, yes.'

Ottone was quiet for a moment. Then he spoke in a low

voice, and Caris could only just hear his words. 'You're a fool, Alençon. And you'll be in hell by nightfall.' Then he turned his horse and rode away.

Caris felt water on her face, and looked up at the sky. It was beginning to rain.

49

THE SHOWER WAS HEAVY but brief and, when it cleared, Ralph looked down over the valley and saw, with a thrill of fear, that the enemy had arrived.

The English occupied a ridge that ran from south-west to north-east. At their backs, to the north-west, was a wood. In front and on both sides the hill sloped down. Their right flank looked over the town of Crécy-en-Ponthieu, which nestled in the valley of the river Maye.

The French were approaching from the south.

Ralph was on the right flank, with Earl Roland's men, commanded by the young prince of Wales. They were drawn up in the harrow formation that had proved so effective against the Scots. To the left and right, triangular formations of archers stood, like the two teeth of a harrow. Between the teeth, set well back, were dismounted knights and men-at-arms. This was a radical innovation, and one which many knights still resisted: they liked their horses and felt vulnerable on foot. But the king was implacable: everyone on foot. In the ground in front of the knights, the men had dug pitfalls – holes in the ground a foot deep and a foot square – to trip the French horses.

On Ralph's right, at the end of the ridge, was a novelty: three new machines called bombards, or cannons, that used explosive powder to shoot round stones. They had been dragged all the way across Normandy but so far had never been fired, and no one was sure whether they would work. Today King Edward needed to use every means at his disposal, for the enemy's superiority was somewhere between four-to-one and seven-to-one.

On the English left flank, the earl of Northampton's men were drawn up in the same harrow formation. Behind the front lines, a third battalion led by the king stood in reserve. Behind the king were two fall-back positions. The baggage wagons formed the first, drawn up in a circle, with non-combatants – cooks, engineers and ostlers – inside the circle with the horses. The second was the wood itself where, in the event of a rout, the remnants of the English army could flee, and the mounted French knights would find it difficult to follow.

They had been here since early morning, with nothing to eat but pea soup with onions. Ralph was wearing his armour and had been sweltering in the heat, so the rainstorm had been welcome. It had also muddied the slope up which the French would have to charge, making their approach treacherously slippery.

Ralph could guess what the French tactics would be. The Genoese crossbowmen would shoot from behind their shields, to soften up the English line. Then, when they had done enough damage, they would step aside, and the French knights would charge on their warhorses.

There was nothing so terrifying as that charge. Called the *furor fransiscus*, it was the ultimate weapon of the French nobility. Their code made them disregard their own safety. Those huge horses, with riders so completely armoured that they looked like iron men, simply rolled over archers, shields, swords and men-at-arms.

Of course, it did not always work. The charge could be repulsed, especially where the terrain favoured the defenders, as it did here. However, the French were not easily discouraged: they would charge again. And they had such enormous superiority in numbers that Ralph could not see how the English could hold them off indefinitely.

He was scared, but all the same he did not regret being with the army. For seven years he had lived the life of action he had always wanted, in which strong men were kings and the weak counted for nothing. He was twenty-nine, and men of action rarely lived to be old. He had committed foul sins, but had been absolved of them all, most recently this morning, by the bishop of Shiring, who was now standing next to his father the earl, armed with a vicious-looking mace – priests were not supposed to shed blood, a rule they acknowledged cursorily by using blunt weapons on the battlefield.

The crossbowmen in their white coats reached the foot of the slope. The English archers, who had been sitting down, their arrows stuck point-first into the ground in front of them, now began to stand up and string their bows. Ralph guessed that most of them felt what he did, a mixture of relief that the long wait was over and fear at the thought of the odds against them.

Ralph thought there was plenty of time. He could see that the Genoese did not have the heavy wooden pavises that were an essential element of their tactics. The battle would not start until the shields were brought, he felt sure.

Behind the crossbowmen, thousands of knights were pouring into the valley from the south, spreading left and right behind the crossbowmen. The sun came out again, lighting up the bright colours of their banners and the horses' coats. Ralph recognized the coat-of-arms of Charles, count of Alençon, King Philippe's brother.

The crossbowmen stopped at the foot of the slope. There were thousands of them. As if at a signal, they all gave a terrific shout. Some jumped up in the air. Trumpets sounded.

It was their war cry, meant to terrify the enemy, and it might have worked on some foes, but the English army consisted of experienced fighting men who were at the end of a six-week campaign, and it took more than shouting to scare them. They looked on impassively.

Then, to Ralph's utter astonishment, the Genoese lifted their crossbows and shot.

What were they doing? They had no shields!

The sound was sudden and terrifying, five thousand iron bolts flying through the air. But the crossbowmen were out of range. Perhaps they had failed to take account of the fact that they were shooting uphill; and the afternoon sun behind the English lines must have been shining in their eyes. Whatever the reason, their bolts fell uselessly short.

There was a flash of flame and a crash like thunder from the middle of the English front line. Amazed, Ralph saw smoke rising from where the new bombards were. Their sound was impressive, but when he returned his gaze to the enemy ranks he saw little actual damage. However, many of the crossbowmen were shocked enough to pause in their reloading.

At that moment, the prince of Wales shouted the order for his archers to shoot.

Two thousand longbows were raised. Knowing they were too distant to shoot in a straight line parallel with the ground, the archers aimed into the sky, intuitively plotting a shallow trajectory for their arrows. All the bows bent simultaneously, like blades of wheat in a field blown by a sudden summer breeze; then the arrows were released with a collective sound like a church bell tolling. The shafts, flying faster than the swiftest bird, rose into the air then turned downwards and fell on the crossbowmen like a hailstorm.

The enemy ranks were densely packed, and the padded Genoese coats gave little protection. Without their shields, the crossbowmen were horribly vulnerable. Hundreds of them fell dead or wounded.

But that was only the beginning.

While the surviving crossbowmen were rewinding their weapons, the English fired again and again. It took an archer only four or five seconds to pull an arrow from the ground, notch it, draw the bow, take aim, shoot and reach for another. Experienced, practised men could do it faster. In the space of a minute, twenty thousand arrows fell on the unprotected crossbowmen.

It was a massacre, and the consequence was inevitable: they turned and ran.

In moments the Genoese were out of range, and the English held their fire, laughing at their unexpected triumph and jeering at the enemy. But then the crossbowmen encountered another hazard. The French knights were moving forward. A dense herd of fleeing crossbowmen came head to head with massed horsemen itching to charge. For a moment there was chaos.

Ralph was amazed to see the enemy begin to fight among themselves. The knights drew their swords and started to hack the bowmen, who discharged their bolts at the knights then fought on with knives. The French noblemen should have been trying to stop the carnage but, as far as Ralph could see, those in the most expensive armour and riding the largest horses were at the forefront of the fight, attacking their own side with ever-greater fury.

The knights drove the crossbowmen back up the slope until

they were again within longbow range. Once again the prince of Wales gave the order for the English archers to shoot. Now the hail of arrows fell among knights as well as bowmen. In seven years of warfare Ralph had seen nothing like this. Hundreds of the enemy lay dead and wounded, and not a single English soldier had been so much as scratched.

At last the French knights retreated, and the remaining crossbowmen scattered. They left the slope below the English position littered with bodies. Welsh and Cornish knifemen ran forward from the English ranks on to the battlefield and began finishing off the French wounded, retrieving undamaged arrows for the longbowmen to reuse, and no doubt robbing the corpses while they were at it. At the same time, boy runners got fresh stocks of arrows from the supply train and brought them to the English front line.

There was a pause, but it did not last long.

The French knights regrouped, reinforced by new arrivals who were appearing in their hundreds and thousands. Peering into their ranks, Ralph could see that the colours of Alençon had been joined by those of Flanders and Normandy. The standard of the count of Alençon moved to the front, then the trumpets sounded, and the horsemen began to move.

Ralph put his faceplate down and drew his sword. He thought of his mother. He knew she prayed for him every time she went to church, and he felt a moment of warm gratitude to her. Then he watched the enemy.

The huge horses were slow to start, encumbered as they were by riders in full plate armour. The setting sun glinted off the French visors, and the flags snapped in the evening breeze. Gradually the pounding of the hooves grew louder and the pace of the charge picked up. The knights yelled encouragement to their mounts and to one another, waving their swords and spears. They came like a wave on to a beach, seeming to get bigger and faster as they got nearer. Ralph's mouth was dry and his heart beat like a big drum.

They came within bowshot, and again the prince gave the order to shoot. Once more, the arrows rose into the air and fell like deadly rain.

The charging knights were fully armoured, and it was a lucky shot indeed that found the weak spot in the joints between plates. But their mounts had only faceplates and chain-mail neck cowls. So it was the horses that were vulnerable. When the arrows pierced their shoulders and their haunches, some stopped dead, some fell, and some turned and tried to flee. The screams of beasts in pain filled the air. Collisions between horses caused more knights to fall to the ground, joining the bodies of Genoese crossbowmen. Those behind were going too fast to take evasive action, so they just rode over the fallen.

But there were thousands of knights, and they kept coming.

The range shortened for the archers, and their trajectory flattened. When the charge was a hundred yards away, they switched to a different type of arrow, with a flattened steel tip for punching through armour instead of a point. Now they could kill the riders, although a shot that hit a horse was almost as good.

The ground was already wet with rain, and now the charge encountered the pitfalls dug earlier by the English. The horses' momentum was such that few of them could step into a hole a foot deep without stumbling, and many fell, pitching their riders on to the ground in the path of other horses.

The oncoming knights shied away from the archers so, as the English had planned, the charge was funnelled into a narrow killing field, fired upon from left and right.

This was the key to the English tactics. At this point, the wisdom of forcing the English knights to dismount became clear. If they had been on horseback they could not have resisted the urge to charge – and then the archers would have had to cease shooting, for fear of killing their own side. But, because the knights and men-at-arms remained in their lines, the enemy could be slaughtered wholesale, with no casualties on the English side.

But it was not enough. The French were too numerous and too brave. Still they came on, and at last they reached the line of dismounted knights and men-at-arms in the fork between the two masses of archers, and the real fighting began.

The horses trampled over the front ranks of English, but their charge had been slowed by the muddy uphill slope, and they were brought up short by the densely packed English line. Ralph was suddenly in the thick of it, avoiding deadly downward blows from mounted knights, swinging his sword at the legs of their horses, aiming to cripple the beasts by the easiest and most reliable method, cutting their hamstrings. The fighting was fierce: the English had nowhere to go, and the French knew that if they retreated they would have to ride back through the same lethal hail of arrows.

Men fell all around Ralph, hacked down by swords and battleaxes, then trampled by the mighty iron-shod hooves of the warhorses. He saw Earl Roland go down to a French sword. Roland's son, Bishop Richard, swung his mace to protect his fallen father, but a warhorse shouldered Richard aside, and the earl was trampled.

The English were forced back, and Ralph realized that the French had a target: the prince of Wales.

Ralph had no affection for the privileged sixteen-year-old heir to the throne, but he knew it would be a crushing blow to English morale if the prince were captured or killed. Ralph moved back and to his left, joining several others who thickened the shield of fighting men around the prince. But the French intensified their efforts, and they were on horseback.

Then Ralph found himself fighting shoulder to shoulder with the prince, recognizing him by his quartered surcoat, with fleurs-de-lis on a blue background and heraldic lions on red. A moment later, a French horseman swung at the prince with an axe, and the prince fell to the ground.

It was a bad moment.

Ralph sprang forward and lunged at the attacker, sliding his long sword into the man's armpit, where the armour was jointed. He had the satisfaction of feeling the point penetrate flesh, and saw blood spurt from the wound.

Someone else straddled the fallen prince and swung a big sword two-handed at men and horses alike. Ralph saw that it was the prince's standard-bearer, Richard FitzSimon, who had dropped the flag over his supine master. For a few moments Richard and Ralph fought savagely to defend the king's son, not knowing if he was alive or dead.

Then reinforcements arrived. The earl of Arundel appeared

with a large force of men-at-arms, all fresh to the fight. The newcomers joined the battle with vigour, and they turned the tables. The French began to fall back.

The prince of Wales got to his knees. Ralph put up his visor and helped the prince to his feet. The boy seemed to be hurt, but not seriously, and Ralph turned away and fought on.

A moment later the French broke. Despite the lunacy of their tactics, their courage had almost enabled them to sever the English line – but not quite. Now they fled, many more falling as they ran the gauntlet of archers, stumbling down the bloody slope back to their own lines; and a cheer went up from the English, weary but jubilant.

Once again the Welsh invaded the battlefield, cutting the throats of the wounded and collecting thousands of arrows. The archers, too, picked up spent shafts to replenish their stocks. From the rear, cooks appeared with jugs of beer and wine, and surgeons rushed to attend injured noblemen.

Ralph saw William of Caster bend over Earl Roland. Roland was breathing, but his eyes were closed and he looked near to death.

Ralph wiped his bloody sword on the ground and put his visor up to drink a tankard of ale. The prince of Wales approached him and said: 'What's your name?'

'Ralph Fitzgerald of Wigleigh, my lord.'

'You fought bravely. You shall be Sir Ralph tomorrow, if the king listens to me.'

Ralph glowed with pleasure. 'Thank you, lord.'

The prince nodded graciously and moved away.

50

CARIS WATCHED THE early stages of the battle from the far side of the valley. She saw the Genoese crossbowmen try to flee, only to be cut down by knights of their own side. Then she saw the first great charge, with the colours of Charles of Alençon leading thousands of knights and men-at-arms.

She had never seen battle, and she was utterly sickened. Hundreds of knights fell to the English arrows, to be trampled by the hooves of the great warhorses. She was too far away to be able to follow the hand-to-hand fighting, but she saw the swords flash and the men fall, and she wanted to weep. As a nun, she had seen severe injuries – men who had fallen from high scaffolding, hurt themselves with sharp tools, suffered hunting accidents – and she always felt the pain and the waste of a lost hand, a crushed leg, a damaged brain. To see men inflicting such wounds on one another intentionally revolted her.

For a long time it seemed the fight could go either way. If she had been at home, hearing news of the war from afar, she might have hoped for an English victory; but after what she had seen in the last two weeks she felt a sort of disgusted neutrality. She could not identify with the English who had murdered peasants and burned their crops, and it made no difference to her that they had committed these atrocities in Normandy. Of course, they would say the French deserved what they got because they had burned Portsmouth, but that was a stupid way to think – so stupid that it led to scenes of horror such as this.

The French retreated, and she assumed they would regroup and reorganize, and wait for the king to arrive to develop a new battle plan. They still had overwhelming superiority in numbers, she could see: there were tens of thousands of troops in the valley, with more still arriving.

But the French did not regroup. Instead, every new battalion that arrived went straight into the attack, throwing themselves suicidally up the hill at the English position. The second and subsequent charges fared worse than the first. Some were cut down by archers even before they reached the English lines; the rest were beaten off by foot soldiers. The slope below the ridge became shiny with the gushing blood of hundreds of men and horses.

After the first charge, Caris looked only occasionally at the battle. She was too busy tending those French wounded who were lucky enough to be able to leave the field. Martin Chirurgien had realized that she was as good a surgeon as he. Giving her free access to his instruments, he left her and Mair to work independently. They washed, sewed and bandaged hour after hour.

News of prominent casualties came back to them from the front line. Charles of Alençon was the first high-ranking fatality. Caris could not help feeling that he deserved his fate. She had witnessed his foolish enthusiasm and careless indiscipline. Hours later, King Jean of Bohemia was reported dead, and she wondered what madness drove a blind man to battle.

'In God's name, why don't they stop?' she said to Martin when he brought her a cup of ale to refresh her.

'Fear,' he replied. 'They're scared of disgrace. To leave the field without striking a blow would be shameful. They would prefer to die.'

'A lot of them have had that wish granted,' said Caris grimly, and she emptied her tankard and went back to work. Her knowledge and understanding of the human body was growing by leaps and bounds, she reflected. She saw inside every part of a living man: the brains beneath shattered skulls, the pipework of the throat, the muscles of the arms sliced open, the heart and lungs within smashed ribcages, the slimy tangle of the intestines, the articulation of the bones at hip and knee and ankle. She discovered more in an hour on the battlefield than in a year at the priory hospital. This was how Matthew Barber had learned so much, she realized. No wonder he was confident.

The carnage continued until night fell. The English lit

torches, afraid of a sneak attack under cover of darkness. But Caris could have told them they were safe. The French were routed. She could hear the calls of French soldiers searching the battlefield for fallen kinsmen and comrades. The king, who had arrived in time to join one of the last hopeless charges, left the field. After that the exit became general.

A fog came up from the river, filling the valley and obscuring the distant flares. Once again, Caris and Mair worked by firelight long into the night, patching up the wounded. All those who could walk or hobble left as soon as they could, putting as much distance as possible between themselves and the English, hoping to avoid tomorrow's inevitable bloodthirsty mopping-up operation. When Caris and Mair had done all they could for the victims, they slipped away.

This was their chance.

They located their ponies and led them forward by the light of a burning torch. They reached the bottom of the valley and found themselves in no-man's-land. Hidden by fog and darkness, they slipped out of their boys' clothing. For a moment they were terribly vulnerable, two naked women in the middle of a battlefield. But no one could see them, and a second later they were pulling their nuns' robes over their heads. They packed up their male garments in case they should need them again: it was a long way home.

Caris decided to abandon the torch, in case an English archer should take it into his head to shoot at the light and ask questions afterwards. Holding hands so that they would not get separated they went forward, still leading the horses. They could see nothing: the fog obscured whatever light might have come from moon or stars. They headed uphill towards the English lines. There was a smell like a butcher's shop. So many bodies of horses and men covered the ground that they could not walk around them. They had to grit their teeth and step on the corpses. Soon their shoes were covered with a mixture of mud and blood.

The bodies on the ground thinned out, and soon there were none. Caris began to feel a deep sense of relief as she approached the English army. She and Mair had travelled hundreds of miles, lived rough for two weeks, and risked their lives for this moment.

She had almost forgotten the outrageous theft by Prior Godwyn of one hundred and fifty pounds from the nuns' treasury – the reason for her journey. Somehow it seemed less important after all this bloodshed. Still, she would appeal to Bishop Richard and win justice for the nunnery.

The walk seemed farther than Caris had imagined when she had looked across the valley in daylight. She wondered nervously if she had become disoriented. She might have turned in the wrong direction and just walked straight past the English. Perhaps the army was now behind her. She strained to hear some noise – ten thousand men could not be silent, even if most of them had fallen into exhausted sleep – but the fog muffled sound.

She clung to the conviction that, as King Edward had positioned his forces on the highest land, she must be approaching him as long as she was walking uphill. But the blindness was unnerving. If there had been a precipice, she would have stepped right over it.

The light of dawn was turning the fog to the colour of pearl when at last she heard a voice. She stopped. It was a man speaking in a low murmur. Mair squeezed her hand nervously. Another man spoke. She could not make out the language. She feared that she might have walked full circle and arrived back on the French side.

She turned towards the voice, still holding Mair's hand. The red glow of flames became visible through the grey mist, and she headed for it gratefully. As she came nearer, she heard the talk more clearly, and realized with immense relief that the men were speaking English. A moment later she made out a group of men around a fire. Several lay asleep, rolled in blankets, but three sat upright, legs crossed, looking into the flames, talking. A moment later Caris saw a man standing, peering into the fog, presumably on sentry duty, though the fact that he had not noticed her approach proved his job was impossible.

To get their attention, Caris said in a low voice: 'God bless you, men of England.'

She startled them. One gave a shout of fear. The sentry said belatedly: 'Who goes there?'

'Two nuns from Kingsbridge Priory,' Caris said. The men

stared at her in superstitious dread, and she realized they thought she might be an apparition. 'Don't worry, we're flesh and blood, and so are these ponies.'

'Did you say Kingsbridge?' said one of them in surprise. 'I know you,' he said, standing up. 'I've seen you before.'

Caris recognized him. 'Lord William of Caster,' she said.

'I am the earl of Shiring, now,' he said. 'My father died of his wounds an hour ago.'

'May his soul rest in peace. We have come here to see your brother, Bishop Richard, who is our abbot.'

'You're too late,' William said. 'My brother, too, is dead.'

*

LATER IN THE morning, when the fog had lifted and the battlefield looked like a sunlit slaughterhouse, Earl William took Caris and Mair to see King Edward.

Everyone was astonished at the tale of the two nuns who had followed the English army all through Normandy, and soldiers who had faced death only yesterday were fascinated by their adventures. William told Caris that the king would want to hear the story from her own lips.

Edward III had been king for nineteen years, but he was still only thirty-three years old. Tall and broad-shouldered, he was imposing rather than handsome, with a face that might have been moulded for power: a big nose, high cheekbones and luxuriant long hair just beginning to recede from his high forehead. Caris saw why people called him a lion.

He sat on a stool in front of his tent, fashionably dressed in two-coloured hose and a cape with a scalloped border. He wore no armour or weapons: the French had vanished, and in fact a force of vengeful troops had been sent out to hunt down and kill any stragglers. A handful of barons stood around.

As Caris told how she and Mair had sought food and shelter in the devastated landscape of Normandy, she wondered if the king felt criticized by her tale of hardship. However, he seemed not to think the sufferings of the people reflected on him. He was as delighted with her exploits as if he were hearing of someone who had been brave during a shipwreck.

She ended by telling him of her disappointment on finding, after all her travails, that Bishop Richard, from whom she hoped for justice, was dead. 'I beg your majesty to order the prior of Kingsbridge to restore to the nuns the money he stole.'

Edward smiled ruefully. 'You're a brave woman, but you know nothing of politics,' he said with condescension. 'The king can't get involved in an ecclesiastical quarrel such as this. We would have all our bishops banging on our door in protest.'

That might be so, Caris reflected, but it did not prevent the king interfering with the church when it suited his own purposes. However, she said nothing.

Edward went on: 'And it would do your cause harm. The church would be so outraged that every cleric in the land would oppose our ruling, regardless of its merits.'

There might be something in that, she judged. But he was not as powerless as he pretended. 'I know you will remember the wronged nuns of Kingsbridge,' she said. 'When you appoint the new bishop of Kingsbridge, please tell him our story.'

'Of course,' said the king, but Caris had the feeling he would forget.

The interview seemed to be over, but then William said: 'Your majesty, now that you have graciously confirmed my elevation to my father's earldom, there is the question of who is to be lord of Caster.'

'Ah, yes. Our son the prince of Wales suggests Sir Ralph Fitzgerald, who was knighted yesterday for saving his life.'

Caris murmured: 'Oh, no!'

The king did not hear her, but William did, and he obviously felt the same way. He was not quite able to hide his indignation as he said: 'Ralph was an outlaw, guilty of numerous thefts, murders and rapes, until he obtained a royal pardon by joining your majesty's army.'

The king was not as moved by this as Caris expected. He said: 'All the same, Ralph has fought with us for seven years now. He has earned a second chance.'

'Indeed he has,' William said diplomatically. 'But, given the trouble we've had with him in the past, I'd like to see him settle down peacefully for a year or two before he's ennobled.'

'Well, you will be his overlord, so you'll have to deal with him,' Edward granted. 'We won't impose him on you against your will. However, the prince is keen that he should have some further reward.' The king thought for a few moments, then said: 'Don't you have a cousin who is eligible for marriage?'

'Yes, Matilda,' said William. 'We call her Tilly.'

Caris knew Tilly. She was at the nunnery school.

'That's right,' said Edward. 'She was your father Roland's ward. Her father had three villages near Shiring.'

'Your majesty has a good memory for detail.'

'Marry Lady Matilda to Ralph and give him her father's villages,' said the king.

Caris was appalled. 'But she's only twelve!' she burst out.

William said to her: 'Hush!'

King Edward turned a cold gaze on her. 'The children of the nobility must grow up fast, sister. Queen Philippa was fourteen when I married her.'

Caris knew she should shut up, but she could not. Tilly was only four years older than the daughter she might have had, if she had given birth to Merthin's baby. 'There's a big difference between twelve and fourteen,' she said desperately.

The young king became even more frosty. 'In the royal presence, people give their opinions only when asked. And the king almost never asks for the opinions of women.'

Caris realized she had taken the wrong tack. Her objection to the marriage was not based on Tilly's age so much as Ralph's character. 'I know Tilly,' she said. 'You can't marry her to that brute Ralph.'

Mair said in a scared whisper: 'Caris! Remember who you're speaking to!'

Edward looked at William. 'Take her away, Shiring, before she says something that cannot be overlooked.'

William took Caris's arm and firmly marched her out of the royal presence. Mair followed. Behind them, Caris heard the king say: 'I can see how she survived in Normandy – the locals must have been terrified of her.' The noblemen around him laughed.

'You must be mad!' William hissed.

'Must I?' Caris said. They were out of earshot of the king

now, and she raised her voice. 'In the last six weeks the king has caused the deaths of thousands of men, women and children, and burned their crops and their homes. And I have tried to save a twelve-year-old girl from being married to a murderer. Tell me again, Lord William, which of us is mad?'

51

IN THE YEAR 1347 the peasants of Wigleigh suffered a poor harvest. The villagers did what they always did in such times: they ate less food, postponed the purchase of hats and belts, and slept closer together for warmth. Old Widow Huberts died earlier than expected; Janey Jones succumbed to a cough that she might have survived in a good year; and Joanna David's new baby, who might otherwise have had a chance, failed to make it to his first birthday.

Gwenda kept an anxious eye on her two little boys. Sam, the eight-year-old, was big for his age, and strong: he had Wulfric's physique, people said, though Gwenda knew that in truth he was like his real father, Ralph Fitzgerald. Even so, Sam was visibly thinner by December. David, named after Wulfric's brother who had died when the bridge collapsed, was six. He resembled Gwenda, being small and dark. The poor diet had weakened him, and all through the autumn he suffered minor ailments: a cold, then a skin rash, then a cough.

All the same, she took the boys with her when she went with Wulfric to finish sowing the winter wheat on Perkin's land. A bitterly cold wind swept across the open fields. She dropped seeds into the furrows, and Sam and David chased off the daring birds who tried to snatch the corn before Wulfric turned the earth over. As they ran, and jumped, and shouted, Gwenda marvelled that these two fully functioning miniature human beings had come from inside her body. They turned the chasing of the birds into some kind of competitive game, and she delighted in the miracle of their imagination. Once part of her, they were now able to have thoughts she did not know about.

Mud clung to their feet as they tramped up and down. A fast-running stream bordered the big field, and on the far bank stood the fulling mill Merthin had built nine years ago. The distant rumble of its pounding wooden hammers accompanied their work. The mill was run by two eccentric brothers, Jack and Eli – both unmarried men with no land – and an apprentice boy who was their nephew. They were the only villagers who had not suffered on account of the bad harvest: Mark Webber paid them the same wages all winter long.

It was a short midwinter day. Gwenda and her family finished sowing just as the grey sky began to darken, and the twilight gathered mistily in the distant woods. They were all tired.

There was half a sack of seed left over, so they took it to Perkin's house. As they approached the place, they saw Perkin himself coming from the opposite direction. He was walking beside a cart on which his daughter, Annet, was riding. They had been to Kingsbridge to sell the last of the year's apples and pears from Perkin's trees.

Annet still retained her girlish figure, although she was now twenty-eight, and had had a child. She called attention to her youthfulness with a dress that was a little too short and a hair style that was charmingly disarrayed. She looked silly, Gwenda thought. Her opinion was shared by every woman in the village and none of the men.

Gwenda was shocked to see that Perkin's cart was full of fruit. 'What happened?' she said.

Perkin's face was grim. 'Kingsbridge folk are having a hard winter just like us,' he said. 'They've no money to buy apples. We shall have to make cider with this lot.'

That was bad news. Gwenda had never known Perkin to come home from the market with so much unsold produce.

Annet seemed unworried. She held out a hand to Wulfric, who helped her down from the cart. As she stepped to the ground she stumbled, and fell against him with her hand on his chest. 'Oops!' she said, and smiled at him as she recovered her balance. Wulfric flushed with pleasure.

You blind idiot, Gwenda thought.

They went inside. Perkin sat at the table, and his wife, Peg, brought him a bowl of pottage. He cut a thick slice from the loaf on the board. Peg served her own family next. Annet, her husband

Billy Howard, Annet's brother, Rob, and Rob's wife. She gave a little to Annet's four-year-old daughter, Amabel, and to Rob's two small boys. Then she invited Wulfric and his family to sit down.

Gwenda spooned up the broth hungrily. It was thicker than the pottage she made: Peg was putting stale bread in, whereas in Gwenda's house the bread never lasted long enough to go stale. Perkin's family got cups of ale, but Gwenda and Wulfric were not offered any: hospitality went only so far in hard times.

Perkin was jocular with his customers, but otherwise a sourpuss, and the atmosphere in his house was always more or less dismal. He talked in a disheartened way about the Kingsbridge market. Most of the traders had had a bad day. The only ones doing any business were those who sold essentials such as corn, meat and salt. No one was buying the now-famous Kingsbridge Scarlet cloth.

Peg lit a lamp. Gwenda wanted to go home but she and Wulfric were waiting for their wages. The boys began to misbehave, running around the room and bumping into adults. 'It's getting near their bed time,' said Gwenda, though it was not really.

At last Wulfric said: 'If you'll give us our wages, Perkin, we'll leave.'

'I haven't got any money,' Perkin said.

Gwenda stared at him. He had never said anything like this in the nine years she and Wulfric had been working for him.

Wulfric said: 'We must have our wages. We've got to eat.'

'You've had some pottage, haven't you?' Perkin said.

Gwenda was outraged. 'We work for money, not pottage!'

'Well, I haven't got any money,' Perkin repeated. 'I went to market to sell my apples, but no one bought them, so I've got more apples than we can eat, and no money.'

Gwenda was so shocked that she did not know what to say. It had never occurred to her that Perkin might not pay them. She felt a stab of fear as she realized there was nothing she could do about it.

Wulfric said slowly: 'Well, what's to be done about it? Shall we go to the Long Field and take the seeds back out of the ground?'

'I'll have to owe you this week's wages,' Perkin said. 'I'll pay you when things get better.'

'And next week?'

'I won't have any money next week, either – where do you think it's to come from?'

Gwenda said: 'We'll go to Mark Webber. Perhaps he can employ us at the fulling mill.'

Perkin shook his head. 'I spoke to him yesterday, in Kingsbridge, and asked if he could hire you. He said no. He's not selling enough cloth. He'll continue to employ Jack and Eli and the boy, and stockpile the cloth until trade picks up, but he can't take on any extra hands.'

Wulfric was bewildered. 'How are we to live? How will you get your spring ploughing done?'

'You can work for food,' Perkin offered.

Wulfric looked at Gwenda. She choked back a scornful retort. She and her family were in deep trouble, and this was not the moment to antagonize anyone. She thought fast. They did not have much choice: eat, or starve. 'We'll work for food, and you'll owe us the money,' she said.

Perkin shook his head. 'What you're suggesting may be fair—'

'It is fair!'

'All right, it is fair, but just the same I can't do it. I don't know when I'll have the money. Why, I could owe you a pound come Whitsun! You can work for food, or not at all.'

'You'll have to feed all four of us.'

'Yes.'

'But only Wulfric will work.'

'I don't know—'

'A family wants more than food. Children need clothes. A man must have boots. If you can't pay me, I will have to find some other way of providing such things.'

'How?'

'I don't know.' She paused. The truth was, she had no idea. She fought down panic. 'I may have to ask my father how he manages.'

Peg put in: 'I wouldn't do that, if I were you – Joby will tell you to steal.'

Gwenda was stung. What right did Peg have to take a supercilious attitude? Joby had never employed people then told them at the end of the week that he could not pay them. But she bit her tongue, and said mildly: 'He fed me through eighteen winters, even if he did sell me to outlaws at the end.'

Peg tossed her head and abruptly began to pick up the bowls from the table.

Wulfric said: 'We should go.'

Gwenda did not move. Whatever advantages she could gain had to be won now. When she left this house, Perkin would consider that a bargain had been struck, and could not be renegotiated. She thought hard. Remembering how Peggy had given ale only to her own family, she said: 'You won't fob us off with stale fish and watery beer. You'll feed us exactly the same as yourself and your family – meat, bread, ale, whatever it may be.'

Peg made a deprecating noise. She had been planning to do just what Gwenda feared, it seemed.

Gwenda added: 'That is, if you want Wulfric to do the same work as you and Rob.' They all knew perfectly well that Wulfric did more work than Rob and twice as much as Perkin.

'All right,' Perkin said.

'And this is strictly an emergency arrangement. As soon as you get money, you have to start paying us again at the old rate – a penny a day each.'

'Yes.'

There was a short silence. Wulfric said: 'Is that it?'

'I think so,' Gwenda said. 'You and Perkin should shake hands on the bargain.'

They shook hands.

Taking their children, Gwenda and Wulfric left. It was now full dark. Clouds hid the stars, and they had to make their way by the glimmer of light shining through cracks in shutters and around doors. Fortunately they had walked from Perkin's house to their own a thousand times before.

Wulfric lit a lamp and built up the fire while Gwenda put the boys to bed. Although there were bedrooms upstairs – they were still living in the large house that had been occupied by Wulfric's parents – nevertheless they all slept in the kitchen, for warmth.

Gwenda felt depressed as she wrapped the boys in blankets and settled them near the fire. She had grown up determined not to live the way her mother did, in constant worry and want. She had aspired to independence: a patch of land, a hard-working husband, a reasonable lord. Wulfric yearned to get back the land his father had farmed. In all those aspirations they had failed. She was a pauper, and her husband a landless labourer whose employer could not even pay him a penny a day. She had ended up exactly like her mother, she thought; and she felt too bitter for tears.

Wulfric took a pottery bottle from a shelf and poured ale into a wooden cup. 'Enjoy it,' Gwenda said sourly. 'You won't be able to buy your own ale for a while.'

Wulfric said conversationally: 'It's amazing that Perkin has no money. He's the richest man in the village, apart from Nathan Reeve.'

'Perkin has money,' Gwenda said. 'There's a jar of silver pennies under his fireplace. I've seen it.'

'Then why won't he pay us?'

'He doesn't want to dip into his savings.'

Wulfric was taken aback. 'But he could pay us, if he wanted to?'

'Of course.'

'Then why am I going to work for food?'

Gwenda let out an impatient grunt. Wulfric was so slow on the uptake. 'Because the alternative was no work at all.'

Wulfric was feeling that they had been hoodwinked. 'We should have insisted on payment.'

'Then why didn't you?'

'I didn't know about the jar of pennies under the fireplace.'

'For God's sake, do you think a man as rich as Perkin can be impoverished by failing to sell one cartload of apples? He's been the largest landholder in Wigleigh ever since he got hold of your father's acres ten years ago. Of course he has savings!'

'Yes, I see that.'

She stared into the fire while he finished the ale, then they went to bed. He put his arms around her, and she rested her head on his chest, but she did not want to make love. She was too angry. She told herself she should not take it out on her husband: Perkin had let them down, not Wulfric. But she *was* angry with Wulfric – furious. As she sensed him drifting off to sleep, she realized that her anger was not about their wages. That was the kind of misfortune that afflicted everyone from time to time, like bad weather and barley mould.

What, then?

She recalled the way Annet had fallen against Wulfric as she stepped down from the cart. When she remembered Annet's coquettish smile, and Wulfric's flush of pleasure, she wanted to slap his face. I'm angry with you, she thought, because that worthless, empty-headed flirt can still make you look such a damn fool.

*

ON THE SUNDAY before Christmas, a manor court was held in the church after the service. It was cold, and the villagers huddled together, wrapped in cloaks and blankets. Nathan Reeve was in charge. The lord of the manor, Ralph Fitzgerald, had not been seen in Wigleigh for years. So much the better, Gwenda thought. Besides, he was Sir Ralph now, with three other villages in his fiefdom, so he would not take much interest in ox teams and cow pasture.

Alfred Shorthouse had died during the week. He was a childless widower with ten acres. 'He has no natural heirs,' said Nate Reeve. 'Perkin is willing to take over his land.'

Gwenda was surprised. How could Perkin think of taking on more land? She was too startled to respond immediately, and Aaron Appletree, the bagpipe player, spoke first. 'Alfred has been in poor health since the summer,' he said. 'He's done no autumn ploughing and sown no winter wheat. All the work is to be done. Perkin will have his hands full.'

Nate said aggressively: 'Are you asking for the land yourself?'

Aaron shook his head. 'In a few more years, when my boys are big enough to help, I'll jump at such a chance,' he said. 'I couldn't handle it now.'

'I can manage it,' Perkin said.

Gwenda frowned. Nate obviously wanted Perkin to have the land. No doubt a bribe had been promised. She had known all along that Perkin had money. But she had little interest in exposing Perkin's duplicity. She was thinking of how she could exploit this situation to her advantage, and get her family out of poverty.

Nate said: 'You could take on another labourer, Perkin.'

'Wait a minute,' Gwenda said. 'Perkin can't pay the labourers he's got now. How can he take on more land?'

Perkin was taken aback, but he could hardly deny what Gwenda was saying, so he remained silent.

Nate said: 'Well, who else can cope with it?'

Gwenda said quickly: 'We'll take it.'

Nate looked surprised.

She added quickly: 'Wulfric is working for food. I have no work. We need land.'

She noticed several nodding heads. No one in the village liked what Perkin had done. They all feared that one day they might end up in the same situation.

Nate saw the danger of his plan going awry. 'You can't afford the entry fee,' he said.

'We'll pay it a little at a time.'

Nate shook his head. 'I want a tenant who can pay right away.' He looked around the assembled villagers. However, no one volunteered. 'David Johns?'

David was a middle-aged man whose sons had land of their own. 'I would have said yes a year ago,' he said. 'But the rain at harvest time knocked me back.'

The offer of an extra ten acres would normally have had the more ambitious villagers fighting among themselves, but it was a bad year. Gwenda and Wulfric were different. For one thing, Wulfric had never ceased to long for land of his own. Alfred's acres were not Wulfric's birthright, but they were better than nothing. Anyway, Gwenda and Wulfric were desperate.

Aaron Appletree said: 'Give it to Wulfric, Nate. He's a hard worker, he'll get the ploughing done in time. And he and his wife deserve some good luck – they've had more than their fair share of bad.'

Nate looked bad-tempered, but there was a loud rumble of assent from the peasants. Wulfric and Gwenda were well respected despite their poverty.

This was a rare combination of circumstances that could get Gwenda and her family started on the road to a better life, and she felt growing excitement as it began to seem possible.

But Nate was still looking dubious. 'Sir Ralph hates Wulfric,' he said.

Wulfric's hand went to his cheek, and he touched the scar made by Ralph's sword.

'I know,' said Gwenda. 'But Ralph's not here.'

52

WHEN EARL ROLAND died the day after the battle of Crécy, several people moved a step up the ladder. His elder son, William, became the earl, overlord of the county of Shiring, answerable to the king. A cousin of William's, Sir Edward Courthose, became lord of Caster, took over the rule of the forty villages of that fiefdom as a sub-tenant of the earl, and moved into William and Philippa's old house in Casterham. And Sir Ralph Fitzgerald became lord of Tench.

For the next eighteen months, none of them went home. They were all too busy travelling with the king and killing French people. Then, in 1347, the war reached a stalemate. The English captured and held the valuable port city of Calais, but otherwise there was little to show for a decade of war – except, of course, a great deal of booty.

In January 1348 Ralph took possession of his new property. Tench was a large village with a hundred peasant families, and the manor included two smaller villages nearby. He also retained Wigleigh, which was half a day's ride away.

Ralph felt a thrill of pride as he rode through Tench. He had looked forward to this moment. The serfs bowed and their children stared. He was lord of every person and owner of every object in the place.

The house was set in a compound. Riding in, followed by a cart loaded with French loot, Ralph saw immediately that the defensive walls had long ago fallen into disrepair. He wondered whether he should restore them. The burgers of Normandy had neglected their defences, by and large, and that had made it relatively easy for Edward III to overrun them. On the other hand, the likelihood of an invasion of southern England was now very small. Early in the war, most of the French fleet had been wiped out at the port of Sluys, and thereafter the English had controlled the sea channel that separated the two countries. Apart from minor raids by freelance pirates, every battle since Sluys had been fought on French soil. On balance it hardly seemed worthwhile to rebuild the compound walls.

Several grooms appeared and took the horses. Ralph left Alan Fernhill to supervise the unloading, and walked towards his new house. He was limping: his injured leg always hurt after a long ride. Tench Hall was a stone-built manor house. It was impressive, he noted with satisfaction, though it needed repairs – not surprisingly, for it had remained unoccupied since Lady Matilda's father died. However, it was modern in design. In old-fashioned houses, the lord's private chamber was an afterthought stuck on to the end of the all-important great hall, but Ralph could see, from the outside, that here the domestic apartments took up half the building.

He entered the hall, and was annoyed to find Earl William there.

At the far end of the room was a large chair made of dark wood, elaborately carved with powerful symbols: angels and lions on the back and arms, snakes and monsters on the legs. It was obviously the chair of the lord of the manor. But William was sitting in it.

Much of Ralph's pleasure evaporated. He could not enjoy his mastery of the new manor under the scrutiny of his own overlord. It would be like going to bed with a woman while her husband listened outside the door.

He masked his displeasure and formally greeted Earl William. The earl introduced the man standing next to him. 'This is Daniel, who has been bailiff here for twenty years, and has taken good care of the place, on my father's behalf, during Tilly's minority.'

Ralph acknowledged the bailiff stiffly. William's message was clear: he wanted Ralph to let Daniel continue in the job. But Daniel had been Earl Roland's man and now he would be Earl William's. Ralph had no intention of letting his domain be managed by the earl's man. His bailiff would be loyal to him alone.

William waited expectantly for Ralph to say something about

Daniel. However, Ralph was not going to have that discussion. Ten years ago he would have jumped feet first into an argument, but he had learned a lot in the time he had spent with the king. He was not obliged to get his earl's approval for his choice of bailiff, so he would not seek it. He would say nothing until William had gone, then he would tell Daniel he was being assigned to other duties.

Both William and Ralph remained stubbornly silent for a few moments, then the deadlock was broken. A large door opened at the domestic end of the hall and the tall, elegant figure of Lady Philippa came in. It was many years since Ralph had seen her, but his youthful passion returned with a shock that felt like a punch, leaving him breathless. She was older – she had to be forty, he guessed – but she was in her prime. Perhaps she was a little heavier than he remembered, her hips more rounded, her breasts fuller, but that only added to her allure. She still walked like a queen. As always, the sight of her made him ask resentfully why he could not have a wife like that.

In the past she had barely deigned to notice his presence, but today she smiled and shook his hand and said: 'Are you getting to know Daniel?'

She, too, wanted him to continue to employ the earl's retainer – that was why she was being courteous. All the more reason to get rid of the man, he thought with secret relish. 'I've just arrived,' he said noncommittally.

Philippa explained their presence. 'We wanted to be here when you met young Tilly – she's part of our family.'

Ralph had commanded the nuns of Kingsbridge Priory to bring his fiancée here to meet him today. Interfering busybodies, the nuns had obviously told Earl William what was happening. 'Lady Matilda was the ward of Earl Roland, rest his soul,' Ralph said, emphasizing that the wardship had ended with Roland's death.

'Yes – and I would have expected the king to transfer her wardship to my husband, as Roland's heir.' Clearly Philippa would have preferred that.

'But he did not,' Ralph said. 'He gave her to me to wed.' Although no ceremony had yet taken place, the girl had immediately become Ralph's responsibility. Strictly speaking, William and Philippa had no business to invite themselves here today, as if playing the role of Tilly's parents. But William was Ralph's overlord, so he could visit whenever he pleased.

Ralph did not want to quarrel with William. It was too easy for William to make Ralph's life difficult. On the other hand, the new earl was overreaching his authority here – probably under pressure from his wife. But Ralph was not going to be bullied. The last seven years had given him the confidence to defend such independence as he was entitled to.

Anyway, he was enjoying crossing swords with Philippa. It gave him an excuse to stare at her. He rested his gaze on the assertive line of her jaw and the fullness of her lips. Despite her hauteur, she was forced to engage with him. This was the longest conversation he had ever had with her.

'Tilly is very young,' said Philippa.

'She will be fourteen this year,' Ralph said. 'That's the age our queen was when she married our king – as the king himself pointed out, to me and to Earl William, after the battle of Crécy.'

'The aftermath of a battle is not necessarily the best moment to decide the fate of a young girl,' Philippa said in a lowered voice.

Ralph was not going to let that pass. 'Speaking for myself, I feel obliged to comply with the decisions of his majesty.'

'As do we all,' she muttered.

Ralph felt he had vanquished her. It was a sexual feeling, almost as if he had lain with her. Satisfied, he turned to Daniel. 'My wife-to-be should arrive in time for dinner,' he said. 'Make sure we have a feast.'

Philippa said: 'I have already seen to that.'

Ralph slowly turned his head until his eyes were on her again. She had overstepped the bounds of courtesy by going into his kitchen and giving orders.

She knew it, and reddened. 'I didn't know what time you would get here,' she said.

Ralph said nothing. She would not apologize, but he was content in having forced her to explain herself – a climbdown for a woman as proud as she.

For a short while there had been the noise of horses outside, and now Ralph's parents came in. He had not seen them for some years, and he hurried to embrace them.

They were both in their fifties, but his mother had aged faster, it seemed to him. Her hair was white and her face was lined. She had the slight stoop of elderly women. His father seemed more vigorous. It was partly the excitement of the moment: he was flushed with pride, and shook Ralph's hand as if pumping water from a well. But there was no grey in his red beard, and his slim figure still appeared spry. They were both wearing new clothes – Ralph had sent the money. Sir Gerald had a heavy wool surcoat and Lady Maud a fur cloak.

Ralph snapped his fingers at Daniel. 'Bring wine,' he said. For an instant, the bailiff looked as though he might protest at being treated like a maidservant; then he swallowed his pride and hurried off to the kitchen.

Ralph said: 'Earl William, Lady Philippa, may I present my father, Sir Gerald, and my mother, Lady Maud.'

He was afraid that William and Philippa would look down their noses at his parents, but they acknowledged them courteously enough.

Gerald said to William: 'I was a comrade-in-arms of your father, may he rest in peace. In fact, Earl William, I knew you as a boy, though you won't remember me.'

Ralph wished his father would not call attention to his glorious past. It only emphasized how far he had fallen.

But William seemed not to notice. 'Well, d'you know, I think I do remember,' he said. He was probably just being kind, but Gerald was pleased. 'Of course,' William added, 'I recall you as a giant at least seven feet tall.'

Gerald, who was short in stature, laughed delightedly.

Maud looked around and said: 'My, this is a fine house, Ralph.'

'I wanted to decorate it with all the treasures I've brought back from France,' he said. 'But I've only just got here.'

A kitchen girl brought a jug of wine and goblets on a tray, and they all took some refreshment. The wine was good Bordeaux, Ralph noticed, clear and sweet. Due credit to Daniel for keeping the house well supplied, he thought at first; then he reflected that for many years no one had been here to drink it – except, of course, Daniel.

He said to his mother: 'Any news of my brother Merthin?'

'He's doing very well,' she said proudly. 'Married with a daughter, and rich. He's building a palace for the family of Buonaventura Caroli.'

'But they haven't made him a *conte* yet, I suppose?' Ralph pretended to be joking, but he was pointing out that Merthin, for all his success, had not gained a noble title; and that it was he, Ralph, who had fulfilled their father's hopes by taking the family back into the nobility.

'Not yet,' said his father gaily, as if it were a real possibility that Merthin might become an Italian count; which annoyed Ralph, but only momentarily.

His mother said: 'Could we see our rooms?'

Ralph hesitated. What did she mean by 'our rooms'? The dreadful thought crossed his mind that his parents might think they were going to live here. He could not have that: they would be a constant reminder of the family's years of shame. Besides, they would cramp his style. On the other hand, he now realized, it was also shameful for a nobleman to let his parents live in a one-room house as pensioners of a priory.

He would have to think more about that. For now he said: 'I haven't had a chance to look at the private quarters myself yet. I hope I can make you comfortable for a few nights.'

'A few nights?' his mother said quickly. 'Are you going to send us back to our hovel in Kingsbridge?'

Ralph was mortified that she should mention that in front of William and Philippa. 'I don't think there's room for you to live here.'

'How do you know, if you haven't yet looked at the chambers?'

Daniel interrupted. 'There's a villager here from Wigleigh, Sir Ralph – name of Perkin. Wants to pay his respects and discuss an urgent matter.'

Ralph would normally have told the man off for butting into a conversation, but on this occasion he was grateful for the diversion. 'Have a look at the rooms, Mother,' he said. 'I'll deal with this peasant.'

William and Philippa went off with his parents to inspect the domestic quarters, and Daniel brought Perkin to the table. Perkin was as obsequious as ever. 'So happy to see your lordship safe and whole after the French wars,' he said.

Ralph looked at his left hand, with three fingers missing. 'Well, almost whole,' he said.

'All the people of Wigleigh are sorry for your wounds, lord, but the rewards! A knighthood, and three more villages, and Lady Matilda to wed!'

'Thank you for your felicitations, but what was the urgent matter you needed to discuss?'

'Lord, it doesn't take long to tell. Alfred Shorthouse died without a natural heir to his ten acres, and I offered to take on the land, even though times have been very hard, after this year's thunderstorms in August—'

'Never mind the weather.'

'Of course. In brief, Nathan Reeve made a decision that I feel you would not approve.'

Ralph felt impatient. He really did not care which peasant farmed Alfred's ten acres. 'Whatever Nathan decided—'

'He gave the land to Wulfric.'

'Ah.'

'Some of the villagers said Wulfric deserved it, as he had no land; but he can't pay the entry fee, and anyway—'

'You don't need to convince me,' Ralph said. 'I will not allow that troublemaker to hold land in my territory.'

'Thank you, lord. Shall I tell Nathan Reeve that you wish me to have the ten acres?'

'Yes,' Ralph said. He saw the earl and countess emerge from the private quarters, with his parents in tow. 'I'll be there to confirm it in person within the next two weeks.' He dismissed Perkin with a wave.

At that moment, Lady Matilda arrived.

She entered the hall with a nun on either side of her. One was Merthin's old girlfriend, Caris, who had tried to tell the king that Tilly was too young to marry. On the other side was the nun who had travelled to Crécy with Caris, an angel-faced woman whose name Ralph did not know. Behind them, presumably acting as their bodyguard, was the one-armed monk who had captured Ralph so cleverly nine years ago, Brother Thomas.

And in the centre was Tilly. Ralph saw immediately why the nuns wanted to protect her from marriage. Her face had a look of childish innocence. She had freckles on her nose and a gap between her two front teeth. She stared about her with frightened eyes. Caris had heightened the childish look by dressing her in a plain white nun's robe and a simple cap, but the clothing failed to hide the womanly curves of the body underneath. Caris had obviously wanted to make Tilly seem too young for wedlock. The effect on Ralph was the opposite of what was intended.

One of the things Ralph had learned in the king's service was that, in many situations, a man could take charge simply by speaking first. He said loudly: 'Come here, Tilly.'

The girl stepped forward and came to him. Her escort hesitated, then stayed where they were.

'I am your husband,' Ralph said to her. 'My name is Sir Ralph Fitzgerald, lord of Tench.'

She looked terrified. 'I'm happy to meet you, sir.'

'This is your home now, as it was when you were a child and your father was lord here. You are now the lady of Tench, as your mother once was. Are you happy to be back in your family home?'

'Yes, lord.' She looked anything but happy.

'I'm sure the nuns have told you that you must be an obedient wife, and do all you can to please your husband, who is your lord and master.'

'Yes, lord.'

'And here are my mother and father, who are your parents, too, now.'

She made a little curtsey to Gerald and Maud.

Ralph said: 'Come here.' He held out his hands.

Automatically, Tilly reached out, then she saw his maimed left hand. She made a disgusted sound and flinched back.

An angry curse came to Ralph's lips, but he suppressed it. With some difficulty he forced himself to speak in a light tone of voice. 'Don't be afraid of my wounded hand,' he said. 'You should be proud of it. I lost those fingers in the service of the king.' He kept both arms stretched out expectantly.

With an effort, she took his hands.

'Now you can kiss me, Tilly.'

He was seated, and she was standing in front of him. She leaned forward and offered her cheek. He put his wounded hand at the back of her head and turned her face, then he kissed her lips. He sensed her uncertainty and guessed that she had not been kissed by a man before. He let his mouth linger on hers, partly because it was so sweet, and partly to enrage those watching. Then, with slow deliberation, he pressed his good hand against her chest, and felt her breasts. They were full and round. She was no child.

He released her and sighed with satisfaction. 'We must get married soon,' he said. He turned to Caris, who was visibly suppressing anger. 'In Kingsbridge Cathedral, four weeks from Sunday,' he said. He looked at Philippa but addressed William. 'As we're getting married by the express wish of His Majesty King Edward, I would be honoured if you would attend, Earl William.'

William nodded curtly.

Caris spoke for the first time. 'Sir Ralph, the prior of Kingsbridge sends you greetings, and says he will be honoured to perform the ceremony, unless of course the new bishop wishes to do so.'

Ralph nodded graciously.

She then added: 'But those of us who have had charge of this child believe she is still too young to live with her husband conjugally.'

Philippa said: 'I concur.'

Ralph's father spoke. 'You know, son, I waited years to marry your mother.'

Ralph did not want to hear that story all over again. 'Unlike you, Father, I have been ordered by the king to marry Lady Matilda.'

His mother said: 'Perhaps you should wait, son.'

'I have waited more than a year! She was twelve when the king gave her to me.'

Caris said: 'Marry the child, yes, with all due ceremony – but then let her return to the nunnery for a year. Let her grow fully into her womanhood. Then bring her to your home.'

Ralph snorted scornfully. 'I could be dead in a year, especially if the king decides to go back to France. Meanwhile, the Fitzgeralds need an heir.'

'She is a child—'

Ralph interrupted, raising his voice. 'She is no child – look at her! That stupid nun's habit can't disguise her breasts.'

'Puppy fat—'

'Does she have a woman's hair?' Ralph demanded.

Tilly gasped at his crude frankness, and her cheeks reddened with shame.

Caris hesitated.

Ralph said: 'Perhaps my mother should examine her on my behalf and tell me.'

Caris shook her head. 'That won't be necessary. Tilly has hair where a woman has it and a child does not.'

'I knew as much. I have seen—' Ralph stopped, realizing that he did not want everyone here to know in what circumstances he had seen the naked bodies of girls of Tilly's age. 'I guessed, from her figure,' he amended, avoiding his mother's eye.

A rarely heard pleading tone entered Caris's voice. 'But, Ralph, in her mind she is still a child.'

I don't care about her mind, Ralph thought, but he did not say so. 'She has four weeks to learn what she does not know,' he said. He gave Caris a knowing look. 'I'm sure you can teach her everything.'

Caris flushed. Nuns were not supposed to know about marital intimacy, of course, but she had been his brother's girlfriend.

His mother said: 'Perhaps a compromise—'

'You just don't understand, Mother, do you?' he said, rudely interrupting her. 'No one is really concerned about her age. If I were going to marry the daughter of a Kingsbridge butcher they wouldn't care if she was nine. It's because Tilly is noble-born, don't you see that? They think they're superior to us!' He knew he was shouting, and he could see the amazed expressions of everyone around him, but he did not care. 'They don't want a cousin of the earl of Shiring to marry the son of an impoverished knight. They want to put off the marriage in the hope that I'll be killed in battle before it's consummated.' He wiped his mouth. 'But this son of an impoverished knight fought at the battle of Crécy, and saved the life of the prince of Wales. That's what matters to the king.' He looked at each of them in turn: haughty William, scornful Philippa, furious Caris and his astonished parents. 'So you might as well accept the facts. Ralph Fitzgerald is a knight and a lord, and a comrade-in-arms of the king. And he's going to marry Lady Matilda, the cousin of the earl – whether you like it or not!'

There was a shocked silence for several moments.

At last Ralph turned to Daniel. 'You can serve dinner now,' he said.

53

IN THE SPRING OF 1348, Merthin woke up as if from a nightmare he could not quite remember. He felt frightened and weak. He opened his eyes to a room lit by bars of bright sunshine coming through half-open shutters. He saw a high ceiling, white walls, red tiles. The air was mild. Reality returned slowly. He was in his bedroom, in his house, in Florence. He had been ill.

The illness came back to him first. It had begun with a skin rash, purplish-black blotches on his chest, then his arms, then everywhere. Soon afterwards he developed a painful lump or bubo in his armpit. He had a fever, sweating in his bed, tangling the sheets as he writhed. He had vomited and coughed blood. He had thought he would die. Worst of all was a terrible, unquenchable thirst that had made him want to throw himself into the river Arno with his mouth open.

He was not the only sufferer. Thousands of Italians had fallen ill with this plague, tens of thousands. Half the workmen on his building sites had disappeared, as had most of his household servants. Almost everyone who caught it died within five days. They called it *la moria grande*, the big death.

But he was alive.

He had a nagging feeling that while ill he had reached a momentous decision, but he could not remember it. He concentrated for a moment. The harder he thought, the more elusive the memory became, until it vanished.

He sat up in bed. His limbs felt feeble and his head spun for a moment. He was wearing a clean linen nightshirt, and he wondered who had put it on him. After a pause, he stood.

He had a four-storey house with a courtyard. He had designed and built it himself, with a flat façade instead of the traditional overhanging floors, and architectural features such as round window arches and classical columns. The neighbours had called it a *palagetto*, a mini-palace. That was seven years ago. Several prosperous Florentine merchants had asked him to build *palagetti* for them, and that had got his career here started.

Florence was a republic, with no ruling prince or duke, dominated by an elite of squabbling merchant families. The city was populated by thousands of weavers, but it was the merchants who made fortunes. They spent their money building grand houses, which made the city a perfect place for a talented young architect to prosper.

He went to the bedroom door and called his wife. 'Silvia! Where are you?' It came naturally to him to speak the Tuscan dialect now, after nine years.

Then he remembered. Silvia had been ill, too. So had their daughter, who was three years old. Her name was Laura, but they had adopted her childish pronunciation, Lolla. His heart was gripped by a terrible fear. Was Silvia alive? Was Lolla?

The house was quiet. So was the city, he realized suddenly. The angle of the sunlight slanting into the rooms told him it was mid-morning. He should have been hearing the cries of street hawkers, the clop of horses and the rumble of wooden cartwheels, the background murmur of a thousand conversations – but there was nothing.

He went up the stairs. In his weakness, the effort made him breathless. He pushed open the door to the nursery. The room looked empty. He broke out in a sweat of fear. There was Lolla's cot, a small chest for her clothes, a box of toys, a miniature table with two tiny chairs. Then he heard a noise. There in the corner was Lolla, sitting on the floor in a clean dress, playing with a small wooden horse with articulated legs. Merthin gave a strangled cry of relief. She heard him and looked up. 'Papa,' she observed in a matter-of-fact tone.

Merthin picked her up and hugged her. 'You're alive,' he said in English.

There was a sound from the next room, and Maria walked in. A grey-haired woman in her fifties, she was Lolla's nurse. 'Master!' she said. 'You got up – are you better?'

'Where is your mistress?' he said.

Maria's face fell. 'I'm so sorry, master,' she said. 'The mistress died.'

Lolla said: 'Mama's gone.'

Merthin felt the shock like a blow. Stunned, he handed Lolla to Maria. Moving slowly and carefully, he turned away and walked out of the room, then down the stairs to the *piano nobile*, the principal floor. He stared at the long table, the empty chairs, the rugs on the floor and the pictures on the walls. It looked like someone else's home.

He stood in front of a painting of the Virgin Mary with her mother. Italian painters were superior to the English or any others, and this artist had given Saint Anne the face of Silvia. She was a proud beauty, with flawless olive skin and noble features, but the painter had seen the sexual passion smouldering in those aloof brown eyes.

It was hard to comprehend that Silvia no longer existed. He thought of her slim body, and remembered how he had marvelled, again and again, at her perfect breasts. That body, with which he had been so completely intimate, now lay in the ground somewhere. When he imagined that, tears came to his eyes at last, and he sobbed with grief.

Where was her grave? he wondered in his misery. He remembered that funerals had ceased in Florence: people were terrified to leave their houses. They simply dragged the bodies outside and laid them on the street. The city's thieves, beggars and drunks had acquired a new profession: they were called corpse carriers or *becchini*, and they charged exorbitant fees to take the bodies away and put them in mass graves. Merthin might never know where Silvia lay.

They had been married four years. Looking at her picture, garbed in Saint Anne's conventional red dress, Merthin suffered an access of painful honesty, and asked himself whether he had really loved her. He was very fond of her, but it was not an all-consuming passion. She had an independent spirit and a sharp tongue, and he was the only man in Florence with the nerve to woo her, despite her father's wealth. In return, she had given him complete devotion. But she had accurately gauged the quality of his love. 'What are you thinking about?' she used to say sometimes, and he would give a guilty start, because he had been remembering Kingsbridge. Soon she changed it to: 'Who are you thinking about?' He never spoke Caris's name, but Silvia said: 'It must be a woman, I can tell by the look on your face.' Eventually she began to talk about 'your English girl'. She would say: 'You're remembering your English girl,' and she was always right. But she seemed to accept it. Merthin was faithful to her. And he adored Lolla.

After a while, Maria brought him soup and bread. 'What day is it?' he asked her.

'Tuesday.'

'How long was I in bed?'

'Two weeks. You were so ill.'

He wondered why he had survived. Some people never succumbed to the disease, as if they had natural protection; but those who caught it nearly always died. However, the tiny minority who recovered were doubly fortunate, for no one had ever caught the illness a second time.

When he had eaten, he felt stronger. He had to rebuild his life, he realized. He suspected that he had already made this decision once, when he was ill, but again he was tantalized by the thread of a memory slipping from his grasp.

His first task was to find out how much of his family was left.

He took his dishes to the kitchen, where Maria was feeding Lolla bread dipped in goat's milk. He asked her: 'What about Silvia's parents? Are they alive?'

'I don't know,' she said. 'I haven't heard. I go out only to buy food.'

'I'd better find out.'

He got dressed and went downstairs. The ground floor of the house was a workshop, with the yard at the rear used for storing wood and stone. No one was at work, either inside or out.

He left the house. The buildings around him were mostly stone-built, some of them very grand: Kingsbridge had no houses to compare with these. The richest man in Kingsbridge, Edmund Wooler, had lived in a timber house. Here in Florence, only the poor lived in such places.

The street was deserted. He had never seen it this way, not

even in the middle of the night. The effect was eerie. He wondered how many people had died: a third of the population? Half? Were their ghosts still lingering in alleyways and shadowed corners, enviously watching the lucky survivors?

The Christi house was on the next street. Merthin's father-in-law, Alessandro Christi, had been his first and best friend in Florence. A schoolmate of Buonaventura Caroli, Alessandro had given Merthin his first commission, a simple warehouse building. He was, of course, Lolla's grandpa.

The door of Alessandro's *palugetto* was locked. That was unusual in itself. Merthin banged on the woodwork and waited. Eventually it was opened by Elizabetta, a small, plump woman who was Alessandro's laundress. She stared at him in shock. 'You're alive!' she said.

'Hello, Betta,' he said. 'I'm glad to see that you're alive, too.'

She turned and called back into the house: 'It's the English lord!'

He had told them he was not a lord, but the servants did not believe him. He stepped inside. 'Alessandro?' he said.

She shook her head and began to cry.

'And your mistress?'

'Both dead.'

The stairs led from the entrance hall to the main floor. Merthin walked up slowly, surprised by how weak he still felt. In the main room he sat down to catch his breath. Alessandro had been wealthy, and the room was a showplace of rugs and hangings, paintings and jewelled ornaments and books.

'Who else is here?' he asked Elizabetta.

'Just Lena and her children.' Lena was an Asiatic slave, unusual but by no means unique in prosperous Florentine households. She had two small children by Alessandro, a boy and a girl, and he had treated them just like his legitimate offspring; in fact Silvia had said acidly that he doted on them more than he ever had on her and her brother. The arrangement was considered eccentric rather than scandalous by the sophisticated Florentines.

Merthin said: 'What about Signor Gianni?' Gianni was Silvia's brother.

'Dead. And his wife. The baby is here with me.'

733

'Dear God.'

Betta said tentatively: 'And your family, lord?'

'My wife is dead.'

'I am so sorry.'

'But Lolla is alive.'

'Thank God!'

'Maria is taking care of her.'

'Maria is a good woman. Would you like some refreshment?'

Merthin nodded, and she went away.

Lena's children came to stare at him: a dark-eyed boy of seven who looked like Alessandro, and a pretty four-year-old with her mother's Asiatic eyes. Then Lena herself came in, a beautiful woman in her twenties with golden skin and high cheekbones. She brought him a silver goblet of dark red Tuscan wine and a tray of almonds and olives.

She said: 'Will you come to live here, lord?'

Merthin was surprised. 'I don't think so – why?'

'The house is yours, now.' She waved a hand to indicate the Christi family's wealth. 'Everything is yours.'

Merthin realized she was right. He was Alessandro Christi's only surviving adult relative. That made him the heir – and the guardian of three children in addition to Lolla.

'Everything,' Lena repeated, giving him a direct look.

Merthin met her candid gaze, and realized that she was offering herself.

He considered the prospect. The house was beautiful. It was home to Lena's children, and a familiar place to Lolla, and even to Gianni's baby: all the children would be happy here. He had inherited enough money to live on for the rest of his life. Lena was a woman of intelligence and experience, and he could readily imagine the pleasures of becoming intimate with her.

She read his mind. She took his hand and pressed it to her bosom. Her breasts felt soft and warm through the light wool dress.

But this was not what he wanted. He drew Lena's hand to him and kissed it. 'I will provide for you and your children,' he said. 'Don't worry.'

'Thank you, lord,' she said, but she looked disappointed, and something in her eyes told Merthin that her offer had not been merely practical. She had genuinely hoped he might be more to her than just her new owner. But that was part of the problem. He could not imagine sex with someone he owned. The idea was distasteful to the point of revulsion.

He sipped his wine and felt stronger. If he was not drawn to an easy life of luxury and sensual gratification, what *did* he want? His family was almost gone: only Lolla was left. But he still had his work. Around the city were three sites where designs of his were under construction. He was not going to give up the job he loved. He had not survived the great death to become an idler. He recalled his youthful ambition to build the tallest building in England. He would pick up where he had left off. He would recover from the loss of Silvia by throwing himself into his building projects.

He got up to leave. Lena flung her arms around him. 'Thank you,' she said. 'Thank you for saying you will take care of my children.'

He patted her back. 'They are Alessandro's grandchildren,' he said. In Florence, the children of slaves were not themselves enslaved. 'When they grow up they will be rich.' He detached her arms gently and went down the stairs.

All the houses were locked and shuttered. On some doorsteps he saw a shrouded form that he presumed was a dead body. There were a few people on the streets, but mostly the poorer sort. The desolation was unnerving. Florence was the greatest city in the Christian world, a noisy commercial metropolis producing thousands of yards of fine woollen cloth every day, a market where vast sums of money were paid over on no more security than a letter from Antwerp or the verbal promise of a prince. Walking through these silent, empty streets was like seeing an injured horse that has fallen and cannot get up: immense strength was suddenly brought to nothing. He saw no one from his circle of acquaintance. His friends were keeping indoors, he presumed – those that were still alive.

He went first to a square nearby, in the old Roman city,

where he was building a fountain for the municipality. He had devised an elaborate system to recycle almost all the water during Florence's long, dry summers.

But, when he reached the square, he could see immediately that no one was working on the site. The underground pipes had been put in and covered over before he fell ill, and the first course of masonry for the stepped plinth around the pool had been laid. However, the dusty, neglected look of the stones told him that no work had been done for days. Worse, a small pyramid of mortar on a wooden board had hardened into a solid mass that gave off a puff of dust when he kicked it. There were even some tools lying on the ground. It was a miracle they had not been stolen.

The fountain was going to be stunning. In Merthin's workshop, the best stone carver in the city was sculpting the centrepiece – or had been. Merthin was disappointed that work had stopped. Surely not all the builders had died? Perhaps they were waiting to see whether Merthin would recover.

This was the smallest of his three projects, albeit a prestigious one. He left the square and headed north to inspect another one. But as he walked he worried. He had not yet met anyone knowledgeable enough to give him a wider perspective. What was left of the city government? Was the plague easing off or getting worse? What about the rest of Italy?

One thing at a time, he told himself.

He was building a home for Giulielmo Caroli, the older brother of Buonaventura. It was to be a real palazzo, a high double-fronted house designed around a grand staircase wider than some of the city's streets. The ground floor wall was already up. The façade was battered, or inclined, at ground level, the slight protrusion giving an impression of fortification; but above were elegant pointed-arch two-light windows with a trefoil. The design said that the people inside were both powerful and refined, which was what the Caroli family wanted.

The scaffolding had been erected for the second floor, but no one was working. There should have been five masons laying stones. The only person on site was an elderly man who acted as caretaker and lived in a wooden hut at the back. Merthin found him cooking a chicken over a fire. The fool had used costly marble slabs for his hearth. 'Where is everyone?' Merthin said abruptly.

The caretaker leaped to his feet. 'Signor Caroli died, and his son Agostino wouldn't pay the men, so they left, those that weren't already dead themselves.'

That was a blow. The Caroli family was one of the richest in Florence. If they felt they could no longer afford to build, the crisis was severe indeed.

'So Agostino is alive?'

'Yes, master, I saw him this morning.'

Merthin knew young Agostino. He was not as clever as his father or his uncle Buonaventura, so he compensated by being extremely cautious and conservative. He would not recommence building until he was sure the family finances had recovered from the effects of the plague.

However, Merthin felt confident his third and largest project would continue. He was building a church for an order of friars much favoured by the city's merchants. The site was south of the river, so he crossed the new bridge.

This bridge had been finished only two years ago. In fact Merthin had done some work on it, under the leading designer, the painter Taddeo Gaddi. The bridge had to withstand fast-flowing water when the winter snows melted, and Merthin had helped with the design of the piers. Now, as he crossed, he was dismayed to see that all the little goldsmiths' shops on the bridge were closed – another bad sign.

The church of Sant' Anna dei Frari was his most ambitious project to date. It was a big church, more like a cathedral – the friars were rich – though nothing like the cathedral at Kingsbridge. Italy had Gothic cathedrals, Milan being one of the greatest, but modern-minded Italians did not like the architecture of France and England: they regarded huge windows and flying buttresses as a foreign fetish. The obsession with light, which made sense in the gloomy north-west of Europe, seemed perverse in sunny Italy, where people sought shade and coolness. Italians identified with the classical architecture of ancient Rome, the ruins of which were all around them. They liked gable ends and round arches, and they rejected ornate exterior sculpture in favour of decorative patterns of different-coloured stone and marble.

But Merthin was going to surprise even the Florentines with this church. The plan was a series of squares, each topped by a dome – five in a row, and two either side of the crossing. He had heard about domes back in England, but had never seen one until he visited Siena cathedral. There were none in Florence. The clerestory would be a row of round windows, or oculi. Instead of narrow pillars that reached yearningly for heaven, this church would have circles, complete in themselves, with the air of earthbound self-sufficiency that characterized the commercial people of Florence.

He was disappointed, but not surprised, to see that there were no masons on the scaffolding, no labourers moving the great stones, no mortar-making women stirring with their giant paddles. This site was as quiet as the other two. However, in this case he felt confident he could get the project restarted. A religious order had a life of its own, independent of individuals. He walked around the site and entered the friary.

The place was silent. Monasteries were supposed to be so, of course, but there was a quality to this silence that unnerved him. He passed from the vestibule into the waiting room. There was usually a brother on duty here, studying the scriptures in between attending to visitors, but today the room was empty. With grim apprehension, Merthin went through another door and found himself in the cloisters. The quadrangle was deserted. 'Hello!' he called out. 'Is anyone there?' His voice echoed around the stone arcades.

He searched the place. All the friars were gone. In the kitchen he found three men sitting at the table, eating ham and drinking wine. They wore the costly clothes of merchants, but they had matted hair, untrimmed beards and dirty hands: they were paupers wearing dead men's garments. When he walked in they looked guilty but defiant. He said: 'Where are the holy brothers?'

'All dead,' said one of the men.

'All?'

'Every one. They took care of the sick, you see, and so they caught the disease.'

The man was drunk, Merthin could see. However, he seemed to be telling the truth. These three were too comfortable, sitting in the monastery, eating the friars' food and drinking their wine. They clearly knew there was no one left to object.

Merthin returned to the site of the new church. The walls of the choir and transepts were up, and the oculi in the clerestory were visible. He sat in the middle of the crossing, amid stacks of stones, looking at his work. For how long would the project be stalled? If all the friars were dead, who would get their money? As far as he knew, they were not part of a larger order. The bishop might claim the inheritance, and so might the pope. There was a legal tangle here that could take years to resolve.

This morning he had resolved to throw himself into his work as a way of healing the wound of Silvia's death. Now it was clear that, at least for the present, he had no work. Ever since he began to repair the roof of St Mark's church in Kingsbridge, ten years ago, he had had at least one building project on the go. Without one, he was lost. It made him feel panicky.

He had woken up to find his whole life in ruins. The fact that he was suddenly very rich only heightened the sense of nightmare. Lolla was the only part of his life he had left.

He did not even know where to go next. He would go home, eventually, but he could not spend all day playing with his three-year-old and talking to Maria. So he stayed where he was, sitting on a carved stone disc intended for a column, looking along what would be the nave.

As the sun rolled down the curve of the afternoon, he began to remember his illness. He had felt sure he would die. So few survived that he did not expect to be among the lucky ones. In his more lucid moments, he had reviewed his life as if it were over. He had come to some grand realization, he knew, but since recovering he had been unable to recall what it was. Now, in the tranquillity of the unfinished church, he recalled concluding that he had made one huge mistake in his life. What was it? He had quarrelled with Elfric, he had had sex with Griselda, he had rejected Elizabeth Clerk ... All these decisions had caused trouble, but none counted as the mistake of a lifetime.

Lying on the bed, sweating, coughing, tormented by thirst, he had almost wanted to die; but not quite. Something had kept him alive – and now it came back to him.

He had wanted to see Caris again.

That was his reason for living. In his delirium he had seen her face, and had wept with grief that he might die here, thousands of miles away from her. The mistake of his life had been to leave her.

As he at last retrieved that elusive memory, and realized the blinding truth of the revelation, he was filled with an odd kind of happiness.

It did not make sense, he reflected. She had joined the nunnery. She had refused to see him and explain herself. But his soul was not rational, and it was telling him that he should be where she was.

He wondered what she was doing now, while he sat in a half-built church in a city nearly destroyed by a plague. The last he had heard was that she had been consecrated by the bishop. That decision was irrevocable – or so they said: Caris had never accepted what other people told her were the rules. On the other hand, once she had made her own decision it was generally impossible to change her mind. There was no doubt she was strongly committed to her new life.

It made no difference. He wanted to see her again. Not to do so would be the second-biggest mistake of his life.

And now he was free. His ties with Florence were all broken. His wife was dead, and so were all his relations by marriage except for three children. The only family he had here was his daughter, Lolla, and he would take her with him. She was so young he felt she would hardly notice that they had left.

It was a momentous move, he told himself. He would first have to prove Alessandro's will, and make arrangements for the children – Agostino Caroli would help him with that. Then he would have to turn his wealth into gold and arrange for it to be transferred to England. The Caroli family could do that, too, if their international network was still intact. Most daunting, he would have to undertake the thousand-mile journey from Florence across Europe to Kingsbridge. And all that without having any idea how Caris would receive him when at last he arrived.

It was a decision that required long and careful thought, obviously.

He made up his mind in a few moments.

He was going home.

54

MERTHIN LEFT ITALY in company with a dozen merchants from Florence and Lucca. They took a ship from Genoa to the ancient French port of Marseilles. From there they travelled overland to Avignon, home of the pope for the last forty years or more, and the most lavish court in Europe – as well as the smelliest city Merthin had ever known. There they joined a large group of clergymen and returning pilgrims heading north.

Everyone travelled in groups, the larger the better. The merchants were carrying money and expensive trading goods, and they had men-at-arms to protect them from outlaws. They were happy to have company: priestly robes and pilgrim badges might deter robbers, and even ordinary travellers such as Merthin helped just by swelling the numbers.

Merthin had entrusted most of his fortune to the Caroli family in Florence. Their relatives in England would give him cash. The Carolis carried on this kind of international transaction all the time, and indeed Merthin had used their services nine years ago to transfer a smaller fortune from Kingsbridge to Florence. All the same, he knew that the system was not completely infallible – such families sometimes went bankrupt, especially if they got involved in lending money to untrustworthy types such as kings and princes. That was why he had a large sum in gold florins sewn into his undershirt.

Lolla enjoyed the journey. As the only child in the caravan, she was much fussed over. During the long days on horseback, she sat on the saddle in front of Merthin, his arms holding her safe while his hands held the reins. He sang songs, repeated rhymes, told stories and talked to her about the things they saw – trees, mills, bridges, churches. She probably did not understand half of what he said, but the sound of his voice kept her happy.

He had never before spent this much time with his daughter. They were together all day, every day, week after week. He hoped the intimacy would make up, in part, for the loss of her mother. It certainly worked the other way around: he would have been terribly lonely without her. She no longer spoke about Mama, but every now and then she would put her arms around his neck and cling to him with desperation, as if frightened to let him go.

He felt regret only when he stood in front of the great cathedral at Chartres, sixty miles outside Paris. There were two towers at its west end. The north tower was unfinished, but the south tower was three hundred and fifty feet high. It reminded him that he had once yearned to design such buildings. He was unlikely to achieve that ambition in Kingsbridge.

He lingered in Paris for two weeks. The plague had not reached here, and it was an immense relief to see the normal life of a great city, with people buying and selling and walking around, instead of empty streets with corpses on the doorsteps. His spirits lifted, and it was only then that he realized how stricken he had been by the horror he had left behind in Florence. He looked at Paris's cathedrals and palaces, making sketches of details that interested him. He had a small notebook made of paper, a new writing material popular in Italy.

Leaving Paris, he teamed up with a noble family returning to Cherbourg. Hearing Lolla talk, the people assumed Merthin was Italian, and he did not disabuse them, for the English were hated passionately in northern France. With the family and their entourage, Merthin crossed Normandy at a leisurely pace, with Lolla on the saddle in front of him and their pack horse following on a leading rein, looking at those churches and abbeys that had survived the devastation of King Edward's invasion almost two years ago.

He could have moved faster, but he told himself he was making the most of an opportunity that might not come again, the chance to see a rich variety of architecture. However, when he was honest with himself he had to admit that he was afraid of what he might find when he reached Kingsbridge.

He was going home to Caris, but she would not be the same Caris he had left behind nine years ago. She might have changed, physically and mentally. Some nuns became grossly fat, their only pleasure in life being food. More likely, Caris might have become ethereally thin, starving herself in an ecstasy of self-denial. By now she could be obsessed with religion, praying all day and flagellating herself for imaginary sins. Or she might be dead.

Those were his wildest nightmares. In his heart he knew she would not be enormously fat or a religious fanatic. And if she were dead he would have heard, as he had heard of the death of her father, Edmund. She was going to be the same Caris, small and neat, quick-witted, organized and determined. But he was seriously concerned about how she would receive him. How did she feel about him after nine years? Did she think of him with indifference, as a part of her past too remote to care about, the way he thought of, say, Griselda? Or did she still long for him, somewhere deep in her soul? He had no idea, and that was the true cause of his anxiety.

They sailed to Portsmouth and travelled with a party of traders. They left the group at Mudeford Crossing, the traders going on to Shiring while Merthin and Lolla forded the shallow river on horseback and took the Kingsbridge road. It was a pity, Merthin thought, that there was no visible sign of the way to Kingsbridge. He wondered how many traders continued on to Shiring simply because they did not realize that Kingsbridge was nearer.

It was a warm summer day, and the sun was shining when they came within sight of their destination. The first thing he saw was the top of the cathedral tower, visible over the trees. At least it had not fallen down, Merthin thought: Elfric's repairs had held for eleven years. It was a pity the tower could not be seen from Mudeford Crossing – what a difference that would make to the numbers visiting the town.

As they came closer, he began to suffer a strange mixture of excitement and fear that made him feel nauseous. For a few moments he was afraid he would have to dismount and throw up. He tried to make himself calm. What could happen? Even if Caris proved to have become indifferent to him, he would not die.

He saw several new buildings on the outskirts of the suburb of Newtown. The splendid new home he had built for Dick

Brewer was no longer on the edge of Kingsbridge, for the town had grown past it.

He momentarily forgot his apprehension when he saw his bridge. It rose in an elegant curve from the river bank and landed gracefully on the midstream island. On the far side of the island, the bridge sprang again to span the second channel. Its white stone gleamed in the sun. People and carts were crossing in both directions. The sight made his heart swell with pride. It was everything he had hoped it would be: beautiful, useful and strong. I did that, he thought, and it's good.

But he suffered a shock when he got closer. The masonry of the nearer span was damaged around the central pier. He could see cracks in the stonework, repaired with iron braces in a clumsy fashion that bore the hallmark of Elfric. He was appalled. Brown dribbles of rust dripped from the nails that fixed the ugly braces in the stonework. The sight took him back eleven years, to Elfric's repairs to the old wooden bridge. Everyone can make mistakes, he thought, but people who don't learn from their mistakes just make the same ones again. 'Bloody fools,' he said aloud.

'Bloody fools,' Lolla repeated. She was learning English.

He rode on to the bridge. The roadbed had been finished properly, he was happy to see, and he was pleased with the design of the parapet, a sturdy barrier with a carved capstone that recalled the mouldings in the cathedral.

Leper Island was still overrun with rabbits. Merthin continued to hold a lease on the island. In his absence, Mark Webber had been collecting rents from tenants, paying the nominal rent due to the priory every year, subtracting an agreed collection fee and sending the balance annually to Merthin in Florence via the Caroli family. After all the deductions it was a small sum, but it grew a little every year.

Merthin's house on the island had an occupied look, the shutters open, the doorstep swept. He had arranged for Jimmie to live there. The boy must now be a man, he thought.

At the near end of the second span, an old man Merthin did not recognize sat in the sun collecting the tolls. Merthin paid him a penny. The man gave him a hard stare, as if trying to recall where he had seen him before, but he said nothing.

The town was both familiar and strange. Because it was almost the same, the changes struck Merthin as miraculous, as if they had happened overnight: a row of hovels knocked down and replaced by fine houses; a busy inn where once there had been a big gloomy house occupied by a wealthy widow; a well dried up and paved over; a grey house painted white.

He went to the Bell inn on the main street next to the priory gates. It was unchanged: a tavern in such a good location would probably last hundreds of years. He left his horses and baggage with an ostler and went inside, holding hands with Lolla.

The Bell was like taverns everywhere: a big front room furnished with rough tables and benches, and a back area where the barrels of beer and wine were racked and food was cooked. Because it was popular and profitable, the straw on the floor was changed frequently and the walls were freshly whitewashed, and in winter a huge fire blazed. Now, in the heat of summer, all the windows were open, and a mild breeze blew through the front room.

After a moment, Bessie Bell came out from the back. Nine years ago she had been a curvy girl; now she was a voluptuous woman. She looked at him without recognition, but he saw her appraise his clothes and judge him an affluent customer. 'Good day to you, traveller,' she said. 'What can we do to make you and your child comfortable?'

Merthin grinned. 'I'd like to take your private room, please, Bessie.'

She knew him as soon as he spoke. 'My soul!' she cried. 'It's Merthin Bridger!' He put out his hand to shake, but she threw her arms around him and hugged him. She had always had a soft spot for him. She released him and studied his face. 'Such a beard you've grown! I would have recognized you sooner otherwise. Is this your little girl?'

'Her name is Lolla.'

'Well, aren't you a pretty thing! Your mother must be beautiful.'

Merthin said: 'My wife died.'

'How sad. But Lolla is young enough to forget. My husband died, too.'

'I didn't know you were married.'

'I met him after you left. Richard Brown, from Gloucester. I lost him a year ago.'

'I'm sorry to hear that.'

'My father's gone to Canterbury, on a pilgrimage, so I'm running this tavern all on my own, at the moment.'

'I always liked your father.'

'He was fond of you, too. He always takes to men with a bit of spirit. He was never very keen on my Richard.'

'Ah.' Merthin felt the conversation had become too intimate, too fast. 'What news of my parents?'

'They're not here in Kingsbridge. They're staying at your brother's new home in Tench.'

Merthin had heard, through Buonaventura, that Ralph had become lord of Tench. 'My father must be very pleased.'

'Proud as a peacock.' She smiled, then looked concerned. 'You must be hungry and tired. I'll tell the boys to take your bags upstairs, then I'll bring you a tankard of ale and some pottage.' She turned to go into the back room.

'That's kind, but . . .'

Bessie paused at the door.

'If you would give Lolla some soup, I'd be grateful. There's something I have to do.'

Bessie nodded. 'Of course.' She bent down to Lolla. 'Do you want to come with Auntie Bessie? I expect you could eat a piece of bread. Do you like new bread?'

Merthin translated the question into Italian, and Lolla nodded happily.

Bessie looked at Merthin. 'Going to see Sister Caris, are you?'

Absurdly, he felt guilty. 'Yes,' he said. 'She's still here, then?'

'Oh, yes. She's guest master at the nunnery now. I'll be surprised if she isn't prioress one day.' She took Lolla's hand and led her into the back room. 'Good luck,' she called over her shoulder.

Merthin went out. Bessie could be a little suffocating, but her affection was sincere, and it warmed his heart to be welcomed back with such enthusiasm. He entered the priory grounds. He paused to look at the soaring west front of the cathedral, almost two hundred years old now and as awe-inspiring as ever.

He noticed a new stone building to the north of the church, beyond the graveyard. It was a medium-sized palace, with an imposing entrance and an upper storey. It had been built close to where the old timber prior's house used to be, so presumably it had replaced that modest building as the residence of Godwyn. He wondered where Godwyn had found the money.

He went closer. The palace was very grand, but Merthin did not like the design. None of the levels related in any way to the cathedral that loomed over it. The details were careless. The top of the ostentatious doorcase blocked part of an upper-storey window. Worst of all, the palace was built on a different axis from that of the church, so that it stood at an awkward angle.

It was Elfric's work, no doubt of that.

A plump cat sat on the doorstep in the sun. It was black with a white tip to its tail. It glared malevolently at Merthin.

He turned away and walked slowly to the hospital. The cathedral green was quiet and deserted: there was no market today. The excitement and apprehension rose again in his stomach. He might see Caris at any moment. He reached the entrance and went in. The long room looked brighter and smelled fresher than he remembered: everything had a scrubbed look. There were a few people lying on mattresses on the floor, most of them elderly. At the altar a young novice was saying prayers aloud. He waited for her to finish. He was so anxious that he was sure he felt more ill than the patients on the beds. He had come a thousand miles for this moment. Was it a wasted journey?

At last the nun said 'Amen' for the last time and turned around. He did not know her. She approached him and said politely: 'May God bless you, stranger.'

Merthin took a deep breath. 'I've come to see Sister Caris,' he said.

*

THE NUNS' CHAPTER meetings now took place in the refectory. In the past they had shared with the monks the elegant octagonal chapter house at the north-east corner of the cathedral. Sadly, mistrust between monks and nuns was now so great that the nuns did not want to risk the monks' eavesdropping on their deliberations. So they met in the long bare room where they took their meals.

The nunnery officials sat behind a table, Mother Cecilia in the middle. There was no sub-prioress: Natalie had died a few weeks ago, at the age of fifty-seven, and Cecilia had not yet replaced her. On Cecilia's right was the treasurer, Beth, and her matricularius, Elizabeth, formerly Elizabeth Clerk. On Cecilia's left were the cellarer, Margaret, in charge of all supplies, and her subordinate Caris, the guest master. Thirty nuns sat on rows of benches facing the senior officials.

After the prayer and the reading, Mother Cecilia made her announcements. 'We have received a letter from our lord bishop in response to our complaint about Prior Godwyn stealing our money,' she said. There was a murmur of anticipation from the nuns.

The reply had been a long time coming. King Edward had taken almost a year to replace Bishop Richard. Earl William had lobbied hard for Jerome, his father's able administrator, but in the end Edward had chosen Henri of Mons, a relative of his wife's from Hainault in northern France. Bishop Henri had come to England for the ceremony, then travelled to Rome to be confirmed by the pope, then returned and settled in to his palace at Shiring, before replying to Cecilia's formal letter of complaint.

Cecilia went on: 'The bishop declines to take any action over the theft, saying that the events took place during the time of Bishop Richard, and the past is past.'

The nuns gasped. They had accepted the delay patiently, feeling confident they would get justice in the end. This was a shocking rejection.

Caris had seen the letter earlier. She was not as astonished as the rest of the nuns. It was not so remarkable that the new bishop did not wish to begin his period of office by quarrelling with the prior of Kingsbridge. The letter told her that Henri would be a pragmatic ruler, not a man of principle. He was no different, in that respect, from the majority of men who were successful in church politics.

However, she was no less disappointed for being unsurprised. The decision meant that she had to abandon, for the foreseeable future, her dream of building a new hospital where sick people could be isolated from healthy guests. She told herself she should not grieve: the priory had existed for hundreds of years without such a luxury, so it could wait another decade or more. On the other hand, it angered her to see the rapid spread of diseases like the vomiting sickness that Maldwyn Cook had brought to the Fleece Fair the year before last. No one understood exactly how these things were transmitted – by looking at a sick person, by touching him or just by being in the same room – but there could be no doubt that many illnesses did hop from one victim to the next, and proximity was a factor. However, she had to forget all that for now.

A rumble of resentful muttering came from the nuns on the benches. Mair's voice rose above the others, saying: 'The monks will be cock-a-hoop.'

She was right, Caris thought. Godwyn and Philemon had got away with daylight robbery. They had always argued that it was not theft for the monks to use the nuns' money, since it was all for the glory of God in the end; and they would now consider that the bishop had vindicated them. It was a bitter defeat, especially for Caris and Mair.

But Mother Cecilia was not going to waste time on regrets. 'This is not the fault of any of us, except perhaps me,' she said. 'We have simply been too trusting.'

You trusted Godwyn, but I did not, Caris thought, but she kept her mouth clamped shut. She waited to hear what Cecilia would say next. She knew that the prioress was going to make changes among the nunnery officials, but no one knew what had been decided.

'However, we must be more careful in the future. We will build a treasury of our own, to which the monks will not have access; indeed, I hope they will not even know where it is. Sister Beth will retire as treasurer, with our thanks for long and faithful service, and Sister Elizabeth will take her place. I have complete faith in Elizabeth.'

Caris tried to control her face so that her disgust would not be seen. Elizabeth had testified that Caris was a witch. It was nine years ago, and Cecilia had forgiven Elizabeth, but Caris never would. However, that was not the only reason for Caris's antipathy. Elizabeth was sour and twisted, and her resentments interfered with her judgement. Such people could never be trusted, in Caris's opinion: they were always liable to make decisions based on their prejudices.

Cecilia went on: 'Sister Margaret has asked permission to step down from her duties, and Sister Caris will take her place as cellarer.'

Caris was disappointed. She had hoped to be made sub-prioress, Cecilia's deputy. She tried to smile as if pleased, but she found it difficult. Cecilia was obviously not going to appoint a sub-prioress. She would have two rival subordinates, Caris and Elizabeth, and let them fight it out. Caris caught Elizabeth's eye, and saw barely suppressed hatred in her look.

Cecilia went on: 'Under Caris's supervision, Sister Mair will become guest master.'

Mair beamed with pleasure. She was glad to be promoted and even happier that she would be working under Caris. Caris, too, liked the decision. Mair shared her obsession with cleanliness and her mistrust of priests' remedies such as bleeding.

Caris had not got what she wanted, but she tried to look happy as Cecilia announced a handful of lesser appointments. When the meeting closed, she went to Cecilia and thanked her.

'Don't imagine it was an easy decision,' the prioress said. 'Elizabeth has brains and determination, and she's steady where you're volatile. But you're imaginative, and you get the best out of people. I need you both.'

Caris could not argue with Cecilia's analysis of her. She really knows me, Caris thought ruefully; better than anyone else in the world, now that my father is dead and Merthin has gone. She felt a surge of affection. Cecilia was like a mother bird, always moving, always busy, taking care of her fledglings. 'I'll do everything I can to live up to your expectations,' Caris vowed.

She left the room. She needed to check on Old Julie. No matter what she said to the younger nuns, no one looked after Julie the way she did. It was as if they believed that a helpless old person did not need to be kept comfortable. Only Caris made sure Julie was given a blanket in cool weather, and got something to drink when she was thirsty, and was helped to the latrine at those times of day when habitually she needed to go. Caris decided to take her a hot drink, an infusion of herbs that seemed to cheer the old nun up. She went to her pharmacy and put a small pan of water on the fire to boil.

Mair came in and closed the door. 'Isn't this wonderful?' she said. 'We'll still be working together!' She threw her arms around Caris and kissed her lips.

Caris hugged her, then detached herself from the embrace. 'Don't kiss me like that,' she said.

'It's because I love you.'

'And I love you, too, but not in the same way.'

It was true. Caris was very fond of Mair. They had become highly intimate in France, when they had risked their lives together. Caris had even found herself attracted by Mair's beauty. One night in a tavern in Calais, when the two of them had had a room with a door that could be locked, Caris had at last succumbed to Mair's advances. Mair had fondled and kissed Caris in all her most private places, and Caris had done the same to Mair. Mair had said it was the happiest day of her life. Unfortunately, Caris had not felt the same. For her the experience was pleasant but not thrilling, and she had not wanted to repeat it.

'That's all right,' Mair said. 'As long as you love me, even just a little bit, I'm happy. You won't ever stop, will you?'

Caris poured boiling water on the herbs. 'When you're as old as Julie, I promise I'll bring you an infusion to keep you healthy.'

Tears came to Mair's eyes. 'That's the nicest thing anyone has ever said to me.'

Caris had not meant it to be a vow of eternal love. 'Don't be sentimental,' she said gently. She strained the infusion into a wooden cup. 'Let's go and check on Julie.'

They crossed the cloisters and entered the hospital. A man with a bushy red beard was standing near the altar. 'God bless you, stranger,' she said. The man seemed familiar. He did not reply to her greeting, but looked hard at her with intense golden-brown eyes. Then she recognized him. She dropped the cup. 'Oh, God!' she said. 'You!'

*

THE FEW MOMENTS before she saw him were exquisite, and Merthin knew he would treasure them all his life, whatever else happened. He stared hungrily at the face he had not seen for nine years, and remembered, with a shock that was like plunging into a cold river on a hot day, how dear that face had been to him. She had hardly changed at all: his fears had been groundless. She did not even look older. She was now thirty, he calculated, but she was as slim and perky as she had been at twenty. She walked quickly into the hospital with an air of brisk authority, carrying a wooden cup full of some medicine; then she looked at him, paused, and dropped the cup.

He grinned at her, feeling happy.

'You're here!' she said. 'I thought you were in Florence!'

'I'm very pleased to be back,' he replied.

She looked at the liquid on the floor. The nun with her said: 'Don't worry about this, I'll clear up. Go and talk to him.' The second nun was pretty, and had tears in her eyes, Merthin noticed, but he was too excited to pay much attention.

Caris said: 'When did you come back?'

'I arrived an hour ago. You look well.'

'And you look ... such a man.'

Merthin laughed.

She said: 'What made you decide to return?'

'It's a long story,' he replied. 'But I'd love to tell it to you.'

'We'll step outside.' She touched his arm lightly and led him out of the building. Nuns were not supposed to touch people, nor to have private conversations with men, but for her such rules had always been optional. He was glad she had not acquired a respect for authority in the last nine years.

Merthin pointed to the bench by the vegetable garden. 'I sat on that seat with Mark and Madge Webber, the day you entered the convent, nine years ago. Madge told me you had refused to see me.'

She nodded. 'It was the most unhappy day of my life – but I knew that seeing you would make it even worse.'

'I felt the same way, except that I wanted to see you, no matter how miserable it made me.'

She gave him a direct look, her gold-flecked green eyes as candid as ever. 'That sounds a bit like a reproach.'

'Perhaps it is. I was very angry with you. Whatever you decided to do, I felt you owed me an explanation.' He had not intended the conversation to go this way, but he found he could not help himself.

She was unapologetic. 'It's really quite simple. I could hardly bear to leave you. If I had been forced to speak to you, I think I would have killed myself.'

He was taken aback. For nine years he had thought she had been selfish on that day of parting. Now it looked as if he had been the selfish one, in making such demands on her. She had always had this ability to make him revise his attitudes, he recalled. It was an uncomfortable process, but she was often right.

They did not sit on the bench, but turned away and walked across the cathedral green. The sky had clouded over, and the sun had gone. 'There is a terrible plague in Italy,' he said. 'They call it *la moria grande.*'

'I've heard about it,' she said. 'Isn't it in southern France, too? It sounds dreadful.'

'I caught the disease. I recovered, which is unusual. My wife, Silvia, died.'

She looked shocked. 'I'm so sorry,' she said. 'You must feel terribly sad.'

'All her family died, and so did all my clients. It seemed like a good moment to come home. And you?'

'I've just been made cellarer,' she said with evident pride.

To Merthin that seemed somewhat trivial, especially after the slaughter he had seen. However, such things were important in the life of the nunnery. He looked up at the great church. 'Florence has a magnificent cathedral,' he said. 'Lots of patterns in coloured stone. But I prefer this: carved shapes, all the same shade.' As he studied the tower, grey stone against grey sky, it started to rain.

They went inside the church for shelter. A dozen or so people were scattered around the nave: visitors to the town looking at the architecture, devout locals praying, a couple of novice monks sweeping. 'I remember feeling you up behind that pillar,' Merthin said with a grin.

'I remember it, too,' she said, but she did not meet his eye.

'I still feel the same about you as I did on that day. That's the real reason I came home.'

She turned and looked at him with anger in her eyes. 'But you got married.'

'And you became a nun.'

'But how could you marry her – Silvia – if you loved me?'

'I thought I could forget you. But I never did. Then, when I thought I was dying, I realized I would never get over you.'

Her anger vanished as quickly as it had appeared, and tears came to her eyes. 'I know,' she said, looking away.

'You feel the same.'

'I never changed.'

'Did you try?'

She met his eye. 'There's a nun...'

'The pretty one who was with you in the hospital?'

'How did you guess?'

'She cried when she saw me. I wondered why.'

Caris looked guilty, and Merthin guessed she was feeling the way he had felt when Silvia used to say: 'You're thinking about your English girl.'

'Mair is dear to me,' Caris said. 'And she loves me. But...'

'But you didn't forget me.'

'No.'

Merthin felt triumphant, but he tried not to let it show. 'In that case,' he said, 'you should renounce your vows, leave the nunnery, and marry me.'

'Leave the nunnery?'

'You'll need first to get a pardon for the witchcraft conviction, I realize that, but I'm sure it can be done – we'll bribe the bishop and the archbishop and even the pope if necessary. I can afford it.'

She was not sure it would be as easy as he thought. But that was not her main problem. 'It's not that I'm not tempted,' she said. 'But I promised Cecilia I would vindicate her faith in me ... I have to help Mair take over as guest master ... we need to build a new treasury ... and I'm the only one who takes care of Old Julie properly...'

He was bewildered. 'Is all that so important?'

'Of course it is!' she said angrily.

'I thought the nunnery was just old women saying prayers.'

'And healing the sick, and feeding the poor, and managing thousands of acres of land. It's at least as important as building bridges and churches.'

He had not anticipated this. She had always been sceptical of religious observance. She had gone into the nunnery under duress, when it was the only way to save her own life. But now she seemed to have grown to love her punishment. 'You're like a prisoner who is reluctant to leave the dungeon, even when the door is opened wide,' he said.

'The door isn't open wide. I would have to renounce my vows. Mother Cecilia—'

'We'll have to work on all these problems. Let's begin right away.'

She looked miserable. 'I'm not sure.'

She was torn, he could see. It amazed him. 'Is this you?' he said incredulously. 'You used to hate the hypocrisy and falsehood that you saw in the priory. Lazy, greedy, dishonest, tyrannical—'

'That's still true of Godwyn and Philemon.'

'Then leave.'

'And do what?'

'Marry me, of course.'

'Is that all?'

Once again he was bewildered. 'It's all I want.'

'No, it's not. You want to design palaces and castles. You want to build the tallest building in England.'

'If you need someone to take care of...'

'What?'

'I've got a little girl. Her name is Lolla. She's three.'

That seemed to settle Caris's mind. She sighed. 'I'm a senior official in a convent of thirty-five nuns, ten novices and twenty-five employees, with a school and a hospital and a pharmacy – and you're asking me to throw all that up to nursemaid one little girl I've never met.'

He gave up arguing. 'All I know is that I love you and I want to be with you.'

She laughed humourlessly. 'If you had said that and nothing else, you might have talked me into it.'

'I'm confused,' he said. 'Are you refusing me, or not?'

'I don't know,' she said.

55

MERTHIN LAY AWAKE MUCH OF the night. He was accustomed to bedding down in taverns, and the sounds Lolla made in her sleep only soothed him; but tonight he could not stop thinking about Caris. He was shocked by her reaction to his return. He realized, now, that he had never thought logically about how she would feel when he reappeared. He had indulged in unrealistic nightmares about how she might have changed, and in his heart he had hoped for a joyous reconciliation. Of course she had not forgotten him; but he could have figured out that she would not have spent nine years moping for him: she was not the type.

All the same, he would never have guessed that she would be so committed to her work as a nun. She had always been more or less hostile to the church. Given how dangerous it was to criticize religion in any way, she might well have concealed the true depth of her scepticism even from him. So it was a terrible shock to find her reluctant to leave the nunnery. He had anticipated fear of Bishop Richard's death sentence, or anxiety about being permitted to renounce her vows, but he had not suspected she might have found life in the priory so fulfilling that she hesitated to leave it to become his wife.

He felt angry with her. He wished he had said: 'I've travelled a thousand miles to ask you to marry me – how can you say you're not sure?' He thought of a lot of biting remarks he might have made. Perhaps it was a good thing they had not occurred to him then. Their conversation had ended with her asking him to give her time to get over the shock of his sudden return and think about what she wanted to do. He had consented – he had no alternative – but it had left him hanging in agony like a man crucified.

Eventually he drifted into a troubled sleep.

Lolla woke him early, as usual, and they went down to the parlour for porridge. He repressed the impulse to go straight to the hospital and speak to Caris again. She had asked for time, and it would do his cause no good to pester her. It occurred to him that there might be more shocks in store for him, and that he had better try to catch up with what had been happening in Kingsbridge. So after breakfast he went to see Mark Webber.

The Webber family lived on the main street in a large house they had bought soon after Caris got them started in the cloth business. Merthin remembered the days when they and their four children had lived in one room that was not much bigger than the loom on which Mark worked. Their new house had a large stone-built ground floor used as a storeroom and shop. The living quarters were in the timber-built upper storey. Merthin found Madge in the shop, checking a cartload of scarlet cloth that had just arrived from one of their out-of-town mills. She was almost forty now, with strands of grey in her dark hair. A short woman, she had become quite plump, with a prominent bosom and a vast behind. She made Merthin think of a pigeon, but an aggressive one, because of her jutting chin and assertive manner.

With her were two youngsters, a beautiful girl of about seventeen and a strapping boy a couple of years older. Merthin recalled her two older children – Dora, a thin girl in a ragged dress, and John, a shy boy – and realized that these were the same, grown up. Now John was effortlessly lifting the heavy bales of cloth while Dora counted them by notching a stick. It made Merthin feel old. I'm only thirty-two, he thought; but that seemed old when he looked at John.

Madge gave a cry of surprise and pleasure when she saw him. She hugged him and kissed his bearded cheeks, then made a fuss of Lolla. 'I thought she could come and play with your children,' Merthin said ruefully. 'Of course they're much too old.'

'Dennis and Noah are at the priory school,' she said. 'They're thirteen and eleven. But Dora will entertain Lolla – she loves children.'

The young woman picked Lolla up. 'The cat next door has kittens,' she said. 'Do you want to see them?'

Lolla replied with a stream of Italian, which Dora took for assent, and they went off.

Madge left John to finish unloading the cart and took Merthin upstairs. 'Mark has gone to Melcombe,' she said. 'We export some of our cloth to Brittany and Gascony. He should be back today or tomorrow.'

Merthin sat in her parlour and accepted a cup of ale. 'Kingsbridge seems to be prospering,' he said.

'The trade in fleeces has declined,' she said. 'It's because of war taxes. Everything has to be sold through a handful of large traders so that the king can collect his share. There are still a few dealers here in Kingsbridge – Petranilla carries on the business Edmund left – but it's nothing like it used to be. Luckily, the trade in finished cloth has grown to replace it, in this town at least.'

'Is Godwyn still prior?'

'Unfortunately, yes.'

'Is he still making difficulties?'

'He's so conservative. He objects to any change and vetoes all progress. For example, Mark proposed opening the market on Saturday as well as Sunday, as an experiment.'

'What possible objection could Godwyn have to that?'

'He said it would enable people to come to market without going to church, which would be a bad thing.'

'Some of them might have gone to church on Saturday too.'

'Godwyn's cup is always half empty, never half full.'

'Surely the parish guild opposes him?'

'Not very often. Elfric is alderman now. He and Alice got almost everything Edmund left.'

'The alderman doesn't have to be the richest man in town.'

'But he usually is. Remember, Elfric employs lots of craftsmen – carpenters, stonemasons, mortar makers, scaffolders – and buys from everyone who trades in building materials. The town is full of people who are more or less bound to support him.'

'And Elfric has always been close to Godwyn.'

'Exactly. He gets all the priory's building work – which means every public project.'

'And he's such a shoddy builder!'

'Strange, isn't it?' Madge said in a musing tone. 'You'd think Godwyn would want the best man for the job. But he doesn't. For him, it's all about who will be compliant, who will obey his wishes unquestioningly.'

Merthin felt a bit depressed. Nothing had changed: his enemies were still in power. It might prove difficult for him to resume his old life. 'No good news for me there, then.' He stood up. 'I'd better take a look at my island.'

'I'm sure Mark will seek you out as soon as he returns from Melcombe.'

Merthin went next door for Lolla, but she was having such a good time that he left her with Dora, and strolled through the town to the riverside. He took another look at the cracks in his bridge, but he did not need to study them long: the cause was obvious. He made a tour of Leper Island. Little had changed: there were a few wharves and storehouses at the west end and just one house, the one he had lent to Jimmie, at the east end, beside the road that led from one span of the bridge to the other.

When he first took possession of the island, he had had ambitious plans for developing it. Nothing had happened, of course, during his exile. Now he thought he could do something. He paced the ground, making rough measurements and visualizing buildings and even streets, until it was time for the midday meal.

He picked Lolla up and returned to the Bell. Bessie served a tasty pork stew thickened with barley. The tavern was quiet, and Bessie joined them for dinner, bringing a jug of her best red wine. When they had eaten, she poured him another cup, and he told her about his ideas. 'The road across the island, from one bridge to the other, is an ideal place to put shops,' he said.

'And taverns,' she pointed out. 'This place and the Holly Bush are the busiest inns in town simply because they are close to the cathedral. Any place where people are continually passing by is a good location for a tavern.'

'If I built a tavern on Leper Island, you could run it.'

She gave him a direct look. 'We could run it together.'

He smiled at her. He was full of her good food and wine, and any man would have loved to tumble into bed with her and enjoy her soft, round body; but it was not to be. 'I was very fond of my wife, Silvia,' he said. 'But, all the time we were married, I kept thinking about Caris. And Silvia knew it.'

Betty looked away. 'That's sad.'

'I know. And I'll never do it to another woman. I won't get married again, unless it's to Caris. I'm not a good man, but I'm not that bad.'

'Caris may never marry you.'

'I know.'

She stood up, picking up their bowls. 'You are a good man,' she said. 'Too good.' She returned to the kitchen.

Merthin put Lolla to bed for a nap, then sat on a bench in front of the tavern, looking down the hillside at Leper Island, sketching on a big slate, enjoying the September sunshine. He did not get much work done because every other person who walked past wanted to welcome him home and ask what he had been doing for the last nine years.

Late in the afternoon he saw the massive figure of Mark Webber coming up the hill driving a cart bearing a barrel. Mark had always been a giant but now, Merthin observed, he was a plump giant.

Merthin shook his enormous hand. 'I've been to Melcombe,' Mark said. 'I go every few weeks.'

'What's in the barrel?'

'Wine from Bordeaux, straight off the ship – which also brought news. You know that Princess Joan was on her way to Spain?'

'Yes.' Every well-informed person in Europe knew that the fifteen-year-old daughter of King Edward was to marry Prince Pedro, heir to the throne of Castile. The marriage would forge an alliance between England and the largest of the Iberian kingdoms, ensuring that Edward could concentrate on his interminable war against France without worrying about interference from the south.

'Well,' said Mark, 'Joan died of the plague in Bordeaux.'

Merthin was doubly shocked: partly because Edward's position in France had suddenly become shaky, but mainly because the plague had spread so far. 'They have the plague in Bordeaux?'

'Bodies piled in the streets, the French sailors told me.'

Merthin was unnerved. He had thought he had left *la moria grande* behind him. Surely it would not come as far as England? He did not fear it personally: no one had ever caught it twice, so he was safe, and Lolla was among those who for some reason did not succumb to it. But he was afraid for everyone else – especially Caris.

Mark had other things on his mind. 'You've returned at just the right time. Some of the younger merchants are getting fed up with Elfric as alderman. A lot of the time he's just a dogsbody for Godwyn. I'm planning to challenge him. You could be influential. There's a meeting of the parish guild tonight – come along and we'll get you admitted right away.'

'Won't it matter that I never finished my apprenticeship?'

'After what you've built, here and abroad? Hardly.'

'All right.' Merthin needed to be a guild member if he was going to develop the island. People always found reasons to object to new buildings, and he might need support himself. But he was not as confident of his acceptance as Mark.

Mark took his barrel home and Merthin went inside to give Lolla her supper. At sundown Mark returned to the Bell, and Merthin walked with him up the main street as the warm afternoon turned into a chilly evening.

The guild hall had seemed like a fine building to Merthin years ago, when he had stood here and presented his bridge design to the parish guild. But it appeared awkward and shabby now that he had seen the grand public buildings of Italy. He wondered what men such as Buonaventura Caroli and Loro Fiorentino must think of its rough stone undercroft, with the prison and the kitchen, and its main hall with a row of pillars running awkwardly down the middle to support the roof.

Mark introduced him to a handful of men who had arrived in Kingsbridge, or had come to prominence, in Merthin's absence. However, most of the faces were familiar, albeit a little older. Merthin greeted those few he had not already encountered in the last two days. Among these was Elfric, ostentatiously dressed in a brocade surcoat made with silver thread. He showed no surprise – someone had obviously told him Merthin was back – but glared with undisguised hostility.

Also present were Prior Godwyn and his sub-prior, Brother Philemon. Godwyn at forty-two was looking more like his uncle Anthony, Merthin observed, with downsloping lines of querulous discontent around his mouth. He put on a pretence of affability that might have fooled someone who did not know him. Philemon, too, had changed. He was no longer lean and awkward. He had filled out like a prosperous merchant, and carried himself with an air of arrogant self-assurance – although Merthin fancied he could still see, underneath the façade, the anxiety and self-hatred of the fawning toady. Philemon shook his hand as if touching a snake. It was depressing to realize that old hatreds were so long-lived.

A handsome, dark-haired young man crossed himself when he saw Merthin, then revealed that he was Merthin's former protégé, Jimmie, now known as Jeremiah Builder. Merthin was delighted to find that he was doing well enough to belong to the parish guild. However, it seemed he was still as superstitious as ever.

Mark mentioned the news about Princess Joan to everyone he spoke to. Merthin answered one or two anxious questions about the plague, but the Kingsbridge merchants were more concerned that the collapse of the alliance with Castile would prolong the French war, which was bad for business.

Elfric sat on the big chair in front of the giant woolsack scales and opened the meeting. Mark immediately proposed that Merthin should be admitted as a member.

Not surprisingly, Elfric objected. 'He was never a member of the guild because he did not finish his apprenticeship.'

'Because he wouldn't marry your daughter, you mean,' said one of the men, and they all laughed. Merthin took a few moments to identify the speaker: it was Bill Watkin, the house builder, the black hair around his bald dome now turning grey.

'Because he is not a craftsman of the required standard,' Elfric persisted stubbornly.

'How can you say that?' Mark protested. 'He has built houses, churches, palaces—'

'And our bridge, which is cracking after only eight years.'

'You built that, Elfric.'

'I followed Merthin's design exactly. Clearly the arches are not strong enough to bear the weight of the roadbed and the traffic upon it. The iron braces I have installed have not been sufficient to prevent the cracks widening. Therefore I propose to reinforce the arches either side of the central pier, on both bridges, with a second course of masonry, doubling their thickness. I thought this subject might come up tonight, so I have prepared estimates of the cost.'

Elfric must have started to plan this attack the moment he heard that Merthin was back in town. He had always seen Merthin as an enemy: nothing had changed. However, he had failed to understand the problem with the bridge, and that gave Merthin his chance.

He spoke to Jeremiah in a low voice. 'Would you do something for me?'

'After all you did for me? Anything!'

'Run to the priory now and ask to speak to Sister Caris urgently. Tell her to find the original drawing I made for the bridge. It should be in the priory library. Bring it here right away.'

Jeremiah slipped out of the room.

Elfric went on: 'I must tell guildsmen that I have already spoken to Prior Godwyn, who says the priory cannot afford to pay for this repair. We will have to finance it, as we financed the original cost of building the bridge, and be repaid out of penny tolls.'

They all groaned. There followed a long and bad-tempered discussion about how much money each member of the guild should put up. Merthin felt animosity building up towards him in the room. This was undoubtedly what Elfric had intended. Merthin kept looking at the door, willing Jeremiah to reappear.

Bill Watkin said: 'Maybe Merthin should pay for the repairs, if it's his design that's at fault.'

Merthin could not stay out of the discussion any longer. He threw caution to the winds. 'I agree,' he said.

There was a startled silence.

'If my design has caused the cracks, I'll repair the bridge at my own expense,' he went on recklessly. Bridges were costly: if he was wrong about the problem, it could cost half his fortune.

Bill said: 'Handsomely said, I'm sure.'

Merthin said: 'But I have something to say, first, if guildsmen will permit.' He looked at Elfric.

Elfric hesitated, obviously trying to think of a reason for refusing; but Bill said: 'Let him speak,' and there was a chorus of assent.

Elfric nodded reluctantly.

'Thank you,' said Merthin. 'When an arch is weak, it cracks in a characteristic pattern. The stones at the top of the arch are pressed downwards, so that their lower edges splay apart, and a crack appears at the crown of the arch on the intrados – the underside.'

'That's true,' said Bill Watkin. 'I've seen that sort of crack many a time. It's not usually fatal.'

Merthin went on: 'This is *not* the type of cracking you're seeing on the bridge. Contrary to what Elfric said, those arches *are* strong enough: the thickness of the arch is one twentieth of its diameter at the base, which is the standard proportion, in every country.'

The builders in the room nodded. They all knew that ratio.

'The crown is intact. However, there are horizontal cracks at the springing of the arch either side of the central pier.'

Bill spoke again. 'You sometimes see that in a quadripartite vault.'

'Which this bridge is *not*,' Merthin pointed out. 'The vaults are simple.'

'What's causing it, then?'

'Elfric did not follow my original design.'

Elfric said: 'I did!'

'I specified a pile of large, loose stones at both ends of the piers.'

'A pile of stones?' Elfric said mockingly. 'And you say that's what was going to keep your bridge upright?'

'Yes, I do,' Merthin said. He could tell that even the builders in the room agreed with Elfric's scepticism. But they did not know about bridges, which were different from any other kind of building because they stood in water. The piles of stones were an essential part of the design.'

'They were never in the drawings.'

'Would you like to show us my drawings, Elfric, to prove your point?'

'The tracing floor is long gone.'

'I did a drawing on parchment. It should be in the priory library.'

Elfric looked at Godwyn. At that moment the complicity between the two men was blatant, and Merthin hoped the rest of the guild could see it. Godwyn said: 'Parchment is costly. That drawing was scraped and reused long ago.'

Merthin nodded as if he believed Godwyn. There was still no sign of Jeremiah. Merthin might have to win the argument without the help of the original plans. 'The stones *would* have prevented the problem that is now causing the cracks,' he said.

Philemon put in: 'You would say that, wouldn't you? But why should we believe you? It's just your word against Elfric's.'

Merthin realized he would have to stick his neck out. All or nothing, he thought. 'I will tell you what the problem is, and prove it to you, in daylight, if you will meet me at the riverside tomorrow at dawn.'

Elfric's face showed that he wanted to refuse this challenge, but Bill Watkin said: 'Fair enough! We'll be there.'

'Bill, can you bring two sensible boys who are good swimmers and divers?'

'Easy.'

Elfric had lost control of the meeting, and Godwyn intervened, revealing himself as the puppetmaster. 'What kind of a mockery are you planning?' he said angrily.

But it was too late. The others were curious now. 'Let him make his point,' said Bill. 'If it's a mockery, we'll all know soon enough.'

Just then, Jeremiah came in. Merthin was pleased to see that he was carrying a wooden frame with a large sheet of parchment stretched across it. Elfric stared at Jeremiah, shocked.

Godwyn looked pale and said: 'Who gave you that?'

'A revealing question,' Merthin commented. 'The lord prior doesn't ask what the drawing shows, nor where it came from – he seems to know all that already. He just wonders who handed it over.'

Bill said: 'Never mind all that. Show us the drawing, Jeremiah.'

Jeremiah stood in front of the scales and turned the frame round so that everyone could see the drawing. There at the ends of the piers were the piles of stones Merthin had spoken of.

Merthin stood up. 'In the morning, I'll explain how they work.'

*

SUMMER WAS TURNING into autumn, and it was chilly on the river bank at dawn. News had somehow got around that a drama would take place and, as well as the members of the parish guild, there were two or three hundred people waiting to see the clash between Merthin and Elfric. Even Caris was there. This was no longer merely an argument about an engineering problem, Merthin realized. He was the youngster challenging the authority of the old bull, and the herd understood that.

Bill Watkin produced two lads of twelve or thirteen, stripped to their undershorts and shivering. It turned out they were Mark Webber's younger sons, Dennis and Noah. Dennis, the thirteen-year-old, was short and chunky, like his mother. He had red-brown hair the colour of leaves in autumn. Noah, the younger by two years, was taller, and would probably grow up to be as big as Mark. Merthin identified with the short redhead. He wondered whether Dennis was embarrassed, as Merthin himself had been at that age, to have a younger brother who was bigger and stronger.

Merthin thought Elfric might object to Mark's sons being the divers, on the grounds that they might have been briefed in advance by their father and told what to say. However, Elfric said nothing. Mark was too transparently honest for anyone to suspect him of such duplicity, and perhaps Elfric realized that – or, more likely, Godwyn realized it.

Merthin told the boys what to do. 'Swim out to the central pier, then dive. You'll find the pier is smooth for a long way down. Then there's the foundation, a great lump of stones held together with mortar. When you reach the river bed, feel underneath the foundation. You probably won't be able to see anything – the water will be too muddy. But hold your breath for as long as you can and investigate thoroughly all around the base. Then come up to the surface and tell us exactly what you find.'

They both jumped into the water and swam out. Merthin spoke to the assembled townspeople. 'The bed of this river is not rock but mud. The current swirls around the piers of a bridge and scours the mud out from underneath the pillars, leaving a depression filled only with water. This happened to the old wooden bridge. The oak piers were not resting on the river bed at all, but hanging from the superstructure. That's why the bridge collapsed. To prevent the same thing happening to the new bridge, I specified piles of large rough stones around the feet of the piers. Such piles break up the current so that its action is haphazard and weak. However, the piles were not installed and so the piers have been undermined. They are no longer supporting the bridge, but hanging from it – and that's why there are cracks where the pier joins the arch.'

Elfric snorted sceptically, but the other builders looked intrigued. The two boys reached midstream, touched the central pier, took deep breaths and disappeared.

Merthin said: 'When they come back, they will tell us that the pier is not resting on the river bed, but hanging over a depression, filled with water, large enough for a man to climb into.'

He hoped he was right.

Both boys stayed under water for a surprisingly long time. Merthin found himself feeling breathless, as it were in sympathy with them. At last a wet head of red hair broke the surface, then a brown one. The two boys conversed briefly, nodding, as if establishing that they had both observed the same thing. Then they struck out for the shore.

Merthin was not completely sure of his diagnosis, but he could think of no other explanation for the cracks. And he had felt the need to appear supremely confident. If he now turned out to be wrong, he would look all the more foolish.

The boys reached the bank and waded out of the water, panting. Madge gave them blankets which they pulled around their shaking shoulders. Merthin allowed them a few moments to catch their breath, then said: 'Well? What did you find?'

'Nothing,' said Dennis, the elder.

'What do you mean, nothing?'

'There's nothing there, at the bottom of the pillar.'

Elfric looked triumphant. 'Just the mud of the river bed, you mean.'

'No!' said Dennis. 'No mud – just water.'

Noah put in: 'There's a hole you could climb into – easily! That big pillar is just hanging in the water, with nothing under it.'

Merthin tried not to look relieved.

Elfric blustered: 'There's still no authority for saying a pile of loose stones would have solved the problem.' But no one was listening to him. In the eyes of the crowd, Merthin had proved his point. They gathered around him, commenting and questioning. After a few moments, Elfric walked away alone.

Merthin felt a momentary pang of compassion. Then he recalled how, when he was an apprentice, Elfric had hit him across the face with a length of timber; and his pity evaporated into the cold morning air.

56

THE FOLLOWING MORNING, a monk came to see Merthin at the Bell. When he pulled back his hood, Merthin did not at first recognize him. Then he saw that the monk's left arm was cut off at the elbow, and he realized it was Brother Thomas, now in his forties, with a grey beard and deep-set lines around his eyes and mouth. Was his secret still dangerous after all these years, Merthin wondered? Would Thomas's life be in danger, even now, if the truth came out?

But Thomas had not come to talk about that. 'You were right about the bridge,' he said.

Merthin nodded. There was a sour satisfaction in it. He had been right, but Prior Godwyn had fired him, and in consequence his bridge would never be perfect. 'I wanted to explain the importance of the rough stones, back then,' he said. 'But I knew Elfric and Godwyn would never listen to me. So I told Edmund Wooler, then he died.'

'You should have told me.'

'I wish I had.'

'Come with me to the church,' Thomas said. 'Since you can read so much from a few cracks, I'd like to show you something, if I may.'

He led Merthin to the south transept. Here and in the south aisle of the choir Elfric had rebuilt the arches, following the partial collapse eleven years ago. Merthin saw immediately what Thomas was worrying about: the cracks had reappeared.

'You said they would come back,' Thomas said.

'Unless you discovered the root cause of the problem, yes.'

'You were right. Elfric was wrong twice.'

Merthin felt a spark of excitement. If the tower needed rebuilding ... 'You understand that, but does Godwyn?'

Thomas did not answer the question. 'What do you think the root cause might be?'

Merthin concentrated on the immediate problem. He had thought about this, on and off, for years. 'This is not the original tower, is it?' he said. 'According to Timothy's Book, it has been rebuilt, and made higher.'

'About a hundred years ago, yes – when the raw wool business was booming. Do you think they made it too high?'

'It depends on the foundations.' The site of the cathedral sloped gently to the south, towards the river, and that might be a factor. He walked through the crossing, under the tower, to the north transept. He stood at the foot of the massive pillar at the north-east corner of the crossing and looked up at the arch that stretched over his head, across the north aisle of the choir, to the wall.

'It's the south aisle I'm worried about,' Thomas said, slightly peevishly. 'There are no problems here.'

Merthin pointed up. 'There's a crack on the underside of the arch – the intrados – at the crown,' he said. 'You get that in a bridge, when the piers are inadequately grounded and start to splay apart.'

'What are you saying – that the tower is moving away from the north transept?'

Merthin went back through the crossing and looked at the matching arch on the south side. 'This one is cracked, too, but on the upper side, the extrados, do you see? The wall above it is cracked, too.'

'They aren't very big cracks.'

'But they tell us what is happening. On the north side, the arch is being stretched; on the south side, it's being pinched. That means the tower is moving south.'

Thomas looked up warily. 'It seems straight.'

'You can't see it with the eye. But if you climb up into the tower, and drop a plumb line from the top of one of the columns of the crossing, just below the springing of the arch, you will see that by the time the line touches the floor it will be adrift of the column to the south by several inches. And, as the tower leans, it's separating from the wall of the choir, which is where the damage shows worst.'

'What can be done?'

Merthin wanted to say: You have to commission me to build a new tower. But that would have been premature. 'A lot more investigation, before any building,' he said, suppressing his excitement. 'We have established that the cracks have appeared because the tower is moving – but *why* is it moving?'

'And how will we learn that?'

'Dig a hole,' Merthin said.

In the end Jeremiah dug the hole. Thomas did not want to employ Merthin directly. It was difficult enough as it was, he said, to get the money for the investigation out of Godwyn, who seemed never to have any money to spare. But he could not give the job to Elfric, who would have said there was nothing to investigate. So the compromise was Merthin's old apprentice.

Jeremiah had learned from his master and liked to work fast. On the first day, he lifted the paving stones in the south transept. Next day, his men started excavating the earth around the huge south-east pier of the crossing.

As the hole got deeper, Jeremiah built a timber hoist for lifting out loads of earth. By the second week he had to build wooden ladders down the sides of the hole so that the labourers could get to the bottom.

Meanwhile, the parish guild gave Merthin the contract for the repair of the bridge. Elfric was against the decision, of course, but he was in no position to claim that he was the best man for the job, and he hardly bothered to argue.

Merthin went to work with speed and energy. He built cofferdams around the two problem piers, drained the dams and began to fill the holes under the piers with rubble and mortar. Next he would surround the piers with the piles of large rough stones he had envisaged from the start. Finally, he would remove Elfric's ugly iron braces and fill the cracks with mortar. Provided the repaired foundations were sound, the cracks would not reopen.

But the job he really wanted was the rebuilding of the tower.

It would not be easy. He would have to get his design accepted by the priory and the parish guild, currently run by his two worst enemies, Godwyn and Elfric. And Godwyn would have to find the money.

As a first step, Merthin encouraged Mark to put himself forward for election as alderman, to replace Elfric. The alderman was elected once a year, on All Hallows' Day, the first of November. In practice, most aldermen were re-elected unopposed until they retired or died. However, there was no doubt that a contest was permitted. Indeed, Elfric himself had put his name forward while Edmund Wooler was still in office.

Mark required little prompting. He was itching to put an end to Elfric's rule. Elfric was so close to Godwyn that there was not much point in having a parish guild at all. The town was in effect run by the priory – narrow, conservative, mistrustful of new ideas, careless of the interests of the townspeople.

So the two candidates began drumming up support. Elfric had his followers, mainly people he either employed or bought materials from. However, he had lost face badly in the argument over the bridge, and those who took his side were downcast. Mark's supporters, by contrast, were ebullient.

Merthin visited the cathedral every day and examined the foundations of the mighty column as they were exposed by Jeremiah's digging. The foundations were made of the same stone as the rest of the church, laid in mortared courses, but less carefully trimmed, as they would not be visible. Each course was a little wider than the one above, in a pyramid shape. As the excavation went deeper, he examined every layer for weakness, and found none. But he felt confident that eventually he would.

Merthin told no one what was in his mind. If his suspicions were correct, and the thirteenth-century tower was simply too heavy for the twelfth-century foundations, the solution would be drastic: the tower would have to be demolished – and a new one built. And the new tower could be the tallest in England ...

One day in the middle of October, Caris appeared at the digging. It was early in the morning, and a winter sun was shining through the great east window. She stood on the edge of the hole with her hood around her head like a halo. Merthin's heart beat faster. Perhaps she had an answer for him. He climbed up the ladder eagerly.

She was as beautiful as ever, though in the strong sunlight he could see the little differences that nine years had made to her face. Her skin was not quite as smooth, and there were now the tiniest of creases at the corners of her lips. But her green eyes still shone with that alert intelligence that he loved so much.

They walked together down the south aisle of the nave and stopped near the pillar that always reminded him of how he had once felt her up here. 'I'm happy to see you,' he said. 'You've been hiding away.'

'I'm a nun, I'm supposed to hide away.'

'But you're thinking about renouncing your vows.'

'I haven't made a decision.'

He was crestfallen. 'How much time do you need?'

'I don't know.'

He looked away. He did not want to show her how badly he was hurt by her hesitation. He said nothing. He could have told her she was being unreasonable, but what was the point?

'You'll be going to visit your parents in Tench at some point, I suppose,' she said.

He nodded. 'Quite soon – they will want to see Lolla.' He was eager to see them, too, and had delayed only because he had become so deeply involved in his work on the bridge and the tower.

'In that case, I wish you would talk to your brother about Wulfric in Wigleigh.'

Merthin wanted to talk about himself and Caris, not Wulfric and Gwenda. His response was cool. 'What do you want me to say to Ralph?'

'Wulfric is labouring for no money – just food – because Ralph won't give him even a small acreage to farm.'

Merthin shrugged. 'Wulfric broke Ralph's nose.' He felt the conversation begin to descend into a quarrel, and he asked himself why he was angry. Caris had not spoken to him for weeks, but she had broken her silence for the sake of Gwenda. He resented Gwenda's place in her heart, he realized. That was an unworthy emotion, he told himself; but he could not shake it.

Caris flushed with annoyance. 'That was twelve years ago! Isn't it time Ralph stopped punishing him?'

Merthin had forgotten the abrasive disagreements he and Caris used to have, but now he recognized this friction as familiar. He spoke dismissively. 'Of course he should stop – in my opinion. But Ralph's opinion is the one that counts.'

'Then see if you can change his mind,' she said.

He resented her imperious attitude. 'I'm yours to command,' he said facetiously.

'Why the irony?'

'Because I'm *not* yours to command, of course, but you seem to think I am. And I feel a bit foolish for going along with you.'

'Oh, for heaven's sake,' she said. 'You're offended that I've asked you?'

For some reason, he felt sure she had made up her mind to reject him and stay in the nunnery. He tried to control his emotions. 'If we were a couple, you could ask me anything. But while you're keeping open the option of rejecting me, it seems a bit presumptuous of you.' He knew he was sounding pompous, but he could not stop. If he revealed his true feelings he would burst into tears.

She was too wrapped up in her indignation to notice his distress. 'But it's not even for myself!' she protested.

'I realize it's your generosity of spirit that makes you do it, but I still feel you're using me.'

'All right, then, don't do it.'

'Of course I'll *do* it.' Suddenly he could no longer contain himself. He turned and walked away from her. He was shaking with some passion he could not identify. As he strode up the aisle of the great church, he struggled to get himself under control. He reached the excavation. This was stupid, he thought. He turned and looked back, but Caris had vanished.

He stood at the lip of the hole, looking down, waiting for the storm inside him to subside.

After a while he realized that the excavation had reached a crucial stage. Thirty feet below him, the men had dug down past the masonry foundations and were beginning to reveal what was beneath. There was nothing more he could do about Caris right now. It would be best to concentrate on his work. He took a deep breath, swallowed and went down the ladder.

This was the moment of truth. His distress over Caris began to ease as he watched the men dig farther down. Shovelful after shovelful of heavy mud was dug up and taken away. Merthin studied the stratum of earth that was revealed below the foundations. It looked like a mixture of sand and small stones. As the men removed the mud, the sandy stuff dribbled into the hole they were making.

Merthin ordered them to stop.

He knelt down and picked up a handful of the sandy material. It was nothing like the soil all around. It was not natural to the site, therefore it must be something that had been put there by builders. The excitement of discovery rose inside him, overmastering his grief about Caris. 'Jeremiah!' he called. 'See if you can find Brother Thomas – quick as you like.'

He told the men to carry on digging, but to make a narrower hole: at this point the excavation itself could be dangerous to the structure. After a while Jeremiah returned with Thomas, and the three of them watched as the men took the hole farther down. Eventually the sandy layer came to an end, and the next stratum was revealed to be the natural muddy earth.

'I wonder what that sandy stuff is,' Thomas said.

'I think I know,' Merthin said. He tried not to look triumphant. He had predicted, years ago, that Elfric's repairs would not work unless the root of the problem was discovered, and he had been right – but it was never wise to say: I told you so.

Thomas and Jeremiah looked at him in anticipation.

He explained. 'When you've dug a foundation hole, you cover the bottom with a mixture of rubble and mortar. Then you lay the masonry on top of that. It's a perfectly good system, as long as the foundations are proportional to the building above.'

Thomas said impatiently: 'We both know this.'

'What happened here was that a much higher tower was erected on foundations that were not designed for it. The extra weight, acting over a hundred years, has crushed that layer of rubble and mortar to sand. The sand has no cohesion, and under pressure it has spread outwards into the surrounding soil, allowing the masonry above it to sink down. The effect is worse on the south side simply because the site naturally slopes that way.' He felt a profound satisfaction at having figured this out.

The other two looked thoughtful. Thomas said: 'I suppose we will have to reinforce the foundations.'

Jeremiah shook his head. 'Before we can put any reinforcement under the stonework, we'd have to remove the sandy stuff, and that would leave the foundations unsupported. The tower would fall down.'

Thomas was perplexed. 'So what *can* we do?'

They both looked at Merthin. He said: 'Build a temporary roof over the crossing, erect scaffolding and take down the tower, stone by stone. Then reinforce the foundations.'

'Then we'd have to build a new tower.'

That was what Merthin wanted, but he did not say so. Thomas might suspect that his judgement had been coloured by his aspiration. 'I'm afraid so,' he said with feigned regret.

'Prior Godwyn won't like that.'

'I know,' Merthin said. 'But I don't think he's got any choice.'

*

Next day Merthin rode out of Kingsbridge with Lolla on the saddle in front of him. As they travelled through the forest, he obsessively ran over his fraught exchange with Caris. He knew he had been ungenerous. How foolish that was, when he was trying to win back her love. What had got into him? Caris's request was perfectly reasonable. Why would he not wish to perform a small service for the woman he wanted to marry?

But she had not agreed to marry him. She was still reserving the right to reject him. That was the source of his anger. She was exercising the privileges of a fiancée without making the commitment.

He could see, now, that it was petty of him to object on these grounds. He had been stupid, and turned what could have been a delightful moment of intimacy into a squabble.

On the other hand, the underlying cause of his distress was all too real. How long did Caris expect him to wait for an answer?

How long was he prepared to wait? He did not like to think about that.

Anyway, it would do him nothing but good if he could persuade Ralph to stop persecuting poor Wulfric.

Tench was on the far side of the county, and on the way Merthin spent a night at windy Wigleigh. He found Gwenda and Wulfric thin after a rainy summer and the second poor harvest in a row. Wulfric's scar seemed to stand out more on a hollowed cheek. Their two small sons looked pale, and had runny noses and sores on their lips.

Merthin gave them a leg of mutton, a small barrel of wine and a gold florin that he pretended were gifts from Caris. Gwenda cooked the mutton over the fire. She was possessed by rage, and she hissed and spat like the turning meat as she talked of the injustice that had been done to them. 'Perkin has almost half the land in the village!' she said. 'The only reason he can manage it all is that he's got Wulfric, who does the work of three men. Yet he must demand more, and keep us in poverty.'

'I'm sorry that Ralph still bears a grudge,' Merthin said.

'Ralph himself provoked that fight!' Gwenda said. 'Even Lady Philippa said so.'

'Old quarrels,' Wulfric said philosophically.

'I'll try to get him to see reason,' Merthin said. 'In the unlikely event that he listens to me, what do you really want from him?'

'Ah,' said Wulfric, and he got a faraway look in his eyes, which was unusual for him. 'What I pray for every Sunday is to get back the lands that my father farmed.'

'That will never happen,' Gwenda said quickly. 'Perkin is too well entrenched. And, if he should die, he has a son and a married daughter waiting to inherit, and a couple of grandsons growing taller every day. But we'd like a piece of land of our own. For the last eleven years Wulfric has been working hard to feed other men's children. It's time he got some of the benefit of his strength.'

'I'll tell my brother he has punished you long enough,' Merthin said.

Next day he and Lolla rode from Wigleigh to Tench. Merthin was even more resolved to do something for Wulfric. It was not just that he wanted to please Caris, and atone for his curmudgeonly attitude. He also felt sad and indignant that two such honest and hard-working people as Wulfric and Gwenda should be poor and thin, and their children sickly, just because of Ralph's vindictiveness.

His parents were living in a house in the village, not in Tench Hall itself. Merthin was shocked by how much his mother had aged, though she perked up when she saw Lolla. His father looked better. 'Ralph is very good to us,' Gerald said in a defensive way that made Merthin think the opposite. The house was pleasant enough, but they would have preferred to live at the hall with Ralph. Merthin guessed that Ralph did not want his mother watching everything he did.

They showed him around their home, and Gerald asked Merthin how things were in Kingsbridge. 'The town is still prospering, despite the effects of the king's French war,' Merthin replied.

'Ah – but Edward must fight for his birthright,' his father said. 'He is the legitimate heir to the throne of France, after all.'

'I think that's a dream, father,' said Merthin. 'No matter how many times the king invades, the French nobility will not accept an Englishman as their king. And a king can't rule without the support of his earls.'

'But we had to stop the French raids on our south coast ports.'

'That hasn't been a major problem since the battle of Sluys, when we destroyed the French fleet – which was eight years ago. Anyway, burning the crops of the peasants won't stop pirates – it might even add to their numbers.'

'The French support the Scots, who keep invading our northern counties.'

'Don't you think the king would be better able to deal with Scottish incursions if he were in the north of England rather than the north of France?'

Gerald looked baffled. It had probably never occurred to him to question the wisdom of the war. 'Well, Ralph has been knighted,' he said. 'And he brought your mother a silver candlestick from Calais.'

That was about the size of it, Merthin thought. The real reason for the war was booty and glory.

They all walked to the manor house. Ralph was out hunting with Alan Fernhill. In the great hall was a huge carved wooden chair, obviously the lord's. Merthin saw what he thought was a young servant girl, heavily pregnant, and was dismayed to be introduced to her as Ralph's wife, Tilly. She went to the kitchen to fetch wine.

'How old is she?' Merthin said to his mother while she was gone.

'Fourteen.'

It was not unknown for girls to become pregnant at fourteen, but all the same Merthin felt that decent people behaved otherwise. Such early pregnancies usually happened in royal families, for whom there was intense political pressure to produce heirs, and among the lowest and most ignorant of peasants, who knew no better. The middle classes maintained higher standards. 'She's a bit young, isn't she?' he said quietly.

Maud replied: 'We all asked Ralph to wait, but he would not.' Clearly she too disapproved.

Tilly returned with a servant carrying a jug of wine and a bowl of apples. She might have been pretty, Merthin thought, but she looked worn out. His father addressed her with forced jollity. 'Cheer up, Tilly! Your husband will be home soon – you don't want to greet him with a long face.'

'I'm fed up with being pregnant,' she said. 'I just wish the baby would come as soon as possible.'

'It won't be long, now,' Maud said. 'Three or four weeks, I'd say.'

'It seems like for ever.'

They heard horses outside. Maud said: 'That sounds like Ralph.'

Waiting for the brother he had not seen for nine years, Merthin had mixed feelings, as ever. His affection for Ralph was always contaminated by his knowledge of the evil Ralph had done. The rape of Annet had been only the beginning. During his days as an outlaw Ralph had murdered innocent men, women and children. Merthin had heard, travelling through Normandy, of the atrocities perpetrated by King Edward's army and, while he did not know specifically what Ralph had done, it would have been foolish to hope that Ralph had held himself aloof from that orgy of rape, burning, looting and slaughter. But Ralph was his brother.

Ralph, too, would have mixed feelings, Merthin was sure. He might not have forgiven Merthin for giving away the location of his outlaw hideout. And, although Merthin had made Brother Thomas promise not to kill Ralph, he had known that Ralph, once captured, was likely to be hanged. The last words Ralph had spoken to Merthin, in the jail in the basement of the guild hall at Kingsbridge, were: 'You betrayed me.'

Ralph came in with Alan, both muddy from the hunt. Merthin was shocked to see that he walked with a limp. Ralph took a moment to recognize Merthin. Then he smiled broadly. 'My big brother!' he said heartily. It was an old joke: Merthin was the elder, but had long been smaller.

They embraced. Merthin felt a surge of warmth, despite everything. At least we're both alive, he thought, despite war and plague. When they had parted he had wondered whether they would ever meet again.

Ralph threw himself into the big chair. 'Bring some beer, we're thirsty!' he said to Tilly.

There were to be no recriminations, Merthin gathered.

He studied his brother. Ralph had changed since that day in 1339 when he had ridden off to war. He had lost some of the fingers of his left hand, presumably in battle. He had a dissipated look: his face was veined from drink and his skin seemed dry and flaky. 'Did you have good hunting?' Merthin asked.

'We brought home a roe deer as fat as a cow,' he replied with satisfaction. 'You shall have her liver for supper.'

Merthin asked him about fighting in the army of the king, and Ralph related some of the highlights of the war. Their father was enthusiastic. 'An English knight is worth ten of the French!' he said. 'The battle of Crécy proved that.'

Ralph's response was surprisingly measured. 'An English knight is not much different from a French knight, in my opinion,' he said. 'But the French haven't yet understood the harrow formation in which we line up, with archers either side of dismounted knights and men-at-arms. They are still charging us suicidally, and long may they continue. But they will figure it out one day, and then they will change their tactics. Meanwhile, we are almost unbeatable in defence. Unfortunately, the harrow formation is irrelevant to attack, so we have ended up winning very little.'

Merthin was struck by how his brother had grown up. Warfare had given him a depth and subtlety he had never previously possessed.

In turn, Merthin talked about Florence: the incredible size of the city, the wealth of the merchants, the churches and palaces. Ralph was particularly fascinated by the notion of slave girls.

Darkness fell and the servants brought lamps and candles, then supper. Ralph drank a lot of wine. Merthin noticed that he hardly spoke to Tilly. Perhaps it was not surprising. Ralph was a thirty-one-year-old soldier who had spent half his adult life in an army, and Tilly was a girl of fourteen who had been educated in a nunnery. What would they have to talk about?

Late in the evening, when Gerald and Maud had returned to their own house and Tilly had gone to bed, Merthin broached the subject Caris had asked him to raise. He felt more optimistic than previously. Ralph was showing signs of maturity. He had forgiven Merthin for what had happened in 1339, and his cool analysis of English and French tactics had been impressively free from tribal chauvinism.

Merthin said: 'On my way here, I spent a night in Wigleigh.'

'I see that fulling mill stays busy.'

'The scarlet cloth has become a good business for Kingsbridge.'

Ralph shrugged. 'Mark Webber pays the rent on time.' It was beneath the dignity of noblemen to discuss business.

'I stayed with Gwenda and Wulfric,' Merthin went on. 'You know that Gwenda has been Caris's friend since childhood.'

'I remember the day we all met Sir Thomas Langley in the forest.'

Merthin shot a quick glance at Alan Fernhill. They had all kept their childish vows, and had not told anyone about that incident. Merthin wanted the secrecy to continue, for he sensed it was still important to Thomas, though he had no idea why. But Alan showed no reaction: he had drunk a lot of wine, and had no ear for hints.

Merthin moved on quickly. 'Caris asked me to speak to you about Wulfric. She thinks you've punished him enough for that fight. And I agree.'

'He broke my nose!'

'I was there, remember? You weren't an innocent party.' Merthin tried to make light of it. 'You did feel up his fiancée. What was her name?'

'Annet.'

'If her tits weren't worth a broken nose, you've only got yourself to blame.'

Alan laughed, but Ralph was not amused. 'Wulfric almost got me hanged, by stirring Lord William up after Annet pretended I'd raped her.'

'But you weren't hanged. And you cut Wulfric's cheek open with your sword when you escaped from the courthouse. It was a terrible wound – you could see his back teeth through it. He'll never lose the scar.'

'Good.'

'You've punished Wulfric for eleven years. His wife is thin and his children are ill. Haven't you done enough, Ralph?'

'No.'

'What do you mean?'

'It's not enough.'

'Why?' Merthin cried in frustration. 'I don't understand you.'

'I will continue to punish Wulfric and hold him back, and humiliate him and his women.'

Merthin was startled by Ralph's frankness. 'For heaven's sake, to what end?'

'I wouldn't normally answer that question. I've learned that it rarely does you any good to explain yourself. But you're my big brother, and from childhood I've always needed your approval.'

Ralph had not really changed, Merthin realized, except insofar as he seemed to know and understand himself in a way he never had when younger.

'The reason is simple,' Ralph went on. 'Wulfric is not afraid of me. He wasn't scared that day at the Fleece Fair, and he's still not scared of me, even after all I've done to him. That's why he must continue to suffer.'

Merthin was horrified. 'That's a life sentence.'

'The day I see fear in his eyes when he looks at me, he shall have anything he likes.'

'Is that so important to you?' Merthin said incredulously. 'That people fear you?'

'It's the most important thing in the world,' said Ralph.

57

MERTHIN'S RETURN AFFECTED the whole town. Caris observed the changes with amazement and admiration. It started with his victory over Elfric in the parish guild. People realized the town could have lost its bridge because of Elfric's incompetence, and that jolted them out of their apathy. But everyone knew that Elfric was a tool of Godwyn, so the priory was the ultimate focus of their resentment.

And people's attitude to the priory was changing. There was a mood of defiance. Caris felt optimistic. Mark Webber had a good chance of winning the election on the first day of November and becoming alderman. If that happened, Prior Godwyn would no longer have things all his own way, and perhaps the town could begin to grow: markets on Saturdays, new mills, independent courts that traders could have faith in.

But she spent most of her time thinking about her own position. Merthin's return was an earthquake that shook the foundations of her life. Her first reaction had been horror at the prospect of abandoning all that she had worked for over the last nine years; her position in the convent hierarchy; maternal Cecilia and affectionate Mair and ailing Old Julie; and most of all her hospital, so much more clean and efficient and welcoming than it had been before.

But as the days became shorter and colder, and Merthin repaired his bridge and began laying out the foundations of the street of new buildings he wanted to create on Leper Island, Caris's resolve to remain a nun weakened. Monastic restrictions that she had stopped noticing began to chafe again. The devotion of Mair, which had been a pleasant romantic diversion, now became irritating. She started to think about what kind of life she might lead as Merthin's wife.

She thought a lot about Lolla, and about the child she might have had with Merthin. Lolla was dark-eyed and black-haired, presumably like her Italian mother. Caris's daughter might have had the green eyes of the Wooler family. The idea of giving up everything to take care of another woman's daughter had appalled Caris in theory, but as soon as she met the little girl she softened.

She could not talk to anyone in the priory about this, of course. Mother Cecilia would tell her she must keep her vows; Mair would beg her to stay. So she agonized alone at night.

Her quarrel with Merthin over Wulfric made her despair. After he walked away from her, she had gone back to her pharmacy and cried. Why were things so difficult? All she wanted was to do the right thing.

While Merthin was at Tench, she confided in Madge Webber.

Two days after Merthin left, Madge came into the hospital soon after dawn, when Caris and Mair were doing their rounds. 'I'm worried about my Mark,' she said.

Mair said to Caris: 'I went to see him yesterday. He had been to Melcombe and come back with a fever and an upset stomach. I didn't tell you because it didn't seem serious.'

'Now he's coughing blood,' Madge said.

'I'll go,' Caris said. The Webbers were old friends: she preferred to attend Mark herself. She picked up a bag containing some basic medicines and went with Madge to her house in the main street.

The living area was upstairs, over the shop. Mark's three sons loitered anxiously in the dining hall. Madge took Caris into a bedroom that smelled bad. Caris was used to the odour of a sick room, a mixture of sweat, vomit and human waste. Mark lay on a straw mattress, perspiring. His huge belly stuck up in the air as if he were pregnant. The daughter, Dora, stood by the bed.

Caris knelt beside Mark and said: 'How do you feel?'

'Rough,' Mark said in a croaky voice. 'Can I have something to drink?'

Dora handed Caris a cup of wine, and Caris held it to Mark's lips. She found it strange to see a big man helpless. Mark had always seemed invulnerable. It was unnerving, like finding an oak tree that has been there all your life suddenly felled by lightning.

She touched his forehead. He was burning up: no wonder he was thirsty. 'Let him have as much to drink as he wants,' she said. 'Weak beer is better than wine.'

She did not tell Madge that she was puzzled and worried by Mark's illness. The fever and the stomach upset were routine, but his coughing blood was a dangerous sign.

She took a vial of rose water from her bag, soaked a small piece of woollen cloth and bathed his face and neck. The action soothed him immediately. The water would cool him a little, and the perfume masked the bad smells in the room. 'I'll give you some of this from my pharmacy,' she said to Madge. 'The physicians prescribe it for an inflamed brain. A fever is hot and humid, and roses are cool and dry, so the monks say. Whatever the reason, it will give him some ease.'

'Thank you.'

But Caris knew of no effective treatment for bloody sputum. The monk-physicians would diagnose an excess of blood and recommend bleeding, but they prescribed that for almost everything, and Caris did not believe in it.

As she bathed Mark's throat, she noticed a symptom Madge had not mentioned. There was a rash of purple-black spots on Mark's neck and chest.

This was an illness she had not come across before, and she was mystified, but she did not let Madge know that. 'Come back with me and I'll give you the rose water.'

The sun was rising as they walked from the house to the hospital. 'You've been very good to my family,' Madge said. 'We were the poorest people in town, until you started the scarlet business.'

'It was your energy and industry that made it work.'

Madge nodded. She knew what she had done. 'All the same, it wouldn't have happened without you.'

On impulse, Caris decided to take Madge through the nuns' cloisters to her pharmacy so that they could talk privately. Lay people were not normally allowed inside, but there were exceptions, and Caris was now senior enough to decide when the rules could be broken.

They were alone in the cramped little room. Caris filled a

pottery bottle with rose water and asked Madge for six pence. Then she said: 'I'm thinking of renouncing my vows.'

Madge nodded, unsurprised. 'Everybody's wondering what you're going to do.'

Caris was shocked that the townspeople had guessed her thoughts. 'How do they know?'

'It doesn't take a clairvoyant. You entered the nunnery only to escape a death sentence for witchcraft. After the work you've done here, you should be able to get a pardon. You and Merthin were in love, and always seemed so right for one another. Now he's come back. You must at least be thinking about marrying him.'

'I just don't know what my life would be like as someone's wife.'

Madge shrugged. 'A bit like mine, perhaps. Mark and I run the cloth business together. I have to organize the household as well – all husbands expect that – but it's not so difficult, especially if you have the money for servants. And the children will always be your responsibility rather than his. But I manage, and so would you.'

'You don't make it sound very exciting.'

She smiled. 'I assume you already know about the good parts: feeling loved and adored; knowing there's one person in the world who will always be on your side; getting into bed every night with someone strong and tender who wants to fuck you ... that's happiness, for me.'

Madge's simple words painted a vivid picture, and Caris was suddenly filled with a longing that was almost unbearable. She felt she could hardly wait to quit the cold, hard, loveless life of the priory, in which the greatest sin was to touch another human being. If Merthin had walked into the room at that moment she would have torn off his clothes and taken him there on the floor.

She saw that Madge was watching her with a little smile, reading her thoughts, and she blushed.

'It's all right,' Madge said. 'I understand.' She put six silver pennies down on the bench and picked up the bottle. 'I'd better go home and look after my man.'

Caris recovered her composure. 'Try to keep him comfortable, and come and fetch me immediately there's any change.'

'Thank you, sister,' said Madge. 'I don't know what we'll do without you.'

*

MERTHIN WAS THOUGHTFUL on the journey back to Kingsbridge. Even Lolla's bright, meaningless chatter did not bring him out of his mood. Ralph had learned a lot, but he had not changed deep down. He was still a cruel man. He neglected his child-wife, barely tolerated his parents and was vengeful to the point of mania. He enjoyed being a lord, but felt little obligation to care for the peasants in his power. He saw everything around him, people included, as being there for his gratification.

However, Merthin felt optimistic about Kingsbridge. All the signs were that Mark would become alderman on All Hallows' Day, and that could be the start of a boom.

Merthin got back on the last day of October, All Hallows' Eve. It was a Friday this year, so there was not the influx of crowds that came when the night of evil spirits fell on a Saturday, as it had in the year that Merthin was eleven, and he met the ten-year-old Caris. All the same the people were nervous, and everyone planned to be in bed by nightfall.

On the main street he saw Mark Webber's eldest son, John. 'My father is in the hospital,' the boy said. 'He has a fever.'

'This is a bad time for him to fall sick,' Merthin said.

'It's an ill-starred day.'

'I didn't mean because of the date. He has to be present at the parish guild meeting tomorrow. An alderman can't be elected in his absence.'

'I don't think he'll be going to any meetings tomorrow.'

That was worrying. Merthin took his horses to the Bell and left Lolla in the care of Betty.

Entering the priory grounds, he ran into Godwyn with his mother. He guessed they had dined together and now Godwyn was walking her to the gate. They were deep in an anxious conversation, and Merthin guessed they were worried about the prospect of their placeman Elfric losing the post of alderman. They stopped abruptly when they saw him. Petranilla said unctuously: 'I'm sorry to hear that Mark is unwell.'

Forcing himself to be civil, Merthin replied: 'It's just a fever.'

'We will pray that he gets well quickly.'

'Thank you.'

Merthin entered the hospital. He found Madge distraught. 'He's been coughing blood,' she said. 'And I can't quench his thirst.' She held a cup of ale to Mark's lips.

Mark had a rash of purple blotches on his face and arms. He was perspiring, and his nose was bleeding.

Merthin said: 'Not so good today, Mark?'

Mark did not seem to see him, but he croaked: 'I'm very thirsty.' Madge gave him the cup again. She said: 'No matter how much he drinks, he's always thirsty.' She spoke with a note of panic that Merthin had never heard in her voice before.

Merthin was filled with dread. Mark made frequent trips to Melcombe, where he talked to sailors from plague-ridden Bordeaux.

Tomorrow's meeting of the parish guild was the least of Mark's worries now. And the least of Merthin's, too.

Merthin's first impulse was to cry out to everyone the news that they were in mortal danger. But he clamped his mouth shut. No one listened to a man in a panic, and besides he was not yet sure. There was a small chance Mark's illness was not what he feared. When he was certain, he would get Caris alone and speak to her calmly and logically. But it would have to be soon.

Caris was bathing Mark's face with a sweet-smelling fluid. She wore a stony expression that Merthin recognized: she was hiding her feelings. She obviously had some idea of how serious Mark's illness was.

Mark was clutching something that looked like a scrap of parchment. Merthin guessed it would have a prayer written on it, or a verse of the Bible, or perhaps a magic spell. That would be Madge's idea – Caris had no faith in writing as a remedy.

Prior Godwyn came into the hospital, trailed as usual by Philemon. 'Stand away from the bed!' Philemon said immediately. 'How will the man get well if he cannot see the altar?'

Merthin and the two women stood back, and Godwyn bent over the patient. He touched Mark's forehead and neck, then felt his pulse. 'Show me the urine,' he said.

The monk-physicians set great store by examination of the patient's urine. The hospital had special glass bottles, called urinals, for the purpose. Caris handed one to Godwyn. It did not take an expert to see that there was blood in Mark's urine.

Godwyn handed it back. 'This man is suffering from overheated blood,' he said. 'He must be bled, then fed sour apples and tripes.'

Merthin knew, from his experience of the plague in Florence, that Godwyn was talking rubbish, but he made no comment. In his mind there was no longer much room for doubt about what was wrong with Mark. The skin rash, the bleeding, the thirst: this was the illness he himself had suffered in Florence, the one that had killed Silvia and all her family. This was *la moria grande*.

The plague had come to Kingsbridge.

*

AS DARKNESS FELL on All Hallows' Eve, Mark Webber's breathing became more difficult. Caris watched him weaken. She felt the angry impotence that possessed her when she was unable to help a patient. Mark passed into a state of troubled unconsciousness, sweating and gasping although his eyes were closed and he showed no awareness. At Merthin's quiet suggestion, Caris felt in Mark's armpits, and found large boil-like swellings there. She did not ask him the significance of this: she would question him later. The nuns prayed and sang hymns while Madge and her four children stood around, helplessly distraught.

At the end Mark convulsed, and blood jetted from his mouth in a sudden flood. Then he fell back, lay still and stopped breathing.

Dora wailed loudly. The three sons looked bewildered, and struggled to hold back unmanly tears. Madge wept bitterly. 'He was the best man in the world,' she said to Caris. 'Why did God have to take him?'

Caris had to fight back her own grief. Her loss was nothing

compared with theirs. She did not know why God so often took the best people and left the wicked alive to do more wrong. The whole idea of a benevolent deity watching over everyone seemed unbelievable at moments such as this. The priests said sickness was a punishment for sin. Mark and Madge loved one another, cared for their children and worked hard: why should they be punished?

There were no answers to religious questions, but Caris had some urgent practical inquiries to make. She was deeply worried by Mark's illness, and she could guess that Merthin knew something about it. She swallowed her tears.

First she sent Madge and her children home to rest, and told the nuns to prepare the body for burial. Then she said to Merthin: 'I want to talk to you.'

'And I to you,' he said.

She noticed that he looked frightened. That was rare. Her fear deepened. 'Come to the church,' she said. 'We can talk privately there.'

A wintry wind swept across the cathedral green. It was a clear night, and they could see by starlight. In the chancel, monks were preparing for the All Hallows dawn service. Caris and Merthin stood in the north-west corner of the nave away from the monks, so that they could not be overheard. Caris shivered, and pulled her robe closer around her. She said: 'Do you know what killed Mark?'

Merthin took a shaky breath. 'It's the plague,' he said. 'La moria grande.'

She nodded. This was what she had feared. But all the same she challenged him. 'How do you know?'

'Mark goes to Melcombe and talks to sailors from Bordeaux, where the bodies are piled in the streets.'

She nodded. 'He's just back.' But she did not want to believe Merthin. 'All the same, can you be sure it's the plague?'

'The symptoms are the same: fever, purple-black spots, bleeding, buboes in the armpits, and most of all the thirst. I remember it, by Christ. I was one of the few to recover. Almost everyone dies within five days, often less.'

She felt as if doomsday had come. She had heard the terrible stories from Italy and southern France: entire families wiped out, unburied bodies rotting in empty palaces, orphaned toddlers wandering the streets crying, livestock dying untended in ghost villages. Was this to happen to Kingsbridge? 'What did the Italian doctors do?'

'Prayed, sang hymns, took blood, prescribed their favourite nostrums and charged a fortune. Everything they tried was useless.'

They were standing close together and speaking in low tones. She could see his face by the faint light of the monks' distant candles. He was staring at her with a strange intensity. He was deeply moved, she could tell, but it did not seem to be grief for Mark that possessed him. He was focused on her.

She asked: 'What are the Italian doctors like, compared with our English physicians?'

'After the Muslims, the Italian doctors are supposed to be the most knowledgeable in the world. They even cut up dead bodies to learn more about sickness. But they never cured a single sufferer from this plague.'

Caris refused to accept such complete hopelessness. 'We can't be utterly helpless.'

'No. We can't cure it, but some people think you can escape it.'

Caris said eagerly: 'How?'

'It seems to spread from one person to another.'

She nodded. 'Lots of diseases do that.'

'Usually, when one in a family gets it, they all do. Proximity is the key factor.'

'That makes sense. Some say you fall ill from looking at sick people.'

'In Florence, the nuns counselled us to stay at home as much as possible, and avoid social gatherings, markets and meetings of guilds and councils.'

'And church services?'

'No, they didn't say that, though lots of people stayed home from church too.'

This chimed with what Caris had been thinking for years. She felt renewed hope: perhaps her methods could stave off the plague. 'What about the nuns themselves, and the physicians, people who have to meet the sick and touch them?'

'Priests refused to hear confessions in whispers, so that they did not have to get too near. Nuns wore linen masks over their mouths and noses so that they would not breathe the same air. Some washed their hands in vinegar every time they touched a patient. The priest-physicians said none of this would do any good, but most of them left the city anyway.'

'And did these precautions help?'

'It's hard to say. None of this was done until the plague was rampant. And it wasn't systematic – just everyone trying different things.'

'All the same, we must make the effort.'

He nodded. After a pause he said: 'However, there is one precaution that is sure.'

'What's that?'

'Run away.'

This was what he had been waiting to say, she realized.

He went on: 'The saying goes: "Leave early, go far and stay long." People who did that escaped the sickness.'

'We can't go away.'

'Why not?'

'Don't be silly. There are six or seven thousand people in Kingsbridge – they can't all leave town. Where would they go?'

'I'm not talking about them – just you. Listen, you may not have caught the plague from Mark. Madge and the children almost certainly have, but you spent less time close to him. If you're still all right, we could escape. We could leave today, you and me and Lolla.'

Caris was appalled by the way he assumed it had spread by now. Was she doomed already? 'And ... and go where?'

'To Wales, or Ireland. We need to find a remote village where they don't see a stranger from one year to the next.'

'You've had the sickness. You told me people don't get it twice.'

'Never. And some people don't catch it at all. Lolla must be like that. If she didn't pick it up from her mother, she's not likely to get it from anyone else.'

'So why do you want to go to Wales?'

He just stared at her with that intense look, and she realized that the fear she had detected in him was for her. He was terrified that she would die. Tears came to her eyes. She remembered what Madge had said: 'Knowing there's one person in the world who will always be on your side.' Merthin tried to look after her, no matter what she did. She thought of poor Madge, blasted by grief at the loss of the one who was always on her side. How could she, Caris, even think of rejecting Merthin?

But she did. 'I can't leave Kingsbridge,' she said. 'Of all times, not now. They rely on me if someone is sick. When the plague strikes, I'm the one they will turn to for help. If I were to flee ... well, I don't know how to explain this.'

'I think I understand,' Merthin said. 'You'd be like a soldier who runs away as soon as the first arrow is shot. You'd feel a coward.'

'Yes – and a cheat, after all these years of being a nun and saying that I live to serve others.'

'I knew you would feel this way,' Merthin said. 'But I had to try.' The sadness in his voice nearly broke her heart as he added: 'And I suppose this means you won't be renouncing your vows in the foreseeable future.'

'No. The hospital is where they come for help. I have to be here at the priory, to play my role. I have to be a nun.'

'All right, then.'

'Don't be too downhearted.'

With wry sorrow he said: 'And why should I not be downhearted?'

'You said that it killed half the population of Florence?'

'Something like that.'

'So at least half the people just didn't catch it.'

'Like Lolla. No one knows why. Perhaps they have some special strength. Or maybe the disease strikes at random, like arrows fired into the enemy ranks, killing some and missing others.'

'Either way, there's a good chance I'll escape the illness.'

'One chance in two.'

'Like the toss of a coin.'

'Heads or tails,' he said. 'Life or death.'

58

HUNDREDS OF PEOPLE CAME TO Mark Webber's funeral. He had been one of the town's leading citizens, but it was more than that. Poor weavers arrived from the surrounding villages, some of them having walked for hours. He had been unusually well loved, Merthin reflected. The combination of his giant's body and his gentle temperament cast a spell.

It was a wet day, and the bared heads of rich and poor men were soaked as they stood around the grave. Cold rain mingled with hot tears on the faces of the mourners. Madge stood with her arms around the shoulders of her two younger sons, Dennis and Noah. They were flanked by the eldest son, John, and the daughter, Dora, who were both much taller than their mother, and looked as if they might be the parents of the three short people in the middle.

Merthin wondered grimly whether Madge or one of her children would be the next to die.

Six strong men grunted with the effort of lowering the extra-large coffin into the grave. Madge sobbed helplessly as the monks sang the last hymn. Then the gravediggers started to shovel the sodden earth back into the hole, and the crowd began to disperse.

Brother Thomas approached Merthin, pulling up his hood to keep the rain off. 'The priory has no money to rebuild the tower,' he said. 'Godwyn has commissioned Elfric to demolish the old tower and just roof the crossing.'

Merthin tore his mind away from apocalyptic thoughts of the plague. 'How will Godwyn pay Elfric for that?'

'The nuns are putting up the money.'

'I thought they hated Godwyn.'

'Sister Elizabeth is the treasurer. Godwyn is careful to be kind to her family, who are tenants of the priory. Most of the other nuns do hate him, it's true – but they need a church.'

Merthin had not given up his hope of rebuilding the tower higher than before. 'If I could find the money, would the priory build a new tower?'

Thomas shrugged. 'Hard to say.'

That afternoon, Elfric was re-elected alderman of the parish guild. After the meeting Merthin sought out Bill Watkin, the largest builder in town after Elfric. 'Once the foundations of the tower are repaired, it could be built even higher,' he said.

'No reason why not,' Bill agreed. 'But what would be the point?'

'So that it could be seen from Mudeford Crossing. Many travellers – pilgrims, merchants and so on – miss the road for Kingsbridge and go on to Shiring. The town loses a lot of custom that way.'

'Godwyn will say he can't afford it.'

'Consider this,' Merthin said. 'Suppose the new tower could be financed the same way as the bridge? The town merchants could lend the money and be repaid out of bridge tolls.'

Bill scratched his monk-like fringe of grey hair. This was an unfamiliar concept. 'But the tower is nothing to do with the bridge.'

'Does that matter?'

'I suppose not.'

'The bridge tolls are just a way of guaranteeing that the loan is repaid.'

Bill considered his self-interest. 'Would I be commissioned to do any of the work?'

'It would be a big project – every builder in town would get a piece of it.'

'That would be useful.'

'All right. Listen, if I design a large tower, will you back me, here at the parish guild, at the next meeting?'

Bill looked dubious. 'The guild members aren't likely to approve of extravagance.'

'I don't think it needs to be extravagant, just high. If we put a domed ceiling over the crossing, I can build that with no centering.'

'A dome? That's a new idea.'

'I saw domes in Italy.'

'I can see how it would save money.'

'And the tower can be topped by a slender wooden spire, which will save money and look wonderful.'

'You've got this all worked out, haven't you?'

'Not really. But it's been at the back of my mind ever since I returned from Florence.'

'Well, it sounds good to me – good for business, good for the town.'

'And good for our eternal souls.'

'I'll do my best to help you push it through.'

'Thank you.'

Merthin mulled over the design of the tower as he went about his more mundane work, repairing the bridge and building new houses on Leper Island. It helped turn his mind away from dreadful, obsessive visions of Caris ill with the plague. He thought a lot about the south tower at Chartres. It was a masterpiece, albeit a little old-fashioned, having been built about two hundred years ago.

What Merthin had liked about it, he recalled very clearly, was the transition from the square tower to the octagonal spire above. At the top of the tower, perched on each of the four corners, were pinnacles facing diagonally outwards. On the same level, at the midpoint of each side of the square, were dormer windows similar in shape to the pinnacles. These eight structures matched the eight sloping sides of the tower rising behind them, so that the eye hardly noticed the change of shape from square to octagon.

However, Chartres was unnecessarily chunky by the standards of the fourteenth century. Merthin's tower would have slender columns and large window openings, to lighten the weight on the pillars below, and to reduce stress by allowing the wind to blow through.

He made his own tracing floor at his workshop on the island.

He enjoyed himself planning the details, doubling and quadrupling the narrow lancets of the old cathedral to make the large windows of the new tower, updating the clusters of columns and the capitals.

He hesitated over the height. He had no way to calculate how high it had to be in order to be visible from Mudeford Crossing. That could be done only by trial and error. When he had finished the stone tower he would have to erect a temporary spire, then go to Mudeford on a clear day and determine whether it could be seen. The cathedral was built on elevated ground, and at Mudeford the road breasted a rise just before descending to the river crossing. His instinct told him that if he went a little higher than Chartres – say about four hundred feet – that would be sufficient.

The tower at Salisbury cathedral was four hundred and four feet high.

Merthin planned his to be four hundred and five.

While he was bent over the tracing floor, drawing the roof pinnacles, Bill Watkin appeared. 'What do you think of this?' Merthin said to him. 'Does it need a cross on top, to point to heaven? Or an angel, to watch over us?'

'Neither,' said Bill. 'It's not going to get built.'

Merthin stood up, holding a straight-edge in his left hand and a sharpened iron drawing-needle in his right. 'What makes you say that?'

'I've had a visit from Brother Philemon. I thought I might as well let you know as soon as possible.'

'What did that snake have to say?'

'He pretended to be friendly. He wanted to give me a piece of advice for my own good. He said it wouldn't be wise of me to support any plan for a tower designed by you.'

'Why not?'

'Because it would annoy Prior Godwyn, who was not going to approve your plans, regardless.'

Merthin could hardly be surprised. If Mark Webber had become alderman, the balance of power in the town would have changed, and Merthin might have won the commission to build the new tower. But Mark's death meant the odds were against him. He had clung to hope, however, and now he felt the deep ache of heavy disappointment. 'I suppose he'll commission Elfric?'

'That was the implication.'

'Will he never learn?'

'When a man is proud, that counts for more than common sense.'

'Will the parish guild pay for a stumpy little tower designed by Elfric?'

'Probably. They may not get excited about it, but they'll find the money. They are proud of their cathedral, despite everything.'

'Elfric's incompetence almost cost them the bridge!' Merthin said indignantly.

'They know that.'

He allowed his wounded feelings to show. 'If I hadn't diagnosed the problem with the tower, it would have collapsed – and it might have brought down the entire cathedral.'

'They know that, too. But they're not going to fight with the prior just because he's treated you badly.'

'Of course not,' said Merthin, as if he thought that was perfectly reasonable; but he was hiding his bitterness. He had done more for Kingsbridge than Godwyn, and he was hurt that the townspeople had not put up more of a fight for him. But he also knew that most people most of the time acted in their own immediate self-interest.

'People are ungrateful,' Bill said. 'I'm sorry.'

'Yes,' Merthin said. 'That's all right.' He looked at Bill, then looked away; and then he threw down his drawing implements and walked off.

*

DURING THE PRE-DAWN service of Lauds, Caris was surprised to look down the nave and see a woman in the north aisle, on her knees, in front of a wall painting of Christ Risen. She had a candle by her side and, in its unsteady light, Caris made out the chunky body and jutting chin of Madge Webber.

Madge stayed there throughout the service, not paying any attention to the psalms, apparently deep in prayer. Perhaps she was asking God to forgive Mark's sins and let him rest in peace –

not that Mark had committed many sins, as far as Caris knew. More likely, Madge was asking Mark to send her good fortune from the spirit world. Madge was going to carry on the cloth business with the help of her two older children. It was the usual thing, when a trader died leaving a widow and a thriving enterprise. Still, no doubt she felt the need of her dead husband's blessing on her efforts.

But this explanation did not quite satisfy Caris. There was something intense in Madge's posture, something about her stillness that suggested great passion, as if she were begging heaven to grant her some terribly important boon.

When the service ended, and the monks and nuns began to file out, Caris broke away from the procession and walked through the vast gloom of the nave towards the candle's glow.

Madge stood up at the sound of her footsteps. When she recognized Caris's face, she spoke with a note of accusation. 'Mark died of the plague, didn't he?'

So that was it. 'I think so,' said Caris.

'You didn't tell me.'

'I'm not sure, and I didn't want to frighten you – not to mention the whole town – on the basis of a guess.'

'I've heard it's come to Bristol.'

So the townspeople had been talking about it. 'And London,' Caris said. She had heard this from a pilgrim.

'What will happen to us all?'

Sorrow stabbed Caris like a pain in the heart. 'I don't know,' she lied.

'It spreads from one to another, I hear.'

'Many illnesses do.'

The aggression went out of Madge, and her face took on a pleading look that broke Caris's heart. In a near-whisper she asked: 'Will my children die?'

'Merthin's wife got it,' Caris said. 'She died, and so did all her family, but Merthin recovered, and Lolla didn't catch it at all.'

'So my children will be all right?'

That was not what Caris had said. 'They may be. Or some may catch it and others escape.'

That did not satisfy Madge. Like most patients, she wanted certainties, not possibilities. 'What can I do to protect them?'

Caris looked at the painting of Christ. 'You're doing all you can,' she said. She began to lose control. As a sob rose in her throat, she turned away to hide her feelings and walked quickly out of the cathedral.

She sat in the nuns' cloisters for a few minutes, pulling herself together, then went to the hospital, as usual at this hour.

Mair was not there. She had probably been called to attend a sick person in the town. Caris took charge, overseeing the serving of breakfast to guests and patients, making sure the place was cleaned thoroughly, checking on those who were sick. The work eased her distress about Madge. She read a psalm to Old Julie. When all the chores were done, Mair still had not appeared, so Caris went in search of her.

She found her in the dormitory, lying face down on her bed. Caris's heart quickened. 'Mair! Are you all right?' she said.

Mair rolled over. She was pale and sweating. She coughed, but did not speak.

Caris knelt beside her and placed a hand on her forehead. 'You've got a fever,' she said, suppressing the dread that rose in her belly like nausea. 'When did it begin?'

'I was coughing yesterday,' Mair said. 'But I slept all right, and got up this morning. Then, when I went in to breakfast, I suddenly felt I was going to throw up. I went to the latrine, then came here and lay down. I think I might have been sleeping ... what time is it?'

'The bell is about to ring for Terce. But you're excused.' It could just be an ordinary illness, Caris told herself. She touched Mair's neck, then pulled the cowl of her robe down.

Mair smiled weakly. 'Are you trying to look at my chest?'

'Yes.'

'You nuns are all the same.'

There was no rash, as far as Caris could see. Perhaps it was just a cold. 'Any pains?'

'There's a dreadfully tender place in my armpit.'

That did not tell Caris much. Painful swellings in the armpits or groin were a feature of other illnesses as well as the plague. 'Let's get you down to the hospital,' she said.

As Mair lifted her head, Caris saw bloodstains on the pillow.

She felt the shock like a blow. Mark Webber had coughed blood. And Mair had been the first person to attend Mark at the start of his illness – she had gone to the house the day before Caris did.

Caris hid her fear and helped Mair up. Tears came to her eyes, but she controlled herself. Mair put her arm around Caris's waist and her head on her shoulder, as if she needed support walking. Caris put her arm around Mair's shoulder. Together they walked down the stairs and through the nuns' cloisters to the hospital.

Caris took Mair to a mattress near the altar. She fetched a cup of cold water from the fountain in the cloisters. Mair drank thirstily. Caris bathed her face and neck with rose water. After a while, Mair seemed to sleep.

The bell rang for Terce. Caris was normally excused this service, but today she felt the need for a few moments of quiet. She joined the file of nuns walking into the church. The old grey stones seemed cold and hard today. She chanted automatically, while in her heart a storm raged.

Mair had the plague. There was no rash, but she had the fever, she was thirsty and she had coughed blood. She would probably die.

Caris felt a terrible guilt. Mair loved her devotedly. Caris had never been able to return Mair's love, not in the way Mair longed for. Now Mair was dying. Caris wished she could have been different. She ought to have been able to make Mair happy. She should be able to save her life. She cried as she sang the psalm, hoping that anyone who noticed her tears would assume she was moved by religious ecstasy.

At the end of the service, a novice nun was waiting anxiously for her outside the south transept door. 'There's someone asking for you urgently in the hospital,' the girl said.

Caris found Madge Webber there, her face white with fear.

Caris did not need to ask what Madge wanted. She picked up her medical bag and the two of them rushed out. They crossed the cathedral green in a biting November wind and went to the Webber house in the main street. Upstairs, Madge's children were waiting in the living room. The two older children were sitting at the table, looking frightened; the young boys were both lying on the floor.

Caris examined them quickly. All four were feverish. The girl had a nose bleed. The three boys were coughing.

They all had a rash of purplish-black spots on their shoulders and necks.

Madge said: 'It's the same, isn't it? This is what Mark died of. They've got the plague.'

Caris nodded. 'I'm sorry.'

'I hope I die, too,' Madge said. 'Then we can all be together in heaven.'

59

In the hospital, Caris instituted the precautions Merthin had told her about. She cut up strips of linen for the nuns to tie over their mouths and noses while they were dealing with people who had the plague. And she compelled everyone to wash their hands in vinegar and water every time they touched a patient. The nuns all got chapped hands.

Madge brought her four children in, then fell ill herself. Old Julie, whose bed had been next to Mark Webber's while he was dying, also succumbed. There was little Caris could do for any of them. She bathed their faces to cool them, gave them cold clear water to drink from the fountain in the cloisters, cleaned up their bloody vomit, and waited for them to die.

She was too busy to think about her own death. She observed a kind of fearful admiration in the townspeople's eyes when they saw her soothing the brows of infectious plague victims, but she did not feel like a selfless martyr. She saw herself as the kind of person who disliked brooding and preferred to act. Like everyone else, she was haunted by the question: Who's next? But she firmly put it out of her mind.

Prior Godwyn came in to see the patients. He refused to wear the face mask, saying it was women's nonsense. He made the same diagnosis as before, overheated blood, and prescribed bleeding and a diet of sour apples and ram's tripes.

It did not matter much what the patients ate, as they threw everything up towards the end; but Caris felt sure that taking blood from them made the illness worse. They were already bleeding too much: they coughed blood, vomited blood and pissed blood. But the monks were the trained physicians, so she had to follow their instructions. She did not have time to be angry whenever she saw a monk or nun kneeling at the bedside of a patient, holding an arm out straight, cutting into a vein with a small sharp knife, and supporting the arm while a pint or more of precious blood dripped into a bowl on the floor.

Caris sat with Mair at the end, holding her hand, not caring if anyone disapproved. To ease her torment, she gave her a tiny amount of the euphoric drug Mattie had taught her to make from poppies. Mair still coughed, but it did not hurt her so much. After a coughing fit, her breathing would be easier for a short while, and she could talk. 'Thank you for that night in Calais,' she whispered. 'I know you didn't really enjoy it, but I was in heaven.'

Caris tried not to cry. 'I'm sorry I couldn't be what you wanted.'

'You loved me, though, in your own way. I know that.'

She coughed again. When the fit ended, Caris wiped the blood from her lips.

'I love you,' Mair said, and closed her eyes.

Caris let the tears come, then, not caring who saw or what they thought. She watched Mair, through a watery film, as she grew paler and breathed more shallowly, until at last her breathing stopped.

Caris remained where she was, on the floor beside the mattress, holding the hand of the corpse. Mair was still beautiful, even like this, white and forever still. It occurred to Caris that one other person loved her as Mair had, and that was Merthin. How strange that she had rejected his love, too. There was something wrong with her, she thought; some malformation of the soul that prevented her from being like other women, and embracing love gladly.

Later that night, the four children of Mark Webber died; and so did Old Julie.

Caris was distraught. Was there nothing she could do? The plague was spreading fast and killing everyone. It was like living in a prison and wondering which of the inmates would be next to go to the gallows. Was Kingsbridge to be like Florence and Bordeaux, with bodies in the streets? Next Sunday there would be a market on the green outside the cathedral. Hundreds of people from every village within walking distance would come to buy and sell and mingle with the townspeople in churches and taverns. How many would go home fatally ill? When she felt like this, excruciatingly helpless up against terrible forces, she understood why people threw up their hands and said everything was controlled by the spirit world. But that had never been her way.

Whenever a member of the priory died there was always a special burial service, involving all the monks and nuns, with extra prayers for the departed soul. Both Mair and Old Julie had been well loved, Julie for her kind heart and Mair for her beauty, and many of the nuns wept. Madge's children were included in the funeral, with the result that several hundred townspeople came. Madge herself was too ill to leave the hospital.

They all gathered in the graveyard under a slate-grey sky. Caris thought she could smell snow in the cold north wind. Brother Joseph said the graveside prayers, and six coffins were lowered into the ground.

A voice in the crowd asked the question that was on everyone's mind. 'Are we all going to die, Brother Joseph?'

Joseph was the most popular of the monk-physicians. Now close to sixty years old and with no teeth, he was intellectual but had a warm bedside manner. Now he said: 'We're all going to die, friend, but none of us knows when. That's why we must always be prepared to meet God.'

Betty Baxter spoke up, ever the probing questioner. 'What can we do about the plague?' she said. 'It is the plague, isn't it?'

'The best protection is prayer,' Joseph said. 'And, in case God has decided to take you regardless, come to church and confess your sins.'

Betty was not so easily fobbed off. 'Merthin says that in Florence people stayed in their homes to avoid contact with the sick. Is that a good idea?'

'I don't think so. Did the Florentines escape the plague?'

Everyone looked at Merthin, standing with Lolla in his arms. 'No, they didn't escape,' he said. 'But perhaps even more would have died if they had done otherwise.'

Joseph shook his head. 'If you stay at home, you can't go to church. Holiness is the best medicine.'

Caris could not remain silent. 'The plague spreads from one person to another,' she said angrily. 'If you stay away from other people, you've got a better chance of escaping infection.'

Prior Godwyn spoke up. 'So the women are the physicians now, are they?'

Caris ignored him. 'We should cancel the market,' she said. 'It would save lives.'

'Cancel the market!' he said scornfully. 'And how would we do that? Send messengers to every village?'

'Shut the city gates,' she replied. 'Block the bridge. Keep all strangers out of the town.'

'But there are already sick people in town.'

'Close all taverns. Cancel meetings of all guilds. Prohibit guests at weddings.'

Merthin said: 'In Florence they even abandoned meetings of the city council.'

Elfric spoke up. 'Then how are people to do business?'

'If you do business, you'll die,' Caris said. 'And you'll kill your wife and children, too. So choose.'

Betty Baxter said: 'I don't want to close my shop – I'd lose a lot of money. But I'll do it to save my life.' Caris's hopes lifted at this, but then Betty dashed them again. 'What do the doctors say? They know best.' Caris groaned aloud.

Prior Godwyn said: 'The plague has been sent by God to punish us for our sins. The world has become wicked. Heresy, lasciviousness and disrespect are rife. Men question authority, women flaunt their bodies, children disobey their parents. God is angry, and His rage is fearsome. Don't try to run from His justice! It will find you, no matter where you hide.'

'What should we do?'

'If you want to live, you should go to church, confess your sins, pray and lead a better life.'

Caris knew it was useless to argue, but all the same she said: 'A starving man should go to church, but he should also eat.'

Mother Cecilia said: 'Sister Caris, you need say no more.'

'But we could save so many—'

'That will do.'

'This is life and death!'

Cecilia lowered her voice. 'But no one is listening to you. Drop it.'

Caris knew Cecilia was right. No matter how long she argued, people would believe the priests, not her. She bit her lip and said no more.

Blind Carlus started a hymn, and the monks began to process back into the church. The nuns followed, and the crowd dispersed.

As they passed from the church into the cloisters, Mother Cecilia sneezed.

*

EVERY EVENING MERTHIN put Lolla to bed in the room at the Bell. He would sing to her, or recite poems, or tell her stories. This was the time when she talked to him, asking him the strangely unexpected questions of a three-year-old, some childish, some profound, some hilarious.

Tonight, while he was singing a lullaby, she burst into tears.

He asked her what the trouble was.

'Why did Dora die?' she wailed.

So that was it. Madge's daughter, Dora, had taken to Lolla. They had spent time together, playing counting games and plaiting one another's hair. 'She had the plague,' Merthin said.

'My mama had the plague,' Lolla said. She switched to the Italian she had not quite forgotten. '*La moria grande.*'

'I had it, too, but I got better.'

'So did Libia.' Libia was the wooden doll she had carried all the way from Florence.

'Did Libia have the plague?'

'Yes. She sneezed, felt hot and had spots, but a nun made her better.'

'I'm very pleased. That means she's safe. Nobody gets it twice.'

'You're safe, aren't you?'

'Yes.' That seemed like a good note on which to end. 'Go to sleep, now.'

'Goodnight,' she said.

He went to the door.

'Is Bessie safe?' she said.

'Go to sleep.'

'I love Bessie.'

'That's nice. Goodnight.' He closed the door.

Downstairs, the parlour was empty. People were nervous about going to crowded places. Despite what Godwyn said, Caris's message had gone home.

He could smell a savoury soup. Following his nose, he went into the kitchen. Bessie was stirring a pot on the fire. 'Bean soup with ham,' she said.

Merthin sat at the table with her father, Paul, a big man now in his fifties. He helped himself to bread while Paul poured him a tankard of ale. Bessie served the soup.

Bessie and Lolla were becoming fond of one another, he realized. He had employed a nanny to take care of Lolla during the day, but Bessie often watched Lolla in the evening, and Lolla preferred her.

Merthin owned a house on Leper Island, but it was a small place, especially by comparison with the *palagetto* he had become used to in Florence. He was happy to let Jimmie go on living there. Merthin was comfortable here at the Bell. The place was warm and clean, and there was plenty of hearty food and good drink. He paid his bill every Saturday, but in other respects he was treated like a member of the family. He was in no hurry to move into a place of his own.

On the other hand, he could not live here for ever. And, when he did move out, Lolla might be upset to leave Bessie behind. Too many of the people in her life had left it. She needed stability. Perhaps he should move out now, before she became too attached to Bessie.

When they had eaten, Paul retired to bed. Bessie gave Merthin another cup of ale, and they sat by the fire. 'How many people died in Florence?' she said.

'Thousands. Tens of thousands, probably. No one could keep count.'

'I wonder who's next in Kingsbridge.'

'I think about it all the time.'

'It might be me.'

'I'm afraid so.'

'I'd like to lie with a man one more time, before I die.'

Merthin smiled, but said nothing.

'I haven't been with a man since my Richard passed away, and that's more than a year.'

'You miss him.'

'How about you? How long is it since you had a woman?'

Merthin had not had sex since Silvia fell ill. Remembering her, he felt a stab of grief. He had been insufficiently grateful for her love. 'About the same,' he said.

'Your wife?'

'Yes, rest her soul.'

'It's a long time to go without loving.'

'Yes.'

'But you're not the type to go with just anybody. You want someone to love.'

'I suppose you're right.'

'I'm the same. It's wonderful to lie with a man, the best thing in the world, but only if you love one another truly. I've only ever had one man, my husband. I never went with anyone else.'

Merthin wondered if that was true. He could not be sure. Bessie seemed sincere. But it was the kind of thing a woman would say anyway.

'What about you?' she said. 'How many women?'

'Three.'

'Your wife, and before that Caris, and … who else? Oh, I remember – Griselda.'

'I'm not saying who they were.'

'Don't worry, everyone knows.'

Merthin smiled ruefully. Of course, everyone did know. Perhaps they could not be sure, but they guessed, and they usually guessed right.

'How old is Griselda's little Merthin now – seven? Eight?'

'Ten.'

'I've got fat knees,' Bessie said. She pulled up the skirt of her dress to show him. 'I've always hated my knees, but Richard used to like them.'

Merthin looked. Her knees were plump and dimpled. He could see her white thighs.

'He would kiss my knees,' she said. 'He was a sweet man.' She adjusted her dress, as if straightening it, but she lifted it, and for a moment he glimpsed the dark inviting patch of hair at her groin. 'He would kiss me all over, sometimes, especially after bathing. I used to like that. I liked everything. A man can do what he likes to a woman who loves him. Don't you agree?'

This had gone far enough. Merthin stood up. 'I think you're probably right, but this kind of talk leads only one way, so I'm going to bed before I commit a sin.'

She gave him a sad smile. 'Sleep well,' she said. 'If you get lonely, I'll be here by the fire.'

'I'll remember that.'

*

THEY PUT MOTHER CECILIA on a bedstead, not a mattress, and placed it immediately in front of the altar, the holiest place in the hospital. Nuns sang and prayed around her bed all day and all night, in shifts. There was always someone to bathe her face with cool rose water, always a cup of clear fountain water at her side. None of it made any difference. She declined as fast as the others, bleeding from her nose and her vagina, her breathing becoming more and more laboured, her thirst unquenchable.

On the fourth night after she sneezed, she sent for Caris.

Caris was heavily asleep. Her days were exhausting: the hospital was overflowing. She was deep in a dream in which all the children in Kingsbridge had the plague, and as she rushed around the hospital trying to care for them all she suddenly realized that she, too, had caught it. One of the children was tugging at her sleeve, but she was ignoring it and desperately trying to figure out how she would cope with all these patients while she was so ill – and then she realized someone was shaking her shoulder with increasing urgency, saying: 'Wake up, sister, please, the Mother Prioress needs you!'

She came awake. A novice knelt by her bed with a candle. 'How is she?' Caris asked.

'She's sinking, but she can still speak, and she wants you.'

Caris got out of bed and put on her sandals. It was a bitterly cold night. She was wearing her nun's robe, and she took the blanket from her bed and pulled it around her shoulders. Then she ran down the stone stairs.

The hospital was full of dying people. The mattresses on the floor were lined up like fish bones, so that those patients who were able to sit upright could see the altar. Families clustered around the beds. There was a smell of blood. Caris took a clean length of linen from a basket by the door and tied it over her mouth and nose.

Four nuns knelt beside Cecilia's bed, singing. Cecilia lay back with her eyes closed, and at first Caris was afraid she had arrived too late. Then the old prioress seemed to sense her presence. She turned her head and opened her eyes.

Caris sat on the edge of the bed. She dipped a rag in a bowl of rose water and wiped a smear of blood from Cecilia's upper lip.

Cecilia's breathing was tortured. In between gasps, she said: 'Has anyone survived this terrible illness?'

'Only Madge Webber.'

'The one who didn't want to live.'

'All her children died.'

'I'm going to die soon.'

'Don't say that.'

'You forget yourself. We nuns have no fear of death. All our lives we long to be united with Jesus in heaven. When death comes, we welcome it.' The long speech exhausted her. She coughed convulsively.

Caris wiped blood from her chin. 'Yes, Mother Prioress. But those who are left behind may weep.' Tears came to her eyes. She had lost Mair and Old Julie, and now she was about to lose Cecilia.

'Don't cry. That's for the others. You have to be strong.'

'I don't see why.'

'I think God has you in mind to take my place, and become prioress.'

In that case he has made a very odd choice, Caris thought. He usually picks people whose view of Him is more orthodox. But she had long ago learned that there was no point in saying these things. 'If the sisters choose me, I'll do my best.'

'I think they'll choose you.'

'I'm sure Sister Elizabeth will want to be considered.'

'Elizabeth is clever, but you're loving.'

Caris bowed her head. Cecilia was probably right. Elizabeth would be too harsh. Caris was the best person to run the nunnery, even though she was sceptical of lives spent in prayer and hymn-singing. She did believe in the school and the hospital. Heaven forbid that Elizabeth should end up running the hospital.

'There's something else.' Cecilia lowered her voice, and Caris had to lean closer. 'Something Prior Anthony told me when he was dying. He had kept it secret until the last, and now I've done the same.'

Caris was not sure she wanted to be burdened with such a secret. However, the death bed seemed to overrule such scruples.

Cecilia said: 'The old king did not die of a fall.'

Caris was shocked. It had happened more than twenty years ago, but she remembered the rumours. The killing of a king was the worst offence imaginable, a double outrage, combining murder with treason, both of them capital crimes. Even knowing about such a thing was dangerous. No wonder Anthony had kept it a secret.

Cecilia went on: 'The queen and her lover, Mortimer, wanted Edward II out of the way. The heir to the throne was a little boy. Mortimer became king in all but name. In the upshot, it didn't last as long as he might have hoped, of course – young Edward III grew up too fast.' She coughed again, more weakly.

'Mortimer was executed while I was an adolescent.'

'But even Edward didn't want anyone to know what had really happened to his father. So the secret was kept.'

Caris was awestruck. Queen Isabella was still alive, living in lavish circumstances in Norfolk, the revered mother of the king. If people found out that she had her husband's blood on her hands there would be a political earthquake. Caris felt guilty just knowing about it.

'So he was murdered?' she asked.

Cecilia made no reply. Caris looked harder. The prioress was still, her face immobile, her eyes staring upward. She was dead.

60

THE DAY AFTER CECILIA DIED, Godwyn asked Sister Elizabeth to have dinner with him.

This was a dangerous moment. Cecilia's death unbalanced the power structure. Godwyn needed the nunnery, because the monastery on its own was not viable: he had never succeeded in improving its finances. Yet most of the nuns were now angry about the money he had taken from them, and bitterly hostile to him. If they fell under the control of a prioress bent on revenge – Caris, perhaps – it could mean the end of the monastery.

He was frightened of the plague, too. What if he caught it? What if Philemon died? Such flashes of nightmare unnerved him, but he succeeded in pushing them to the back of his mind. He was determined not to be distracted from his long-term purpose by the plague.

The election of the prioress was an immediate danger. He had visions of the monastery closing down, and himself leaving Kingsbridge in disgrace, being forced to become an ordinary monk in some other place, subordinate to a prior who would discipline and humiliate him. If that happened he thought he might kill himself.

On the other hand, this was an opportunity as well as a threat. If he handled things cleverly he might get a prioress sympathetic to him who would be content to let him take the lead. And Elizabeth was his best bet.

She would make an imperious leader, one who would stand on her dignity. But he could work with her. She was pragmatic: she had proved that, the time she had warned him that Caris was planning to audit the treasury. She would be his ally.

She walked in with her head held high. She knew she had suddenly become important, and she was enjoying it, Godwyn

816

realized. He wondered anxiously if she would go along with the plan he was about to propose. She might need careful handling.

She looked around the grand dining hall. 'You built a splendid palace,' she said, reminding him that she had helped him get the money for it.

She had never been inside the place, he realized, although it had been finished a year ago. He preferred not to have females in the monks' part of the priory. Only Petranilla and Cecilia had been admitted here, until today. He said: 'Thank you. I believe it wins us respect from the noble and powerful. Already we have entertained the archbishop of Monmouth here.'

He had used the last of the nuns' florins to buy tapestries showing scenes from the lives of the prophets. She studied a picture of Daniel in the lions' den. 'This is very good,' she said.

'From Arras.'

She raised an eyebrow. 'Is that your cat under the sideboard?'

Godwyn tutted. 'I can't get rid of it,' he lied. He shooed it out of the room. Monks were not supposed to have pets, but he found the cat a soothing presence.

They sat at one end of the long banqueting table. He hated having a woman here, sitting down to dinner as if she were just as good as a man; but he hid his discomfort.

He had ordered an expensive dish, pork cooked with ginger and apples. Philemon poured wine from Gascony. Elizabeth tasted the pork and said: 'Delicious.'

Godwyn was not very interested in food, except as a means of impressing people, but Philemon tucked in greedily.

Godwyn got down to business. 'How do you plan to win this election?'

'I believe I'm a better candidate than Sister Caris,' she said.

Godwyn sensed the suppressed emotion with which she uttered the name. Clearly she was still angry that Merthin had rejected her in favour of Caris. Now she was about to enter another contest with her old rival. She would kill to win this time, he thought.

That was good.

Philemon said to her: 'Why do you think you're better?'

'I'm older than Caris,' Elizabeth said. 'I've been a nun longer, and a priory officer longer. And I was born and brought up in a deeply religious household.'

Philemon shook his head dismissively. 'None of that will make any difference.'

She raised her eyebrows, startled by his bluntness, and Godwyn hoped Philemon would not be too brutal. We need her compliant, he wanted to whisper. Don't get her back up.

Philemon went on remorselessly. 'You've only got one year of experience more than Caris has. And your father, the bishop – rest his soul – will count against you. After all, bishops aren't supposed to have children.'

She flushed. 'Priors aren't supposed to have cats.'

'We're not discussing the prior,' he said impatiently. His manner was insolent, and Godwyn winced. Godwyn was good at masking his hostility and putting on a façade of friendly charm, but Philemon had never learned that art.

However, Elizabeth took it coolly. 'So, did you ask me here to tell me I can't win?' She turned to Godwyn. 'It's not like you to cook with costly ginger just for the pleasure of it.'

'You're quite right,' said Godwyn. 'We want you to become prioress, and we're going to do everything we can to help you.'

Philemon said: 'And we're going to start by taking a realistic look at your prospects. Caris is liked by everyone – nuns, monks, merchants and nobility. The job she does is a great advantage to her. Most of the monks and nuns, and hundreds of townspeople, have come to the hospital with ailments and been helped by her. By contrast, they rarely see you. You're the treasurer, thought of as cold and calculating.'

'I appreciate your frankness,' Elizabeth said. 'Perhaps I should give up now.'

Godwyn could not tell whether she was being ironic.

'You can't win,' Philemon said. 'But she can lose.'

'Don't be enigmatic, it's tiresome,' Elizabeth snapped. 'Just tell me in plain words what you're getting at.'

I can see why she's not popular, Godwyn thought.

Philemon pretended not to notice her tone. 'Your task in the next few weeks is to destroy Caris,' he said. 'You have to transform her, in the nuns' minds, from a likeable, hard-working, compassionate sister into a monster.'

A glint of eagerness came into Elizabeth's eye. 'Is that possible?'

'With our help, yes.'

'Go on.'

'Is she still ordering nuns to wear linen masks in the hospital?'

'Yes.'

'And wash their hands?'

'Yes.'

'There is no basis for these practices in Galen or any other medical authority, and certainly none in the Bible. It seems a mere superstition.'

Elizabeth shrugged. 'Apparently the Italian doctors believe the plague spreads through the air. You catch it by looking at sick people, or touching them, or breathing their breath. I don't see how—'

'And where did the Italians get this idea?'

'Perhaps just by observing patients.'

'I have heard Merthin say that the Italian doctors are the best – except for the Arabs.'

Elizabeth nodded. 'I've heard that.'

'So this whole business of wearing masks probably comes from the Muslims.'

'Possibly.'

'In other words, it is a heathen practice.'

'I suppose so.'

Philemon sat back, as if he had proved a point.

Elizabeth did not yet get it. 'So we outmanoeuvre Caris by saying she has introduced a heathen superstition into the nunnery?'

'Not exactly,' said Philemon with a crafty smile. 'We say she is practising witchcraft.'

She saw it then. 'Of course! I had almost forgotten about that.'

'You testified against her at the trial!'

'It was a long time ago.'

'I would think you'd never forget that your enemy was once accused of such a crime,' Philemon said.

Philemon himself certainly never forgot such things, Godwyn reflected. Knowing people's weaknesses, and exploiting them shamelessly, was his speciality. Godwyn sometimes felt guilty about the sheer depth of Philemon's malice. But that malice was so useful to Godwyn that he always suppressed his misgivings. Who else could have dreamed up this way of poisoning the nuns' minds against the beloved Caris?

A novice brought apples and cheese, and Philemon poured more wine. Elizabeth said: 'All right, this makes sense. Have you thought about how, in detail, we should bring this up?'

'It's important to prepare the ground,' Philemon said. 'You should never make an accusation such as this formally until it's already believed by large numbers of people.'

Philemon was very good at this, Godwyn thought admiringly. Elizabeth said: 'And how do you suggest we achieve that?'

'Actions are better than words. Refuse to wear the mask yourself. When asked, shrug and say quietly that you have heard it is a Muslim practice, and you prefer Christian means of protection. Encourage your friends to refuse the mask, as a sign of support for you. Don't wash your hands too often, either. When you notice people following Caris's precepts, frown disapprovingly – but say nothing.'

Godwyn nodded agreement. Philemon's slyness sometimes approached the level of genius.

'Should we not even mention heresy?'

'Talk about it as much as you like, without connecting it directly to Caris. Say that you've heard of a heretic being executed in another city, or a devil worshipper who succeeded in depraving an entire nunnery, perhaps in France.'

'I wouldn't wish to say anything that was not true,' Elizabeth said stiffly.

Philemon sometimes forgot that not everyone was as unscrupulous as he. Godwyn said hastily: 'Of course not – Philemon just means that you should repeat such stories if and when you hear them, to remind the nuns of the ever-present danger.'

'Very good.' The bell rang for Nones, and Elizabeth stood up.

'I mustn't miss the service. I don't want someone to notice my absence and guess that I've been here.'

'Quite right,' said Godwyn. 'Anyway, we've agreed our plan.'

She nodded. 'No masks.'

Godwyn could see that she was nursing a doubt. He said: 'You don't imagine they're effective, do you?'

'No,' she replied. 'No, of course not. How could they be?'

'Exactly.'

'Thank you for dinner.' She went out.

That had gone well, Godwyn reflected, but he was still worried. He said anxiously to Philemon: 'Elizabeth on her own might not be able to convince people that Caris is still a witch.'

'I agree. We may need to help with the process.'

'Perhaps with a sermon?'

'Exactly.'

'I'll speak about the plague from the cathedral pulpit.'

Philemon looked thoughtful. 'It might be dangerous to attack Caris directly. That could backfire.'

Godwyn agreed. If there were open strife between himself and Caris, the townspeople would probably support her. 'I won't mention her name.'

'Just sow the seeds of doubt, and let people come to their own conclusions.'

'I'll blame heresy, devil worship and heathenish practices.'

Godwyn's mother, Petranilla, came in. She was very stooped, and walked with two canes, but her large head still jutted forward assertively on her bony shoulders. 'How did that go?' she said. She had urged Godwyn to attack Caris, and had approved Philemon's plan.

'Elizabeth will do exactly as we wish,' Godwyn said, feeling pleased. He enjoyed giving her good news.

'Good. Now I want to talk to you about something else.' She turned to Philemon. 'We won't need you.'

For a moment, Philemon looked hurt, like a child unexpectedly smacked. Brutally abrasive himself, he was easily wounded. However, he recovered quickly, and pretended to be untroubled and even a bit amused by her high-handedness. 'Of course, madam,' he said with exaggerated deference.

Godwyn said to him: 'Take charge of Nones for me, will you?'

'Very good.'

When he had gone, Petranilla sat at the big table and said: 'I know it was me who urged you to foster that young man's talents, but I have to admit that nowadays he makes my flesh crawl.'

'He's more useful than ever.'

'You can never really trust a ruthless man. If he will betray others, why should he not betray you?'

'I'll remember that,' Godwyn said, though he felt he was now so bound up with Philemon that it was hard to imagine operating without him. However, he did not want to tell his mother that. Changing the subject, he said: 'Would you like a cup of wine?'

She shook her head. 'I'm already too liable to fall over. Sit down and listen to me.'

'Very well, Mother.' He sat beside her at the table.

'I want you to leave Kingsbridge before this plague gets much worse.'

'I can't do that. But you could go—'

'I don't matter! I'm going to die soon anyway.'

The thought filled Godwyn with panic. 'Don't say that!'

'Don't be stupid. I'm sixty years old. Look at me – I can't even stand upright. It's time for me to go. But you're only forty-two – and you've got so much ahead! You could be bishop, archbishop, even cardinal.'

As always, her limitless ambition for him made Godwyn feel dizzy. Was he really capable of becoming a cardinal? Or was it just a mother's blindness? He did not really know.

'I don't want you to die of the plague before you've achieved your destiny,' she finished.

'Mother, you're not going to die.'

'Forget about me!' she said angrily.

'I can't leave town. I have to make sure the nuns don't make Caris prioress.'

'Get them to hold the election quickly. Failing that, get out anyway and leave the election in God's hands.'

He was terrified of the plague, but he feared failure too. 'I could lose everything if they elect Caris!'

Her voice softened. 'Godwyn, listen to me. I have only one child, and that's you. I can't bear to lose you.'

Her sudden change of tone shocked him into silence.

She went on: 'Please, I beg you, get out of this city and go to some place where the plague can't reach you.'

He had never known her to plead. It was unnerving. He felt scared. Just to stop her, he said: 'Let me think about it.'

'This plague,' she said. 'It's like a wolf in the forest. When you see it, you don't think – you run.'

※

GODWYN GAVE THE sermon on the Sunday before Christmas.

It was a dry day with high pale cloud roofing the cold vault of heaven. The central tower of the cathedral was covered by a bird's nest of rope-and-branch scaffolding where Elfric was demolishing it from the top down. At the market on the green, shivering traders did desultory business with a few preoccupied customers. Beyond the market, the frozen grass of the cemetery was quilted with the brown rectangles of more than a hundred fresh graves.

But the church was full. The frost that Godwyn had noticed on the inside walls during Prime had been dispersed by the warmth of thousands of bodies by the time he entered the church to perform the Christmas service. They huddled in their heavy earth-coloured coats and cloaks, looking like cattle in a pen. They had come because of the plague, he knew. The congregation of thousands of townspeople had been augmented by hundreds more from the surrounding countryside, all in search of God's protection against an illness that had already struck at least one family in every city street and rural village. Godwyn sympathized. Even he had been praying more fervently lately.

Normally only the people at the front solemnly followed the service. Those behind chatted to their friends and neighbours, and the youngsters amused themselves at the back. But today there was little noise from the nave. All heads were turned to the monks and nuns, watching with unusual attention as they performed the rituals. The crowd murmured the responses scrupulously, desperate to acquire what defensive holiness they could. Godwyn studied their faces, reading their expressions. What he saw there was dread. Like him, they were wondering fearfully who would be the next to sneeze, or suffer a nosebleed, or come out in a rash of purple-black spots.

Right at the front he could see Earl William with his wife Philippa, their two grown sons, Roland and Richard, and their much younger daughter, Odila, who was fourteen. William ruled the county in the same style as his father, Roland, with order and justice and a firm hand that was occasionally cruel. He looked worried: an outbreak of plague in his earldom was something he could not control, no matter how harsh he was. Philippa had her arm around the young girl, as if to protect her.

Next to them was Sir Ralph, lord of Tench. Ralph had never been any good at hiding his feelings, and now he looked terrified. His child-wife was carrying a tiny baby boy. Godwyn had recently christened the child Gerald, after its grandfather, who stood nearby with the grandmother, Maud.

Godwyn's eye moved along the line to Ralph's brother, Merthin. When Merthin had returned from Florence, Godwyn had hoped that Caris would renounce her vows and leave the nunnery. He thought she might be less of a nuisance as the mere wife of a citizen. But it had not happened. Merthin was holding the hand of his little Italian daughter. Next to them was Bessie from the Bell inn. Bessie's father, Paul Bell, had succumbed to the plague already.

Not far away was the family Merthin had spurned: Elfric, with his daughter, Griselda, the little boy they had named Merthin – now ten – and Harry Mason, the husband Griselda had wed after she gave up hope of the original Merthin. Next to Elfric was his second wife, Godwyn's cousin Alice. Elfric kept looking up. He had built a temporary ceiling over the crossing while he tore down the tower, and he was either admiring his work or worrying about it.

Conspicuously absent was the bishop of Shiring, Henri of Mons. The bishop normally gave the sermon on Christmas Day. However, he had not come. So many clergy had died of the plague that the bishop was frantically busy visiting parishes and searching for replacements. There was already talk of easing the requirements for priests, and ordaining under-twenty-fives and even illegitimate men.

Godwyn stepped forward to speak. He had a delicate task. He needed to whip up fear and hatred of the most popular person in Kingsbridge. And he had to do it without mentioning her name, indeed without even letting people think he was hostile to her. They must turn on her with fury but, when they did, they had to believe it was their own idea, not his.

Not every service featured a sermon. Only at major solemnities, attended by large crowds, did he address the congregation, and then he did not always preach. Often there were announcements, messages from the archbishop or the king about national events – military victories, taxes, royal births and deaths. But today was special.

'What is sickness?' he said. The church was already quiet, but the congregation became very still. He had asked the question that was on everybody's mind.

'Why does God send illnesses and plagues to torment and kill us?' He caught the eye of his mother, standing behind Elfric and Alice, and he was suddenly reminded of her forecast that she would die soon. For a moment he froze, paralysed with fear, unable to speak. The congregation shifted restlessly, waiting. Knowing he was losing their attention, he felt panicky, and that made his paralysis worse. Then the moment passed.

'Sickness is a punishment for sin,' he resumed. Over the years he had developed a preaching style. He was not a ranter, like Friar Murdo. He spoke in a more conversational manner, sounding like a reasonable man rather than a demagogue. He wondered how suitable that was for whipping up the kind of hatred he wanted them to feel. But Philemon said it made him sound more convincing.

'The plague is a special sickness, so we know God is inflicting a special punishment on us.' There was a low collective sound, between a murmur and a moan, from the crowd. This was what they wanted to hear. He was encouraged.

'We must ask ourselves what sins we have committed, to merit such punishment.' As he said this he noticed Madge

Webber, standing alone. Last time she came to church she had had a husband and four children. He thought of making the point that she had enriched herself using dyes concocted by witchcraft, but he decided against that tactic. Madge was too well liked and respected.

'I say to you that God is punishing us for heresy. There are people in the world – in this town – even in this great cathedral today – who question the authority of God's holy church and its ministers. They doubt that the sacrament turns bread into the true body of Christ; they deny the efficacy of masses for the dead; they claim that it is idolatry to pray before statues of the saints.' These were the usual heresies debated among student priests at Oxford. Few people in Kingsbridge cared about such arguments, and Godwyn saw disappointment and boredom on the faces in the crowd. He sensed he was losing them again, and he felt the panic rise. Desperately, he added: 'There are people in this city who practise witchcraft.'

That got their attention. There was a collective gasp.

'We must be vigilant against false religion,' he said. 'Remember that only God can cure sickness. Prayer, confession, communion, penance – these are the remedies sanctioned by Christianity.' He raised his voice a little. 'All else is blasphemy!'

This was not clear enough, he decided. He needed to be more specific.

'For if God sends us a punishment, and we try to escape it, are we not defying His will? We may pray to Him to forgive us, and perhaps in his wisdom he will heal our sickness. But heretical cures will only make matters worse.' The audience was rapt, and he warmed up. 'I warn you! Magic spells, appeals to the fairy folk, unchristian incantations, and especially heathen practices – all are witchcraft, all are forbidden by God's holy church.'

His real audience today was the thirty-two nuns standing behind him in the choir of the church. So far only a few had registered their opposition to Caris, and their support for Elizabeth, by refusing to wear the mask against the plague. As things stood, Caris would easily win next week's election. He needed to give the nuns the clear message that Caris's medical ideas were heretical.

'Anyone who is guilty of such practices –' he paused for effect, leaning forward and staring at the congregation – 'anyone in town –' he turned and looked behind him, at the monks and nuns in the choir. '– or even in the priory –' he turned back. 'I say, anyone guilty of such practices should be shunned.'

He paused for effect.

'And may God have mercy on their souls.'

61

PAUL BELL WAS BURIED three days before Christmas. All those who stood at his frosty graveside in the December cold were invited to the Bell to drink to his memory. His daughter, Bessie, now owned the place. She did not want to grieve alone, so she poured the tavern's best ale generously. Lennie Fiddler played sad tunes on his five-stringed instrument, and the mourners became tearful and maudlin as they got drunker.

Merthin sat in the corner with Lolla. At yesterday's market he had bought some sweet raisins from Corinth – an expensive luxury. He was sharing them with Lolla, teaching her numbers at the same time. He counted nine raisins for himself, but when he was counting out hers he missed every other number, saying: 'One, three, five, seven, nine.'

'No!' she said. 'That's not right!' She was laughing, knowing that he was only teasing.

'But I counted nine each,' he protested.

'But you've got more!'

'Well, how did that happen?'

'You didn't count them right, silly.'

'You'd better count them, then, and see if you can do better.'

Bessie sat with them. She was wearing her best dress, which was a bit tight. 'Can I have some raisins?' she said.

Lolla said: 'Yes, but don't let Daddy count them.'

'Don't worry,' Bessie said. 'I know his tricks.'

'Here you are,' Merthin said to Bessie. 'One, three, nine, thirteen – oh, thirteen is too many. I'd better take some away.' He took back three raisins. 'Twelve, eleven, ten. There, now you've got ten raisins.'

Lolla thought this was hysterically funny. 'But she's only got one!' she said.

'Did I count them wrong again?'

'Yes!' She looked at Bessie. 'We know his tricks.'

'You count them, then.'

The door opened, letting in a blast of icy air. Caris came in, wrapped in a heavy cloak. Merthin smiled: every time he saw her, he felt glad she was still alive.

Bessie looked at her warily, but spoke a welcome. 'Hello, sister,' she said. 'It's kind of you to remember my father.'

Caris said: 'I'm very sorry you have lost him. He was a good man.' She, too, was being formally polite. Merthin realized that these two women saw themselves as rivals for his affections. He did not know what he had done to deserve such devotion.

'Thank you,' Bessie said to Caris. 'Will you have a cup of ale?'

'That's very kind, but no. I need to speak to Merthin.'

Bessie looked at Lolla. 'Shall we roast some nuts on the fire?'

'Yes, please!'

Bessie took Lolla away.

'They get on well together,' Caris said.

Merthin nodded. 'Bessie has a warm heart, and no children of her own.'

Caris looked sad. 'I have no children ... but perhaps I haven't got the warm heart.'

Merthin touched her hand. 'I know better,' he said. 'You have such a warm heart you have to take care of not just one or two children but dozens of people.'

'It's kind of you to see it that way.'

'It's true, that's all. How are things at the hospital?'

'Unbearable. The place is full of people dying, and I can't do anything for them except bury them.'

Merthin felt a surge of compassion. She was always so competent, so reliable, but the strain told on her, and she was willing to show it to him, if to no one else. 'You look tired,' he said.

'I am, God knows.'

'I suppose you're worrying about the election, too.'

'I came to ask for your help with that.'

Merthin hesitated. He was torn by contradictory feelings. Part of him wanted her to achieve her ambition and become prioress.

But then would she ever be his wife? He had a shamefully selfish hope that she would lose the election and renounce her vows. All the same, he wanted to give her whatever help she asked for, just because he loved her. 'All right,' he said.

'Godwyn's sermon yesterday hurt me.'

'Will you never be rid of that old accusation of witchcraft? It's so absurd!'

'People are stupid. The sermon had a big impact on the nuns.'

'As was intended, of course.'

'No doubt of it. Few of them believed Elizabeth when she said that my linen masks were heathenish. Only her close friends discarded the mask: Cressie, Elaine, Jeannie, Rosie and Simone. But when the others heard the message from the pulpit of the cathedral, it was different. The more impressionable sisters have all now discarded the mask. A few avoid making an obvious choice by never coming into the hospital. Only a handful still wear it: me and four nuns I'm close to.'

'I was afraid of this.'

'Now that Mother Cecilia, Mair and Old Julie are dead, there are only thirty-two nuns eligible to vote. Seventeen votes are all you need to win. Elizabeth originally had five sworn supporters. The sermon has given her eleven more. With her own vote, that makes seventeen. I have only five, and even if all the waverers came over to me, I would lose.'

Merthin felt angry on her behalf. It must be hurtful to be rejected like this after all she had done for the nunnery. 'What can you do?'

'The bishop is my last hope. If he sets his face against Elizabeth, and announces that he will not ratify her election, some of her support may fall away, and I could have a chance.'

'How can you influence him?'

'I can't, but you could – or, at least, the parish guild could.'

'I suppose so...'

'They have a meeting this evening. You'll be there, I imagine.'

'Yes.'

'Think about it. Godwyn already has the town in a stranglehold. He's close to Elizabeth – her family are tenants of the priory, and Godwyn has always been careful to favour them.

If she becomes prioress, she will be as compliant as Elfric. Godwyn will have no opposition in or out of the priory. It will be the death of Kingsbridge.'

'That's true, but whether the guildsmen will agree to intercede with the bishop...'

Suddenly she looked terribly disheartened. 'Just try. If they turn you down, so be it.'

Her desperation touched him, and he wished he could be more optimistic. 'I will, of course.'

'Thank you.' She stood up. 'You must have conflicting feelings about this. Thank you for being a true friend.'

He smiled wryly. He wanted to be her husband, not her friend. But he would take what he could get.

She went out into the cold.

Merthin joined Bessie and Lolla at the fireside and sampled their roasted nuts, but he was preoccupied. Godwyn's influence was malign, but all the same his power never ceased to grow. Why was that? Perhaps because he was an ambitious man with no conscience – a potent combination.

As darkness fell he put Lolla to bed and paid a neighbour's daughter to watch her. Bessie left the barmaid, Sairy, in charge of the tavern. Wearing heavy cloaks, they walked up the main street to the guild hall for the midwinter meeting of the parish guild.

At the back of the long room there was a seasonal barrel of ale for the members. The merrymaking seemed to have a driven quality this Christmas, Merthin thought. They had been drinking hard at Paul Bell's wake, and some of those people now followed Merthin in and filled their tankards again as eagerly as if they had not tasted ale for a week. Perhaps it took their minds off the plague.

Bessie was one of four people introduced as new members. The other three were eldest sons of leading merchants who had died. Godwyn, as overlord of the townspeople, must be enjoying a rise in his income from inheritance tax, Merthin realized.

When the routine business had been dealt with, Merthin raised the subject of the election of the new prioress.

'That's none of our business,' Elfric said immediately.

'On the contrary, the result will affect commerce in this town for years to come, perhaps decades,' Merthin argued. 'The prioress is one of the richest and most powerful people in Kingsbridge, and we ought to do what we can to get one who will do nothing to fetter trade.'

'But there's nothing we can do – we have no vote.'

'We have influence. We could petition the bishop.'

'It's never been done before.'

'That's not much of an argument.'

Bill Watkin interrupted. 'Who are the candidates?'

Merthin replied: 'Sorry, I thought you'd know. Sister Caris and Sister Elizabeth. I think we should support Caris.'

'Of course you do,' said Elfric. 'And we all know why!'

There was a ripple of laughter. Everyone knew about the longstanding on-off love affair between Merthin and Caris.

Merthin smiled. 'Go on, laugh – I don't mind. Just remember that Caris grew up in the wool business and helped her father, so she understands the problems and challenges that merchants face – whereas her rival is the daughter of a bishop, and more likely to sympathize with the prior.'

Elfric was looking red in the face – partly because of the ale he had drunk, Merthin thought, but mainly through anger. 'Why do you hate me, Merthin?' he said.

Merthin was surprised. 'I thought it was the other way around.'

'You seduced my daughter, then refused to marry her. You tried to prevent my building the bridge. I thought we'd got rid of you, then you came back and humiliated me over the cracks in the bridge. You hadn't been back more than a few days before you tried to get me ousted as alderman and replaced by your friend Mark. You even hinted that the cracks in the cathedral were my fault, although it was built before I was born. I repeat, why do you hate me?'

Merthin did not know what to say. How could Elfric not know what he had done to Merthin? But Merthin did not want to have this argument in front of the parish guild – it seemed childish. 'I don't hate you, Elfric. You were a cruel master when I was an apprentice, and you're a slipshod builder, and you toady to Godwyn, but all the same I don't hate you.'

One of the new members, Joseph Blacksmith, said: 'Is this what you do at the parish guild – have stupid arguments?'

Merthin felt hard done by. It was not he who had introduced the personal note. But for him to say that would be seen as continuing a stupid argument. So he said nothing, and reflected that Elfric was ever sly.

'Joe's right,' said Bill Watkin. 'We didn't come here to listen to Elfric and Merthin squabbling.'

Merthin was troubled by Bill's willingness to put him and Elfric on the same level. Generally, the guildsmen liked him and felt mildly hostile to Elfric, since the dispute over the bridge cracks. Indeed, they would have ousted Elfric if Mark had not died. But something had changed.

Merthin said: 'Can we return to the matter in hand, which is petitioning the bishop to favour Caris as prioress?'

'I'm against it,' Elfric said. 'Prior Godwyn wants Elizabeth.'

A new voice spoke up. 'I'm with Elfric. We don't want to quarrel with the Father Prior.' It was Marcel Chandler, who had the contract to supply wax candles to the priory. Godwyn was his biggest customer. Merthin was not surprised.

However, the next speaker shocked him. It was Jeremiah Builder, who said: 'I don't think we should favour someone who has been accused of heresy.' He spat on the floor twice, left and right, and crossed himself.

Merthin was too surprised to reply. Jeremiah had always been fearfully superstitious, but Merthin would never have imagined it would lead him to betray his mentor.

It was left to Bessie to defend Caris. 'That charge was always ludicrous,' she said.

'It was never disproved, though,' said Jeremiah.

Merthin stared at him, but Jeremiah would not meet his eye. 'What's got into you, Jimmie?' Merthin said.

'I don't want to die of the plague,' Jeremiah said. 'You heard the sermon. Anyone practising heathen remedies should be shunned. We're talking about asking the bishop to make her prioress – that's not shunning her!'

There was a murmur of assent, and Merthin realized that the tide of opinion had turned. The others were not as credulous as

Jeremiah, but they shared his fear. The plague had spooked them all, undermining their rationality. Godwyn's sermon had been more effective than Merthin had imagined.

He was ready to give up – then he thought of Caris, and how weary and demoralized she had looked, and he gave it one more try. 'I've lived through this once, in Florence,' he said. 'I warn you now, priests and monks won't save anyone from the plague. You'll have handed the town to Godwyn on a plate, and all for nothing.'

Jeremiah said: 'That sounds awfully close to blasphemy.'

Merthin looked around. The others agreed with Jeremiah. They were too scared to think straight. There was nothing more he could do.

They decided to take no action on the election for prioress, and soon afterwards the meeting broke up in somewhat bad humour, the members taking burning sticks from the fire to light their way home.

Merthin decided it was too late to report to Caris – the nuns, like the monks, went to bed at nightfall and got up in the early hours of the morning. However, there was a figure wrapped in a big wool cloak waiting outside the guild hall, and to his surprise his torch revealed the troubled face of Caris. 'What happened?' she said anxiously.

'I failed,' he said. 'I'm sorry.'

In the torchlight she looked wounded. 'What did they say?'

'They won't intervene. They believed the sermon.'

'Fools.'

Together they walked down the main street. At the priory gates, Merthin said: 'Leave the nunnery, Caris. Not for my sake, but for your own. You can't work under Elizabeth. She hates you, and she'll block everything you want to do.'

'She hasn't won yet.'

'She will, though – you said so yourself. Renounce your vows, and marry me.'

'Marriage is a vow. If I break my vow to God, why would you trust me to keep my promise to you?'

He smiled. 'I'll risk it.'

'Let me think about it.'

'You've been thinking about it for months,' Merthin said with resentment. 'If you don't leave now, you never will.'

'I can't leave now. People need me more than ever.'

He began to feel angry. 'I won't keep asking for ever.'

'I know.'

'In fact, I won't ask you again, after tonight.'

She began to cry. 'I'm sorry, but I can't abandon the hospital in the midst of a plague.'

'The hospital.'

'And the people of the town.'

'But what about yourself?'

The flame of his torch made her tears glisten. 'They need me so badly.'

'They're ungrateful, all of them – nuns, monks, townspeople. I should know, by God.'

'It makes no difference.'

He nodded, accepting her decision, suppressing his selfish anger. 'If that's how you feel, you must do your duty.'

'Thank you for understanding.'

'I wish this had turned out differently.'

'So do I.'

'You'd better take this torch.'

'Thank you.'

She took the burning branch from his hand and turned away. He watched her, thinking: Is this how it ends? Is this all? She walked away with her characteristic stride, determined and confident, but her head was bowed. She passed through the gateway and disappeared.

The lights of the Bell shone cheerfully through the gaps around the shutters and the door. He went inside.

The last few customers were saying drunken farewells, and Sairy was collecting tankards and wiping tables. Merthin checked on Lolla, who was fast asleep, and paid the girl who had been watching her. He thought of going to bed, but he knew he would not sleep. He was too upset. Why had he run out of patience tonight, as opposed to any other time? He had got angry. But his anger came from fear, he realized as he calmed down. Underneath it all, he was terrified that Caris would catch the plague and die.

He sat on a bench in the parlour of the inn and took off his boots. He stayed there, staring into the fire, wondering why he could not have the one thing in life that he wanted most.

Bessie came in and hung up her cloak. Sairy left, and Bessie locked up. She sat opposite Merthin, taking the big chair that her father had always used. 'I'm sorry about what happened at the guild,' she said. 'I'm not sure who's right, but I know you're disappointed.'

'Thank you for supporting me, anyway.'

'I'll always support you.'

'Perhaps it's time for me to stop fighting Caris's battles.'

'I agree with that. But I can see that it makes you sad.'

'Sad and angry. I seem to have wasted half my life waiting for Caris.'

'Love is never wasted.'

He looked up at her, surprised. After a pause, he said: 'You're a wise person.'

'There's no one else in the house, except for Lolla,' she said. 'All the Christmas guests have left.' She got up from her chair and knelt in front of him. 'I'd like to comfort you,' she said. 'Any way I can.'

He looked at her round, friendly face and felt his body stir in response. It was such a long time since he had held the soft body of a woman in his arms. But he shook his head. 'I don't want to use you.'

She smiled. 'I'm not asking you to marry me. I'm not even asking you to love me. I've just buried my father, and you've been disappointed by Caris, and we're both in need of someone warm to hold on to.'

'To dull the pain, like a jug of wine.'

She took his hand and kissed the palm. 'Better than wine,' she said. She pressed his hand to her breast. It was big and soft, and he sighed as he caressed it. She turned her face up, and he leaned down and kissed her lips. She gave a little moan of pleasure. The kiss was delicious, like a cold drink on a hot day, and he did not want to stop.

Eventually she broke away from him, panting. She stood upright and pulled her woollen dress over her head. Her naked body looked rosy in the firelight. She was all curves: round hips, round belly, round breasts. Still seated, he put his hands on her waist and drew her to him. He kissed the warm skin of her belly, then the pink tips of her breasts. He looked up at her flushed face. 'Do you want to go upstairs?' he murmured.

'No,' she said breathlessly. 'I can't wait that long.'

62

THE ELECTION FOR PRIORESS WAS held on the day after Christmas. That morning, Caris felt so depressed she could hardly get out of bed. When the bell rang for Matins in the early hours, she was strongly tempted to put her head under the blankets and say that she did not feel well. But she could not pretend when so many were dying, so in the end she forced herself.

She shuffled around the ice-cold flagstones of the cloisters side by side with Elizabeth, the two of them at the head of the procession to the church. This protocol had been agreed because neither would yield precedence to the other while they were competing in the election. But Caris no longer cared. The result was a foregone conclusion. She stood yawning and shivering in the choir through the psalms and readings. She was angry. Later today, Elizabeth would be elected prioress. Caris resented the nuns for rejecting her, she hated Godwyn for his enmity, and she despised the town's merchants for refusing to intervene.

She felt as if her life had been a failure. She had not built the new hospital she had dreamed of, and now she never would.

She also resented Merthin, for making her an offer she could not accept. He did not understand. For him, their marriage would be an adjunct to his life as an architect. For her, marriage would have to *replace* the work to which she had dedicated herself. That was why she had vacillated for so many years. It was not that she did not want him. She longed for him with a hunger that she could hardly bear.

She mumbled the last of the responses and then, mechanically, walked out of the church at the front of the line. As they walked around the cloisters again, someone behind her sneezed. She was too dispirited even to look and see who it was.

The nuns climbed the stairs to their dormitory. When Caris

entered the room she heard heavy breathing, and realized that someone had stayed behind. Her candle revealed the novice mistress, Sister Simone – a dour middle-aged woman, normally a conscientious nun, not one to malinger. Caris bound a strip of linen around her own face then knelt by Simone's mattress. Simone was perspiring and looking scared.

Caris said: 'How do you feel?'

'Awful,' Simone said. 'I've had strange dreams.'

Caris touched her forehead. She was burning hot.

Simone said: 'Can I have something to drink?'

'In a moment.'

'It's just a cold, I expect.'

'You're certainly running a fever.'

'I haven't got the plague, though, have I? It's not that bad.'

'We'll take you to the hospital anyway,' Caris said evasively. 'Can you walk?'

Simone struggled to her feet. Caris took a blanket off the bed and wrapped it around Simone's shoulders.

As they were heading for the door, Caris heard a sneeze. This time she could see that it came from Sister Rosie, the plump matricularius. Caris looked hard at Rosie, who appeared scared.

Caris picked another nun at random. 'Sister Cressie, take Simone to the hospital while I look at Rosie.'

Cressie took Simone's arm and led her down the stairs.

Caris held her candle up to Rosie's face. She, too, was perspiring. Caris pulled down the neck of her robe. There was a rash of small purple spots over her shoulders and breasts.

'No,' Rosie said. 'No, please.'

'It may be nothing at all,' Caris lied.

'I don't want to die of the plague!' Rosie said, her voice cracking.

Caris said quietly: 'Just keep calm and come with me.' She took Rosie's arm firmly.

Rosie resisted. 'No, I'll be all right!'

'Try saying a prayer,' Caris said. 'Ave Maria, come on.'

Rosie began to pray, and a moment later Caris was able to lead her away.

The hospital was crammed with dying people and their

families, most of them awake despite the hour. There was a strong odour of sweaty bodies, vomit and blood. The place was dimly lit by tallow lamps and the candles on the altar. A handful of nuns attended to the patients, bringing water and cleaning up. Some wore the mask, others did not.

Brother Joseph was there, the oldest of the monk-physicians and the most well liked. He was giving the last rites to Rick Silvers, the head of the jewellers' guild, bending to hear the man's whispered confession, surrounded by the children and grandchildren.

Caris made a space for Rosie and persuaded her to lie down. One of the nuns brought her a cup of clear fountain water. Rosie lay still, but her eyes shifted restlessly this way and that. She knew her fate, and she was frightened. 'Brother Joseph will come and see you shortly,' Caris told her.

'You were right, Sister Caris,' said Rosie.

'What do you mean?'

'Simone and I were among the original friends of Sister Elizabeth who refused to wear the mask – and look what has happened to us.'

Caris had not thought of this. Would she be proved horribly right by the deaths of those who disagreed with her? She would rather be wrong.

She went to look at Simone. She was lying down and holding the hand of Cressie. Simone was older and calmer than Rosie, but there was fear in her eyes, and she was gripping Cressie's hand hard.

Caris glanced at Cressie. There was a dark stain above her lip. Caris reached out and wiped it with her sleeve.

Cressie, too, was among the original group who had abandoned the mask.

She looked at the mark on Caris's sleeve. 'What is it?' she said.

'Blood,' said Caris.

*

THE ELECTION TOOK PLACE in the refectory an hour before dinner time. Caris and Elizabeth were side by side behind a table at one end of the room, and the nuns sat on benches in rows.

Everything had changed. Simone, Rosie and Cressie lay in

the hospital, stricken by the plague. Here in the refectory the other two who had originally refused the mask, Elaine and Jeannie, were both showing early symptoms, Elaine sneezing and Jeannie sweating. Brother Joseph, who had been treating plague victims without a mask since the beginning, had at last succumbed. All the remaining nuns had resumed wearing the masks in the hospital. If the mask was still a sign of support for Caris, she had won.

They were tense and restless. Sister Beth, the former treasurer and now the oldest nun, read a prayer to open the meeting. Almost before she had finished, several nuns spoke at once. The voice that prevailed was that of Sister Margaret, the former cellarer. 'Caris was right, and Elizabeth was wrong!' she cried. 'Those who refused the mask are now dying.'

There was a collective rumble of agreement.

Caris said: 'I wish it were otherwise. I'd rather have Rosie and Simone and Cressie sitting here voting against me.' She meant it. She was sick of seeing people die. It made her think how trivial everything else was.

Elizabeth stood up. 'I propose we postpone the election,' she said. 'Three nuns are dead and three more are in the hospital. We should wait until the plague is over.'

That took Caris by surprise. She had thought there was nothing Elizabeth could do to avoid defeat – but she had been wrong. No one would now vote for Elizabeth, but her supporters might prefer to avoid making any choice at all.

Caris's apathy vanished. Suddenly she remembered all the reasons why she wanted to be prioress: to improve the hospital, to teach more girls to read and write, to help the town prosper. It would be a catastrophe if Elizabeth were elected instead.

Elizabeth was immediately supported by old Sister Beth. 'We shouldn't hold the election in a panic, and make a choice we might regret later when things have calmed down.' Her statement sounded rehearsed: Elizabeth had obviously planned this. But the argument was not unreasonable, Caris thought with some trepidation.

Margaret said indignantly: 'Beth, you only say that because you know Elizabeth is going to lose.'

Caris held back from speaking, for fear of prompting the same argument against herself.

Sister Naomi, who was not committed to either side, said: 'The trouble is, we have no leader. Mother Cecilia, rest her soul, never appointed a sub-prioress after Natalie died.'

'Is that so bad?' Elizabeth said.

'Yes!' Margaret said. 'We can't even make up our minds who is to go first in the procession!'

Caris decided to risk making a practical point. 'There is a long list of decisions that need to be taken, especially about inheritance of nunnery properties whose tenants have died of the plague. It would be difficult to go much longer with no prioress.'

Sister Elaine, one of the original five friends of Elizabeth, now argued against postponement. 'I hate elections,' she said. She sneezed, then went on: 'They set sister against sister and cause acrimony. I want to get this over with so that we can be united in the face of this dreadful plague.'

That raised a cheer of support.

Elizabeth glared angrily at Elaine. Elaine caught her eye and said: 'You see, I can't even make a pacific remark like that without Elizabeth looking at me as if I've betrayed her!'

Elizabeth dropped her gaze.

Margaret said: 'Come on, let's vote. Whoever is for Elizabeth, say: "Aye."'

For a moment, no one spoke. Then Beth said quietly: 'Aye.'

Caris waited for someone else to speak, but Beth was the only one.

Caris's heart beat faster. Was she about to achieve her ambition?

Margaret said: 'Who is for Caris?'

The response was instant. There was a shout of 'Aye!' It seemed to Caris that almost all the nuns voted for her.

I've done it, she thought. I'm prioress. Now we can really begin.

Margaret said: 'In that case—'

A male voice suddenly said: 'Wait!'

Several nuns gasped, and one screamed. They all looked at

the door. Philemon stood there. He must have been listening outside, Caris thought.

He said: 'Before you go any farther—'

Caris was not having this. She stood up and interrupted him. 'How dare you enter the nunnery?' she said. 'You do not have permission and you are not welcome. Leave now!'

'I'm sent by the lord prior—'

'He has no right—'

'He is the senior religious in Kingsbridge, and in the absence of a prioress or a sub-prioress he has authority over the nuns.'

'We are no longer without a prioress, Brother Philemon.' Caris advanced towards him. 'I have just been elected.'

The nuns hated Philemon, and they all cheered.

He said: 'Father Godwyn refuses to permit this election.'

'Too late. Tell him *Mother* Caris is now in charge of the nunnery – and she threw you out.'

Philemon backed away. 'You are not prioress until your election has been ratified by the bishop!'

'Out!' said Caris.

The nuns took up the chant. 'Out! Out! Out!'

Philemon was intimidated. He was not used to being defied. She took another step towards him, and he took another back. He looked amazed by what was happening, but also scared. The chanting got louder. Suddenly he turned around and scurried out.

The nuns laughed and cheered.

But Caris realized that his parting remark had been true. Her election would have to be ratified by Bishop Henri.

And Godwyn would do everything in his power to prevent that.

*

A TEAM OF volunteers from the town had cleared an acre of rough woodland on the far side of the river, and Godwyn was in the process of consecrating the new land as a cemetery. Every churchyard within the town walls was full, and the available space in the cathedral graveyard was shrinking fast.

Godwyn paced the borders of the plot in a biting cold wind,

sprinkling holy water that froze when it hit the ground, while monks and nuns marched behind him, singing a psalm. Although the service was not yet over, the gravediggers were already at work. Humps of raw earth stood in neat lines beside straight-sided pits, placed as close together as possible to save space. But an acre would not last long, and men were already at work clearing the next patch of woodland.

At moments such as this, Godwyn had to struggle to keep his composure. The plague was like an incoming tide, submerging everyone in its path, unstoppable. The monks had buried a hundred people during the week before Christmas and the numbers were still rising. Brother Joseph had died yesterday, and two more monks were now ill. Where would it end? Would everyone in the world die? Would Godwyn himself die?

He was so scared that he stopped, staring at the gold aspergillum with which he was sprinkling the holy water as if he had no idea how it had got into his hand. For a moment he was so panicked that he could not move. Then Philemon, at the head of the procession, pushed him gently from behind. Godwyn stumbled forward and resumed his march. He had to thrust these frightening thoughts from his mind.

He turned his brain to the problem of the nuns' election. Reaction to his sermon had been so favourable that he had thought Elizabeth's victory secure. The tide had turned with shocking rapidity, and the infuriating revival in Caris's popularity had taken him by surprise. Philemon's last-ditch intervention had been a desperate measure taken just too late. When he thought of it, Godwyn wanted to scream.

But it was not yet over. Caris had mocked Philemon, but the truth was that she could not consider her position safe until she had Bishop Henri's approval.

Unfortunately, Godwyn had not yet had a chance to ingratiate himself with Henri. The new bishop, who spoke no English, had visited Kingsbridge only once. Because he was so new, Philemon had not yet learned whether he had any fatal weaknesses. But he was a man, and a priest, so he ought to side with Godwyn against Caris.

Godwyn had written to Henri saying that Caris had bewitched

the nuns into thinking she could save them from the plague. He had detailed Caris's history: the accusation of heresy, the trial and sentence eight years ago, the rescue by Cecilia. He hoped Henri would arrive in Kingsbridge with his mind firmly prejudiced against Caris.

But when would Henri come? It was extraordinary for the bishop to miss the Christmas service in the cathedral. A letter from the efficient, unimaginative Archdeacon Lloyd had explained that Henri was busy appointing clergy to replace those who had died of the plague. Lloyd might be against Godwyn: he was Earl William's man, owing his position to William's late brother Richard; and the father of William and Richard, Earl Roland, had hated Godwyn. But Lloyd would not make the decision, Henri would. It was hard to know what might happen. Godwyn felt he had lost control. His career was threatened by Caris and his life was threatened by a remorseless plague.

A light snowfall began as the ceremony of consecration came to an end. Just beyond the cleared plot, seven funeral processions were at a standstill, waiting for the cemetery to be ready. At Godwyn's signal, they moved forward. The first body was in a coffin, but the rest were in shrouds on biers. In the best of times coffins were a luxury for the prosperous, but now that timber had become expensive and coffin-makers were overworked it was only the very rich who could afford to be buried in a wooden casket.

At the head of the first procession was Merthin, with snowflakes caught in his copper-red hair and beard. He was carrying his little girl. The wealthy deceased in the coffin must be Bessie Bell, Godwyn deduced. Bessie had died without relatives and left the tavern to Merthin. Money sticks to that man like wet leaves, Godwyn thought sourly. Merthin already had Leper Island and the fortune he had made in Florence. Now he owned the busiest tavern in Kingsbridge.

Godwyn knew about Bessie's will because the priory was entitled to an inheritance tax and had taken a fat percentage of the value of the place. Merthin had paid the money in gold florins without hesitation.

The one good consequence of the plague was that the priory suddenly had plenty of cash.

Godwyn conducted one burial service for all seven bodies. This was now the norm: one funeral in the morning and one in the afternoon, regardless of the number of dead. There were not enough priests in Kingsbridge to bury each person individually.

That thought renewed Godwyn's feeling of dread. He stumbled over the words of the service, seeing himself in one of the graves; then he managed to take hold of himself and continue.

At last the service was over, and he led the procession of monks and nuns back to the cathedral. They entered the church and fell out of formation in the nave. The monks returned to their normal duties. A novice nun approached Godwyn nervously and said: 'Father Prior, would you kindly come to the hospital?'

Godwyn did not like to receive bossy messages via novices. 'What for?' he snapped.

'I'm sorry, father, I don't know – I was just told to ask you.'

'I'll come as soon as I can,' he said irritably. He did not have anything urgent to do, but just to make the point he delayed in the cathedral, speaking to Brother Eli about the monks' robes.

A few minutes later he crossed the cloisters and entered the hospital.

Nuns were crowded around a bedstead that had been set up in front of the altar. They must have an important patient, he thought. He wondered who it was. One of the attendant nuns turned to him. She wore a linen mask over her nose and mouth, but he recognized the gold-flecked green eyes that he and all his family shared: it was Caris. Although he could see so little of her face, he read an odd expression in her look. He expected dislike and contempt, but instead he saw compassion.

He moved closer to the bed with a feeling of trepidation. When the other nuns saw him they moved aside deferentially. A moment later, he saw the patient.

It was his mother.

Petranilla's large head lay on a white pillow. She was sweating, and there was a steady trickle of blood from her nose. A nun was in the act of wiping it away, but it reappeared. Another nun offered the patient a cup of water. There was a rash of purple spots on the wrinkled skin of Petranilla's throat.

Godwyn cried out as if he had been struck. He stared in horror. His mother gazed at him with suffering eyes. There was no room for doubt: she had fallen victim to the plague. 'No!' he shouted. 'No! No!' He felt an unbearable pain in his chest, as if he had been stabbed.

He heard Philemon, beside him, say in a frightened voice: 'Try to stay calm, Father Prior,' but he could not. He opened his mouth to scream, but no sound came. He suddenly felt detached from his body, with no control over his movements. Then a black mist arose from the floor and engulfed him, gradually rising up his body until it covered his nose and mouth, so that he could not breathe, and then his eyes, so that he was blind; and at last he lost consciousness.

*

GODWYN WAS IN BED for five days. He ate nothing and drank only when Philemon put a cup to his lips. He could not think straight. He could not move, for it seemed he had no way of deciding what to do. He sobbed, and slept, then woke up and sobbed again. He was vaguely aware of a monk feeling his forehead, taking a urine sample, diagnosing brain fever and bleeding him.

Then, on the last day of December, a scared-looking Philemon brought him the news that his mother was dead.

Godwyn got up. He had himself shaved, put on a new robe and went to the hospital.

The nuns had washed and dressed the body. Petranilla's hair was brushed and she wore a dress of costly Italian wool. Seeing her like that, with the pallor of death on her face and her eyes forever closed, Godwyn felt a resurgence of the panic that had overwhelmed him; but this time he was able to fight it down. 'Take her body to the cathedral,' he ordered. Normally the honour of lying in state in the cathedral was reserved for monks, nuns, senior clergymen and the aristocracy; but Godwyn knew that no one would dare to contradict him.

When she had been moved into the church and placed in front of the altar, he knelt beside her and prayed. Prayer helped him calm his terror, and gradually he figured out what to do. When at last he stood up, he ordered Philemon to call a meeting in the chapter house immediately.

He felt shaky, but he knew he had to pull himself together. He had always been blessed with the power of persuasion. Now he had to use it to the utmost.

When the monks had gathered, he read to them from the Book of Genesis. 'And it came to pass after these things that God did tempt Abraham, and said unto him, Abraham: and he said, Behold, here I am. And he said, Take now thy son, thine only son Isaac, whom thou lovest, and get thee into the land of Moriah; and offer him there for a burnt offering upon one of the mountains which I will tell thee of. And Abraham rose up early in the morning, and saddled his ass, and took two of his young men with him, and Isaac his son, and clave the wood for the burnt offering, and rose up, and went unto the place of which God had told him.'

Godwyn looked up from the book. The monks were watching him intently. They all knew the story of Abraham and Isaac. They were more interested in him, Godwyn. They were alert, wary, wondering what would come next.

'What does the story of Abraham and Isaac teach us?' he asked rhetorically. 'God tells Abraham to kill his son – not just his eldest son, but his only son, born when he was a hundred years old. Did Abraham protest? Did he plead for mercy? Did he argue with God? Did he point out that to kill Isaac would be murder, infanticide, a terrible sin?' Godwyn let the question hang for a moment, then looked down at the book and read: 'And Abraham rose up early in the morning, and saddled his ass...'

He looked up again. 'God may tempt us, too. He may order us to perform acts which seem wrong. Perhaps he will tell us to do something that appears to be a sin. When that happens, we must remember Abraham.'

Godwyn was speaking in what he knew was his most persuasive preaching style, rhythmic yet conversational. He could tell that he had their rapt attention by the quiet in the octagonal chapter house: no one fidgeted, whispered or shuffled.

'We must not question,' he said. 'We must not argue. When

God leads us, we must follow – no matter how foolish, sinful or cruel his wishes may seem to our feeble human minds. We are weak and humble. Our understanding is fallible. It is not given to us to make decisions or choices. Our duty is simple. It is to obey.'

Then he told them what they had to do.

*

THE BISHOP ARRIVED after dark. It was almost midnight when the entourage entered the precinct: they had ridden by torchlight. Most of the priory had been in bed for hours, but there was a group of nuns at work in the hospital, and one of them came to wake Caris. 'The bishop is here,' she said.

'Why does he want me?' Caris asked sleepily.

'I don't know, Mother Prior.'

Of course she didn't. Caris pulled herself out of bed and put on a cloak.

She paused in the cloisters. She took a long drink of water, and for a few moments she breathed deeply of the cold night air, clearing her head of sleep. She wanted to make a good impression on the bishop, so that there would be no trouble about his ratifying her election as prioress.

Archdeacon Lloyd was in the hospital, looking tired, the pointed tip of his long nose red with cold. 'Come and greet your bishop,' he said crossly, as if she ought to have been up and waiting.

She followed him out. A servant stood outside the door with a burning torch. They walked across the green to where the bishop sat on his horse.

He was a small man in a big hat, and he looked thoroughly fed up.

Caris said in Norman French: 'Welcome to Kingsbridge Priory, my lord bishop.'

Henri said peevishly: 'Who are you?'

Caris had seen him before but had never spoken to him. 'I am Sister Caris, prioress-elect.'

'The witch.'

Her heart sank. Godwyn must have already tried to poison

Henri's mind against her. She felt indignant. 'No, my lord bishop, there are no witches here,' she said with more acerbity than was prudent. 'Just a group of ordinary nuns doing their best for a town that has been stricken by the plague.'

He ignored that. 'Where is Prior Godwyn?'

'In his palace.'

'No, he's not!'

Archdeacon Lloyd explained: 'We've been there. The building is empty.'

'Really?'

'Yes,' the archdeacon said irritably. 'Really.'

At that moment, Caris spotted Godwyn's cat, with the distinctive white tip to its tail. The novices called it Archbishop. It walked across the west front of the cathedral and looked into the spaces between the pillars, as if searching for its master.

Caris was taken aback. 'How strange ... perhaps Godwyn decided to sleep in the dormitory with the other monks.'

'And why would he do that? I hope there's no impropriety going on.'

Caris shook her head dismissively. The bishop suspected unchastity, but Godwyn was not prone to that particular sin. 'He reacted badly when his mother caught the plague. He had some kind of fit and collapsed. She died today.'

'If he's been unwell I should have thought he was all the more likely to sleep in his own bed.'

Anything might have happened. Godwyn was slightly unhinged by Petranilla's illness. Caris said: 'Would the lord bishop like to speak to one of his deputies?'

Henri answered crossly: 'If I could find one, yes!'

'Perhaps if I take Archdeacon Lloyd to the dormitory...'

'As soon as you like!'

Lloyd got a torch from a servant, and Caris led him quickly through the cathedral into the cloisters. The place was silent, as monasteries generally were at this time of night. They reached the foot of the staircase that led up to the dormitory, and Caris stopped. 'You'd better go up alone,' she said. 'A nun should not see monks in bed.'

'Of course.' Lloyd went up the stairs with his torch, leaving her in darkness. She waited, curious. She heard him shout: 'Hello?' There was a strange silence. Then, after a few moments, he called down to her in an odd voice: 'Sister?'

'Yes?'

'You can come up.'

Mystified, she climbed the stairs and entered the dormitory. She stood beside Lloyd and peered into the room by the unsteady light of the burning torch. The monks' straw mattresses lay neatly in their places along either side of the room – but not one of them was occupied. 'There's no one here,' Caris said.

'Not a soul,' Lloyd agreed. 'What on earth has happened?'

'I don't know, but I can guess,' said Caris.

'Then enlighten me, please.'

'Isn't it obvious?' she said. 'They've run away.'

Part Six

January 1349 to January 1351

Part Six

63

WHEN GODWYN LEFT, he took with him all the valuables from the monks' treasury and all the charters. This included the nuns' charters, which they had never succeeded in retrieving from his locked chest. He also took the sacred relics, including the bones of St Adolphus in their priceless reliquary.

Caris discovered this on the morning afterwards, the first day of January, the Feast of the Circumcision of Christ. She went with Bishop Henri and Sister Elizabeth to the treasury off the south transept. Henri's attitude to her was stiffly formal, which was worrying; but he was a peevish character, so perhaps he was like that with everyone.

The flayed skin of Gilbert Hereford was still nailed to the door, slowly turning hard and yellow, and giving off a faint but distinct whiff of rottenness.

But the door was not locked.

They went in. Caris had not been inside this room since Prior Godwyn stole the nuns' one hundred and fifty pounds to build his palace. After that they had built their own treasury.

It was immediately obvious what had happened. The flagstones that disguised the vaults in the floor had been lifted and not put back, and the lid of the ironbound chest stood open. Vaults and chest were empty.

Caris felt that her contempt for Godwyn was vindicated. A trained physician, a priest and the leader of the monks, he had fled just at the moment when the people needed him most. Now, surely, everyone would realize his true nature.

Archdeacon Lloyd was outraged. 'He took everything!'

Caris said to Henri: 'And this is the man who wanted you to annul my election.'

Bishop Henri grunted noncommittally.

Elizabeth was desperate to find an excuse for Godwyn's behaviour. 'I'm sure the lord prior took the valuables with him for safekeeping.'

That stung the bishop into a response. 'Rubbish,' he said crisply. 'If your servant empties your purse and disappears without warning, he's not keeping your money safe, he's stealing it.'

Elizabeth tried a different tack. 'I believe this was Philemon's idea.'

'The sub-prior?' Henri looked scornful. 'Godwyn is in charge, not Philemon. Godwyn is responsible.'

Elizabeth shut up.

Godwyn must have recovered from the death of his mother, Caris thought, at least temporarily. It was quite an achievement to persuade every single one of the monks to follow him. She wondered where they had gone.

Bishop Henri was thinking the same thing. 'Where did the wretched cowards go?'

Caris remembered Merthin trying to persuade her to leave. 'To Wales, or Ireland', he had said. 'A remote village where they don't see a stranger from one year to the next.' She said to the bishop: 'They will be hiding out in some isolated place where no one ever goes.'

'Find out exactly where,' he said.

Caris realized that all opposition to her election had vanished with Godwyn. She felt triumphant, and made an effort not to look too pleased. 'I'll make some inquiries in the town,' she said. 'Somebody must have seen them leave.'

'Good,' said the bishop. 'However, I don't think they're coming back soon, so in the meantime you're going to have to manage as best you can with no men. Continue the services as normally as possible with the nuns. Get a parish priest to come into the cathedral for mass, if you can find one still alive. You cannot perform the mass, but you can hear confessions – there has been a special dispensation from the archbishop, because so many clergymen have died.'

Caris was not going to let him slide past the question of her election. 'Are you confirming me as prioress?' she said.

'Of course,' he said irritably.

'In that case, before I accept the honour—'

'You have no decision to make, Mother Prioress,' he said indignantly. 'It is your duty to obey me.'

She wanted the post desperately, but she resolved to pretend otherwise. She was going to drive a hard bargain. 'We live in strange times, don't we?' she said. 'You've given nuns authority to hear confessions. You've shortened the training for priests, but you still can't ordain them fast enough to keep up with deaths from the plague, I hear.'

'Is it your intention to exploit the difficulties the church is facing for some purpose of your own?'

'No, but there is something you need to do to make it possible for me to carry out your instructions.'

Henri sighed. Clearly he did not like being spoken to in this way. But, as Caris had suspected, he needed her more than she needed him. 'Very well, what is it?'

'I want you to convene an ecclesiastical court and reopen my trial for witchcraft.'

'For heaven's sake, why?'

'To declare me innocent, of course. Until that happens, it could be difficult for me to exercise authority. Anyone who disagrees with my decisions can all too easily undermine me by pointing out that I stand condemned.'

The tidy secretarial mind of Archdeacon Lloyd liked that idea. 'It would be good to have the issue disposed of once and for all, my lord bishop.'

'Very well, then,' said Henri.

'Thank you.' She felt a surge of delight and relief, and bowed her head for fear that her triumph would show in her face. 'I will do my best to bring honour to the position of prioress of Kingsbridge.'

'Lose no time in inquiring after Godwyn. I'd like some kind of answer before I leave town.'

'The alderman of the parish guild is a crony of Godwyn's. He'll know where they've gone if anyone does. I'll go and see him.'

'Right away, please.'

Caris left. Bishop Henri was charmless, but he seemed

competent, and she thought she could work with him. Perhaps he would be the kind òf leader who made decisions based on the merits of the case, instead of siding with whomever he perceived as an ally. That would be a pleasant change.

Passing the Bell, she was tempted to go in and tell Merthin her good news. However, she thought she had better find Elfric first.

In the street in front of the Holly Bush she saw Duncan Dyer lying on the ground. His wife, Winnie, was sitting on the bench outside the tavern, crying. Caris thought the man must have been hurt, but Winnie said: 'He's drunk.'

Caris was shocked. 'It isn't even dinner time yet!'

'His uncle, Peter Dyer, caught the plague and passed away. His wife and children died too, so Duncan inherited all his money, and he just spends it on wine. I don't know what to do.'

'Let's get him home,' Caris said. 'I'll help you lift him.' They each took an arm and got Duncan to his feet. Holding him upright, they half dragged him down the street to his house. They put him on the floor and covered him with a blanket. Winnie said: 'He's like this every day. He's says it's not worth working, because we're all going to die of the plague. What shall I do?'

Caris thought for a moment. 'Bury the money in the garden, now, while he's sleeping. When he wakes up, tell him he lost it all gambling with a chapman who left town.'

'I might do that,' Winnie said.

Caris crossed the street to Elfric's house and went inside. Her sister, Alice, was sitting in the kitchen sewing stockings. They had not been close since Alice married Elfric, and what little was left of their relationship had been destroyed by Elfric's testifying against Caris in the heresy trial. Forced to choose between sister and husband, Alice had been loyal to Elfric. Caris understood that, but it meant her sister had become like a stranger to her.

When Alice saw her she stood up and dropped her sewing. 'What are you doing here?' she said.

'The monks have all disappeared,' Caris told her. 'They must have left in the night.'

'So that was what it was!' Alice said.

'Did you see them?'

'No, but I heard a whole crowd of men and horses. They weren't loud – in fact, now that I think of it, they must have been making an effort to be quiet – but you can't keep horses silent, and men make a noise just walking along the street. They woke me, but I didn't get up to see – it was too cold. Is that why you've entered my house for the first time in ten years?'

'You didn't know they were going to run off?'

'Is that what they've done, run off? Because of the plague?'

'I assume so.'

'Surely not. What's the use of physicians who flee from sickness?' Alice was troubled by this behaviour on the part of her husband's patron. 'I can't understand it.'

'I was wondering if Elfric knew anything about it.'

'If he does, he hasn't told me.'

'Where will I find him?'

'St Peter's. Rick Silvers left some money to the church, and the priest decided to pave the floor of the nave.'

'I'll go and ask him.' Caris wondered if she should make an attempt to be courteous. Alice had no children of her own, but she had a stepdaughter. 'How is Griselda?' Caris said.

'Very well and happy,' Alice said with a touch of defiance, as if she thought Caris might prefer to hear otherwise.

'And your grandson?' Caris could not bring herself to use the child's name, which was Merthin.

'Lovely. And another grandchild on the way.'

'I'm pleased for her.'

'Yes. It's just as well she didn't marry your Merthin, the way things have turned out.'

Caris refused to be drawn. 'I'll go and find Elfric.'

St Peter's church was at the western end of the town. As Caris was threading her way through the winding streets, she came upon two men fighting. They were shouting curses at one another and punching wildly. Two women, presumably their wives, were screeching abuse, while a small crowd of neighbours looked on. The door of the nearest house had been broken down. On the ground nearby was a cage made of twigs and rushes containing three live chickens.

Caris went up to the men and stepped between them. 'Stop it this instant,' she said. 'I command you in the name of God.'

They did not take much persuading. They had probably expended their wrath with the first few blows and might even be grateful for an excuse to stop. They stepped back and dropped their arms.

'What's this about?' Caris demanded.

They both started speaking at once, and so did their wives.

'One at a time!' Caris said. She pointed at the larger of the two men, a dark-haired fellow whose good looks were spoiled by a swelling around his eye. 'You're Joe Blacksmith, aren't you? Explain.'

'I caught Toby Peterson stealing Jack Marrow's chickens. He broke down the door.'

Toby was a smaller man with a gamecock bravado. He spoke through bleeding lips. 'Jack Marrow owed me five shillings – I'm entitled to those chickens!'

Joe said: 'Jack and all his family died of the plague two weeks ago. I've been feeding his chickens ever since. They'd be dead but for me. If anyone should take them, it ought to be me.'

Caris said: 'Well, you're both entitled to them, aren't you? Toby because of the debt, and Joe because he kept them alive at his own expense.'

They looked taken aback at the thought that they might both be right.

Caris said: 'Joseph, take one of the chickens out of the cage.'

Toby said: 'Wait a moment—'

'Trust me, Toby,' Caris said. 'You know I wouldn't treat you unjustly, don't you?'

'Well, I can't deny that...'

Joe opened the cage and picked up a scrawny brown-feathered chicken by its feet. The bird's head turned jerkily from side to side, as if it was bewildered to see the world upside down.

Caris said: 'Now give it to Toby's wife.'

'What?'

'Would I cheat you, Joseph?'

Joe reluctantly handed the chicken to Toby's wife, a pretty, sulky type. 'There you are, then, Jane.'

Jane took it with alacrity.

Caris said to her: 'Now thank Joe.'

Jane looked petulant, but she said: 'I thank you, Joseph Blacksmith.'

Caris said: 'Now, Toby, give a chicken to Ellie Blacksmith.'

Toby obeyed, with a sheepish grin. Joe's wife, Ellie, who was heavily pregnant, smiled and said: 'Thank you, Toby Peterson.'

They were returning to normal, and beginning to realize the foolishness of what they had been doing.

Jane said: 'What about the third chicken?'

'I'm coming to that,' Caris said. She looked at the watching crowd and pointed at a sensible-looking girl of eleven or twelve. 'What's your name?'

'I'm Jesca, Mother Prior – the daughter of John Constable.'

'Take the other chicken to St Peter's church and give it to Father Michael. Say that Toby and Joe will be coming to ask forgiveness for the sin of covetousness.'

'Yes, sister.' Jesca picked up the third chicken and went off.

Joe's wife, Ellie, said: 'You may remember, Mother Caris, that you helped my husband's baby sister, Minnie, when she burned her arm in the forge.'

'Oh, yes, of course,' Caris said. It had been a nasty burn, she remembered. 'She must be ten now.'

'That's right.'

'Is she well?'

'Right as rain, thanks to you, and God's grace.'

'I'm glad to hear it.'

'Would you care to step into my house for a cup of ale, Mother Prioress?'

'I'd love to, but I'm in a hurry.' She turned to the men. 'God bless you, and no more fighting.'

Joe said: 'Thank you.'

Caris walked away.

Toby called after her: 'Thank you, mother.'

She waved without looking back.

She noticed several more houses that appeared to have been broken into, presumably to be looted after the occupants died. Someone ought to do something about it, she thought. But with

Elfric as alderman, and a disappearing prior, there was no one to take the initiative.

She reached St Peter's and found Elfric with a team of paviours and their apprentices in the nave. Stone slabs were stacked all around, and the men were preparing the ground, pouring sand and smoothing it with sticks. Elfric was checking that the surface was level, using a complicated piece of apparatus with a wooden frame and a dangling cord with a lead point at its end. The apparatus looked like a miniature gallows, and it reminded Caris that Elfric had tried to get her hanged for witchcraft ten years ago. She was surprised to find that she felt no hatred for him. He was too mean-spirited and small-minded for that. When she looked at him, she felt nothing but contempt.

She waited for him to finish, then said abruptly: 'Did you know that Godwyn and all the monks have run away?'

She intended to surprise him, and she knew by his look of astonishment that he had no foreknowledge. 'Why would they...? When...? Oh, last night?'

'You didn't see them.'

'I heard something.'

'I saw them,' said a paviour. He leaned on his spade to talk. 'I was coming out of the Holly Bush. It was dark, but they had torches. The prior was riding, and the rest walking, but they had a sight of baggage: wine casks and wheels of cheese and I don't know what.'

Caris already knew that Godwyn had emptied the monks' food stores. He had not tried to take any of the nuns' supplies, which were kept separately. 'What time was that?'

'Not late – nine or ten o'clock.'

'Did you speak to them?'

'Just to say goodnight.'

'Any clue as to where they might have been headed?'

The paviour shook his head. 'They went over the bridge, but I didn't see which road they took at Gallows Cross.'

Caris turned to Elfric. 'Think back over the past few days. Did Godwyn say anything to you that, with hindsight, might relate to this? Mention any place names – Monmouth, York, Antwerp, Bremen?'

'No. I had no clue.' Elfric looked grumpy about not having been forewarned, which made Caris think he was telling the truth.

If Elfric was surprised, it was unlikely that anyone else had known what Godwyn planned. Godwyn was fleeing from the plague, and clearly he did not want anyone to follow him, bringing the disease with them. 'Leave early, go far and stay long,' Merthin had said. Godwyn could be anywhere.

'If you hear from him, or any of the monks, please tell me,' Caris said.

Elfric said nothing.

Caris raised her voice to make sure the workmen heard. 'Godwyn has stolen all the precious ornaments,' she said. There was a rumble of indignation. The men felt proprietorial about the cathedral ornaments – indeed, the wealthier craftsmen had probably helped pay for some of them. 'The bishop wants them back. Anyone who helps Godwyn, even just by concealing his whereabouts, is guilty of sacrilege.'

Elfric looked bewildered. He had based his life on ingratiating himself with Godwyn. Now his patron had gone. He said: 'There may be some perfectly innocent explanation...'

'If there is, why did Godwyn tell no one? Or even leave behind a letter?'

Elfric could not think of anything to say.

Caris realized she was going to have to speak to all the leading merchants, and the sooner the better. 'I'd like you to call a meeting,' she said to Elfric. Then she thought of a more persuasive way of putting it. 'The bishop wants the parish guild to meet today, after dinner. Please inform the members.'

'Very well,' said Elfric.

They would all be there, Caris knew, agog with curiosity.

She left St Peter's and headed back towards the priory. As she passed the White Horse tavern, she saw something that made her pause. A young girl was talking to an older man, and there was something about the interaction that raised Caris's hackles. She always felt the vulnerability of girls very sharply – perhaps because she remembered herself as an adolescent, perhaps because of the daughter she had never had. She drew back into a doorway and studied them.

The man was poorly dressed except for a costly fur hat. Caris did not know him, but she guessed he was a labourer and had inherited the hat. So many people had died that there was a glut of finery, and you saw odd sights like this all the time. The girl was about fourteen years old, and pretty, with an adolescent figure. She was trying to be coquettish, Caris saw with disapproval; though she was not very convincing. The man took money from his purse, and they seemed to be arguing. Then the man fondled the girl's small breast.

Caris had seen enough. She marched up to the pair. The man took one look at her nun's habit and walked quickly away. The girl looked both guilty and resentful. Caris said: 'What are you doing – trying to sell your body?'

'No, mother.'

'Tell the truth! Why did you let him feel your breast?'

'I don't know what to do! I haven't got anything to eat, and now you've chased him away.' She burst into tears.

Caris could believe the girl was hungry. She looked thin and pale. 'Come with me,' Caris said. 'I'll give you something to eat.'

She took the girl's arm and steered her towards the priory. 'What's your name?' she asked.

'Ismay.'

'How old are you?'

'Thirteen.'

They reached the priory and Caris took Ismay to the kitchen, where the nuns' dinner was being prepared under the supervision of a novice called Oonagh. The kitchener, Josephine, had fallen to the plague. 'Give this child some bread and butter,' Caris said to Oonagh.

She sat and watched the girl eat. Ismay obviously had not had food for days. She ate half of a four-pound loaf before slowing down.

Caris poured her a cup of cider. 'Why were you starving?' she asked.

'All my family died of the plague.'

'What was your father?'

'A tailor, and I can sew very neatly, but no one is buying

864

clothes – they can get anything they want from the homes of dead people.'

'So that's why you were trying to prostitute yourself.'

She looked down. 'I'm sorry, Mother Prioress. I was so hungry.'

'Was that the first time that you tried?'

She shook her head and would not look at Caris.

Tears of rage welled up in Caris's eyes. What kind of man would have sexual congress with a starving thirteen-year-old? What kind of God would drive a girl to such desperation? 'Would you like to live here, with the nuns, and work in the kitchen?' she said. 'You would have plenty to eat.'

Ismay looked up with eagerness. 'Oh, yes, mother, I'd like that.'

'Then you shall. You can begin by helping to prepare the nuns' dinner. Oonagh, here's a new kitchen hand.'

'Thank you, Mother Caris, I need all the help I can get.'

Caris left the kitchen and went thoughtfully into the cathedral for the service of Sext. The plague was not just a physical sickness, she was beginning to realize. Ismay had escaped the disease, but her soul had been in peril.

Bishop Henri took the service, leaving Caris free to think. At the parish guild meeting she needed to talk about more than just the flight of the monks, she decided. It was time to get the town organized to deal with the effects of the plague. But how?

She mulled over the problems through dinner. For all sorts of reasons, this was a good time to make big decisions. With the bishop here to back up her authority, she might be able to push through measures that could otherwise meet with opposition.

This was also a good moment to get what she wanted from the bishop. That was a fertile thought...

After dinner she went to see the bishop in the prior's house, where he was staying. He was at table with Archdeacon Lloyd. They had been fed by the nuns' kitchen and were drinking wine while a priory servant cleared the table. 'I hope you enjoyed your dinner, my lord bishop,' she said formally.

He was a little less peevish than usual. 'It was fine, thank you, Mother Caris – a very tasty pike. Any news of the runaway prior?'

'He seems to have been careful to leave no clue as to his destination.'

'Disappointing.'

'As I walked through the town, making inquiries, I saw several incidents that disturbed me: a thirteen-year-old girl prostituting herself; two normally law-abiding citizens fighting over a dead man's property; a man dead drunk at midday.'

'These are the effects of the plague. It's the same everywhere.'

'I believe we must act to counter those effects.'

He raised his eyebrows. It seemed he had not thought of taking such action. 'How?'

'The prior is overlord of Kingsbridge. He is the one to take the initiative.'

'But he has vanished.'

'As bishop, you are technically our abbot. I believe you must stay here in Kingsbridge permanently, and take charge of the town.'

This was in fact the last thing she wanted. Fortunately, there was little chance of the bishop agreeing: he had far too much to do elsewhere. She was just trying to back him into a corner.

He hesitated, and for a moment she worried that she might have misjudged him, and he might accept her suggestion. Then he said: 'Out of the question. Every town in the diocese has the same problems. Shiring is worse. I have to try to hold together the fabric of Christianity here while my priests are dying. I have no time to worry about drunks and prostitutes.'

'Well, somebody must act as prior of Kingsbridge. The town needs a moral leader.'

Archdeacon Lloyd put in: 'My lord bishop, there is also the question of who is to receive monies owed to the priory, maintain the cathedral and other buildings, manage the lands and the serfs...'

Henri said: 'Well, you will have to do all that, Mother Caris.'

She pretended to consider the suggestion as if she had not already thought of it. 'I could handle all the less important tasks – managing the monks' money and their lands – but I could not do what you can do, my lord bishop. I could not perform the holy sacraments.'

'We've already discussed that,' he said impatiently. 'I'm creating new priests as fast as I can. But you can do everything else.'

'It almost seems as if you're asking me to be acting prior of Kingsbridge.'

'That's exactly what I want.'

Caris was careful not to show her elation. It seemed too good to be true. She was prior for all purposes except those she did not care about. Were there any hidden snags she had not thought of?

Archdeacon Lloyd said: 'You'd better let me write her a letter to that effect, in case she needs to enforce her authority.'

Caris said: 'If you want the town to abide by your wishes, you may need to impress upon them that this is your personal decision. A meeting of the parish guild is about to begin. If you're willing, bishop, I'd like you to attend it and make an announcement.'

'All right, let us go.'

They left Godwyn's palace and walked up the main street to the guild hall. The members were all waiting to hear what had happened to the monks. Caris began by telling them what she knew. Several people had seen or heard the exodus yesterday after dark, although no one had realized or even suspected that every single one of the monks was leaving.

She asked them to be alert for talk among travellers about a large group of monks on the road with a lot of baggage.

'But we have to accept the likelihood that the monks will not return soon. And in connection with that, the lord bishop has an announcement.' She wanted the words to come from him, not her.

Henri cleared his throat and said: 'I have confirmed the election of Caris as prioress, and I have appointed her acting prior. You will all please treat her as my representative and your overlord in all matters, excepting only those reserved to ordained priests.'

Caris watched the faces. Elfric was furious. Merthin smiled faintly, guessing that she had manoeuvred herself into this position, pleased for her and for the town, the rueful twist to his mouth showing that he knew this would keep her out of his arms. Everyone else seemed glad. They knew and trusted her, and she had won even more loyalty by staying while Godwyn fled.

She would make the most of it. 'Three matters I want to take care of urgently on my first day as acting prior,' she said. 'First, drunkenness. Today I saw Duncan Dyer unconscious in the street before dinner time. I believe this contributes to an atmosphere of debauchery in the town, which is the last thing we need during this dreadful crisis.'

There were loud sounds of approval. The parish guild was dominated by the older and more conservative of the town merchants. If they ever got drunk in the morning, they did it at home where no one could see.

Caris went on: 'I want to give John Constable an extra deputy and instruct him to arrest anyone found drunk in daylight. He can put them in the jail until they sober up.'

Even Elfric was nodding.

'Second is the question of what happens to the property of people who die without heirs. This morning I found Joseph Blacksmith and Toby Peterson fighting in the street over three chickens belonging to Jack Marrow.'

There was laughter at the idea of grown men fighting over such trifles.

Caris had thought out her solution to that problem. 'In principle, such property reverts to the lord of the manor, which for Kingsbridge residents means the priory. However, I don't want the monastery buildings filled up with old clothes, so I propose to waive the rule for anyone whose possessions are worth less than two pounds. Instead, the two nearest neighbours should lock up the house, to make sure nothing is taken; then the property should be inventoried by the parish priest, who will also hear the claims of any creditors. Where there is no priest they can come to me. When any debts have been paid, the deceased's personal possessions – clothing, furniture, food and drink – will be divided up among the neighbours, and any cash given to the parish church.'

There was widespread approval for this, too, most people nodding and murmuring agreement.

'Finally, I found a thirteen-year-old orphan girl trying to sell her body outside the White Horse. Her name is Ismay, and she did it because she had nothing to eat.' Caris looked around the room with a challenging stare. 'Can anyone tell me how such a thing could possibly happen in a Christian town? All her family are dead – but did they have no friends or neighbours? Who allows a child to starve?'

Edward Butcher said in a low voice: 'Ismay Taylor is a rather badly behaved child.'

Caris was not accepting excuses. 'She's thirteen!'

'I'm just saying that she might have been offered help and spurned it.'

'Since when did we allow children to make such decisions for themselves? If a child is orphaned, it is the duty of every one of us to take care of her. What does your religion mean, if not that?'

They all looked shamefaced.

'In future, whenever a child is orphaned, I want the two nearest neighbours to bring the child to me. Those who cannot be placed with a friendly family will move into the priory. The girls can live with the nuns, and we will turn the monks' dormitory into a bedroom for boys. They can all have lessons in the morning and do suitable work in the afternoon.'

There was general approval for that, too.

Elfric spoke up. 'Have you finished, Mother Caris?'

'I think so, unless anyone wants to discuss the details of what I have suggested.'

No one spoke up, and the members began to move in their seats as if the meeting was over.

Then Elfric said: 'Some of the men here may remember that they elected *me* as alderman of the guild.'

His voice was full of resentment. Everyone fidgeted impatiently.

'We have now seen the prior of Kingsbridge accused of theft and condemned without trial,' he went on.

That went down badly. There was a rumble of dissent. No one thought Godwyn innocent.

Elfric ignored the mood of the room. 'And we have sat here like slaves and let a woman dictate the laws of the city to us. By whose authority are drunks to be imprisoned? Hers. Who is the ultimate judge of inheritance? She is. Who will dispose of the city's orphans? She will. What have you come to? Are you not men?'

Betty Baxter said: 'No.'

The men laughed.

Caris decided not to intervene. It was unnecessary. She glanced at the bishop, wondering if he would assert himself against Elfric, and saw that he was sitting back, mouth clamped shut: plainly he, too, had realized that Elfric was fighting a losing battle.

Elfric raised his voice. 'I say we reject a female prior, even acting prior, and we deny the right of the prioress to come to the parish guild and issue commandments!'

Several muttered mutinously. Two or three stood up, as if about to walk out in disgust. Someone called out: 'Forget it, Elfric.'

He persisted. 'And this is a woman who was convicted of witchcraft and sentenced to death!'

All the men were standing, now. One walked out of the door.

'Come back!' Elfric shouted. 'I haven't closed the meeting!'

No one took any notice.

Caris joined the group at the door. She made way for the bishop and the archdeacon. She was the last to leave. She turned back at the exit and looked at Elfric. He sat alone at the head of the room.

She went out.

64

IT WAS TWELVE YEARS SINCE Godwyn and Philemon had visited the cell of St-John-in-the-Forest. Godwyn remembered being impressed by the neatness of the fields, the trimmed hedges, the cleared ditches and the apple trees in straight lines in the orchard. It was the same today. Evidently Saul Whitehead had not changed, either.

Godwyn and his caravan crossed a chequerboard of frozen fields towards the clustered buildings of the monastery. As they came closer, Godwyn saw that there had been some developments. Twelve years ago the little stone church with its cloister and dormitory had been surrounded by a scatter of small wooden structures: kitchen, stables, dairy, bakery. Now the flimsy timber outbuildings had gone, and the stone-built complex attached to the church had grown correspondingly. 'The compound is more secure than it used to be,' Godwyn remarked.

'Because of the increase in outlawry by soldiers coming home from the French wars, I'd guess,' Philemon said.

Godwyn frowned. 'I don't recall being asked for my permission for the building programme.'

'You were not.'

'Hmm.' Unfortunately, he could hardly complain. Someone might ask how it was possible for Saul to have carried out such a programme without Godwyn's knowledge, unless Godwyn had neglected his duty of supervision.

Besides, it suited his purpose now for the place to be easily closed to intruders.

The two-day journey had somewhat calmed him. The death of his mother had thrown him into a frenzy of fear. Every hour he remained in Kingsbridge, he had felt he was sure to die. He had got just enough grip on his emotions to address the meeting in the chapter house and organize the exodus. Despite his eloquence, a few of the monks had had misgivings about fleeing. Fortunately, they were all sworn to obedience, and the habit of doing as they were told had prevailed. Nevertheless, he had not begun to feel safe until his group had crossed the double bridge, torches blazing, and headed off into the night.

He still felt close to the edge. Every now and again he would be mulling something over and would decide to ask Petranilla what she thought, then he would realize he could not ask her advice ever again, and panic would rise like bile in his throat.

He was fleeing from the plague – but he should have done it three months ago, when Mark Webber died. Was he too late? He fought down terror. He would not feel safe until he was locked away from the world.

He wrenched his thoughts back to the present. There was no one in the fields at this time of year, but in a yard of beaten earth in front of the monastery he saw a handful of monks working: one shoeing a horse, another mending a plough, and a small group turning the lever of a cider press.

They all stopped what they were doing and stared, astonished, at the crowd of visitors approaching them: twenty monks, half a dozen novices, four carts and ten pack horses. Godwyn had left nobody behind but the priory servants.

One of those at the cider press detached himself from the group and came forward. Godwyn recognized him as Saul Whitehead. They had met on Saul's annual visits to Kingsbridge, but now for the first time Godwyn noticed touches of grey in Saul's distinctive ash-blond hair.

Twenty years ago they had been students together at Oxford. Saul had been the star pupil, quick to learn and agile in argument. He had also been the most devoutly religious of them all. He might have become prior of Kingsbridge if he had been less spiritual, and had thought strategically about his career instead of leaving such matters to God. As it was, when Prior Anthony had died and the election was held, Godwyn had easily outmanoeuvred Saul.

All the same, Saul was not weak. He had a streak of stubborn righteousness that Godwyn feared. Would he go along obediently with Godwyn's plan today, or would he make trouble? Once again Godwyn fought down panic and struggled to remain cool.

He studied Saul's face carefully. The prior of St John was surprised to see him, and clearly displeased. His expression was carefully composed into a look of polite welcome, but he was not smiling.

During the election campaign, Godwyn had made everyone believe that he himself did not want the job, but he had eliminated every other reasonable candidate including Saul. Did Saul suspect how he had been hoodwinked?

'Good day to you, Father Prior,' Saul said as he approached. 'This is an unexpected blessing.'

So he was not going to be openly hostile. No doubt he would think that such behaviour conflicted with his vow of obedience. Godwyn was relieved. He said: 'God bless you, my son. It is too long since I have visited my children at St John.'

Saul looked at the monks, the horses and the carts loaded with supplies. 'This appears to be more than a simple visit.' He did not offer to help Godwyn down from his horse. It was as if he wanted an explanation before he would invite them in – which was ridiculous: he had no right to turn away his superior.

All the same, Godwyn found himself explaining. 'Have you heard about the plague?'

'Rumours,' Saul said. 'There are few visitors to bring us news.'

That was good. The lack of visitors was what drew Godwyn here. 'The disease has killed hundreds in Kingsbridge. I feared it might wipe out the priory. That's why I've brought the monks here. It may be the only way to ensure our survival.'

'You are welcome here, of course, whatever the reason for your visit.'

'It goes without saying,' Godwyn said stiffly. He felt angry that he had been nudged into justifying himself.

Saul looked thoughtful. 'I'm not sure where everyone's going to sleep...'

'I shall decide that,' Godwyn said, reasserting his authority. 'You can show me around while your kitchen is preparing our supper.' He got down from his horse unaided and walked into the monastery.

Saul was obliged to follow.

The whole place had a bare, scrubbed look that expressed how serious Saul was about the monkish vow of poverty. But today Godwyn was more interested in how readily the place could be closed to outsiders. Fortunately, Saul's belief in order and control had led him to design buildings with few entrances. There were only three ways into the priory: through the kitchen, the stable or the church. Each entrance had a stout door that could be firmly barred.

The dormitory was small, normally accommodating nine or ten monks, and there was no separate bedroom for the prior. The only way to fit twenty extra monks in was to let them sleep in the church.

Godwyn thought of taking over the dormitory for himself, but there was nowhere in the room to hide the cathedral treasures, and he wanted to keep them close. Fortunately, the little church had a small side chapel that could be closed off, and Godwyn took that for his own room. The rest of the Kingsbridge monks spread straw on the stamped-earth floor of the nave and made the best of it.

The food and wine went to the kitchen and the cellar, but Philemon brought the ornaments into Godwyn's chapel-bedroom. Philemon had been chatting to the St John monks. 'Saul has his own way of running things,' he reported. 'He demands rigid obedience to God and the Rule of St Benedict, but they say he doesn't set himself up on a pedestal. He sleeps in the dorm, eats the same food as the others, and in general takes no privileges. Needless to say, they like him for that. But there's one monk who is constantly being punished – Brother Jonquil.'

'I remember him.' Jonquil had always been in trouble while a novice at Kingsbridge – for lateness, slovenliness, laziness and greed. He was without self-control, and had probably been drawn to the monastic life as a way of getting someone else to enforce the restraint he could not impose on himself. 'I doubt that he will be much help to us.'

'He will break ranks, given half a chance,' Philemon said. 'But he doesn't carry any authority. No one will follow him.'

'And they have no complaints about Saul? Doesn't he sleep

late, or dodge unpleasant chores, or take the best wine for himself?'

'Apparently not.'

'Hmm.' Saul was as upright as ever. Godwyn was disappointed, but not very surprised.

During Evensong, Godwyn noted how solemn and disciplined the St John men were. Over the years, he had always sent problem monks here: the mutinous, the mentally ill, those inclined to question the church's teachings and take an interest in heretical ideas. Saul had never complained, never sent anyone back. It seemed he was able to turn such people into model monks.

After the service, Godwyn sent most of the Kingsbridge men to the refectory for supper, keeping only Philemon and two strong young monks behind. When they had the church to themselves, he told Philemon to guard the door that gave entrance from the cloisters, then ordered the youngsters to move the carved wooden altar and dig a hole beneath where it normally stood.

When the hole was deep enough, Godwyn brought the cathedral ornaments from his chapel, ready to be buried beneath the altar. But before he could complete the job Saul came to the door.

Godwyn heard Philemon say: 'The lord prior wishes to be alone.'

Next came Saul's voice. 'Then he may tell me so himself.'

'He has asked me to say so.'

Saul's voice rose. 'I will not be shut out of my own church – least of all by you!'

'Will you offer violence to me, the sub-prior of Kingsbridge?'

'I will pick you up and throw you in the fountain, if you continue to stand in my way.'

Godwyn intervened. He would have preferred to keep Saul in ignorance, but it was not to be. 'Let him in, Philemon,' he called.

Philemon stepped aside and Saul marched in. He saw the baggage and, without asking permission, opened the neck of a sack and looked inside. 'My soul!' he exclaimed, drawing out a silver-gilt altar cruet. 'What's all this?'

Godwyn was tempted to tell him not to interrogate his

superiors. Saul might have accepted such a reproof: he believed in humility, at least in principle. But Godwyn did not want to let suspicion ferment in Saul's mind, so he said: 'I've brought the cathedral treasures with me.'

Saul made a face of distaste. 'I realize that such gewgaws are thought appropriate in a great cathedral, but they will seem out of place at a humble cell in the forest.'

'You won't have to look at them. I'm going to hide them. There's no harm in your knowing where, though I intended to spare you the burden of that knowledge.'

Saul looked suspicious. 'Why bring them at all?'

'For safekeeping.'

Saul was not so easily reassured. 'I'm surprised the bishop was willing to let them be taken away.'

The bishop had not been asked, of course, but Godwyn did not say that. 'At the moment, things are so bad in Kingsbridge that we're not sure the ornaments are safe even at the priory.'

'Safer than here, though, surely? We are surrounded by outlaws, you know. Thank God you didn't meet them on the road.'

'God is watching over us.'

'And over His jewellery, I hope.'

Saul's attitude amounted almost to insubordination, but Godwyn did not reprimand him, fearing that an overreaction would suggest guilt. However, he noted that Saul's humility had its limits. Perhaps after all Saul did know that he had been hoodwinked twelve years ago.

Now Godwyn said: 'Please ask all the monks to stay in the refectory after supper. I will address them as soon as I have finished here.'

Saul accepted this dismissal and went out. Godwyn buried the ornaments, the priory charters, the relics of the saint, and almost all the money. The monks replaced the soil in the hole, tamped it down and put the altar back in its place. There was some loose earth left over, which they took outside and scattered.

Then they went to the refectory. The little room was crowded now, with the addition of the Kingsbridge men. A monk stood at the lectern, reading a passage from Mark's gospel, but he fell silent when Godwyn walked in.

Godwyn motioned the reader to a seat and took his place. 'This is a holy retreat,' he began. 'God has sent this terrible plague to punish us for our sins. We have come here to purge those sins far away from the corrupting influence of the city.'

Godwyn had not intended to open a discussion, but Saul sang out: 'What sins in particular, Father Godwyn?'

Godwyn improvised. 'Men have challenged the authority of God's holy church; women have become lascivious; monks have failed to separate themselves completely from female society; nuns have turned to heresy and witchcraft.'

'And how long will it take to purge these sins?'

'We will know we have triumphed when the plague dies away.'

Another St John monk spoke up, and Godwyn recognized Jonquil, a large, uncoordinated man with a wild look in his eyes. 'How will you purge yourself?'

Godwyn was surprised that the monks here felt so free to question their superiors. 'By prayer, meditation and fasting.'

'The fasting is a good idea,' said Jonquil. 'We haven't got much food to spare.'

There was a little laughter at that.

Godwyn was worried that he might lose control of his audience. He banged the lectern for quiet. 'From now on, anyone who comes here from the outside world is a danger to us,' he said. 'I want all doors to the precinct barred from the inside day and night. No monk is to go outside without my personal permission, which will be granted only in emergency. All callers are to be turned away. We are going to lock ourselves in until this terrible plague is over.'

Jonquil said: 'But what if—'

Godwyn interrupted him. 'I haven't asked for comments, brother.' He glared around the room, staring them all into silence. 'You are monks, and it is your duty to obey,' he said. 'And now, let us pray.'

*

THE CRISIS CAME the very next day.

Godwyn sensed that his orders had been accepted by Saul

and the other monks in a provisional way. Everyone was taken by surprise, and on the spur of the moment they could think of no great objections; and so, in default of a strong reason for rebellion, they instinctively obeyed their superior. But he knew the time would come when they would have to make a real decision. However, he did not expect it so soon.

They were singing the office of Prime. It was freezing cold in the little church. Godwyn was stiff and aching after an uncomfortable night. He missed his palace with its fireplaces and soft beds. The grey light of a winter dawn was beginning to appear in the windows when there was a banging on the heavy west door of the church.

Godwyn tensed. He wished he had been given an extra day or two to consolidate his position.

He signalled that the monks should ignore the knocking and continue with the service. The knocking was then augmented by shouting. Saul stood up to go to the door, but Godwyn made sit-down signs with his hands and, after a hesitation, Saul obeyed. Godwyn was determined to sit tight. If the monks did nothing, the intruders must go away.

However, Godwyn began to realize that persuading people to do nothing was extraordinarily difficult.

The monks were too distracted to concentrate on the psalm. They were all whispering to one another and looking back over their shoulders towards the west end. The singing became ragged and uncoordinated and eventually petered out until only Godwyn's voice was left.

He felt irate. If they had followed his lead, they could have ignored the disturbance. Angered by their weakness, he at last left his place and walked down the short nave to the door, which was barred. 'What is it?' he shouted.

'Let us in!' came the muffled reply.

'You can't come in,' Godwyn shouted back. 'Go away.'

Saul appeared at his side. 'Are you turning them away from the church?' he said in a horrified tone.

'I told you,' Godwyn replied. 'No visitors.'

The banging resumed. 'Let us in!'

Saul shouted: 'Who are you?'

There was a pause, then the voice said: 'We are men of the forest.'

Philemon spoke up. 'Outlaws,' he said.

Saul said indignantly: 'Sinners like us, and God's children too.'

'That's no reason to let them murder us.'

'Perhaps we should find out whether that's what they intend.' Saul went to the window on the right of the door. The church was a low building, and the window ledges were just below eye level. None of them was glazed: they were closed against the cold by shutters of translucent linen. Saul opened the shutter and stood on tiptoe to look out. 'Why have you come here?' he called.

Godwyn heard the reply. 'One of our number is sick.'

Godwyn said to Saul: 'I will speak to them.'

Saul stared at him.

'Come away from the window,' Godwyn said.

Reluctantly, Saul obeyed.

Godwyn shouted: 'We cannot let you in. Go away.'

Saul looked at him with incredulity. 'Are you going to turn away a sick man?' he said. 'We are monks and physicians!'

'If the man has the plague, there is nothing we can do for him. By admitting him, we will kill ourselves.'

'That is in God's hands, surely.'

'God does not permit us to commit suicide.'

'You don't know what is wrong with the man. He may have a broken arm.'

Godwyn opened the corresponding window on the left of the door and looked out. He saw a group of six rough-looking characters standing around a stretcher that they had put down in front of the church door. Their clothes were costly but dirty, as if they were sleeping rough in their Sunday best. This was typical of outlaws, who stole fine clothes from travellers and made them shabby very quickly. The men were heavily armed, some with good-quality swords, daggers and longbows, which suggested they might be demobilized soldiers.

On the stretcher lay a man who was perspiring heavily – even though it was a frosty January morning – and bleeding from his nose. Suddenly, without wishing it, Godwyn saw in his imagination that scene in the hospital when his mother lay dying, and the trickle of blood on her upper lip kept returning, no matter how often the nun wiped it away. The thought that he might die like that made him so distracted that he wanted to throw himself from the roof of Kingsbridge Cathedral. How much better it would be to die in one brief instant of overwhelming pain than over three, four or five days of mad delirium and agonizing thirst. 'That man has the plague!' Godwyn exclaimed, and he heard in his own voice a note of hysteria.

One of the outlaws stepped forward. 'I know you,' he said. 'You're the prior of Kingsbridge.'

Godwyn tried to pull himself together. He looked with fear and anger at the man who was evidently the leader. He carried himself with the arrogant assurance of a nobleman, and he had once been handsome, though his looks had been marred by years of living rough. Godwyn said: 'And who are you, that comes banging on a church door while the monks are singing psalms to God?'

'Some call me Tam Hiding,' the outlaw replied.

There was a gasp from the monks: Tam Hiding was a legend. Brother Jonquil shouted: 'They will kill us all!'

Saul rounded on Jonquil. 'Be silent,' he said. 'All of us will die when God wills it, and not before.'

'Yes, father.'

Saul returned to the window and said: 'You stole our chickens last year.'

'I'm sorry, father,' said Tam. 'We were starving.'

'Yet now you come to me for help?'

'Because you preach that God forgives.'

Godwyn said to Saul: 'Let *me* deal with this!'

Saul's internal struggle was evident on his face, which looked alternately ashamed and mutinous; but at last he bowed his head.

Godwyn said to Tam: 'God forgives those who truly repent.'

'Well, this man's name is Win Forester, and he truly repents all his many sins. He would like to come into the church to pray for healing or, failing that, to die in a holy place.'

One of the other outlaws sneezed.

Saul came away from his window and stood facing Godwyn, hands on hips. 'We cannot turn him away!'

Godwyn tried to make himself calm. 'You heard that sneeze –

don't you understand what it means?' He turned to the rest of the monks, to make sure they heard what he said next. 'They've *all* got the plague!'

They gave a collective murmur of fear. Godwyn wanted them frightened. That way they would support him if Saul decided to defy him.

Saul said: 'We must help them, even if they have got the plague. Our lives are not our own, to be protected like gold hidden under the earth. We have given ourselves to God, to use as he wishes, and he will end our lives when it suits his holy purpose.'

'To let those outlaws in would be suicide. They'll kill us all!'

'We are men of God. For us, death is the happy reunion with Christ. What do we have to fear, Father Prior?'

Godwyn realized that he was sounding frightened, whereas Saul was speaking reasonably. He forced himself to appear calm and philosophical. 'It is a sin to seek our own death.'

'But if death comes to us in the course of our holy duty, we embrace it gladly.'

Godwyn realized he could debate all day with Saul and get nowhere. This was not the way to impose his authority. He closed his shutter. 'Shut your window, Brother Saul, and come here to me,' he said. He looked at Saul, waiting.

After a hesitation, Saul did as he was told.

Godwyn said: 'What are your three vows, brother?'

There was a pause. Saul knew what was happening here. Godwyn was refusing to engage with him as an equal. At first, Saul looked as if he might refuse to answer, but his training took over, and he said: 'Poverty, chastity, obedience.'

'And who must you obey?'

'God, and the Rule of St Benedict, and my prior.'

'And your prior stands before you now. Do you acknowledge me?'

'Yes.'

'You may say: "Yes, Father Prior."'

'Yes, Father Prior.'

'Now I will tell you what you must do, and you will obey.' Godwyn looked around. 'All of you – return to your places.'

There was a moment of frozen silence. No one moved and no one spoke. It could go either way, Godwyn thought: compliance or mutiny, order or anarchy, victory or defeat. He held his breath.

At last, Saul moved. He bowed his head and turned away. He walked up the short aisle and resumed his position in front of the altar.

All the others did the same.

There were a few more shouts from outside, but they sounded like parting shots. Perhaps the outlaws had realized they could not force a physician to treat their sick comrade.

Godwyn returned to the altar and turned to face the monks. 'We will finish the interrupted psalm,' he said, and he began singing.

> Glory be to the Father
> And to the Son
> And to the Holy Ghost

The singing was still ragged. The monks were far too excited to adopt the proper attitude. All the same, they were back in their places and following their routine. Godwyn had prevailed.

> As it was in the beginning
> Is now
> And ever shall be
> World without end
> Amen.

'Amen,' Godwyn repeated.

One of the monks sneezed.

65

SOON AFTER GODWYN FLED, Elfric died of the plague.

Caris was sorry for Alice, his widow; but aside from that she could hardly help rejoicing that he was gone. He had bullied the weak and toadied to the strong, and the lies he had told at her trial almost got her hanged. The world was a better place without him. Even his building business would be better off run by his son-in-law, Harold Mason.

The parish guild elected Merthin as alderman in Elfric's place. Merthin said it was like being made captain of a sinking ship.

As the deaths went on and on, and people buried their relatives, neighbours, friends, customers and employees, the constant horror seemed to brutalize many of them, until no violence or cruelty seemed shocking. People who thought they were about to die lost all restraint and followed their impulses regardless of the consequences.

Together, Merthin and Caris struggled to preserve something like normal life in Kingsbridge. The orphanage was the most successful part of Caris's programme. The children were grateful for the security of the nunnery, after the ordeal of losing their parents to the plague. Taking care of them, and teaching them to read and sing hymns, brought out long-suppressed maternal instincts in some of the nuns. There was plenty of food with fewer people competing for the winter stores. And Kingsbridge Priory was full of the sound of children.

In the town things were more difficult. There continued to be violent quarrels over the property of the dead. People just walked into empty houses and picked up whatever took their fancy. Children who had inherited money, or a warehouse full of cloth or corn, were sometimes adopted by unscrupulous neighbours greedy to get their hands on the legacy. The prospect of something for nothing brought out the worst in people, Caris thought despairingly.

Caris and Merthin were only partly successful against the decline in public behaviour. Caris was disappointed with the results of John Constable's crackdown on drunkenness. The large numbers of new widows and widowers seemed frantic to find partners, and it was not unusual to see middle-aged people in a passionate embrace in a tavern or even a doorway. Caris had no great objection to this sort of thing in itself, but she found that the combination of drunkenness and public licentiousness often led to fighting. However, Merthin and the parish guild were unable to stop it.

Just at the moment when the townspeople needed their spines stiffened, the flight of the monks had the opposite effect. It demoralized everyone. God's representatives had left: the Almighty had abandoned the town. Some said that the relics of the saint had always brought good fortune, and now that the bones had gone their luck had run out. The lack of precious crucifixes and candlesticks at the Sunday services was a weekly reminder that Kingsbridge was considered doomed. So why not get drunk and fornicate in the street?

Out of a population of about seven thousand, Kingsbridge had lost at least a thousand by mid-January. Other towns were similar. Despite the masks Caris had invented, the death toll was higher among the nuns, no doubt because they were continually in contact with plague victims. There had been thirty-five nuns, and now there were twenty. But they heard of places where almost every monk or nun had died, leaving a handful, or sometimes just one, to carry on the work; so they counted themselves fortunate. Meanwhile, Caris had shortened the period of novitiate and intensified the training so that she would have more help in the hospital.

Merthin hired the barman from the Holly Bush and put him in charge of the Bell. He also took on a sensible seventeen-year-old girl called Martina to nursemaid Lolla.

Then the plague seemed to die down. Having buried a hundred people a week in the run-up to Christmas, Caris found that the number dropped to fifty in January, then twenty in February. She allowed herself to hope that the nightmare might be coming to an end.

One of the unlucky people to fall ill during this period was a dark-haired man in his thirties who might once have been good-looking. He was a visitor to the town. 'I thought I had a cold yesterday,' he said when he came through the door. 'But now I've got this nosebleed that won't stop.' He was holding a bloody rag to his nostrils.

'I'll find you somewhere to lie down,' she said through her linen mask.

'It's the plague, isn't it?' he said, and she was surprised to hear calm resignation in his voice in place of the usual panic. 'Can you do anything to cure it?'

'We can make you comfortable, and we can pray for you.'

'That won't do any good. Even you don't believe in it, I can tell.'

She was shocked by how easily he had read her heart. 'You don't know what you're saying,' she protested weakly. 'I'm a nun, I must believe it.'

'You can tell me the truth. How soon will I die?'

She looked hard at him. He was smiling at her, a charming smile that she guessed had melted a few female hearts. 'Why aren't you frightened?' she said. 'Everyone else is.'

'I don't believe what I'm told by priests.' He looked at her shrewdly. 'And I have a suspicion that you don't either.'

She was not about to have this discussion with a stranger, no matter how charming. 'Almost everyone who falls ill with the plague dies within three to five days,' she said bluntly. 'A few survive, no one knows why.'

He took it well. 'As I thought.'

'You can lie down here.'

He gave her the bad-boy grin again. 'Will it do me any good?'

'If you don't lie down soon, you'll fall down.'

'All right.' He lay on the palliasse she indicated.

She gave him a blanket. 'What's your name?'

'Tam.'

She studied his face. Despite his charm, she sensed a streak of cruelty. He might seduce women, she thought, but if that failed he would rape them. His skin was weathered by outdoor living, and he had the red nose of a drinker. His clothes were costly but dirty. 'I know who you are,' she said. 'Aren't you afraid you'll be punished for your sins?'

'If I believed that, I wouldn't have committed them. Are *you* afraid you'll burn in hell?'

It was a question she normally sidestepped, but she felt that this dying outlaw deserved a true answer. 'I believe that what I do becomes part of me,' she said. 'When I'm brave and strong, and care for children and the sick and the poor, I become a better person. And when I'm cruel, or cowardly, or tell lies, or get drunk, I turn into someone less worthy, and I can't respect myself. That's the divine retribution I believe in.'

He looked at her thoughtfully. 'I wish I'd met you twenty years ago.'

She made a deprecatory noise. 'I would have been twelve.'

He raised an eyebrow suggestively.

That was enough, she decided. He was beginning to flirt – and she was beginning to enjoy it. She turned away.

'You're a brave woman to do this work,' he said. 'It will probably kill you.'

'I know,' she said, turning to face him again. 'But this is my destiny. I can't run away from people who need me.'

'Your prior doesn't seem to think that way.'

'He's vanished.'

'People can't vanish.'

'I mean, no one knows where Prior Godwyn and the monks have gone.'

'I do,' said Tam.

*

THE WEATHER AT the end of February was sunny and mild. Caris left Kingsbridge on a dun pony, heading for St-John-in-the-Forest. Merthin went with her, riding a black cob. Normally, eyebrows would have been raised by a nun going on a journey accompanied only by a man, but these were strange times.

The danger from outlaws had receded. Many had fallen victim to the plague, Tam Hiding had told her himself before he died.

Also, the sudden drop in population had brought about a countrywide surplus of food, wine and clothing – all the things outlaws normally stole. Those outlaws who survived the plague could walk into ghost towns and abandoned villages and take whatever they wanted.

Caris had at first felt frustrated to learn that Godwyn was no farther than two days' journey from Kingsbridge. She had imagined him gone to a place so distant that he would never return. However, she was glad of the chance to retrieve the priory's money and valuables and, in particular, the nunnery's charters, so vital whenever there was a dispute about property or rights.

When and if she was able to confront Godwyn, she would demand the return of the priory's property, in the name of the bishop. She had a letter from Henri to back her up. If Godwyn still refused, that would prove beyond doubt that he was stealing it rather than keeping it safe. The bishop could then take legal action to get it back – or simply arrive at the cell with a force of men-at-arms.

Although disappointed that Godwyn was not permanently out of her life, Caris relished the prospect of confronting him with his cowardice and dishonesty.

As she rode away from the town she recalled that her last long journey had been to France, with Mair – a real adventure in every way. She felt bereft when she thought of Mair. Of all those who had died of the plague, she missed Mair the most: her beautiful face, her kind heart, her love.

But it was a joy to have Merthin to herself for two whole days. Following the road through the forest, side by side on their horses, they talked continuously, about anything that sprang to mind, just as they had when they were adolescents.

Merthin was as full of bright ideas as ever. Despite the plague, he was building shops and taverns on Leper Island, and he told her he planned to demolish the tavern he had inherited from Bessie Bell and rebuild it twice as big.

Caris guessed that he and Bessie had been lovers – why else would she have left her property to him? But Caris had only herself to blame. She was the one Merthin really wanted, and

Bessie had been second best. Both women had known that. All the same, Caris felt jealous and angry when she thought of Merthin in bed with that plump barmaid.

They stopped at noon and rested by a stream. They ate bread, cheese and apples, the food that all but the wealthiest travellers carried. They gave the horses some grain: grazing was not enough for a mount that had to carry a man or woman all day. When they had eaten, they lay in the sun for a few minutes, but the ground was too cold and damp for sleep, and they soon roused themselves and moved on.

They quickly slipped back into the affectionate intimacy of their youth. Merthin had always been able to make her laugh, and she needed cheering up, with people dying every day in the hospital. She soon forgot to be angry about Bessie.

They were taking a route that had been followed by Kingsbridge monks for hundreds of years, and they stopped for the night at the usual half-way point, the Red Cow tavern in the small town of Lordsborough. They had roast beef and strong ale for supper.

By this time, Caris was aching for him. The last ten years seemed to have vanished from memory, and she longed to take him in her arms and make love to him the way they used to. But it was not to be. The Red Cow had two bedrooms, one for men and one for women – which was no doubt why it had always been the choice of the monks. Caris and Merthin parted company on the landing, and Caris lay awake, listening to the snores of a knight's wife and the wheezing of a spice-seller, touching herself and wishing the hand between her thighs was Merthin's.

She woke up tired and dispirited, and ate her breakfast porridge mechanically. But Merthin was so happy to be with her that her mood soon lifted. By the time they rode away from Lordsborough, they were talking and laughing as merrily as yesterday.

The second day's journey was through dense woodland, and they saw no other travellers all morning. Their conversation became more personal. She learned more about his time in Florence: how he had met Silvia, and what kind of person she was. Caris wanted to ask: What was it like to make love to her?

Was she different from me? How? But she held back, feeling that such questions would trespass on Silvia's privacy, even though Silvia was dead. Anyway, she could guess a lot from Merthin's tone of voice. He had been happy in bed with Silvia, she sensed, even if the relationship had not been as intensely passionate as his with Caris.

The unaccustomed hours on horseback were making her sore, so she was relieved to stop for dinner and get off the pony. When they had eaten they sat on the ground with their backs to a broad tree trunk, to rest and let their food go down before resuming the journey.

Caris was thinking about Godwyn, and wondering what she would find at St-John-in-the-Forest, when suddenly she realized that she and Merthin were about to make love. She could not have explained how she knew – they were not even touching – but she had no doubt. She turned to look at him and saw that he sensed it, too. He smiled at her ruefully, and in his eyes she saw ten years of hope and regrets, pain and tears.

He took her hand and kissed her palm, then he put his lips to the soft inside of her wrist, and closed his eyes. 'I can feel your pulse,' he said quietly.

'You can't tell much from the pulse,' she breathed. 'You'll have to give me a thorough examination.'

He kissed her forehead, and her eyelids, and her nose. 'I hope you won't be embarrassed by my seeing your naked body.'

'Don't fret – I'm not taking my clothes off in this weather.'

They both giggled.

He said: 'Perhaps you would be kind enough to lift the skirt of your robe, so that I may proceed with the check-up.'

She reached down and took hold of the hem of her dress. She was wearing hose that came up to her knees. She lifted her dress slowly, revealing her ankles, her shins, her knees, and then the white skin of her thighs. She was feeling playful, but in the back of her mind she wondered if he could detect the changes wrought in her body by the last ten years. She had got thinner, yet at the same time her bottom had spread. Her skin was a little less supple and smooth than it had been. Her breasts were not as firm and upright. What would he think? She suppressed the worry and played the game. 'Is that sufficient, for medical purposes?'

'Not quite.'

'But I'm afraid I'm not wearing underdrawers – such luxuries are considered inappropriate for us nuns.'

'We physicians are obliged to be very thorough, no matter how distasteful we find it.'

'Oh, dear,' she said with a smile. 'What a shame. All right, then.' Watching his face she slowly lifted her skirt until it was around her waist.

He stared at her body, and she could see that he was breathing harder. 'My, my,' he said. 'This is a very severe case. In fact –' he looked up at her face, swallowed, and said – 'I can't joke about this any more.'

She put her arms around him and pulled his body to her own, squeezing as hard as she could, clinging to him as if she were saving him from drowning. 'Make love to me, Merthin,' she said. 'Now, quickly.'

*

THE PRIORY OF St-John-in-the-Forest looked tranquil in the afternoon light – a sure sign that something was wrong, Caris thought. The little cell was traditionally self-sufficient in food, and was surrounded by fields, moist with rain, that needed ploughing and harrowing. But no one was at work.

When they got closer, they saw that the little cemetery next to the church had a row of fresh graves. 'It seems the plague may have reached this far,' Merthin said.

Caris nodded. 'So Godwyn's cowardly escape plan failed.' She could not help feeling a glow of vengeful satisfaction.

Merthin said: 'I wonder if he himself has fallen victim.'

Caris found herself hoping he had, but was too ashamed to say so.

She and Merthin rode around the silent monastery to what was obviously the stable yard. The door was open, and the horses had been let out and were grazing a patch of meadow around a pond. But no one appeared to help the visitors unsaddle.

They walked through the empty stables into the interior. It

was eerily quiet, and Caris wondered if all the monks were dead. They looked into a kitchen, which Caris observed was not as clean as it should be, and a bakery with a cold oven. Their footsteps echoed around the cool grey arcades of the cloisters. Then, approaching the entrance to the church, they met Brother Thomas.

'You found us!' he said. 'Thank God.'

Caris embraced him. She knew that women's bodies did not present a temptation to Thomas. 'I'm glad you're alive,' she said.

'I fell ill and got better,' he explained.

'Not many survive.'

'I know.'

'Tell us what happened.'

'Godwyn and Philemon planned it well,' Thomas said. 'There was almost no warning. Godwyn addressed the chapter, and told the story of Abraham and Isaac to show that God sometimes asks us to do things that appear wrong. Then he told us we were leaving that night. Most of the monks were glad to get away from the plague, and those that had misgivings were instructed to remember their vow of obedience.'

Caris nodded. 'I can imagine. It's not hard to obey orders when they are so strongly in your own self-interest.'

'I'm not proud of myself.'

Caris touched the stump of his left arm. 'I meant no reproof, Thomas.'

Merthin said: 'All the same, I'm surprised no one leaked the destination.'

'That's because Godwyn didn't tell us where we were going. Most of us didn't know even after we arrived – we had to ask the local monks what place this was.'

'But the plague caught up with you.'

'You've seen the graveyard. All the St John monks are there except Prior Saul, who is buried in the church. Almost all the Kingsbridge men are dead. A few ran away after the sickness broke out here – God knows what happened to them.'

Caris recalled that Thomas had always been close to one particular monk, a sweet-natured man a few years younger than he. Hesitantly she said: 'And Brother Matthias?'

'Dead,' Thomas said brusquely; then tears came to his eyes, and he looked away, embarrassed.

Caris put a hand on his shoulder. 'I'm very sorry.'

'So many people have suffered bereavement,' he said.

Caris decided it would be kinder not to dwell on Matthias. 'What about Godwyn and Philemon?'

'Philemon ran away. Godwyn is alive and well – he hasn't caught it.'

'I have a message for Godwyn from the bishop.'

'I can imagine.'

'You'd better take me to him.'

'He's in the church. He set up a bed in a side chapel. He's convinced that's why he hasn't fallen ill. Come with me.'

They crossed the cloisters and entered the little church. It smelled more like a dormitory. The wall painting of the Day of Judgement at the east end seemed grimly appropriate now. The nave was strewn with straw and littered with blankets, as if a crowd of people had been sleeping here; but the only person present was Godwyn. He was lying face down on the dirt floor in front of the altar, his arms stretched out sideways. For a moment she thought he was dead, then she realized this was simply the attitude of extreme penitence.

Thomas said: 'You have visitors, Father Prior.'

Godwyn remained in position. Caris would have assumed he was putting on a show, but something about his stillness made her think he was sincerely seeking forgiveness.

Then he got slowly to his feet and turned round.

He was pale and thin, Caris saw, and he looked tired and anxious.

'You,' he said.

'You've been discovered, Godwyn,' she said. She was not going to call him 'father'. He was a miscreant and she had caught him. She felt deep satisfaction.

He said: 'I suppose Tam Hiding betrayed me.'

His mind was as sharp as ever, Caris noted. 'You tried to escape justice, but you failed.'

'I have nothing to fear from justice,' he said defiantly. 'I came here in the hope of saving the lives of my monks. My error was to leave it too late.'

'An innocent man doesn't sneak away under cover of night.'

'I had to keep my destination secret. It would have defeated my purpose to allow anyone to follow us here.'

'You didn't have to steal the cathedral ornaments.'

'I didn't steal them. I took them for safekeeping. I shall return them to their rightful place when it's safe to do so.'

'So why did you tell no one that you were taking them?'

'But I did. I wrote to Bishop Henri. Did he not receive my letter?'

Caris felt a growing sense of dismay. Surely Godwyn could not wriggle out of this? 'Certainly not,' she said. 'No letter was received, and I don't believe one was sent.'

'Perhaps the messenger died of the plague before he could deliver it.'

'And what was the name of this vanishing messenger?'

'I never knew it. Philemon hired the man.'

'And Philemon is not here – how convenient,' she said sarcastically. 'Well, you can say what you like, but Bishop Henri accuses you of stealing the treasure, and he has sent me here to demand its return. I have a letter ordering you to hand everything to me, immediately.'

'That won't be necessary. I'll take it to him myself.'

'That is not what your bishop commands you to do.'

'I'll be the judge of what's best.'

'Your refusal is proof of theft.'

'I'm sure I can persuade Bishop Henri to see things differently.'

The trouble was, Caris thought despairingly, that Godwyn might well do just that. He could be very plausible, and Henri, like most bishops, would generally avoid confrontation if he could. She felt as if the victory trophy was slipping through her hands.

Godwyn felt he had turned the tables on her, and he permitted himself a small smile of satisfaction. That infuriated her, but she had no more to say. All she could do now was return and tell Bishop Henri what had happened.

She could hardly believe it. Would Godwyn really return to Kingsbridge and resume his position as prior? How could he possibly hold his head up in Kingsbridge Cathedral? After all he had done to damage the priory, the town and the church? Even if the bishop accepted him, surely the townspeople would riot? The prospect was dire, yet stranger things had happened. Was there no justice?

She stared at him. The look of triumph on his face must be matched, she supposed, by the defeat on her own.

Then she saw something that turned the tables yet again.

On Godwyn's upper lip, just below his left nostril, there was a trickle of blood.

*

NEXT MORNING, GODWYN did not get out of bed.

Caris put on her linen mask and nursed him. She bathed his face in rose water and gave him diluted wine whenever he asked for a drink. Every time she touched him, she washed her hands in vinegar.

Other than Godwyn and Thomas, there were only two monks left, both Kingsbridge novices. They, too, were dying of the plague; so she brought them down from the dormitory to lie in the church, and she took care of them as well, flitting around the dim-lit nave like a shade as she went from one dying man to the next.

She asked Godwyn where the cathedral treasures were, but he refused to say.

Merthin and Thomas searched the priory. The first place they looked was under the altar. Something had been buried there, quite recently, they could tell by the looseness of the earth. However, when they made a hole – Thomas digging surprisingly well with one hand – they found nothing. Whatever had been buried there had since been removed.

They checked every echoing room in the deserted monastery, and even looked in the cold bakery oven and the dry brewery tanks, but they found no jewels, relics or charters.

After the first night, Thomas quietly vacated the dormitory – without being asked – and left Merthin and Caris to sleep there alone. He made no comment, not even a nudge or a wink. Grateful for his discreet connivance, they huddled under a pile of blankets and made love. Afterwards, Caris lay awake. An owl lived somewhere in the roof, and she heard its nocturnal hooting, and occasionally the scream of a small animal caught in its talons. She wondered if she would become pregnant. She did not want to give up her vocation – but she could not resist the temptation of lying in Merthin's arms. So she just refused to think about the future.

On the third day, as Caris, Merthin and Thomas ate dinner in the refectory, Thomas said: 'When Godwyn asks for a drink, refuse to give it to him until he's told you where he hid the treasure.'

Caris considered that. It would be perfectly just. But it would also amount to torture. 'I can't do that,' she said. 'I know he deserves it, but all the same I can't do it. If a sick man asks for a drink I must give it to him. That's more important than all the jewelled ornaments in Christendom.'

'You don't owe him compassion – he never showed any to you.'

'I've turned the church into a hospital, but I won't let it become a torture chamber.'

Thomas looked as if he might be inclined to argue further, but Merthin dissuaded him with a shake of the head. 'Think, Thomas,' he said. 'When did you last see this stuff?'

'The night we arrived,' Thomas said. 'It was in leather bags and boxes on a couple of horses. It was unloaded at the same time as everything else, and I think it was carried into the church.'

'Then what happened to it?'

'I never saw it again. But after Evensong, when we all went to supper, I noticed that Godwyn and Philemon stayed behind in the church with two other monks, Juley and John.'

Caris said: 'Let me guess: Juley and John were both young and strong.'

'Yes.'

Merthin said: 'So that's probably when they buried the treasure under the altar. But when did they dig it up?'

'It had to be when nobody was in the church, and they could be sure of that only at mealtimes.'

'Were they absent from any other meals?'

'Several, probably. Godwyn and Philemon always acted as if the rules didn't really apply to them. Their missing meals and services wasn't unusual enough for me to remember every instance.'

Caris said: 'Do you recall Juley and John being absent a second time? Godwyn and Philemon would have needed help again.'

'Not necessarily,' Merthin said. 'It's much easier to re-excavate ground that has already been loosened. Godwyn is forty-three and Philemon is only thirty-four. They could have done it without help, if they really wanted to.'

That night, Godwyn began to rave. Some of the time he seemed to be quoting from the Bible, sometimes preaching, and sometimes making excuses. Caris listened for a while, hoping for clues. 'Great Babylon is fallen, and all the nations have drunk of the wrath of her fornication; and out of the throne proceeded fire, and thunder; and all the merchants of the earth shall weep. Repent, oh, repent, all ye who have committed fornication with the mother of harlots! It was all done for a higher purpose, all done for the glory of God, because the end justifies the means. Give me something to drink, for the love of God.' The apocalyptic tone of his delirium was probably suggested by the wall painting, with its graphic depiction of the tortures of hell.

Caris held a cup to his mouth. 'Where are the cathedral ornaments, Godwyn?'

'I saw seven golden candlesticks, all covered with pearls, and precious stones, and wrapped in fine linen, and purple, and scarlet, and lying in an ark made of cedar wood, and sandalwood, and silver. I saw a woman riding upon a scarlet beast, having seven heads and ten horns, and full of the names of blasphemy.' The nave rang with the echoes of his ranting.

On the following day the two novices died. That afternoon, Thomas and Merthin buried them in the graveyard to the north of the priory. It was a cold, damp day, but they sweated with the effort of digging. Thomas performed the funeral service. Caris stood at the grave with Merthin. When everything was falling apart, the rituals helped to maintain a semblance of normality. Around them were the new graves of all the other monks except Godwyn and Saul. Saul's body lay under the little chancel of the church, an honour reserved for the most highly regarded priors.

Afterwards Caris came back into the church and stared at Saul's grave in the chancel. That part of the church was paved with flagstones. Obviously the flags had been lifted so that the grave could be dug. When they had been put back, one of the stones had been polished and carved with an inscription.

It was hard to concentrate, with Godwyn in the corner raving about beasts with seven heads.

Merthin noticed her thoughtful look and followed her gaze. He immediately guessed what she was thinking. In a horrified voice he said: 'Surely Godwyn can't have hidden the treasure in Saul Whitehead's coffin?'

'It's hard to imagine monks desecrating a tomb,' she said. 'On the other hand, the ornaments wouldn't have had to leave the church.'

Thomas said: 'Saul died a week before you arrived. Philemon disappeared two days later.'

'So Philemon could have helped Godwyn dig up the grave.'

'Yes.'

The three of them looked at one another, trying to ignore the mad mumblings of Godwyn.

'There's only one way to find out,' Merthin said.

Merthin and Thomas got their wooden shovels. They lifted the memorial slab and the paving stones around it, and started digging.

Thomas had developed a one-handed technique. He pushed the shovel into the earth with his good arm, tilted it, then ran his hand all the way down the shaft to the blade and lifted it. His right arm had become very muscular as a result of this kind of adaptation.

Nevertheless, it took a long time. Many graves were shallow, nowadays, but for Prior Saul they had dug down the full six feet. Night was falling outside, and Caris fetched candles. The devils in the wall painting seemed to move in the flickering light.

Both Thomas and Merthin were standing in the hole, with only their heads visible above floor level, when Merthin said: 'Wait. Something's here.'

Caris saw some muddy white material that looked like the oiled linen sometimes used for shrouds. 'You've found the body,' she said.

Thomas said: 'But where's the coffin?'

'Was he buried in a box?' Coffins were only for the elite: poor people were interred in a shroud.

Thomas said: 'Saul was buried in a coffin – I saw it. There's plenty of wood here in the middle of the forest. All the monks were put in coffins, right up until Brother Silas fell ill – he was the carpenter.'

'Wait,' said Merthin. He pushed his shovel through the earth at the feet of the shroud and lifted a shovelful. Then he tapped with the blade, and Caris heard the dull thud of wood on wood. 'Here's the coffin, underneath,' he said.

Thomas said: 'How did the body get out?'

Caris felt a shiver of fear.

Over in the corner, Godwyn raised his voice. 'And he shall be tormented with fire and brimstone in the sight of the holy angels, and the smoke of his torment will rise up for ever and ever.'

Thomas said to Caris: 'Can't you shut him up?'

'I've got no drugs with me.'

Merthin said: 'There's nothing supernatural here. My guess is that Godwyn and Philemon took the body out – and filled the coffin with their stolen treasures.'

Thomas pulled himself together. 'We'd better look in the coffin, then.'

First they had to move the shrouded corpse. Merthin and Thomas bent down, grabbed it by the shoulders and knees, and lifted it. When they had raised it to the level of their shoulders, the only way they could get it farther was to toss it out on to the floor. It landed with a thump. They both looked fearful. Even Caris, who did not believe much of what she was told about the spirit world, felt frightened by what they were doing, and found herself glancing nervously over her shoulder into the shadowed corners of the church.

Merthin cleared the earth from the top of the coffin while Thomas went to fetch an iron bar. Then they lifted the lid of the casket.

Caris held two candles over the grave so that they could see better.

Inside the coffin was another shrouded body.

Thomas said: 'This is very strange!' His voice was distinctly shaky.

'Let's just think sensibly about this,' Merthin said. He was sounding calm and collected, but Caris – who knew him extraordinarily well – could tell that his composure was taking a big effort. 'Who is in the coffin?' he said. 'Let's look.'

He bent down, grabbed the shroud in two hands, and ripped it open along the stitched seam at the head. The corpse was a week dead, and there was a bad smell, but it had not deteriorated much in the cold ground under the unheated church. Even in the unsteady light from Caris's candles, there was no doubt about the identity of the dead man: the head was fringed with distinctively ash-blond hair.

Thomas said: 'That's Saul Whitehead.'

'In his rightful coffin,' said Merthin.

Caris said: 'So who is the other corpse?'

Merthin closed the shroud around Saul's blond head and replaced the coffin lid.

Caris knelt by the other corpse. She had dealt with many dead bodies, but she had never brought one up from its grave, and her hands were shaky. Nevertheless she opened the shroud and exposed the face. To her horror, the eyes were open and seemed to be staring. She forced herself to close the cold eyelids.

It was a big young monk she did not recognize. Thomas stood on tiptoe to look out of the grave and said: 'That's Brother Jonquil. He died the day after Prior Saul.'

Caris said: 'And he was buried ... ?'

'In the cemetery ... we all thought.'

'In a coffin?'

'Yes.'

'Except that he's here.'

'His coffin weighed enough,' Thomas said. 'I helped carry it...'

Merthin said: 'I see what happened. Jonquil lay here in the church, in his coffin, prior to burial. While the other monks were at dinner, Godwyn and Philemon opened the coffin and took the body out. They dug up Saul's tomb and tumbled Jonquil in on top of Saul's coffin. They closed the grave. Then they put the cathedral treasures in Jonquil's coffin and closed it again.'

Thomas said: 'So we have to dig up Jonquil's grave.'

Caris glanced up at the windows of the church. They were dark. Night had fallen while they were opening the tomb of Saul. 'We could leave it until morning,' she said.

Both men were silent for a long moment, then Thomas said: 'Let's get it over with.'

Caris went to the kitchen, picked two branches from the firewood pile, lit them at the fire, then returned to the church.

As the three of them went outside they heard Godwyn cry: 'And the winepress of the wrath of God was trodden outside the city, and the grapes gave forth blood, and the land was flooded to the height of the horses' bridles.'

Caris shuddered. It was a vile image from the Revelation of St John the Divine, and it disgusted her. She tried to put it out of her mind.

They walked quickly to the cemetery in the red light of the torches. Caris was relieved to be away from that wall painting and out of earshot of Godwyn's mad ravings. They found Jonquil's headstone and began to excavate.

The two men had already dug two graves for the novices and re-dug Saul's. This was their fourth since dinner time. Merthin looked tired and Thomas was sweating heavily. But they worked on doggedly. Slowly the hole got deeper and the pile of earth beside it rose higher. At last a shovel struck wood.

Caris passed Merthin the crowbar, then she knelt on the edge of the pit, holding both torches. Merthin prised open the coffin lid and threw it out of the grave.

There was no corpse in the box.

Instead it was packed tightly with bags and boxes. Merthin opened a leather bag and pulled out a jewelled crucifix. 'Hallelujah,' he said wearily.

Thomas opened a box to reveal a row of parchment rolls, packed tightly together like fish in a crate: the charters.

Caris felt a weight of worry roll off her shoulders. She had got the nunnery charters back.

Thomas put his hand into another bag. When he looked at what he had got hold of, it was a skull. He gave a fearful cry and dropped it.

'St Adolphus,' Merthin said in a matter-of-fact voice. 'Pilgrims travel hundreds of miles to touch the box that holds his bones.' He picked up the skull. 'Lucky us,' he said, and put it back into the bag.

'If I may make a suggestion?' said Caris. 'We have to carry this stuff all the way back to Kingsbridge in a cart. Why don't we leave it in the coffin? It's packed already, and the casket may serve to deter thieves.'

'Good idea,' Merthin said. 'We'll just lift the coffin out of the grave.'

Thomas returned to the priory and brought ropes, and they lifted the coffin out of the hole. They re-fixed the lid, then tied the ropes around the box in order to drag it across the ground and into the church.

As they were about to start, they heard a scream.

Caris let out a cry of fear.

They all looked towards the church. A figure was running towards them, eyes staring, blood coming from its mouth. Caris suffered a moment of utter terror when she suddenly believed every foolish superstition she had ever heard about spirits. Then she realized she was looking at Godwyn. Somehow he had found the strength to rise from his death bed. He had staggered out of the church and seen their torches, and now in his madness he was running towards them.

They watched him, transfixed.

He stopped and looked at the coffin, then at the empty grave, and in the restless torchlight Caris thought she saw a glimmer of understanding on his grimacing face. Then he seemed to lose his strength, and he collapsed. He fell on the mound of earth beside Jonquil's empty grave, then he rolled down the mound and into the pit.

They all stepped forward and looked into the grave.

Godwyn lay there on his back, looking up at them with open, sightless eyes.

66

As soon as Caris got back to Kingsbridge, she decided to leave again.

The image of St-John-in-the-Forest that stayed with her was not the graveyard, nor the corpses Merthin and Thomas had dug up, but the neat fields with no one tilling them. As she rode home, with Merthin beside her and Thomas driving the cart, she saw a lot of land in the same state, and she foresaw a crisis.

The monks and nuns got most of their income from rents. Serfs grew crops and raised livestock on land belonging to the priory and, instead of paying a knight or an earl for the privilege, they paid the prior or prioress. Traditionally they brought a portion of their harvest to the cathedral – a dozen sacks of flour, three sheep, a calf, a cartload of onions – but nowadays most people paid cash.

If no one was cultivating the land, there would be no rent paid, obviously. And then what would the nuns eat?

The cathedral ornaments, the money and the charters she had retrieved from St-John-in-the-Forest were stashed safely in the new, secret treasury that Mother Cecilia had commissioned Jeremiah to build in a place where no one could easily find it. All the ornaments had been found except one, a gold candlestick given by the chandlers' guild, the group that represented the wax-candle makers of Kingsbridge. That had disappeared.

Caris held a triumphant Sunday service featuring the rescued bones of the saint. She put Thomas in charge of the boys in the orphanage – some of them were old enough to require a strong male presence. She herself moved into the prior's palace, thinking with pleasure how appalled the late Godwyn would be that it was occupied by a woman. Then, as soon as she had dealt with these details, she went to Outhenby.

The vale of Outhen was a fertile valley of heavy clay soil a day's journey from Kingsbridge. It had been given to the nuns a hundred years ago by a wicked old knight making a last-gasp attempt to win forgiveness for a lifetime of sins. Five villages stood at intervals along the banks of the river Outhen. On either side the great fields covered the land and the lower slopes of the hills.

The fields were divided into strips allocated to different families. As she had feared, many strips were not being cultivated. The plague had changed everything, but no one had had the brains – or perhaps the courage – to reorganize farming in the light of the new circumstances. Caris herself would have to do that. She had a rough idea of what was required, and she would work out the details as she went along.

With her was Sister Joan, a young nun recently out of her novitiate. Joan was a bright girl who reminded Caris of herself ten years ago – not in appearance, for she was black-haired and blue-eyed, but in her questioning mind and brisk scepticism.

They rode to the largest of the villages, Outhenby. The bailiff for the whole valley, Will, lived there in a large timber house next to the church. He was not at home, but they found him in the farthest field, sowing oats; a big, slow-moving man. The next strip had been left fallow, and wild grass and weeds were poking up, grazed by a few sheep.

Will Bailiff visited the priory several times a year, usually to bring the rents from the villages, so he knew Caris; but he was disconcerted to meet her on his home ground. 'Sister Caris!' he exclaimed when he recognized her. 'What brings you here?'

'I'm Mother Caris now, Will, and I've come to make sure the nuns' lands are being properly husbanded.'

'Ah.' He shook his head. 'We're doing our best, as you see, but we've lost so many men that it's very, very difficult.'

Bailiffs always said that times were difficult – but in this case it was true.

Caris dismounted. 'Walk with me and tell me about it.' A few hundred yards away, on the gentle slope of a hillside, she saw a peasant ploughing with a team of eight oxen. He halted the team and looked at her curiously, so she headed that way.

Will began to recover his composure. Walking alongside her, he said: 'A woman of God, such as yourself, can't be expected to know much about tilling the soil, of course; but I'll do my best to explain the finer points.'

'That would be kind.' She was used to being condescended to by men of Will's type. She had found that it was best not to challenge them, but rather to lull them into a false sense of security. That way, she learned more. 'How many men have you lost to the plague?'

'Oh, many men.'

'How many?'

'Well, now, let me see, there was William Jones, and his two sons; then Richard Carpenter, and his wife—'

'I don't need to know their names,' she said, controlling her exasperation. 'How many, roughly speaking?'

'I'd have to think about that.'

They had reached the plough. Managing the eight-ox team was a skilled job, and ploughmen were often among the more intelligent villagers. Caris addressed the young man. 'How many people in Outhenby have died of the plague?'

'About two hundred, I'd say.'

Caris studied him. He was short but muscular, with a bushy blond beard. He had a cocksure look, as young men often did. 'Who are you?' she asked.

'My name is Harry, and my father was Richard, holy sister.'

'I am Mother Caris. How do you work out that figure of two hundred?'

'There's forty-two dead here in Outhenby, by my reckoning. It's just as bad in Ham and Shortacre, making about a hundred and twenty. Longwater escaped completely, but every soul in Oldchurch is dead but old Roger Breton, which is about eighty people, making two hundred.'

She turned to Will. 'Out of about how many in the whole valley?'

'Ah, now, let me see . . .'

Harry Ploughman said: 'A thousand, near enough, before the plague.'

Will said: 'That's why you see me sowing my own strip, which should be done by labourers – but I have no labourers. They've all died.'

Harry said: 'Or they've gone to work elsewhere for higher wages.'

Caris perked up. 'Oh? Who offers higher wages?'

'Some of the wealthier peasants in the next valley,' Will said indignantly. 'The nobility pay a penny a day, which is what labourers have always got and always should; but there are some people who think they can do as they please.'

'But they get their crops sowed, I suppose,' Caris said.

'But there's right and wrong, Mother Caris,' said Will.

Caris pointed to the fallow strip where the sheep were. 'And what about that land? Why has it not been ploughed?'

Will said: 'That belonged to William Jones. He and his sons died, and his wife went to live with her sister in Shiring.'

'Have you looked for a new tenant?'

'Can't get them, mother.'

Harry interjected again. 'Not on the old terms, anyhow.'

Will glared at him, but Caris said: 'What do you mean?'

'Prices have fallen, you see, even though it's spring when corn is usually dear.'

Caris nodded. That was how markets worked, everyone knew: if there were fewer buyers, the price fell. 'But people must live somehow.'

'They don't want to grow wheat and barley and oats – but they have to grow what they're told, at least in this valley. So a man looking for a tenancy would rather go elsewhere.'

'And what will he get elsewhere?'

Will interrupted angrily: 'They want to do as they please.'

Harry answered Caris's question. 'They want to be free tenants, paying cash rent, rather than serfs working one day a week on the lord's land; and they want to be able to grow different crops.'

'What crops?'

'Hemp, or flax, or apples and pears – things they know they can sell at the market. Maybe something different every year. But that's never been allowed in Outhenby.' Harry seemed to recollect himself, and added: 'No offence to your holy order, Mother Prioress, nor to Will Bailiff, an honest man as everyone knows.'

Caris saw how it was. Bailiffs were always conservative. In good times, it hardly mattered: the old ways sufficed. But this was a crisis.

She assumed her most authoritative manner. 'All right, listen carefully, now, Will, and I'll tell you what you're going to do.' Will looked startled: he had thought he was being consulted, not commanded. 'First, you are to stop ploughing the hillsides. It's foolish when we've got good land uncultivated.'

'But—'

'Be quiet and listen. Offer every tenant an exchange, acre for acre, good valley bottom instead of hillside.'

'Then what will we do with the hillside?'

'Convert it to grazing, cattle on the lower slopes and sheep on the higher. You don't need many men for that, just a few boys to herd them.'

'Oh,' said Will. It was plain that he wanted to argue, but he could not immediately think of an objection.

Caris went on: 'Next, any valley-bottom land that is still untenanted should be offered as a free tenancy with cash rent to anyone who will take it on.' A free tenancy meant that the tenant was not a serf, and did not have to work on the lord's land, or get his permission to marry or build a house. All he had to do was pay his rent.

'You're doing away with all the old customs.'

She pointed at the fallow strip. 'The old customs are letting my land go to waste. Can you think of another way to stop this happening?'

'Well,' said Will, and there was a long pause; then he shook his head silently.

'Thirdly, offer wages of two pence a day to anyone who will work the land.'

'Two pence a day!'

Caris felt she could not rely on Will to implement these changes vigorously. He would drag his feet and invent excuses. She turned to the cocksure ploughman. She would make him the champion of her reforms. 'Harry, I want you to go to every market in the county over the next few weeks. Spread the word that anyone who is on the move can do well in Outhenby. If there are labourers looking for wages I want them to come here.'

Harry grinned and nodded, though Will still looked a bit dazed.

'I want to see all this good land growing crops this summer,' she said. 'Is that clear?'

'Yes,' said Will. 'Thank you, Mother Prioress.'

*

CARIS WENT THROUGH all the charters with Sister Joan, making a note of the date and subject of each. She decided to have them copied, one by one – the idea Godwyn had proposed, though he had only pretended to be copying them as a pretext for taking them away from the nuns. But it was a sound notion. The more copies there were, the harder it was for a valuable document to disappear.

She was intrigued by a deed dated 1327 which assigned to the monks the large farm near Lynn, in Norfolk, that they called Lynn Grange. The gift was made on condition the priory took on, as a novice monk, a knight called Sir Thomas Langley.

Caris was taken back to her childhood, and the day she had ventured into the wood with Merthin, Ralph and Gwenda, and they had seen Thomas receive the wound that had caused him to lose his arm.

She showed the charter to Joan, who shrugged and said: 'It's usual for such a gift to be made when someone from a wealthy family becomes a monk.'

'But look who the donor is.'

Joan looked again. 'Queen Isabella!' Isabella was the widow of Edward II and the mother of Edward III. 'What's her interest in Kingsbridge?'

'Or in Thomas?' said Caris.

A few days later she had a chance to find out. The bailiff of Lynn Grange, Andrew, came to Kingsbridge on his biannual visit. A Norfolk-born man of over fifty, he had been in charge of the grange ever since it was gifted to the priory. He was now white-